THE FLINT SAGA

THE FLINT SAGA

TREASURE HERNANDEZ

www.urbanbooks.net

Urban Books, LLC
78 East Industry Court
Deer Park, NY 11729

ISBN 13: 978-1-60162-434-5
ISBN 10: 1-60162-434-4

First Printing February 2011
Printed in the United States of America

10 9 8 7 6 5 4 3 2 1

This is a work of fiction. Any references or similarities to actual events, real people, living, or dead, or to real locales are intended to give the novel a sense of reality. Any similarity in other names, characters, places, and incidents is entirely coincidental.

Distributed by Kensington Publishing Corp.
Submit Wholesale Orders to:
Kensington Publishing Corp.
C/O Penguin Group (USA) Inc.
Attention: Order Processing
405 Murray Hill Parkway
East Rutherford, NJ 07073-2316
Phone: 1-800-526-0275
Fax: 1-800-227-9604

Chapter One

"There go your boy," Nikki whispered to Halleigh as they sat in the cafeteria watching Malek Johnson lope into the room.

Halleigh glanced up, and her thin, glossy lips were instantly graced with a smile at just the sight of him. Malek stood out like a Hollywood celebrity against the crowd of Flint Central High School students milling about the lunchroom. At six feet, five inches tall and well-built, it wasn't just his clean-cut, Sean John look. He also had a charismatic presence that commanded nothing but the utmost respect, and he received it. He also had a smile that melted the panties off many females throughout the school, with the exception of Halleigh Walters.

Yeah, Mr. Malek might have looked good and all, draped in his blue, gray, and white plaid Sean Jean button-up and his midnight blue Sean John jeans. Any other girl would have been happy to stitch his name on her "Vickie" panties, but Halleigh, in her own gentle presence, demanded her own respect. She couldn't get it by becoming just another shoestring hole in his Jordan's, to be laced up with all those other tricks he'd been with. She had to show that she was a different kind of breed and unlike those other hoodrats he'd fucked with before.

After realizing that she was smiling just like some of those other groupies that couldn't wait for him to pass them by just so they could get high off of his lingering scent, Halleigh quickly got rid of it and replaced it with the twisting up of her lips and a shrug of her shoulders. "Yeah, I see him," she said nonchalantly. She poked at the entrée that the school cook referred to as spaghetti, but from what she could see, it was just a bunch of noodles with a couple hunks of ground burger here and there. The last time she checked, spaghetti had sauce.

Nikki told her, "Girl, all I can say is that you crazy. I would've gave that nigga some, if I was you. You know he's going to the league. You need to be trying to have his baby. That NBA money will have you set for life."

As she spoke, Nikki watched Malek's every move. His popularity was evident. His confident swagger not only demanded Halleigh's and Nikki's attention, but everyone grinned and called out his name as he passed, like the act of saying his name alone made them part of his dream—the one to escape the ghetto. He was the number one high school basketball prospect in the state. In the world, for all they knew.

The students acted like paparazzi or would-be agents.

"Waddup? Malek, you the man."

"Malek, did you decide where you gon' go yet?"

"Malek, you gon' sign if you get drafted?"

Malek worked the crowd, slapping hands with some of his team-mates that stood in his path; a path that one would think should have been laid out with a red carpet. He gave dap to other classmates and pounds to a few of his friends he'd grown up with. Without missing a beat, he bobbed his head to an invisible rhythm, as a five-person BET camera crew followed his every move.

Malek was expected to be the number one pick in the upcoming draft, and he was high from all the attention he had been receiving over the past couple of weeks. Malek hadn't decided if he would enter the league or if he would try his hand at college first. The anticipation over his decision was killing sports fans all across the country. Malek was the man of the hour. Everybody wanted a piece of him. Even Halleigh wanted a piece of him, literally. She could just taste him, but would never dare to let that little fact be known.

"Shut up, Nikki," Halleigh snapped. "It's not like that with me and him. I'm not trying to trap anybody. I just like being around him."

"Just like being around him? Girl, you better do more than just be around that nigga. Hell, a fly buzzing around his head is just being around him.

You better give him some of that thing right there"—Nikki pointed to Halleigh's girlhood—"before the next chick steals on your man." Nikki looked around the cafeteria at the damn-near drooling chicks. "These scandalous bitches don't just see a good-looking brotha when they look at Malek. They see dollar signs. They practically begging him to fuck with them." Nikki was seriously trying to put her friend up on game. *Shit, I'd throw some pussy his way if I thought he would take it,* she thought to herself.

Nikki flipped her long hair out of the way before taking a bite of her roll that accompanied the spaghetti. Her dark brown locks were wavy now, after having worn her hair in French braids for the last week. Against her dark brown, smooth skin her hair made her look exotic, like she was from the islands or something. She was gorgeous, a chocolate delight, to say the least. Standing at average height, around five feet, six inches, Nikki was also of average size, a twelve in winter months and a ten in the summer months. She made it a point to shed any extra pounds she had accumulated in the winter months by the time the school year was up. She had to look good in a two-piece for whenever she went to the pool. All the ballers hung out at the pool, on the prowl for a summer bunny, which meant for some lucky female, three months of shopping, eating out, and as a bonus, maybe they'd even get a tennis bracelet. She had managed to earn two since her ninth grade year. If her best friend played her cards right with Malek, she too could begin her collection. That's why she had to come to her from the hip, letting her know that if she didn't show her hand, an-other bitch might trump her ass.

"I'm not worried about the next girl," Halleigh said. "I know what me and Malek got. He ain't worried about nobody else but me. It's me and him against the world."

Halleigh was, in fact, as confident as she sounded. Ever since she first met Malek back in eighth grade, long before he became the high school basketball star that he was today, he had always been nothing but kind and respectful to her. Back then, they had shared a history class together when the two of them, along with two other students, were placed in a group to work on a project together. At the time, Malek was kicking it with some girl named Nessa, but his attraction to Halleigh was evident from the way he stared at her whenever she was discussing something about the project. Malek was fine. Any girl in her right mind would have had a mutual attraction, but what really drew Halleigh to him was the fact that he never came on to her. She assumed it was because he respected his relationship with Nessa.

After their history class together, Malek and Halleigh didn't really talk much, but whenever they passed each other in the halls, the unspoken attraction took up the space between them. Even after Malek and Nessa broke up, when other girls would swarm him, trying to be his next chick, Halleigh never pushed up on him. She figured if he wanted her, he'd come to her; she shouldn't have to chase after any man.

By the same token, with all the girls chasing after him, Malek felt that if Halleigh was interested in being his girl, then she would show her interest by doing the same thing the other girls were doing, but she didn't. So Malek did go on to kick it with plenty of other girls before finally, in eleventh grade, putting his pride aside and going after Halleigh and making her his one and only.

When they first got together all kinds of whispers and rumors made the rounds of the school. "Girl, he just gon' screw you and dump you like he did all them other girls."

"Don't get comfortable. He loves 'em and leaves 'em."

"If all the other chicks didn't have what it takes to keep him, what makes you think you do?"

"I hear he's sleeping with you and every other girl in the school."

Although, in most cases, the gossip might have gotten to other couples and put a dent in their relationship, it only made Halleigh and Malek more bound and determined to prove everybody wrong.

Halleigh never let the rumors that Malek was fucking so-and-so get to her. Some of the girls started the rumors themselves, just to try and break up the couple so that they could have dibs, but it never worked. Also, it never convinced Halleigh to give up her own virginity just so she could keep her man.

"Yeah, all that is cool, but you never gonna lose that cherry if you keep waiting for shit to happen. You have to make shit happen." Nikki eyeballed Halleigh with a knowing look.

"Yeah, whateva." Halleigh tossed her hair flippantly. Her hair wasn't as long as Nikki's, but it was a good length, to her shoulders. Halleigh always wore it flat-iron straight with feathered side bangs down her face. Light skinned and not as gorgeous as Nikki or as tall, she was still cute in the face; cute enough to have Malek sniffing behind her for all those years, anyway. On top of that, she had a nice figure that was lean and toned, but meaty and thick in all the right places.

Somewhat peeved, Halleigh arose from the table and made her way over to Malek. Halleigh didn't care what Nikki said. She didn't see her with any steady boyfriend, so what did she know? All those drawers she had dropped, and where was her man? Doesn't matter how beautiful a girl is on the outside, if niggas know that everybody done been inside, they ain't trying to make her wifey. Although Halleigh loved Nikki like a stepsister, she was the prime example of why she hadn't given it up. She wanted to make sure that when she did have sex, it would be with someone who she knew loved her for her and not for what was between her legs. Last night, she had come to the conclusion of who that person was.

After making her way to Malek, Halleigh quickly took her place under one of his arms. As he gazed into the cameras, he introduced her to the world. "This is my girl, Halleigh." He looked down at her and kissed her on the forehead. "This is my boo."

This time, Halleigh let the smile stay painted on her lips as she mouthed, "Hi", to the cameras and waved. Standing by Malek's side while he was being interviewed, she was so glad she'd worn her orange designer dress to school that day. She couldn't stop smiling if someone had paid her. Every time she was around him, she felt lucky to be a part of his life.

Standing there together in front of the cameras, they were in sharp contrast to one another. He was tall and slim; she was short and thick. He was dark sienna brown, and she was a rich persimmon color. He was full of personality and animated, and she was laid-back and plain.

Even though Halleigh looked innocent, a lot of people thought that she was a freak behind doors, since usually it was the quiet ones that you had to look out for. They figured Malek was probably only with her for what she could do for him behind closed doors. A lot of people also thought that she was only with Malek because of his promising future, but she knew the deal. She was with him because she loved him. They had been dating since their junior year and were friends long before that, not to mention he knew her like no one else did.

Halleigh stood by him until the end of his interview. Then they strolled out of the cafeteria together. He kissed the top of her head as they made their way down the hallway. "So what's all that you were talking on the phone last night?" Malek asked. He couldn't wait for the opportunity to bring up that conversation today. He needed to make

sure that his conversation last night with her wasn't just a dream, or that she hadn't been half 'sleep when she'd called him up late last night.

Halleigh blushed. She thought back to the conversation she'd had with him the night before. She'd made the phone call after coming to the conclusion that Malek really did love her for her and not just for the sex. She hadn't given him any, but now she wanted to. She knew deep down inside that she didn't have to have sex to keep him. She wanted to have sex with him because she loved him. So, before she could coward out and second-guess herself, after midnight she'd made this call telling him how much she loved him. After he confirmed his love for her, something she already knew, she promised him that she would give him her virginity the night of the championship game, which was that night.

She'd held out for the entire two years that they had been dating and felt like it was time to take their relationship to the next level. They would be graduating soon. They would be adults and would no longer have to put up with all the childish he-said, she-said and rumors that high school life entailed. Although she hated to admit it, Halleigh was also beginning to take heed to Nikki's warnings.

Now that they would be leaving the high school life behind, there would be the real world. She'd be up against real women. She didn't want to give another girl room to take her place. She wanted Malek to be completely satisfied with her, mind and body. "Can I ask you a question?" she inquired right when the school bell rang.

Malek stopped walking when the two stood at his locker. "You know you can ask me anything." He fumbled around with his lock, trying to put in his combination, but was unsuccessful.

Halleigh, who knew the combination, operated the lock for him and successfully unlocked it. While Malek opened up his locker and began sifting through it, she glimpsed around at the throngs of students flowing throughout the high school corridor. She made sure no one was within earshot then said, "I'm not saying that I don't want to, because I do." She inhaled a deep breath. "But . . . if we didn't have sex, if I never called you last night and told you that I would, you know . . . would you leave me?" Halleigh's face scrunched up and worry tinged her voice. "I mean, with all those college girls out there, or just women, period. . . ."

Malek looked down at her as she lowered her head and tried to avert his stare. He placed his finger on her lips to silence her. "Is that what you really think? I mean, is that what *you* think"—he gently poked her heart with his finger—"and not what somebody is putting in your ear?" Malek knew how other broads were, how they liked to get into the ears of other girls who weren't out sexin' everybody like they were.

Halleigh didn't reply.

Malek, after getting everything he needed from his locker, closed it and continued talking. "Hal, you don't have to do nothing you don't want to do."

"I know, I know, but I don't want none of these other chicks offering you something that I'm not giving you. Eventually, you will get what you want from someone else," she whispered, clutching her books to her chest. "It's not like you ain't gotten it before." She turned to walk toward her next class, her eyes watering from the very thought of Malek choosing another girl over her. None of that stuff had ever bothered her before, but now, all of a sudden, and now that life after high school was approaching, she couldn't shake off the thoughts as easily as before.

"It's not like that with us," Malek tried to assure her, as they walked side by side. "I thought I've shown you that by now. I'm not trying to fuck with nobody but you. These girls only chasing after me because they think I'm about to come into some money. I know where your head is at. I had to chase after you, remember?" he said in a playful manner. He lifted her chin while the two continued walking down the hall. "I'm gon' be with you always. I'm with you for you, the same way that you are with me for me. I know that if all the material shit that comes along with being a basketball star is gone tomorrow, you would still be here holding me down." Malek stopped walking. Then his tone became serious. "You the only one who really cares about me on the inside. Everyone else just wants to use me and get a piece of me."

Halleigh stood still next to her man, absorbing his every word.

"I love you, Halleigh, and I'll wait as long as you need me to. I'm not going to lie, I know you mentally and emotionally, but I'm trying to know you physically too. But, baby girl, I'll wait until you are comfortable. You're my world, you know that. At least, I thought you did."

Halleigh stared into her man's eyes, searching for congruency between what his eyes said and the words his mouth uttered. His eyes didn't crinkle teasingly like they did when he was joking with her. He was dead serious. It was more than just his eyes that told the truth. Halleigh could hear the sincerity behind his words, and in her heart. She knew that after the game that night, she would be in his bed. "I know, I know," she replied.

"So you gon' let me get up in that or what?" he whispered in her ear, pushing her hair behind her double-pierced ears that held the diamond studs he'd purchased for her as a birthday gift.

She hit him in the stomach and laughed.

"You know I'm just playing with you," he offered. Malek continued walking with Halleigh right by his side.

"Okay, let's make a bet," she proposed. "If you score over 40 points

in the championship, then I got you guaranteed, if not, you just gon' have to wait a little bit longer."

Malek's eyes lit up. He liked the game she was playing. "How much longer?"

"Until graduation."

"That's four months away!" he exclaimed.

Just then, they stopped walking and stood in the doorway to Halleigh's next class.

"Then you better get off tonight if you don't want to wait," she said in a flirtatious and challenging tone. She smiled mischievously, hinting at their night of pleasure to come.

As Malek leaned over and kissed her lightly on the lips, Halleigh's teacher, Ms. Gulley, announced, "That's enough, Mr. Johnson," interrupting their intimate moment.

Halleigh laughed and pushed Malek, feigning not having anything to do with the kiss.

"Sorry, Ms. Gulley," Malek said, throwing two fingers in the air and winking at Halleigh before he strolled up the hallway.

"And pull up those pants!" Ms. Gulley bellowed. She smiled and shook her head. "Nobody wants to see your behind."

Speak for yourself. Halleigh smiled then turned and headed into the classroom.

"Malek Johnson is having one of the best ball games of his life, ladies and gentlemen," the ESPN sports commentator said as he watched the game in awe. "This is amazing. It is only the third quarter and he already has 32 points. Talent like this doesn't come around too often. This is his last game before the NBA draft in a couple of months. I think he's trying to show the pros what he's working with."

Cameras were positioned everywhere. From local news stations to national coverage, every media outlet was there to witness Malek's last game of his high school career. He was considered the nation's top basketball recruit. The spectators jumped to their feet and roared with excitement every time he got the ball in his hands.

Everyone thought that Malek was showing out because it was his last game, but Halleigh knew the real motivation behind his extreme performance that night. After every basket he scored, he pointed to her in the stands.

"Girl, he's pointing at you." Nikki bumped Halleigh's shoulder as she sat there in the stands right next to her.

Halleigh cheered loudly throughout the game and admired her man as he brought the packed crowd to their feet time and time again. With every point he scored she thought, *I'm really about to give it up now. He's working hard for this.* She almost felt honored that her high school would have her to thank if they won tonight's game. A tremor of exhilaration mixed with fear shivered up her back.

By the last few seconds of the game, Malek had managed forty-seven points and fifteen assists, and his team had a ten-point lead. During his final moments on the floor, he simply dribbled the ball, showing off his handling skills as the crowd began to chant his name in unison. Malek scanned the crowd until his eyes met Halleigh's. Then he smiled at her as the final buzzer sounded off. The crowd went absolutely crazy as they rushed the floor.

Halleigh eventually made her way down to the court, and Malek made a beeline over to her, bypassing all of the flocking reporters. Once he reached her, he picked her up and hugged her tightly, kissing her as he celebrated his team's championship victory.

"I love you," she whispered in his ear.

"I know," he said. "And I can't wait for you to show me just how much." Then he quickly ran back onto the floor to whoop and holler with his team.

Chapter Two

After the game, Halleigh leaned on Malek's beat-up Ford Tempo and waited patiently for him to exit the school. One dude yelled, "Hal, tell Malek I said good game!"

"Yeah, he did his thang out there!" a girl added.

Halleigh smiled. "Yeah, he gon' be feeling thick tonight."

She had to admit that Malek did play a good game. She was proud of him for everything that he was accomplishing and felt blessed to know that he'd chosen her to share his future with. On the outside, Halleigh Walters looked like a regular, carefree teenager without a worry in the world, but on the inside, she had come up in a harsh environment. Growing up in a single-parent household, it had always been hard for her mother, Sharina, to take care of and provide for her. Sharina had never had a real relationship with Halleigh's father. He never played a role in his daughter's life, so the sole support for Halleigh fell on her mother's shoulders. In Halleigh's early years, Sharina had worked as a line worker at the General Motors plants. Many people say that shop jobs aren't meant for women because of the strenuous labor that comes with it, but Sharina did what she had to do to make ends meet. Making pretty decent money, she took care of Halleigh, and although her long work hours left Halleigh alone most

of the time, they never needed for anything. Unfortunately, Sharina had become another casualty of economics and was one of thousands to lose her job when the hiring of cheap, overseas labor took its toll and General Motors decided to downsize their plants. General Motors was the livelihood of Flint, so the loss of these jobs hit everybody hard. For Halleigh, it seemed to have hit her mother the hardest.

Out of work, and depressed because she wasn't having any luck finding another job, Halleigh's mother fell victim to her circumstance. She ended up turning to drugs as her daughter sat by helplessly and watched. A strong drug habit quickly formed, and Sharina became addicted to heroin, which affected Halleigh's entire outlook on life.

Once unemployment and government assistance would no longer do the trick, instead of turning tricks herself, Sharina started boosting clothes, not to feed her daughter, but to feed her habit instead. It was that same skill of boosting that Sharina had mastered that kept people from being able to tell just how bad Halleigh's upbringing really was.

Halleigh stayed fly in the latest fashions, because her mother's closet looked like the local Macy's. Sharina always made sure she boosted some nice pieces for both herself and her daughter. Just like a Mary Kay consultant, she had to be a representative of her product. In fact, Sharina was a walking advertisement for her craft. As for Halleigh, dressing nice was her way of hiding her predicament from the world.

Nobody knew how tough she had it, nobody but Malek anyway. Halleigh tried to hide it from him at first, never allowing him to come to her house, making up the excuse that her mother would flip the script if she knew her baby girl had a boyfriend. After a while, and after Halleigh ran out of excuses, he finally got her to keep it real. She told him what was so bad at her house that she didn't want him to be witness to it. The last thing Halleigh wanted her new man to know, her new man that lived in a house with both of his parents and dressed nice because both of his parents were employed, was that her mother was a drug addict whose occupation was stuffing pieces of clothing down a girdle.

One night, Halleigh confessed on the phone to Malek. He wanted to stop by and just see her, and her refusal led to a huge argument. After Halleigh confessed,, his feelings for her didn't change. As a matter of fact, he was relieved. For some reason, he thought that Halleigh might have been ashamed of him, although he couldn't imagine why, or even worse, that she had another nigga that she didn't want to get busted with.

Malek loved her unconditionally and didn't look down on her because of how she had come up. He knew that her circumstance wasn't that uncommon. He truly admired and respected her. Even when his boys told him that he could do better than her, he begged to differ. Far from the prettiest girl in Flint, he thought she was the sweetest and

most innocent girl he had ever been with and liked how she carried herself. He also liked a girl with some meat on her bones.

Malek definitely wasn't going to hold Halleigh's being poor against her. Hell, Flint was a dead city. Most of the people who lived there were poor, not because they wanted to be, but because it was the only way to be. Flint had literally become a war zone.

With an 18% unemployment rate and the cost of living steadily rising, people from Flint developed a dog-eat-dog mentality. Everybody was out for self. It got so bad that people felt like if you were stupid enough to let somebody get you, then you deserved to get got. Crime swept over the city like a plague, and Flint became notorious as the murder capital.

Even the hustlers weren't getting it like they were supposed to, unless they had a good connect. Then it was a completely different story. A city where people were once proud to be called a "Flintstone," had quickly been transformed into a city where dreams were lost. Everybody who came up in Flint knew the game. With its ruthless atmosphere, the city produced some of the grimiest dudes, the sheistiest females, the most strategic hustlers, the baddest bitches, and the most talented authors. Whatever a person's game was, they were usually the best at it because survival depended on it.

In a city like that, how could Malek look down on Halleigh for being a part of the majority? Even his parents struggled every now and then. Most folks were only a paycheck away from being homeless, so when an unexpected financial situation occurred, it hit everybody's pockets hard.

Malek's parents weren't rich by any means, but they had a roof over their heads, food on the table, and clothes on their backs. His father even ended up working two jobs to make sure that his family didn't go without anything, and his mother's paycheck as a nurse's aide helped too. They stood on the hope that their son would make it in life. Having the number one draft pick for a son added extra motivation, of course. They knew that their hard work would eventually pay off. When it came to Halleigh, it could eventually pay off for her too.

Malek spotted Halleigh leaning up against his car. "You ready?"

Nervous energy filled her stomach when she saw him come out of the building with a gym bag hanging from his shoulder. A Colgate smile was the only way to describe the look that was on his face.

"Y'all sho' look good together," an older man commented as he passed by. "Y'all make a nice-looking young couple."

"Thank you, sir," Halleigh replied, feeling like this was a good omen. They already looked like a settled young married couple. She couldn't wait until the day she said, "I do." She turned to Malek. "Yes, I'm ready."

Malek reached over and opened the passenger door for her, and

she slid into the car. Then he drove off, blowing his horn for their victory at a couple of his teammates and fans.

Halleigh asked, "Babe, can you drop me off at home?"

Malek turned to her with a puzzled look on his face.

"I just want to freshen up a little bit. I've been sitting in there on those bleachers for the past couple of hours all sweated up and stuff." Though she'd never had sex before, she'd heard rumors about fishy-smelling chicks. Even though her hygiene was always up to par, she still wanted to make sure she was just right for her man.

Earlier, she wanted to pick up a throwaway douche for internal cleansing, but she decided against doing so. She didn't want her mother to find the box. As much as Sharina had deteriorated over the last couple of years due to her drug habit, Halleigh still gave her mother her respect.

Also, she didn't want to break her hymen. She'd heard that could happen from taking douches or using tampons. She wanted Malek to be the one to break her in. She wanted everything to be perfect.

Malek cruised the city streets until he finally made it to her house on the north end of town.

Before getting out of the car, Halleigh asked, "Are you sure your parents aren't coming home tonight?"

"Yeah, Moms won't be home until tomorrow morning. She's working the graveyard shift at the hospital tonight. My pops is on a business trip that he couldn't get out of, so we have the whole night to ourselves. I'll have you back home by the time my moms gets in. How about your mom?"

Halleigh shrugged. "You know her." Her mother was known to stay out all night and disappear at any given moment. She changed the subject. "You get the condoms? I don't want to get pregnant."

"Yeah, I got this. Don't worry, baby."

Suddenly Betty Wright's song, "Tonight is the Night," came on the radio.

Malek glanced at Halleigh. "Baby, they playing our song. Tonight I'ma make you a woman and I will be gentle with you."

Halleigh didn't reply. The seriousness of her choice hit her. She'd no longer be a little girl. In fact, she was just moments away from being a woman.

As she reached for the door, Malek stopped her.

"You sure you down for this? I love you, Hal, and I want you more than anything in the world, but it's still your choice."

Halleigh thought for a minute. "Even the NBA?"

"Huh?"

"Do you want me more than going to the NBA?"

Malek leaned over and kissed her softly on the lips. "Even the NBA."

Halleigh hesitated, before nodding. "Yes, baby, I'm sure that I'm down for this." She opened the car door.

"You want me to wait for you or what?"

Halleigh looked over to her man before stepping out of the car and going into her house. "No, baby, you've waited for me long enough. I'll be over in an hour."

Chapter Three

H alleigh sauntered into her house and headed straight to her bedroom. She looked around their two-bedroom bungalow but didn't see her mother. "Dang!" she groaned.

The house was so cluttered it looked like a cyclone had hit it. Their current housekeeping standards were lower than when her mother used to work sixty hours a week in the plant. Then, her mother kept a cleaner, more organized house than she did now. Seems like she would have had all the time in the world to clean now that she didn't hold down a job, but that would have been too much like right. Instead, the house looked like she had turned it upside down looking for a hit.

Halleigh had to admit that she kept her room on point. It was the rest of the house that was an embarrassment. No matter how much Halleigh cleaned, Sharina and her junkie friends would come in behind her hard work, filling ashtrays and leaving beer bottles and drug paraphernalia lying around the house.

At first, Halleigh would just continue to do the best she could to clean up again, but her mother would run through the house during the day while she was at school and tear everything back up, looking for any loose change to cop some more junk. After a while, Halleigh came to the conclusion that her efforts to keep the place looking even halfway decent were in vain, so she didn't even like to invite Malek over anymore. Tonight though, Halleigh decided to ignore the disarray and just get ready for her intimate evening with Malek.

She opened up her panty drawer to see what she would wear that night. Even though, as Betty Wright would tell it, tonight Malek was going to make her a woman, as a high schooler, she didn't have anything along the lines of lingerie. She figured that a cute bra-and-panty set would have to do the trick. Since black was sexy, she picked out a

black one her mother had boosted from Victoria's Secret. She also picked out a short denim Azzure skirt and a blue shirt that hung loosely off her shoulders.

Halleigh was relieved that her mother wasn't home. She figured once she was already gone, that her mother wouldn't miss her presence. She hurried into the bathroom to take a shower. The water felt good on her skin. As she thought about the way that she was about to give herself to Malek; her nipples hardened and tingled from the hot water pelting them. Though extremely nervous, she got excited just thinking about her man and how she was going to become a woman, Malek's woman. Would it hurt? She'd heard from Nikki that the first time hurt, and that sometimes the girl would even bleed. Her vagina contracted, just thinking of it. Would she enjoy sex as much as she enjoyed just spending time with Malek?

The funny thing was that her body had been craving and wanting to have sex with Malek for the past few months, but her mind always gave her hands the order to push him away, once he tried to go beyond her bra or panties. She would allow him to kiss her, but never go too far. No grinding, no dry sex, no fingering, no titty-fucking. None of that stuff high school kids made famous. He seemed to respect her all the more for setting this boundary.

In the past, Malek had told her he'd been with a lot of "technical virgins," who would let him finger them, or who would even do blowjobs on him, just so they could still claim they were virgins. But Halleigh . . . now that girl truly was a virgin. She'd never even masturbated.

Oddly enough, Halleigh wasn't raised to put a premium on being a virgin when she got married. In fact, before her mother got on the drugs, the only warning she used to give her daughter regarding sex was just to make sure her first time was special, that it should be with someone she loved. Sharina had also told Halleigh to come to her and inform her when she was ready to become sexually active so she could put her on birth control pills. Her mother used to be cool like that. In fact, before Sharina became addicted, she used to take relatively good care of Halleigh. Now, it seemed Halleigh had to take care of her.

Nowadays, the truth be known, Sharina didn't care what her daughter did. If Halleigh hadn't disciplined herself, she could really have run the streets wild. That's why it wouldn't be any problem to spend most of the night over at Malek's house tonight. Sometimes, she didn't like to think about how different her once-caring mother had become, but tonight she would use it to her advantage.

The good thing that came out of a bad situation was that after her mother got on drugs, Halleigh started wanting a better life for herself. She saw what happened when you gave up on life and didn't practice self-control. At seventeen, unlike many of the youths she'd grown up

with, she'd never smoked, drank, or tried any type of drugs. She truly didn't want to be another teen mother, like so many of the girls in her neighborhood, so she'd purposely abstained from having sex. It never swayed her that many of her friends had been having sex since they were twelve.

Although she did not want to escape from the steady massage of the running water, after rinsing the soap off her body Halleigh exited the shower,. Next, she sprayed on some of her mother's *Incidence* perfume that she had lifted from the Genesee Valley Shopping Center. Then she stood in front of the mirror and carefully shaved her na-na. She'd read about this in magazines and wanted to tame the hairs running wild between her young legs. She sprayed the scent on her neatly trimmed vagina and applied a sweet-scented body lotion from head to foot.

The sound of the door slamming made her jump. *Damn! Now I got to lie about where I'm going,* Halleigh thought. *I'll just tell her that I'm staying the night at Nikki's crib.* She exited the bathroom and proceeded to get dressed. "Hey, Ma!" she yelled as she dressed, but she got no response.

"Ma!" she yelled again. *I know she heard me.* She finished putting on her clothes, then made her way to her mother's room down the hallway from hers. When she opened the bedroom door, her mother was holding a soiled brown paper bag and frantically looking for a place to hide it.

"What are you doing, Ma?"

"Nothin', baby. Just go in your room." Her mother's eyes darted around the room. "Go back to your room." She quickly pushed Halleigh out of her bedroom and closed the door in her face.

Sharina seemed nervous, but Halleigh was too preoccupied to worry about her. Nowadays her mother always acted skittish, so she was used to her strange behavior of either being in a trying-to-get-high mode, or in an already high nod. There was no in-between. Tonight, though, she was glad that her mother had other things on her mind. *It shouldn't be too hard to get out of the house. She ain't paying me no mind, anyway.* Halleigh made her way back to her room.

A few minutes after Halleigh went into her room, closing the door behind her, a loud crash echoed throughout the house. It sounded as if it had come from the living room. She heard a male voice shout, "Bitch, you gon' try to steal from me?"

"No, Riq, it wasn't me," her mother pleaded. "You know I wouldn't take nothing from you, Riq."

The sound of her mother's screams alarmed Halleigh. She opened her bedroom door and followed the ruckus into the living room. "Ma!" she yelled, seeing two men beating on her mother. "Stop it!" Halleigh cried. "Ma!"

Startled, the two men paused from their beat-down on Sharina and looked in Halleigh's direction. They didn't even seem to consider that someone else could have been in the house. A twisted smile formed on one guy's face. He left his accomplice, who had Sharina pinned up against the wall by the throat, and approached Halleigh.

Sharina called out to the guy who was approaching her daughter. "Tariq," she said, calling the man by his full name, "leave her alone. That's my baby. She's only seventeen!"

"That's old enough to pay back your debt." Riq then turned to his partner. "Mad Dog, can you help?"

Sharina, palms held up in appeal, turned to look at Mad Dog, who was busy eyeballing the fresh meat that stood before them. Lust already shining in his eyes, he held his hand up in the "talk-to-the-hand" sign and shook his head, letting Riq know that he was down for it.

Riq began backing Halleigh up in a corner, his hands roaming all over her young body. He pressed his hardening manhood against her.

"Ma!" Halleigh cried.

Riq turned and looked over his shoulder at Sharina, while he continued to fondle her daughter's body. "What's it gon' be, Sharina? You can either give me back my package with interest, or you can let me fuck your daughter here and we'll call it even." Riq put his hands up Halleigh's short skirt.

Sharina thought about the monkey that was on her back. She had an entire package that would take her into ecstasy. There would be no way she would be able to feed her habit if she gave it back to him. *Halleigh is about to be a woman anyway. It's not like he gon' hurt her,* Sharina thought selfishly. *Besides, even if I do give the package back, their dicks are already hard. They probably gonna do her anyway.*

"Mama, please, make him stop!" Halleigh screamed, snapping Sharina out of her thoughts. "Maaaaaa!" she wailed, as the tears glistened and fell from her eyes.

"What's it gon' be, Rina?" Riq asked, rubbing himself.

"That's my baby, Riq." Sharina figured she'd give one last-ditch effort to save her daughter from the pending sexual attack.

"Okay. Then where's my shit?"

"Like I said, I don't—"

Before Sharina could even finish her sentence, Riq's partner punched her in her lying mouth, spilling blood and loosening teeth.

Sharina held up her hands to block the oncoming blows, but it was useless. She began to see stars, and her head began to pound and throb. She knew if she didn't do something quick, one of those blows would be fatal. One of her eyes had already swollen shut and was filled with blood. With her other eye, when she didn't see a fist coming to-

ward it, she saw her daughter standing in complete fear of a rampaging Riq. At that moment, she knew what she had to do.

"Okay, okay! Wait!" Sharina held up her hand. "I don't have your money, but"—she saw the same fist that had been beating her mercilessly making its way toward her again—"but you can have her instead," she quickly shouted, halting the fist before it landed on her flesh.

Riq looked from Sharina to her daughter, who was standing, there all dressed, up as if she knew tonight she would have a debt to pay for her mother. Halleigh looked at her mother in shock. She couldn't believe the words that had just come out of her mouth. No! She had to be hearing things. No!

When Sharina took one last look at her daughter with apologetic eyes, and then put her head down so as not to witness the rape of her own child, Halleigh knew she'd heard right. Her instincts told her to do one thing—run like hell!

She took off for the door, but Riq caught her and tackled her to the hard floor. "Uh-uh, sweetness. Where you think you going?" He forced his hands up her skirt.

Halleigh could feel his fingers invading her space. Her jaws tightened as she cringed in pain. "Ma!" Halleigh cried out in anguish as she fought back by beating Riq on his back. That was all she could do, with the weight of his body pinning her to the ground.

"Shut up!" Riq ordered as he brought his open hand down across her face. She clawed and kicked, but when his accomplice came and helped him hold her down, she was overpowered and didn't have a chance in the world to escape their clutches.

They were about to take, in an instant, what she'd made Malek wait for for years. Her virginity was what had made her different from the other girls to him. It was what made her special. Moreover, it was what had made their relationship valuable to both of them. She just couldn't let them take what wasn't theirs. She just couldn't.

Halleigh took a deep breath and tried with all of her might to loosen herself from the grip of her attacker. The next thing she knew, Mad Dog spread and held her legs apart, while Riq pinned her hands behind her head. With one hard shove, Riq penetrated her, plowing into her young body as though she were a seasoned hooker. Once inside her narrow canal, the drug dealer took long, hard strokes.

Halleigh must have blacked out because, when she came to, suddenly she saw herself drifting near the top of the ceiling, looking down on the two men going at her body like two rapacious vultures picking over a dead carcass. Halleigh could have sworn she was having an out-of-body experience, but she was in such pain. Although she knew it was herself lying there, she hurt so badly, she became this disembod-

ied figure, floating above the men's sexual assault, to be able to endure it.

Dispassionately, she looked down from the ceiling and watched Riq, pants wiggled down below his hips, hump up and down, up and down, like a disjointed caterpillar.

"Oooh, buddy," he gasped between moans, "this shit is tight. I mean, damn, it's good. This young girl know she got some good-ass pussy."

Still holding Halleigh's legs apart, Mad Dog licked his lips salaciously. "Oooh, hurry up, man, so I can get some of that sweet young stuff."

Finally, Riq shuddered and let out a loud groan of pleasure. "Owwww!" He collapsed on top of Halleigh and heaved deep breaths.

Mad Dawg pulled out his erected manhood. "Dawg, get the fuck up so I can get mines."

Pushing his penis back into his pants, Tariq stood up. "Eee-ooo-wee! That cherry was in there so tight. I'm already sore. But, man, that was the best cherry I ever busted." He looked down at the blood between Halleigh's legs. Her eyes were glazed. She appeared to be semiconscious at this point. He scratched his head in disbelief. "I didn't think they made no virgins over ten around here no more."

Both he and Mad Dog shared a laugh.

"Well, I guess I'll just help break her in some more." Mad Dog rushed in and climbed on top of Halleigh, and she passed out again.

When she came to, he had turned her over and was sodomizing her. When he got through, Riq took another turn, all of this while Sharina had snuck off to the bedroom to get high.

Sharina had never thought her habit would push her to do something so horrible as to trade her very own flesh and blood for a fix. It was so awful. She couldn't bear to watch them take her daughter's innocence. That's when she went into her room, removed the package from her closet, and wrapped a leather belt around her arm, ignoring Halleigh's screams. She hurriedly put the heroin into a tablespoon and lit a flame to it, causing the contents to melt down. She filled the syringe and located a large vein.

When she felt the drug go into her system, she knew that her decision was well worth it. *Shit, Halleigh will be all right. Truth be told, she was probably already fucking anyway.*

Sharina didn't even realize how much damage she had just caused. The last thing she heard before drifting into a nod was the sound of Halleigh calling her name over and over again as the two men brutally raped her.

Chapter Four

Barefoot Halleigh, crying her young eyes out, stumbled aimlessly down the street. In throbbing pain, she gripped her hand over her stomach. She felt like her coochie and her ass were both going to fall out and hit the ground. The streets were deserted, and she'd never felt more alone in her life. Feeling discombobulated, she could hardly see because she was so blinded by her own tears.

"I can't believe this just happened to me," she muttered to herself. *This has to be a nightmare,* she tried to convince herself, but the pain that she clearly felt proved otherwise. This couldn't be happening to Halleigh. This wasn't the night's plan. She was supposed to be wrapped up in Malek's arms, but then the sound of her feet scraping the glass-splattered, needle-scattered sidewalk of the empty street would bring her back to reality. This was really happening, and it was happening to her.

Her innocence had been viciously stripped from her at the expense of her mother's drug habit. Her womanhood ached and bled under her skirt as she headed towards Malek's house. She didn't know where else to go. He was the only one that she could ever confide in; the only one who ever made her feel loved and protected. She had to get to him.

Once upon a time it was her mother who she felt she could confide in, who could protect her, but that was a thing of the past. She couldn't believe that her mother had just tricked her out. As badly as that betrayal cut her to the bone and had her body wracked with pain, her heart ached the most. Who could a girl trust if she couldn't trust her own mother?

She'd never felt more desolate in her life, walking through the only city she'd known as home. Flint's streets were so cold, in more ways than one, and the streets were pitch-black, because the city's hoodlums had busted out the streetlights.

As the thoughts of those two grown men taking turns with her body would revisit Halleigh's mind, she would mumble, "No, no, no," over and over as she shook her head. She felt so defiled, so humiliated, so cheated. She kept thinking about what she and Malek could have had tonight, if only the rape hadn't happened. Those men could have taken anything in the house, the TV, the DVD, the CD player, the only things of value they had left that her mother hadn't already hocked. Those were material items that could have easily been replaced. Instead they chose to take something that was irreplaceable, something Halleigh could never get back.

What she and Malek would have had would have been so innocent,

so pure, so unlike what she'd experienced with those two animals who she felt had pissed in and on her. They not only robbed her of her innocence, but in so doing, they had stolen her right to choose. The two men had taken turns, both turning deaf ears to her pleas and ignoring her tears of outrage over being violated.

They didn't care that she had saved herself all these years for the man she loved. All they wanted was to fulfill their own lustful desires. To think she'd waited seventeen years for it to all wind up like this. Now she was just another ghetto statistic.

Suddenly a fine drizzle began to fall and quickly turned into large raindrops, which blended into Halleigh's tears. Oblivious to the rain swirling around her, Halleigh pushed forward with one destination in mind.

As soon as she approached Malek's small, Cape Cod-style house, she began to cry even harder. When she made it to his doorstep, she stood still for a moment before knocking. What should she say? What would she do? Would he even believe her? She weighed her options. Should she just go back home and pretend this whole thing never happened and try to just move on, or should she stay? What if Malek tried to make her call the police and tell them what happened? What would happen to her mother? Would they take her to jail too for allowing it to happen? Then where would that leave Halleigh? Where would she go, to a foster home for someone to turn around and abuse her again? What if she went back home and Riq and Mad Dog were still waiting to repeat the entire act all over again?

Absently, Halleigh shook her head. She was too afraid Tariq and Mad Dog might come back, and she never wanted to experience that again. She felt both embarrassed and abandoned as she contemplated knocking on her boyfriend's door. *Will he look down on me for this?* she thought as she stood there, drenched and shivering from the cold rain that fell from the black sky.

Finally, she made up her mind. Malek was all she had. She knew deep in her heart that he would be there for her. He had never looked down on her, so why would he start now? She knocked on the door and crossed her arms tightly around her stomach, her head down.

Seconds later, Malek opened the door, and the sounds of Usher lightly played in the background. Halleigh's knees buckled, and she fell into his arms.

Right away, he knew there was something wrong. Halleigh was crying, her hair was soaking wet, and her shirt was torn. He gently grabbed her by the shoulders and pulled her inside, closing the door behind them. "What's wrong, baby?" He held her against his chest. "Talk to me, Hal."

She couldn't speak. She only cried.

Malek pulled her away from him, and his heart nearly dropped when she looked him in the eyes.

They were filled with humiliation, anguish, and pain. Her tears were flowing, and he could feel her body trembling. "Hal, what's wrong?" he asked again.

"They raped me, Malek," she said in a low voice in between her cries, a tremor rippling through her body.

"Whaaaat?" Malek stuttered. He wasn't sure he'd heard her right.

"They raped me." She embraced him and buried her head in his chest.

"Who? What? I mean . . ." Malek's words trailed off. He couldn't believe what he was hearing. "What happened, Halleigh? Who did this to you?"

Halleigh's mouth opened, but no words came out.

For a minute, Malek didn't realize that he was shaking his girlfriend. He was angry and seemed like he was going to lose his temper. Then he pulled himself into check and just shook his head. He wrapped his arms around her and hugged her tightly, never wanting to let her go. He was confused and angry at the same time. He was at a loss for words and didn't know what to say to her. His fist clenched tightly as he thought about someone hurting her. Her heartbeat began to pick up as he rocked her back and forth in his arms.

Finally he released her. "Who touched you, Halleigh?" he questioned again, but all Halleigh did was cry. "Who?" he shouted, frustrated with not knowing who had done this to his girl. He grabbed her by the shoulders and peered into her eyes.

Halleigh was so distraught, she just couldn't answer him. Her hysterical cries muffled her speech.

"Come on." Malek guided her over to the couch and sat her down to console her.

After finally getting her calmed down, Halleigh was able to tell Malek everything that had gone down back at her house. It brought tears to his eyes. He continued to hug her for the longest time.

After a while, he broke his embrace then went to the bathroom and ran a tub of hot water. He helped his girlfriend into the bathroom and aided her in easing off her bloody skirt and underwear. Slowly, he helped her ease down into the tub. Fresh tears filled his eyes when he saw the water between Halleigh's legs and behind her turn red with her blood. He could see the bruises on her back and around her neck, but they weren't open wounds. He knew, without Halleigh saying a word, that she was bleeding vaginally and from her anus. He knew this wasn't menstrual blood. Once again, Malek just shook his head as tears fell, tears of anger. He wanted to take somebody's head off, but first he knew he had to tend to a broken and bruised Halleigh.

Although they had planned to use a condom, they had also planned to have sex at the safest time in her cycle. She'd just had her period the weekend before. Plus, he'd never doubted that Halleigh had been a virgin before these animals took what rightfully should have been hers to give to whoever she chose.

What kind of men would take turns raping a young girl? he wondered. Malek had never had to force any girl to have sex with him. As horny as Halleigh used to get him when they kissed, he'd never tried to take advantage of her against her will. Tonight, when his girl had finally been willing to have sex with him, the only way he would've wanted it, these animals seemed like they'd gotten off on forcing their way on her.

He gently sponged Halleigh's body and spoke in a low, hushed tone. "You're safe now, baby. I'm here. You're safe."

Halleigh could smell Malek's cologne, but it wasn't strong enough to cover the smell that had seemed to dwell in her nostrils. She couldn't stand the smell, the smell of the men's nasty sperm mixed with her blood. It smelled worse than when she was on her cycle. She started crying all over again.

"Shhhh. Don't cry, baby. Everything's gonna be all right."

Even though it was the first time Malek had ever seen Halleigh naked, he didn't think of anything sensual. In fact, sex was the last thing on his mind. He just wanted to soothe her and be there for her.

Halleigh had no shame in her nudeness. It almost seemed like a bad dream to her as she kept visualizing herself being raped.

Malek slowly rubbed his hands through her hair while she sat in the tub. He wanted to call the police, but in Flint the police were just as crooked as the criminals they chased down. Contacting them would only bring doom to themselves.

The same thoughts that had crossed Halleigh's mind while she stood on the porch contemplating her next move crossed his mind too. What if they took her mother to jail? Then where would that leave Halleigh? Where would that leave him and her? At this point, Malek was just ready to take Halleigh as far away from Flint as possible and take care of her.

"Hal, I swear I'm going to get you away from all of this. I'm going to enter the draft, and you won't have to worry about anything. I won't let anything like this happen to you again," Malek said with confidence.

Halleigh looked up into his sincere eyes. "You promise?"

He wiped a streaming tear from her cheek. "I promise."

After the bath, he wrapped her in a large bath towel. He found one of his T-shirts for her to put on. "Here, put this on then come on and

lay down," he said, pulling back the spread on his twin bed. "You need to sleep."

Still dazed, Halleigh lumbered into the bed. They didn't speak. They just lay in each other's arms, wanting to shut out the world. They lay on top of the bed like that for hours, and he could feel her pain as he held her in his arms.

Malek held Halleigh all through the night and watched her as she cried herself to sleep. He himself fell asleep with her spooned in his arms and didn't wake up until he heard a familiar voice screaming at him.

"Malek Lamont Johnson, what in the name of God is going on here?"

Malek sat up with a startled look on his face. It was early morning already, and his mother was off work and standing over his bed, a look of shock and disgust on her face. She had come in from work and found a half-naked girl and her son laid up. The fact that Halleigh wore a T-shirt didn't mean anything, because her bare breasts and nipples protruded beneath the shirt.

"Boy, I know you ain't got some li'l heifer laid up in my house!" She put both of her hands on her hips. "I know you must be out of your mind. What do you think your father is going to say about this?"

When she recognized the girl as Halleigh, she became even more upset. She'd never cared for Halleigh too much. Not that they were rolling in dough or anything, but she'd heard about Halleigh's upbringing and about her mother's habit and illegal career of boosting. She always thought that Halleigh just wanted Malek because of his potential NBA future. Like any mother, she was just being protective of her only child.

Malek was completely taken off guard. Before he could even respond, his mother began yelling again, forcing Halleigh to rustle out of her sleep.

"This is a house of God. I will not allow you to disrespect me up in here." Mrs. Johnson then focused her attention on Halleigh. "And you, you li'l fast wench, up in here half-naked, trying to trap my baby, get out!"

"Momma, hold up. It's not what it looked like. Calm down for a sec." Malek pleaded as his mother hollered, quoting Bible scriptures at the top of her lungs.

Halleigh was so embarrassed, so lost, and so confused. Even though she and Malek hadn't done anything sexually, she knew it didn't look good. While Malek was trying to calm his mother down, she just sat there, not knowing what to say.

Mrs. Johnson pointed her finger in Halleigh's face. "Get the hell out!"

"I'm so sorry, Mrs. Johnson."

Mrs. Johnson wasn't trying to hear anything coming out of her mouth.

Halleigh got up, and with nothing on but the T-shirt, hurried out of the house while Malek and his mother argued.

Malek tried to run after her, but his mother blocked his path. As bad as he wanted to snatch his mother up and push her out of the way, he didn't.

Oh my God, where am I going to go? Halleigh thought as she stood outside on Malek's porch and the reality sunk in further. She was too afraid to return to her mother's home. The truth of the matter was, she never wanted to return to her mother's house again. Sharina had gone too far this time. Malek was the only other person she had, so she just stood there, not knowing which way to go.

After a moment, she began walking. Just as she reached the sidewalk, Malek came darting out of the house running after her.

"Halleigh, Halleigh! Wait!" he said, clutching his Air Jordan shoes and running toward her. They both stood face to face with rain pouring down on them. "I love you, Halleigh. Just wait, let me calm my moms down. Let me tell her. Let me explain to her what happened."

"Malek, it's okay," Halleigh said, hopelessness filling her heart.

Just before Malek could respond, his mother stood in the doorway and yelled, "Malek, get back in here!"

He looked at his mother and then back at Halleigh. He didn't want to disobey his mother, but at the same time, he couldn't leave Halleigh. She needed him.

Then his mother went from quoting Bible scriptures to cursing. "Malek, get yo ass in here now!"

Malek rarely heard his mother curse, so he knew she was upset. He froze up, looking back and forth from his mother to his girl.

Halleigh looked into his eyes. "Go on, Malek. I'll be okay." Then she kissed him on his lips and walked away. *There's nothing you can do for me anyway.*

Malek just stood there and watched Halleigh walk away. Hearing his mother yell his name again brought him out of his daze. Angrily, he trekked back to the front door and stood in front of his mother. "Ma, I can't leave her out here like this. I can't," he said almost in a whisper.

"You're going to pick some little ghetto girl to be disobedient over your own mother's word? Not even my word, but God's words. The Book of Proverbs says—"

"Ma, I don't care about the Book of Proverbs. I care about Halleigh."

Mrs. Johnson crossed her arms tightly and tapped her foot against

the ground. "Okay, you wanna go running after some hoodrat? After all me and your daddy has done for you? After all we've sacrificed? Fine, go! As a matter of fact, you get out! You can go ahead with her. I work at all hours of the night and your father works two jobs trying to keep a roof over your head, and you got the audacity to even consider going against me! Get out!"

In a flurry of frenetic motion, his mother reached inside and grabbed his varsity jacket and hat and hurled them at him. With that, she slammed the door in his face, leaving Malek staring at the steel screen door.

She knew her boy. She knew he wouldn't turn on everything his parents had done for him to go chasing after some panties. She sat waiting on the living room couch, just knowing her son would come walking back through that door at any second.

For a moment, Malek stood on the other side of the door like an ice statue. It hurt his heart to go against his mother's wishes, but he knew that Halleigh needed him more than ever. If his mother knew why Halleigh needed him she would support him. He wanted to go back inside and make one last effort to explain to his mother what was going on. When he finally willed himself to move, it was in the direction of Halleigh.

All those "suicides" his coach made him do were paying off now as he sprinted to catch up with Halleigh. Finally catching up with her, he ran up behind her, his sprints now long trots. "Halleigh! Halleigh!"

She turned around just in time to see her man approaching. "Oh, Malek," she said, touching his face. She was so glad and relieved to see him. "Thank you for letting me stay with you last night," she said. "I didn't mean to drag you into all of this." Her voice began to crack. "I just didn't have anywhere else to go."

"Everything is going to be all right." He wrapped his leather varsity coat around her shoulders. "Don't worry about it. I'm always here for you."

Hearing Malek's words and feeling his arms around her made her believe that everything, in fact, would be all right, but unfortunately it wouldn't be.

Chapter Five

It was around five-thirty AM, still pitch-black outside, and Malek and Halleigh trudged down the streets, wondering where they were going to crash. Malek knew that he could go back home if he wanted to, but he couldn't go and take Halleigh with him. Since he wasn't going to leave her hanging like that either, he decided to stay with her.

Halleigh definitely didn't want to go back to her mother's home. She'd rather sleep in the street or at a homeless shelter. What a joke! Her mother was no longer a parent who was there to guide and protect her as a young woman. Her mother had morphed into this walking-dead monster, who now saw Halleigh as a commodity she could exchange for her drugs. Halleigh sensed that if she went back home, the rape that had happened the night before was only a harbinger of what was to come at her mother's hands. Tariq and Mad Dog would only be the beginning of one long train of men her mother would bring in to use her body so that she could get her drugs for free. Hell no! Halleigh had to face the cold truth. Sharina's god wasn't the same god that Mrs. Johnson had been speaking of. Sharina's god was the heroin she shot in her veins. What she had done to Halleigh was so foul, that her daughter could never forgive her for it. As the couple made their way down the street, Malek thought about all his options as to where he and Halleigh could go. He thought about all the people who had been jocking him at school, but came up with nothing. There was no true friend whose house they could crash at, no teacher and no relative. He had no money, didn't have the keys to his car, and no plan. What were they going to do?

It was pouring rain and nearly thirty degrees outside. The two began shivering. The swirling rain lashed at both of their bodies, drenching them, as lightning flashed across the sky, the loud thunder frightening them.

Malek knew that they needed shelter or they would freeze to death. If only they had just a few dollars, they could surely find a cheap motel to crash at. They walked past the twenty-four-hour corner store on the corner of Clio Road. Malek suddenly got an idea of just how they could get money. Malek ran his plan by her. He stuck the small beer bottle under his shirt, pretending it was a gun.

Although Halleigh didn't agree that robbing the corner store was a good idea, she didn't have a better one. Here she was walking around half-naked. It would be daylight soon. They needed a place to stay. "Malek, you don't have to do this," she said.

"I'm just going to take enough for a hotel room for us, that's all. I

promise. It'll be quick and easy." He kissed her on the cheek and went into the store with his hat pulled low over his eyes.

"Be careful," Halleigh whispered as Malek made his way to the door. She watched through the store's glass windows while she stood in the nearby alley. She wanted to stop Malek, but he was too determined to make sure they would be okay. Besides, what other options did they have, to go back and ask his mother to loan them some money for a hotel room? Yeah, right!

She watched as Malek slowly walked up in the empty store, an Asian man standing behind the counter, his hands in his hoody. Moments later, the Asian man put both of his hands in the air, a terrified look on his face. Halleigh knew that Malek had gone through with it.

Her heart began to pound, and her limbs shook as she watched Malek attempt to rob the owner with a beer bottle. She got a bad feeling in the pit of her stomach. A feeling that told her that Malek should just get the hell out of there right now—whether he had the money or not. "Just leave, Malek, please. Just leave," she whispered to herself as she watched the scene unfold.

Malek's hand began to shake. Obviously, he was nervous. Suddenly she saw both men turn their heads toward the back of the store as if they'd heard a startling noise or something. She turned her attention toward the direction both Malek and the Asian man were looking, and saw another store clerk come from out back. The Asian man behind the counter reached under and pulled out a chrome handgun and pointed it toward Malek's head. By the time he turned back around, he was staring at the barrel of a gun.

Terrified, Halleigh barreled toward the store. Upon entering the bell hanging over the door rang.

Malek looked over at Halleigh, and just then a shot rang out as he tried to put his hands up to signal Halleigh to get out of the store. Boom!

A single bullet went through Malek's head in one side and out the other. That was the last thing Halleigh saw before she saw his lifeless body drop to the ground.

"No!" Halleigh exclaimed, snapping back to reality from the horrible vision that had just played out in her head. She took a shuddering breath.

Malek stood in front of her, staring at her. He had the bottle tucked in his hoody. "What? What's wrong? It doesn't look like a real burner?" He looked down at the bottle. "You don't think I can pull this thing off with it?"

"Malek, I have a bad feeling about this one. Don't do it!" Halleigh held on to his arm, trying to persuade him not to go through with it. She kept visualizing her brief daydream of him being shot and didn't

want it to become a reality. Malek reconsidered the act he was about to commit. He thought about his NBA career for a moment, and how getting caught doing something like this could ruin his professional basketball career before it ever even took off. A Maurice Clarett he didn't want to be.

Every time he looked at Halleigh, she gave him the adrenaline he needed to do it. He'd promised her that he would take care of her, and now was the time for him to make good on his word. "Don't worry." He kissed her on the cheek and pulled away from her.

He pulled his hat low over his eyes as he went into the convenience store. He kept looking over his shoulder at the camera monitor lodged in the ceiling's right-hand corner.

Feeling helpless, Halleigh looked on through the glass windows of the store as the scenario unfolded. Her heart began to pound, and her limbs shook as she watched Malek attempt to rob the storeowner with a beer bottle.

"Just leave, Malek, please, just leave," she whispered to herself as she watched the scene unfold. She watched as Malek's hand began to shake, obviously he was nervous. Moments later she saw the Asian man empty the cash register and hand Malek the money from the drawer.

"Come on. Come on. Get out of there," she whispered urgently as if Malek could hear her. No sooner had she finished her sentence, a police car pulled up. Halleigh didn't know what to do. She acted on her first impulse.

"Help! Help, please," she screamed while running toward the officer, trying to divert his attention. "A man just attacked and robbed me in the alley. He stole my purse!"

The officer got out of the car with both of his hands in front of him, trying to calm Halleigh down. "Hold on, ma'am. Calm down. Where did he go?"

"That way!" She pointed in the opposite direction of the store. She peeked over at the store at the same time that Malek was coming out with a handful of money.

Suddenly a loud shotgun blast erupted, followed by the sound of shattered glass. The Asian man had reached for his weapon while Malek was escaping, the blast from the shotgun just missing Malek's head. Malek quickly ran toward Halleigh, not realizing she was talking to a cop.

Hearing the ruckus, the cop quickly ducked down and reached for his pistol. He saw Malek running with money in his hand and saw the Asian man running toward the front door with his weapon still in hand. He put two and two together—a young black man running out of a store with money in his hand and a storeowner brandishing a gun

in hot pursuit. In his mind, Malek was already guilty. The officer pointed his service revolver to Malek's face. "Freeze, muthafucka! Put your hands where I can see them! Now!"

Malek halted. For a moment, he looked as stunned as a rabbit caught in a snare. Finally, realizing he could get shot in the back, or worse, shot numerous times by the trigger-happy cop, he put up his hands in surrender. He instantly looked over at Halleigh, who stood there with her hand over her mouth in an attempt to trap the wailing that wanted to escape her lips. Her boyfriend had almost been shot dead right before her eyes. Malek let out a groan of regret for his dumb actions.

"Get outta here, miss!" the cop yelled to Halleigh, his gun pointed at Malek. "Back up!"

Halleigh didn't obey the officer's command.

"Ma'am, is this the man who attacked and robbed you?"

She just shook her head slowly. "No."

"Then go. Get out of here before you get hurt."

Halleigh looked into Malek's eyes and began to cry. Malek moved his eyes quickly, signaling her to go.

Halleigh didn't want to go, but she knew she couldn't do anything if she got arrested with him.

With his gun still aimed at Malek, the cop called for backup and then inched over to Malek. Once he reached Malek, he grabbed him and spun him around, hurtling Malek onto the ground, causing his head to hit the pavement forcefully. "You're under arrest," the police officer informed him. "You have the right to remain silent. Anything you say can and will be used against you in a court of law. You have the right to—"

"Noo, what's happening?" Halleigh put both of her hands on her mouth as she cried out frantically. In a matter of hours she had gone from one bad nightmare to another.

Malek hissed at Halleigh, "Go! Get outta here!"

With his hands cuffed behind his back, he kept motioning for her to get away from the crime scene by jerking his head, which in turn, made his entire body jerk.

This gave the officer grounds to say that Malek was resisting arrest. Suddenly the cop began to bludgeon Malek with his club to settle him down.

Guilt overcame Halleigh as she ran away, looking over her shoulder to see the cop beat Malek the way her mother had been beaten. She knew she was the cause of all of this. She should have just left Malek out of it, but it was too late. Now he was in far too deep.

Chapter Six

"Wait!" Halleigh screamed out as she ran out from the alley she had run down and hid in. Her calls went unheard. The police car drove away with Malek handcuffed in the back seat and damn near unconscious.

"Malek!" she called out once more at the top of her lungs. She didn't know if Malek heard her over the sirens or if he just felt her presence, but he slowly turned back and stared at her with haunting eyes. She watched the taillights turn the corner, her heart beating like a drum in her ear. She had no clue what to do. *They are probably taking him downtown,* she thought fearfully. She couldn't believe this was happening.

In spite of the hot bath, her body still ached as a result of being her mother's tradeoff. Her heart hurt from the thought of Malek being removed from her life by the law. Her mind hurt as she tried to think of a way to deal with the situation. The only thing that she could think of doing was contacting Malek's mother. The fear of telling Mrs. Johnson that her son was in jail was enough to make Halleigh tremble.

At last, the rain slowed and settled back into a soft drizzle. She was relieved she wasn't out in the downpour as they had been earlier. She was still wearing Malek's jacket, but she was soaking wet from her head to her bare feet. Totally oblivious to how she looked though, she headed toward Malek's house.

When she arrived she could see Mrs. Johnson inside through the living room picture window. Mrs. Johnson's head was in her hands as she sat on the couch, and a wine glass sat on the table in front of her. Halleigh could tell that she was worried about her son. Filled with trepidation, Halleigh reluctantly marched up the sidewalk that led to Malek's house. Her hands felt like they weighed a ton as she reached up and knocked on the door. Halleigh's breaths became hollow. She wanted to leave the doorstep, just as she had contemplated the night before.

Without warning, the door opened and Mrs. Johnson saw Halleigh standing there. His mother's cheeks were ashy from the many tears that had dried up on her face.

The sight of Halleigh standing in front of her brought fresh tears to Mrs. Johnson's eyes. "Where is my son?" she asked.

Halleigh couldn't speak. The cat had her tongue. She was in shock and was beginning to feel like Mrs. Johnson had been right all along, that she was indeed bad news for Malek.

"Halleigh, where is my son?" Mrs. Johnson asked, raising her voice a bit.

"He-he was arrested, Mrs. Johnson," she finally responded.

Mrs. Johnson's heart dropped to her stomach when the words left Halleigh's mouth. *Not my baby,* she thought as tears came to her eyes. "Arrested? Oh, Lord." Mrs. Johnson put her hand over her chest.

"They took him," Halleigh cried, staring in the eyes of the woman who had brought her only love into the world.

"Arrested?" Mrs. Johnson repeated. She looked at Halleigh, who had tears running down her face. Instead of feeling sorry for her, she felt angry. "I knew that you were bad news from the moment I laid eyes on you."

Mrs. Johnson's words cut like a knife, but Halleigh had to agree with Malek's mother's perception of her.

Mrs. Johnson began to pace back and forth. "I need to call his father." She grabbed her cell phone. "No, wait, I need to get my baby," she mumbled frantically as she grabbed her purse and keys. "I need to get my baby!" she screamed, just imagining what those Flint cops might be doing to her son.

Halleigh followed Mrs. Johnson to the car. As Mrs. Johnson went to the driver's side, Halleigh waited at the passenger side with her hand on the doorknob. Mrs. Johnson looked at her like she was crazy. "Where do you think you're going?"

"Mrs. Johnson, please . . . I love him," Halleigh pleaded. "I need to go see about him. Please, Mrs. Johnson. After this, you never have to lay eyes on me again, but please . . . I just need to know that he's okay." Halleigh stood there biting down on her bottom lip in anticipation, her eyes begging Mrs. Johnson to just this once put her feeling for her aside.

"Listen to me, Halleigh. I don't even know what took place to land my son in jail, but my spirit of discernment tells me that you have everything to do with it. If I've said it before, I'll say it again—you are not good enough for my son. Malek has a future, and I am going to make sure that you're not a part of it." She paused then held her hand to her chest, as if overcome by so much emotion she couldn't go on. Finally she growled through clenched teeth, "Stay away from him and this house before I hurt you, little girl." The look in Mrs. Johnson's eyes showed that her threat was not an idle one.

All of a sudden, Mrs. Johnson stormed around the car to the passenger side. Halleigh backed away from the car while putting her arms up, not knowing what this crazed woman was going to do to her.

"Give me back my son's jacket." With that, Mrs. Johnson snatched the jacket off Halleigh's back, pushed past her, and went and climbed into her vehicle. She backed out of the driveway, wheels squealing.

"Mrs. Johnson, please!" Halleigh begged as she ran after the car and pounded on the hood desperately. All she wanted to do was get to Malek, but Mrs. Johnson ignored her cries and sped away, leaving Halleigh behind.

"What's your name?" Officer Cornwell asked with a smug expression on his face. *These street thugs coming in here with their diamond necklaces and their fancy cars. Cocky sons of bitches, I hope we lock all of their drug-dealing asses up.* He watched Malek remove all of the personal items from his pockets. He tilted his head from left to right, getting a better look at Malek. *He looks familiar. He must be a repeat offender.*

Malek didn't respond to the officer. He'd barely heard a word that he had said. He couldn't stop thinking about Halleigh. *Where is she? I hope she's all right,* he thought. *I should've never taken her home after the game. But how was I to know? I mean, I knew that her moms was fiended out, but I never thought she would stoop so low as to turn her daughter over as payment to get high.* Even though he himself was in a bad position, Malek could only think about helping his Halleigh. He loved her that much. Her well-being came before his own.

"Name?" the white officer repeated loudly, pounding the top of the table to get the young kid's attention.

Malek looked up at the officer. "Malek Johnson."

"Malek Johnson?" It was at that moment that Officer Cornwell realized where he had seen the boy's face before. Malek Johnson was Flint Central's starting shooting guard and the biggest thing to hit basketball since LeBron James. *What the hell is he doing here?* he thought to himself.

After realizing that Malek wasn't the average stick-up kid, he figured he could get some money for allowing the reporters to get photographs of Malek while he was locked up. *This will be a helluva story,* Cornwell thought greedily to himself. He hurriedly processed him into the system and then handed him off to another officer so he could get busy. He picked up the phone and dialed the number to the local news stations. If Malek hadn't been well-known before, now he was about to be.

Chapter Seven

Mrs. Johnson parked her car in an illegal zone and hopped out as she ran into the police station as fast as she could. As soon as she slammed her door shut, her cell phone rang. "Hello?" she answered in a frantic tone.

Alex Wilson, Malek's agent, screamed into the phone, "Denise, what the hell is going on?"

"Alex, I can't talk to you right now. I'm busy."

"Not busy doing what you're supposed to be doing. All I asked you to do is make sure Malek graduates and keeps a clean image until the draft. He's out here knocking over fucking convenience stores?"

"How do you know what's going on?" she commented in confusion. "I'm in front of the police station now, but I don't even know exactly what's going on yet."

"Then obviously you haven't watched the early morning news, seven o'clock edition," Alex told her. "Malek is the golden boy right now. Someone made a phone call and tipped off the news stations. Those vultures are probably on their way down to the station right now."

"Oh, no." Mrs. Johnson put her hand over her forehead. "Is this going to affect his chances of getting into the league?"

"If those news cameras get to Malek, there will be no league for him. They don't take too kindly to players coming out of high school with tarnished images. If the press gets the facts, Malek will be finished before he starts."

Mrs. Johnson hung up the phone and rushed into the police station. "I need to see my son," she stated to the white officer, whose badge identified him as Officer Cornwell. She had no idea that he was the officer who had checked Malek in and sold him out to the press.

"What's his name, ma'am?" he asked, feigning ignorance.

"Malek, uh, Malek Johnson," she whispered, looking around nervously for prying ears.

"Right this way." Officer Cornwell led her toward the visitors' room. He knew that Malek wasn't supposed to have any visitors, but he figured that the scene would make for some good pictures for the press and a big payday for him.

He brought Malek out in handcuffs and sat him in the chair in front of his mother. "You've got fifteen minutes, ma'am," Officer Cornwell told Mrs. Johnson.

She nodded her head in acknowledgment, and he left the room. "Malek, son, baby," she cried as she placed his face in her hands and

observed his bruises from the beating he had taken from the arresting officer.

The beating itself had looked more brutal than it actually was. Although right after he was handcuffed and thrown into the back of the squad car Malek felt as if he was about to go unconscious, most of that feeling derived from the fact that he was in shock that everything was going down.

"You all right?" Mrs. Johnson caressed his bruises and the slight knot on his head. "What happened? Why have they arrested you? What did you do?" The questions poured out of Mrs. Johnson's mouth one after the other.

"Yeah, Ma, I'm fine," he told her, pulling back his face from her hands. He then proceeded to tell her about the prior night's events that led to his arrest.

Mrs. Johnson stared at her son for a minute before taking her purse and letting him have one upside the head. "What the hell were you thinking, boy?" Malek flinched, but Mrs. Johnson whacked him one more time with her purse. "Do you know what this is going to do to your father? All of this for some whore who probably would have given it up to them, just like her mother, for a crack rock?"

Malek ignored his mother's insults against Halleigh. That was nothing new, and he had learned not to speak on it, not wanting to give his mother even more ammunition to spit, but he was concerned about what she'd said about his father. Malek imagined how his father would feel knowing that the son he had sacrificed so much for and raised to be a good man was now sitting in jail. "Does Dad know?"

"No, he doesn't know. I decided to wait and find out what was going on. It would break his heart . . ." Mrs. Johnson's words trailed off and tears trailed down her face.

"Please don't tell Dad about this, Ma. Everything is going to be all right. I'll be out before you know it."

"Well, not soon enough. Not before the whole world knows it."

Malek thought for a second. "How did you even know I was here?"

Mrs. Johnson sucked her teeth. "Your little girlfriend came and told me. The one I warned would bring you down." She looked her son up and down. "And just look at you."

"I know I messed up, Ma." Malek dropped his head in shame. "But it's not Halleigh's fault. Where is she anyway?"

"You don't need to be asking about her right now. I don't know where the little fast heifer is, but you are not to see her again. She is the last thing you should be worried about." Mrs. Johnson's voice was stern. "You're about to throw your entire life away on that gold-digger. She only wants you for the money, boy. Can't you see that?"

"You don't even know her," Malek said, defending his girlfriend.

"You never even gave her the chance, Ma. I love her. I know her. She doesn't care about any of this NBA stuff." He shook his head from side to side, scratching it in confusion.

He was right. Halleigh didn't care about all that NBA stuff, but he did. For the first time, it was starting to set in that he could have ruined his chances at everything he had worked so hard for all through high school. "I messed up, Ma. What am I gon' do? I messed up," he kept repeating. Tears threatened to fall from his eyes. Holding his hands together in his handcuffs, he laced and unlaced his fingers nervously.

Mrs. Johnson was about to walk over and embrace her son. "Oh, son—"

The door suddenly clanged open. Right before them were flashes and clicks from ten different news cameras rushing into the room.

Mrs. Johnson immediately went over to her son and hugged him, turning his back against the camera crews in an attempt to shield him from them. "Malek, this is not good, baby," she whispered in his ear.

Malek buried his face down to shield his face from the reporters and their probing lenses.

"Your agent called me to inform me that if the press got wind of this little mishap your chances of getting drafted were over. Now look at what's happening," she said, her voice cracking. "Look at what's happening."

Mrs. Johnson couldn't hold in the river of tears that streamed out of her eyes. Nor could she tolerate the insensitiveness of the media. "And what are y'all looking at?" She screamed at the police officers who stood idly around the room and watched the drama unfold, "Get these reporters out of here!"

The cameras continued to flash in her son's face. She tried her best to shield him from them, but he had dug his own grave. She couldn't save him this time. The paparazzi were onto his scent. They smelled scandal and were as bloodthirsty as sharks.

Malek buried his chin in his chest, trying to hide his face, but that didn't stop the reporters from flashing away. Eventually, after Mrs. Johnson's continuous protesting, the officers got up and escorted Malek back to the bull pen.

As Officer Cornwell walked next to Malek, he couldn't have been more pleased with what he had done. He had a five-thousand-dollar check waiting on him from at least three different TV stations, just for giving them the tip. "Well, son, looks like you're a star." He chuckled.

Malek knew that Cornwell was the one who'd sold him out, just by the look on his face and the tone of his voice. He was eating this whole thing up.

Before he was thrown back into the pen he decided to call Officer Cornwell on it. "Was it the money? How much did they offer you?"

"Excuse me, boy," Officer Cornwell said. He was not happy with Malek's knowing and accusing tone.

"If it was about the money, I would have given you double what they gave you just to keep your mouth shut."

His words rattled Officer Cornwell's feathers a bit, but he quickly regained his composure. After looking Malek up and down, he said, "Boy, right about now you ain't even got a quarter in your pocket. Otherwise, you wouldn't have been out trying to commit robbery. You know that is a felony, right, son?" He let out a wicked chuckle to complement his grin and then walked away.

Under his breath Malek replied, "But I could have been worth millions."

Chapter Eight

Halleigh had walked for what seemed like hours in the freezing weather before she finally reached the large jailhouse building. She was exhausted, but she knew that she had to get to Malek. She just wanted to see him, to know that he was okay. She pulled her damp T-shirt down below her knees and entered the building.

"Are you okay, young lady?" an officer asked her as she entered through the Flint precinct's glass double doors. He couldn't help but notice her bare feet as his eyes stayed glued on them momentarily.

Halleigh followed the officer's eyes down to her own bare feet. She hadn't even realized she had been walking around barefoot all of this time. The fact that her shoes had come off during her kicking and trying to get away from the assailants quickly reminded her of the ordeal she had gone through. She shuddered at the thoughts. It was at that moment that she wanted to say to the officer, "No, I'm not okay. I've been raped," but she wasn't there for herself. She was there for Malek, the boy who might have lost everything because he was trying to be there for her.

Halleigh shook off her selfish thoughts and replied to the officer, "I'm looking for my boyfriend," she said in an almost inaudible tone. "He was arrested earlier."

The officer took his position behind a desk and flicked on his computer. "What's his name?"

"Malek Johnson."

The officer didn't even need to finish typing in the name. The jail had been a circus ever since the young man had arrived. "We can't allow anyone else in to see Mr. Johnson," he stated firmly. "The next person that sees Mr. Johnson better have bail money."

"No! I need to get him out of here," she pleaded.

"Malek Johnson can't go anywhere until he sees a judge, which ain't gonna be until Monday morning. I wouldn't be surprised if the judge sets his bail at a million dollars for the little stunt he pulled. Just imagine all those kids from the projects that looked up to "the pull" and this is how their role model pays them back." The officer shook his head. "Crying shame, crying shame." The officer began shuffling papers, dismissing Halleigh as if she wasn't important.

Halleigh put her hands over her face and sighed deeply as she tried to keep her composure.

The officer looked up and saw she was still standing in front of him. He frowned in concern. "Young lady, how old are you anyway? Why are you up here like this by yourself?"

She lied as she walked away from the desk, "I'm grown." With nowhere to go, she found a seat in the waiting area.

"Seems to me someone as grown as you would at least be able to afford a pair of shoes then," he called out.

Halleigh didn't respond. She just sat there thinking, *I'll just stay here until Monday if I have to. I have to see Malek. I want to be here when he gets out.* In her heart she knew that she had no other place to go.

Taking pity on her, the officer approached her. "Here," he said, extending her a pair of jail-issued flip-flops, "at least put something on your feet."

"I'm tired of y'all pig mu'fuckas always locking a bitch up! Damn! Get on my nerves. Got me in this musty mu'fucka."

Halleigh had been leaned up against the precinct wall, trying to ease her mind, when the loud voice snapped her out of her restless sleep.

"Give me my shit!" The girl snatched her belongings from the officer sitting behind the desk. She sat down and pulled a pair of stilettos and some cheap jewelry out of the bag that the officer had given her. She put the shoes on her feet, applied her bracelets to her arm, and sashayed out the door. "Fuck y'all!" she yelled, slamming the door closed behind her.

After all the commotion died down, a female officer, the one who had just been handling the screaming woman, walked over to Halleigh. She had noticed that Halleigh had been there for quite a while now. "Excuse me, young lady, but can we help you with something?"

"I'm just waiting for Malek Johnson." Halleigh tried to sound grown-up and undaunted by authority.

"Well, you can't wait here . . . unless you want to get arrested for loitering."

Now she could see why that woman had been going off. These cops were jerks. As bad as Halleigh wanted to show her ass, the only words that came out of her mouth were, "Whatever." She sighed under her breath as she got up and left the station.

The late winter air was colder than normal. The weather had shifted from a slight drizzle, to a downpour, to a thunderous shower with lightning and everything. Heavy rain drops pelted against Halleigh's skin so hard, she felt like she was lost in a hailstorm. Here she was, standing outside wearing nothing, but the flimsy T-shirt. The flip-flops on her feet were soaked and didn't keep her toes warm. She was freezing and didn't know where she could possibly go until Monday morning.

Then she heard a familiar voice say, "Damn, Tash! Come the fuck on!"

When she looked up, it was that same girl who had caused the commotion earlier in the police precinct. She was pacing, switching her hips back and forth as if she were trying to create some type of friction between her legs. She was fidgeting just to stay warm.

"Come on, Tash. It's cold out here," she complained to herself out loud. Just then she noticed Halleigh walking by. She held up her hand and halted her as if she were hailing a taxi cab. "Ay, yo, you got a light?" she asked Halleigh.

Halleigh shook her head.

"Fuck," the girl snapped.

Just then, Halleigh watched as the girl walked to a car that was parked on the side of the street, looked around to make sure no one was coming, and then tried the door, which opened. Halleigh peeped her surroundings nervously. *I know this girl is not breaking into a car right in front of the police station.*

The girl popped in the car lighter and stood outside the car waiting a couple minutes for it to heat up. She lit her cigarette and then quickly closed the door and took her place back on the street to wait for her ride.

The girl looked Halleigh up and down and noticed her disheveled appearance. "Damn, girl, what happened to you?"

"You don't even want to know," Halleigh replied, blowing hot air from her mouth into her hands.

"You waiting for a ride or something?" The girl puffed her cigarette.

"No. I don't know what I'm doing. My boyfriend is locked up. They talking about he has to wait until Monday to get a bail set." Halleigh

looked defeated. "Even then, I don't know how I'm going to come up with that. He's in all of this mess because of me, trying to look out for me. I don't know what to do." Halleigh's hands dropped to her sides as the rain washed her tears away.

"Where you stay?"

Halleigh looked around. "Right now, where I stand. I just need a place to think. I have to figure out what I'm gon' do."

"Well, it's colder than a bitch out here," the girl commented. "You ain't gon' figure nothing out waiting outside, especially in this cold-ass rain." She sucked her teeth. "What's your name?"

"Halleigh."

"I'm Mimi." She noticed that Halleigh was shivering and took pity on the girl. "Look, girl, you can crash at my spot if you need to, at least for the night. My daddy will probably be able to help you out too. He can help you get your boy out of jail if you want him to."

Halleigh didn't know Mimi from the man on the moon, but as of now, she had officially run out of options. Anything would be better than being on the streets, she figured, so she decided to accept Mimi's offer. "You sure your daddy won't mind?"

Mimi smirked and looked Halleigh up and down and then licked her lips. "Nah, he won't mind, trust me."

Halleigh stood next to Mimi on the street as they waited for Mimi's ride to pick them up. She didn't want to seem like a charity case, but she didn't have anywhere else to go. For a moment she thought about going to Nikki's house. Nikki had a single mother too, but her mother was stricter on Nikki than Halleigh's mother was on her. Nikki had the type of mother who made phone calls to make sure a situation was kosher. Halleigh couldn't go and stay for two nights at Nikki's without raising suspicion. Besides, she didn't want Nikki to know about the disasters that had happened to her and to Malek. She knew that, underneath, Nikki had envied their relationship, and she would be glad to know all their plans had been shipwrecked.

Malek was locked up, so of course, staying with him wasn't an option. Her mother was so strung-out that she had sacrificed her relationship with her daughter just to get high. Halleigh knew that she would never walk into her mother's house again. There was no repairing their relationship. *I hate her,* Halleigh thought, feeling bombarded with mixed emotions of hatred, anger, and disgust for her mother.

Mimi paced up and down Saginaw Street puffing on her cigarette. She kept looking up and down the block to see if her ride was nearing. She looked down at the girl that she had befriended and could tell that she was carrying a large burden on her shoulders. "Here, hit this. It'll calm your nerves." Mimi offered Halleigh a drag of her Newport.

Halleigh shook her head. "I don't smoke."

Mimi shrugged her shoulders and took a long pull of the nicotine as

she continued to pace back and forth, the silver stilettos that laced up her slim legs clicking back and forth. She wore a short silver halter dress. Her hair was braided straight to the back, her extensions causing it to fall right above her butt. Baby hair rested along her edges.

"Where the hell is this girl at?" Mimi muttered impatiently.

"Are you sure this is all right? Your daddy won't mind it if I stay the night?" Halleigh furrowed her eyebrows together in worry. She pondered over her situation. Who was this woman whose father would allow her to bring a stranger home? He must be a nice man, or why would Mimi even offer to allow this?

Mimi looked her up and down again and smirked. "Nah, like I said before, he won't mind. My daddy will be happy to have you. He'll help you figure everything out." Mimi's last sentence was said in a sing-song tone.

Just as Halleigh was about to reply, a caramel-colored girl with long layered hair pulled up in a Toyota and honked the horn. "Mimi, get in!" she yelled.

Halleigh anxiously waited near the curb while Mimi strolled over to the car. "Come on, Hal," Mimi called.

Instantly Halleigh picked up on the fact that Mimi had already used her nickname, as if they were friends, as if she'd known her forever. A sense of security swept over Halleigh, like everything would be okay. She began taking steps toward the car.

"Mimi, get your ass in the car!" the girl shouted from inside the car just as she noticed Halleigh making her way over to the car too. "And where the fuck she think she going?" Halleigh stopped in her tracks as she looked helplessly at Mimi.

"Tasha, chill! She needs our help. She needs to meet Daddy." Mimi spoke through clenched teeth.

Tasha peered out at the girl who was standing beside her car. It was obvious that the girl had been crying. Her eyes were red and puffy. She was shivering, and her arms were wrapped around herself as if she were afraid. "Tell her to get in," Tasha said with an attitude. Heaving a sigh of resignation, she put the car in drive.

"See, I told you everything would be cool. Get in," Mimi said to Halleigh as she opened the back door for her.

Halleigh got into the car and rode silently as she watched the city streets pass her by. She could feel Tasha's eyes on her as she glared at her from the rearview mirror. She kept feeling her stare and started feeling uncomfortable in the confinement of the car.

"You know Manolo about to trip on you, right?" Tasha asked as they pulled into the driveway of a ranch-style home on the city's South Side.

"He'll be cool once he sees what I got for him." Mimi shuffled dollars together from inside her purse.

The three girls exited the car and entered the house. There were several girls scattered throughout the house. Some were lounging in the large living room, others were getting dressed and rushing about as they prepared to leave, still others walked freely throughout the house wearing nothing but their underclothes. Most of them had high-perched breasts, smooth thighs without cellulite, and round cantaloupe-shaped hips. There appeared to be about five women in all.

"This your daddy's crib?" Halleigh asked, scanning the large rooms with wonder.

"Yeah, he probably in the back," Mimi replied.

Halleigh noticed Tasha roll her eyes as she followed them down a long hallway in the five-bedroom house. They entered the room, and Halleigh saw a tall, well-built man sitting in a recliner in the corner of the room and puffing on a blunt. The first thing that she noticed was his long, perfectly manicured fingernails.

"How did you get locked up?" was his first question as he stared directly at Mimi.

"It was all a misunderstanding, Daddy. I promise it will never happen again," Mimi replied. She didn't give him a chance to respond. She just rambled right into her next sentence. "This is my friend, Halleigh. I met her outside of the jail when I was waiting on slow-ass Tasha to come pick me up." Mimi stroked a piece of Halleigh's hair and then pushed it behind her ear. "She is in a bind right now, and I told her that you might be able to help her out."

The man didn't even look Halleigh's way. Instead, he looked at Tasha. "What do you think?"

She looked over at Halleigh and, once again, rolled her eyes. "I don't know." She shrugged. "But I guess it could be a good move." Tasha made her way over to the man and began to massage his defined shoulders. "What do you think?"

Mimi noticed the way he was now looking at Halleigh. It was the same look he gave her when she'd first met him, so she knew that it was a done deal. She had done good.

Slowly, without Halleigh even noticing, Mimi backed up and began to ease out of the room. Just as she was about to close the door, the man called out to her, "Mimi, you gon' work double to pay me back that bail money," never taking his eyes off Halleigh.

Damn, this mu'fucka could've let me slide since I brought his ass some fresh pussy. Niggas don't appreciate shit, I swear. Mimi walked out of the room without responding, and Tasha followed, leaving Halleigh in the room alone.

Now completely alone with this stranger and under his steely gaze, Halleigh pulled at the T-shirt that she wore, feeling uncomfortable in her own skin. She felt goose bumps rise on her arms. The room was

smoky from the weed, and Halleigh could tell that he was as high as a kite.

"What did you say your name was?" he asked as he continued to smoke on his blunt.

"Halleigh," she replied, then took a gulp, trying to swallow the huge knot in her throat.

"Halleigh. Your name fits you." He looked at her high-yellow skin tone and licked his lips as if he could taste her. Yeah, Mimi had done good.

Being in the pimping game for over ten years Manolo knew a lost soul when he saw one. Halleigh's eyes revealed her sadness. He didn't know what path she had followed that brought her to his doorstep, but he knew that he was about to lead her in a new direction. His eyes admired the proportioned curves of her young body. He had to mentally tame his dick down when he noticed her hard nipples poking through her T-shirt.

"So why do you need Manolo's help?" he asked, referring to himself in the third person.

Her thoughts instantly went back to Malek, and tears came to her eyes.

Manolo nodded his head toward his bed. "Take your time, baby girl. Have a seat. I won't bite you, I promise."

Halleigh sat on the bed near his chair. "It's my boyfriend, Malek. He was arrested, and I need money to get him out."

"What they holding him for?" Manolo tapped the blunt against an ashtray that sat on a glass table beside him.

Although hesitant at first because she didn't just want to be telling this stranger all of her business, she knew that if she was going to get him to help her, she needed to tell him everything. "He robbed a store . . . but he's not like that. He only did it because I needed the money." Halleigh even told Manolo about the awful attack that took place at her mother's house and why she couldn't go back there. In fact, she revealed everything that had occurred, up to the point of stepping foot in his house.

"Sounds to me like your boyfriend ain't gon' want nothing to do with you when he gets out." Manolo knew to begin planting the seeds of doubt into this fresh soil. "Sitting in jail has a way of making people think about things. He's probably thinking about you right now and how you've probably fucked things up for him."

Manolo's words were harsh, but Halleigh wasn't about to kid herself. She knew there was plenty of truth to them, and that Malek probably was sitting in jail right now thinking how none of this would be happening had he never met her.

"Now I want to help you," Manolo continued, "but I've got to be truthful. I'm not a liar, so I'm gon' keep it gully with you."

Halleigh nodded eagerly, wondering what he would say next. Here she was traumatized, perhaps expecting a little empathy, but Manolo dished out anything but.

"I know you believe your man is probably just thinking it, but I'm going to tell you straight up—this is all your fault. If it wasn't for you, your man wouldn't be locked up right now."

Flabbergasted, Halleigh's mouth flew open. Manolo's words shocked her as sharply as an unexpected slap. With his harsh words, she began to let her tears flow freely. Believing it was all her fault was one thing, but hearing it was another.

Halleigh stood there doing what it seemed she'd been doing for the last twenty-four hours, crying. She was tired of crying though. Those tears weren't getting her anywhere. It was time to do something about the messy bed that was made.

"What do I do?" she asked, wiping her tears away roughly, as if she was angry at them for even falling from her eyes. As quickly as she wiped them, more would fall.

Manolo stood up and began to help her wipe her tears away. He knew that he had her in the palm of his hand. His main agenda was to get a woman to become and remain his ho. He called that "the pimp's creed." Having taken advantage of some of the toughest bitches that Flint had ever bred, he knew this was going to be a piece of cake. He knew how to break a grown-ass woman down, so he knew it wouldn't be any problem with such a naïve teen.

"It's your fault that this happened, so you have to fix it," he told her. "How you fix it is up to you."

"But how can I fix it? Even when they set bail, I don't have the money to get him out. His parents work hard and everything, but it's not their fault he's in there, it's mine." Halleigh knew that if Malek's parents had to come up off that bail money, Mrs. Johnson would do everything in her power to see to it that Malek never saw her again, and she couldn't let that happen. Manolo was right. It was her fault. She had to come up with the bail money.

Manolo questioned Halleigh the same way Satan had questioned Eve in the garden. "You don't have any money?"

"I don't even have a roof over my head right now."

Manolo put his index finger to his chin and thought for a minute. "He's in for robbery, did you say?"

Halleigh nodded.

"Is this his first offense ever?"

Once again, Halleigh nodded.

"Let me see . . ." Manolo, with his street wisdom, figured out how much Malek's bail would probably be for a first-time offender. "Ten stacks," he finally said.

Halleigh hadn't the slightest idea what he was talking about. "Huh?"

"Ten thousand dollars. That's my estimate on what your boyfriend's bail is probably going to be." Manolo thought for another moment. "Yeah, that is a lot of money"—he looked back at Halleigh—"especially for a girl who has nothing."

Halleigh's head fell, her chin to her chest.

"I could help you get that money." Manolo was glad to see he had the girl's undivided attention again. "But it won't be easy. It'll take a couple days, but I think we could do it if you work hard," he stated, throwing out the bait.

Relieved, Halleigh said, "I'll do anything. I just want to fix this."

"You can even stay here until you find your own spot," he said, knowing Halleigh would accept the offer.

Truth was, Halleigh really didn't have a choice but to rest her head under his roof. Any ho that had ever worked for him always lived in his house. *My roof, my rules,* Manolo thought to himself. He felt that it was easier to control his girls if he knew their whereabouts at all times.

"Halleigh, why did you come to me for help? Where are your people? I mean, I know the deal with your mom, but haven't you anyone else you can turn to?" Manolo wanted to make sure that she didn't have anybody that could come and save her from the life she was about to get into. He knew that there would come a time when she would want out. By that time he would make her feel so hopeless that she would think that he was the only one who cared about her.

"I don't have anybody. Malek is the only person I can count on." Halleigh lowered her head at the thought of her mother. *She let them rape me.*

He took her hand and lifted her to her feet. "You can count on me, Sunshine," he whispered softly in her ear as he wrapped his hands around her waist.

"Sunshine?" Halleigh stated.

"Yeah, Sunshine." Manolo looked deep into Halleigh's eyes. "When I look into your eyes, I see a rainstorm. There's been so much pain in your life, so much thunder, I know you've felt as though a black rain cloud has just been following you around."

Tears began to fall from Halleigh's eyes. Manolo couldn't have been more right. Not only had it been raining on her, literally, for the last twenty-four hours, but her entire life was like one bad, pouring-down shower in which the rain just wouldn't seem to let up.

"Well, the rain is about to dry up, and there'll be nothing but sunshine in your life from this day forward." He then embraced her like a father would a daughter. Halleigh broke down in tears as she appreciated his embrace.

"Shhh. I will help you get what you need." Manolo began rocking her back and forth in his arms.

He had sucked her in so deep that she was hanging on to, and be-

lieving his every word. He spat out so many broken promises and manipulated her young mind to the point that she didn't even realize that his hands had found a comfortable place on her ass while he was grinding his crotch slowly against her.

"Shh, that's right. Get it all out, Sunshine," he repeated over and over again.

Just like Halleigh had once felt, only in Malek's arms, she felt that same way in Manolo's arms—safe.

Chapter Nine

M alek took a seat on the same bench Jamaica Joe was sitting on. Everyone else in the bullpen was terrified of Joe, but Malek's mind was elsewhere. He didn't even have the energy to be terrified of a man. The only thing he was afraid of was what Halleigh could possibly be going through right now; not to mention what would become of his basketball career.

He didn't even notice that everyone else in the room kept their distance as they tried to avoid Joe. The truth was he really didn't know who Jamaica Joe was or what he stood for. He'd heard of his reputation, but he'd never seen him in person.

As a single parent, his mother had done the best she could to shield him from the malevolent streets. Then when he was eight years old, she married his stepfather, who as far as Malek was concerned, was his father. Kind of like how Shaq feels about his stepfather. It was Malek's stepfather who was behind his involvement in basketball camps every summer since he was nine years old. The camps not only developed his skills, but also contributed to him burning up a lot of energy. He was always too tired to get into trouble.

Over the past five years, while his friends were going to Maxey Boys Training School for juvenile offenders, Malek had been too busy dribbling basketballs to get involved in crime. There were generally male mentors at the camp who spoke out against young black men getting caught up in drug dealing, crime, or substance abuse.

Up until his arrest last night, Malek had never had any trouble with the law. Now he'd just turned eighteen. He wondered, with this being his first offense, if the judge would be lenient on him and give him probation. He sure didn't want a felony on his record. He wondered if

this would affect his chances of getting into the NBA. What a mess he had made of things.

In disgust, Malek buried his face in the palms of his hands as he blocked everything out that was going on around him. He was so busy regretting his foolish act he was oblivious to all the noise and chatter of the jail cell. Suppose he had gotten enough money from the robbery for a night at a hotel, then what? Would he have to keep knocking off corner stores to pay for additional nights? He hadn't even bothered to think that far in advance. All he was worried about at the time was Halleigh. Speaking of which, he was worried about her now.

Malek took a deep breath as he stared down at his feet. All of a sudden some words his stepfather had spoken to him some time ago came back to haunt him. *"You don't even know how much danger is out there in the streets. You don't want to be in the wrong place at the wrong time and wind up in jail or prison, which is no place for a Black man."* His father may not have been in the home as much as Malek would have liked him to be. He may not have been able to attend his basketball games as much as he wanted him to, but his love for Malek went without question. He had done nothing but work hard since marrying Malek's mother.

Before Malek was even two years old, his real father was shot dead in a drug deal gone bad. In an unrelated incident, his stepfather's dad had been sentenced to life in jail for a murder that took place during a drug deal gone badly. Prior to their deaths, the men had played no role at all in their son's lives, choosing the streets over their own flesh and blood. So Mr. Johnson knew what it was like to need and desperately want a man in the home to teach him how to be a man, to teach him how to be a provider and to take care of his family the right way. For that, Malek had the utmost respect for the man his mother married, the man he called Dad.

Once again, Malek sighed and shook his head thinking about what his father would possibly think about him if he saw him right now; sitting in a jail cell for robbery. A blitz of reporters suddenly stood on the opposite side of the bars, and cameras were flashing away once again. Once the word that Malek was in there leaked to the media, the reporters flocked to the jailhouse to get a photo of the jailed star, first to the visiting room with him and his mother, and now right there in the jail cell. They were relentless and wouldn't let up. "Not this shit again," Malek said. He put up his hands up to shield his face. Jamaica Joe discreetly turned his back, trying to avoid being photographed. After three straight minutes of constant flashing, the second wave of reporters left satisfied.

The criminals and drunks in the bullpen began an uproar. In spite of the stench coming from the one backed-up toilet in the corner and the crowded conditions, they all felt as important and as special as a

group of rappers, several even posing for the cameras. Others threw up gang signs. They'd never seen anything like it.

One particular Latino man was the first to speak to Malek. He wore a tight T-shirt over his ripped, muscular upper body and had at least ten tattoos on his neck alone. He was obviously intoxicated. In his mind, for some reason, he felt that Malek thought he was better than the rest of them. Well, that's what he told himself. He didn't want to admit that it was pure jealousy that caused him to dislike Malek.

"You must be somebody important, huh?" the Latino man yelled across the room.

Malek looked around and then focused on the man. "You talking to me?" he asked, placing his index finger on his chest.

"Yeah, I'm talking to you," the Latino man yelled in a drunken slur. "I don't see no other bitches in here."

The other men began to laugh at his comment, gassing him up more. Malek stared at the man for a second to see if he was serious and then dropped his head in an attempt to ignore him. He ran his hands over the top of his head, feeling the ripples of the few waves in his hair that still remained in spite of the rain.

The man wasn't done with Malek though. He hated pretty boys and felt obligated to tell Malek about himself. He staggered over to Malek to give him a piece of his mind.

Before Malek even realized that the man was headed over his way, the Latino man was standing directly over him. "You's a ol' bitch-ass, pretty boy. Who the fuck is you anyway? You got these mu'fuckas snapping photos and shit. You ain't nobody. You in here just like the rest of us. You ain't no better than none of us."

Malek looked up at the man, with a confused look on his face and thought, *What is this mu'fucka's problem?* He watched as the man swayed from side to side and struggled to keep his balance. "Look, man, I don't want any trouble, fam," Malek told him.

The man must have felt that Malek was trying to be disrespectful, because out of nowhere, he swung on him. Before the man could connect, Malek moved to the side, causing the man to spin around and almost fall. Malek quickly rose to his feet and caught the man with two swift punches. The man didn't know what hit him. Jamaica Joe slightly grinned as he stepped to the side to give the two men room to get their brawl on. Malek followed up with another punch, connecting with the man's nose.

The Latino man held his nose in agony as he fell flat on his back. Malek smiled when he realized how quickly he had dropped the man. The smile quickly dropped when he saw two other Latinos that closely resembled the man he had just beaten down emerge from the crowd. From the way the men were dressed alike, it was obvious that they were from the same gang or set.

"Ay, homes, you done fucked up," one of the men said just before he ran up on Malek.

Malek shifted his stance and put up his dukes. He kept his eyes steady, and he stood his ground, refusing to back down.

Jamaica Joe just sat back and watched as Malek showed no fear. *Li'l man got mad heart,* Joe thought to himself as he leaned against the brick wall.

The men in the bullpen gathered around the fight to witness the unexpected entertainment.

"Get him."

"Fuck him up, *hombre*."

"Fight, fight," the sideliners instigated.

Just like the first man, Malek laid the second one down in a matter of seconds, without as much as a scratch on himself even though the second one didn't seem to be as drunk as the first one. Now, both men lay on the ground next to each other. The third Latino man sized Malek up and circled him as he contemplated the best way to get at Malek. His chest heaved up and down from trying to catch his breath. Malek was tired from the scuffle with the two previous men, but he didn't show it. He was ready to drop this one the same way he had dropped the rest. The first man that Malek dropped returned to his feet, blood dripping from his nose. He might have been injured, but he was still ready to fight. Malek was outnumbered at that point and prepared himself for the worst.

"That's enough," a calm voice said. It was Jamaica Joe. He had seen enough and respected Malek's braveness. "Leave li'l man alone," Joe demanded of the Latinos, not even respecting them enough to look at them.

The men's demeanor totally changed at Joe's request. They all dropped their fists as they looked at Joe nervously. It was evident that Joe had control of the situation, because the three Latino men weren't even focused on Malek anymore. They were worried about Jamaica Joe.

Malek, on the other hand, didn't drop his guard and was ready to knock out whoever ran up on him.

"Ay, Joe, I didn't know he wuz with chu," one of them said in broken English.

Malek balled up his fist, his adrenaline pumping. "Run up, nigga!"

As much as the Latino crew wanted to, they did nothing. Malek finally realized why everyone was on the opposite side of the room from Joe when he first came in. They feared him.

"Joseph Holland!" the guard yelled as he approached the cell.

A middle-aged white man with a neat tailored suit walked alongside the guard. It was Jamaica Joe's attorney, Anderson Wallace, one of the most prestigious and sought-after attorneys in the Midwest.

File in hand, Wallace was noticeably upset. "Release my client immediately! This is preposterous!"

Jamaica Joe headed out of the cell after it was opened for him, but not before Malek called out to him, "Thanks."

Joe simply nodded his head in acknowledgment and exited the cell. Malek watched as the guard closed the steel gate behind Joe, and then he focused his attention back on the bullpen. He was sure that the Latino gang would try to finish what they'd started, but to Malek's surprise, they didn't do as much as look at him.

After an hour of keeping his eye on the gang, Malek figured that they weren't going to try anything, so once again, he began to think about his current predicament. He knew he had acted on impulse by trying to knock over the convenience store; an impulse that could change his life forever. What else could he have done? What other choices did he have? Should he have gone and tried to retaliate against the drug dealers who raped his girl? That type of people didn't play, and they would have come after both of them and probably killed them. Absently, he shook his head. He was caught in a quandary. What else could he have done? What was he going to do now? He dropped his head in defeat. His whole world was tumbling down. When it rains, it pours.

Chapter Ten

"What am I gon' do?" Halleigh asked aloud. She was sitting in the bedroom that she now shared with Mimi. The room was just big enough to fit two twin beds, but she was grateful just to have a place to lay her head. She had taken a shower, and Mimi had loaned her some old clothes.

Manolo had told Halleigh that she could stay as long as she needed to, and he had assured her that he would help her make the money she needed to get Malek out of jail. The fact that she still had four more months of high school to complete crept into her thoughts. How on God's earth was she going to be able to get back and forth from school, let alone, be able to focus on things once she was back at school? After a couple of minutes of sifting a few options and ideas, she decided that she couldn't worry about that now. Perhaps she could go back to school once she got a job and saved up some money.

Mimi sat on her bed with her back against the wall, painting her toe nails. "How much did you say ol' boy's bail is probably going to be?"

"Ten thousand," Halleigh replied.

"Damn! He gon' rot in that mu'fucka." Mimi let out a low whistle. "He ain't got no family that can get him out?" she asked. "I wouldn't be spending my hard-earned money on nobody's bail. His family would be going half or something." Mimi blew on her toes, attempting to dry the wet paint.

"His moms don't like me. She can't stand me. She won't even talk to me, so I don't know what is going on. His pops, I don't even know if he knows what went down yet. He was out of town for his job. He's always out of town working hard."

"Good. Then let his hardworking ass pay the bail, and you hit the Genesee Mall and go shopping."

Halleigh just shrugged her shoulders. She had already decided that she couldn't put that burden on Malek's parents' shoulders. Her heart was heavy. Whenever she thought about Malek sitting locked up in jail, she felt as great a pain as when the two men had pulled the train on her and raped her.

At Halleigh's silence, Mimi continued her reasoning. "It ain't about you, it's about their son. They want him out of there just as much as you do. That's who I would be going to see if I were you." Mimi hopped up off the bed and left the room.

Halleigh tried not to let Mimi's words override her own thoughts on the situation, but she couldn't help it. *It will take me forever to make ten G's by myself. I don't even know what type of job Manolo gon' give me. What if it's only making minimum wage or something? Maybe I should go to Malek's parents and let them know that I can at least pay half of his bail. It will probably be a whole lot easier for me to come up with half of the money rather than all of it. Besides, if they can put up half, we can get Malek out faster. On top of that, maybe my sacrifice to get the money will finally show Mrs. Johnson how much I love her son. Then she'll finally accept me.*

The next day, Halleigh found herself breathing erratically as she stood on Mrs. Johnson's doorstep. She was nervous, and she knew she looked a mess, but she hoped that Mrs. Johnson would put their beef to the side and agree to help her get Malek out of jail.

I'm just gon' tell her that this is not about us. Her son is sitting downtown in jail, and if we work together, we can get him out. I love him, and so does she. I know she won't just let him sit in there. She has to help me.

At first, when Halleigh asked Mimi to take her to Malek's house, she realized that it was Sunday and that Mrs. Johnson would probably be in church praying for her son to get out of jail. To Halleigh's surprise,

when they pulled up in front of the house, Mrs. Johnson's car was parked right outside.

Mrs. Johnson had decided against going to church for two reasons. One, the reporters were still outside her doorstep early in the morning They only vacated the premises when they realized that she wasn't going to answer the door to comment on her son's situation. Secondly, the last thing she wanted was for all those gossiping heifers at her church to pretend to comfort her and pray for her, just so they could have something to talk about. Hell, she might as well have talked to the reporters in that case. Just as Halleigh was about to knock on the door, she saw Mrs. Johnson look through the curtains. Halleigh thought once she saw her that she would answer the door, but she didn't. *I know she knows I'm out here*, Halleigh thought in frustration. Tired of playing games, she knocked on the door with force. She shouted, "Mrs. Johnson, please open the door. We need to talk!" She heard the bolt lock click.

Mrs. Johnson opened the door with a stone face. "Stop beating on my door," she said without emotion in her voice. Her eyes were red, and she still wore her house coat, even though it was one o'clock in the afternoon.

Halleigh looked the woman in the eyes. "I'm sorry, but please . . . I need to talk to you."

"What do you want, little girl? Haven't you done enough damage?" Mrs. Johnson said coldly. Her eyes pierced Halleigh's soul like a pair of machetes, her glare was so cold. "You've already ruined my son's life, now what?"

"Listen, I love Malek, and I know you think I'm a gold-digger and that I'm only with him because he's going to the NBA, but that's not true."

Halleigh could see that Mrs. Johnson was about ready to close the door on her, so she quickly put her cards on the table. "Look, I know you don't like me, but this is not about me. I'm here because I want to help Malek. I know that you and Mr. Johnson work hard just to maintain, and probably don't have money stored away to get him out of jail, and I can't help him by myself. I think I can come up with half of the money for his bail. If you all can put up the other half, we can help him together."

Mrs. Johnson just stared at Halleigh without any expression on her face. Her heart hated the girl that stood before her. In a way she was jealous of the way that Malek felt about Halleigh. For so long it had just been her and her son, until her husband came into her life. Before him, they never had much, but as long as they had each other, it always seemed to be enough. Mr. Johnson did some telemarketing sales work, but was mostly in and out of town with his second job as a Kirby

Sweeper salesman, going to different conventions and traveling afar in search of new clients. So even now, it was still pretty much her and Malek in the house. If Mrs. Johnson was being honest with herself, Mr. Johnson only married her out of guilt from his own childhood.

After meeting Malek and befriending him, and Malek so quickly taking to him as if he were his biological father, Mr. Johnson couldn't imagine exiting the boy's life. So he did what was right and committed himself to the family.

When Malek met Halleigh, Mrs. Johnson had to share her son's heart, and it hurt her dearly. She felt as if Malek had given up so much just to be with her, and that he didn't even know that the young girls these days were all alike. They come a dime a dozen. They come running when their so-called man is on top, but are the first to get ghost when things look as though they're about to crumble. That's why Mrs. Johnson was a little surprised herself that Halleigh was trying to stick around, now that her son was obviously at his worst. Even that didn't melt the hard ice around her heart as she looked at Halleigh and thought, *I will never let her get her claws in my son's back again.*

She figured this was the perfect opportunity to get rid of Halleigh and she took it. Mrs. Johnson burst into patronizing laughter right in Halleigh's face. "Sweetheart, do you really think that I would let my son stay in jail? That his father would let him stay in jail? Malek came home this morning," she lied. "Being a future NBA star has its perks."

A smile spread across Halleigh's face. "Can I see him, please?" she asked. "I just want to make sure he's all right."

"Halleigh, I'm sorry to be the one to break this to you, but Malek left this morning. His father came into town and thought that it would be good for him if he got away from all this madness until things died down." Mrs. Johnson was starting to believe the fable herself, and so she continued to add yeast to make it rise. "He didn't want to see you, honey. He said that you were the reason why his chance of getting in the NBA is now jeopardized. He'll be lucky to even get a decent college to accept him after this little stunt."

Tears built up in Halleigh's eyes from the news she had just received. "Mrs. Johnson, can you please just call him? Just let me talk to him?"

"I'm sorry, honey, but he asked me not to give you or anyone else his number, and I have to respect his wishes. I know that you and I have had our days, but I truly am sorry that you had to hear this from me, the same way I had to hear about my son being in jail from you." Mrs. Johnson cleared her throat, forcing down the sarcasm stuck there. "He just feels that it's time to move on with his life, a life that no longer includes you."

On the inside, Mrs. Johnson was smiling, pleased with her decep-

tion. She could tell that her words were breaking the young girl's heart into a thousand pieces. *Anything to take care of my baby. He doesn't need her in his life,* she thought.

Mrs. Johnson knew that Malek's arraignment was set for the next morning, but she refused to let Halleigh know that. *I'll do anything to keep this girl away from my son.* Mrs. Johnson banked on her perception about the girl being correct, thinking that by later that night the hoodrat would already be sticking her claws into the next boy.

Halleigh was too shocked to move. She was too shocked to speak, so she just watched in desperation as Mrs. Johnson shut the door in her face. Her heart and mind couldn't quite grasp what Malek's mother had told her. *Why would he do this to me?* she thought. Since she didn't have Mimi wait on her she began the long trek back to the South Side of town. She had thought only positive thoughts. She'd go talk to Mrs. Johnson, and then the two of them would work things out. Halleigh wasn't surprised that Mr. Johnson would scoop Malek up like that. After all, he'd always been the voice of reason in the home. Of course, he didn't care for Halleigh all that much either, but he didn't dislike her as Mrs. Johnson did. Halleigh couldn't help thinking that things would have turned out different if she'd gotten to Mr. Johnson earlier.

Halleigh tried to hold her tears inside as she treaded through the city, often stopping just to get her thoughts together. It was like she was in a trance. Before she knew it, light became dark, and confidence became insecurity when she thought about her relationship with Malek. She was so sure that he would never leave her. *He promised me that he would take care of me. What am I going to do without him?*

Feeling like her world had come to an end, Halleigh lost all perspective of her circumstances. Her mind went numb, and she headed back toward the new place that she hoped she would be able to call home.

Chapter Eleven

Two days after witnessing the brutal rape of her own daughter, Sharina had shot up a week's worth of products and was in need of a new fix. Actually, she hadn't noticed that Halleigh was gone until she needed her services again.

She ranted and raved through the house, "Halleigh, where the hell are you?" tossing furniture over as if Halleigh was hiding under it.

In a fit, and with a monkey on her back, she tore the house up, searching under tossed pillows on the sofa, under the bed, and in the closets. She even groveled on the carpet with a straw when she thought she saw a white dash of powder. Unfortunately, it wasn't crank (amphetamine) or crack, but a piece of lint.

"Where the hell is that heifer?" she grumbled, scratching an open sore on her arm. "She know I need her. Much as I done did for her, she better be glad I ain't callin' the law on her. If Flint PD wasn't so crooked, I'd report her underage ass. But, hell, the damn cop would probably fuck her too before they even made it to the station."

After what seemed like hours of destruction for Sharina, she had finally worn herself out. The last place she had searched was the bathroom, removing everything from under the sink and the medicine cabinets, and tearing down towels and washcloths from the racks that held them. Sweaty, funky, and exhausted, she slumped down the wall and onto the floor. She stared at the toilet across from her, feeling like a piece of shit, wanting to just dunk her head in and drown herself.

All of a sudden, it was as if she was having an epiphany. Her eyes lit up as she crawled over to the toilet. She found a little bit of blow that she'd hidden from her friends a few weeks earlier in the bathroom commode. She'd forgotten all about it until now. "Thank you, God," she cried out. "Thank you, Lord," she added, giving God thanks for the devil's work.

Elated at the discovery of the drugs, Sharina snorted some then shot up the rest. "I can quit any time I want," she murmured to herself as her high settled throughout her body, "but I don't wanna." She smiled. "Shit feels too good."

She slumped, and her eyes closed. "I'm gonna get high forever," were the last words she spoke out loud. The last words she thought were, *and Halleigh's going to help me to be able to do it*.

Chapter Twelve

Manolo watched Mimi step her skinny legs into a purple thong. Her body was slim, but stacked just right. Her ass cheeks filled out voluptuously, causing him to lust after her. He asked her, "Where she go?"

"She went to see the young boy's mama." Mimi studied his facial expression to see if he was upset, but saw no sign of anger in his eyes. "Don't worry, she'll be back," she said, once again studying his facial expressions. "You upset?"

"Nah, I ain't mad. We haven't given her a reason not to want to come back. She doesn't know the deal yet. I still got to break li'l mama in." He thought about how easy it was going to be to get into Halleigh's head.

Tasha walked into the room, strutting as if she belonged on a runway. Her layered hair was held out of her face with a pair of large Chloe glasses, and her manicured feet were covered in red flip-flops. She struggled with the many bags in her hand.

"Did you get what I asked you to?" Manolo asked.

Tasha nodded her head, removing outfit after outfit from large shopping bags. The outfits were all revealing, short mini skirts with low-cut tops, and a pair of matching stilettos for each outfit.

Manolo had sent her on a shopping trip for Halleigh. He had big plans for her; she just didn't know it yet.

Mimi observed some of the items, measuring them. "Yeah, she should be able to fit this stuff." She then frowned. "But you sure she's gon' be down for this? She seem kind of timid to me."

Tasha chimed in, "She's taken a bath and cleaned up, but her clothes still look pretty bad. She gonna be able to work it?" Tasha snapped her fingers with the twitch of her ass.

"I gave her something to wear for now," Mimi told her. "She a'ight."

Manolo was tired of hearing the girls go back and forth over his latest project, and whether he could pull off getting her right where he wanted her. He said, "Don't worry about it. I'll handle it." He looked at Tasha. "When I first got a hold of your ass, you was the deacon's daughter, now you the baddest bitch in Flint." He slapped her on the ass. His dick swelled a bit at the thought of Tasha's sweet pussy, and how he had broken her in.

Although only twenty-three, Tasha knew how to please a man. She was a freak and had no problem giving Manolo the goods anytime he wanted it. That's one of the reasons why he'd made her the madam of the house. He preferred to have her all to himself and didn't want her working niggas anymore. He wasn't trying to share her pussy. Tasha thought about Manolo's comment. Halleigh did remind her of herself a little bit when she first got into the game, which is why a part of her was a little intimidated. She was going to make sure that Halleigh didn't dare try to come after her crown as the queen of that there throne.

Mimi rolled her eyes at both Manolo and Tasha. *Bitch always getting special treatment.* She finished dressing as she watched Manolo pull Tasha toward him, grinding his swollen dick into her backside.

All of a sudden, they heard the front door slam. They saw Halleigh

run past Manolo's bedroom and into her own. They could hear her crying.

Tasha shook her head and sighed. "You better save that for her." She rubbed Manolo's crotch. "It looks like you gon' have your work cut out for you." She then maneuvered herself out of his grasp and left the room, taking Mimi with her. "We'll be at the hotel," she said, knowing Manolo would want privacy while he entertained the young girl.

Manolo paid for hotel rooms on a weekly basis for his girls to turn their tricks. This way he could more easily keep an eye on them and their johns. On a regular basis, he would show up there unannounced, so the girls had to be on their toes at all times.

Manolo wore some sea-green slacks with matching gators, and a white wife-beater that showed his tattooed arms. He had a button-up shirt to match the slacks, but it was thrown across the chair in his room. He walked into the hallway and knocked lightly on the frame of Halleigh's door, announcing his presence, even though the door was already ajar. He walked inside over to where Halleigh lay across the bed sobbing. Halleigh was crying so hard, she didn't even notice he was standing beside her.

"You a'ight?" he asked in his well-rehearsed tone of fake concern.

Halleigh quickly tried to brush her tears away, turning her head toward the wall and away from Manolo. "Yeah, I'm good," she replied. Her voice cracked in mid-sentence. She broke down in sobs at the thought of all of the words Mrs. Johnson had said to her earlier that day.

Manolo sat down next to her. He put his hand on her back and guided her head into his lap. He then gently began to rub her head, massaging her neck as he listened to her cry. "Shhh, tell Nolo what's wrong, baby girl," he whispered. He blew air into her ear in a seemingly innocent way.

Halleigh couldn't respond. Every time she attempted to speak, her words got caught in her throat, and she found herself weeping even harder.

"Don't talk, baby," Manolo said, trying to soothe her. "Just get it all out."

Halleigh cried and cried until she felt emptied out. She eventually stopped crying but still couldn't speak. Her eyes burned as she stared blankly at the wall.

Afterwards, Manolo and Halleigh sat in silence in the same spot for an hour. He asked her, "So are you ready to talk yet?"

Halleigh sniffed. "He left me," she said, her voice cracking again. "You were right. He blamed me for getting arrested, and he left me." Just hearing herself say it made more tears spill down Halleigh's face.

"It's okay, baby girl. You'll be okay."

"He was all I had," she said, her voice breaking up from the thought of being alone in the world.

Manolo could hear the pain in her voice, a pain that put a devious smile on his insides, but he had to stay in character. He eased her head down in his lap and massaged her scalp and her hair. He kept smoothing back her hair. "You've got me, baby girl. Fuck that nigga. He just up and left you. He don't know how to hold you down. I bet he promised he would always take care of you, huh?"

Just like clockwork, Halleigh nodded.

"And now when you need him most, he gets ghost on you." Manolo paused. "And besides, he let somebody else touch you, baby girl. If he was really your man, he would've handled that for you. Fuck robbing a store with a bottle. He should have been shoving that bottle up the mu'fuckas' asses that did that shit to you."

Manolo spoke in a low, hypnotic voice. He slowly ran his hands all over Halleigh's body, sending chills up her spine. Suddenly tears flooded Halleigh's vision. She had a flashback as to how powerless she felt when she was being raped and began to shake uncontrollably. He lifted her head out of his lap and looked into her eyes. "They hurt you, didn't they?"

She nodded her head and dropped it shamefully into her chest.

"It makes me crazy just thinking about somebody hurting someone as sweet and innocent as you. That nigga should've protected you."

Halleigh gazed up in surprise at how upset Manolo had become.

"Fuck that, Halleigh," he continued, going for the Oscar nomination. "Any nigga put his hands on you, they gotta die." He stood up and motioned for Halleigh to follow him into his bedroom, where he pulled a .45 out of his closet.

Halleigh's eyes bucked at the sight of the pistol. She put her hands up to calm Manolo down. "No, wait a minute," she said. "I don't even know who did it. I don't know who they are."

The way he had erupted in anger scared her, but excited her at the same time. Her mother didn't protect her, Malek didn't protect her, but here someone who barely knew her was willing to protect her. He was willing to make sure that the two bastards who had raped her never had the opportunity to touch her again.

"Fuck! If you don't know the cats who did this to you, then I'm going for the next best thing—that nigga Malek. That mu'fucka should've held you down, Halleigh. Fuck basketball and the NBA. You was supposed to be his girl. I'm murking that stupid nigga for letting them get away with it," he yelled, inserting the clip and pulling back the chamber of the gun.

"No!" Halleigh yelled as she rushed to Manolo to grab the pistol from his hand. "No, don't!" She couldn't even fathom the thought of Manolo harming Malek. She especially didn't want to be the cause of

it. She had already been the cause of enough bad luck in Malek's life. She removed the gun from Manolo's hands.

He closed his eyes and wrapped his arms around her waist. "I'm sorry, baby girl. I'm sorry if I scared you. I just want to keep you safe, baby girl, that's all." His voice took on a syrupy tone. He held on to her tight. "I want you to feel safe," he repeated, as if he had known her all his life and it was his duty to keep her secure.

Halleigh held on tightly to Manolo. The truth was, he did make her feel safe. The fact that he wanted revenge on the dudes who'd hurt her made her feel special, like he truly cared for her.

"He doesn't love you. He wasn't treating you right, Halleigh," he whispered in her ear and then kissed it.

For a moment, his touch reminded her of Malek's. For a moment, she closed her eyes and envisioned that it was Malek's touch.

"He promised you all that, but he left you here in Flint while he's living it up without you."

Once again, Manolo was right. Why was she shedding tears over Malek when he had picked up and left her for dead? "Why did he do this to me?" she asked him in dismay.

"Because he doesn't know what he had," Manolo told her. "He don't deserve you." As he continued to speak, he could feel Halleigh dropping her guard. Her body loosened up as he held on to her, and she began to breathe heavily as she, too, brought her body closer to his.

Her broken heart had left her vulnerable to Manolo's manipulation. Her broken heart, as well as being thrown away and discarded by everybody who she felt should have loved and protected her and did-n't—her father, her mother, and now Malek. She needed to hear the words that Manolo was speaking. She needed to know that there was still one person in the world who hadn't thrown her away, even if it was a damn-near stranger. Every girl needed to be loved and to feel the way that he was making her feel. Any emotion felt better than the pain that everyone else had caused her. Any direction was better than being lost, and being wanted by somebody, anybody, was better than being discarded by everyone. How could she turn down Manolo's offer of protection?

"Let me take care of you, baby girl," he whispered, bringing his lips from her ear to her lips. Only inches away from her face, he was holding her so tight, not wanting her to have the option of backing away from him. "Nobody wants you, baby. Nobody loves you. But I see something in you. I want you. Can I make you mine?" He put his finger under her chin then kissed the tears rolling down her face.

Halleigh nodded her head as Manolo moved in to kiss her softly on the lips. She was hesitant at first, but he kissed her so deeply that she convinced herself that he was being sincere.

Manolo's kisses made their way from her lips to her breasts, to her stomach, and finally to her belt buckle, where he lingered, while her hands rested on his neatly waved taper.

"Baby girl, I want you. Do you belong to me?" he asked her. He unzipped the loose-fitting Baby Phat pants that she'd borrowed from Mimi. When she didn't respond, he said, "Tell me that you're mine, baby girl." He softly pushed Halleigh back on the bed, and with the precision of a heart surgeon, pulled her panties off.

She gasped as her heart beat uncontrollably. *What is he doing to me?* she thought.

"Tell me," he repeated.

He parted her legs, and let his tongue roll softly over her throbbing clitoris. She was still hesitant. He could tell that she was holding back, but when he inserted two fingers into her vagina, he knew she was willing. *I've just got to get her to say it,* he thought. *I've got to make her think my feelings for her are real.* He caressed her thick thighs and plump ass as he buried his tongue into her pussy. He lifted her hips up and fucked her with his tongue.

"Hmm," she moaned. She began to grind her hips on his face, gripping his processed hair and holding on for dear life. "Hmm, hmm," she moaned as he went to work.

"Tell me, who's Daddy? Who do you belong to?" he asked between licks.

"I'm yours," she moaned, moving her hips in circle eights, as if she was at a rodeo. "I belong to you."

"Who am I? What's my name?" he demanded. "Whose are you?"

"I'm yours, Daddy."

"Whose pussy is this?" he asked. He knew he was the man when it came to eating pussy. His head game was fierce, so he knew what her answer would be, even before she moaned back her response.

"Yours, Nolo. I'm yours, Daddy."

Got her. He positioned her in the middle of the bed, spread her legs even farther apart, and put his body on top of hers. His manhood stood at attention, her seventeen-year-old body drawing him to her like a magnet to steel. He couldn't wait to enter her. He groped her blossoming titties and took her dark nipples into his mouth.

Halleigh looked down at what she was inviting between her legs, fear gripping her as she thought about how badly it hurt when Riq had entered her walls for the very first time, busting through her like a football team would a banner on homecoming night.

Manolo felt her body tense up, and saw tears resurface on her face. He licked her face, wiping the tears away with his hot tongue like a mother cat cleans her kittens. "What them niggas did to you don't count," he said, knowing exactly what to say to make her feel better.

"Baby girl, *this* is your first time, and I'm going to make it right for you. I'm not going to hurt you."

She didn't say another word, relaxing her legs to allow him to enter her easily. Pain was what hit her first as his thick nine inches eased into her. She felt like her insides were once again being ripped out of her. She arched her back and tried to scoot her body away from him.

"Relax," he whispered as he began to pump in and out of her in a slow rhythm, as if he was moving to a silent melody.

Halleigh closed her eyes and dug her nails into his back, moving her hips in unison with his, as pain transformed into pleasure.

She didn't know it yet, but by giving her body to Manolo first, she was also giving him her head. She, like most women, equated love with sex. It wasn't going to be hard for Manolo to have his way with her, to create and control her little world.

Afterwards, her body was sore as she lay beside Manolo. She was quiet because she didn't know what to say. She hoped that it was good enough for him to want to keep her around. She knew that this was probably the reason all the other girls got to stay around. She had nowhere else to go, so if this is what it took, so be it. He'd promised to keep her safe, and she believed he would make good on his promise, unlike all the other liars in her life.

"Are you sore?" he asked her as he held her from behind.

"A little bit," she answered in a low voice. Her mind drifted back to Malek. *Why did he leave me?* she thought.

I got to get the kid off her mind. Manolo asked, "What's on your mind?" already knowing the answer to his question.

"Nothing."

He sat up and pulled her into his lap, and she sat between his legs, her back against his chest and her head resting on his shoulder.

"Look, Halleigh," he stated firmly, "I know what you been through, and I know you've got feelings for ol' boy. But I got to be honest with you. I can't be involved with no bitch—excuse me, baby girl. I don't need to refer to you like that, because you are anything but that. But when I think of you having feelings for another dude, I just get . . ." His words trailed off, and then he continued without finishing his original thought. "Point is, if you gon' be here with me, you've got to be loyal. Loyalty is important. If I can't trust you, I don't want you. Now, I'm not trying to do you like everybody else in your life and leave you, but I need to know this now before I get all caught up in you and end up being hurt by you leaving me."

Quickly, she responded like Tina Turner in the movie *What's Love Got to Do with It*, "I would never leave you." Halleigh knew what it felt like to be walked out on by her own blood, by people who she thought would be there to take care of her.

She wasn't about to do that same thing to someone else and walk out on them. *Never*, she thought.

"I just need to know who you gon' ride for?" he asked.

"You," she replied without hesitation.

"Are you sure?" He turned her chin so he could see into her eyes. "Because if I see you or even hear about you messing with another nigga, especially that nigga you *was* fucking with, I'ma kill 'em, you dig?"

"I understand," she replied. Her thoughts kept finding their way back to Malek, but he had hurt her beyond forgiveness. She knew that Manolo would never hurt her.

"So tell me who Daddy is, my little Sunshine," He tongue-kissed her sloppily on the lips.

"You are. You're Daddy," she responded with a grateful smile, happy that for the first time in her life she had a "daddy."

Chapter Thirteen

Jamaica Joe and his attorney strolled out of the police precinct toward a white Bentley parked right out front. Joe's head henchman, Tariq, was sitting on the hood, waiting for his boss.

Once Joe reached the bottom of the steps, he said to his attorney, "Thanks for coming so quickly. Those mu'fuckas fuck with me any chance they get." Joe was still upset about the Flint police and the petty traffic stop they'd made that led to his arrest.

"No problem, Joe," Wallace flashed a slight grin. "That's what you pay me for."

Joe looked over at Tariq and nodded his head. Tariq immediately went into his all-black hoody and pulled out a wad of money in a rubber band. He tossed it to Wallace, making it land right in the palm of his hands.

"Have a nice night, gentlemen," Wallace said. He shook Joe's hand then turned and headed to his own Bentley.

"Let's get the fuck outta here, fam," Joe said as he slid into the passenger side of his own car.

Tariq jumped into the driver's side and pulled off. He began to put Joe up on the latest. "Yo, you know that nigga Sweets is talking big shit about the Berston Park Battle. I heard he even recruited some NBA

players to play on his team this year," Tariq said, referring to the basketball game that was held every year at Berston Park.

"Oh yeah?" Joe's interest was piqued, although he tried to act indifferent.

It was the only time that Joe and Sweets would be in the same vicinity and not trying to kill each other. It was like an unspoken oath to the city—no violence at the Berston Park Battle. Berston Park was like a sacred ground to the city, and both sides respected it.

Joe and Sweets had been enemies for years and had a mutual hatred toward each other. Both of them wanted control of the city's drug trade and were standing in each other's way. Joe ran the North Side of Flint, and Sweets ran the South Side. Once a year, they sponsored a basketball team for the Berston game, and their teams battled it out on the court. For the last four years, Sweets had been victorious, enabling him to carry bragging rights over from one year to the next, plus any money that was put up on the game.

Very few people knew that Jamaica Joe had come from a middle-class Christian family in Fayetteville, North Carolina. His father used to be a principal, and his mother, a school teacher. Every one of his three sisters had graduated from college. Jamaica Joe, the youngest in the family, was an only son. From the time he was born, he was spoiled rotten to the bone, but it wasn't his upbringing that had made him a drug kingpin. It was just something in his blood. He loved the streets from the time he was a teenager. After doing a one-year stint in a juvenile camp for armed robbery, he was released at the age of eighteen and moved to Flint. He'd heard the drug trade was really jumping off there. He'd now been living there for the past twenty years in relative wealth and wielded some power.

Joe was noticeably bothered by the mention of Sweet's name. "Fuck that faggot-ass mu'fucka," he said. He searched through his phone to see what messages he'd received while locked up. He continued, "Send word to his crew that I'm willing to put up fifty thousand; winner take all."

"I'll put the news out in the streets," Tariq said, maneuvering the luxury car through downtown Flint.

Joe suddenly thought about Malek. The Latino man in the jail cell might not have known who Malek was, but he did. He knew Malek's skills; that he was an NBA prospect. *I need that nigga on my squad. Li'l man got heart.* He remembered how Malek held his own in the bullpen. *I know that young cat got some street-ball skills in him too.*

Joe was very familiar with Malek's ball game. He frequently gambled on Malek's high school games and whether Malek knew it or not, he'd made Joe a lot of money through his phenomenal plays. He pulled out his cell and dialed Wallace's number. "Yo, I need a favor," he said as he lay back in his seat.

Chapter Fourteen

Attorney Wallace stood next to Malek before Judge William Kennedy. "Your Honor," he said, "we move to have the case dismissed due to lack of evidence."

It was Monday morning, and the first case on Judge Kennedy's docket. The courtroom was filled to capacity with press, cameras, news reporters, and spectators. The judge had to call the court to order more than once.

Loyal fans just couldn't bring themselves to believe that someone with such a bright future ahead of them would throw it all away like that. They kept chanting, "Free Malek, free Malek, free Malek," only stopping their chants when the judge threatened to close the courtroom and put everybody out.

Wallace continued, "Your Honor, I submit that Malek Johnson has been the victim of the most heinous form of racism. This young man has no priors, is a model student, and is the number one national prospect for the NBA. For the life of me, I don't understand how Mr. Chiu could slander my client like this. This has to be a miscarriage of justice."

Malek's mother sat in the front row, her lip trembling, tears glazing her eyes. His stepfather sat next to her. Mrs. Johnson had kept her promise to her son by not calling her husband to inform him about Malek's arrest. She'd hoped and prayed that her son would be free from jail and at home before his father found out. That way, things wouldn't have seemed so bad. After seeing footage of his son on ESPN, Mr. Johnson made a beeline home.

Malek couldn't believe how Anderson Wallace shredded the prosecution to pieces, making it seem like he'd done no wrong. Wallace even produced an eyewitness who claimed to have seen the whole ordeal. The witness, a retired cop to boot, testified that he was taking his regular jog, when the streets were quiet and clear, and saw with his very own eyes Malek get racially profiled and discriminated against by the Asian storeowner. He testified how Malek had just been walking by, when, out of nowhere, the storeowner came running from the store and pointed him out as the man who'd just robbed his store.

"Any black man walking by would have been accused of the robbery that night," the witness said in an ever so convincing tone. "Hell, it could have been me." He claimed that the overzealous store-owner jumped the gun.

Anderson Wallace flipped the script and made Malek look like the victim, rather than the criminal. That's why Wallace was the best.

Malek didn't understand how this attorney had come to his parents

and volunteered to defend him for free. It had only been two days since the botched robbery, and already he was on the verge of having his image being restored.

The DA's office was too worried about Anderson Wallace filing a civil suit against them and just wanted to end the case as soon as possible. The prosecuting attorney, Jack Byrne, stood up and cleared his throat. He said, "Uhh, Your Honor, uhh, we too request that the case be dismissed."

Wallace looked over at the prosecution and smiled as he relished in another victory. He had fifty-two wins and no losses, to be exact.

The judge looked at Byrne skeptically. "Are you sure?"

"Yes, sir, we're quite sure," the prosecutor affirmed.

The judge bellowed in a stentorian voice, "Case dismissed!" and banged his gavel resolutely.

Malek smiled and looked back at his mother and his father with relief and joy. His father held his fist up and shook it in victory, as if to say, "The truth will always prevail. I knew my boy wasn't capable of making such a stupid decision." Malek then looked at his mother, who knew the truth, but had kept her word in not telling his father what had really gone down, that he really did hold up the convenience store. It was their secret. Malek noticed too that his agent/adviser was sitting in the courtroom. He had a look on his face as if, all of a sudden, a Good Samaritan had just returned the suitcase with a million dollars that someone had stolen. He was cheering louder for Malek than he ever had at one of his basketball games.

As Wallace guided Malek and his parents out of the courtroom, Malek then turned back to Wallace and gratefully shook his hand. Cameras flashed away as soon as they opened the double doors. ESPN reporters were frantically trying to get a comment from the newly acquitted NBA prospect.

Malek's agent acted as security, helping his client through the massive crowd. "No comment, no comment."

Once they reached the front steps of the courthouse Malek looked at Wallace. "I don't know who you are, but thank you." He breathed a sigh of relief.

"Yes, thank you," Mr. Johnson said, shaking Wallace's hand nonstop. "Thank you for getting the truth out about my boy." He turned to his wife and son. "You two, wait here. I'm going to go ahead and pull the car around."

"Thank you, honey." Mrs. Johnson watched her husband walk off to go retrieve their car. She then turned to Wallace. "Like my husband, I can't thank you enough for what you did for our son, but I do make one heck of a pineapple upside down cake," she smiled.

"You are all quite welcome," Wallace said, "but I'm not the one you should be thanking." He motioned his head to a tinted Bentley parked

across the street. Malek was confused. He was relieved to be out of jail and having his case dismissed completely, but he still was confounded as to how he got off. He wanted to see who was responsible for his miraculous exoneration. "I'll be right back." He kissed his mother and shook his agent's hand before jogging across the street to the car, where a young man with an iced-out chain and long braids was sitting on the hood.

Once he reached the car, Tariq acknowledged him, slowly throwing his head up. "What up?"

Malek nodded his head in response.

Before Tariq could say anything else, the back window of the car slowly rolled down, and Jamaica Joe's face emerged. "Get in," he said as he hit the unlock button.

Malek turned and looked at his mother, who was standing on the steps and chatting with his agent as she waited for his father. "Ma," he shouted. When he got her attention, he said, "You and Dad go ahead home. I'll catch up with you in a minute."

Mrs. Johnson wanted to disagree, fearing he might be going to try to see that hoodrat girlfriend of his. He hadn't even noticed yet that she wasn't there to support him. Malek had already climbed into Joe's car before she could say anything.

Tariq also got in the car and looked at Joe through the rearview.

"Wanna take a ride?" Joe asked Malek.

"Cool."

As the reporters circled the car, trying to take pictures through the tinted glass, Joe nodded his head, and Tariq pulled away from the chaos.

Malek had heard a lot about Jamaica Joe, most of which was bad. He couldn't understand why Joe had helped him out. The first thing on his mind was extortion. *This nigga must gon' try to ask for ten times more when I get drafted.* Malek looked around at the soft leather interior and then at Joe's presidential Rolex. *The way things look I know he ain't hurting for cash.* "Thanks for having your lawyer on my case. He saved me, for real."

"No doubt," Joe replied. "You're young, black, and talented. Them white folks would love to keep you down." He lit a blunt and let the smoke curl out of the corner of his mouth.

"What's the catch?" Malek asked, trying to get straight to the point.

"See, that's what's wrong with our people. We don't believe in helping our own out without expecting something in return. How do you know I'm not just lending a helping hand?"

"Because ain't shit in this world free."

"You a smart man. That's why I like you." Joe took another puff of his blunt. "Li'l nigga smart." He tossed the comment at Tariq as though Malek wasn't present. "This weekend my team is playing in the annual

Berston charity game. I would appreciate if you would play on my squad." Malek remained silent for a second. He knew about the tournament. It was the biggest event of the year, and he always went to watch it. He wanted to play in it, but after his popularity soared, his agent advised him not to play in non-school athletics to avoid getting injured.

"I don't know. My agent—"

"You a man, right?" Joe said calmly.

"No doubt." Malek lifted his chin and puffed out his chest.

"Stand on ya own two. Take your balls out your socks. It's just a one-day tournament. You gon' let some agent punk you?"

Malek pondered his situation for a moment. First, he took into consideration Joe's act of kindness. He knew that if it wasn't for Joe, he would be in jail facing robbery charges. After all, what was one game?

"I'll play," he said, evenly, and without flinching.

Chapter Fifteen

Manolo sexed Halleigh crazy for a week in celebration of her eighteenth birthday, breaking her in, teaching her how to drive a nigga crazy with her body. He showed her how to do the Kegel exercises, sticking his finger inside of her and having her tighten up a hundred times, to keep her vaginal muscles taut. He taught her how to suck dick, how to take it from the back, and how to be seductive without being trashy.

She didn't know she was being groomed for every other man in the world. She just thought she was being groomed for Manolo. After all, he had expressed his anger at just the thought of her being with another man. So why would she think he would be training her to do just that?

During that first week, Manolo showed all the concern of a loving man. He sent Halleigh to Planned Parenthood to make sure she hadn't caught a disease from the train the two men pulled on her. Even when the clinic said she didn't have any infections or anything, Manolo gave her some of Mimi's STD antibiotics to take for a week. Next, he gave her the morning-after pills until her period came.

After she had her menstrual cycle, Manolo sat her on the side of the

bath tub and showed her how to take a douche. "That's just to clean out all the toxins," he told her.

He also showed her how to properly wash her body after having sex with him. "Front to the back," he would say, pointing to her vaginal area. "I like clean women."

As a precaution, he also put Halleigh on birth control pills. Manolo became like the mother she sorely missed, providing her with the things a mother would, to usher her into young womanhood; right down to teaching her how to use a tampon properly. Before she only used Maxi pads.

Even while on her period she had to make money, so he had to show her how to plug it up and take care of business without a trick knowing she was on the rag. Some niggas didn't care. They were grimy like that, but some were disgusted by just the thought of a woman having the curse.

All along, Halleigh thought that he was teaching her how he wanted his woman to be. She didn't think twice about the freaky things he did to her. She couldn't tell him no. Even though she knew that she wasn't his only girl, she felt like they had a connection. As the days passed, she became aware that Manolo was somewhat of a pimp. That all the girls weren't just for his selfish pleasures, even though he didn't mind helping himself if the price was right. She noticed how the other women sashayed around naked or wearing only boa feathers around their necks, but at dinner time, whenever everyone was present, they sat down and ate like one big, happy family.

In return for offering his place to his girls, they worked for him out of the Best Western, trading sexual favors for cash. He also was part-owner of a strip club called Wild Thangs, where some of his girls worked for extra ducats.

His profession and what he did with the other girls didn't bother Halleigh though, as long as he kept his promise to her. She was too far-gone on Manolo's loving to care.

She was so enthralled with Manolo, she figured that she was just as important to him as Tasha appeared to be. They were the only two girls in the house that he never put to work, and she loved the attention. She had no idea that pretty soon, she would be old news and would have to pay later for all of the things he was doing for her now.

Halleigh stared at herself in the mirror as Tasha stood behind her and flat-ironed her shoulder-length hair. She wore light denim Dereon shorts. Her white and gold halter top revealed her newly pierced navel. The M•A•C cosmetics that Tasha applied to her face gave her a mature look instead of the schoolgirl look. Halleigh liked the change in appearance. She had never been more secure in herself in her entire life; the sexier style giving her a boost in confidence.

"Y'all ready?" Manolo asked. He stepped into the room. He exam-

ined Mimi, Halleigh, and Tasha from head to toe. His eyes lingered on Halleigh. Her denim shorts were so short you could see where her ass cheeks darkened. Manolo licked his lips at the voluptuous sight. *This bitch gon' make me some money.*

This would be the first time Manolo put Halleigh to work. He knew that the Berston Park annual game was the perfect place for her to make her debut. Niggas from all over Flint, and even major players from Detroit, would be in attendance, all looking for pussy. Dollars would flow like wine from a vineyard, and Manolo made sure that his bitches would be there to drink it up.

"Yeah, we almost ready, Nolo." Tasha watched through the mirror as he approached Halleigh. *I hope she's ready.* She was aware of Halleigh's illusions that Manolo loved her and didn't even want her looking at another man. *Wait until she finds out that not only he don't give a damn if another man looks at her, but that he wants her to fuck them.* She chuckled to herself as she tossed on more makeup.

"You look good, Sunshine," Manolo whispered to Halleigh.

Halleigh blushed. She loved when Manolo called her Sunshine. It literally brightened her mood. She lowered her head and replied in a low tone, "Thanks."

"You know it's gon' be a lot of niggas there trying to step to you—"

Halleigh interrupted him. "You don't have to worry 'bout that. I'm with you."

"Nah, baby girl. Niggas gon' be tryin'a see you. Put your game down and do you. It's time for you to make Daddy proud."

Across Halleigh's face flashed a look of confusion.

He could see the reluctance in her eyes as she realized what he was trying to say. "You with me? You down for Daddy, right?"

She nodded.

"Then it's time for you to make me a proud poppa." He turned her toward him by her shoulders. "Look, I done showed you how a nigga like to be treated. Now I need you to use what I taught you and make it work for you. Bring Daddy that paper," he said, kissing her on the neck.

Halleigh just stood there like a frozen popsicle. Was she really hearing what she was hearing? He kissed her on the cheek and then stroked her cheek with the back of his hand, sending sensual chills through her body.

He leaned into her ear. "You're not Daddy's little girl anymore," he whispered, his lips lightly brushing up against her ear. "It's time to grow up and earn your keep; earn your spot in this house and in my life."

The last thing Halleigh wanted was to lose her place in Manolo's heart, not to mention a bed to sleep in at night. She thought about how alone, cold, and afraid she was the night of the rape. Then Mimi

took her out of the rain and home to Manolo. Now, they were all her family, and she never wanted to be out on the streets alone and cold again. With that thought, Halleigh nodded her head in agreement. She was so lost she didn't even second-guess what Manolo was asking her to do. How could she tell him no after all that he had done for her? She didn't see that she was being used. She only saw that Manolo wanted her, which was more than she could say about anyone else in her life.

Manolo, Tasha, and Mimi left the room, Halleigh trailing slowly behind them. They all got into an old-school Monte Carlo. It was sitting on "grown man's" and had a fresh money-green paint job. Manolo got into the car.

Before the girls entered, Tasha turned around and whispered to Mimi and Halleigh, "Sweets gon' be there, so make sure y'all are about that paper today. If a nigga ain't talking money, keep it pushing."

Mimi didn't respond. She already knew what was up. Although Manolo took care of them, and he was the one they were indebted to, he reported to Sweets.

Sweets had the South Side of Flint on smash and had a notorious reputation in the hood. With Sweets behind him, Manolo was able to keep the sex game on lock, recruiting the baddest bitches in town. As long as he split his profits with Sweets, he had the muscle he needed to run his business however he pleased. Sweets respected Manolo's hustle so much he even went in on a strip joint with him. Mimi knew that whenever Sweets was around, she had to be about her money if she didn't want his foot in her ass.

Halleigh nodded her head, and Tasha got on into the car. Before Halleigh got in, she grabbed Mimi's arm and quietly asked, "Who's Sweets?"

With a matter-of-fact look on her face, Mimi replied, "You don't want to know."

Chapter Sixteen

Berston Park was packed for the first day of the big game. The sun was shining brightly, and the sky was a clear blue with no signs of clouds anywhere on the horizon. Both young and old were present. Flint families were happy to bring their children out to a decent out-

ing, and they all eagerly anticipated a good game. They'd heard that Malek, the number one high school prospect, would be playing. Some of the top gamblers in town had a lot riding on the game. The odds were 2-1 in favor of Sweets' team, since he'd won the past few years.

The excited onlookers in the bleachers kept cheering, "Malek! Malek! Malek!"

Malek warmed up for the game by dribbling the ball on the court, his eyes all the while scanning the crowd in search of Halleigh. He had desperately searched for her in spite of his mother telling him that she had showed up on their doorstep confessing that she had ruined his life and had decided to break up with him.

"I told you that little tramp only wanted you for your money," Mrs. Johnson told Malek. "Now that the chips are down and she thinks you don't have a chance in the world at the NBA, she's left you hanging."

That statement was only confirmed after Malek realized and thought about the fact that Halleigh hadn't bothered to show up for his court date.

It was hard for Malek to believe that Halleigh had left him hanging. He had even gone to her mother's home looking for her, just so that he could hear it coming straight from her mouth that she didn't want to be with him anymore. But he arrived only to find drug junkies scattered throughout the living room, and no sign of Halleigh.

"Miss Walters, have you seen Halleigh?" he asked Sharina.

"No. I don't know where that heifer is," her mother said, scratching her pus-cratered arms. "I thought she was with you."

"You mean she hasn't been home?"

"No. But if you see that li'l bitch, tell her to get her ass home. I got things for her to do."

He smirked. *Yeah, right. Like being your little trick?*

Malek really was beginning to get worried as the days passed. Where could she have gone off to if she didn't go back home? She didn't have anybody else. Nikki hadn't seen her since the night of the championship game. Malek shook his thoughts about Halleigh and tried to focus on the game that was about to take place. As both teams filled the court and the game was about to start, all eyes were on him. Malek's sports agent had begged him not to play in the game, but Malek believed that he owed Joe this one favor. So being very big on loyalty, he kept his word to Joe and played in the game.

Jamaica Joe stood in the middle of his team wearing a white Sean Jean polo shirt and a crisp pair of Air Force Ones. Sweets emerged from the limo with a Sean John wife-beater, crisp jeans, and new Timberlands, his tattooed body on display and his ripped body shining.

Looking at Sweets, one would never know he was homosexual. Actually, he was bisexual. He slept with both men and women. The ladies lusted after him, but he had no desire to have a relationship with them

unless they were moving dope for him. Sweets was a bonafide hustler and ran the South Side single-handedly.

Everyone, from pro athletes to rappers to street legends, was in attendance at the park. Every year the same two teams made it to the championship game: Joe's versus Sweets', north versus south. Every year it was an all-out battle, and the entire city was there to see who would come out victorious.

Sweets took his place on the bench as his players scurried over next to him. He then took a quick glance over at Jamaica Joe, who now waited with his team under a tent across the park. He hated Joe with a passion, and even though they had an unspoken pact not to war at Berston, he still took every precaution. His young hit squad was scattered throughout the park, each one carrying twin pistols. They called themselves the Shottah Boyz. The Shottah Boyz are four young killers who Sweets had practically raised, since their mothers were on crack. They all were between the ages of sixteen and twenty-two. Although young, they had a notorious reputation. It was rumored that between the four of them, they had fifty murders under their belt. Rah-Rah was reported to be the craziest. They said at seventeen, he was a stone-cold killer.

The announcer announced that the game was about to start, and the two teams filed back onto the court.

Joe's team huddled around him as he gave them a pep talk. "Let's bring the trophy back to the north. Fuck them niggas! Show 'em how we get down. Bring the title back to the hood."

Joe stuck his fist out, and the whole team put their fist on top of his and yelled, "North Side," in unison.

The game started, and immediately Malek began to take over the game. He had the whole crowd in awe as he played like a man among boys. Even the NBA players on Sweets' team had a problem stopping Malek. They may have been professionals, but Malek was at home, playing on that very same court practically all his life.

Joe sat on the bench watching his team blowout Sweet's. He couldn't believe how Malek took over the game and single-handedly made Sweet's team look bad. "Yeah, baby!" He clapped loudly, grinning and looking over at Sweets, who was obviously irritated. *Today is a good day, baby. It's gon' be easy taking that faggot mu'fucka's money,* Joe thought as he re-focused his attention on the game.

Meanwhile, Manolo's focus was on how much money his bitches was gon' clock today.

"Damn, look at all this money," Mimi said as the car pulled up to the park. She peeped the massive crowd that had occupied Berston Field House. "It's packed."

Tasha and Manolo stepped out first. Mimi and Halleigh trailed behind them. Dudes with iced-out neck pieces, and chicks with ass and

titties hanging out were all that could be seen. The fact that north and south were in the same place at one time had everyone on edge, so everybody was clicked up.

Mimi and Halleigh went their own way as they split up from Tasha and Manolo. It was so crowded in the small space that Halleigh and Mimi couldn't even see the players on the court.

"Yo, ma, where you going?" a dude asked Halleigh as she walked by him. He was standing with his arms folded across his chest; a white bath towel draped over his head to shield his face from the hot sun. The guy and all of his friends watched her backside; the natural sway of her hips commanding their attention.

Halleigh smiled as she continued to maneuver her way past them. Mimi stopped in mid-step, causing Halleigh to bump into her. Mimi looked at her like she was crazy.

"What?" Halleigh asked.

"Girl, you better go back over there and make that money." Mimi glanced back at the group of dudes. "I'm trying to get down too. Them niggas is crazy paid. So go on and hook it up." Mimi gave her a light shove.

Halleigh strutted back over to the group of dudes. She stammered to the guy that had called out to her, "Y-y-you, uhh, checking for me?" She tried to look confident, placing her hand on her hip and tilting her head to the side.

He grabbed her hand and held it above her head, commanding her to walk in a full circle while he peeped her up and down. Her juicy ass cheeks shifted from side to side as she turned around. "What's your name, ma?" he asked.

Before Halleigh could respond, Mimi cut in, "What's your government? You all into my girl's shit. How about you let her know who you are and what you're about, then she'll decide if you worth fucking with."

Mimi was arrogant and smart-mouthed, but her looks allowed her to be. The dude smiled and rubbed his goatee as he looked at the two young girls that stood in front of him. He figured they had to be only seventeen or eighteen. He was twenty-six and loved young pussy. "Chill, shorty. I'm Mitch," he said.

Mimi arched her eyebrows. "Well, what's up? What *you* working with?"

"Damn! What are you, her pimp or something? Can I kick it to your girl for a minute?" he asked politely, but obviously irritated.

"Do you, baby. All I'm saying is, time is money, ya feel me?" Mimi rubbed her fingers together as if she were flipping through bills.

"For real? Y'all getting down like that? You mean all I got to do is pay for this pussy?" He stared at Halleigh in disbelief.

Mimi nudged her.

Meantime, Halleigh's heart was beating out of her chest. "That's all it takes," she said in an embarrassed whisper.

"Shit. Take a walk with me then, shorty." He grabbed Halleigh's hand.

Before she walked away Mimi grabbed her hand and whispered, "Get the money first. Make sure he uses a condom too."

Halleigh nodded, and then she followed him to an '07 Cadillac DeVille.

He opened the door for her. "Get in," he stated.

"You got the cash?" she asked nervously. She looked over her shoulder and looked around. Somehow Mimi's aggressiveness made her feel better. She wished Mimi had followed behind them or something.

"How much you taxing?" he asked. He couldn't believe that the gorgeous young girl in front of him was tricking. She really looked innocent and clean-cut.

How much am I supposed to charge this nigga? she thought. That was the one thing she hadn't been schooled on.

"Two fifty," she said, hoping that she wasn't short-changing herself.

He pulled out three hundred-dollar bills and handed it to her.

As she nestled into the back seat of the car, she felt her chest heave up and down as the small space became hot. Her hands began to sweat when she felt Mitch put his tongue on her neck.

"Come here, ma. Why you all over there?" he asked, pulling out his manhood.

Halleigh psyched herself up. *Just do it. Close your eyes and do what you got to do.* She unbuttoned her shorts and eased out of them. *I'm doing this for Manolo. I'm going to make Daddy proud.* She straddled him and grinded her hips as he touched her breasts, squeezing them a little bit too hard. He slid her thong to the side, pulled out a condom, and slid it on to his throbbing dick.

Halleigh looked down at it. He was a decent size. In fact, he wasn't any bigger than Manolo, and she was grateful because she didn't want it to hurt. She felt as if she was selling her soul to the devil when he put himself inside of her.

When he felt her tight walls, he said, "Shit! Ma, you a virgin?"

She gripped him. From the way he moaned she could tell that he loved the way the inside of her felt. At the same time, a tear fell from her eyes as she stared out of the rear windshield and rode his dick.

"Damn, ma, you working it. Umm . . ." he stated as she performed her new job.

She couldn't stop the tears from rolling down her eyes. *I can't believe I'm doing this,* she thought.

He finally came and she got off of him. Feeling disgraced, she wiped her eyes, put her shorts back on, and quickly exited the vehicle.

Even though she'd used the feminine wipes Mimi told her to use, she still never felt dirtier in her life.

Chapter Seventeen

With only thirty seconds remaining in the game, Joe's team was ahead 84-52. Joe knew that they had a pact to keep beef away from the charity game, but he wasn't going to let this opportunity to demean Sweets slip away. He stood up and looked at Sweets. He then put up his middle finger and cracked a small smile.

Sweets was steaming hot. He hated to lose, and to lose to Joe made it that much worse. Sweets stared at Joe as he openly disrespected him in front of the entire audience.

Someone in the crowd stood up and yelled, "North Side!"

Other members of the crowd began to chant, "North Side!" giving respect to Joe's side of the city.

Sweets, totally humiliated, wasn't going to let Joe's disrespect ride. He looked over at the members of the Shottah Boyz, and Rah-Rah nodded his head, to signal that he would take care of the problem.

Malek dribbled the ball, waiting for the final buzzer to sound. He had easily led his team to a victory. When the final buzzer went off, everyone cleared the stands and rushed the court, chanting, "North Side, North Side, North Side."

Malek smiled and scanned the crowd. He went over to Joe and gave him a brief hug, and the team joined him, huddling around and jumping up and down.

Joe embraced Malek and locked hands with him. "Good game, fam. You did ya thing out there. You ever need something or a favor, holla at me."

"Thanks."

The crowd had begun to break up, but in the midst of everything, Malek spotted her. He spotted Halleigh and his heart dropped.

"I'm 'bout to let that bitch-ass nigga have it," Rah-Rah said under his breath. He gripped on his .45 pistol that he had tucked under his shirt. The youngest of the Shottah Boyz, he was by far the nuttiest of the clique. Rah-Rah watched Jamaica Joe as he embraced one of the players from his team and knew that it was the perfect time to get at him. He had the go-ahead from Sweets to let him have it and was more than

happy to put in the work. Rah-Rah got within five feet of Joe, pulled out his pistol and pointed it at him, while he was still embracing Malek.

Halleigh felt dirty as she rushed away from the car, and it seemed as though people were staring at her. It was like they knew what she'd just done.

Mitch emerged from the car and ran after her. He yelled, "Yo, ma!"

She stopped walking and turned around to face him, but didn't respond. She knew that she had hit a new low. In her wildest dreams, she never thought she would turn a trick. What was happening to her? Who was she becoming? She didn't even know herself anymore.

"Where can I reach you, you know, if I'm trying to see you again?" Mitch asked. "I mean, you working for somebody, or is this a private hustle?"

"I work for Manolo." She hated what she had just said. *I work for Manolo.* She never wanted to work for him. She just wanted him to love and protect her from the very mean streets he now had her working. Tears flooded her eyes.

"Word? You a Manolo 'mami'?" he asked. Before she could respond, he continued, "Damn, that nigga is moving up. Let him know Mitch said you good for business, baby. He ain't had a bitch like you since Tash retired." Mitch pulled off another hundred-dollar bill and placed it in her hand. "I'ma get at you again, ma, for real."

Halleigh placed the money down in her short's pocket with the other bills as she stood on the curb. Just as she was getting ready to go find Mimi, gunshots rang out through the park. *Boom! Boom! Boom!*

The park suddenly turned into a frenzy as everybody began ducking low and running for cover. Pandemonium reigned. The thunder of feet stampeding and hysterical shouts could be heard all over the park.

Oh, God! Where is Mimi? She looked frantically for Tasha, Manolo, and Mimi, anybody. When she didn't find them, she made a run for the car.

Boom! Boom! More shots rang out.

Mimi spotted Halleigh running toward the car, which she had already made her way to. She yelled, "Hal! Hal! Come on. Them niggas started shooting. Somebody got shot! The police on they way."

Manolo, who was sitting in the driver's side of the car, along with Tasha in the front passenger side, yelled, "Halleigh, let's go!"

Halleigh finally hopped into the car. Tasha was sitting calmly on the passenger's side, and when everyone was safely inside, she called out, "All right, let's go." Manolo pulled away from the curb and headed toward the house.

After they all calmed down, Tasha turned toward the back seat. She could tell by the look on Halleigh's face that she'd been crying. Her

eyes were red. Tasha knew that those tears had nothing to do with the fear of bullets traveling. *She turned her first trick.* Tasha recognized the lost look that every girl had after they turned their first trick.

As if Manolo had read Tasha's mind, he said pointedly, "Hal, I saw you handling your business out there. You got my money?"

Halleigh pulled the money from her pocket and handed it to Manolo.

He looked at the four crisp hundred-dollar bills. "Damn, Hal! How much you charge the nigga?"

"Two fifty. He just told me to keep the rest," she answered in a whisper. Dazed, she stared blankly out of the window.

Manolo laughed and looked in the rearview at the young girl. Then he looked at Mimi, who sat next to her. "You see that? You better take notes." Manolo was pleased with himself for grooming a bitch like Halleigh. He knew she was guaranteed to make him money.

Looking at her through the rearview mirror as she stared out of the window, he knew that out of all the girls, she really wasn't cut out for this business. For a brief moment, a little bit of guilt seeped into his veins. Then he thought about his mother, eloquently referred to as Lady. Lady. She resembled the legendary Lady Day, Billie Holiday, before heroin took its toll on her looks. His mother was a high-yellow hustler, and Manolo's father was her pimp. So if hoeing was good enough for his mother, it was certainly good enough for any bitch. With that thought, the guilt evaporated from his veins as he visualized just how much money his little Sunshine was really worth.

Chapter Eighteen

The shots rang out as Malek was embracing Joe.
Boom! Boom!

"What the fuck was that?" Joe hollered. He let Malek go, but Malek's body acted as if it didn't want to part from Joe's, as if it was just heavy and couldn't move.

Just then, Malek, clinging to Joe, said as loudly as he could, which turned out to be a whisper, "Man, I've been hit!"

His tone was so low, and the whole park had fallen into such chaos, Joe didn't hear him. "Get up off me!" Joe exclaimed, unaware that Malek had been hit. Once again, he tried to push Malek off him.

Bullets that were, in fact, meant for Joe, had caught Malek in the calf and in his hip, but no one noticed, as people emerged from every direction, running and hiding. Screams rang out and echoed throughout the park. The cacophony of gunfire piercing the summer day made it sound like the Fourth of July, except, these were no firecrackers. The park had erupted into a war zone. People fell to the ground, and some hid behind cars as they called out to one another to try to get to safety.

"Hit the ground."

"Run!"

"Get Nay-Nay and them."

Instantly, Joe's henchmen came to their boss's defense, and they began to return fire. Laying there in the midst of gunfire, Malek listened to the curses of Joe's men. "Aw, hell naw!" one called out. "No, these bitch-ass niggas didn't start no shit today of all days."

"Open fire on these mu'fuckas," another spat.

"I swear on everything I love, it's on," another one said.

Rah-Rah shouted, "Y'all niggas is dead." He maneuvered through the crowd holding a smoking gun in his hand. He'd heard shots fired and knew that they were coming for him. He saw his older brother, Lynch, another member of the Shottah Boyz, trading shots with one of Joe's henchmen.

Boom! Boom!

Rah-Rah rose up and fired two shots at Tariq, who was shooting it out with his brother. Rah-Rah bust his gun like a madman, not caring who he hit, as he continued to fire in Tariq's direction carelessly. Meanwhile, women, children, and men scattered in a frenzy, trying not to get caught by stray bullets.

"Yo, I'm hit," Malek whispered, holding his leg in agony. It felt like a missile had hit him. He had fallen on top of Joe when he got hit.

After pushing Malek off him, Joe held the young man in his arms. He looked at his leg and noticed that the bullet had gone in and out, and that blood was pouring out of his calf. "It went in and out. You good. Stay right here!"

Joe then reached into his waist and pulled out his all-black .45 pistol. He cocked it and rose up. Without even ducking for cover, he walked straight toward Rah-Rah, who was too busy busting at Tariq to see him coming. With one shot, Joe sent a hollow-tip through Rah-Rah's torso, causing him to drop his gun and fall to the pavement. He then walked over to Rah-Rah as he spat up blood and clenched his stomach.

As Rah-Rah struggled to get air, Joe stared at the young boy. He pointed his gun at Rah-Rah's head, his index finger on the trigger, and his conscience pricked him. *This kid doesn't even look a day older*

than seventeen, he thought to himself. Mayhem happening all around him, he blocked all of it out and just stared deep into Rah-Rah's eyes as the young boy tried to stay conscious. Joe looked at the tattoo on the boy's neck—*Shottah Boyz*. He then realized that the young boy wasn't an average kid. He was a killer, a killer who had just tried to take his life. Joe let off two bullets into Rah-Rah's chest, leaving him staring into space forever. Joe saw the rest of the members of the Shottah Boyz jump into a black tinted SUV and speed off. He ran back toward Malek, who was on the ground in pain. He yelled to his henchmen across the park, "Yo, come over here!"

His workers, along with Tariq, ran over to him and picked up Malek so they could rush him to the hospital. When the screeching tires of the black SUV that the Shottah Boyz had jumped into came back around, Joe and his men immediately began to fire shots at the truck, but the bullets didn't penetrate.

"It's bulletproof!" Joe yelled. He stopped firing. He knew he'd just be wasting shots. He was very familiar with bulletproof whips, since all of his were equipped with the feature.

The back door opened, and a young man that strongly resembled Rah-Rah came out with his hands up and no shirt on, to let them know he wasn't strapped. Tears ran down his eyes as he slowly walked toward his dead brother.

Joe signaled his crew to take Malek to the car and to not shoot at Lynch. He understood the game.

"No! Oh, my God. Rah-Rah!" Lynch held both hands above his head and made his way over to his younger brother. He wasn't even focused on the men who had been shooting at him with their guns. He just wanted to come and get his heart—his brother. He didn't notice that Rah-Rah wasn't in the car, until they reached the corner and he knew that something had gone wrong. Rah-Rah was the fastest of them all and was always the first to jump in the car when they exited a crime scene, but not this time. He had an inevitable appointment with his maker.

Lynch had come back, unconcerned for any danger to him, and found his brother lying dead. He kneeled next to his brother's lifeless body and gently scooped him into his arms and rocked back and forth. He hadn't cried since adolescence, but now he was crying a river for Rah-Rah, another soul lost to the game.

Malek heaved deep breaths and squirmed in the back seat as Tariq sped through Flint's streets, headed toward McLaren Hospital. The bullet wound felt like fire.

Joe, sitting next to Malek, tried to keep him calm. "You gon' be all right, fam. Just hold steady."

Malek tried to block out the pain, but it was too much to bear. The

only thing he could think about was how his basketball future and life with Halleigh were doomed. His life was going in a fast downward spiral. This was the beginning of the end for him.

Chapter Nineteen

Malek rested in his hospital bed as his mother sat next to him with her Bible open. His father had just left after Mrs. Johnson insisted he go home and get some rest. He agreed, but only upon the promise that, once he returned to the hospital, she would go home and get some rest too. Mrs. Johnson had been right there by Malek's side for days straight. She hadn't even changed clothes because she was so worried about her son.

The room was filled with flowers from Jamaica Joe and his crew.

"Even though I walk through the valley of the shadow of death, I fear no evil," Mrs. Johnson read from Psalm 23:4.

"Ma, stop reading all that stuff about dying. I'm gon' be fine," Malek assured her.

"I know. The doctor said you were lucky. This has always been one of my favorite scriptures, though. It's comforting."

Mrs. Johnson had been reading him her favorite scriptures for the past three days. She'd almost had a heart attack when she got news that her only son had been shot. She was relieved when the doctor informed her that both wounds had been in-and-out and no major organs had been punctured. Malek was very lucky to not have any permanent damage.

One reason Mrs. Johnson had been continuously reading scripture was because she felt that if she kept talking, Malek wouldn't have time to ask her what she knew he had been wondering about for the past three days. Finally, she had worked up the nerve to tell Malek what she knew was his greatest fear.

"Baby," Mrs. Johnson started, "your, uh, agent called me this morning." She swallowed the knot in her throat.

Malek sat up at attention. "What did he say?" Malek had wondered why his agent hadn't been up to the hospital to see him. This absence made him fear the worst, that he was no longer interested in agenting him.

"He, uh, said that, uh—"

"Come on, Ma," Malek said, starting to get agitated, "just spit it out."

"Okay, son, he said that all the NBA teams have lost interest in you," Mrs. Johnson reluctantly informed Malek, and it just broke her heart to do so. She knew that the news would hurt his heart just as well, but she had to tell him the truth.

"What?" Malek said as he sat there in shock. The words felt like daggers straight through his heart.

"Baby, I'm sorry," Mrs. Johnson said. "He said it doesn't look too good. He doesn't even want to represent you anymore."

A single tear slid down Malek's face as his childhood dreams began to evaporate. All he knew was basketball. If you took that away from him, in his mind, he was nothing.

"Let's just thank the Almighty Lord that you are still breathing." Mrs. Johnson grabbed her only child's hand.

Malek was too devastated to speak. He just threw his head back in the pillow, bit his bottom lip, and let the tears flow. He didn't have Halleigh, he didn't have basketball, and he didn't have any hope. College basketball was out of the question, because he'd hired an agent, which made him ineligible to play college ball. The bullet holes in his body weren't helping matters, either.

"Ma, the only thing I ever wanted to do was play ball. That's all I ever knew. What am I supposed to do now, huh? I was supposed to buy you and Dad that big brick house. I'm just like my real daddy now, a failure."

"Malek, hush that nonsense. You ain't nothing like that man. You are an intelligent young man with all the opportunities in the world. This little mishap isn't going to stop you. With God on our side, we gon' make it through this, hear?"

"Yes, ma'am." Malek gripped his mother's hand. "Ma, I never forgot how you worked so hard all these years, and how Pops worked those two jobs selling sweepers and doing telemarketing sales just to feed and clothe me. Y'all found the money to send me to basketball camp every summer, even if y'all had to go without. Mama, I will try to find some way to pay you and Dad back, I promise." Malek just broke down in a heaving sob.

"Don't worry about it. Everything is going to work out. You don't owe me or your father anything. Just be a good man and make something out of your life. I don't know why this happened to you, son, but we are going to get through it."

Malek didn't tell his mother that he knew the man who the bullet was really intended for. He just told her that he was at the wrong place at the wrong time and caught a stray bullet, trying to spare her all that worrying.

The painkillers the doctor had Malek on were starting to make him

kind of drowsy. As he began to doze off, the thoughts of the news about his future were eating him up.

"I love you, baby," Mrs. Johnson said, rubbing her son's forehead.

"I love you too," Malek answered, closing his eyes.

Malek's thoughts were consumed by his ugly reality. Why hadn't he listened to his agent, or to his own gut feelings for that matter? He'd had a bad feeling about playing in the Berston game, but felt that he owed it to Joe. Now his career had ended before it even began.

I fucked up. I fucked up, Malek thought to himself. Wishing that the recent events had never happened he realized Mrs. Johnson was right. At least he had his life, unlike Rah-Rah, whose brother, Lynch, could only wish for at this point. Three days after the shooting, Malek might have been laying up in the hospital, but Lynch's brother was about to be laying six feet under.

Lynch walked out of the funeral home with revenge on his mind. He just had to do the most difficult task he'd ever been faced with— pick out his brother's casket. He didn't know how he would even make it through the funeral. It had always been Rah-Rah and Lynch, since they were little boys. He didn't know how he was going to be able to go on.

Although grief-stricken, all he could think about for the last three days was getting back at Jamaica Joe. He kept picturing him hugging and cheering along with Malek after the game. The more he thought about it, the angrier he became.

Still feeling incensed, he joined Sweets and the rest of the Shottah Boyz in Sweet's Hummer. He wanted Jamaica Joe's blood. "Where you say ol' dude live again?" Lynch asked. He loaded up his automatic assault rifle, a.k.a., the street sweeper.

Sweets hadn't been able to find out where Joe lived, so he suggested the next best thing. He was going to make Joe look for them. "Yeah, when you wanna bring out a rat, you gotta lay out the cheese," Sweets told Lynch. "Don't worry, we gon' get these niggas. I swear on everything I love, and I swear on your brother's grave."

Sweets was also devastated by the loss. Rah-Rah had been like a son to him. He had raised the boy up since he was nine years old. After their mother's crack habit had caused her to dissipate into a strawberry, Rah-Rah and Lynch were just two homeless little waifs.

Although they had been placed in foster care, the boys kept running away due to the physical and emotional abuse. When Sweets found them, they had just run away from their latest foster home placement and were eating out of the garbage. He took them into his home and taught them a trade. Eventually, the authorities, their caseloads swollen with too many drug babies, too many broken families, and too much dysfunction to worry about two little black boys,

stopped looking for them. They became just another statistic that had fallen into the cracks.

From the start, Sweets became their provider, their protector, and their mentor. Sweets never forgot the foster home he had been raised in, where he had been sexually molested. That is why he had always provided a safe haven for "his boys." Although bisexual, Sweets wasn't a pedophile. He never messed with any of his boys. That's why they were all so loyal to him. In return, they became his little killing squad; Rah-Rah being the baddest.

Sweets never went along with his Shottah Boyz when handling business, but this time it was personal. He was ready to kill anyone associated with Joe, and that meant Malek was in danger now too.

After some convincing from the nurses on staff, Mrs. Johnson went home to get some rest. They told her that the medication would have Malek out for quite some time, so while he was asleep, it was as good a time as any for her to sleep as well. At first, she insisted that she do what she had been doing, sleeping right there in the hospital chair, but after further convincing she headed on home.

Mrs. Johnson pulled up to her house and prepared to walk in to change clothes. She wanted to get back to her son's side as quickly as possible. She knew that he was in pain. She didn't show Malek, but she was hurting inside also. The thought of a big house was nice to her. She didn't say it, but she had also been banking on Malek getting drafted by the pros.

She had worked hard for so many years. She thought that Malek would change all of that but reality finally set in. She now knew the chances of him going pro were slim and next to nothing.

It took all her strength not to break down and cry when she pulled up in front of their little Cape Cod-style house. Malek just didn't know what his success had represented for her. He'd been her entire life, and his success had become hers.

Now, she could see the dark days that lay ahead for her son. She was a realist. It was a crushing defeat for her to see Malek throw away his one opportunity to get out of Flint.

Nineteen years earlier, she had missed her chance when she chose not to go away to college, hooking up instead with Malek's biological father. That turned out to be one of the worst decisions, considering he never was a father to her son. Determined not to raise her child on welfare, she worked at a string of low-paying jobs, never the career she could have had as a school teacher, had she not chosen love. That's why she didn't want Malek to throw everything away on a hoodrat like Halleigh, who was no longer in the picture anyhow.

Mrs. Johnson was consumed by her thoughts as she shambled up the stairs on her front porch and unlocked her front door. She didn't

see the black SUV pull up with Lynch hanging out of the window, his weapon cocked.

Shots rang out as Lynch sprayed the house like an insane man. He didn't care that he was shooting at an innocent bystander. He just wanted to send a message to Joe. Bullets ripped through Mrs. Johnson's back, and she fell to the ground, gripping her Bible to her chest.

"Lord, help me," were her last words spoken.

Lynch made the Johnson house look like Swiss cheese and laughed as he let off his whole clip. He was trying to start a war, and indeed that's what he did. The war had just begun—North versus South Flint.

Chapter Twenty

"You got another john on his way up," Tasha said into the phone. "Okay, I'm ready." Halleigh watched her last customer leave the room. She hung up the phone and took a long, deep breath. She walked over to the hotel's bathroom so she could freshen up before her next customer arrived. She glanced in the mirror and didn't recognize the face that was staring back at her.

The past weeks had flown by like a blur and she hated the person that she had become. What would her momma think if she saw her little girl now? What would Malek think? she wondered. Was he even thinking about her at all? One thing she knew, not a day went by when Malek didn't cross her mind.

I can't believe he just up and left me like that. He promised me he would always be here for me. I should've never told him about what happened that night. He probably thought less of me because— Before Halleigh could complete her thoughts, the sound of knocking on the door filled the air. She dropped her head and rested her hands on the sink as she remembered how much she hated exchanging sex for money. But it was the only way she knew to survive.

Halleigh wiped the semen from her cheek as she finished up her last job for the day. The overweight black man was looking at her with goo-goo eyes as he stroked his manhood until all of his juices were out.

"You something else, Sunshine!" he said, calling her by her working

name, the one Manolo had branded her with. He pulled up his pants and zipped them up.

Halleigh looked at Barry and smiled as she stood to her feet. Barry was a regular customer of hers who loved to frequently call upon her to get a blowjob after work. She was totally disgusted by him, but she would never let him know that. Let Barry tell it, Halleigh enjoyed hitting him off just as much as he loved receiving it.

"Eighty dollars, Daddy." Halleigh walked over to the bathroom sink totally nude, her voluptuous cakes shifting sides with every step.

Barry enjoyed the view and left a hundred-dollar bill on the bed, giving her a twenty-dollar tip. "See you next week, baby," he said, admiring Halleigh's body. He headed for the door to return to his wife and children across town.

"I'll be waiting for you, Daddy," she said, leaning halfway out of the bathroom and displaying her pretty smile. She glanced at the bed to make sure he had left her the cash and then focused back on him as he exited the hotel room.

As soon as the door closed behind him, she dropped her fake smile and went over to pick up her cash. She was glad that it was the end of the day so she could rest. She'd turned eight tricks that day, and her body was tired. After turning her first trick with Mitch, she had started keeping count. Now there had been so many, she'd lost count of how many tricks she'd turned in the past weeks.

She turned on the shower and flopped on the bed. She picked up the phone and called Tasha to let her know she had finished up with her last client. Tasha instructed her to meet her in her room when she finished showering.

After getting fresh, Halleigh walked to Tasha's room and knocked on the door.

"Come in. It's open!" she heard Tasha yell.

Halleigh opened the door and saw Tasha on the bed counting money. She had money stacks placed all over the bed as she sat Indian-style adding up the day's total. Halleigh couldn't understand why Tasha didn't have to turn tricks anymore, but although Tasha was only twenty-three, she had put in a lot of work for Manolo. She had been turning tricks since she was sixteen, and Manolo had a sweet spot for her.

"Hey, girl," Tasha said as she looked at Halleigh with a smile. "How did you do tonight?"

"Not too bad. I made nearly eight hundred," Halleigh replied, digging into her purse and pulling out a wad of money.

Tasha, still counting the money, replied, "Toss it on the bed."

Following Tasha's instructions, Halleigh stated, "Girl, I'm tired as hell. I hate when you send stanky-ass Barry to me."

"That nigga is fat and ugly as hell, but the nigga always request you. That's a part of the game though." Tasha briefly stopped counting the money and looked at Halleigh. "Nolo gon' be happy with you. You made a killing tonight."

"Yeah, they were tipping good."

Mimi came storming in, a Newport hanging out of her mouth. "What's up, bitches?" Mimi said jokingly. She kicked off her stilettos. "These mu'fuckas are killing my feet."

"Hey, Mimi," Halleigh said as she watched Mimi dig into her bra and pull out wrinkled bills.

"Hey, girl," Tasha said while she counted the money.

"I made five hundred tonight," Mimi said, tossing money onto the bed near Tasha. "Damn, I'm good!" She looked at Halleigh. "How much you make?"

Tasha replied on Halleigh's behalf, "Eight hundred."

Mimi got a salty look on her face and smacked her lips in jealousy. Tasha and Halleigh giggled at the sight of Mimi's bubble getting busted.

"Anyways!" Mimi said as she snapped her head and rolled her eyes. She and Tasha began a conversation while Halleigh's mind was elsewhere.

Halleigh couldn't believe the life she was leading. She could've been preparing to graduate from school and be with the love of her life. Instead she was laid up in a cheap hotel, fucking anybody who was willing to throw her a little cash. *I can't believe I was stupid enough to fall for Manolo's game. He took advantage of my situation, and now I can't get out. I wish I would have run away from his ass the day I met him,* she thought sadly to herself. Halleigh, ashamed of the things she was doing, knew that she had to get by any way that she could.

"Y'all coming to watch my set tonight?" Mimi asked. She often doubled up and made money in Manolo's and Sweets' strip club. She was all about her paper and figured that if she was gon' sell pussy, she might as well get extra customers from Wild Thangs.

Halleigh was so engrossed in her own thoughts that she didn't even hear Mimi. The only thing on her mind at that particular moment was Malek. She missed him, and the thought of him hurt so badly, she tried to suppress the fact that she ever had him in her life. *Ain't no point in thinking about what I can't have,* she thought.

"Damn, Hal, what you thinking about?" Tasha asked. "You good, girl?"

"Yeah, I'm good," she replied.

Mimi just stared at her. That wasn't the first time she'd seen Halleigh just completely blank out. She knew what the cause was too. Halleigh was heartbroken. "Fuck that nigga, Hal," Mimi remarked. "He

didn't deserve you anyway. I bet you his ass ain't losing no sleep over you."

Tasha looked at Halleigh. "What nigga?"

Halleigh lowered her eyes to the floor and shook her head. "Nobody," she said.

"It better be nobody. I hope you not talking about the kid, Malek. Manolo will kill both you and him if he even finds out you even thinking about him."

"But he's not gon' find out," Mimi cut in quickly. "Right, Tash?"

Tasha looked at Halleigh. "Yeah, I'll keep my mouth shut, but you get your head together, Hal."

Halleigh tried to dismiss thoughts of Malek. "Ain't nothing to get together, Tasha. Don't worry, I'm okay."

Tasha almost felt bad for Halleigh as she watched her drift back into wishful thinking. She knew that Halleigh wasn't built for the lifestyle she was leading. *It takes a strong bitch to make this money. You can't let it make you,* Tasha thought. She knew that Halleigh looked down on herself for what she had become, and it was the first time that she felt guilty for keeping one of Manolo's girls in line.

"Let's get out of here." Tasha stood and walked out of the room, heading toward home.

When they arrived at the house, Tasha went to give Manolo their earnings for the night. She tapped on his door lightly and then entered without waiting for a response. When she opened the door she saw Manolo kicked back on his king-size bed, one hand down his sweat pants, the other on the remote control.

"Bring that ass over here," he ordered.

Tasha chortled and then walked over to the bed. She could tell that he had blown a couple trees from the scent of marijuana that still lingered in the air.

"You already know what I want," he said, patting a spot on the bed next to him.

"Yeah, I know." She pulled out and then dumped the rolled-up wads of money onto the bed beside him.

Manolo grabbed the cash and began counting, *twenty, forty, sixty, sixty-five, seventy . . .* until he reached two thousand seven hundred.

"How much Mimi bring in?" he asked, a look of confusion on his face.

Tasha noticed. "Five—why you ask that?"

He ignored her question, but in his head he thought, *That bitch been shaving money off the top. She usually brings in at least seven bills a night.*

Once Tasha saw that he wasn't going to respond to her, she got up to leave.

Before she reached the door, he said, "Send Halleigh in here. I feel like getting my dick sucked."

Tasha turned up her face. She hated when Manolo got beside himself. He usually treated his girls decent, but when something was bothering him, he would get to smelling hisself and start degrading his girls. She nodded and then walked out of the room.

Tasha entered the room Halleigh and Mimi shared in time to see Mimi standing with her back to the mirror and her head turned around as she watched herself work her ass muscles. She wore only a thong and was making her booty clap.

"Them other hoes don't got shit on me. Them bitches better hope my set ain't first, cuz it ain't gon' be no tip money left," Mimi mumbled conceitedly.

Mimi was a different type of chick. She was confident and felt like she chose to do what she was doing. Her motto was, "If I'm a ho, I'm a top-dollar ho," and she didn't mind sleeping with a different man every night as long as his pockets were heavy.

Tasha wished that Manolo had asked her to get Mimi for him instead of Halleigh, since she was beside herself as well. She knew that Halleigh wasn't built for hoeing and sooner or later it would break her. She didn't need Manolo throwing her no extra work. "Hal, Nolo wants you," Tasha stated.

Halleigh nodded and then left the room. She walked into Manolo's room and she could see the print of his hard dick through his baggy sweat pants. "Tasha said you wanted me." Her tone was dead as she walked over and sat on the bed next to him.

He pulled out his manhood and began to stroke himself. "Hook me up, baby girl."

The thought of pleasing Manolo almost made her gag. Now that she realized how he had played her, she was disgusted by him. She hated to be in the same room with him because he reminded her of all the things that had gone wrong in her life since losing Malek. Now whenever she looked at Manolo he reminded her of the rape because he left her feeling just as powerless. At least when she was raped, she fought back until the two men overpowered her. Now, it was like she was getting screwed in the ass, straight up, with no Vaseline. It was like she had given him permission. As bad as her mother's drug habit was, as far as Halleigh knew, Sharina had never turned tricks for a living. She mainly got her money through boosting.

"Nolo, I have to get ready to go to the club," she said in avoidance.

"I own the mu'fucka. That can wait." He grabbed the back of her neck and slowly pulled her head into his lap. When she pulled in the opposite direction, he applied more force. "What are you running from, Halleigh? I said put your mouth on it!" he whispered through

clenched teeth. As the words came out, he gripped her hair and pulled roughly.

"Oww! Manolo, you hurting me!" she yelled as she resisted more.

A few minutes later, Tasha and Mimi heard an ear-piercing scream that came out of Manolo's room. "Agghhh!!!"

"What is he doing to her?" Mimi asked.

Tasha hurried into Manolo's room. Halleigh was laid over the bed fighting against Manolo as he grabbed for her panties.

"Daddy, Daddy, wait!" Tasha reached for Manolo's raised fist as he prepared to strike Halleigh.

He pushed Tasha off of him and continued his rage against Halleigh. "You telling me no? How you gon' tell me I can't have what's mine?" he yelled.

He bitch-slapped Halleigh in the mouth before she knew what had happened.

Tasha flung herself over Halleigh, blocking Manolo's blow, just as he was about to hit her again,. "Wait, Daddy, she didn't mean it. Halleigh hasn't been feeling too good. She's just tired. She made you eight hundred dollars today all by herself. She just don't want you to be in no stanky pussy, Daddy. She just wanna be fresh for you. She worked hard for you today." Tasha was rambling and talking so fast, Manolo actually bought the bullshit that she was selling.

Halleigh was sniffling and crying violently.

"Go help her fix her shit up. We got to be at the club in thirty minutes!" he yelled.

Tasha quickly pulled Halleigh out of the room.

Manolo slammed the door behind them, but not before they heard him mumble, "Ungratefulass bitch!"

"Are you all right?" Mimi asked Halleigh when they came back into her room.

Halleigh couldn't stop crying. She hated her life. *How did I get here?* she asked herself.

"She's fine. Help me clean her up," Tasha said.

Halleigh had a busted lip, and Mimi quickly went to retrieve a washcloth to wipe up the blood. She also grabbed Tasha's makeup kit.

"What were you thinking," Tasha asked her, "boss'n up on Manolo? When he asks for something, you give it to him—plain and simple."

"I can't," Halleigh choked out words in between her tears.

"What you mean, you can't? You better." Mimi began to put makeup on Halleigh. "And quit crying. You fucking up my work."

Halleigh held the tears inside. "I can't do this no more. This is not me. This is not how my life was supposed to be."

Tasha turned Halleigh's head toward her so she could look her in the eyes. "Listen, Hal, you have to get yourself together. This may not be what you had planned, but this is what you got. You better deal

with whatever you going through before you get yourself hurt. Manolo don't play that shit. You the one told him that he could do this to you. Now you got to live with your decision."

"I told him? I didn't tell him he could pimp me," Halleigh said in a harsh whisper. Visions of how she could have been at the prom with Malek, or how she could now be walking across the stage at her graduation to get her diploma danced through her mind.

"You told him that he was Daddy. You gave him permission to do this to you. You have to just accept it and get used to it. There is no way out, Hal. He will kill you before he lets you leave. All you have to do is do what he tells you, and you will be fine, I promise," Tasha stated. "Okay?"

Halleigh nodded, and both girls embraced her to make her feel better.

"Okay, okay! Let's go, so y'all bitches can watch me work," Mimi stated with a smile, trying to lighten the mood.

Chapter Twenty-one

When Manolo and the girls had first entered the club, 50 Cent's "Hustler's Ambition" was blasting. The crowd swayed back and forth to the rhythm.

Meanwhile, people addressed Mimi as though she were a hood celebrity. One patron called out, "Mimi, you on tonight?"

Mimi nodded and then went straight to the dressing room to prepare for her set. Manolo, Tasha, and Halleigh sat in the large booth of the strip joint as they all waited for Mimi to come on stage.

The club was crowded, and everyone seemed to be having a good time. The club's patrons consisted of many of the major Flint players, hustlers, pimps and whores. The women wore mini dresses, jumpsuits, and capri pants, and the men wore anything from suits to casual wear. All the pimps wore bright colors, from canary yellow to parakeet green, carried gold canes, and wore different styles of hats to distinguish themselves.

"You okay, Hal?" Tasha asked as she leaned in toward her to whisper the words in her ear.

Halleigh nodded, but Tasha knew differently. She could tell that Halleigh was uncomfortable. Her body language said it all. She sat

with her hands tucked tightly in between her legs and she hadn't said a word all night. Tasha hoped that the young girl would develop a thick skin. Otherwise, she'd never make it. *She has to if she wants to survive in this game.* Tasha stared at Halleigh with a sympathetic look in her eyes. *As much money as she is pulling in, Manolo ain't trying to cut her loose no time soon.*

Tasha was familiar with Manolo's tactics. First, he lured the young girls in. He made them feel as if he would take care of them even though no one else wanted them. Although his girls knew that he was a pimp, he always made each one feel as if she was more special than the next. After he was sure that he was inside their head, he would flip the script on them. He would remind them of all the things that he'd done for them and make them feel indebted to him. It was never too long before he put a girl to work. He also knew how to keep them pitted against each other with suspicion and envy. By the time these girls realized they were being pimped, it was too late. Manolo had them so afraid of him that they did it just to avoid upsetting him.

Tasha knew the game well because she had been through it. She was different than the other girls, though. She was strong-minded and let Manolo know up front that she wasn't trying to trick her entire life. They came up with the agreement that if she watched over the other girls and helped him keep them in line, then he wouldn't put her to work. Tasha was twenty-three and hadn't turned a trick in almost three years. In fact, she was instrumental in Manolo's operation, helping to instill the fear in the rest of his girls. With Halleigh it was different, though. She now felt guilty for trapping the young girl.

A half-hour had gone by before Mimi finally came on stage. That's when the DJ, on cue, began to spin T-Pain's "I'm N Love (Wit A Stripper)." She was wearing a "Catwoman" outfit and glasses before she slowly stripped down to her thong. All eyes were on her as she hopped to the top of the pole, intertwining her legs through it and spinning seductively to the bottom. She worked the pole like the professional that she was, seducing the pole like she was handling a hard dick. She also knew how to clap her ass cheeks without missing a beat.

Tasha smirked as she looked around the club and noticed how the men practically worshiped Mimi. She had to admit, *That bitch is good.*

Mimi rolled her stomach as she held onto the pole with one hand. She walked around picking up as many dollar bills as she could without interrupting her entrancing dance. She then turned toward the crowd and did the move she'd practiced at home. Men crowded the stage when her thick ass and thighs jiggled as she made her ass clap. Mimi wrapped one leg around the neck of one of the spectators and grinded her pussy in his face. It didn't surprise Tasha when the man stuck his tongue out and took a taste of Mimi's spot. She continued to dance in front of him as she held out her hand, waiting for him to bless

her with some cash. By the end of the song, she'd made about three hundred easily.

Mimi sashayed off stage and went over to Manolo's table. "How I do, Daddy?" she asked.

"I don't know. You tell me," he responded, referring to how much money she'd just made.

Mimi discreetly rolled her eyes and pulled out the crumbled bills. Manolo took his cut and then handed the rest back to her. The split was always the same, 80/20 in Manolo's favor.

This nigga always taking all the money, but he don't put in no work, Mimi complained silently.

They all knew that the way the money was cut up was unfair, but no one was stupid enough to say anything to Manolo about it. They signed on to be his mami, and unfortunately, what he said was law.

Manolo sat back, and with Mimi on one side and Halleigh on the other, wrapped his arms tightly around their shoulders. Tasha sat next to Halleigh.

A bright-skinned girl with shoulder-length, kinky hair came walking by. She stopped at the table. "Hey, Daddy, what you drinking?" she asked Manolo.

Tasha rolled her eyes and Mimi gave the girl a dirty look. The girl's name was Keesha. She'd been trying to get down for the longest. She wanted to be a Manolo mami so bad, whenever one of Manolo's girls did something wrong, she was the first to report it to him, hoping he'd get rid of them and allow her to take their place. Her little trick hadn't benefited her thus far, though.

Big nose, snitchin'-ass, stanky-pussy bitch. Mimi crossed her legs. *She want to get down. That bitch is a dirty trick, and her pussy stank, that's why she only serving drinks. Ain't nobody trying to fuck her.*

"Yeah, bring us all some Long Islands, top-shelf, and keep 'em coming. I feel like getting loose tonight," Manolo said.

They all kicked back.

They were having a good time, and even Halleigh began to chill. When she got that liquor in her, she let her guard down and actually forgot about her current circumstances. For a moment, she felt like she was on top of the world. The way Keesha kept pushing up on Manolo, it made her feel like she was a member of an exclusive club. The whole world was the fools and Manolo's mamis were the ones who really had it going on. *Maybe life wasn't so bad after all*, she thought, when the liquor oozed into her bloodstream.

"Uh-oh, here comes this bitch again," Mimi mumbled. She moved over and sat between Tasha and Halleigh.

"Why y'all don't like her?" Halleigh whispered as she watched Keesha approach.

"Uh-um, ain't no *y'all*. Bitch, you don't like her either," Mimi stated.

"That bitch is a snitch and a wannabe." Mimi's lips curled into a sneer of hatred. Manolo ignored their conversation, but he tightened up when he saw a male approach Mimi. He knew exactly who the bald-head dude was. "What can I do for you, Troy?" he asked, obviously irritated.

"You can't do shit for me," Troy told him. "My business is with li'l mama."

Halleigh looked at Tasha, who looked at Manolo. They all waited for a response.

"She is my business, player. So what can I do for you today, my man?" Manolo took a sip of his drink.Suddenly, a level of unrest overtook the room. Tension was high at the table, and the girls kept looking back and forth, waiting to see how the situation would play out.Troy pulled out a badge and flipped it open, along with a hundred-dollar bill. "Look, man, I come in peace. I'm just looking for"—he paused to kiss Mimi's shoulder—"a little entertainment, that's all."

Manolo nodded his head and thought about what he could gain out of having a cop in his pocket. *This dumb mu'fucka will risk his entire career for some pussy. I'ma make sure I tape this shit.* "I think we can waive the payment under these circumstances." Manolo said. "I'm a man who likes to form business relationships, you know? A favor for a favor. You can have all the entertainment you'd like if you are willing to overlook certain things."

"Consider it done," Troy responded.

Mimi looked on in astonishment. *I know this nigga ain't serious,* she thought to herself. *He 'bout to make me give this pussy up for free?*

Manolo nodded his head as a signal for Mimi to leave with Troy.

She smacked her lips loudly and said, "Fuck that. I ain't messing with no cop. Especially if the mu'fucka ain't paying. Y'all got me fucked up. I'm about to get back to work." She rose from the booth.

Halleigh could see Manolo's temperature rise at Mimi's disrespect.

"Bitch!" he yelled. "You gon' do whatever the fuck I tell you to." He grabbed Mimi's arm forcefully and bent it backwards, as if he was trying to break it.

"Awww!" Mimi cried out.

Tasha immediately jumped up and pulled Mimi into her side of the booth. She stepped over to Troy and whispered in his ear, causing a smile to spread across his face.

"I'll take her," Troy stated, looking Tasha up and down as if he could taste between her legs already.

"I'll take care of him, Daddy," she said to Manolo, getting Mimi off the hook. "Calm down and enjoy your night."

Tasha held on to Troy, who was now palming her ass, and mean-mugged Mimi as she walked away with him. She hadn't had to turn a trick in years and now here she was saving Mimi's ass—literally. *What's*

happening to me? Tasha thought. *Since when do I have feeling for these bitches and care whether or not they get their ass kicked by Manolo?*

Tasha could tell by the way Manolo was gritting his teeth that he was furious at Mimi though, and that an ass-kickin' might still be in store for her. Tasha's thoughts continued as she walked away to handle her business with Troy. *This dumb bitch, she don't even know what she just got herself into. Why would she do that shit after what happened earlier with Halleigh telling the nigga no? Now she got me out here about to hit this nigga off just to keep shit peaceful. I ain't tryin' a fuck with this blue-vested mu'fucka either, but it's all a part of the game.*

Once they were back in the so-called VIP (Very Important Pussy) room, Tasha thought as she lifted her dress and guided Troy's face to her vagina, *Me doing this is gon' keep Mimi's dumb ass out of jail next time. This nigga ain't about to get shit from me. He gon' eat my pussy and beat his own dick. My shit so good, he won't know the difference. If Mimi was as bad as she thinks she is, she wouldn't have to fuck the nigga. Real bitches do real things. You can't be a street diva if you don't know how to make the game work for you.* That's just what Tasha did, make the game work for her.

Chapter Twenty-two

The tension was so thick for the remainder of the night that Halleigh was thankful when it was over.

Manolo had retired to his upstairs office at the club with Tasha, who was more than likely watching him count up the evening's profits, if not counting it herself while he watched over her.

Halleigh and Mimi walked around silently as they helped Keesha clean up. Halleigh was exhausted. It was three in the morning and the club had been dead for about an hour. She couldn't wait to get home, take a shower, and go to bed.

They all looked up when they heard Manolo's footsteps echo through the quiet room. He walked slowly down the steps and approached Mimi. Without saying one word, he smacked her clear across the room; his hand making a loud clapping sound when it made contact with Mimi's skin.

"Nolo!" Mimi yelled. "Stop! Don't, Daddy!" She put her hands up to block her face.

Halleigh looked on and witnessed Manolo become a madman. All the nicey-nice façade disappeared and the real Manolo emerged as his raging fit took over.

"Bitch, don't you ever," he yelled as his open hand became a fist and he rained punches all over Mimi's body, "in your life . . . disrespect me!"

Halleigh stood frozen in fear; her feet glued to the floor and her mouth as dry as cotton.

Meanwhile, Keesha smirked as Manolo beat Mimi mercilessly, connecting with blow after blow to her body. He hit her repeatedly and made it worse when he grabbed her by her braids so she couldn't block her face. "Bitch, you . . . do . . . what . . . I say do!" he said almost in a patterned rhythm, pausing every time he swung. He was so enraged he was foaming at the mouth. When his fists became too sore, he stood up and kicked and stomped her.

"Aghh!" she howled from the pain that pierced her small body.

"Manolo!" Tasha yelled, descending the steps two at a time. She'd heard the commotion all the way from upstairs, but she wasn't prepared for the bloody mess that she found downstairs.

Troy ran out behind her, but when he saw Manolo's act, he dismissed himself and left the club. He didn't want to get involved if the police were called in. As an officer, he knew he would be called in to question if he was caught in the red-light district.

"Fuck, Manolo!" Tasha stated as she pulled him off of Mimi. "What did you do to her? How she gon' make you any money now lookin' like this?"

Halleigh was frozen in fear. She watched as Manolo pulled Mimi up by her neck and held her out for everyone to see. "This is what happens to you if you disrespect me." He let Mimi's body drop to the floor.

Tasha rushed to his side. "It's okay, Daddy. Calm down. You taught her. She won't do it again." Tasha pulled Manolo away and led him back up the stairs.

Dumbfounded, Halleigh stared in disbelief at Mimi, who was squirming and moaning in pain on the floor. She was barely conscious.

Tasha snapped her fingers in Halleigh's direction to get her attention. Halleigh finally snapped out of it and looked at Tasha with nothing but pure fear in her eyes. Tasha threw her car keys at Halleigh. "Take her to the house and make sure she's okay." She then turned her attention to Keesha. "And, Keesha, clean this mess up."

Halleigh ran to Mimi's side. "Oh my God! Mimi!" she whispered. "You'll be okay, Mimi. Come on, let's get you out of here."

"Fuck him," Mimi cried uncontrollably as she spit blood from her mouth.

"Shhh." Halleigh picked Mimi up and put her head underneath her shoulder to support her weight. "We've got to get you out of here."

Mimi limped and could barely walk as they headed to the car, and when they finally made it, she passed out in the back seat from the pain of her beatdown. Halleigh got in the car and looked in her rearview at Mimi's beaten body. Tears rushed to her eyes. *He could've killed her,* she thought to herself. "It'll be all right. Everything is gon' be okay," she kept repeating; not only trying to convince Mimi, but herself as well. It was times like this that Halleigh wished she'd had a father. If she had one, there was no way she would have been so gullible, getting caught up with the likes of Manolo. That night in their bedroom, she whispered back and forth with Mimi. "How did you get caught up with Manolo?" she asked her.

"I was just like you, young and dumb. I was trying to get to Hollywood. I wanted to be a dancer. First, he got me in his club, then the next thing I know, he had me on the stroll."

"Do you think we can get away?"

"Only if we leave feet first."

"What's that?"

"Six feet under."

Chapter Twenty-three

ONE YEAR LATER

When Malek was in the hospital recovering from the two bullet wounds he had suffered at the Berston Park Battle annual basketball game he'd learned of his parents' fate. Bullets from the drive-by shooting had riddled his house, killing his mother and also killing his stepfather, who lay asleep on the front living room couch. When Malek was released from the hospital, he had nowhere to go. He was of adult age, but he was still in high school. How in the hell was he supposed to pay the house note that his parents had left behind? He

got a little bit of change from a life insurance policy his parents had, but after he gave them a proper burial, there was hardly enough money left to pay for a night at a hotel, let alone pay a mortgage. It wasn't long before the bank foreclosed on the house and Malek ended up on the streets.

With no other family in Flint, Malek turned to the one source that always seemed to be a last option; one that doesn't discriminate . . . the streets. With a broken spirit and broken dreams, it wasn't long before Malek fell into the street life full force. Jamaica Joe, whose street credentials were much validated on the streets of Flint, took Malek under his wing and put him on the block in search of the American dream. Now that it was obvious that his basketball talents weren't going to get him in the pros, Malek was getting money the only way he knew how.

"Take it or leave it, mu'fucka. It is what it is." Malek held one hand in his pants and looked up the block to make sure the coast was clear as he interacted with the dope fiend. "You can take yo ass over to the South Side and cop some of that bullshit dope if you want to, or be satisfied with what I just gave your ass." Malek waited for his customer to respond, although he knew that eventually the man would see things his way, because Jamaica Joe had the best connect in the city of Flint.

The dope fiend examined the bag of heroin, holding it up high and thumbing it in an attempt to make all of the contents fall to the bottom. He could get a better picture of just how much dope he had if it was all heaped together in one pile. The fiend had been complaining about the pack's size. Whether Malek obliged his complaint or not, he knew that he had the best dope in town in the palm of his hands and he wasn't going to pass up that good high for nothing. The customer nodded with approval and then walked off with the bag of dope with him after leaving Malek with fifty dollars.

Malek sat on the stoop as he waited for his next customer. He wouldn't be surprised if it turned out to be the same fiend that had just walked off. Ever since Malek started slinging that premium, the term "repeat customer" had a new definition. Hell, some fiends would only get as far as their automobile, smoke up their dope, then hit Malek right back up again. It was crazy like that.

As Malek sat waiting, all types of thoughts crossed his mind. Not for one moment did he think about how quickly he had gone from becoming a potential NBA star athlete to a fuckin' corner boy. Standing six feet and five inches tall, Malek was built for the NBA, but when his mother and stepfather were killed in a drive-by shooting, his dream of having a basketball career died with them. They had been his strength, his rock, his reason for wanting it so bad. They had sacrificed their entire lives for him, and Malek wanted nothing more than to reward their

efforts by seeing to it that, through his skills and talents, they would never need to work again a day in their lives.

Although Malek's bullet wounds might not have been life-threatening, one just happened to bury itself in his leg. He had barely been checked into the hospital before NBA teams, and even colleges, lost interest in him. He knew he didn't have a chance in the world when even his agent abandoned him in the hospital bed. They all feared the inevitable: that his leg would never allow him to play ball like he once did before the ill-fated shooting. He now walked with a very slight limp, which he camouflaged as part of a smooth swagger.

Malek took to the streets like a duck took to water. It turned out that he was a natural-born hustler. He had only been hustling for a year, but quickly moved up in the ranks. Joe had given him his own block in the Fifth Ward, which was the most profitable block on the North Side of Flint.

Every day Malek thought about his mother and stepfather and missed them dearly. To date, the police had not found the person responsible for the fatal shootings, and that hurt him even more. Revenge and hatred toward the unknown perpetrator was buried in his bones, just waiting to be resurrected. The shooter had taken away every person he had ever loved. Almost everybody, with the exception of Halleigh, who just seemed to walk away on her own free will, left Malek for dead, it seemed.

Halleigh was about the only girl Malek had ever loved. As a matter of fact, it was the night that he had decided to keep his promise to her and stand by her side and be there for her that his entire life changed for the worse. Yet, it seemed she hadn't so much as thought twice about him since. He had put his entire life on the line and ruined it for her; someone who didn't even love him back enough to come see about him in the hospital after the shooting. At the end of the day, Malek had to admit that losing Halleigh hurt more than losing his dreams.

Malek rubbed his neck, which had his deceased mother's name tattooed on it, as he scanned the block. When he saw a silver Lexus turning the corner, he smiled and threw his hands up, knowing that it was Joe. The car pulled up and stopped in front of Malek. The back passenger's side window rolled down.

"What's good, son?" Joe asked as he rolled down the window and looked at Malek.

Malek walked over to the car and extended his hand to show Joe love.

"What up, fam?" he replied, greeting Joe with a handshake and a snap.

"Get in." Joe threw his head in the direction of the empty seat next to him. Malek walked around to the other side, opened the door, and

slid in next to Joe. When Malek got in, Tariq, who was driving, gave him an envious stare through the rearview mirror.

Although he had never verbally expressed it, Tariq didn't care for Malek too much. It was safe to say that he was a little envious of how his boss had taken to the youngster, putting his trust and loyalty in this kid so quickly. The fact that after only a year Malek was running his own block was evidence that for some reason, Joe favored this young buck. Tariq had to be a corner boy for years before Joe gave him his own block. This gave him envy in his heart toward Malek, who moved up in the ranks after only a few months of putting in work, not just for Joe, but in the game, period. For Malek to have the busiest block of them all only added to Tariq's jealousy.

Joe lit his blunt while they sat in the idle car. He took a puff and then asked Malek, "How you do this week?"

"I need to re-up again," Malek said as he spotted one of his workers and waved him over.

Trap, a heavyset hustler about the same age as Malek, scanned the block and then reached under the porch of the house he sold from and grabbed a brown paper bag. He then ran over to the car and handed it to Malek. Malek took the bag, opened it, looked inside, then turned and handed it to Joe.

Joe opened the bag to see money rolls filling it up to the top. A smile crept across his face as he nodded proudly. Through the rear-view mirror, Tariq watched, boiling inside, knowing that this kid was about to receive accolades from the boss.

Joe closed the bag and set it in between him and Malek. Shaking his head, he said to Malek, "You never cease to amaze me, Malek."

The compliment made Malek feel good as Joe spoke to him just as proudly as his stepfather would have congratulated him on winning the NBA championship.

"If you keep this up, you're going to be great in this game," Joe added, referring to the dope game.

Joe had never seen anyone move dope like Malek moved it. From the moment Joe had first seen Malek in that county jail cell, he knew this kid had a bigger hustle in him than the petty crime he was being held for. His instincts had steered him right, because the way Malek had been putting in work lately, Joe knew that without a doubt, just like himself, Malek was born to hustle.

Malek remained silent as he took in Joe's compliments. He glanced up at Tariq, who was mugging him through the mirror.

What's that niggas problem? Malek thought as he returned a mean stare for a brief moment. Malek felt uneasy around Tariq. Not that he was a threat or anything; Malek just sensed that Tariq was light-weight offended by his presence. Malek knew that because he was so young, the older cats that had been in the game would be intimidated by a

young hustler getting his grind on. That never stopped Malek from doing what he had to do. What Malek did sometimes worry about was another hatin'-ass nigga trying to stop him.

I'm going to have to keep an eye on that nigga Tariq, Malek surmised. *He might just be a problem.*

Joe interrupted Malek's thoughts. "You ran through a whole brick in two days?" Joe asked him, not believing the obvious.

"Yeah. That shit is like clockwork 'round here. I be hittin' niggas off proper. I don't be cutting my shit heavy." Malek shared with Joe his technique that kept the fiends coming back. "I might not make as much on the flip, but I run through the dope faster, re-upping more. So, in the long run, I make more money."

"If more mu'fuckas thought like you, then everybody could eat off this game." Joe looked to his head henchman. "Ain't that right, Tariq? Not even your ass ever came up with that type of logic." He turned his attention back to Malek, leaving Tariq's ego wounded. "Niggas get greedy and try to stretch they dope so much that it doesn't even get their customers high anymore." Joe inhaled the smoke into his lungs. "I'll have someone drop off a brick in an hour."

"No doubt," Malek said. He then immediately turned the conversation to some more important business. "Have you found out anything about the shooting?" he asked Joe for the millionth time. Joe told Malek that niggas in the street talked; they were worse than broads sometimes. He assured him that he would have his soldiers keep their ears to the street and he would find out just exactly who was behind it. When they did, payback would be a mutha.

Joe's reassurance wasn't enough for Malek. Time was of the essence. The spirit of revenge was embedded deep inside Malek's bones. Every day that went by was another day that the culprit got to breathe and Malek wasn't having that. Every time he got a chance, he asked Joe that very same question. He was worse than Celie in *The Color Purple*, asking Mister every day if any mail had come for her.

"No, not yet, but trust me, I am going to handle that for you. We're going to make whoever did that pay," Joe answered.

"Yeah, I hear you, man," Malek said as he exited the car.

Joe could hear the disappointment and doubt in Malek's tone. "Don't worry. We gon' find that shit out. You feel me?" Malek gave a doubtful nod. "You trust me on this one?"

Malek stood outside of the car and looked up to the heavens, where he knew that as much as his mother loved and served the Lord, she was watching down on him. He then looked back down at Joe. "Yeah, I trust you, man."

"That's what I'm talking about." Joe stuck out his hand to give Malek some dap and then signaled for Tariq to drive off.

Ever since the death of Malek's parents, Joe and Malek had formed

a close bond. After losing all potential to go pro, Malek fell into the arms of the streets. With Joe there grooming him and now turned out by the streets, there was no turning back for Malek. He was deep into the game, and everybody knew that there were only two ways out: death or jail. Now it was all about the survival of the fittest, and he was in for keeps.

Chapter Twenty-four

Halleigh waited inside the hotel room for her next john to show up. Business was slow, but Halleigh wasn't complaining. She needed the break. Her body was tired from the constant sexing of men over the last year.

She sat in front of the vanity mirror, and tears began to flow as she looked into her soulless pupils. She hated the woman that she'd become. She had once been a plain Jane high school honors student with a positive future. She was even dating what the world thought was a shoo-in future NBA star. No one would believe—hell, she didn't believe—that that same girl was now selling her body and her soul to any man with the right amount of cash.

Her mascara ran down her cheeks as she reached into her blouse and pulled out a small plastic baggie. She emptied the contents of the baggie onto the vanity table and made it into a straight line with her pinky fingernail. Halleigh looked down at the white substance that had become her "acquaintance" over the last six months. She'd started snorting as an escape from the reality she was living. She hoped that, like Calgon, the feeling would take her away; that it wouldn't be her laying there while every Tom, Dick, and Kwalie got on top of her and did their business. Halleigh couldn't believe she was heading down the same path of drug abuse as her fiended-out mother

"I hate my life. It wasn't supposed to be like this," Halleigh whispered as she lowered her head and sniffed the cocaine into her nostrils. She immediately jerked her head back to prevent her nose from running. She had picked up this bad habit from a john she serviced frequently. He'd convinced her that the drug was an escape, the much-needed escape her mind desired. She needed to escape from the pain. She needed to escape from life itself.

After her initial introduction to the vice, she had developed a steady

habit for the drug. Whenever she was feeling down or needed a boost to cope with her profession, she leaned on her "new friend," cocaine. She had to admit, ever since she started using the drug, her clientele had picked up and became more regular. High on coke, she got lost in herself, in the moment, willing to do things that she would not have done otherwise. Sexual exploration was like a side effect of the drug.

The phone rang, startling Halleigh as she was trying to enjoy her high. She wiped her runny nose and walked over to the phone.

"Hello?" she sniffed.

"You got another john coming up. He wants a number two," Tasha said, referring to vaginal sex. They called oral sex *number one* and vaginal sex *number two*. *Twelve* was the total package, meaning the client paid double for anything his heart desired, or on some occasions, her heart desired.

The business of trickin' wasn't just exclusive for men out to throw away some cash for a few moments of pleasure. There were female clients every now and then also. A couple of the women were married with children, but secretly had desires to be with other women. They didn't want to chance getting into a serious relationship with a woman and being found out, so this was the only other way they could think to cure the craving inside of them. One time Halleigh had two female clients at once. Fortunately, all they wanted Halleigh to do was watch them. Another time, when they showed up as repeat customers and were assigned to Mimi, they wanted the third wheel to roll with them. Of course, Mimi didn't play when it came to gettin' money, so she was down for whatever. Every act had a price tag on it as far as she was concerned.

Halleigh took a deep breath and shook her head from side to side. She was sore, worn-out, and needed a while to recoup. Her last client had paid for a number twelve and she thought he'd never leave. As long as the money kept coming, no pun intended, Halleigh had to keep him comin'.

Halleigh sighed as a stalling technique. "Tash, I just came on my period. I can't do it," Halleigh lied, trying to avoid having to take the job. Not even high off the cocaine could she force her body to cooperate with the next trick's request.

What Halleigh failed to realize was that as the madam, Tasha made it her business to know every single girl's cycle like clockwork. She even had a calendar; that way she knew to send the johns who only wanted oral sex performed on them to the girls who were on their periods. So she was very much aware of the fact that Halleigh's period wasn't due for a week or so. Just to double check, though, Tasha opened her calendar in the back of her appointment book and scanned down until she found Halleigh's name.

"What you talking about, Hal? You know and I know that you ain't

on the rag yet," Tasha replied in a confident tone after verifying such on her calendar. "Don't even try that bullshit. Trust me, many a girl before you have tried that same lame-ass excuse. There is no time for laziness. In this business, a girl's gotta put her stilettos on and hustle-hustle." Tasha snapped her finger twice. "This is about making that dough. You know what happens when someone tries to fuck with Manolo's cash flow. Now, with all that said, do you want that trick's dick up in your pussy, or Daddy's foot up in your ass?"

Halleigh knew that Tasha was right. She thought about that time when she'd first started in the business and Manolo had beaten her down after she refused to please him orally. Then, just like now, she had been worn out and tired after spending an entire day with johns. Even as she reflected back on the beating, as tired as she was now, she thought the beat-down just might be worth it.

"My body has been acting funny lately. I haven't been getting a lot of rest, Tash. You know that," Halleigh replied in a whiny voice, hoping to gain her madam's sympathy.

Tasha felt bad for Halleigh and knew that she needed a break, but she also knew that Manolo would have a problem with that and take it out on Halleigh's ass. If it wasn't for Tasha coming to her rescue that time Manolo beat Halleigh, the nineteen-year-old might not even be alive today. Tasha couldn't help but fear what would happen if Manolo got a hold of her again and she wasn't there to protect her this time.

"Look, you can take the rest of the day off and get yourself together," Tasha told her, "but you have to stay in the room so Manolo won't find out. I'll send your clients to some of the other girls."

"Thank you so much, Tash. I owe you." Halleigh was glad that she had found favor in Tasha's sight.

When Halleigh first started working for Manolo, she saw Tasha as some hardcore, unfeeling broad who cared about two things only— Manolo and Manolo. This meant that she carried the whip, making sure that bitches followed his orders so that he stayed happy, and that no bitch tried to take her place. Getting paid and taken care of without giving up the pussy was a position Tasha was not willing to give up. On top of that, she got five percent profit off of whatever the girls made for Manolo. Being the madam over the Manolo Mamis definitely had its perks.

"Oh, please believe, you still working today. I'm just not going to send you any clients. I need you to make store runs for me today. So come next door and get some money and run to the store and grab some condoms and douches." Tasha was in the room right next to Halleigh's.

"No problem." Halleigh smiled at the thought of a day off. She hung up the phone and went over to finish her coke before leaving for the store, glad to play the role of errand girl over whore any day.

Scratch, the neighborhood crackhead, sat in the alley next to a store, the place he had called home for the past two weeks after losing his bed at the homeless shelter. His body was yearning for another fix of crack, heroin, something. He'd been without a shot since earlier that day, and now here it was nighttime and it was like he was turning into a werewolf. His body throbbed as he clenched his stomach tightly. He frantically scratched his itchy and irritated arms, which felt like something was trying to burst up out of his skin. He stood up. His legs were as weak as a boxer's in the twelfth round who had taken some hard punches. He had to try and think of a way he could get some money for his next fix. Scratch walked out of the alley, where the streetlights illuminated the sidewalk.

In his forty-one years, he had been through hell and back, and his near death appearance showed it. He had once been Flint's "push man," but now he was nothing more than a junkie. In the late eighties, he'd tried a dose of his own supply, and ever since then, he had been on the opposite side of the game, hooked on heroin and crack co-caine. Karma wasn't no joke. Scratch paced back and forth in front of the store, desperately seeking a way to get right.

"Ay, brotha," he said to a man walking out of the store. "Look out for Scratch. Spare me a dollar, young blood."

The man ignored him and proceeded to his car.

"Come on, man," Scratch continued to plead, legs wobbling, "I know you got it. I know you got some change back up in there."

The man got into his car, shaking his head in disgust.

Scratch wanted to fire off a string of curse words at the man, but a pain shot through Scratch's stomach as his body went through with-drawal. The only thing that came out of his mouth was a sigh of pain. Once the pain began to let up, Scratch slowly eased up back into standing position. Still clenching his stomach, he saw a beautiful girl in high heels and a miniskirt walking by him toward the store. "Ay, baby girl, can you spare a dolla? Come on, baby girl. Hook Scratch up."

The bell over the door rang as the girl, her head hung low, walked right past him and entered the store without paying him a bit of mind. It wasn't as if she was trying to ignore him like the man before her had so blatantly done. It was just that she was so consumed with her own personal thoughts that she hadn't heard a word Scratch had said to her.

Scratch watched through the store's glass door as the girl stood in line at the counter, dug into her bra, and pulled out wrinkled bills. His mind began to work overtime. "Bingo!" he whispered. He now had a plan.

Chapter Twenty-five

Halleigh had just walked down the street and into the corner store, still high from the line she had inhaled minutes earlier. High as a kite, she kept her head down as she picked up a few items and then stood in line.

As she had aimlessly strolled to the store, her thoughts, just as they always managed to do, landed on Malek. Now she stood in the line consumed by thoughts of her past boyfriend, whom she thought was going to be her future.

I miss that boy so much. I wonder if he ever thinks about me. Halleigh's eyes watered as Malek's mother's words filled her head, reminding her that there was probably no way on earth Malek was thinking about her. Halleigh caught a tear that had managed to escape her eye and wiped it away. She couldn't believe Malek had just up and left her like that. Her mind understood the words Mrs. Johnson had spoken, but her heart just couldn't believe them.

Lost in her thoughts, Halleigh didn't even notice the crackhead eyeballing her through the glass door from outside the store. In all actuality, she'd never even noticed him when he tried to bum money from her as she was entering the store, but she would certainly notice him in a few minutes.

Scratch searched frantically throughout the alley. He needed to find some sort of weapon so that he could rob the girl he'd been scoping out inside the store. He felt bad about what he planned to do, but he had to get the monkey off his back, and quick. At the time, the dead presidents she kept stashed in her brasierre seemed like his only option right now. Since opportunity was knocking, he'd be a fool not to answer the door. He grabbed a short but thick stick off the ground and quickly put it up under his shirt. He then proceeded to arrange it so that it poked through his shirt to look like a gun. He leaned against the side of the building in the alley and awaited his prey.

"Give me yo mu'fuckin' money!" he whispered, trying to practice his approach. For years he had managed to get high without ever having to knock an old lady upside the head; ironically, something he was proud of. The girl he was preparing to rob wasn't no old lady, but still, he was doing something he thought he'd never have to do and he felt ashamed. As an addict, Scratch had always comforted himself with the logic that he wasn't hurting anybody but himself by getting high. Now that was about to change.

He looked down at the stick and knew that it wouldn't pass as a gun. "Damn! This shit ain't gon' work," he said to himself. He threw

the stick down in frustration and became agitated as he sought out another weapon in the litter-filled alley.

Scratch's eyes focused on a broken beer bottle. "Yeah, that right there will do it." He walked over and picked up the bottle. He then rehearsed his line again. "Give me yo mu'fuckin' money!" he spat softly. "Or I'll cut your fuckin' throat." Scratch smiled, figuring he had found the right approach, but then his smile quickly faded. "What if she tries to run?" Scratch looked down at his wobbling legs and knew that he wasn't up for a chase. "Damn," he said, throwing down the broken bottle.

Scratch knew that the girl would be walking out of the store any minute. He had to think quickly. He looked down at his feet and then got an idea. He took off his worn-out shoe and then pulled off his soiled, stinky sock. He gathered up a bunch of rocks from the ground and filled the sock with them. He held up the sock, and the most horrendous odor reeked off of it.

"Well, goddamn!" He grimaced as the foul odor invaded his nose. "Whew! If the rocks won't knock her out, the smell sho' in the hell will," he said, quickly distancing the sock from his face.

Once again, he leaned up against the wall and practiced his approach, which seemed even less threatening with a sock. "Fuck!" He knew that the "sock and rock" method wouldn't scare anybody and decided to resort back to using the stick as a fake gun. He shuffled around real quick and found the stick that he'd discarded earlier. that's when he noticed an even bigger one. "Just in case I do have to knock her ass out," he told himself. He threw down the smaller one and took the bigger stick and placed it underneath his shirt, as if he had a burner. "Yeah." He shook his head, finally satisfied with his choice. "That's what Scratch talking about."

At that moment, Scratch heard the doorbell jingle, signaling that his would-be victim was exiting the store. Then he heard the clicking of the girl's high-heeled shoes. Just as he had anticipated, the girl came strutting out with a bag in her hand. He quickly ducked and leaned into the alley and waited for her to pass so he could grab her. However, his guilty conscience began to set in. In just those few seconds while he waited for her to cross his path, he went back and forth with himself about going through with his plan. The little red devil with the pitchfork sitting on his left shoulder got the better of him. When he saw the girl walk past, he went for it. He quickly grabbed her from the back and placed his hands over her mouth, dragging her into the alley and slamming her against the wall. "Give me all yo money!" Scratch was shaking just as much as the girl was.

"Please don't hurt me!" she screamed, dropping the items in her hands, then raising her arms in surrender.

Scratch pushed her against the wall and pointed his fake gun at her. "Give me yo cash and you won't get hurt," he whispered harshly.

"Please don't kill me," she said, her knees shaking uncontrollably. One would think she was going through withdrawal as well.

"Just give me all the dough and I won't shoot."

Just as Scratch had watched her do before, she anxiously went into her bra to pull out all the money she had. Scratch looked into the young girl's eyes and thought she looked familiar. As he stared into her eyes a little longer, he frowned. "Halleigh?" he whispered, lowering his fake gun.

Afraid to say anything, she nodded her head, not wanting to give him a reason to pop off.

"You Sharina's daughter, ain't you?" Scratch asked. He knew Halleigh's face well, because of Sharina. The two looked more like sisters than mother and daughter, and he knew that since it wasn't Sharina, it had to be her baby girl.

"Well, I'll be damned," Scratch said as he smiled. "I can't believe I'm standing here looking dead at Sharina's baby girl."

Sharina had been one of Scratch's get-high buddies, and he'd seen pictures of Halleigh over at Sharina's house whenever he was over there getting high. He had even seen Halleigh in person a couple of times, but of course she never paid her mother's dope partners any mind.

Halleigh nodded her head again, confirming that in fact she was Sharina's daughter. A small glimmer of hope ran through her. Since he knew her mother, maybe he really wouldn't hurt her. For the first time since Halleigh could remember, she had never been more glad to be Sharina's daughter. She knew it had to come in handy and do her some good at one point in her life, and what better time than now?

"Can you let me go?" Halleigh asked Scratch, her back still pressed against the wall.

Scratch looked down and forgot about the fake gun. "Oh yeah," he said. He pulled the stick out from under his shirt and then threw it to the ground.

"You out here robbing people with sticks?" Halleigh asked, a sense of relief passing through her. She couldn't help but chuckle, although what she really wanted to do was take that stick and crack him upside the head; not for trying to rob her with it, but just for the pure stupidity of him thinking he could rob anybody with it.

"It almost worked, didn't it?" Scratch let out a slight chuckle himself. "What is a girl like you doing out here on these mean streets this time of night anyway?" Sudden concern now seemed to take over Scratch's mind.

The last thing Halleigh wanted to do was stand out there having a conversation with a man who'd just tried to rob her. She wanted to

leave the raggedy man in the alley, but she knew he had a jones. She could tell, because she'd seen the same look in her mother's eyes many a night. With that, thoughts of her mother and this man's relationship piqued her curiosity.

"I was just running to the store," Halleigh told the man. "How do you know my mother?"

"Me and Sharina used to get high together." Scratch thought back to the days when he and Sharina used to do more than just get high together. Back before Scratch was so strung out, he and Sharina used to kick it. Back then, neither one of them were users. He remembered how Sharina used to look up to him for being such a major player in the game. Once she learned of his drug use, she looked at him the same way a sinner would look at her pastor who done fell from grace. She felt like, hell, if Scratch could do it, then why couldn't she?

Scratch tried to tell Sharina that the shit wasn't for her; but who was he to tell her that when, by then, he had started using pretty heavy himself? Still looking up to him, Sharina wanted to be on that same high. Before they knew it, the two found themselves no longer hooking up to keep each other company, but hooking up to get high together.

"How's Sharina doing these days?" Scratch asked, thinking about their pre-addict times together.

"I don't know. I don't fuck with her like that no more." Bitterness laced Halleigh's tone. "Last time I saw her she was more worried about a fix than she was me."

Scratch could sense Halleigh's feeling of disgust toward her mother and made an attempt to comfort her. "Aaah, that's just Sharina. But you know what? High or not, she sure did love her some you." Scratch smiled. "She loved her baby girl; talked about you all the time." Scratch wasn't exaggerating. Sharina did love her daughter with all of her heart, and she still did to this day. It's just that her mind had power over her heart; and her mind needed the drug.

"Oh yeah," Halleigh spat. "Well, actions speak louder than words."

"Look, you don't understand, baby girl. That crack rock ain't no joke. Scratch know that shit. It ain't just no little monkey either. It's more like a gorilla; like King Kong, you know. It overpowers everything. So don't be too hard on your moms."

"Tuh, that's an understatement." Halleigh begged to differ.

Scratch could see that he wasn't going to get anywhere with the subject of Halleigh and her mother, so he switched it back to himself. "Anyway, speaking of that monkey-gorilla thing . . ." Scratch turned on his smooth, convincing tone. "Why don't you hook Scratch up, Li'l Rina?" Scratch begged. "Let me hold something so I can get right."

Halleigh was about to walk away and leave him there, but the fact

that he knew her mother softened her up a bit. As much as she wanted every vein in her body to pump nothing but pure hatred for her mother, there was just a little part of her that still loved Sharina. At the same time, though, Halleigh was still a little scared of what Scratch might try to put himself up to next. Having witnessed firsthand what a person was willing to do for a hit, she wouldn't be surprised if he'd try something even worse. Yeah, he'd spared her, but what about the next person?

Halleigh looked down at her money, and before she handed some to Scratch, she asked, "What do you get from getting high off of crack? I never understood why my mother did it." Halleigh never even considered that using cocaine really wasn't any better than using crack. She didn't see herself as being anything like the dope fiends she'd encountered. Getting high wasn't something she felt she needed to do. It was something she just *wanted* to do.

"So much fucked-up shit has happened to me in my life, Li'l Rina. It's like when you're high, all that goes away."

Halleigh could feel that. She knew exactly what Scratch was speaking about. Halleigh peeled a twenty-dollar bill from her stack of money and handed it to Scratch. Then she began to walk away. Suddenly, she stopped in her tracks and turned around. "What did you say your name was again?"

Scratch's eyes lit up as he gazed at the money, knowing that he could finally get the monkey off his back. He looked up at Halleigh with his gap-toothed smile. "Scratch. Everybody knows me as Scratch."

"Well, Scratch, don't get yourself killed out here robbing people with sticks," Halleigh said with a slight grin.

"You betta count yo blessings, baby girl. A stick is the least of your worries. I was going to unleash my stankingass sock on you with the ol' 'sock and rock,' " Scratch said jokingly. He looked down at his one bare foot. He hadn't had time to put his sock and shoe back on.

Halleigh grinned and started walking away.

"If you ever need to talk, come and holla at me, good ol' Scratch. The rest of me might not be right, but I got good ears for listening. I'll be right here," Scratch yelled as he watched Halleigh walk away into the darkness.

Chapter Twenty-six

Halleigh leaned back on her bed and closed her eyes. She was tired, and her body felt extremely drained. She had swooped her shoulder-length hair, which she usually wore flat-ironed straight with feathered side bangs, into a ponytail. The fairly new blonde highlights complemented her light skin.

Halleigh was cute, but she never saw herself as beautiful, or anything close to it, especially when she was next to her former high school best friend, Nikki. Halleigh hadn't seen Nikki in more than a year, and although every now and then she thought about kickin' it with her old friend, on the flip side, Halleigh was glad of it. It wasn't because she didn't miss her friend or want to see her, but she didn't want her friend to see her now. Turning over to look at the clock, Halleigh saw that it read 8:00 P.M. She let out a loud sigh, knowing that she was supposed to be over at the hotel at 11:30 P.M. *I just want to get some rest before then,* she thought as she balled up on the bed, put the pillow on top of her head, and turned to face the wall. The only thing that she could think of was the comfortable sleep that she was drifting into.

Less than five minutes after Halleigh closed her eyes, Mimi came bursting into the room and sat down on the bed. "Hal, you awake?" Mimi whispered, gently nudging her. "Hal, you up?" She ran her hands down her braided hair extensions, which she wore straight back, with baby hair surrounding the edges, the braids falling right above her butt.

Halleigh heard Mimi, but she tried to ignore her in hopes that she would let her get some sleep.

"Halleigh, wake up, girl. I need a favor."

Halleigh sighed loudly and removed the pillow from her eyes. She looked up at the girl she once saw as her savior.

Mimi continued to shake Halleigh. "You up?" Mimi repeated once again.

"I am now," Halleigh snapped. "Damn, girl, that sleep was feeling good. What you want?"

"I need a favor." Mimi stopped and waited to see Halleigh's reaction.

Halleigh looked at her as if to say, *And?*

Mimi continued, "I got this private party lined up. It pays one thousand dollars for each girl."

Halleigh could see the dollar signs forming in Mimi's greedy eyes. Once the idea of getting some paper set in, Mimi was unstoppable. Nothing came between her and her paper. Halleigh had often won-

dered why Manolo had chosen Tasha to be the madam versus Mimi, who stayed on the paper chase and made sure her money was right. Then again, Halleigh surmised, with that much paper flowing through Mimi's hands, she was too stuck on herself to be that damn loyal to the game. And it wasn't no secret amongst the girls that Mimi was forever trying to hook up gigs that paid her behind Manolo's back.

"They want two girls for just a couple of hours."

"When?" Halleigh asked hesitantly.

Mimi then delivered the catch. "Tonight."

"Oh, hell nah," Halleigh replied quickly, shaking her head from side to side.

"Come on, Hal, please. You know I can't miss this money," Mimi pleaded. "I'd do it for you."

"Like hell you would." Halleigh rolled her eyes.

Halleigh knew better than to fall for Mimi's "I'd-do-it-for-you" look of pity. On top of that, Halleigh was almost certain that Manolo knew nothing about this little private party. Mimi was always doing side jobs that Manolo didn't know about. She kept a tight leash on her regulars just for that simple fact. Mimi had her game set up so tight that she'd schooled her loyal regulars to call up Tasha and request one thing: something simple like a blow job. Once the john showed up in her hotel room, she'd have him pay her directly for the service that he really wanted.

To date, none of Mimi's little schemes had ever backfired on her, but when it did, the last thing Halleigh wanted to do was to be there, caught up in the midst of it all. Halleigh knew just as well as Mimi did that if Manolo ever found out, there'd be hell to pay.

"No, fuck that, Mimi. I know you ain't forgotten that ass-whupping Manolo put on you at Wild Thangs," Halleigh said, trying to jog Mimi's memory of the beat-down at the strip club.

Mimi got this salty look on her face after Halleigh's smart remark. Hell yeah, she remembered being beaten nearly unconscious and she thought that Halleigh was trying to be a smart ass by throwing it back in her face. All Halleigh was really doing was trying to make sure that Manolo hadn't knocked her upside her head so hard that she had lost her mind. After all, Halleigh figured Mimi had to have lost her mind in order to keep trying to do her own thing on the side; cutting Manolo out completely. Although Mimi wanted to remind Halleigh about the ass-whippin' she too had endured at the hands of Manolo, she decided not to start a verbal war with the person whose help she needed so desperately right about now.

"Please, Hal, you know I wouldn't even be asking you to do this if I didn't need you there." Mimi used the most sincere tone she could muster up to try to convince her fellow comrade to help her out.

Halleigh stayed strong. "Uh-uh. Nope." She shook her head adamantly.

"You better ask Keesha or somebody. You ain't about to pull me into no bullshit." Halleigh knew that if anybody else was out to make paper like Mimi, it was Keesha. That's why it was the first name that had popped into Halleigh's head. She felt sure if presented with the opportunity, Keesha would do it, and therefore Halleigh would be off the hook.

Mimi stood up, trying to convince Halleigh to roll with her. "Come on, now. Girl, you know I can't get Keesha to do it with me. That snitching-ass bitch, she can't hold water. She'd be the first one running to tell Manolo, to try to get a bitch in trouble so that she can take my place. You know I can't trust her ass." Mimi cuddled next to Halleigh and brushed her hair with the back of her hand. "You know you my girl. I need you there. Come on, Halleigh. Just have my back this one time," Mimi begged.

Halleigh sighed in frustration. *I know if I don't roll with her, she gon' do it anyway. I can't let her go solo.* Halleigh knew that Mimi wouldn't let a dollar slip through her fingers. With or without her, she was going. If the girls had learned anything, it was to be paired up when hustling.

A few years ago, one of the dancers at Wild Thangs left with a customer who wanted to do a little more than stick money down her thong. The customer had been buying the girl twenty-dollar drinks all night long. He was dressed in a suit and just appeared to be paid.

The customer ended up taking her back to his condo, where two more of his dudes were waiting for her. All three men ended up having their way with her for the next four hours. They paid her money, throwing it to her afterwards as if she were less than human. All the things they had her doing, she did out of complete fear because they were so drunk and high and dominating that she was afraid what might happen to her if she refused. It went without saying that no amount of money was worth it.

After that incident, Tasha set a house rule that the girls had to work in pairs if they were going to turn tricks outside of the club or hotel atmosphere. Even though Mimi's hustle wasn't one of Manolo's assignments, Halleigh knew she still had to be there for Mimi.

"All right, girl . . . damn, I'll do it." Halleigh sighed. "You know you get on my nerves, don't you?" Halleigh sat up in the bed, surrendering to Mimi's pleas.

"Thank you, thank you, thank you," Mimi whispered eagerly as she hugged Halleigh and then got up from the bed. She pulled out a tube of lip gloss and began coating her lips as if she were preparing on the spot.

"Who are these niggas anyway?" Halleigh inquired.

"Jamaica Joe and his people," Mimi said under her breath. She

turned toward the full-length mirror and applied another coat of lip gloss.

"Jamaica Joe and his people?" Halleigh abruptly got up out of the bed, realizing that this was, in fact, the actual catch. "Hell no, Mimi! Are you out of your mind? Jamaica Joe?" Halleigh began pacing. "Manolo will kill both of us. You know Sweets and Manolo don't fuck with them North Side niggas. And what if Joe finds out we down with Manolo? That nigga might pop off just because. He might try to use us as ransom or something. I'm sorry, Mimi, but you are on your own with this one."

"Come on, Hal. You already said yes," Mimi reminded her.

"But that's before I knew who the dudes that hired us were." Halleigh couldn't believe that Mimi still expected her to lend a helping hand after dropping Jamaica Joe's name. Hell, she couldn't believe Mimi had even given it a second thought. Maybe Manolo had hit her upside her head too hard, because she had definitely lost her marbles. "You done lost your mind. Manolo will have our heads on a platter and you know it."

Halleigh wasn't saying anything that Mimi hadn't already thought of. She was well aware of the beef between Sweets and Joe and this scenario was nothing but trouble. If Sweets ever found out that Mano-lo's girls were associated with Joe in any kind of way, then he would make Manolo teach them a lesson they wouldn't soon forget.

Mimi was a risk-taker. At the end of the day, she knew that together, they made too much money for Manolo to ever get rid of them, or to hurt them bad enough that they couldn't eventually make him more money.

"Please, Halleigh? Look, it'll be short and quick. We can be in and out of there in an hour. One hour and we'll be a thousand dollars richer, and you ain't even gon' have to split that shit." Of course, when dealing with Mimi, she always had a scheme inside of her original scheme.

Jamaica Joe was actually paying $1,500 per girl. He knew that in order to get Mimi to take such a risk and fuck with him, he'd have to be willing to pay the price. He didn't mind at all. He got a thrill knowing that he had the power to get a couple of his rival team's cheerleaders to come cheer for his team for a little while. Even though he was willing to pay each girl $1,500 Mimi decided, that she was entitled to a $500 finder's fee. This was a $2,000 come-up for her. She needed Halleigh to come through for her.

The more Halleigh thought about it, the more she realized that she, too, could use that money. Working for Manolo, she barely made enough money to take care of her personal needs. If she went with Mimi on this little one-hour gig, she could pocket the money without Manolo getting a cut.

"All right, I'll go. One hour and then I'm out," Halleigh said matter-of-factly.

"One hour, I promise!" Mimi exclaimed with excitement, running over and hugging and kissing Halleigh on the cheek. "We'll drop by the party at around ten o'clock. We're not set to go on until eleven-thirty, so that gives us an hour to do what we got to do and a half hour to check in with Tasha so that she won't know what's up."

"Where are we going to tell Tasha that we are at?" Halleigh asked, making sure that Mimi had crossed all the Ts and dotted all the Is.

"I don't know . . . we'll just tell her a john wanted a private at his house or something and that we paired up for safety. I'll check in the money for a blow job or something out of my share. Don't worry, Hal. Your girl's got this."

"You better know what you're doing." Halleigh walked by Mimi and lightly swatted her on the ass as she headed to the shower to get ready.

"Oh, I know what I'm doing all right," Mimi was talking to herself because Halleigh had already left the room. She rubbed her hands together in greed. "I'm about to get paid is what I'm doing." Mimi tapped herself on the shoulder for a job well done in getting Halleigh to roll with her. Next, she said a small prayer. "Lord, please get us through this night without anything going wrong." Mimi then left the room, not realizing that tonight she'd need more than just a prayer to get her out of the situation she had gotten herself, and now Halleigh, into. She'd need a miracle.

Chapter Twenty-seven

Tariq maneuvered the '99 Chevy Suburban into the Valley, one of Flint's South Side neighborhoods. His windows were tinted, so he didn't have to worry about anyone seeing his face. Still, he was nervous about being out of his own territory.

This nigga bullshitting, having me meet him on the South, Tariq thought. *I done murked too many niggas on this side of town to be riding around this bitch solo.* Tariq kept checking his rearview mirror to make sure no one was tailing him. The last thing he was trying to do was to get caught slipping. He put his hand on the snub-nosed pistol tucked at his waistline for reassurance. *This is all the back-up I need.* He bobbed his head to Tupac's "Me and My Girlfriend."

Tariq turned onto Tebo Street and parked his truck at the curb in front of the small blue-and-white house. He turned off the ignition and sat nervously inside the car for a couple of minutes. He had to get his head right, to make sure that he was prepared to do what he was about to do; because one thing he knew for sure was that once he stepped foot out of that car and went up to that house, there would be no turning back. He looked around cautiously before he unlocked his car door and stepped out. He kept his hand on his pistol the entire time as he walked swiftly up the driveway and knocked on the back door.

Tap, tap, tap!

He knocked on the steel screen door. A few seconds passed, but it felt like hours as Tariq continuously looked over his shoulder. *This mu'fucka better come on,* he thought, stepping nervously from side to side.

Tariq knocked a little more forcefully this time.

Sweets finally appeared at the door. "Fuck you beating down my door for, nigga?" He was shirtless and wore only jean shorts and Nike flip-flops. His tattooed, hardcore body was ripped like LL Cool J's. It was a body most women would die for, and some men, too, considering Sweets was a "homo thug".

"Man, you gon' let me in or what?" Tariq looked around, still observing his surroundings.

Sweets smiled coyly and replied "Oh yeah, I forgot. You scared of us South Side niggas. Only time y'all North Siders got heart is when you cliqued up."

"Just open the door," Tariq responded impatiently.

Sweets opened the door and stepped to the side as Tariq walked into his house. "We in the basement," he said and began to walk down the stairs.

"Who the fuck is *we*?" Tariq asked. "I don't need more than your ears hearing what I got to say, nah mean?"

"Nah, don't worry about it. I understand what's up. My man down here ain't a street nigga. He ain't worried 'bout what you talking."

Tariq reluctantly walked down the steps behind Sweets, patting his weapon for reassurance just in case something did jump off.

The basement was arranged more like a den, with a sofa, love seat, and a seventy-two-inch plasma TV all positioned comfortably in the small space. Sweets took a seat on the sofa. His company, who was a dark-skinned dude with a striped button-up shirt on, snuggled up against him.

Tariq almost gagged at the sight. *This gay mu'fucka,* he thought, turning his nose up. Tariq was disgusted, not only because of the sight before him, but because it reminded him of how his own pops was living.

Tariq's mom thought she was the luckiest woman in the world

when Tariq Sr. chose to make a home with her. Although the two never married, they were together for ten years total. His pops left him and his mom when Tariq was eight years old. Tariq never knew what happened. He just came home from school one day to find all of his father's things gone. When he asked his mother where his father was, her only reply was, "He's left."

Until Tariq was about twelve years old, he hated his father for abandoning them. He wondered how he could just pick up and leave without even saying good-bye. Tariq would spend hours in his room alone, blaming himself for his father up and leaving. His relationship with his mother, which had once been closeknit and healthy, became severed and weak. Thinking that it might help pull Tariq out of his slumping funk of depression, his mother decided it might be a good idea to tell Tariq the truth about his father. She decided to do it before it was too late for them to even be able to mend their own mother and son relationship.

The day Tariq's mother sat him down and told him that his father didn't just up and leave, but that she had put him out and ordered him to never come around them again, Tariq immediately shifted his hate from his father to his mother. He couldn't imagine why she would do such a thing. He began to disrespect her by cursing and yelling. It was then she knew that she had to tell him the full reason why she had done so.

Tariq's mother explained to him that his father had used her; had used both of them to paint an image in order to cover up who he really was. While on the outside he looked like the typical husband and father, on the inside, he truly desired men. Convinced that some homosexual spirit was on him, she put him out and told him that if he ever came around her or her son, she would expose him for who he really was. Tariq's father wasn't willing to come out of the closet and face the prejudice of society or his family and friends, from whom he had managed for so many years to keep the truth. So he agreed, packing up all of his things and leaving, knowing he'd never be able to see his son again. Within months of leaving Tariq and his mother, he found another woman whom he impregnated. She gave him another child, behind whom he hid his true self.

Upon hearing that his father was homosexual, the only thing that came to Tariq's mind was how people would always tell him how he was just like his father, how he looked just like his father and how when he grew up, he was probably going to be just like his father. This made Tariq sick to his stomach. After hearing the bomb his mother had dropped on him, the last person he wanted to be like was his dad.

From that point on, Tariq felt he had to do everything possible to prove himself as a real man, and not some soft-ass punk buried in a man's body like his father. So he took to acting out; acting hard and

getting into trouble. He hooked up with the hardest cats in school to prove he wasn't a sissy. He went through girls one after another to prove that he liked girls and not men. The night he raped Halleigh, it was just another way of proving his manhood; having control and power over someone else.

His father's lifestyle had messed up his head in more ways than one. Now seeing Sweets hugged with another man so openly made him want to vomit.

Sweets picked up an Xbox controller and resumed the Madden game he'd been playing with his manfriend before Tariq arrived. "What you got for me?" Sweets asked as his friend licked his neck teasingly.

Tariq looked at Sweets in disbelief. "Yo, man, can we handle this in private?" Tariq didn't mask the irritation in his voice.

Sweets whispered in his companion's ear. The dude rose from the couch, mean-mugging Tariq, smacking his lips and rolling his eyes before leaving the room.

Tariq just shook his head and waited until the man left the room. One thing he could say about Sweets, though; he definitely wasn't on the down low. He kept his shit wide and out in the open. His reputation and credential on the street let cats know that in spite of what things looked like, he was a real nigga when it came to handling his business.

"What you got for me?"

"What you got for me?" Tariq asked right back. He was about to give Sweets some valuable information, but it wouldn't come without a price. Hell, nothing in this world came for free.

"It depends on what you tell me," Sweets replied. "I'm trying to murder this nigga. He hit my li'l man, Rah-Rah, at the Berston Park shootout last year. It's about time we got back at him, you know. Can't let that shit rest . . . no, no," Sweets stated to himself more than to Tariq.

Certain members of Sweets' crew had wanted to retaliate right after the shooting. Sweets knew how the game worked, though. He knew that Jamaica Joe and his crew would be expecting immediate retaliation and would certainly have their guards up. He felt that it would be better to wait it out and catch them fools off guard. With the help of Tariq, it looked as though they were about to do just that.

A streak of guilt ran through Tariq as he thought about exactly what it was he was planning to do to his comrade. Then he thought about how his comrade had been so quick to put the young boy Malek on. *This nigga been acting like Malek is his right hand instead of me, the nigga that done had his back for all these years. That li'l nigga ain't put in no work, but Joe got this dude in the cut like he belongs.*

"Joe having a get-together tonight at his crib on Coldwater," Tariq began to sing.

Sweets didn't take his eyes off the game he was playing when he said, "What I'm supposed to do with that information, fam?"

"I'm just letting you know there's a window of opportunity, if you trying to take it."

"Yo' mama ain't never teach you not to take your fight to your enemy's house? Ain't no telling what he got in that mu'fucka," Sweets stated. "What they looking like anyway, as far as heat is concerned? They gon' have the burners on 'em?"

"That's just it," Tariq said in a tone that told Sweets if he'd just shut up and let him finish, he'd have all his questions answered. "Ain't nobody allowed to take no heat in Joe's house. Niggas be leaving them shits in their whips. Joe gon' be the only one holding."

"I don't know," Sweets replied, shaking his head as he operated the remote control. "This might not be too valuable. Sounds kind of risky to me."

Tariq felt that Sweets might be trying to play him by pretending that the information was of little use, so that he didn't have to pay Tariq for it. Tariq knew Sweets would still use the info, so he decided to throw in a little extra incentive, just to make sure that Sweets sealed the deal. "I know where the bricks at too. I can put you up on them, if the split is right."

Sweets paused the game system. "The bricks in his house?" he asked. He had now given Tariq his full, undivided attention.

Tariq nodded. "In the basement. Fifteen joints in the safe. You get in, hit Joe, and then take the bricks."

All of this sounded too good to be true, so he had to question Tariq's intentions. "What you getting out of all this?" Sweets asked suspiciously.

Tariq knew that he better pick his words carefully. He didn't want Sweets to think that he was trying to play both sides of the fence. "It's time for a new era, baby. I ain't making that much paper under Joe. He put this new kid on, and it seems to me that the li'l nigga making more moves than me. So, to make a long story short, it's time to take what I'm owed."

Sweets thought for a minute. Tariq was the type he feared most on his own team: a jealous nigga. He knew how they operated. Their loyalty was only as good as the dough coming their way that paid for their loyalty. Now that it seemed that another nigga was cutting into Tariq's paper, he was ready to turn against the captain. It always added salt to the wound when the next player in line was some young cat who still had milk behind his ears.

"You mean that kid Malek? Is that who you feel is steppin' on your toes?" Sweets had been hearing about Malek on the streets. The kid was definitely coming up in the game.

"Yeah."

"Yeah, I been hearing 'bout the little nigga. Used to hoop, right? My li'l nigga shot up his ol' miss a while back. He stopped one of my soldiers from hitting Joe at Berston. That was the only time we had a chance to get him, too," Sweets said, regretting that his crew missed Joe that time.

Tariq was surprised to hear that the Shottah Boyz were responsible for killing Malek's mother, and obviously his stepfather too. The shooters had been unknown to him until that moment. Even though Jamaica Joe had put money on the table for anyone who brought back information on the shooting, nothing had surfaced.

Tariq quickly got back on task and cut to the chase. "This is your chance to get Joe, fam. It might not be another chance. He doesn't put down his guard a lot," Tariq said, getting frustrated.

Sweets nodded his head in understanding. He reached under his sofa and pulled out a roll of money: five thousand dollars, to be exact. Tossing it to Tariq, he asked, "So what time should I crash the party?"

Tariq flipped through the rolls and then replied, "Party start at eleven o'clock. Joe lives on Coldwater, between Jennings and Clio, not that spot over there on Harriet Street where everybody think he lays his head. Come through around midnight. I'll make sure that I'm at the door by then, and I'll let you slide through."

"You do that," Sweets told him, nodding his head because he knew it was on. Revenge was finally about to be served.

Chapter Twenty-eight

Halleigh looked around nervously as she and Mimi walked up the long circular driveway to Jamaica Joe's luxury house. It was a sand-colored, five-level stucco house with a brick front. There were no flowers or anything like that planted, but the landscape was immaculate. All of the bushes were evenly trimmed, surrounded by black mulch. The house had to be around 4,500 square feet, not including the attached three-car garage.

"Damn," Mimi said, admiring the mini-castle. "Shit, I should have charged they asses two grand each." She looked around. "After all, what's another five hundred each to this nigga?"

"You mean a thousand each," Halleigh corrected her. Mimi thought for a moment, realizing that she almost blew her cover by revealing the

fact that Joe was really paying $1,500 per girl instead of the $1,000 she had told Halleigh he was paying. "Oh yeah, that's right, girl. You know I'm not good at math."

"Not when it comes to other people's money you're not," Halleigh said sarcastically. "But I will agree that from the looks of this house," Halleigh stated as she too admired the dwelling, "they could have afforded it, that's for sure."

The two women made their way to the back door, which Mimi had been instructed by Joe to use. When they got there, the only thing that stood between them and the man on the other side was a glass storm door.

"Y'all the dancers?" the man asked, opening the door for them.

"Naw, we here to deliver pizza," Mimi said sarcastically as she made her way past the man. Halleigh followed close behind.

Instantly the women's nostrils were filled with the smell of weed as they peeped out their surroundings. Mimi appeared to be confident that the gig would go down without a hitch and that Manolo would never find out about it. After all, no one who associated with the North Side crews associated with the South Side crews, so she knew that there was no mutual player to go back and run his mouth. Halleigh, on the other hand, wasn't as convinced as Mimi that Manolo would never find out. She couldn't stop the butterflies from fluttering in her stomach.

"Mimi, are you sure about this?"

"Yeah. Just chill, Hal." Mimi spotted Joe standing at the bottom of the basement steps. "There's Joe right there."

Joe ascended the steps and hugged Mimi as if they were old friends.

Halleigh took a deep breath to calm her nerves. *One hour and then we're out,* she reminded herself. Now that she stood there, she couldn't believe that she had let Mimi talk her into this madness.

"Joe, this is my girl, Sunshine," Mimi said, using the name Manolo had branded Halleigh with. "But you can call her Sunny." Mimi turned to Halleigh. "Sunny, this is Joe."

Joe nodded a "what up" at Halleigh and then stepped out of the landing and up onto the main level of his luxurious home. Mimi grabbed Halleigh's hand, and they followed Joe toward the back of the house, where the bedrooms were located.

Joe looked Halleigh up and down, admiring her curves for the first time. "Yeah, you gon' heat things up quite a bit with your rays, Sunshine." Joe smiled at Halleigh, caressing her chin with his index finger. "My boy gon' love you, ma." He licked his lips and turned to Mimi. "You, princess, come with me." Looking over at Halleigh, he said, "And you can wait in here for my boy. Just chill out and relax. My man should be here any minute. Get yourself a drink or something in the meantime. But take care of my young boy for me, all right?"

Halleigh nodded her head in agreement and then watched as Mimi and Joe left the room.

Tariq and Malek pulled up to Jamaica Joe's house and noticed the group of people headed inside. Everyone who was invited to the party was a close friend or associate of Joe's. They were people he trusted, so Malek wasn't worried about any drama popping off inside. He knew that he couldn't take his gun inside of Joe's house—house rule— so he took it out of his waistline and stored it under Tariq's passenger's seat. Malek got out of the car and followed Tariq up the driveway, limping slightly, making him seem a bit more gangster than he actually was. Malek had been anything but gangster up until a year ago when circumstances changed his situation.

Before getting into the drug game, the only game Malek had ever concerned himself with was the game of basketball. Although new to the game, the bullet he had taken for Jamaica Joe was getting him much respect from the entire North Side of Flint.

Tariq and Malek walked up to the back door, where they were greeted by a member of their crew. They walked inside and greeted Jamaica Joe, who had just returned from the back bedroom. Mimi was on his arm.

Joe released Mimi and then slapped hands with Malek and embraced him tightly. "I got a surprise for you, baby," he stated. He slapped hands with Tariq and said, "Get on the door. You know who gets in and out."

Tariq sniffed loudly as he scratched his nose and nodded his head. He was tired of being treated like a flunky. It was like Malek had become Joe's favorite soldier. Tariq kept his feelings inside and stood by the back door as he was instructed, while he watched Malek join the party inside.

Joe threw his arm around Malek and led him through the house, toward the back bedroom. "How that leg feeling?"

"It's all right," Malek responded, tapping his leg. "It keeps me standing. I guess that's all that matters, that I'm still standing. Some ain't so lucky." Malek put his head down.

It was obvious to Joe that he was referencing his mother and stepfather. "I heard that," Joe said. "And, yo, you know we gon' handle that shit with your moms and pops and shit. I'm sorry your family got pulled into all this."

Malek simply nodded, not wanting to think anymore about the great loss he'd suffered. He had already lost a part of his heart when Halleigh disappeared. The other part had been stripped from him the day his mother and stepfather were taken from this earth.

"I got something to cheer you up, though," Joe stated with a mischievous smile. "It's right in this room." He pointed to one of the bedroom doors then patted Malek on the shoulder. "Don't hurt yourself,

li'l man," he added as he walked away, knowing that the young girl was about to put it on Malek.

Malek opened the door and saw a girl sitting on the bed. She was bent over, her face buried in her hands. He could see her body trembling, and she seemed to be in deep thought. Feeling a presence in the room, the girl looked up and straight into Malek's eyes. Malek couldn't believe the sight before him. He stood there in complete disbelief. *This isn't real.* Then finally he spoke. "Halleigh?" Malek called out in astonishment.

The sound of his voice let her know that her eyes hadn't deceived her. As she ran to him tears flooded her line of sight. He hugged her tightly, picking her up off her feet.

Halleigh pulled back and touched his face, allowing her rich persimmon-complected fingers to run the course of his dark sienna-brown skin. She ran her hands down the ripples of waves in his hair. She just wanted to make sure that he was real. Once she was completely convinced, she pressed herself back up against him.

For all this time, Halleigh had felt so much anger toward Malek. She wanted to be mad at him forever. As he stood in front of her in the flesh, that deep-seated love she had for him outweighed every other emotion.

As Malek held her, she felt relief swarm over her body. Just being in his arms again made everything okay. He was the answer to all of her prayers. For a minute, Halleigh forgot all about the past year. She forgot all about the life she was living, and that she was at that house on an assignment. She felt like the smart high school girl that she had once been; untainted by the streets.

"Baby," was all Malek said as he kissed her on top of her head, which was buried in his chest. Halleigh began to sob hysterically as he held onto her and tears came to his own eyes. Malek squeezed her even tighter against him, as if she might disappear any second.

"I thought you left me," she cried hysterically. "You left me."

"Shhh. I would never leave you, Hal. I thought you left me," he told her. "Do you know that? I looked for you every day for weeks." He rubbed her hair softly, trying to soothe her soul. He had no idea of the things she had experienced since he'd last seen her, but he could feel that there was something different about her.

He put her back down to her feet and looked her in the eyes. She was still the most beautiful girl he had ever seen, but she looked tired and worn down, the small bags underneath her eyes revealing nothing but sadness and despair.

"What happened to you? Where have you been?" he asked. "I thought I saw you one day, but . . ." Malek's words just trailed off. He was still in disbelief.

Halleigh stared at him blankly. She knew he was about to start ask-

ing her twenty questions. Halleigh didn't know if she should lie or tell the truth. She couldn't help but wonder if she told him about the person she was now, would he still love her?

"You just up and dipped on me," Malek stated when Halleigh never responded.

"I dipped on you?" Halleigh couldn't believe he had just fixed his lips to say that. "You're the one who left me stuck here while you ran off out of town without me." That old anger began to rear its ugly head in Halleigh's tone. She poked Malek in the chest as she spoke her next words. "You promised me you would take me away from here. You promised you would be there for me. You lied and it's been hell. I've been out here all alone trying to survive. You have no idea what I've been through since you left me. No idea." Halleigh's eyes flooded with tears.

Malek tried to reach out to her, but she pulled from his reach. "You hurt me, Malek." She flopped down on the bed hopelessly as hot tears flowed uncontrollably. Her spirit felt so broken and confused that she couldn't think straight. She had imagined the moment that she would be reunited with Malek so many times, but now that he was in her presence, she didn't know what to say or do.

Malek let out an "are you kidding me?" chuckle.

"What are you talking about, Hal? I never left town." Malek kneeled down in front of her.

"Then why didn't you come for me? I came to your house and your mother told me everything."

A perplexed look covered Malek's face. "What do you mean, *everything*?"

"That you were gone. She said that you didn't want to see me, that you blamed me for losing your shot at going pro. Malek, you don't know half the things I've had to go through this past year." Halleigh stood up and walked away in shame. She didn't even want Malek to be able to look into her eyes and see who she was now. "You have no idea." Halleigh just shook her head and continued to cry.

Malek took a deep breath and swallowed the disappointment that was stirring up in him. The last thing he wanted to do was to feel anger toward his deceased mother, but he could only imagine the conversation that took place between her and Halleigh. He could only imagine the lies his mother had fed her just to keep the two of them apart, but he loved his mother dearly. He couldn't get upset with her, especially now that she was dead. All the good his mother had done for him in his life could never outweigh the bad. All his mother ever wanted was what was best for Malek, and she had worked hard to make sure that he got it.

One day when Malek's mother was in first grade, she experienced what she thought was the most embarrassing moment in her life. She

was in the grocery store line with her mother when one of her class-mates got in line behind them with her mother. When it was their turn to get checked out, Malek's mother wanted to disappear when her mother pulled out all of those books of food stamps to pay for the grocery bill. By the time Malek's mother arrived at school the next morning, the entire class knew that she was on food stamps. The jokes followed her all the way through elementary. It was a childhood scar she carried with her all through her life, right up to the birth of Malek.

She swore that she would do whatever it took to stay off of welfare. So, not once in her life did she ever receive government assistance. On top of working so hard, she still managed to be there to support Malek in everything he did. Some days she didn't get a moment's rest. It was something that wore her body out physically, but more than anything, it was something she was proud of. Not one time did she ever fuss, holler or complain about the sacrifices she had made. She knew that Malek making it into the NBA and making enough money to take care of her for the rest of her life was her reward. That's when she would rest. Now, she was resting in peace, and Malek would respect that rest by instantly forgiving his mother for keeping him away from Halleigh.

Malek put his hands on both sides of Halleigh's face and made her look him in the eyes. "Look, Hal, a lot of shit has happened in my life since the last time I saw you." He paused for a moment. "I met Jamaica Joe while I was in the county jail that day of the robbery. He hooked me up with a lawyer that took care of the case for me. It was thrown out. Me and Joe been tight ever since. I mean, if it hadn't been for him, I could still be rotting in jail somewhere. Because I'm associated with him, I've made some enemies." Malek paused for a moment and then continued. "I got popped last year during the Berston game in a shoot-out between Joe and this nigga named Sweets from the North Side."

Halleigh interrupted. "I was there that day. Oh my God. I was there," she exclaimed. She couldn't believe she had been in the same vicinity as Malek and didn't even know it. She had always felt as though they were soul mates, and that she would just be able to sense that he was around, but after all, her mind was cloudy that day. That would be the first time Halleigh worked as a Manolo Mami. She was set to turn her first trick that day. If only she had found Malek that day, so much in her life could have been different. She would never have turned that first trick; a trick that led to another and then another, getting her to the point where she was today . . . a bonafide whore.

"You were there at the park that day?" Malek said as a gleam shot across his face. "I knew it. I thought I saw you there. I thought that was you. I knew it."

"Then why didn't you say anything?"

"Because when I saw you, that's when all that shit start jumpin' off, you know. One of Sweets' li'l niggas got hit." Malek paused again,

fighting back tears. "Well, I got hit in my calf and the hip. They didn't hit no major arteries or nothing, so I was good. After hearing about my injuries, my basketball career wasn't good, if you know what I'm saying. My agent dropped me; not a single school was interested in me any longer. It was a trip."

"I'm sorry to hear that, Malek," Halleigh said sincerely. "I know making it to the pros was everything for you."

"Yeah, well, at least I still have my life." Malek sighed. "I can't say the same for moms and pops."

"What–what happened?" Halleigh stammered.

"To top off everything that was going on, someone sprayed my house, and my moms and pops got hit. They, uh, they, uh, they dead."

Halleigh's mouth dropped in shock. She couldn't help but allow her mind to go back to the root of the chain reaction of bad stuff that had taken place in Malek's life. She shook her head, knowing that Malek's life had turned out badly because of her. That one night she went to Malek for help turned out to be what catapulted a life of destruction for both of them. All of this stemmed from her running to Malek for help that night after those two men raped her. *Why didn't I just run to the police?* Halleigh blamed herself.

"I'm sorry, Malek. I'm so sorry."

Halleigh walked back over to Malek, who was now sitting on the bed with his hands buried in his face. "I should have never even told you about me being raped that night. I should have just gone to the police and let them handle it. I mean, what was I thinking? You were just a high school kid. If you didn't try to help me, you wouldn't be where you are right now. You would be off somewhere playing hoop, and Mr. and Mrs. Johnson would still be alive. Maybe your mother was right—I was bad for you . . . I am bad for you."

Malek quickly uncovered his face. "That's the one thing that my moms was wrong about," he stated. "You're nothing but good for me." He finally got a smile from Halleigh, and a sexy smirk appeared on his lips as he pulled her wet face toward his and kissed her lips gently.

Halleigh escaped into good thoughts of her and Malek again as Malek made love to her with his mouth. His kiss felt like pure ecstasy to her. It had been a long time since a man kissed her the way Malek kissed her . . . and didn't have to pay for it.

Malek's kisses now felt different to Halleigh. He was more mature and had developed a thug demeanor. Halleigh liked it. She loved it. She loved her some Malek, and that was just something that would never go away. After their kiss ended, Halleigh turned her back to him. "Things are different now, Malek. You don't know how much has happened to me," she mumbled, knowing that Malek wouldn't want her if he knew the truth; if he knew how many men she had let conquer her body, something he had never done. Not once had she and Malek ever

been intimate together, and she just knew he wouldn't be able to deal with hearing how many men had touched her in a way that he had never touched her.

"Then tell me." Malek turned Halleigh back around to face him. "Make me understand."

Halleigh opened her mouth, but nothing came out. She just shook her head. "I can't. You won't want me," she whispered painfully as shameful tears continued to flow freely.

"I'll always want you. I've always wanted you," he assured her. "You don't know how long I looked for you after I got out of jail and the hospital. I love you, Halleigh. I'll always want you in my life. Don't be afraid to share who you are with me. I mean, I'm not the same Malek you knew either. You may not agree with some of the stuff I've been into, but if we are going to make this thing work, we have to share with each other who we are. Now tell me. What's going on with you, Halleigh?" He looked deep into her eyes. "Tell me who you are."

Halleigh's body shook as she thought about all the different men, all the abuse, and all the manipulation she went through because of Manolo. She opened her mouth, and this time, she proceeded to tell Malek everything about the life she was now living.

"Pimp?" Malek exclaimed.

Halleigh didn't respond.

"Some nigga out here putting you up for sale?" he asked angrily.

"I didn't know, Malek. It was too late. I got trapped in the life. After I thought you had abandoned me, I just felt so lost and alone that I didn't even care anymore. I didn't care about myself." Halleigh swallowed and continued. "He promised to take care of everything for me, and he put a roof over my head. I swear to you, Malek, I didn't realize what I was getting myself into until it was too late. Now I can't get out. He'll kill me."

Her story brought tears of anger to Malek's eyes. For him, all of this was like dèja vu. Once again, someone had taken advantage of Halleigh's innocence, the innocence that had rightfully belonged to him. The innocence he waited for until she was ready. The thought of her being manipulated into selling her body to other men, any man, sickened and angered Malek. He balled his hands into fists and leaned over the bed, hitting himself in the head out of frustration.

Finally, through gritted teeth, he asked Halleigh, "How many niggas?"

Halleigh was stunned by Malek's question. She couldn't understand why he would want to know the intimate details. It would only hurt him the same way it hurt her just thinking about it. Although Halleigh felt that her mother held a big part of the blame for her being on the streets, she somehow felt like she was worse than her mother. She had watched her mother do a lot of things to get high. She lied, cheated

and stole. She was such a good booster that she could steal the Pope's hat off of his head on national television without anyone noticing. But not once . . . not once had Sharina sold her own body to get high. *No, she just sold mine,* Halleigh reasoned, *and now I'm keeping it going.*

"Answer me. How many men, Halleigh?" Malek repeated, trying to maintain his composure.

Halleigh just stood there shaking her head.

"How many men?" Malek finally yelled.

Malek's booming tone startled Halleigh and she quickly said, "I don't know. I don't know how many, Malek. I lost count," Halleigh confessed. "When I'm doing it, I just blank out and try to imagine that I'm somewhere else." She closed her eyes. "Somewhere else . . . with someone else . . . like with you."

Malek was silent as he tried to process what she had just told him. "What's the nigga's name that got you out here like this?" he asked. He knew that he could call in a favor from Joe and get the situation handled, but this shit was personal. Malek was gonna take care of the dude that had Halleigh trickin' on the streets himself, he thought as his nose flared.

Halleigh could practically hear his thoughts. "No, Malek. Please . . . I don't want to pull you into anything else. I've already messed up your life."

"What's his name?" Malek asked her again, his tone hard. "What's his name, Halleigh?" he yelled.

"Manolo," she whispered.

The look on Malek's face said it all. "You a Manolo Mami?" he asked in disgust. He knew Manolo's reputation in the pimp game. He knew Manolo was all about the paper and kept his girls working. He couldn't help but think of all the niggas that Halleigh had given herself to. *How did I let this happen to her?*

"I'm sorry," she whispered. "I'm so sorry. Please don't hate me. I know you probably think I'm dirty now, but please, Malek, please . . ."

Malek wanted to embrace Halleigh, but he couldn't move. He was sick just thinking about how many niggas had been with her. He gagged inside as tears rolled down his face.

"Malek?" Halleigh said. "Please say something . . . anything."

Malek swallowed his tears and regained his composure. He wiped his face dry and then sniffed, standing there as if he had never been crying. He then looked over to Halleigh and softly summoned her. "Come here."

Halleigh almost didn't hear him, so he said it again.

"Come here, girl. You don't have nothing to be sorry about." They met each other halfway, and once again, he held her tightly in his arms. "I shouldn't have let this happen to you. Don't you worry. I said I'd always be here for you. That ain't changed. I'ma handle this," he re-

sponded, glaring off with a look of hatred and revenge in his eyes. "You best believe I'ma handle this."

"Malek, can we get out of here? I can't do this anymore. I can't do this."

"I got you, Halleigh. You leaving with me. I'ma take care of you this time," and he meant it. He pulled her close to him. If he had to use every dime he had saved up since working for Joe, he was going to take care of Halleigh. He wiped the tears from her face, and she rested her head against his chest. "I'ma take you far away from Flint. Ain't nobody gon' hurt you again."

Chapter Twenty-nine

"I'm about to murder this nigga." Lynch leaned up from the back seat, in between the front car seats, where Sweets and Manolo were seated.

"Yeah, whatever. Just make sure you don't pop off before I get the combo to the safe," Sweets stated calmly to Lynch as they prepared to head to Joe's.

The Shottah Boyz, Sweets' young hit squad, sat in the back seat.

Everyone's eyes were concentrated on the luxury house in front of them. The lights were on throughout the house, and they could hear the loud music coming from within. The loud music seemed awkward in the suburban neighborhood.

The only person standing outside was Tariq. Every so often, he stepped outside and walked around to scope things out. When he came around the house and spotted Sweets in an SUV, he nodded, giving them the green light to bring it on.

They all felt the adrenaline pumping in their veins. The group of men made sure that the safeties were disabled on their weapons. They didn't want to take any chances. Whoever got in the way would get popped that night.

Lynch was especially ready. Since the death of his brother, he hadn't been the same. His murder game had become out of control as he tried to quench his thirst for death. He was taking out niggas left and right just for looking at him funny. He felt as though he didn't have anything to lose. When he lost his brother, he lost everything, as far as

he was concerned. Even though he had been leaving a path of death behind him, the only death that would truly mean something to him was Jamaica Joe's. He wanted Joe's head and knew that nothing would stop him from getting his revenge. Joe had been extremely careful, but Lynch knew that sooner or later he would get at him. The day had finally come.

"Yo, you sure this ain't a set-up?" Manolo asked Sweets as he stared suspiciously at the house, with Tariq casing back and forth.

"Shit, there's only one way to find out. Either way, I'm trying to get to what Joe got in that safe." Sweets pulled out a Blow Pop and stuck it in his mouth.

They slipped on their black ski masks and hopped out of the stolen SUV, leaving the ignition running for an easy getaway. They strolled up to the back door where Tariq was standing guard and eased right past him.

Tariq smirked and entered the house behind them, but instead of following them down the steps, he made his way upstairs and went into the bathroom. He waited patiently for shit to pop off.

With his hit squad behind him, Sweets bum-rushed the basement.

As soon as Joe and his guests saw the masked intruders, screams erupted and the party came to a standstill.

"Put your mu'fuckin' hands up. Y'all already know what time it is," Sweets stated in a nonchalant tone as he pointed his 9 mm at Joe and his guests. Manolo and the Shottah Boyz held all the guests at gunpoint.

Caught slipping, Joe gritted his teeth furiously. He immediately regretted throwing the party at his spot.

Sweets snatched Joe off the leather sectional and put the pistol to his head. "Where's the safe?"

Twenty minutes earlier, Mimi would have been sitting there clinging to Joe's arm, but she had to run out and get condoms. She had brought regular condoms with her, but Joe required Magnums, of which she had none. If she'd learned anything from her years of trickin', it was never to let a nigga run up raw . . . no matter how much he was willing to pay.

"What you talking about, man? Ain't no safe in here." Joe was sweating bullets on the inside, but he wouldn't give anybody the pleasure of seeing him panic.

"Okay, so you wanna do this the hard way?" Sweets jammed his gun in Joe's neck and jerked him by the collar as he turned to face Lynch. "You see that nigga right there? He's waiting for me to give him the go-ahead. He is trying to get at you, for real. You took something away from him that he can't get back, nah mean?"

Joe stared at the man before him, but he couldn't see his face. It

wasn't until he looked at his forearms that he saw the word *Shottah* tattooed in black ink. *Fuck,* he thought, knowing that the young boy before him was the brother of the nigga he'd murdered at Berston.

"Now, let's try this again. Where's the safe?"

Joe stood strong and still didn't respond.

Lynch, growing tired of Jamaica Joe's games, ran up on him and split his nose with the butt of his gun. "Nigga, you thinks this a game? Where the mu'fuckin' safe?" He whipped Joe across the face with the pistol two more times.

Jamaica Joe dropped to his knees in pain. He held his face and blood seeped in between his fingers. He weighed his options and knew that he would have to reveal his safe to his intruders. *I got a pistol in that safe,* he thought. He knew that he was outnumbered greatly and began to regret not letting his boys enter his house with their pistols. One gun didn't amount to much, but he knew that it gave him a better chance of walking out of the situation with his life.

"It's underneath the floor," he stated as he got up and walked toward a bookshelf in the corner of the room.

"Hurry up." Sweets pushed Joe slightly, urging him to speed up the process.

Jamaica Joe pulled up some loose floorboards in his basement and revealed a steel combination safe. He paused, trying to buy more time. *How the fuck am I gon' get out of this? And where the fuck is Tariq?*

"Open it!" Sweets demanded.

Joe twisted the knob to the safe and opened the door, revealing the crystal-white cocaine inside.

"Load that shit up," Sweets ordered Joe then looked over to Lynch. "Handle your business, man," he stated, giving him the okay to shoot Joe.

Lynch raised his arm and aimed the .357 at Joe's head. Just as he was getting ready to pull the trigger, they heard a loud banging on the back door.

"Flint Police Department! Is anyone home?" the voice yelled loudly.

Sweets, Manolo, and the other two Shottah Boyz looked at each other nervously. They quickly snatched off their masks. "Block that mu'fucka," Sweets whispered, referring to the open safe, and Lynch quickly pushed the bookshelf over the missing floorboards. Sweets put his finger to his lips, signaling for everyone in the basement to keep quiet.

Jamaica Joe never thought he would be so happy to have the cops at his door.

"Flint Police! We're coming in!" they shouted.

Jamaica Joe heard his back door open and shut. Sweets and his crew tried to hide their guns as the police came down the steps.

Two white cops came into the room. One immediately went to the

home stereo system and cut the volume, and the other one looked around the room, his hand on his holster, looking for an excuse to open fire.

Even though Jamaica Joe's guests were afraid of Sweets and his crew, snitching was a no-no in Flint, so everyone kept their mouths shut and waited to see how the scene would play out.

"What seems to be the problem, officers?" Sweets asked, removing all traces of slang from his vocabulary.

"Are you the owner of this house?" one of the officers asked.

"No, sir," Sweets responded.

"Then who is?"

"I am," Jamaica Joe stated with a smile.

The officer frowned when he saw Joe's busted nose and asked, "Is everything all right here? What's going on?" He eyed the group of men suspiciously.

"I don't know." Jamaica Joe turned to Sweets. "Is everything all right?"

"Yeah, everything's cool, officer," Sweets responded. "Just a small gathering amongst friends, you know."

"Well, your gathering is disturbing your neighbors. We got a noise complaint, and it looks like we came just in time," one of the officers stated. The officers began their routine, separating Sweets and Jamaica Joe and questioning them to get to the bottom of the situation.

Jamaica Joe stared into the eyes of the white man as he used his shirt to wipe the blood from his nose.

"Now, if there is something going on here, you can tell me. If you need our assistance, all you have to do is nod your head," the officer stated.

"No, sir, our party just got a little out of control. I'm not feeling too well, though. I would appreciate it if you and your partner could clear this out for me." Joe stared intently across the room at Sweets and his crew. He was heated that they had the audacity to run up on him in his crib. The situation could have easily ended badly for him, so he was grateful for the lawful interruption.

"All right, it's time to clear this out. Party's over!" the officer yelled.

Joe's guests flew up the steps as quickly as possible. Nobody was trying to be a part of the bloodbath. Joe was so infuriated that he didn't realize that he was standing with his fists balled at his side.

The police officers stood and watched as Jamaica Joe walked over to Sweets and held up his hand, as if he were showing him love. Sweets looked at Joe's hand and then at the cops and decided that he would play along with Joe's little game. *Nigga, you got lucky this time, but next time I'ma make sure there are no interruptions.* He slapped Joe's hand.

Joe pulled Sweets toward him discreetly, but with force. "You niggas is dead."

Sweets and Joe stared each other down as they came out of their embrace. Sweets nodded his head to his crew, who were scared shitless. They all walked up the basement steps, while Joe remained in the basement, a cop on either side of him.

Rage overcame Joe as he witnessed Sweets and his crew walking out of his home with his bricks. He wasn't in a position to try to stop them, and his insides were boiling. He knew that he couldn't protest because of the cops' presence. Sweets gave Joe a small smirk like, *Yeah, I'm walking out with yo shit and you can't do anything about it.* It took all of Joe's willpower not to grab Sweets up and take back what was his.

The cops were too busy directing people out of the house. They didn't notice the evil stares that Sweets and Joe were exchanging. If looks could kill, Joe and Sweets would both be circled in chalk.

As Sweets and his crew exited the door, Sweets looked back and held up the bags. "Yo, Joe, thanks for the party favors. That was very nice of you, buddy. Appreciate the hospitality," he said sarcastically as he made his way out of the door.

Just as Sweets, Manolo, and the Shottah Boyz reached the top of the steps, Malek and Halleigh walked out of the bedroom and through Joe's kitchen. With the loud music playing and their deep conversation, they hadn't heard the initial chaos and were clueless to the fact that robbery and murder had been about to go down.

Malek and Halleigh were prepared to exit through the back door when they bumped into Sweets, Manolo, and the Shottah Boyz. Halleigh stopped dead in her tracks when she saw Manolo's face. She tried to turn around, but it was too late.

"What the fuck are you doing here?" Manolo asked Halleigh, trying to disguise his anger because he knew the police were within earshot. He attempted to snatch Halleigh up.

But Malek slapped his hand with force. "Whoa, homeboy, you might want to calm that down if you know what's good for you. You don't got no business here no more." He pulled Halleigh close to him to show Manolo that he was serious. Malek could feel Halleigh's hand become moist as he held it in his.

"This one of our bitches?" Sweets asked Manolo as he eyed Halleigh, looking her up and down, making her feel as if she were naked. The disapproving tone in Sweets' voice let Manolo know he wasn't handling his business, embarrassing him.

Halleigh's breaths became shallow as she looked for an explanation. Finally she said, "Nolo, this is Malek. This is the guy that I needed the money for," she tried to explain.

Manolo leaned in close to her. "You remember what I told you

when I first met you? You already know how I get down. You might get out of here tonight, but I'ma get at you, and when I do, I'm gon' kill the nigga right in front of you. I'm the Grim Reaper, baby girl. *If you want this little nigga breathing, you better let him know who Daddy is.*"

Backed up on the stairs because of the scene that was occurring at the doorway, the police finally emerged from the basement. "Let's move it! Time to go!"

"Please, Manolo, don't do this," Halleigh begged.

Malek held onto her hand tightly as he waited for her to make a decision.

"You already know what it is," Manolo stated coldly as he walked out the door with Sweets, the Shottah Boyz, and the police following. "The ball is in your court now, Sunshine," he said, looking back at her over his shoulder.

Tears accumulated in Halleigh's eyes as she let go of Malek's hand. She knew that Manolo would kill him if she stayed. "I have to go," she whispered. "I'm sorry," she cried as she walked out the door.

"Halleigh!" Malek yelled as he stepped outside and watched her walk down the driveway, her head down. "Halleigh!"

The sound of his voice calling her name broke her heart. She looked back one last time. For a brief moment she contemplated running back into Malek's arms. He said he would take care of her, protect her, but he'd also said it the last time and didn't make good on his word. Could she trust him to protect her this time?

"Bitch, get in the car." Manolo got into the front seat of the SUV.

Halleigh's tears poured out of her eyes like flood waters as she hopelessly got into the SUV. She watched Malek stand there in disbelief as Sweets drove away.

"Halleigh!" Malek started running toward the SUV in one last-ditch effort to get his girl.

Joe stopped him before he could get past him and just said, "Not now, kid. But don't worry. We gon' take care of this."

Halleigh had her face buried in her hands as she wept. She'd just done the hardest thing she ever had to do in her life. Turning her first trick wasn't even this hard. She loved Malek with all of her heart, from the depths of her soul, but out of fear for his well-being, she left with Manolo. She knew Manolo would follow up on his threat about killing Malek and didn't want that. What she didn't know was that Malek was no longer green to the streets and could hold his own. Nonetheless, she left the love of her life standing in heartbroken disbelief.

Chapter Thirty

Jamaica Joe came out of the house to make sure that Sweets didn't try to double back. He walked to the end of his driveway and looked up and down the street, making sure that no odd cars were parked on the block.

Tariq and Mimi came running out of the house. Mimi had heard Manolo's voice when she came back in from the store after getting the condoms, so she ran for cover into one of the bedrooms. She'd thought about turning around and running back out of the house, but something inside of her just wouldn't let her leave Halleigh there. Actually, when she ran into the bedroom, she thought it was the one Joe had showed them to earlier, but it wasn't. Mimi stayed put and hid anyway until she thought the coast was clear.

"And where the fuck you been, mu'fucka?" Joe snapped. "How the fuck they ass get in my house? You was supposed to be guarding the door!" Jamaica Joe yelled furiously as he pointed at Tariq's head.

Tariq's face showed surprise when he saw that Jamaica Joe was still alive. "I had to go take a shit, nigga. Damn! I had the bubble guts. How was I supposed to know that somebody was gon' run up in the spot?" Tariq asked. "Niggas ain't ever been that bold before." If Tariq hadn't really had the bubble guts before, he had them now. He couldn't believe the plan didn't go down smoothly, and now he was left standing with the possibility of Joe finding out that he was behind it all.

"How did they know where I lived?" Joe pretty much asked himself.

"You ain't been too cautious with that, fam," Tariq jumped in. "I mean, look how many niggas was up in your spot tonight. You used to be on it all the time, making sure just any and everybody didn't know where you rest at. But look, you throwing parties and shit. He could have found out easily," Tariq stated quickly, making sure that no suspicion was directed his way. He even went so far as to point a finger at Malek, who was sitting on the back steps, his head on his fists. "This nigga in love with one of the enemy's hoes, wifeying the bitch. She could've set the shit up."

"Shut the fuck up, nigga!" Malek jumped to his feet. "Don't speak my name, for real. That's just a warning for your best interests. Don't even speak her name."

"Oh shit!" Mimi said. "Where the fuck is Halleigh? Did she leave with them?" Mimi wrapped her arms around herself. She already knew the answer to her question, and she felt guilty because she knew that Halleigh was in for the beating of her life, and her too, if Halleigh told Manolo that it was Mimi who set up the entire thing.

"Yeah, ma, your girl left with them. It's time for you to bounce too." Joe pulled out three Gs and placed them in Mimi's hand.

Mimi stared at the money and then looked up at Joe. "Listen, I didn't have nothing to do with them coming here tonight."

"I know," Joe stated as he walked into his house.

"And how do you know that shit?" Tariq was quick to mention in an attempt to direct Joe's suspicions elsewhere.

" 'Cause my gut instincts tell me so," Joe said to Tariq. "The same instincts that done kept me around this long." Joe looked over at Mimi. "Go on, ma."

Right away, Mimi left, headed back to Manolo's house.

"Yo, Joe, man, I got to go get her." Malek was pacing, as if he wanted to follow Mimi to Manolo's and get Halleigh. "She needs my help. I can't just leave her."

"Man, fuck that bitch! You ain't Daddy no more, nigga," Tariq said. "Manolo pimpin' her ass all over town. She chose that life. We got bigger things to worry about for right now."

Joe hated to agree, but they had bigger fish to fry with Sweets' crew. "Yeah, I got to get back at them niggas. If I don't, South Side mu'fuckas gon' be trying to test me all the time. I got to make an example."

Malek thought about what Tariq and Joe had just said, and the longer he contemplated the situation, the angrier he became. He thought about all the things he had given up to be with Halleigh: forfeiting his future, trying to be her man and stand by her. His NBA career was non-existent because of his commitment to her. He'd even chosen to love her when his own mother hated her. He had sacrificed all those things, and she had the audacity to choose another nigga over him.

Maybe my moms was right. I can't fuck with Halleigh. I'm through. He joined Joe and Tariq in the house so that they could plan their next move.

Chapter Thirty-one

"Manolo! She has to eat!" Tasha yelled as she walked behind him and pleaded on Halleigh's behalf. "You can't starve her, Manolo." She wanted desperately for him to ease up on his punishment of

Halleigh, but every time Tasha came to Halleigh's defense, he would become even angrier.

"Shut the fuck up, Tasha, before you end up down there with her. I got to teach that bitch some discipline," he shot back. "Do you not understand what the fuck just went down last night? For a little bit of paper, this bitch turned on us. She fucking with your reputation now, Tasha," Manolo said, trying to turn the tables on Tasha for not having the girls in check.

On that note, Tasha decided to fall back. She knew that she could be more of a help to Halleigh if she remained in Manolo's good graces.

Manolo was a cruel man and was showing exactly how devious he could be. After the botched robbery attempt at Joe's house he didn't say anything to her. Not one word. His silence was more threatening than his actual actions, though, because Halleigh knew that at any moment, when she was least expecting it, he could snap. That's just what he did.

The morning after the party, while Halleigh was sitting down, preparing to eat the breakfast Tasha had prepared for the girls, Manolo snatched her up from the dining room table by her hair and dragged her to the basement, where he tossed her down the steps as if she were a rag doll. That was three days ago, and he hadn't let her out since.

Halleigh's stomach growled violently as a sign that she needed nourishment. She'd been in the damp, dark basement for days, and the only thing that she had to drink was the filthy water from the laundry basin. Halleigh had never experienced hunger pangs like the ones that raged throughout her body. She was famished and cried all day and all night for her punishment to end. Manolo forbade her to come up those steps and turn on the light switch at the top, so the only time she could see anything was during the day, when sunlight came through the sublevel windows.

At night, the basement was darker than dark. She couldn't even see her own hand when she held it out in front of her. She constantly scratched her arms and legs as the dark played games on her. She always felt as if something was crawling on her. *All these spiders,* Halleigh thought as she scratched her body, breaking her skin and causing her arms to bleed. It was like being trapped in a dungeon.

"Manolo, please let me out," she pleaded from the bottom of the steps, just hoping and praying that the door would open, freeing her from the pits of hell. "Please, open the door!" she screamed.

Her cries were futile, because Manolo didn't budge. He kept her down there, locked up for her disloyalty. Halleigh was going crazy in her confinement. She began to talk to herself, pretending that she was having conversations with Malek.

As the days passed, she became weaker, and all she did was sleep. It

was during that time that she began to dream of Malek. Thoughts of him were the only thing keeping her sane; thoughts of him coming to rescue her, and he didn't even know it.

Halleigh was aware that Malek would never be able to forgive her for what she had done. Her dreams would be the only place where they would ever be together, and she had to accept that. Her heart was shattered, and her spirit was broken. A part of her wished that she would just die down there. Manolo had made her feel worthless; the same tactic he'd used to trick her into becoming one of his girls in the first place.

Mimi could hear Halleigh crying at night when she slept in her bed, and the guilt was eating her alive. Halleigh hadn't even thought about ratting Mimi out to Manolo, so she took the punishment all herself. Her agonizing cries made Mimi's skin crawl. She couldn't even imagine what Halleigh was going through.

After a while, Tasha began sneaking food and water down to Halleigh when she felt the coast was clear, which was only a couple of times. The smell down there almost made Tasha sick to her stomach from Halleigh having to relieve herself in the corner of the basement like she was a dog, but Tasha was never bold enough to free Halleigh from the basement.

Tasha would simply place food and water at the bottom of the steps. She knew that Manolo had gone crazy on Halleigh for making him look bad in front of Sweets. If he found out that Tasha was feeding Halleigh, he might lock her up too, but Tasha couldn't let Halleigh die from starvation, so she took the risk anyway.

After almost two weeks of torture, Manolo finally opened the door to the basement. "Halleigh?" he called as he made his way down the steps.

Tasha and Mimi stood in the kitchen as they waited anxiously for Halleigh to emerge.

"Halleigh?"

"Hmm?" she moaned.

Manolo saw her in a corner of the basement, balled into a fetal position with her eyes closed.

"Halleigh!" he yelled, trying to get her attention. He walked over to her and picked her up.

She was too weak to object, even though she didn't want his hands on her.

Her body flopped almost lifelessly as he carried her up the steps. She stunk badly. Her monthly cycle had come and gone, but the traces of blood were dried up on her thighs and legs. The sun burned her eyes when he stepped into the kitchen with her. It was like a thousand needles were being stuck into them.

Mimi's hard exterior melted away when she saw her friend. She

began to sob uncontrollably as Manolo carried Halleigh past her and into their room, where he just threw her down on the bed and left her.

Once Mimi saw Manolo exit the room, she immediately went back there. When she saw Halleigh, all she could do was just stand there and cry. She wanted to run over and hug Halleigh, but she looked so fragile that she might break if Mimi so much as touched her.

Tasha came into the room and comforted Mimi. She looked over at Halleigh in disbelief. *How could he do this to her?*

Manolo's deep voice startled both Tasha and Mimi as it boomed from the other room. "Clean her up for work tonight," he said then he left the house.

Mimi released herself from Tasha and then finally made her way over to Halleigh and kneeled by the head of the bed. "I'm so sorry, Hal. I'm so sorry."

Halleigh didn't respond. She couldn't speak as Mimi just kept apologizing over and over.

Mimi took a deep breath and then reached down into her bra. She pulled out the exact same hundred dollar bills that Joe had handed her the night of the party. "I got something for you," Mimi told Halleigh. "It's your pay from the party."

Halleigh just looked at Mimi, too weak to say anything.

"It's three thousand dollars," Mimi said truthfully. "I'll put it under your pillow. Okay?" As much as Mimi loved money, her conscience would not allow her to spend one dime of that money Jamaica Joe had paid her that night. After all that Halleigh had endured at the hands of Manolo just because she was trying to help her out, Mimi felt that she owed it to Halleigh. That could have easily been her down there in that basement with Halleigh. If Mimi had learned anything in the game, it was that loyalty had a price. This time, the loyalty that Halleigh had showed her would cost Mimi three thousand dollars, which she gladly paid.

Just then, Tasha came over and instructed Mimi to help her lift Halleigh. They carried her into the bathroom. Tasha ran bathwater while Mimi held Halleigh up. The two eventually got her clothes off and placed her into the water-filled tub. Tasha began to bathe Halleigh as if she were a baby. Halleigh just sat there with her eyes closed while Tasha rinsed the soap off of her. Tasha had to close her own eyes to stop the tears from falling.

When Halleigh finally did open her eyes, silent tears fell. She stared directly in front of her as Tasha tried to wash away her pain.

"Forget about that boy, Halleigh," Tasha told her. "Manolo will never let you leave now that he knows who you want to be with. I mean, that kid runs with Jamaica Joe for Christ's sake. Now you know he is off limits."

Halleigh was non-responsive.

"Manolo will never let you go," Tasha added. "He is jealous and crazy like that. He'll kill you before he gives you up to that boy. I'm not trying to see you in a box, Halleigh. Get it together before you leave him with no choice, sweetheart. You have to learn how to cope, baby, and learn fast, before you get seriously hurt." Tasha kissed the top of Halleigh's head and prayed to God that the young girl was listening.

Chapter Thirty-two

"*You have to learn how to cope, baby, and learn fast, before you get seriously hurt.*"

Tasha's words echoed through Halleigh's head as she remembered their previous conversation. Halleigh had definitely found a way to cope, but now she was stepping her game up a notch, hoping for an even greater escape than her casual cocaine use had been providing her.

Halleigh tied the leather belt around her arm and found a large vein. She shook eagerly as she inserted the heroin needle into her arm. As she pumped the syringe into her system, her head fell back in satisfaction. All the ills of the world escaped her thoughts as she let the drug work its magic. Her heartbeat began to speed up, and all her worries went out of her body as she indulged in the most addictive drug ever created.

"Damn, Li'l Rina. You betta take it easy," Scratch said as he impatiently waited for his turn.

"Shut up, Scratch!" Halleigh shot back. "You said that it would make all the pain go away. Well, that's all I want to do." She passed the dirty needle back to Scratch.

Scratch didn't want to take it, but the urge was too strong. He felt guilty for turning Halleigh on to the poison, but she had come to him desperately seeking an escape from the world she was living in. Next to death itself, Scratch didn't know a better escape than heroin.

"This ain't for you, Li'l Rina. This ain't for you," he said as he filled the needle to the top and joined in on the party. Scratch looked at the beautiful young girl, and his conscience began to eat at him.

When Halleigh came to him crying about her life and how she had ended up living the life she was now living, just like Scratch had prom-

ised, he provided a listening ear. After Halleigh told him of her latest fiasco with Manolo, Scratch convinced Halleigh that drugs would help her through the pain. He did it for his own selfish reasons. He needed a hit badly, and his listening ears only heard one thing while Halleigh spoke: an opportunity for himself. He knew that if he talked Halleigh into trying the drug, he could manage to get a free high out of the deal as well. Looking at Halleigh right now, none of it seemed worth it to Scratch anymore.

When Scratch looked at Halleigh, it was like déjà vu. He remembered how, years ago, it was her mother he had turned out on the drug. Unfortunately for Halleigh, history was repeating itself in a cruel way.

"You know you're too good for this life. You let Manolo go all upside yo head, knowing that fool ain't no good. You don't need to be here with an ol' man like me. I already fucked up my life; I can't let you fuck up yours." Scratch tossed the needle down the alley. He was overcome with guilt and knew he wasn't right for feeding her poison.

"Scratch! What the fuck is wrong with you?" Halleigh yelled. Her eyes scanned the alley for the needle, and she quickly jumped up to fetch it. "I paid for that shit, and you throw it." Halleigh tried to scramble away, but Scratch grabbed her arm and pulled her back down. His eyes were watering, and Halleigh had never seen anyone look so sincere.

"Look, baby girl, this ain't for you. Look at yourself," Scratch told her. "I know I told you this shit would make you feel better, but I lied. Look at you. You're only worse."

"But I do feel better," Halleigh tried to convince Scratch. "It makes me better."

Scratch just looked at the monster he had created in Halleigh and shook his head. "I feel so bad for introducing this to you." Scratch dropped his head in shame. "Don't make the same mistakes that your momma made. She let life get the best of her, and now look at her. Get away from all this. Get away from me. Ol' Scratch ain't gon' do you no good. Scratch do more harm than good to anybody that comes into his life, it seems."

Scratch's words hit home for Halleigh, and it felt like her high left as the words came out of his mouth. The mention of her mother made Halleigh listen to what Scratch was saying. Was she like her mother? Was she letting this thing get to her and take over?

Halleigh was reminded of all the times she had witnessed her mother high; all the times her mother went out boosting clothes to keep up her habit; all the times her mother never came home after consecutive days of getting high; all the times her mother hadn't been there for her. Most importantly, she remembered the time her mother chose drugs over protecting her own daughter.

Scratch's words were, indeed, hitting Halleigh hard in the heart. She usually hated when he called her Li'l Rina because as far as she was concerned, she was nothing like her mother. Today she felt closer to her mother than she had in a long time. For the first time ever, she understood why her mother couldn't beat her addiction.

It took all Halleigh's might not to run and get the needle that Scratch had tossed, but she took a step back and looked at herself. *What the fuck am I doing? Am I an addict now? I can't help it, though. It feels so good. I just don't want to feel bad anymore. I just want to feel good.*

"I have to go, Scratch. Time to get back to work," Halleigh said as she left Scratch alone in the alley. She hated her new habit, but it helped her get through the day. When she was high, it made the tricks she turned seem like a blur. She liked it better that way. The demons that haunted her nineteen-year-old soul were enough to drive a sane person crazy. Halleigh had fallen at the hands of the game.

As Halleigh walked off, Scratch watched, feeling lower than ever. It hurt him to his heart that he'd turned another woman onto his preferred drug. He was responsible for starting Halleigh's mother on drugs. Although he hadn't seen Sharina in ages, it still bothered him to this day that he had ruined her life. Scratch watched Halleigh until she faded away. Then ran over to retrieve the heroin needle he had thrown.

"I'm sorry, Halleigh," he whispered.

Chapter Thirty-three

As Halleigh headed back to the hotel, she tried to conjure up an excuse for being gone so long. She couldn't tell Tasha that she was out doing drugs with Scratch in an alley, so her mind raced, trying to figure out a legit story. Manolo kept close tabs on his girls, and if the money didn't add up at the end of the night, there would definitely be a price to pay. As far as Halleigh was concerned, she had paid her share to the piper, and there was no way she was going to set herself up to endure any more torment at the hands of Manolo.

What the fuck can I tell her? I've been gone for hours and shot all of my money up in my veins? I don't know . . .

Before Halleigh could finish her thought, she got an idea. She turned around and headed back to the alley. When she got there, she

found Scratch pushing the last of the drug from the needle into his
veins. "Want to make some money?" she asked Scratch.

"Do pigs oink?" was his reply. "Hell yeah, Scratch wanna make some
money!"

"I got an idea. Follow me," Halleigh said as she led him back to her
hotel.

Halleigh rested her hand on the telephone, making sure that Scratch
understood what to say. "Make sure you repeat it just like I told you,"
Halleigh instructed.

"Scratch got it, baby girl."

"Tell her that you've got a thousand dollars for a bitch with a mean
head job and to meet you in the lobby," she said, coaching Scratch.

"Cool."

Halleigh picked up the phone and dialed Mimi's room number and
quickly handed the phone to Scratch.

Scratch cleared his throat and waited to hear a voice on the other
end. After the fifth ring, Scratch heard a woman's voice answer the
phone. "Looky here, baby girl," Scratch started. "I'm looking for a
bitch with a mean head game. Dig this: I got a thousand dollars for
whoever can show me a good time."

Halleigh stood there watching intensely as Scratch tried to sound as
smooth as he could in his short conversation with Mimi. Halleigh
could tell that back in the day, Scratch definitely had game. She could
tell by the look on his face that he enjoyed pretending to go back in
time and play the role.

After he finished his conversation, Scratch hung up the phone and
licked his lips, feeling good about what he had just done. He thought
he still had game, and in his mind, his slick talking confirmed it.

"What did she say?" Halleigh asked impatiently as she threw her hands
up.

"You know ol' Scratch is nice with the ladies. She was hanging off
my every—"

"What the fuck did she say? Damn!" Halleigh snapped, cutting Scratch
off, hoping that he would just get to the point.

"She said she'll meet me in the lobby in five minutes," Scratch said
smoothly. He continued to smile and rub his hands together like a
1980s pimp.

"Good." Halleigh ran to her peephole and waited to see Mimi walk
past, on her way down to the lobby. She knew that Mimi secretly took
calls to do side jobs without Tasha knowing. Mimi was too greedy, she
figured, to let the opportunity pass to make that much money.

Right on cue, Mimi rushed down to the lobby. Halleigh knew she
didn't have a lot of time before Mimi would get tired of waiting for the
john that would never come, and she would eventually return back to
her room.

Halleigh rushed to the door that joined their two rooms and entered Mimi's room. She searched Mimi's drawers, underneath the bed, and her purse, looking for Mimi's money.

"Damn!" Halleigh yelled after a few minutes of searching and not coming up with anything. Her eyes nervously scanned the room, trying to figure out just where Mimi's stash could be. She knew Mimi hadn't taken it with her.

The girls knew better than to carry their money on them. More than a few johns had tried to rob their tricks before, and Mimi was in the game long enough to know better.

Halleigh picked up the mattress and flipped it over and still found nothing. *Damn! I know she didn't take her money with her, this time of all times,* she thought as the realization sunk in. Her plan had failed. She would have no money to turn over to show that she'd been working all day. She would have to suffer the consequences with Manolo. Hopefully it wouldn't be more time in the basement.

Just as Halleigh turned to exit the hotel room, she saw a bulky Newport cigarette box on the dresser and thought, *Bingo!* Halleigh rushed over to the box and opened it up, feeling like she'd hit a Vegas jackpot. There was Mimi's money, rolled up and stuffed into that cigarette box.

"Ooh, Mimi, girl, I told you smoking was bad for your health." Halleigh shrugged as she scooped the box up from the dresser and rushed out of Mimi's hotel room and back over to her own, through the same connecting door she had entered.

There, Scratch was waiting, hoping that Halleigh's scheme had worked, so that at least this time he wouldn't have to worry about where the money for his next hit was coming from.

Halleigh closed the door and walked over to Scratch. "Here!" she said as she pulled the money out of the box and handed him two balled-up twenties.

Scratch's face lit up. He hadn't had that much money all at one time in weeks. "Good lookin' out, Li'l Rina," Scratch said, holding one of the twenties up in the air, examining it and then plucking it.

Halleigh rushed Scratch out of the room so that she could make her way over to Tasha's room to show her just how much money she had made since she'd been gone. She told him, "Look, I'll see you later."

When Halleigh got to Tasha's door, she flattened down her clothes and relaxed her shoulders. She then held her hand up to the door. Just before she knocked, a streak of guilt went through her like lightning. *How can I do this to Mimi?* she asked herself. Halleigh knew what was going to happen to Mimi if she didn't have any money to show for her time today. Knowing darn well that Tasha had tabbed all of her tricks, Manolo wasn't going to accept any excuses as to why she didn't have his money. Then Halleigh thought about another day in that basement.

Next she thought about how Mimi, knowing she was the one to blame, didn't have any problem letting her ass stay down there to be tortured. *I didn't see her ass stepping up to my rescue.* Halleigh knocked on Tasha's door.

Tasha yelled, "Come in."

As Halleigh walked in, another one of Manolo's girls was heading out. There were about five other girls in the room, including Tasha. Halleigh brushed past the girl who was leaving and walked over to Tasha. She was sitting at the table counting money.

"You in trouble," Tasha said in a low voice, never even taking her eyes off the money she was counting. "I told you about disappearing." She pushed her bangs off her forehead and allowed them to blend in with her layered hair.

Before Halleigh could respond, Manolo came out of the bathroom, making Halleigh's heart skip a beat. She didn't expect him to be there

"Where the fuck have you been all day?" Manolo spat. "Tasha said you didn't check in or nothing." He walked over to Halleigh, chest puffed up in an intimidating manner.

Halleigh pulled Mimi's earnings out of her pocket and said, "I've been working. I went to the store to get something to eat and I got approached by a couple of johns. I made the money right then and there because they weren't trying to come back to the hotel."

"That's my bitch," Manolo said proudly. *Maybe she's finally coming around,* he thought.

He looked down at his watch. "It's time for me to wrap it up for the night. I'll meet y'all at home. Tasha, collect the money and have it counted before y'all get home, baby." He pulled Tasha up and kissed her passionately on the lips, smacking her ass when he finished.

He walked over to Halleigh and did the same to her. He thought about the wad of money she'd just turned over. "You made Daddy proud today, Sunshine."

When Manolo left the room, Tasha returned her full attention to Halleigh. She noticed that something was different about her. Her eyes were moving fast, and she couldn't stay still. "Are you okay, Hal?" Tasha asked in a soft, concerned tone. "You don't look so good."

"Yeah. Why you ask that? I'm good." Halleigh said, trying to look as normal as she possibly could. *Damn! Can she tell that I'm high? I don't look high, do I?*

Boom!

The door banged against the wall as Mimi stormed in the room totally enraged. "Somebody stole my mu'fuckin' money!" she yelled as she balled up her fist. "I know it was one of y'all bitches!" she said loud enough for all the girls to hear, even the one who went into the bathroom when Manolo had come out.

"Calm down yo voice! Don't bring that shit up in here," Tasha said low, but stern.

"Tash, my fault," Mimi said. "But my money is gone. I just made a run to the store, and when I came back, it was gone."

"I don't have anything to do with that. You have to explain that shit to Manolo." Tasha continued to count the money.

"I swear to God, it's some fake-ass bitches in here! When I find out who got my shit, I'm beating a bitch's ass!" Mimi stormed out of the room, knowing she had to try to make some money before she saw Manolo. She didn't want him to beat her ass, so she knew she had to get her hustle on.

Halleigh took a deep breath. She hated that she'd smoked up all her money and had to steal Mimi's, putting her in jeopardy. Just as quickly as the last wave of guilt had disappeared, so did this one.

Whatever. Just like when she left me on stuck at Jamaica Joe's house, I'ma let her ass take the fall for this one. I got to do whatever I got to do to get by. Halleigh took another deep breath and returned to her room.

Chapter Thirty-four

Mimi and Tasha started to notice a drastic change in Halleigh's behavior and appearance. She was always so edgy and "noided" and was losing weight by the hour, it seemed.

The three of them had grown close living under the same roof together, but lately, Halleigh was acting all paranoid. She was acting withdrawn, and seemed spaced-out all the time. She was often depressed, and when she thought no one was paying attention, she cried silently to herself.

"I mean, let's just leave her alone. Let her do her. Maybe she ain't trying to have us all up in her face," Mimi stated one day when Tasha asked her opinion on the situation. She figured that Halleigh would eventually snap out of whatever it was she was going through.

Tasha knew that there was much more to the story. Her heart went out to Halleigh because she could see what the streets were doing to her. Ho'ing was sucking the life right out of Halleigh. Tasha could see Halleigh's innocence fading, and the youthful sparkle in her eye had disappeared completely.

Since Halleigh's run-in with Malek, she had lost all hope. Not once had he come for her. It wasn't that she really wanted him to come knocking down the door and making a scene. The last thing she wanted was for him to once again put his life on the line for her, but if Julia Roberts could dream about her Prince Charming in the movie *Pretty Woman*, couldn't Halleigh?

After all, Malek was real to her. He was once her Prince Charming. He was all that she had ever wanted, but the reality was, they would never be together. After all that had happened, it was impossible for them to reconnect. Things would never go back to the way they used to be. Manolo had made it clear that she was not to associate herself with Malek, and if she disobeyed, he would kill both her and Malek.

Halleigh's appreciation for Manolo had long ago turned into contempt. She hated the sight of him, and the sound of his voice made her sick to her stomach. In her eyes, he was the root of all evil. He held her life in his hands and was unwilling to let her go. Halleigh knew that getting away from him would be one hell of a fight—a fight she just didn't have the energy for.

"I should just kill Manolo's ass." Halleigh thought out loud in desperation as she lay in bed in one of her depressed states.

Mimi exited the bathroom just in time to hear Halleigh's outburst. She snapped her head in Halleigh's direction, a look of shock on her face. Then she rushed to their bedroom door and closed it. *I hope Manolo didn't hear that,* she thought.

Mimi walked back over to Halleigh and sat next to her. "Girl, you better stop talking reckless before somebody hears you," she whispered. "Have you lost your mind?"

Halleigh didn't say a word to Mimi. She just sat Indian-style and closed her eyes, like it was too painful for her to see her life as it was.

"What is wrong with you?" Mimi asked.

"I just want to be with him. Malek is all that I know. He is my heart. We had plans that always included each other. He's all I've ever really wanted." She dropped her head and played with her fingernails. "He's how I ended up here in the first place. I was just trying to help him, earn a little money to help put up toward his bail, but look at me now, Mimi. Look at me now. I'm a whore! Who wants to spend the rest of their life with a whore who almost every nigga in Flint done ran up in, huh?"

Mimi looked at Halleigh with sympathy, but she couldn't feel empathy. She knew that Halleigh was in love with Malek. She could always tell when Halleigh was thinking about that boy, and that was usually day in and day out, but Mimi couldn't fathom having love for another person. The only person she cared about was herself, not because she was selfish, but because she knew no other way.

Mimi's mother had abandoned her when she was just a child, send-

ing her into the foster care system at the tender age of three. Never having a stable environment took its toll on Mimi. She never stayed in the same place long enough to develop any attachments. She practically raised herself.

"Shit, I can't really speak on that because I don't know nothing about love. The only thing I love is money. If a nigga got money, I guess I could learn to love him too."

Halleigh shook her head. "No, you don't know anything about the way I feel because money can't compare to Malek. I would die for him."

"You are basically dying for him. The only reason you still here is to stop Manolo from hurting that boy. You saving his life and he don't even know it."

Yeah, if only he knew, Halleigh thought. *If only he knew.*

Chapter Thirty-five

Sweets sat back and watched one of his many boyfriends as he counted his money. He had quickly unloaded all of the bricks that he had stolen from Jamaica Joe, and the profit was incredible. He hated to admit it, but Joe had a nice connect and the quality of his cocaine was better. *No wonder I can't keep up with this nigga,* Sweets thought as he concentrated on the different denominations that he flipped through his hands. The process was lengthy because most of the bills were wrinkled fives, tens, and twenties. It was money that had probably been everywhere, from stuck down in a sock to the crotch of a G-string, but he couldn't complain. He knew that dirty money was the best money, and he loved getting it.

What he could complain about was Joe. He was tired of sharing the city with Joe and knew that it was only a matter of time before he crushed Joe's North Side empire.

What gave Sweets the advantage in the battle was that Jamaica Joe wasn't even aware that there was a snake in his camp. *He should've made sure he was feeding his soldiers. If niggas ain't eating, they start creeping. Disloyal-ass nigga,* Sweets thought. He hated workers like Tariq. He felt that a side needed to be chosen. Either you were North or South. He despised dudes that tried to ride the fence. Usually, Sweets would have murked any nigga who tried to step to him

with any type of proposition such as the one Tariq had presented him with, but Tariq was different. He was Joe's right-hand man, not just some disgruntled corner boy, and he knew the ins and outs of Joe's operation. So Sweets used it to his advantage. He was going to get as much information from Tariq as he could and then dispose of him afterwards.

Sweets sucked on the Blow Pop in his mouth as he reached for his twin Desert Eagle pistols and looked around his bedroom. He placed one pistol in his lap and put the other on the nightstand next to him.

"Ay, go check the door," Sweets instructed his lover.

I just did an hour ago," was the man's reply.

"Then get your ass up and do it again and shut them dick suckers up."

Sweets had been on edge ever since hitting Joe's spot. He knew that Joe wasn't going to let the situation go easily. He would try to retaliate. When he did, Sweets planned on being prepared. *He won't catch me slipping,* Sweets thought.

Most dudes who were out in the open with their attraction to other men would have been underestimated when it came to gunplay, but Sweets was amongst the feared in Flint. It wasn't a secret that he had been with both men and women, but preferred men to women any day. He had been gay ever since he was a child. Although, as a child, he was molested by one of his foster mother's boyfriends, that wasn't the cause of him being like he was today.

Sweets grew up knowing that he was different than the other little knuckleheads that ran around his block, and it was apparent to everyone else that he had feminine characteristics. Kids his age taunted him daily, and it wasn't until he hit high school that he began to accept himself.

When he was in the tenth grade, Sweets met one of Flint's most notorious gangsters, Smitty Jake. Smitty was a smooth OG and a retired hustler, but he was still respected around the city. He was married with three children at home, but he still found time to mess around with men. His fascination with men, young and old, was what drew him to Sweets. The two had a love affair that introduced Sweets to an entirely different perspective of the homosexual lifestyle.

Smitty would take Sweets out of town to gay underground clubs, where they would partake in all types of sexual acts. Looking at Smitty, one wouldn't know that he was gay, and even in his own eyes, he wasn't. He was married and had a family, which is how he justified his sexuality. "Gay men don't have wives and kids," he told himself. Anyone who ever said otherwise always came up missing.

Smitty was a killer, and hustling was second nature to him. He groomed Sweets into the young hustler that he was today. He once told Sweets, "You don't have to be a straight man to be a gangster.

That's something that's just in you. Either you got it, or you don't. Either you built for the streets, or you ain't, simple as that. Don't hide who you are, Sweet Tooth."

Smitty was the one who had nicknamed Sweets in the first place, initially calling him Sweet Tooth. Sweets shortened the name himself.

"Do you, and stay true to yourself," Smitty told his young prodigy. "You blast on any nigga who got something to say about it. I've lived a double life for so long that I don't know which life is real. Don't be like me. Don't let another man's judgment dictate how you want to live your life."

Once Smitty uttered those words, Sweets ran with them. He came out of the closet, and any dude that talked that slick shit or tried to test him because of his sexual preference found himself six feet underneath the earth. *And if Jamaica Joe think he's any different,* Sweets thought, *I'll put the steel to his dome.*

Jamaica Joe called a meeting for all his workers and block lieutenants. He wanted to discuss the recent events with Sweets' crew and the beef that seemed to have taken itself to a whole 'nother level. Malek and Tariq, his two most trusted soldiers, stood next to him as he addressed the roomful of hustlers.

How does this young nigga get to stand armored guard at the front of the table? I been putting in work for years and I just got to the front, ol' pretty-boy mu'fucka, Tariq thought. *I see this nigga is going to be a problem. I should be running the Fifth Ward block, not this li'l nigga.* Tariq discreetly gave Malek cold stares. He hated the way that Joe took Malek under his wing so quickly.

Honestly, Tariq wished that he and Joe had the same relationship that Malek had with him. Jamaica Joe knew that Malek was a kingpin in the making. Joe would always say, "You don't learn to be a hustla. Hustlas are born." True indeed, Malek was just that, a born hustla.

"We just gon' fall back for a minute," Joe said, sitting at the head of the long red oak table.

One of the hustlers from Selby stood and said, "Why haven't we clapped back yet? Sweets over there feeling good about that caper he pulled. We've already been laying low for two weeks now. Let's get at that nigga."

"We want him to start feeling himself. I'm playing mental chess with that nigga," Joe replied. "You have to know when to strike and when to fall back. Once he start thinking that everything is all good, then we get at his ass. Smell me? Sweets is over there thinking that I'm just going to chalk it up as a loss, but I got tricks for that nigga." Joe clenched his fist. "Just when he thinks shit is sweet, we gon' swoop on 'em." Joe tried to speak calmly, but they could hear the anxiousness in his voice.

Malek just stood back and listened. He had been reaping the re-

wards of being down with Jamaica Joe's empire. Now it was time for him to prove himself and put in some real work.

Joe pulled out his gun and laid it on the table. "Y'all ready to bring the heat to this mu'fucka?"

Malek nodded.

Tariq replied, "No doubt. That's what I do best."

Everyone in the room was in agreement, and the tension could be felt in the air.

"Good," Joe stated, "because blood is about to flow. Anybody who is caught associating with a South Side mu'fucka can get it. I don't care if the mu'fucka is your uncle, your cousin, or your gotdamn daddy. Niggas gon' have to choose. Either you South Side or North Side. I got to show this nigga who he fuckin' with . . . and soon."

Chapter Thirty-six

"I'll be back, Tash," Halleigh announced as she walked into Tasha's hotel room. "I'm about to run to the store. You want me to pick up some more condoms?"

Tasha, on the phone setting up a meeting for one of Mimi's johns, put her finger up to signal for Halleigh to hold on. "I told you we don't do that *pissing* shit," Tasha stated into the phone, a disgusted look on her face.

After a few seconds, she said, "All right, she's in room eight-ten. We don't carry change, so have your shit correct." She hung up the phone and turned toward Halleigh. "Them white mu'fuckas be on some freaky-ass shit." She laughed.

"Hell yeah." Halleigh giggled. She'd had her share of them, but if she knew Mimi, for an extra twenty spot, she was about to be drinking a full glass of water and then releasing it on her next john.

Tasha looked at Halleigh and noticed that her appearance still continued to deteriorate as each day passed. She looked tired and run-down, her eyes were red as if she hadn't slept in weeks, and her skin had lost its healthy, youthful glow.

Tasha reached into the nightstand near the bed and pulled out a ten dollar bill. "You been ripping and running to the store a lot lately. What? You trying to avoid making this money here? You know if you need a break, all you got to do is tell me. I'll find a way to cover for you

with Manolo. I'd rather you take a break and get your shit together than get to the point where you can't make no money at all. Trust me, you don't want to see that day."

Halleigh yawned and rubbed her eyes. "Nah, I'm good, Tasha," she said, lying to Tasha and herself. "I don't even give a fuck anymore, you know. Once you've fucked one, you've fucked 'em all. I've accepted the fact that this is my life. Like you said, there is no way out. Besides, the same predicament that landed me here in the first place is the one that's keeping me here. I ain't got no other place to go."

Tasha frowned. She'd never heard Halleigh talk like that, and she was genuinely concerned. "Hal, girl, are you okay?" She had grown to care for her and Mimi as if they were her little sisters. Those were the only two Manolo Mamis she ever fraternized with.

"Like I said, I'm good." Halleigh held the door open and waited for Tasha's response. "Anyway, do you need something from the store?"

Tasha extended her hand with the ten dollar bill in it.

"Yeah, bring me back some condoms and a bag of hot Cheetos."

Halleigh took the money and put it in her pocket. She hurried through the hallway and caught the elevator down to the lobby. She was almost running, she was so eager to get to her destination.

She made her way to the alley up the street, where her new best friend was waiting for her.

"Hey, Li'l Rina." Scratch knew that Halleigh would be coming. She always visited him around the same time, and he always had the drug waiting for her. He pulled open the top flap on his cardboard box and offered her a seat in his very humble abode.

She watched eagerly as he pumped poison into his arms. "Hurry up, Scratch," she whined.

He closed his eyes as the drug took him to a state of pure bliss.

"Come on, quit hogging it." Halleigh scratched her forearm. She attempted to snatch the belt and needle from him.

"Come on now, Li'l Rina," Scratch said, pulling away. "I done told you that this ain't for you." Scratch repeated the same line he always repeated to Halleigh before he'd give in. "You too good for this. Look at yourself." He pointed to her. "You got your whole life ahead of you." Scratch was feeling guilty that he'd introduced her to the deadly habit, even though he saw to it that she got it on a regular, taking the cliché "misery loves company" to a whole new level.

"Look at you!" Halleigh snapped back. "You out here doing the same thing, so don't try to give me the you-better-than-this speech! Don't judge me. I'm tired of hearing that shit, Scratch. You need to live right yourself." She grabbed the belt violently from him.

"I'm an old man. My life is almost over anyway. I've lived, you haven't. You can still beat this."

Halleigh didn't even let her brain absorb the words. She disre-

garded him as she always did, grabbed the needle, and put it into her arm. Scratch shook his head, knowing she was going to do what she wanted to do, so he shut up about it before he blew his high arguing with her.

A few minutes later, Halleigh was so gone off her high, she forgot that she was supposed to be back at the hotel. She had messed around and stayed in the alley with Scratch for more than an hour.

Once the high began to wear down some, she came to her senses. "Gotta go, Scratch," she said quickly as she kissed Scratch on the cheek and then stood up. He was in the middle of a lean and didn't respond.

Halleigh jumped up and walked quickly back to the hotel. She ran into Tasha's room and announced, "I'm back," like she'd only been gone a hot second.

"Damn, Hal! It took your ass almost two hours to hit the corner store?" Tasha asked in irritation. She had girls who couldn't take johns because she didn't have any condoms, so waiting on Halleigh to return had her missing money.

"The store on this street was closed. I had to go all out the way to find the next one."

Tasha held her hand out to Halleigh. "Well, where the condoms at?"

Halleigh just looked at her empty palm in confusion. *Damn! I did tell her I was gon' bring those back. I forgot all about that.* She didn't even have time to think of an excuse. "I forgot all about them, Tash. Sorry, girl. It slipped my mind."

Tasha said, "And my Cheetos?" her hand still extended. From the look on Halleigh's face, it was evident that she'd forgotten those too. Tasha smacked her lips and dropped her hand.

Tasha frowned as she peeped Halleigh's demeanor. She was dazed and could barely keep her eyes open. Her words came out one on top of the other in a slurring fit. Tasha could see the signs clear as day, but she didn't want her assumption to be right. *She's been getting high. I know she ain't noddin'.*

Tasha didn't want to outright ask, so she took an indirect approach. "Well, what you get?"

"Damn! What is this? An interrogation? I told you I forgot your shit! I ate my shit up before I came back!" she yelled.

"Look, Ms. Halleigh, you need to calm the fuck down. You ain't foolin' nobody. I've been around the block more times than you can count. I know you out there." She looked Halleigh up and down. "And from the looks of it, you out there bad."

Halleigh rolled her eyes up in her head, trying to keep tears from falling out of them.

"Look, Hal, you getting high ain't gon' solve your problems. And I'm not trying to ride you. I'm just looking out for you, girl. That shit ain't no good. Trust me. I've seen that monkey beat the best."

Halleigh heard what Tasha was saying, but she wasn't trying to. As far as she was concerned, all Tasha wanted to do was make sure Halleigh didn't get so far gone that she couldn't make any more money. "I'm straight, Tasha," Halleigh told her, "so just get off my back. I'm a grown-ass woman. You may not think so, but from the first time I opened my legs for Manolo's lying ass, I grew up, so I can handle my shit just fine." A single tear managed to escape Halleigh's eyes, but she quickly and forcefully knocked it away, practically smacking herself in the face.

It hurt Tasha's heart to see Halleigh go out like so many other young girls had done. There used to be thirteen Manolo Mamis, but three had been lost to their drug addiction. Loita died as a result of an overdose. That's why Tasha always made it a point not to get close with any of the girls. Tasha and Loita, the half-Hispanic–half-white girl who used to pull in over a thousand dollars a night, had been tight like the fist on an Afro pick. Men used to love her exotic look, calling up and requesting her specifically, sometimes booking her a full weekend in advance.

Tasha loved Loita's honesty and loyalty to the game. Dudes would tip her twenty, fifty, sometimes a hundred dollars, and she would always turn it in to Tasha, along with her regular earnings. Tasha always let her keep it, to reward her honesty. In turn, Loita would always throw Tasha half of the tip for her pocket. The two looked out for each other. That's just how it was between them. Even though Loita ran circles around the other girls when it came to checking in loot, she had no enemies. No one was jealous or envious of her because she had such a beautiful spirit. There was nothing to hate.

If another girl came up short on dough or didn't make enough money to please Manolo, Loita was known, on occasion, to give her tip money to make the difference. She just got down like that. The same couldn't be said for any other girl in the crew.

But when Loita started going MIA after a gig with a regular, Tasha sensed something was wrong. Turned out, the john got her hooked on heroin and started to pay Loita for her services with drugs instead of cash. Her appearance started to deteriorate, and so did her loyalty. She stopped checking in tips to Tasha, and just like Halleigh was doing now, spent more time at the corner store than in the hotel room.

The signs were there, but Tasha never stepped up and spoke on it. She wished she had; especially the night she had to go get the hotel manager to open Loita's hotel room door after not hearing from her, only to find her lying dead on the bed, a needle in her arm.

Tasha couldn't let the same thing happen to Halleigh, not under her watch. "Why are you doing this to yourself, Halleigh?" she asked.

"Why else? Because I have to. It's the only way I know how to do

this thing. It's the only way I can keep laying on my back every day and let you send ten different niggas in my hotel room to fuck me."

This was the boldest Halleigh had ever been with Tasha, but she was on an emotional overload right now.

"I'm only nineteen, Tash, and I'm on the track for Manolo. All I wanted was to be with my man, you know." Tears rolled down Halleigh's face. "Do you know how it feels, not being able to be with someone who your heart just burns for?" Halleigh wiped her nose with the back of her hand. "I have to get high to get by, and that's my business, not yours. Your business is making sure I turn all my money over to you." Halleigh was throwing a guilt trip on Tasha so Tasha would feel her pain.

"You in my face day and night, acting like you care, but you don't. All you care about is how many niggas I suck and fuck. That's how it has always been, and that's how it's always going to be, so squash the act about you being all concerned about me and shit," she screamed. Halleigh was upset with the world and was letting the heroin speak for her. She knew that Tasha had grown quite close to her, but she didn't care. She needed to vent, so she continued with her rant. "No, you aren't the one who put me on the ho stroll, but you're the one who helped him get in my head. So don't be trying to act all innocent, like you didn't have shit to do with it."

Halleigh wiped every last teardrop away. Hell, she was tired of crying. She had no more tears left. Her sadness had transformed into resentment and hatred, and she was taking it all out on Tasha.

Halleigh attempted to leave the room, but Tasha jumped up and blocked the doorway. "No, Halleigh, wait!" Tasha begged. She knew that Halleigh was telling the truth. She did help Manolo manipulate his young girls, but this time she wished she hadn't participated. Halleigh was too pure for what Manolo had in store for her, and Tasha knew that almost from the first time she'd set eyes on her. Halleigh couldn't handle the game, and Tasha felt obligated to get the monkey off her back, especially since she had participated in the cause that put the monkey there in the first place.

"Just calm down, sweetheart," Tasha said, holding her hands up in surrender. "You know that I would never intentionally hurt you. You are like my sister." Tasha choked up, her eyes filled with tears. She imagined saying the same thing to Loita. If she had, maybe Loita would still be alive today. "I know this lifestyle ain't healthy for you. If I can get you to Malek, will you promise me you will stay off the drugs?"

Halleigh couldn't believe her ears. Had Tasha just made her the offer she thought she heard?

"Okay, Hal?" Tasha placed a hand on either side of Halleigh's face.

Halleigh nodded her head. "Yes," she replied, sounding like a hope-

ful child. "Tasha, I swear I will. I swear to God. Just get me to Malek. Get me out of this life. Help me. Please help me."

Tasha hugged Halleigh tightly, looked up toward the ceiling and said a short prayer. *Please help me with this, God. I don't know how I'm gon' do it, but I have to help her out of this.*

It was the first time that Tasha had prayed since she was a child. She just hoped God was listening.

Tasha pulled away from Halleigh and put her hands on her shoulders. "Listen, stay here. I'll be back in a while. Do not leave this room, Hal. If the phone rings, just answer it and direct the traffic to the other girls. You got that?"

Halleigh nodded.

"Good. I'll be back," Tasha said as she exited the room.

After Tasha closed the door behind her, she stood there with her back against it, still holding the knob. She exhaled. Because Halleigh was a genuinely good person, Tasha's heart ached for her. Tasha knew that she was partly to blame for Halleigh's disposition. Being the madam of the house, it was her job to make the girls feel as if they had nowhere else to go. The situation with Halleigh had gone too far, however, with her resorting to heroin as an escape, just like Loita.

I have to find Malek for her.

Tasha knew there was a possibility that Manolo would harm Halleigh if he ever found out that she reunited with Malek, but she knew for sure that drugs would kill her. Tasha couldn't just sit back and watch her girl send herself into an early grave. So she had a job to do. She had made a promise that she intended to keep.

She released the doorknob and began her trek in search of Malek.

Chapter Thirty-seven

Tasha pulled her car up to Joe's home on Coldwater and turned off her ignition. She was down with Sweets, Manolo, and the South Side, but she was also well known throughout the entire city. She and Joe had enjoyed some mind-blowing nights together a couple years ago, and she was confident that she was safe on his side of town.

She stared up at his four-bedroom home and butterflies entered her stomach. She wasn't afraid of Jamaica Joe, but she was afraid of what

Manolo would do to her if he ever found out that she was in the presence of his enemy.

She pulled down the sun visor and looked at herself in the mirror attached to it. She checked her M•A•C makeup to make sure her shit was tight. Then she stepped out of the car, gracing the cold Flint streets with her Jimmy Choo stilettos. Most hoes in Flint didn't even know what the hell Jimmy Choo was. It was more like, "Jimmy who?"

These whack chicks probably thinking it's a new Chinese joint or something, no-class-having-ass bitches, Tasha thought arrogantly as she adjusted the strap on her shoe and then made her way to Joe's front porch.

Tasha was a top-notch ho, and she knew it. So did everybody who knew her. She kept up with all the latest fashions. If she'd been born in a big city, her dreams of becoming a model might have been realistic, but in a small city like Flint, it just wasn't happening. As she walked up to Joe's, she quickly caught the attention of the group of men posted around his back entryway. They lusted blatantly, commenting on her five-foot–nine-inch stature, slim waist, and wide hips. Her calf muscles were defined from years of walking up and down Flint's tracks, and her perky C cups set her figure off just right. Tasha was damn near perfect.

The only thing she didn't like about herself was the scars on her back, left by the last john she'd serviced. The psycho had almost taken her life when he became upset that he had to pay extra money for some extra acts that Tasha had performed for him. He ended up pulling a box cutter on her, eventually getting the extra acts he wanted, cutting her and taking them by force. She fought back with every ounce of strength she had in her, ignoring the burning stings from the blade. She was lucky to leave with her life. After the incident, she convinced Manolo to put her on as the madam of the house.

Tasha adjusted her bra strap and licked her lips. She didn't mind at all the slick comments that Joe's associates made as she stood before them. She was used to lame niggas spitting whack lines to get down. Little did they know, if they started talking the right amount of money, they could have her. *Broke niggas don't never want to put their money where their mouth is.*

She came right out and said, "I'm looking for Malek. Does anybody know where I can find him?" She stood at the bottom of the porch steps, waiting on a reply, glancing from one dude to the next..

One of the guys said, "Damn, this li'l mu'fucka got bad bitches like you checking for him?"

Tasha ignored the comment.

One of the other men tapped lightly on the door and yelled through the screen, "Yo, Joe, tell Malek he got a bad bitch looking for him out here."

Jamaica Joe came to the screen and peered out. He instantly recognized Tasha. "Aw shit, Tash! Come on in," he stated, happy to see her.

As soon as she walked through the door, he embraced her. He looked over his shoulders and nodded for his guys to go check out shit, to make sure she didn't bring anybody else with her who might be trying to set him up.

"How you been doing, Joe?" Tasha tried to pull away from Joe's embrace, but was unable to, as he caressed her like a long-lost friend, feeling her up. "Look, Joe, you can stop it with the body search. I ain't got nothin' on me. I ain't come bringing no shit. I'm just looking for somebody, one of your homeboys, all right?"

Joe eased up and released her. He knew Tasha was good peoples, but with some of the shit going down lately, he could never be too sure. For all he knew, Manolo and Sweets had sent her to catch a nigga slippin' again.

"All right. You good, ma." He looked her up and down. "And still lookin' good too. By the way, how's that chump nigga treating you? You still running the Manolo Mamis, right?"

"I'm good, Joe."

"Yeah, that's what your mouth say. I don't know why you still in that game anyway. You know if you ever need something—"

"I'm good," she answered again.

Joe and Tasha had a nice little rapport going on between them. They always had, despite the beef between the two rival gangs. Joe had tried to pull her from underneath Manolo plenty of times, but Tasha wasn't trying to be the atomic bomb in a war that was already explosive enough. She knew the game, and she knew her place. Loyalty was important to her, even though she did enjoy spending time with Joe.

"Okay, okay. You killing me, though, coming to my spot, looking for my boy." Joe placed a hand on his heart, as if he'd been shot there.

His charming smile made Tasha laugh. "Come on now," she said. "You know me better than that. I need to talk to your boy about my girl Halleigh."

Before Jamaica Joe could respond, Malek walked into the room.

"Speak of the devil," Joe said.

Tasha stared up at the tall, handsome young boy who stood before her. He was far from a boy, though. The nineteen-year-old was nice, with a body that had Tasha's eyes wandering. *Damn, this is why Hal's head is so gone off of him.*

"What about Halleigh?" Malek asked. Hearing her name had piqued his interest.

Tasha could sense the concern and anxiety in his voice and thought that it might be easier than she expected to hook them up. "She needs you," Tasha said simply. "Your girl is on some other shit right now. I don't want to put her business out like that, so I'm just gon' say it's

bad. You're the only person she talks about. She is going crazy without you," Tasha stated in a serious tone. "Maybe you can talk some sense into her, 'cause as of now, she ain't trying to hear me."

Jamaica Joe interjected, "I know y'all ain't talking about that little trick from the party, Manolo's ho."

Tasha nodded, never taking her eyes off Malek.

"Yo, fuck that shit right now." Jamaica Joe put his hand on Malek's shoulder. The last thing he wanted was for Malek's head to be far gone on some broad while they had bigger things to tend to. He needed his soldier focused on the real business at hand—catching Sweets and his crew slipping.

Jamaica Joe had seen how fucked up Malek was after Halleigh chose Manolo over him the night of the party. His pain was evident from the look in his eyes. As far as Joe was concerned, his business took priority over Malek's business with some high school girlfriend. "That's Manolo's pussy, man," Joe said to Malek then turned his attention to Tasha. "She straight ho'ed my boy for that nigga. She deserves to be where she's at."

Tasha yelled when she saw Malek's expression turn cold. "Joe, it's not like that. You know how Manolo can get in these girls' heads. He told her that he would kill her *and* Malek."

"Nah. He can touch her, but this nigga right here can't be touched." Joe patted Malek on the shoulder, letting him know he had his back.

"Malek?" Tasha asked, her voice pleading with him to help Halleigh.

Jamaica Joe stared intently at him to see what his decision would be. He'd already made it clear that there was no riding the fence anymore. Malek had to choose. He was either North or South.

The light of hope Tasha had initially seen in Malek was now dimming. "Just come see her," Tasha said. "Please . . . that's all I'm asking."

Malek hesitated. The thought of Halleigh being in trouble bothered him, but he couldn't get past the fact that she'd put another nigga before him.

Joe got in his ear. "What's it gonna be, homie, North or South?" His tone was laced with a discreet warning that Malek better make the right choice or he might not even make it out of that house alive to go talk to Halleigh.

Malek looked up at Joe, even though he was replying to Tasha, and said, "I don't fuck with no South Side bitch." Then he walked away.

A smirk appeared on Joe's face. He nodded his head, pleased that Malek had made the right decision—money over bitches—and watched his boy walk away.

"Joe?" Tasha said as she looked his way for help.

Joe shrugged. *I know this ho don't think I'ma talk my boy into choosing her crew over mine.*

"Come on, Joe. Go talk to him."

"He a grown-ass man. That's his business."

"Yeah, but this is a matter of life and death. You have no idea how far gone this chick is. I ain't asking him to disregard his loyalty to you. I just want him to have one lousy gotdamn conversation with her, a conversation that could possibly save her life."

Joe simply shrugged again and then kissed Tasha on the cheek, letting her know it was still good between them.

Tasha sighed and threw her hands up in despair. She stormed out of the house. It was the first time in a long time that she felt like crying. *What do I tell this girl? I can't just walk in there and say, "He don't want your ass no more."*

Tasha drove slowly back to the hotel, trying to decide if she should lie to Halleigh and say that she couldn't find Malek but would keep trying. Perhaps that would buy her some time.

When Tasha got back to the hotel, she wasn't even in the room more than a few seconds before Halleigh jumped up, eager to find out if she'd tracked down Malek.

"Hey, Tash," Halleigh said excitedly. She kept peering behind Tasha, hoping Malek would walk through the door. "Where is he? What did he say?"

Tasha shook her head, but she was unable to form the words.

"Well, come on, tell me. Since when have you ever been at a loss for words?" Halleigh said, trying to keep the mood light. Tasha's mood was a sure sign that her attempt was unsuccessful. "You didn't find him, did you?"

At that moment, Tasha could have easily lied to Halleigh. She could have been persistent and kept going back at Malek until he gave in and talked to Halleigh; even if she had to throw some pussy at him just to get him to do it. Instead, the truth prevailed. "No, I found him."

There was a pregnant silence.

"And?" Halleigh finally said.

Tasha looked up with her saddened eyes.

"And he's not coming, is he?"

Before Tasha could even speak, Halleigh's excitement had turned to complete despair. She could only imagine what Malek said to Tasha. "He doesn't love me anymore." Halleigh fell weakly to her knees.

The sound that erupted from her body was enough to bring Tasha to tears as she fell to the floor with her friend and held her tightly. Despite what Halleigh thought, Tasha really did care about her.

"It's okay. It's going to be okay," Tasha repeated over and over in her attempt to comfort Halleigh.

Her words fell on deaf ears, though. Halleigh couldn't stop the pain she was feeling. She just sat on the floor hopelessly and cried enough tears to cleanse the entire city.

Tasha stroked Halleigh's hair and thought about her next move.

Chapter Thirty-eight

Tasha, I don't know about y'all living at the hotel. That would be double the cost just for the rooms. Instead of paying for the rooms for a couple of hours, I would be paying full price," Manolo said, skepticism in his voice.

"Come on, Daddy. Think about it. We are missing out on so much money. By us being here at the hotel twenty-four hours, we could make twice as much money. It's a win-win situation," Tasha said convincingly as she talked into the phone in her hotel room. She hoped that Manolo would fall for the little trick she had up her sleeve, because she knew that she would need time to get Halleigh back right. If Manolo saw her in the state she was in, his method of detox would probably be another two weeks in the basement.

Manolo listened closely on the other end of the phone, while one of the girls filed his fingernails for him. Fortunately for Tasha, the more she talked, the more he began to see things her way. The mention of making more money had him game.

"All right, Tasha, but if the cash flow don't double up, I'ma take it out on that ass, hear me?" Manolo said sternly.

"Yeah, Daddy, I hear you. I'ma make you proud." With that, Tasha hung up the phone and focused her attention over to her bed. She knew the other girls weren't going to take too kindly to the new arrangement she'd just made with Manolo, but if she had to sacrifice their time and happiness to save one, then her mind was made up: she was going to do it.

Tasha knew that she had bought herself some time. She wanted to keep Manolo away from Halleigh for as long as possible, until she got better. Seeing her would be a dead giveaway. He would easily see that Halleigh was fiending for one of two things: either dope or Malek. Neither one would please him.

Now that Tasha had taken care of phase one of the plan with Manolo, it was time to take care of phase two with Halleigh. She went into one of the dominatrix bags that the girls sometimes used on their customers. She then made her way over to Halleigh, who was coming out of a dope coma.

"Let me go, you crazy bitch!" Halleigh yelled as she tried to avoid being handcuffed to the bed. She was too weak to stand a chance against Tasha.

"Look, Halleigh, I'm sorry about this. I don't want to have to leave you tied up like this, but I can't sit here and watch you continue to hurt yourself. You are killing yourself slowly on that needle. Believe me, I've seen that shit destroy some of the toughest chicks. Let me

help you, okay?" Tasha said in a comforting tone. She looked into Halleigh's baggy eyes and felt sorry for her. Determined to help Halleigh shake her habit, she wasn't about to let the streets swallow her whole like they did Loita.

"Bitch, I said let me go!" Halleigh screamed as she continued to squirm and jerk to no avail.

Tasha had to head out and take care of some business, and she didn't want Halleigh to hit the streets looking for another fix. Unfortunately, part of her plan meant that she herself would have to come out of retirement and hit the track to compensate for Halleigh. While out tricking, she knew she had to keep Halleigh restrained, or else the first thing she'd do was go out and get a hit.

"I will let you go, Hal, but you have to kick this shit first. I'm so sorry, but it's for your own good." Tasha looked at her, hoping that Halleigh could see in her eyes how sincere she was about helping her.

"Aghh! Aghh! Help me!" Halleigh screamed, hoping her cries for help would grab someone's attention.

Tasha let her scream, knowing that no one would come and check on her. They were at a "whore motel," and screaming and begging was a common sound coming from their rooms.

"Go ahead and scream all you like," Tasha told her, "but I'm not going to let you go until I get back. I know you don't believe me when I say it, but I really do care about you and what happens to you. I don't want to see you end up like . . ." Tasha's words trailed off. "Look, I love you, girl, and I know that you are going to beat this shit." Tasha sat on the bed next to Halleigh and began to rub her head.

"I don't need your help!" Halleigh forcefully yanked away from Tasha. "I need a hit!"

"That shit is going to kill you, Halleigh," Tasha yelled as she looked down at her with tears in her eyes. Why couldn't Halleigh see that all she was trying to do was help her? Tasha could have easily just let her fall off and become like some of the other girls, but she wouldn't be able to live with herself. She just couldn't understand why Halleigh wouldn't want the help somebody was trying to offer her.

"Maybe I want to die, Tasha. You ever thought about that? Malek doesn't want me. What man would? There's no point in living," she said, staring at the ceiling.

"Fuck him, Halleigh, and anybody else, for that matter." She grabbed Halleigh by the face. "Do this for you! Don't end up like your mother. Fight this."

Halleigh was offended that Tasha would even insinuate that she was anything like her mother. "I'm not going to end up like my mother. I'm nothing like that bitch."

Tasha realized that she'd hit a nerve, and so she decided to go for the jugular. She let out a menacing chuckle. "Huh? Nothing like her?

Have you looked in the mirror lately? You're just like her. Matter of fact . . ."—Tasha got up and went over to her purse, pulled out a M•A•C makeup compact, opened it up and held the mirror in front of Halleigh—"See. Look at yourself. Just look at you."

Halleigh turned. She didn't want to see herself. She could only imagine what her reflection looked like. "Stop it! No!" Halleigh continued to struggle.

Tasha grabbed her tightly by the chin to hold her face steady and rammed the mirror in front of her. "I said look! Look at you. If you're not your mother, then who are you?"

Halleigh began to weep, but it didn't stop Tasha from making her point. "Who are you then?"

When Halleigh's eyes met those looking back at her in the mirror, she shut them tight and began to cry. "I don't know," she finally answered. "I don't know who I am anymore. Oh, God," she cried with heaving shoulders.

Tasha uttered a sigh of relief, figuring she'd made her point and that Halleigh had had enough. Tasha took Halleigh into her arms and rocked her.

Just then, a thought came into Halleigh's mind. "I hear what you're saying, Tasha,"—She rattled the handcuffs—"about me being locked down and all, but what will Manolo say? He'll know that I'm fucked up when he sees that I'm not bringing in any money. I'm better off killing myself with drugs anyway after he gets a hold of me."

But Tasha knew that was just a last-ditch drug addict tactic to convince her to let Halleigh go.

Halleigh was right about Manolo's cash, though. If he sensed that the money was coming short, he would definitely put a foot in their asses. That's why Tasha decided to come out of retirement. She didn't want to go back to ho'ing, but she knew that she had to, to keep Halleigh's condition a secret from Manolo. She'd promised herself that she would never turn a trick again, but desperate times called for desperate measures. This was definitely one of those times. Halleigh was like a little sister to her, and she refused to let her continue down the path she was taking.

You have to make this game your hustle, not your life. Tricks get in this game for the wrong reasons.

Tasha released Halleigh and then stood up to head for the door. "I've taken care of that." She opened the compact she already had in her hands and touched up her face with the powder puff.

Tasha knew being a prostitute wasn't easy. It was best to get money and then get out because in this game, if you stay in it too long, it becomes you. When the streets become you, there is no turning back.

Tasha had on her four-inch stilettos and a black miniskirt. Before walking out the door, she walked over to the dresser mirror to apply

some mascara. She could hear Halleigh moaning in the background in obvious pain, and she wanted so badly to uncuff her, but that would only be enabling her friend to go and do more drugs.

"Sorry, Hal," Tasha whispered as Halleigh continued to moan loudly, "but this is for your own good." Tasha finished applying her mascara then headed for the door.

"Please help me, Tasha. I hurt so badly," Halleigh said, tears streaming down her face. Her body was craving the drug, and sharp pains shot through her stomach as the monkey jumped on her back.

It's for her own good. Tasha exited the room. Somebody had to fill in for Halleigh, and Tasha was taking one for the team.

"Please! Please, Tash, help me out. I need a fix. I swear this will be the last time," Halleigh begged.

If Tasha looked back at Halleigh, she would give in, so she just exited the room with tears in her eyes and never looked back.

Chapter Thirty-nine

"You like that, Daddy?" Tasha asked the john seductively as she massaged his balls with one hand and gripped his pipe with the other. Tasha peeked up at the man, and he was in pure bliss. He was about to cum, and she hadn't even put her mouth on his dick yet. This is what she called "easy money." As she continued to massage his balls and blow on his manhood, she felt his legs stiffen up. She gave him one good stroke and licked his head, and that was it. Game over.

Tasha hadn't lost her touch. She made that fool cum in under a minute. She wasn't the best for nothing.

"That's a hundred and fifty dollars, Daddy." Tasha got off her knees and held out her palm. She had charged him for a head job, when in actuality he only got jerked off. The fool was so in love, he didn't know the difference. Tasha could peep vulnerable men from a mile away. The way he was moaning and looking into Tasha's eyes, she knew from jump that she could overcharge him.

The man handed Tasha two crisp hundred dollar bills. "Keep the change."

Tasha got the money and then hopped out of his two-door Cadillac. She walked the track, trying to pick up her next john. She had only

been on the ho stroll for a couple of hours, and she almost had six hundred dollars, just that quick.

Tasha was a veteran. She knew which johns to service and which johns not to. If a john didn't look like he was spending big dough, she passed on him. For her, being out there all night fucking with small-timers just wasn't worth it.

Tasha grew hungry and stopped at the chicken spot on the corner of Clio and Stewart to grab a bite to eat and to use their bathroom to freshen up a little. She picked up two chicken dinners then walked out of the spot.

"Hey, miss."

She turned and saw the store owner coming her way. He was the one who had just waited on her.

Once he finally caught up with her, he said, "You uh, you uh, forgot your change." The way he said it was kind of peculiar, and he seemed to be looking around to make sure no one was watching him.

"Oh, did I?" Tasha could have sworn that he'd given it to her. She started to check her purse, but then he extended his hand to her. Inside of it was a hundred dollar bill.

Tasha took it out of his hand and looked at it like it was nothing but a dollar bill. "And what's this for?"

"Oh, yeah, I, uh, just was wondering if you could do something for me."

Once again, Tasha looked at the hundred dollar bill like it was nothing.

The man continued. "I was just, uh, wondering if you could come with me to my truck. It's, uh, right over there."

Tasha's eyes followed his finger to the black SUV with tinted windows. "And?"

"And just watch me."

A puzzled look came across Tasha's face. Seeing her confusion, the man went on. "And just watch me, you know, take care of my business."

"Ohhh," Tasha said, nodding her head. She smiled and then licked her lips. Once again, a vulnerable one. She loved how she attracted his kind. She knew that she could have easily manipulated him out of more money if she threw in a couple of extra treats, but to watch him jerk off for a bill was good enough. Besides, she didn't want her food to get cold, so she obliged him, joining him over in his truck and watching him, while he watched her watch him jerk off.

Three minutes tops was all it took. Now that was easy money!

Tasha's feet were killing her as she headed back to the hotel. She hadn't strolled in stilettos in almost two years and was paying the price. When Tasha made it to the room, her heart dropped when she opened the door. Halleigh was gone. She'd found a way to slither out

of the handcuffs. Tasha flopped on the bed and buried her face in her hands, knowing that she'd failed Halleigh.

A noise from the bathroom startled Tasha, and she quickly looked in the direction of the commotion. She walked to the bathroom and opened the door to find Halleigh with her head over the toilet bowl.

"Halleigh, are you okay, girl?" Tasha dropped to her knees and pulled Halleigh's hair away from her face. Halleigh looked horrible, like she had lost even more weight within the past couple of hours. Her body was soaking wet because of all of the sweating she was doing. Halleigh trembled as a chill ran through her body.

"I stayed in the room. I didn't go anywhere. I didn't go," Halleigh said in a child-like, whiny voice. "See? You can trust me."

"I know, baby, I know." Tasha continued to rub her hair. She understood that Halleigh was actually trying to beat her addiction because she didn't leave the room when she had a chance.

"Come on, girl." Tasha helped Halleigh up and began to pull off her sweaty clothes.

Tasha helped her into the shower and let the water hit her face and body. She stood right by her side, washing her and holding her up. Halleigh's body was so weak. The dependence on the drug had gotten the best of her.

She's so young. I can barely handle this life and I'm twenty-four, Tasha thought.

Tasha had been involved in the pimp game for years. Just seeing Halleigh in this position and being reminded of Loita, whom she herself had introduced to the game, Tasha decided that she couldn't do this anymore. It was time for a change. The first chance she got, she would come up with a plan to do something better with her life. When she did finally decide to make the move, she promised herself that she would take Halleigh with her.

Chapter Forty

Halleigh's eyes darted frantically around the room as she tried to gather her bearings. She felt like she was dying. Her body hurt so badly. No matter what she did, nothing eased the pain. She couldn't believe that her life had gotten so bad in such a short period of time, and she was ashamed of herself for losing control. All of those years

she'd watched her mother's condition deteriorate because of drugs. Now she was following in her footsteps. What would Malek think if he saw her now?

Halleigh's body shook violently as the draft in the room sent cold shivers up her spine. She was freezing, and nothing she did could warm her body. She broke out in constant cold sweats as she squirmed and wrapped herself with the covers on the bed. The slightest touch hurt her skin, and she felt like the sun was burning out her eyes every time she attempted to open them. She'd been trying to kick her habit for weeks, and it just didn't seem to be working. The only time she could ever seem to pull herself together was when Tasha warned her that Manolo might be dropping by. Of course, Tasha always told him that Halleigh was with a john, but how much longer would that little stunt of theirs work before he started getting suspicious?

Just last week, when Manolo dropped by the hotel to check things out, Tasha was sure her little plan was about to be discovered. It was the motel keeper who almost made the plan backfire. The skinny, gray-haired man, his skin the color of coffee with a hint of cream, said to Manolo when he saw him entering the motel and heading over to the elevators, "Business picking up, I see."

Manolo simply nodded. He wasn't into talking about his business with strangers. As far as he was concerned, old dude could have recently been bought by the feds to try to trap him, or something. On second thought, Manolo knew that if anything was in the works, his hired cop, Troy, would have tipped him off. After all, that's why Troy got his pick of the litter of free pussy from the Manolo Mamis, plus a little green on the side.

Right before the elevator door opened to welcome Manolo's presence, the motel keeper added, "Yeah, when your girl came down a few weeks ago and added another room to your already-set block of five, I knew things must be picking up for you."

Manolo had already gotten inside the elevator and the doors were about to close, but hearing the man's last comment, he held his hand out, stopping the doors. "What did you say?" Manolo inquired. "Another room?"

"Well, yeah," the clerk said with a tone and expression on his face that said maybe he had spoken on something that he shouldn't have. "You, uh, have the six rooms now, right?"

When Manolo's facial expression clearly showed that he knew nothing about adding another room to their block of five, the clerk tried to clean things up. After all, he didn't want to mess up his money by spilling the beans on something he shouldn't have. "Maybe I made a mistake."

"Nah," Manolo said. "You don't look like the type of fella who makes mistakes. Just to be sure, why don't you double-check your records?"

"Uh, well, uh, yes, sir," the man stammered as he shuffled through some paperwork and receipts. After resting on one piece of paper in particular, he held it up and said, "You're right. I didn't make a mistake. Six rooms as of last month."

Fire shot out of Manolo's nostrils as he snatched the paper from the man and read the receipt that showed Tasha had been paying for an extra room. *What the fuck is going on, and why is my money being spent on shit without my prior consent?*

He had agreed with Tasha as far as paying for the rooms twenty-four/seven, but she hadn't said anything about adding an extra room to the block. Tasha, he was sure, never made mistakes. That's why she held the rank with him that she did. So he was almost one hundred percent certain that this wasn't an oversight on her part, but deliberate deception instead. But why? Why would Tasha decide to play him after all these years? Not once was the money ever short. She'd never beat him for one red cent, and now here she was trying to do something extra on the side without his knowledge. He expected this type of thing from Mimi, but not Tasha.

Is she trying to start up her own thing on the side, steal my business?

If she was, she wouldn't have been the first. The madam Manolo had before Tasha tried to pull that exact same stunt. All the while she was supposed to be minding the Manolo Mami business, she was minding her own on the side, forming a prostitution ring so that once she slipped out from under Manolo, she would already have her own thing set up.

Of course, that didn't sit too well with Manolo, and unfortunately for her—but fortunate for Tasha—the woman went missing right on time for Tasha to take her spot in Manolo's ring. If Tasha called herself doing the same thing, who would he get to replace her when she went missing?

With the paper in hand, Manolo turned back toward the elevator with every intention of going to confront Tasha with this newfound information. As he stood there waiting on the elevator, he had a second thought. He wouldn't outright confront her just yet. Instead, he would test her and watch her, to see if anything seemed out of the ordinary with her. He didn't want to believe that Tasha would try to double-cross him. Hell, even Tina Turner stuck it out with Ike, and Manolo treated Tasha way better than Ike treated Tina. If he'd learned anything about putting his trust in someone, it was not to—no exceptions. Manolo simply folded the paper, placed it in his pocket and got on the elevator, heading up to check in with Tasha, to make sure it was business as usual. For her sake, it better be.

Tasha had just returned from trickin' with a john when Manolo entered the hotel room. "Oh shit!" she exclaimed.

"What's the matter, baby girl? Did I scare you?" Manolo walked over to her, grabbed her by the back of her hair, and stared her in the eyes.

She tried her best not to tremble. "What?" she asked Manolo, wondering why he was just standing there looking down at her like she'd stolen something from him.

Manolo didn't speak. He just tightened his grip and then proceeded to ram his tongue down her throat.

Tasha wanted to throw up. Manolo's touch used to reassure her of her role in his life, but now it only sickened her. Besides, if he only knew what she'd just done with that tongue of hers, he'd reconsider sticking his in her mouth.

After tonguing Tasha down for a few seconds, Manolo pulled her away from him and stared in her eyes again.

"What, Daddy? What is it?"

Manolo just stood there searching her eyes. Usually, if someone was deceiving him, their eyes were a dead giveaway, but when he looked at Tasha, he saw the same thing that he always saw in her eyes—loyalty. "Nothing," Manolo finally replied. "I just missed you, is all."

Tasha relaxed a little. For a minute there, she was afraid that Manolo might have heard something about her from the street. She showed no fear as she maintained her composure. "I missed you too." Tasha pulled away from Manolo and headed toward the bathroom.

"Where you going?" Manolo looked her up and down. He noticed that she was a little bit more dressed up than usual.

"Uh, just to the bathroom. I just got back from walking to the store. I didn't know you were stopping by."

"Well, aren't you a little overdressed for the store?"

"You know when I step out I always gotta do it right. After all, I'm a walking advertisement for the Manolo Mamis. Niggas see me, and like stray little puppies, they wanna follow me home, and home is where the money is," Tasha said, thinking quick on her feet.

She walked back over toward Manolo and said seductively, "Anyway, like I was saying, I didn't know you were stopping by. Otherwise, I wouldn't have gotten myself all sweaty and stuff down there. I would have kept it crisp for you." She ran her fingers across Manolo's lips. "You know, with me running this spot twenty-four hours now, I never get to see you as often, and a girl has needs too, Daddy. I know you ain't gon' leave me hanging. You gotta hit me off with a little something because God knows when I'll get the chance to be alone with you again."

Manolo closed his eyes and moaned as Tasha cupped his manhood and began to massage it.

"Oh shit, baby. You know Daddy wouldn't do you like that."

"Good." Tasha backed away from him slowly and sensually toward the bathroom. "Then you stay right there. Promise me you won't leave me, Daddy," Tasha begged.

"Promise." Manolo watched her disappear behind the bathroom door. "Mm-mm-mm," he said to himself. He began to undress, and reasonable doubt regarding Tasha's loyalty to him slowly began to vacate his mind. *Maybe business was booming, and she had to get an extra room and just didn't worry about telling me, since it's not going to be a regular thing. Yeah, that's probably it.*

Manolo lay down on the bed, caressing his manhood and waiting on Daddy's favorite little girl to come please him. *Hell, even if she's up to no good after all, I don't see no reason why I can't get one last fuck-and-suck before I see to it that she or anyone who decides to jump camp with her, like Toni Braxton said, never breathes again.*

Chapter Forty-one

As Halleigh lay there in pain, she didn't know what to do. "God, help me," she moaned, grabbing her stomach. She lifted herself up and tried to crawl out of the hotel bed, but ended up landing on her knees beside the bed. As if her knees were magnetized to the floor, she remained in that spot.

A few weeks ago, after convincing Manolo to allow the girls to run business twenty-four/seven in the motel, Tasha had gone down and paid the clerk for an extra room to house Halleigh. She didn't want any of the other girls getting wind that Halleigh wasn't putting in any work at all. That alone would've given them cause to run back and start complaining to Manolo. So Tasha just got Halleigh her own room, away from the ones where the other girls tricked, so that she could get better.

Tasha even used her own money to pay for the room. In all the years she'd dealt with Manolo, she'd never burned him when it came to "the ends." Even though she was starting to hate the ground he walked on, she still wasn't about to start spending his money without his say. That would have sent up a red flag. Then what excuse would she have given him? Instead, she turned an extra trick when she could, just to cover the cost of the additional room she'd added to their tab.

"God help me!" Halleigh cried out once again, gripping her stom-

ach in agony. That's when the irony of it all hit. She was exactly where God probably wanted her to be in order for Him to get her to call out to Him: on her knees.

In all of the mess she had been in since the night of the rape, she had not once gone to God and asked Him for help. She went to Malek, Mimi, Manolo, and, regretfully, she'd gone to Scratch. Not once did she just go to the one who was in charge of everything and ask Him to show her the right way to go about life.

As Halleigh began to call out to God with what seemed to be her last breath, she only hoped it wasn't too late. Figuring that she didn't have anything to lose since she had given up everything, right down to her soul, she began to pray. Hopefully she could convince God to talk to Satan and order him to give her back her soul.

Halleigh folded her hands and leaned over the bed. Her healing bones ached with every movement. She was willing to try anything now to take the pain away, though. Since all else failed, perhaps prayer wouldn't. The pressure on her knees was too much to take. She fell down on her side and began to cry. She figured that she didn't have to be on her knees in order for God to hear her, so she let the tears come as she put her hands up to her face.

God, please help me. I know that you shouldn't, and I am probably not worth saving, but haven't I suffered enough? You blessed my life when You brought Malek into it. Before him, I didn't know love. I would have never imagined knowing another person better than I know myself. You already know how my mother gets down, so I don't have to go into that whole situation, and I'm not looking for a pity party, because I know that I did this to myself. Life just hurts so bad, God. It hurts. Malek doesn't want me anymore. He won't even see me. He was my everything, God, my reason for breathing. What did I do to deserve losing him?

I don't know if I can handle life without him. That's why I'm lying here on this floor with a drug-infested body. I poisoned myself trying to soothe my heart, shooting dope, free-basing. I did whatever I had to do to forget about Malek and the life I'm living. I'm killing myself slowly, but I know that I'm wrong. I can't fix it by myself. It hurts so bad. My body hurts all day. It feels like I can't breathe.

I'm begging You, God, to take this burden away from me. I can't handle it. I'm not strong enough. I know I've never come to You before. I don't go to church every Sunday like some of the other people who call on You might, but I do believe that You can save me. If I am Your child, why does my life hurt so badly? Why me? Please save me from this because I don't think I'm strong enough to do this without Your support. I don't want to do this to myself anymore. I'm dying.

Halleigh became too weak to even think. Her prayer stopped short

as her eyes became too heavy for her to keep them open. Her arms fell to her sides as she just lay there.

Tasha entered the hotel room and saw Halleigh sprawled out on the floor near the bed. "Oh God!" She dropped her purse and ran over to Halleigh. "God, please don't let her be dead. Please don't let her be dead."

Tasha made it over to Halleigh, got on her knees, and grabbed her wrist to check for a pulse. She then placed her ear against Halleigh's nose, trying to see if she could feel any life coming out of her, something she'd seen on television.

Halleigh coughed.

"Oh Jesus!" Tasha said with a sigh of relief. "Hal, why are you laying out on the floor like this?" Tasha sat beside her on the floor and rubbed her hair softly.

Halleigh opened her eyes and replied, "No, Tasha, don't touch me. It hurts." She was too fatigued to even cry. Tears just drained from her eyes and rolled down the side of her face. "It just hurts so bad," she whispered.

"I know, I know, Hal. I'm so sorry for this. I know that this ain't for you. This isn't for anybody. You don't deserve this. I don't deserve this. I'm going to get us out of here. Just let me come up with a plan. I just need to think of a way to get us away from Manolo safely. Just hang in there. Give me time. I swear, I'm going to find a way out."

"I thought you said there is no way out," Halleigh replied, feeding Tasha's own words back to her.

"I'll find a way, Halleigh. I'll find a way," Tasha muttered as she tried to think of a possible escape plan for them. She pulled a cover and two pillows off the bed and lay right beside Halleigh. She snuggled close to her, wrapped her arms around her, and let the tears fall without shame.

It had been so long since she had cried. She'd trained herself not to be emotional from the day she turned her first trick. She didn't want anyone to think she was weak or that she could be easily manipulated, so she told herself that crying was a sure way to lose control over her own life. Now she felt weak, trapped underneath Manolo's selfish reign, and all she really felt like doing was crying.

As Tasha lay next to Halleigh, she cried for all of the times that she'd let strange men have her body. For all of the souls of the girls she'd helped Manolo lure in. For her parents, whom she knew she'd hurt when she started tricking. And for Loita. When Loita died, she didn't even cry then, so she was crying for her now too.

She released her entire life's heartache while she lay next to Halleigh. More, now than ever before, she felt close to her. Tasha knew that it was time for her to get strong—on her own. She didn't want to feel powerful by preying on the weakness of others, She wanted to em-

power both herself and Halleigh so that they could live the life that they deserved.

God surely must have taken these two women to the bottom this day, to a point where they both realized that they had nowhere to go to and no one to go to but Him. It seemed that prayer was moving in Tasha's heart that day as well. She asked God for the strength she needed to get them out of their current situation, and to give her a better direction in life.

Chapter Forty-two

Two weeks passed by, and each day God answered Halleigh's prayers by gradually taking the pain away. Halleigh was no longer in unbearable pain, but she was still very weak. She honestly didn't know what it was that was causing her pain to be less severe; whether it was prayer, God, or if her body was just getting better on its own now that she wasn't feeding it heroin anymore.

Also, to help ease her pain, Tasha had tricked with a doctor who gave her a prescription of methadone for Halleigh that made her body think it was getting a hit, but it really wasn't.

Now that she was getting better, Halleigh was tired of being locked up in the hotel room. Before, she could barely move, so staying in that hotel room wasn't an issue. Now she felt cooped up and nauseated all the time. She had polluted her body with drugs. Now that she wasn't on them anymore, she felt weird, and was grateful to be alive. She realized what a stupid mistake she'd made and didn't want to be addicted to drugs anymore. For her entire life, she had tried to differentiate herself from her mother. She wanted to show people that she wouldn't follow in her mother's footsteps, but indeed, she had fallen victim to the trials and tribulations of the streets.

Halleigh knew that she was very lucky to have her life. She had been spared. For what reason? She didn't know, but she promised herself that she would never take her life for granted again, not for Malek, not for anyone.

Tasha promised Halleigh that she would still try to help her see Malek again, if that's what she really wanted, even if it was just for closure. First things first, Tasha had to get her and Halleigh out of Manolo's clutch. Halleigh knew that Tasha was trying to get her out of the game, but

what she didn't know was that Tasha herself wanted out of the life as well.

"How do you feel?" Tasha asked Halleigh, who was sitting on the bed playing a game of solitaire. Tasha had just finished up a long night of work.

"Better." Halleigh continued her game, not looking up at Tasha. Not only was Halleigh ashamed that Tasha was out turning tricks because of her, but she was embarrassed by her own behavior.

Tasha noticed her disposition. "Ain't no need to feel no type of way around me. You're my sister. I did what I had to do to make sure you were okay, so don't look down on yourself. You know these past few weeks we've sort of switched places. Turning tricks will tear you down mentally and physically. I understand how it broke you, Hal, but you have to promise me that you are going to take care of yourself. You've got to stay strong from here on out. No more drugs. Having to cover for you and turn tricks to make sure that Manolo's money was consistent made me realize that this lifestyle ain't for me either. Now I realize it was never for you. We'll get away from Manolo. I don't know how yet, but we will. Just give me some time to figure it out, okay?"

Halleigh nodded her head. "Okay," she stated, still not looking up.

"Now, you ready to get out of this hotel to get some fresh air? I know you have to be starving."

Halleigh didn't think that she would be able to hold down any food. Given the way her stomach felt, the food would probably make her sick. She was also still having a hard time controlling her bowels. She stood up and looked at herself in the mirror. What she saw disgusted her. She'd lost about twenty-five pounds, and her skin was sickly-looking. She barely recognized the person staring back at her.

"Yeah, from the looks of it, I need to eat," she said, figuring she'd at least give it a try. If nothing else, she would at least enjoy some fresh air. She felt like a prisoner in solitary confinement, although she was the one who'd created her own prison.

"Then let me go get cleaned up real quick," Tasha told her, "and then we'll head out." Tasha headed over to the bathroom.

"Cool," Halleigh replied.

At that exact moment, Mimi came banging on Tasha's door, stopping Tasha right in her tracks at the doorway. "Tasha, open up!" Mimi yelled. "I know you in here."

Halleigh looked at Tasha nervously.

Tasha whispered, "Don't worry about it. I didn't tell her anything about what's been going on. She just thinks you've been sick."

Halleigh breathed a sigh of relief. She didn't want her business to be out there like that, and was grateful that Tasha hadn't spread the news. Halleigh liked Mimi, but she knew Mimi's relationship with Benjamin Franklin took precedence over any friendship.

Tasha nodded at Halleigh to go ahead and open the door for Mimi, which she obliged.

When the door opened, Mimi practically knocked Halleigh down when she saw her. "Bitch, where the hell have you been?" she asked as she hugged her tightly.

"Ow, Mimi!" Halleigh whined, grimacing slightly from Mimi's tight grasp.

"Take it easy, Mimi," Tasha said. "She's still a little under the weather."

"Um, no offense," Mimi said, looking Halleigh up and down, "but you do look bad." She then walked over to Tasha to talk about the business at hand: the fresh gossip that had her anxious to spill.

"Girl! Keesha lying ass been spreading all types of rumors around this bitch about where Halleigh been. First, she was talking about Halleigh was pregnant, and I was like uh-uh, 'cause I knew you wouldn't have kept that from me." Mimi turned to Halleigh. "Then she started talking about how Halleigh had caught something from one of her johns and gave it to Manolo. She said that he had her taken care of. I knew that shit was a lie too, though."

Halleigh and Tasha were cracking up at Mimi, who couldn't stop talking. She was going on and on about how much drama Halleigh had missed and how much she hated Keesha.

"Tasha, will you please let me beat that bitch's ass for lying on my girl?" Mimi said, getting even more amped at the thought of fighting Keesha.

"No, let it go, Mi," Tasha told her. "She ain't worth it. Anyway, I'm about to freshen up. Hal and I are about to go grab something to eat."

Tasha continued into the bathroom, but before she closed the door, Mimi mocked, "Hal and I are about to go grab something to eat," and threw Tasha a nasty look.

"You got a problem?" Tasha said, stepping to her.

"No, just that you are all of a sudden treating me like some step-child, like I ain't a part of y'all's little clique." She turned back to Halleigh and said, "I asked her a thousand times about what was going on with you, and she wouldn't tell me anything except that you were sick. Well, what kind of sick?"

"That's 'cause you didn't need to know nothing, bitch," Tasha said playfully. "And don't get jealous, ho. You can come eat with us too if you want," Tasha said, closing the bathroom door.

"You paying?" Mimi asked through the door, her hands on her hips.

"Yeah, it's on me." Tasha shook her head from side to side at Mimi's cheap self.

A few minutes later, Tasha came out of the bathroom and grabbed her purse. "Y'all ready to eat or what? Come on, let's go celebrate." Tasha winked at Halleigh.

"What are we celebrating?" Mimi asked, feeling like she was on the outside of an inside joke.

"We are celebrating that our Halleigh's health is coming back and that everything is good now." She turned to Halleigh. "So where you want to eat, guest of honor?"

"It ain't got to be nothing all big. Let's just go to Atlas Coney Island," she replied. "Hopefully I can get a hot dog down at least."

Tasha smiled, and the girls headed out of the room, Mimi leading the way and Halleigh behind her.

"I'm proud of you," Tasha whispered to Halleigh as she put her arm around her shoulders and they headed out. Tasha was also proud of herself for pulling Halleigh out of the gutter. Now all she had to do was make sure that they both kept their heads above water until they found rescue.

Chapter Forty-three

Jamaica Joe, Tariq, and Malek loaded up the black Navigator with several duffle bags containing twenty kilos of pure cocaine. Joe had a buyer in Detroit who wanted to get hit off. Joe usually never made transactions face to face with his buyers, but because of the big order, he decided to make the trip himself. He couldn't afford to take any risk with some other cat fucking up his money.

Sweets' little caper had set Joe back, and he was trying to get his paper back up to par. He needed this flip desperately, and wasn't going to trust anyone else with that amount of money. He would make $350,000 on the transaction, and didn't want any funny business with one of his mules, or some nigga getting caught slippin' and getting robbed. He asked Malek and Tariq to come along for added security, and made sure they were prepared before they hit the road.

Joe loaded the last bag into the trunk. "Yo, you strapped up?" he asked Malek.

"You know it," Malek said in a low tone as he patted his waist.

"You?" Joe asked Tariq as he looked over in his direction.

"Yep!" Tariq lifted his shirt and displayed his twin 9 mm pistols.

They all jumped into the truck and took off. Malek drove, and Tariq sat up front in the passenger's seat, while Joe sat in the back and lit up a blunt.

'Bout time this nigga chauffeured my ass around for a change, Tariq thought as he pulled out his Sidekick. *Now, this shit is more like it.* He leaned back and got comfortable, reclining his seat a little. He looked over at Malek. *Although it's too little, too late, as far as I'm concerned. But still, I'ma milk this shit for all it's worth.*

"Yo, let's stop at Atlas restaurant and grab something to eat before we hit the road. I'm hungry as hell," Joe said as he leaned back in his chair and inhaled the weed smoke into his lungs.

As they headed toward the restaurant ,they all bobbed their heads in unison to Jay-Z's Reasonable Doubt, which was pumping lightly out of the subwoofers in the trunk.

Malek kept noticing how Tariq was continuously typing on his Sidekick. He was wondering if Joe had peeped it, but then his question was answered when he heard Joe say, "Nigga, you always on that mu'-fucka, sweet-talking them hoes."

Tariq hurriedly put his Sidekick away. "Man, ain't nobody sweet-talking nobody."

"Yeah right, nigga. You probably over there caking it, paying car notes and all," Malek added.

"Yeah right," Tariq responded, noticeably irritated. *I'ma be caking, all right, nigga. Just wait and see.*

"Please don't kill me, Sweets! Please. I got three kids at home. I'm sorry," the man pleaded while on his knees. Sweets had found out that he was skimming off of the top and stepping on the dope to make more money. The man had been stealing from Sweets for years and had finally gotten caught.

"You stupid mu'fucka, why would you steal from me, huh?" Sweets slapped dude upside the head, like he was some young schoolboy getting popped by his mama for not cleaning up his room. "Don't I treat you good? When yo bitch-ass ex-wife took yo house, who helped you get on yo feet? I gave you a job, and this is how you repay me. You stepping on my dope, having fiends run to the North Side because my product is weak. That's bad business, my nigga! You fuckin' with my money. Now you gotta pay. It ain't a game, fam!" Sweets grabbed his long machete from behind his desk.

The grown man began to cry like a little child, begging and pleading for his life. The sight of the long machete made his limbs shake uncontrollably. He knew something bad was about to happen to him, and he instantly began to regret skimming money from Sweets.

"Pick his ass up and turn him around!" Sweets ordered two of his soldiers, who stood in the room with him.

Lynch and another one of Sweets' henchmen grabbed the man and turned him around to face the wall.

"Don't move, mu'fucka!" Sweets said as he raised his machete.

The man knew that Sweets was about to cut his ass up. He'd heard stories about how crazy Sweets was. His body tensed up as he waited for his life to end. He kept visualizing Sweets chopping off his head with that long machete.

"Please, Sweets, don't kill me." The man decided to plead one last time as he faced the wall, not knowing how he was about to die. He began to sweat profusely. All he could do was beg for his life. "Please, Sweets, please, man. I'll never steal another thing in my life."

The sound of plastic being ripped filled the air as Sweets stood behind the man. He didn't know what it was, but he would soon find out. All of a sudden, the man heard the sound of the machete slicing through the air. The man closed his eyes, preparing himself to be decapitated. When he didn't feel a knife pierce his skin, he slowly opened his eyes and saw that Sweets had other plans in mind. Sweets had cut the man's belt off, causing his pants to fall to his ankles. The man finally got the picture. He begged Sweets to stop, but the pleas fell on deaf ears. The ripping sound that he'd heard was Sweets opening a condom wrapper.

"You take my money, I take your manhood. If you move, I'm going to slice yo mu'fuckin' throat." Sweets pulled down the man's boxers and grabbed himself.

Lynch turned his back to avoid witnessing the scene. Sweets often degraded men who stole from him in that sort of way. *I hate when he do this shit. This is some twisted gay shit, fam.* Lynch walked out of the room.

Sweets bent the man over and rested his dick on the man's back. "If you move, I'ma slice yo' mu'fuckin' throat. You got that?" Sweets took the knife and slightly punctured the man's neck. Blood trickled from the crying man's flesh as Sweets prepared to force himself in.

Just before Sweets could enter, his phone began to vibrate on his hip. He smacked his lips, irritated with the interruption, and pulled the phone off his hip. He had a new text message that read: ATLAS IN TEN MINUTES—20 BRICKS IN DA TRUNK.

"Oh shit!" Sweets said out loud gleefully. A huge smile covered his face as he immediately pulled up his pants and pushed the man forcefully to the ground. "You got lucky this time, mu'fucka. You steal from me again, though, and I guarantee you won't get off so easy the next time," Sweets said as he grabbed his gun and jacket. He had someone to meet.

"Thank you, Sweets, thank you," the man said while tears ran down his eyes. He'd just escaped an ass-thrashing, literally. "I promise it will never happen again. God bless you, Sweets. God bless you," the man repeated as he pulled up his pants.

"Nigga, get the fuck out of here with all that crying," Sweets said. He thought to himself, *Damn! And I was gon' tear that ass up. But hell,*

money over dick. "Load up! Joe at Atlas. Let's get 'em!" Sweets yelled loud enough for his soldiers to hear him in the next room.

Lynch rushed into the room, not believing what he'd just heard. He was itching to get at Joe, to avenge the death of his little brother.

"His man just hit me up saying that they're going to be at Atlas in ten minutes. Let's roll." Sweets zipped up his pants.

"What you going to do with ol' dude?" Lynch said, throwing his head in the thief's direction.

Sweets looked at the man and contemplated what to do with him. He knew he couldn't just let him get out of there scot-free, with no consequences whatsoever. That would be bad for business. He finally said, "Give 'im a limp." Sweets headed out the door.

"No doubt." Lynch pulled out his gun, pointed it at the man's leg, and left two bullets in it. *Bang! Bang!* "Hope you wasn't an NBA prospect too." Lynch chuckled.

The man screamed in agony while Sweets and the Shottah Boyz rushed over to Atlas restaurant to give Joe's crew a rude awakening.

Chapter Forty-four

Halleigh entered the twenty-four-hour restaurant along with Tasha and Mimi. The Manolo Mamis were in the building, and all eyes were on them as they strolled in. Halleigh was still beautiful, although her recent struggles showed in her face and loss of weight. She looked tired and worn out, but she was proud of herself for being brave enough to fight her drug addiction. Although she hated what Tasha did to her at the time, she loved her for it now and understood exactly why she had done it. Had she not, as far as Halleigh was concerned, she could be lying dead in an alley somewhere.

Among the patrons who looked their way when the girls entered the restaurant was Malek. His heart sank into his stomach when he saw Halleigh. She wasn't the same Halleigh he'd seen just a few months ago. She looked as though she'd taken an ass-whippin' from the streets.

What the fuck happened? Malek looked her up and down. Then he heard the sound of Tasha's words echoing through his head. *"She needs you,"* he remembered her telling him, and from the looks of things, he knew that it was true.

Malek couldn't take his eyes off of her. His heart beat so loudly in his chest that he was sure Jamaica Joe and Tariq could hear it. His heart dropped at the sight of Halleigh. He noticed that she had lost weight, and her eyes looked baggy. Something wasn't right with her, and that's probably what Tasha had been trying to warn him about. His pride wanted him not to stare, but his heart made his eyes stick on her.

No matter what Halleigh and Malek had gone through, he still loved her. Halleigh might have been able to shake drugs, but Malek couldn't seem to shake her.

For the last couple of months, Malek, trying to keep Halleigh off his mind, was just getting with chicks for the hell of it. Whenever he was inside one of them, he couldn't help but picture Halleigh's face.

"Who the fuck is Halleigh?" one of the girls spat to him as she sat butt naked on top of him, riding the hell out of him.

She was putting her back into it when all of a sudden he had yelled, "Oh, Halleigh, baby, don't stop!"

Halleigh finally looked in the direction where Malek and his crew were sitting, and when she saw him, her eyes almost popped out of her head. She stopped suddenly in her tracks.

"You all right, girl?" Tasha asked her. She followed Halleigh's eyes and saw Malek.

"Yeah," Halleigh lied. She wanted to believe that she was okay, but she wasn't.

"Come on," Tasha said, grabbing her arm. "Just let him be over there with his boys. If he wants to step to you, then so be it. Otherwise, let 'im be."

When Halleigh and Malek had locked eyes, it felt as if the two of them were the only ones in the room.

"Yeah, you're right," Halleigh said as she took a couple more steps. She peeled her eyes off of Malek and let them fall on the two guys he was with. Once again she stopped dead in her tracks, but this time, she began to tremble.

"What is it, Hal?" Tasha asked, her eyes darting back and forth from Halleigh to Malek and his boys. "You okay?" Tasha could feel Halleigh's body trembling.

Halleigh just stood there with her mouth dropped open as she stared at Tariq. That's him, Halleigh thought. She would never forget the faces of the men who raped her

Her heart began to beat rapidly. She couldn't believe that Malek was sitting there with him—the man he was supposed to protect her from, the man he said he would kill if he ever found him. Now here the two of them were, about to break bread together.

Halleigh pulled her arm away from Tasha and hurried to the back of the restaurant, where the restrooms were located. She could barely breathe. The sight of Malek with Tariq made her want to throw up.

She burst into the bathroom and rested both of her arms on the sink. She was tormented by horrific memories of the night her virginity was ripped away from her. The fact that Malek was sitting next to her rapist made her heart sink deeper in her chest. She couldn't believe it. "How could he?" she whispered as the tears in her eyes built up. "How could he?"

Chapter Forty-five

"I'll be back," Malek said to Joe and Tariq as he made his way to the back of the restaurant. He knew Jamaica Joe probably had something to say about him going after Halleigh, but he couldn't hold off any longer. He had to talk to her.

He paced outside of the bathroom, waiting for Haleigh to come out.

"Yo, come on, man," Joe called out. "We got business."

Malek acted like he didn't hear him and just continued pacing until he heard the women's bathroom door open. He caught Halleigh on her way out. "Halleigh!" he whispered as he grabbed her arm.

"Get away from me, Malek," she said, trying to pull away.

"No, I need to talk to you. Just listen to me for a minute," Malek said while Halleigh struggled to get away from his grip, using up the little bit of energy left in her body.

Malek got tired of struggling with her and ended up pushing her into the men's bathroom and into one of the stalls.

"Don't touch me," she said weakly. His touch hurt her sensitive body, but she also didn't want his hands on her since he was associating with the person who'd raped her. In her mind, Malek was just as lowdown as the hoodlum he was sitting with.

"Are you okay?" Malek cupped her face in his hands and stared into her lost eyes. "What happened to you? Baby, I'm sorry. I should've come to you," Malek said as he got an up close and personal look at just how bad Halleigh appeared. She was "Whitney Houston skinny."

"Stop touching me," Halleigh said. "I can't believe this. How could you be with him? How could you?"

"What? Who? What are you talking about?"

Just then, the men's bathroom door opened. "Yo, Malek!" Tariq called out as he entered the bathroom.

Malek closed the stall door and replied, "What up?"

"It's time to go," Tariq said. "Joe trying to get on the road."

The sound of Tariq's voice sent chills up Halleigh's spine. The same way she could never forget his face, she could never forget his voice.

"All right, I'll be out in a minute," Malek said in an irritated tone. The only thing on his mind was Halleigh. When Tariq left the restroom, Halleigh snatched away from Malek once again.

"Just let me go, Malek!"

"I will let you go, but on one condition . . ." Malek paused before continuing. "Leave with me, Hal."

Halleigh let out a sarcastic laugh.

"I'm serious. You're not looking too good. Let me take care of you. We can start over, just me and you."

"Let you take care of me?" Halleigh repeated. "Let you take care of me? You mean the same way you been taking care of me? Fuck you, Malek!"

"Fuck me? You the one who picked that other nigga over me, and you got the nerve to have an attitude with me?"

"It looks like you picked your niggas over me," she replied, her eyes flooded with tears. Malek's betrayal hurt more than anything she'd ever felt.

"What the fuck are you talking about?"

"Let me ask you one question, Malek. Since when did you start fucking with the nigga that raped me? Huh? He's what started all this. He raped me, and you're running around here with him like y'all best friends," Halleigh yelled, the warm tears gracing her cheeks.

Her words hit Malek like a ton of bricks.

"Y'all cut from the same cloth, Malek?" She began beating on Malek's chest. "You a rapist too? Huh? Is that what you were going to do to the girl in that room the night of that party before you saw that it was me?"

"Whoa, hold up," Malek said, putting up his hands.

"You trying to say my boy Joe was one of the dudes that raped you?"

"I don't know his fuckin' name. The one you just told you'd be out in a minute," Halleigh said furiously. "What? Are you two on your way to rape somebody else?"

Malek tried to digest everything Halleigh was spitting at him. Finally, Halleigh mustered up every ounce of strength she had in an attempt to shove Malek out of her way, but Malek grabbed her.

"Get your hands off me," she said. "Don't touch me! Don't you ever touch me again," Halleigh screamed with so much rage that Malek released her. Then she squeezed past him and stormed out of the bathroom.

"Wait, Halleigh!" he yelled out, but Halleigh never looked back. Still in a daze, Malek exited the bathroom stall and began pacing again. "I

can't believe this shit." He balled his fist and began punching the walls in the restroom as he tried to calm down.

Halleigh's words had hit him like a dagger. He was determined to make things right for them. She was his soul mate, and he wasn't going to lose her again. The thought of Tariq raping Halleigh emerged in his mind. He pulled out his gun and cocked the hammer back. *I'ma murder that nigga.*

Just like Halleigh had accused him, he felt guilty, as if he were one of the men who'd raped her. All of this time he'd had no clue that Tariq was one of the men who'd hurt Halleigh on that horrible night, but now that he knew, he was going to make Tariq pay.

Chapter Forty-six

M alek stormed out of the restroom with rage in his eyes, his temple pulsating from the range of emotions he was experiencing. He watched as Halleigh, the woman he loved from the depths of his soul, rushed out of the restaurant with Tasha and Mimi.

He then focused his attention on Tariq, who was seated next to Jamaica Joe. His blood boiled as he closed his eyes and envisioned the hurtful expression that had covered Halleigh's face. Things had definitely shifted from what Malek thought they seemed. All along, he had been thinking that it was Halleigh who was, in fact, sleeping with the enemy by fucking with Manolo, when it was actually Malek himself that was cliqued up with one of the dudes that had raped her.

Just then, Malek became suspicious of everybody who was assigned under Tariq. Was it one of them who had gone to Halleigh's mom's apartment that night and participated in the assault? Malek's mind was twisted. He didn't know what his next move should be. Should he find out who the other cat was that helped Tariq and take them both out, or should he just kill Tariq's ass and ask questions later? Malek looked out the window and saw Halleigh hop into the passenger's side of Tasha's car. He had to admit, he did love her. He felt like a traitor for associating with people who had harmed her. Now wasn't the time for him to stand there and beat himself up. He had a vendetta to take care of.

When Jamaica Joe saw Malek heading back their way, he stood and threw a fifty dollar bill on the table. He then walked over to Malek.

"Everything's good?" Joe asked, noticing the distressed look on his face.

Malek nodded. He wasn't sure if he should tell Joe about the situation. He knew that Tariq was Joe's man way before he'd entered the picture, so he wasn't trying to create bad business by spitting venom on Joe's right-hand man. *I'ma handle that nigga myself when the time is right,* Malek assured himself and then turned to Joe and said, "Yeah, man, everything is good."

"Good, then let's get out of here. Time is money and—" Before Joe could finish his sentence, the sound of his car alarm going off caught his attention. "Fuck is going on?" he asked as he hurried outside.

Malek ran out behind him and exchanged cold stares with Tariq as he passed.

"'Sup, dude?" Tariq asked him aggressively, peeping out how Malek had just mean-mugged him like he had a problem with him or something.

Malek stopped in his tracks as Joe kept moving. Joe wasn't concerned about what was happening between his two soldiers. He was only concerned about his car, or better yet, the goods he had inside his car.

Malek stepped into Tariq's space. "What, mu'fucka?" he said, blatantly showing him disrespect as he stared down at him. "You got a problem?"

Before the confrontation could escalate, gunshots rang out in the air.

"Oh shit! Joe!" Malek pushed past Tariq and ran outside, his pistol drawn.

Tariq ran out after him, and they both started busting, no questions asked, at Jamaica Joe's truck, his Viper car alarm blaring loudly as bullets whizzed through the air.

The back of Jamaica Joe's truck was open, and by the time they made their way over to the truck, blasting the entire way, Malek immediately peeped that the duffel bag full of bricks was missing. The gunfire was so hectic that everybody had to take cover. Joe, Tariq, and Malek were tucked behind a car in the parking lot, while Sweets, Manolo, and the Shottah Boyz ducked behind Joe's truck.

"Fuck! They got the joints," Joe stated in a frustrated tone. He pulled a full clip out of his pants pocket and loaded it into his gun. "I'm tired of playing around with this gay mu'fucka!"

Boom! Boom!

Bullets crashed the windows of the car they were crouched behind, sending glass flying everywhere.

Boom! Boom! Boom!

Malek shot back. He saw Manolo peek from behind Joe's truck and shot relentlessly at him.

Boom! Boom! Boom! Boom! Boom!

Jamaica Joe looked at Tariq, who was crouched low, hiding from the bullets, while Malek was a true soldier, standing his own against the hit squad. "Nigga, fuck you doing?" he yelled to Tariq. "Go get my bricks!" Joe reached over the car hood and fired a shot.

By now Joe's truck looked like Swiss cheese, but that was the last thing on his mind. He couldn't afford to take this loss. He had to get his dope back.

Tariq stood up and pulled out his gun. He shot in Sweets' direction, making sure not to hit any of his crew, firing shots indirectly.

Malek was a madman, taking out all of his anger on Sweets and his crew. What he really wanted to do was blast on Tariq's ass, but that opportunity would have to present itself at a later date. Right now his target was Manolo. He'd hurt Halleigh too. From this point on, Malek was getting ready to get at any nigga who had even looked at her wrong in the past.

His gun spat, *Boom! Boom! Boom!*

All of a sudden, Tariq stepped into Malek's line of view. Malek's gun was already aimed to hit him. All he had to do was pull the trigger. *This nigga raped my girl,* he thought as his finger twitched violently. *This nigga took what should've been mine.*

Malek had never killed a man, but he was tempted to let Tariq have his whole clip. He froze and stared at Tariq, his gun pointed at his back. Tariq had no idea that Malek was behind him with deadly intentions.

Jamaica Joe heard the sirens of the approaching police cars. They sounded as if they were right around the corner. He peered from behind the car, and his eyes bucked when he saw Malek aiming his pistol at the back of Tariq's head. *Fuck is he doing?* Joe thought.

Malek closed his eyes and pulled the trigger.

CLICK! The sound of the empty clip rang out, but Tariq didn't hear it.

Sweets ran and jumped back into his truck when he heard the police sirens, and was pulling wildly out of the parking lot as Tariq feigned to bust wildly at him.

Tears filled Malek's eyes. He regretted wasting his bullets on Sweets. *CLICK! CLICK!* He continued to squeeze the trigger anyway, even though he knew he had no ammunition.

Jamaica Joe ran up and put his hand on Malek's shoulder. "Whoa," he stated in Malek's ear as he took the gun from his hand. He didn't ask any questions, but he definitely wanted to know what was going on between Tariq and Malek. "Jacob!" he shouted, signaling to Tariq that the police were on their way.

Since their truck was all shot up, tires and all, Tariq busted out a window to another car in the restaurant parking lot. He quickly hot-wired

the car and pulled off with Jamaica Joe in the front seat and Malek in the back.

Riding shotgun as Tariq maneuvered away from the shootout scene, Jamaica Joe turned around and eyed Malek suspiciously. "You a'ight, partna?"

Malek leaned across the back seat and nodded his head, murderous thoughts racing through his mind as he sat behind Tariq. "Don't like to leave business unfinished, that's all."

"Oh, we gon' finish that shit," Tariq stated, referring to the beef with the South Side. He tossed his pistol in the back seat and threw his head back in relief. He took a deep breath, knowing he had just sparked some deep shit. "This shit ain't over," he added, pretending he was ready to retaliate.

"No doubt," Malek responded, referring to his unresolved beef with Tariq. Malek's blood was boiling. He couldn't control himself anymore. He slowly picked up Tariq's banger and put it in his lap.

Tupac's song, "Hail Mary," was in the CD player. Malek asked Tariq to turn it up a notch, but it wasn't because he wanted to hear the song. Once the music was up loud enough to conceal the sound, Malek cocked the pistol and pointed it to the back of Tariq's dome.

Chapter Forty-seven

Halleigh looked in the mirror and saw a person who bore no resemblance to the young woman she used to be. It seemed like just yesterday she was an excelling senior in high school and dating the most popular boy at school.

As Halleigh stood there, her mind wandered off to her first day on the job.

"What happened to me?" Halleigh asked herself. She shook her head in shame as she recalled her recent past.

Halleigh felt the tears flow down her face. They weren't tears of force that came from heaving and overreacting. They were true tears of a broken, hopeless spirit, and they stained her face as she looked down at the gun in her hand.

The day Halleigh copped the gun, she had actually intended to ask her get-high buddy, Scratch, to cop her some heroin. Then, on her way

to meet Scratch at their spot in the alley, people were looking at her. The way they grimaced, she felt as if she were deformed or something,

Having been nothing short of a dime-piece, Halleigh was used to turning the heads of gawking men. She was used to the envious glares of women, but this time, the attention she was receiving was different. They were stares of disgust and pity. As she walked by a used appliance store, she caught a glimpse of her reflection in the window. She stopped in her tracks and gasped at the frail sight before her. Slowly, her hands began to roam her face, just to confirm that the reflection was actually hers. Were those really her eyes she was looking into? Once upon a time those eyes had been full of life and energy, no matter how much negativity they had witnessed.

Halleigh allowed her hands to roam down her body. Wearing tight-fitting jeans with knee-high stiletto boots and a sequined top, she thought she looked just fine, but underneath her hands she could feel almost every bone in her body, every rib. Taking a long, hard look at herself, Halleigh, too, was disgusted by what she saw.

The storeowner interrupted her when he came out of the store and asked if he could help her with anything. Without saying a word, she walked off crying. As far as Halleigh was concerned, what she had just seen wasn't her, but a disintegrating corpse of her former self. She was as good as dead. She felt like death anyway. Hell, she couldn't remember the last time she had felt free and alive. That was the moment she decided she was better off dead than living the way she had been living.

By the time she met up with Scratch, she had a plan all mapped out. As long as Scratch was willing to be her accomplice, she didn't see how the plan could fail.

When she asked Scratch to help her cop a gun, he wasn't for it at first. He was trying to get high with Halleigh's money, not waste it on a cold piece of metal. After realizing that he could cop a gun and still have money left over to get a hit for himself, he obliged her. She hadn't told him what she intended to do with the weapon. He never asked. Now, here Halleigh stood in the bathroom of what she called home, which was nothing more than another prison, as far as she was concerned. Manolo, a.k.a. Daddy, told them when they could leave, when they couldn't, and how long they could stay gone. He needed to know where his money was at all times.

If only I could see the look on that motherfucker's face when he finds me, Halleigh thought with a half-witted smile, the gun to her temple. *His greedy ass probably won't even see my brains splattered all over the walls; he'll see a pile of useless currency.*

Halleigh trembled as the cold steel pressed against her clammy skin. Her body began to break out into a cold, nervous sweat.

Moments from her life flashed before her eyes—all the heartache

and tragedy she'd experienced—and she had a drastic decision to make. Live or die? Fight or retreat? Win or lose? She was tired of struggling to survive in a city that had no love for her. She was choosing death, and there was no turning back.

Halleigh put her finger just above the trigger. She squinted her eyes closed tight, and just when she was about to squeeze, there was a knock on the door.

"Hal, what are you doing in there? Open the door!" Mimi's voice came from the other side of the bathroom door, where she stood in the hallway. "You've been in there forever. What's going on?" This was the second time in the past half hour Mimi had knocked on the door to check on Halleigh. She felt as though something wasn't kosher.

Halleigh, who had actually been locked in the small bathroom for the past forty-five minutes, didn't respond.

"Halleigh?" Mimi called again. "Open the door. Why you locking doors around this mu'fucka anyway? You know Manolo will have a fit."

The last time one of Manolo's girls called herself "locking a door," Manolo made it so that she never wanted to be locked up behind a closed door again in her life. For hours Manolo kept her locked inside a dark closet. The girl lost her mind and had to be committed to an institution afterwards. As hard as Mimi had tried to calm the girl down, it was to no avail. Come to find out, the girl's stepfather used to lock her in the closet when she was twelve, but not before running up in her like she was a grown woman.

Mimi had relayed the story to Halleigh, so she hoped Halleigh would take heed and unlock that door quickly.

Halleigh's arm shook uncontrollably as Mimi continued knocking. "Just pull the trigger," she whispered to herself. "All of the pain will go away if you just pull the goddamn trigger. Just end it." A small cry escaped her lips. She lowered the gun.

"Halleigh? Are you all right? You crying?" Mimi said, her tone now filled with concern.

"Open the damn door." The fear in her voice translated as if she was angry.

When Halleigh failed to respond, Mimi sensed that something was terribly wrong. "Tasha!" she turned around and yelled. "There's something wrong with Halleigh!"

Wearing only a bra and panties, Tasha appeared from behind her bedroom door. "What do you mean, something's wrong with her?" she asked.

"I mean she's in this mu'fucka with the door locked and she's crying and shit." Mimi then began to whisper. "I don't want the bitch to do nothing crazy. You know she just been through all that shit with Malek." Mimi then got an I-told-you-so attitude. "I told y'all she wasn't cut out for this shit."

"Fuck you whispering for? Like she can't hear you." As far as Tasha was concerned, this was not the time for Mimi to gloat about her call on Halleigh.

Tasha came out of her bedroom and walked up to the door. She put her ear against it. She, too, could hear Halleigh whimpering. "Hal, open up the door so we can talk," she urged. She picked up from where Mimi left off and began knocking on the door. "Halleigh, listen, just open up the door." Tasha, her eyes wide with fright, turned around and stared at Mimi.

"I told you," Mimi said, folding her arms pretzel-style. After all the drama and heartache that Halleigh had experienced, Mimi wasn't surprised that she was flipping out. As a matter of fact, the only thing that did surprise her was that she hadn't done it sooner.

In all honesty, Mimi thought that Halleigh wouldn't last after her first trick. She didn't care, considering she had already gotten her $500 finder's fee for bringing the new girl home.

Halleigh could hear Tasha and Mimi calling for her, but ignored them. She knew what she had to do, and she wasn't going to let anything distract her from doing it. She lifted the semi-automatic to her head again and cocked it. No matter how hard Halleigh had tried to convince herself over the past few months things would get better, they hadn't. She felt that shooting her brains out would be a quick end to what felt like a long, miserable life.

Click! Click!

"Oh shit!" Mimi panicked. "Was that a fuckin' gun?"

Before Tasha could reply, they heard loud sounds coming from the bathroom.

Bam!

Mimi and Tasha hit the deck, faces buried in the brown carpet.

"Does that answer your question?" Tasha said to Mimi.

"That crazy bitch is trying to shoot us," Mimi whispered.

After a few seconds of silence, Tasha stood up and pounded her open hand frantically against the door. "Halleigh, if you trying to fuck with our minds, it worked. Now open the damn door!"

There was no reply from the other side.

"Say 'Boo,' fart or do something, damn it. Just at least let us know that you're okay."

That's when it hit Mimi what was really going on. She immediately stood up from the floor. "Oh my God! She shot herself, didn't she?" she asked Tasha. "The broad done shot herself!" Mimi shouted in a panic. "Tasha, do something! Ain't there a key to this motherfucker?" Mimi tried to turn the knob.

Tasha felt helpless. As the madam of the house, she was supposed to keep all of the Manolo Mamis in line. That was why Manolo had appointed her to the job. As a woman, Tasha also felt like she was sup-

posed to protect them. She hated the fact that she might not have been able to protect one of the girls from her own self.

Tasha stepped back a couple of feet and mustered up all the strength she had in her body. Next, she charged toward the bathroom door and threw her body against it. When she finally broke it off its hinges, she raced into the bathroom to find Halleigh laid out on the floor with blood behind her head.

"Halleigh, baby girl, what have you done?" Tasha said as she kneeled down next to Halleigh's body.

The moan that was released from Halleigh's lips startled her.

"My head . . ." Halleigh moaned. "I think I hit my head when I fell." Halleigh grabbed the back of her head.

The sound of the gunshot had been deafening as it ricocheted off the bathroom wall. On top of that, the force of pulling the trigger on the weapon had been so great that it knocked Halleigh off her feet and onto the floor.

Tasha didn't know whether to be happy that Halleigh was alive, or pissed that she had scared them half to death.

"Fuck is you doing?" Tasha screamed, deciding to be mad. Her shoulder throbbed from the impact of breaking into the bathroom door, but she disregarded the pain as she picked the gun up from the floor and handed it over her shoulder to Mimi.

"Hey, watch how you handling that thing," Mimi said, carefully taking it from Tasha's hand. She then disappeared to get rid of the gun.

Tasha didn't pay Mimi any mind. She focused her attention on Halleigh, who began to shake life a leaf.

Halleigh looked down at the blood on her hand then at the bullet hole in the wall. "I could have . . ." Halleigh hesitated. "I could have . . ." Her cries built up in her throat as she struggled to contain her emotions.

"Shhh. Come here," Tasha said, pulling Halleigh close and comforting her. "It's okay, Hal. Everything is gon' be all right."

After a few moments, Tasha pulled away from Halleigh and looked at her. "I've told you that everything is going to be all right. You just gotta hold on, ma." She put her arms around her friend again and rocked her slowly.

Mimi reappeared at the doorway after burying the gun in a drawer full of lingerie. She looked down at a visibly shaken Halleigh. "Is she all right?" she asked Tasha.

"Yeah, she's okay. She's gon' be fine," Tasha replied, still holding Halleigh tightly.

Mimi was never one to get emotional. The only thing that made her cry was missing out on money, so when Tasha looked up and noticed Mimi's eyes full of tears, she outstretched her other arm to invite Mimi

into the embrace. Mimi quickly bent down and filled in the circle and hugged Halleigh as well.

"It's time for this to stop," Tasha stated, her voice cracking. "We can't do this to ourselves anymore. Manolo is the only person getting something out of all this." Tasha looked around. "So he keeps a roof over our heads—we can get that shit on our own." She shook her head. "I can't believe we've been selling ourselves short all this time. I mean, he's beaten Hal down to the point where she feels she needs to take her own life. This is bullshit. Nobody should have that much power over us. Nobody!" Tasha had to fight back her own tears. "You and me, Mimi, we're a different breed. We're strong. We can handle this life better than Halleigh, but look at her. Look what this is doing to her."

Mimi nodded.

Tasha shook her head. "First she was trying to kill herself by shooting that shit into her body, and now she's trying to shoot herself, period. This is crazy."

"When black people start killing themselves, oh yeah, you know shit done got too crazy," Mimi agreed.

Halleigh was too distraught to reply. She had just attempted to take her own life—and she might have succeeded if not for the fact that her heroin-wasted muscles couldn't even hold the weight of the gun to aim properly. Otherwise, her two friends would've been weeping over a bleeding corpse. That's what Halleigh felt like, anyway—dead, and bleeding on the inside.

"I hear what you saying, Tash," Mimi stated, "but you know as well as I do that there ain't no way we leaving Manolo and living to tell about it. Ya heard me?" Mimi stood up. "You already know how he is, Tasha. You've been around longer than any of us. So you tell us what happens when a chick tries to walk away from Manolo."

Tasha relaxed her arms to her side and just swallowed.

"Exactly!" Mimi said, smacking her lips. "So you can give your 'Obama speeches' all day long, telling us what we need to do, but I want you to show me how we're supposed to do it. Tell me, Tasha, how are we supposed to get out of this situation? If we do make it out, how we gon' survive? All we used to doing is selling pussy. So what's the difference whether we're selling it for ourselves or Manolo? Selling pussy is selling pussy."

They couldn't just walk away from Manolo without recourse. He was Daddy, and would kill them before he let them leave. Even if Tasha found a way to pull the girls out from under Manolo's clutches, what would be their means of survival? She was stuck between a rock and a hard place, but that didn't deter her from wanting to escape from Manolo's iron-fisted rule.

"What are we gon' do?" Mimi asked again.

"Let me think. Damn!" Tasha replied, aggravated that she didn't have all of the answers to Mimi's queries. She had never thought this through about trying to dip out on Manolo, so, no, the answers weren't at the top of her head. "For right now, just shut up and help me get Halleigh up from the floor."

Mimi gave her a questioning look, still wanting answers.

Tasha told her, "Look, all I know is that I'm gonna have us out of here by the end of the week, I promise. That's my word."

Upon hearing Tasha's promise, an emotion finally registered on Halleigh's face. It was a look of surprise laced with disbelief.

Tasha noticed Halleigh's expression, and she wanted to remove her doubt. "I promise, Hal," Tasha reaffirmed. She didn't know how she was going to pull it off, but she knew she had to at least try . . . for the sake of them all.

Chapter Forty-eight

Tariq sat breaking down the buds of weed on the table as the hustlers that worked for him crowded around. They were listening to him talk mad shit about his superior.

"Fuck Jamaica Joe!" Tariq spat. "I'm the next big thing 'round this mu'fucka." He filled the blunt with the goods, lit it, and continued to put on a show for his crew. "Just stick wit' me and you're gonna go places," he stated.

They were all inside the crack house that Jamaica Joe had assigned Tariq to run. Drug addicts filed in to buy their preferred drug as Tariq sat at the table in the middle of the dope spot. For the past fifteen minutes, he'd been bragging about how he was going to take over the North Side drug game, and how nothing or no one would get in his way.

"Yo, and that ho-ass nigga Malek is done, nah mean? That nigga ain't a hustla anyway. Before Joe took that nigga in, he was a soft-ass ballplayer who didn't know shit about the streets of Flint. Now that nigga think he Rich Porter or somebody. I'm telling you, son, I got some shit about to pop off soon, and when it do pop off, that nigga Joe and Malek are gonna be outta dis bitch. Trust that!" Tariq said, jealousy overtaking his emotions.

For the past week, Tariq had been creating a plan to get Joe and

Malek out of the picture. Unfortunately, his last two attempts to set up his former comrade had failed miserably.

Tariq's level of confidence was high. He was so confident he had no fear in expressing himself, knowing that Jamaica Joe wouldn't be around long enough to find out about it anyway.

Tariq and Jamaica Joe went way back in the street game, always playing on the same team. Until recently, Tariq had always been loyal to his superior, but now, as far as he was concerned, Joe shit on that loyalty thing when he let some punk-ass teen who hadn't put in no work in the streets come in and try to play his position.

As Tariq began to fill one of his closest workers in on the plan to take down Joe, a fiend approached the table, looking to cop a fix. Tariq was in mid-sentence when the fiend interrupted him.

"Excuse me, youngblood. Can I get a dime?" The crack-head stood before Tariq with a handful of quarters, dimes, and pennies.

Tariq slapped the change out of the crackhead's hands, causing all of the coins to scatter across the hardwood floor. The other users scrambled for the change and eventually left the man with only a few cents.

"Didn't you see me over here talking to my mans?" Tariq spat. "Don't interrupt me for a mu'fuckin' dime rock. You betta go and holla at one of them li'l niggas out front and cop," Tariq said as he watched the man scramble for any of his change that hadn't already been confiscated.

Tariq and the worker he had been discussing his plan with laughed as they watched the fiend walk out of the crackhouse with no money and no drugs, a crackhead's nightmare. Tariq continued explaining his plan to take out Jamaica Joe, once the fiend left

By the end of the night, he was high off the bomb weed he had been tootin' and the anticipation that he would soon reign the North Side drug game.

Jamaica Joe and Malek sat in the spacious back seat of the all-black Bentley as they were chauffeured by one of Joe's henchmen. The curtains on the windows hid their faces from the public, but unless they had been under a rock or were new to the city, everyone knew who was inside the luxury vehicle.

Malek looked through the back window and then at Joe. "Yo, Joe, I think someone is following us. That car been on us since Ballenger Road," Malek said in reference to the blue Ford Taurus with tinted windows behind them.

"Ah, don't worry about them. That's just the Feds," Joe said nonchalantly. "They been on me for the last couple of weeks. But I ain't pressed. They don't have anything on a nigga. They're just waiting for me to slip up. But it ain't gon' happen, feel me?" Joe didn't even look back once. Everything about him reflected that he wasn't the least bit

worried. It showed in his actions and the tone of his voice. He knew that the FBI were on him closely, and he understood that the war he had with the South Side and Sweets was what brought the attention his way.

"Damn, fam, it's like that?" Malek couldn't believe how casual Joe was, considering that the authorities were just waiting for the opportunity to put him under the jail.

"Yeah. They can follow me all they want, though. My hands stay clean. I stay one step ahead of them mu'fuckas at all times." Joe fixed his cufflinks. "They couldn't catch me if they wanted to anyway."

Joe looked at the rearview mirror and locked eyes with his driver. He nodded slowly, signaling for his driver to speed up. He was ready to have a little fun with his tail.

The driver put the pedal to the floor, and the luxury vehicle weaved in and out of traffic at 100 miles per hour. The speed of the car was far too much for the Ford Taurus to keep up with, and within seconds, the FBI was MIA.

Joe pulled out a pre-rolled blunt and looked over at Malek. "See, I told you they can't fuck with me!" He lit the blunt and took a pull. Circles of smoke billowed from his mouth as he exhaled.

Malek grinned at how easy it was for them to shake the other car. "You a crazy mu'fucka."

They pulled onto the block that Joe had assigned to Tariq. The next thing Joe and Malek knew, the driver hit his brakes abruptly, causing the tires to screech. Within seconds, they noticed the skinny man who had jumped in the middle of the street in an attempt to flag down Joe's car.

"What the fuck?" Joe's eyes darted toward the front.

The driver immediately put the car in park and jumped out with his gun in palm. He rushed over to the man, grabbed him by the neck, and pressed the gun to his temple. "What the fuck is yo problem? I should blow yo brains out."

"Now hold up, youngblood. I just want to talk to Jamaica Joe for a second," the man stated nervously.

Joe looked closer as his henchman pinned the man down on the hood of the car. That's when he recognized the familiar face. "Oh, that ain't nobody but Scratch, that crazy-ass fiend," Joe said as he relaxed back on his seat. He knew Scratch from back in the day. Joe actually used to look up to Scratch in the '80s. Scratch used to be the dope man, but when he hit his own pack, he switched sides in the game. Instead of being the pusher, he became the user.

Figuring it was time to come to Scratch's rescue, Joe cracked his window a little bit and signaled for his henchman to let Scratch come over to the car. "It's all good, man. Bring him over."

When the henchman released his grip, Scratch immediately rose up

and massaged his neck. "Damn, youngblood, you didn't have to do Scratch like that," he said, talking about himself in third person, a habit that he always had.

Scratch walked over to the back door, and Joe rolled down his window, exposing his face.

"Scratch, you could've gotten yourself killed, fam," Joe told him.

"Ah, nah. You know it take a lot more than a car to kill good ol' Scratch." He smiled, displaying his rotted teeth—what he had left of them anyway. "Look, man, I got some valuable information for you, ya dig?" Scratch said, scratching his arms and neck.

"Some valuable information, huh?" Joe asked skeptically.

"That's right. You know I wouldn't come at you with no bullshit, Joe."

Joe thought for a minute and then nodded. "Get in."

In all of Joe's dealings with him, Scratch had never tried to play or run game, so if Scratch said he had some valuable information, then nine times out of ten, he did. All Joe had to do was determine just who the information was most valuable to.

Jamaica Joe and Malek slid over, making room for Scratch to sit down. As soon as Scratch entered the car, a foul stench filled their nostrils as the horrendous body odor punched them in the face.

Malek frowned his face and put his hand over his nose, trying to avoid the smell. "Damn, man," he said, waving his hand and then rolling his window down a bit. "I got some priceless information for your ass too—soap and water works." Malek stuck his head out the window.

Jamaica Joe grew irritated at the odor and couldn't wait to rid himself of Scratch's presence, but he had to see what info the fiend had for him. He wasn't trying to make small talk with or smell Scratch for longer than he had to. "Yo, what you got to talk to me about, fam? Make it quick, 'cause you smell like death," he barked.

"Look, youngblood, Scratch was in the dope house, ya dig. And that cat, Tariq, was talking all greasy and stuff, saying he was the next big thang on the North Side and that you ain't gon' be the boss for much longer. He didn't notice Scratch, though. He was too busy talking. I heard everything he was saying. He said he was going to set you up to get you killed so that you'd be out of the way . . . and some other li'l nigga you been joined at the hip wit' these past days."

That last comment had gotten Malek's attention. He knew just what li'l nigga Tariq had been yapping about. He turned and faced Joe and Scratch.

An angry expression covered Joe's face. "What the fuck you talkin' 'bout, Scratch?" Joe grabbed Scratch by his collar.

"I ain't say it," Scratch said, raising his hands in surrender. "Don't

kill the messenger. Scratch just repeating what that nigga Tariq said. He gon' set you up, man."

The thought of someone setting him up instantly enraged Joe. Malek remained calm and silent as he watched the scenario unfold.

Scratch was shaking uncontrollably as his eyes shot wide open. "You know me, Joe. Scratch wouldn't lie to you, man. You know that. Scratch ain't never came to you wit' no bullshit. You know that, man. You know that, right?" Scratch swallowed hard as he tried to read the expression on Joe's face. Unable to, he decided to keep talking. "Tariq was saying something about setting you up with a fake buyer from Detroit and taking you out once you got there. Scratch is keeping it real, man. You've got to believe me, Joe," Scratch pleaded, talking so quickly that his words ran together.

Joe paused and thought about everything Scratch had said. Just earlier that week, Tariq had informed Joe that he had a potential buyer that was looking to cop heavy weight from him. He said it was a cat from Detroit, and he mentioned that the dude insisted he wasn't gon' fuck with nobody but Joe in closing the deal.

"What is this nigga talking about?" Malek finally asked as he looked at Joe.

"I don't know, but I'm about to find out." Joe took out his cell phone and pushed the speed dial button for Tariq. The phone rang a couple of times before Tariq picked up.

"What's good, fam?" Tariq answered.

"Ain't nothin'," Joe said, trying his best to keep his cool until he got to the bottom of things. "Yo, about that trip this weekend, though, I can't make it. I'ma send one of the little niggas with you to watch your back, just in case some shit jump off. You know what I'm saying?"

There was a pause. Joe could hear Tariq take a deep breath, as if his brain was churning, trying to come up with his next words to say.

All Tariq knew was that he had to make the deal go down as planned. He had already lined up his soldiers that he was going to take with him to the top. What would he look like if his word wasn't bond? As far as he was concerned, Joe not coming through was not an option. He had to make it happen.

"Fam, I'm telling you, he ain't fucking with nobody else." Tariq used the most convincing tone he could muster. "He said he wants to deal directly through you. He a real paranoid mu'fucka, nah mean?" Tariq lied. "You know how it is when niggas be hatin'. He gotta watch his back, so he only wants to deal with the head, not some cat who might be trying to take his spot."

The irony of Tariq's words killed Joe, but he maintained his composure. "Yeah, fam." Joe chuckled. "I know exactly what you mean. Nonetheless, I can't fuck with it. I got to shoot to Miami for the weekend on business."

"Joe, I really think this cat is a major player. He upped his order to fifty bricks, rather than thirty," Tariq said, thinking fast.

"Word?" Joe said, hearing the nervousness that laced Tariq's voice. Hell, he was even starting to talk just as fast as Scratch, if not faster.

"For real. You gon' do it?" Tariq asked. "I mean, I can get at dude and let him know you got bigger business going on besides him and that y'all can reschedule the meeting, but I don't know, man. He might feel a little slighted and not want to fuck with you after that. And we talkin' about fifty bricks."

Joe grew a very suspicious look on his face and glanced over at Malek, who had been listening to the conversation intensely. Joe didn't want to believe that his man was setting him up, but he knew that the game didn't breed real niggas anymore, so anything was possible. Anybody could become an enemy, and his suspicions were now set on Tariq.

Malek whispered, "It's a setup, man. I can feel it."

Joe nodded his head in agreement, knowing that Tariq had tried to backdoor him.

"All right, I'll meet you at Atlas on Saturday morning," Joe stated just before he flipped down his cell phone. He shook his head in disbelief and then took a long pull of the blunt that he'd set in the ashtray earlier.

Joe then looked over to Scratch. "I guess you were telling the truth, man." He shook his head, still unable to grasp the fact that his man had turned on him. "Tariq ain't never asked me to go meet a buyer with him until now. He knew that I wouldn't let a fifty-brick sell bypass me either. Niggas playin' fo' keeps," Joe said, disappointment on his face.

Joe let out a deep sigh. "Get out." He leaned over Scratch and opened the door so that he could make his exit.

Scratch started to get out, but then hesitated. "Well, I was wondering, ya know, since I, uh," Scratch stammered, "looked out fo' you . . ." He swallowed hard then continued. "Why don't you, uh, you know, look out fo' Scratch?" He scratched his arms and avoided looking in Joe's eyes.

"I knew there was a catch." Joe reached into his pocket and pulled out a diamond-encrusted money clip shaped in the initial J. He peeled off two hundred-dollar bills and placed them in Scratch's lap.

Scratch's eyes lit up when he saw Benjamin Franklin's face. Just as quickly as Joe dropped the cash, Scratch scooped it up and slid out of the car. "Thanks, man. Scratch 'preciate it! Yeah, Scratch sho' 'preciate it."

They could hear him still shouting as they drove off.

Malek, finally able to inhale fresh air now that Scratch was gone,

took a deep breath. "I knew Tariq was a bitch-made nigga. I knew it," Malek said as his mind began to spin.

After the shootout, out of respect for Joe, Malek fell back. He knew that Tariq had been Joe's right-hand man for some years, and he didn't want his beef with Tariq to fuck up business for Joe. Regardless of how tight or cool Malek and Joe were, Malek knew that things changed when one person fucked up the other's money. Now it was time for Malek to get vengeance on Tariq for raping Halleigh.

"So, what you thinkin', man?" Malek inquired as they pulled up in front of the dope house where Tariq was.

Joe shook his head as he stared out of the window at the house. "It's always the people who are closest to you that want to cross you." Joe slammed his hand down on the seat. "Fuck!" Joe gritted through his teeth. "Should kill that nigga."

"Yeah, and I wish I had took that mu'fucka out when—" Malek paused.

Joe was silent for a minute and then said, "Is that why, during that shootout, your aim was a little, how should I say, off?"

Malek looked at Joe in surprise. "You saw that?" Since Joe had never spoken on it, Malek hadn't been sure whether Joe was fully aware of his intentions with Tariq that day at the shootout.

Joe nodded. He could tell by the expression on Malek's face that he was wondering why he hadn't said anything before now, so Joe put his mind to rest. "I didn't say anything because I figured your mind was all twisted. I mean, you had just run into your old girlfriend and shit, and I know how she be having a nigga's mind fucked up, so I let it go. Besides, I figured, if you had wanted that nigga dead, you would have handled yours right then and there. You had a perfect, clear shot."

Malek sighed. He was glad that Joe hadn't held that against him and placed him under the microscope of suspicion.

"But don't worry," Joe said as he puffed and exhaled, "this time I'm going to handle the situation. I got something for his ass." Joe reclined in his chair and signaled for his driver to pull off.

Chapter Forty-nine

Tasha pulled down the sun visor in her car to check her makeup in the mirror. She released a deep sigh before she flipped the visor

back up. Butterflies had the nerve to be fluttering around in her stomach.

"Get it together," she told herself. "Since when have your skills failed you?"

Tasha was the queen of manipulation, which is one of the reasons why she had done her job of looking after the girls so successfully. Whatever Manolo hadn't been able to convince the girls of doing, she stepped in and made shit happen. Well, now, once again it was up to her to make shit happen, and, this time, lives were on the line.

Taking a deep breath, Tasha exited the car. As she walked into the Flint Police Department, a look of contempt crossed her face. She hated the police and everything associated with them, but desperate times called for desperate measures. Heads turned as the police officers admired her shapely legs, which stretched out beneath the red shirtlike dress she had ordered from a Frederick's of Hollywood catalog. It fit just tightly enough to reveal the outline of her round behind.

As Tasha walked by officers who were just standing around shooting the breeze or updating one another on police business, she noticed the lustful stares, and a smirk crossed her face. *Your pockets can't afford this pussy. Fuckin' pigs,* she thought while turning her nose up and making her way over to the front desk.

"What can I do for you?" an officer asked. He was reading the *Daily Journal* and barely even looked up to acknowledge Tasha.

"I'm here to see Detective Troy Davis," she responded.

"Have a seat. I'll see if I can track him down," the officer behind the desk responded to Tasha, reading one more line before putting the paper down and picking up the phone.

Tasha nodded and went and sat down. She crossed her legs and massaged them suggestively as she waited for Officer Troy to come into sight. She had to make sure that he caught her getting her sexy on. She needed his help and knew that she would have to give a little to get a little. Tasha had to admit, not being conceited but convinced, that with her "work-'em" attitude, Officer Troy shouldn't be a problem. She knew that she looked good, and if the attitude didn't do the trick, then with her "fuck-'em" dress on, she was sure that Detective Troy Davis would take the bait.

"Miss Tasha."

She looked up to see none other than Officer Troy standing there, looking his usual lame, baldhead self.

Why couldn't he have at least laid off the doughnuts since the last time I saw him? Tasha thought, turned off by his protruding gut. *But fuck it. This is 'bout business.*

"Well, well, well," he chimed, "to what do I owe this unexpected surprise?" Troy rubbed his hands together and approached her, licking

his lips as he looked her up and down. He knew firsthand that Tasha tasted as good as she looked.

This cornball-ass nigga. Tasha flicked her hair behind her shoulders. She did all she could to ignore the fact that Troy's bald head was shaped funny, that he'd had one doughnut too many, and, worst of all, that he was part of Flint PD—a stinkin' cop. She needed something, so she'd have to put on her game face and play her hand right.

"Is there somewhere we can go to talk, you know, privately?" she asked, batting her eyes then allowing them to travel down to his crotch, which was only partially visible due to his bulging gut hanging over his belt.

"Yeah, let me show you to my office," he replied.

Tasha stood.

"After you." He held out his hand, allowing her to walk through the doorway first.

She walked with him through the precinct. When he put his hand on the small of her back and massaged it gently, she knew that she had him right where she needed him to be. Now she just had to go in for the kill.

They went into a small, messy office. He closed the door behind them, leaving on the other side a few drooling fellow officers who wished they could be in his shoes. He pulled out a chair for Tasha and then took a seat behind his desk.

"So . . . what can I do for you, Tasha? What is it that you want from me?" He leaned back in his chair and put his hands behind his head. He, too, had intentions of getting her right where he wanted her. It was an open playing field right about now, and anyone's game to win.

"Why does a girl have to want something?" she asked sweetly, giving him a genuine smile. Something about Officer Troy's tone let Tasha know that he wasn't as naïve as she'd assumed he was. She knew that she would have to play her cards right in order to get him to help her out.

"Because you haven't said one word to me since our little rendezvous at Wild Thangs. And that was, what, over a year ago?" He rocked back and forth in his office chair. "I even been up in there a few times. I figured since your boss owns the strip club, I'd maybe catch you in there. Guess I was wrong."

"Well, you know how it is in my line of work. A girl gets busy."

"Oh, but now all of a sudden your busy schedule has permitted you to just show up here out of the blue looking for me?"

Tasha shrugged as if to say, "That's what it looks like."

"Well, I got news for you—my luck ain't that fuckin' good, sweetheart. So let's try this again. What can I do for you?"

Tasha knew it was time to change her strategy. She didn't want to insult Troy any further by making him think she was taking him for a

fool. She was confident, however, that by the end of the day he'd be playing the fool anyway.

She let her shoulders drop, and with a serious look on her face, she began her spiel. "Okay, I'm not gon' try to game you because I know you ain't falling for the bullshit anyway."

"You damn right about that, shorty, so let's just be real."

Tasha smiled because she had Troy thinking that he was in control. Using reverse psychology, she was still gaming his ass, making it seem like he had the upper hand. She had to give herself a pat on the back because she was truly one of a kind. There wasn't a man alive who could outsmart her. Not even Manolo, and she'd soon enough prove it.

"Okay, I need a favor," Tasha just came out and said to Troy.

"So the plot thickens," he replied sarcastically.

She raised her eyebrows and looked at him like he was crazy. "Are you gon' let me finish?"

"I'm sorry, sexy. Go ahead. I mean, what else do I have to spend my time doing?" He spoke with sarcasm. "There are only a few hundred criminals I could be out there busting."

"Well, speaking of criminals . . . I need you to raid Manolo's club," Tasha said bluntly.

"What do you mean, you want me to raid his spot? For show or something?" Troy asked with a puzzled look on in his face.

Manolo had been allowing him a free supply of pussy from the Manolo Mamis in exchange for "overlooking certain things." So Troy couldn't imagine why else Tasha, whom he had known to be clearly on Manolo's team, would want him to raid Wild Thangs.

"No, not for show," Tasha corrected him. "For real." She moved in closer to Troy as if she were about to tell him something top secret. "He's got ten bricks and a little over fifty thousand dollars in a wall safe in his office." She bit her tongue and knew that it was because she was snitching. Under any other circumstance, she wouldn't even be caught in a police station, but she figured Manolo had this coming to him, having watched him manipulate the minds of young girls for years.

Tasha knew she played a role in the manipulation too, which was why she felt a responsibility to help Halleigh, and Mimi get their lives back on track. This was the reason she was abandoning her principles, snitching to bring down Manolo. She couldn't take back the heartache, pain, and even the death that some of the prostitutes had suffered in the trick game, but she could at least save others from it. If ever there was a time she needed redemption in her life, it was now. She hoped that her efforts wouldn't be in vain.

Troy sat up in his seat and looked Tasha directly in the eyes. "This ain't news to me. I know what goes on in that club. The thing is, Manolo laces my pockets here and there, if you know what I mean. Or

have you forgot?" He winked at Tasha and rubbed her thigh. "So I'm already getting my cut," he stated frankly, giving her one hard smack on the leg and then turning his chair away to let her know that he wasn't interested.

As far as Troy was concerned, Tasha hadn't brought any better deal to the table than he was already getting with Manolo. In addition to free pussy from the Manolo Mamis, Manolo himself threw Troy some cash on the side.

"Believe me, that little bit of paper Manolo throwing you ain't got shit on what's sitting inside that safe." Tasha knew she had to butter up the deal to make it just a tad more tasty so that Troy would want to take a bite. "I figure we could split the take fifty-fifty. That's twenty-five stacks each . . . not to mention the potential profit from the bricks." She looked Troy up and down. "That's what, two years' salary for you?" Tasha stated, hoping to convince the crooked officer to see things her way. Otherwise, she'd have to walk out of his office with the risk of him ratting her out to Manolo, and she knew what the end result for her would be if he did.

Troy got a little curious and asked Tasha, "Why would you be telling me this? Manolo's pimpin' your pretty ass. I mean, no offense, but you Manolo's bitch. What do you have to gain?" Tasha thought long and hard about the question Troy had just posed to her.

"My freedom," Tasha finally replied. "My freedom is what I have to gain." She stood from her chair and walked over to lock the office door.

Troy watched her every move. He turned his chair to face her as she closed the blinds and walked behind his desk. She lifted one knee to open his legs wide, her hands massaging the bulge growing in his groin.

"I'm chasing my freedom, Troy, and I'll do anything to get it," she whispered in his ear.

"Anything?" he whispered back, the lust making his voice seem deeper as he received the gentle massage in his private area.

"Anything," she replied.

He slipped a finger between her legs and smiled when he discovered that she wasn't wearing any panties. He had to admit, Tasha was a woman determined to get what she wanted.

Tasha's beauty had always enabled her to hustle men, and right now, Troy was merely another victim to be added to her long list of conquests.

Troy stood up and bent Tasha over his desk. Her voluptuous ass was calling for him. He began to grind against her as he undid his belt buckle.

Tasha played in her pussy, opening herself up for Troy and massag-

ing her clitoris. She pulled a condom out of her bra and slid it to him. "Put the safety belt on it, daddy . . . and let's ride."

Troy, working with a good nine inches, rubbed his bare thickness against her vaginal walls. He wanted to feel just a touch of her rawness before slipping on the condom. "Put it on for me, baby," he ordered Tasha.

She turned around, took the condom package out of Troy's hand, then used her teeth to rip open the packet. She then stared Troy dead in the eyes as she teasingly slipped the condom on him. After making sure the condom was on just right, Tasha turned around and assumed the position. Troy played with Tasha's womanhood with the tip of his penis.

With Troy behind her, she didn't have to look at his face, and she was getting hot. She licked on her own nipples as she anticipated Troy's nine inches entering her. He slid into her with ease and pumped her so hard that he caused her to crash against the desk. As she bucked against him, contracting her pussy on his shaft, items flew to the floor. He gripped her ass and opened and closed her cheeks as he rocked in and out of her. The sight of her slim waist, round behind, and the sound of her titties bouncing and making slapping sounds only excited him more. He began to moan in delight.

Tasha had to give it up to Troy. The nigga was fucking her right. If she had known that he was getting down like that, she might have given his ass some pussy the last time they'd connected at the strip club. Instead, Troy had left the club with Tasha's pussy juice on his face only. At the time, that was enough to make her feel disgusted by what she had to do.

Now, Tasha was actually enjoying herself. She closed her eyes and bit her lip when Troy reached around and pinched her nipples. It turned her on, and before she knew it, she too was trying to silence her moans.

"Damn, this pussy so good," he whispered as his hips moved in circles, causing him to go even deeper inside of her. "Them other tricks ain't got nothing on your fine ass." Troy slapped her ass and stroked deeper.

"Mmmm, they learned from the best, Big Poppa," Tasha replied.

They were so loud that they had attracted a crowd outside of Troy's office. Someone knocked loudly, but Troy ignored it. They heard a voice from the other side.

"Everything all right?"

Still ignoring the interruption, Troy didn't respond. He just pulled out of Tasha, turned her toward him, then picked her up. He placed his stiff dick inside her again and pumped in and out of her while holding her in midair.

"Oh my God," she whispered in delight as he carried her around his office.

He reached his office door and pressed her against it as he continued to sex her.

"Damn, baby," Troy huffed and puffed.

He got so loud that Tasha had to put her hand over his mouth.

"I'm about to nut," he exclaimed.

"Nut for me, baby," she whispered, popping her pussy even harder, trying to get hers in too. She felt the gush between her legs as she came.

A few seconds later, Troy gripped her ass tightly as he experienced the best orgasm of his life.

After quickly releasing Tasha, he put his hand around his length and pumped every single ounce of cum out of himself and into the tip of the condom.

Tasha pulled her dress down and straightened it out. "So . . . do we have a deal?" she asked.

"Are you crazy? Hell yeah, we got a deal." He breathed heavily, trying to catch his breath after that workout. "Whatever you want," he replied breathlessly as he began to clean himself up with some napkins he removed from around a paper cup of coffee.

Tasha, accustomed to getting her way, smiled. "Good. I need you to do it tonight."

"Tonight?" Troy questioned. "I need a little bit more time for that. I have to make sure I get the right men for the job, if you know what I'm saying. How about tomorrow night?"

"Tomorrow night will be too late," Tasha told him. "You know how the game is. Anything can change between now and tomorrow night. You need to make that hit tonight, or it might not even be worth it." Tasha walked up to Troy seductively. "And you know damn well it was worth it. Might even be worth a little somethin'-somethin' extra . . . if you know what I mean."

"Oh, I know what you mean all right, sweet thang." He looked Tasha up and down. "Tell you what—let me make a few calls. Now that I'm looking at things from another perspective," he gave Tasha the once-over. "I think tonight is doable."

"Good." Tasha smiled. "I'm glad you took another look at things." She winked and then said, "So tonight, after you do your part, we'll split everything up sixty-forty, my favor."

Troy frowned as he pulled up his slacks. "Sixty-forty? What happened to fifty-fifty?"

"Well, Officer Troy, I, too, had to take another look at things. And, well, you know"—She looked down at herself—"this pussy ain't free." Tasha blew him a kiss as she sashayed away. She opened the door to

find a group of men standing there and eyeing her as if they were imagining what it would be like to be in Troy's shoes.

"Gentlemen," she greeted them, maneuvering between the men and exiting the building. She couldn't help the smile that spread across her face. She was about to gain her independence from Manolo. That was definitely something to smile about.

Tasha also knew that afterwards, she, Halleigh, and Mimi would have to lay low. She decided that she would go back to her hometown of New York for a while until things cooled off. She thought about the bricks she would soon have on her hands to unload and turn into cash. That wasn't her forte, but she knew just who could help her do it. She was looking forward to the future now. After tonight, she hoped to be on the first flight out of Flint to New York. She couldn't wait to share the good news with Halleigh and Mimi as she made her way back to the house.

As Tasha drove, she thought momentarily about Manolo and what her betrayal would do to him. The more she thought about her relationship with him, the more she realized that Manolo had never done her wrong, not even once, since she'd known him. He'd always treated her like his main bitch, even before she ever officially was. As a matter of fact, it wasn't even his idea to put Tasha on the ho stroll in the first place; it was her own. She was paper-driven at the time, and whoring was just another way to add to the hustle. Unlike the other girls, Tasha had been picky regarding who she would trick with. Not that the majority of the men were fine anyway, but there was a fine line between unattractive, plain ol' ugly, and completely disgusting. So if one of her johns would show up looking like he could make her throw up, Tasha would pass on the money, and not once did Manolo ever reprimand her for it. If any other bitch had tried that, he would have been upside her head quick, fast and in a hurry.

Although Tasha had witnessed Manolo beat a couple of the girls senseless, he'd never laid a hand on her, except to embrace her or make love to her. Come to think of it, Manolo was the first man in Tasha's life who hadn't hurt her, and setting him up was how she was about to repay him.

All of a sudden, the sound of the tires rolling off the paved highway lane and onto the berm startled Tasha out of her thoughts. "Oh, shit!" she said as she regained control of the car and positioned the vehicle back in its lane. Now she just needed to get control of herself because there was no turning back at this point.

As Tasha continued driving, fond thoughts of Manolo were suppressed by visions of everything she had witnessed him doing to the other girls

Tasha realized that all the girls who had ever come through that house had taken one for the team by means of physical or mental abuse.

Everyone but her. So, as she weighed her loyalty to Manolo against her sympathy for the girls, it was a no-brainer. She stepped on the gas and said, "Fuck you, Manolo. I'm out for self now."

Chapter Fifty

Tariq waited anxiously at Atlas Restaurant. Today was the day that he would become boss by default. He had spent the last few weeks mapping out his master plan, and now it was all about to go down. Tariq hadn't been shy about bragging of his efforts, before they were even played out, to any member of his team that had been willing to listen. Still, he felt comfortable bringing only one of his workers into the actual scheme.

Poppa, one of Tariq's workers, would wait for them to arrive at a rest stop halfway between Detroit and Flint. That was the spot where Tariq decided to take out both Joe and Malek, and Poppa was going to be the triggerman. Tariq was counting on Joe bringing Malek along. He knew that Malek already had a thing against him, and if Joe turned up dead on a run he had set up, Tariq knew that it wouldn't take long for Malek to put two and two together. Then a war would be on between the two of them. By the same token, Tariq knew that Malek was like Joe's little shadow, and more likely than not, he would be tagging along. The plan was one that couldn't fail, let Tariq tell it. After Poppa took out Joe and Malek, Tariq was going to leave their bodies there to rot, and take off with not only the bricks of cocaine, but with his new-found boss status. It was cut and dried. The only thing for him to do now was to wait.

After leaving the restaurant, Tariq sat out in the parking lot in his Suburban. That was the spot where he was supposed to meet up with Jamaica Joe and Malek. Any other time, he would have been bitter about the young buck rolling with them to handle grown folks' business, but this time, he was glad that Joe was bringing Malek along with them, so that he could kill two birds with one stone.

Tariq looked in his rearview mirror and saw his man in the rear hatch with a pistol gripped tightly. He looked straight ahead as he gave nineteen-year-old Poppa some last-minute instructions. "Yo, fam, you have to stay quiet, and don't do anything until I give you the signal."

"I got you, man," the young gun assured Tariq.

"Remember, when I pull into the rest area and turn the music up, bang them."

"Ain't they gon' think it strange when you pull over and shit?"

"I'm going to tell them I have to pull over to piss. That's when you do it, man." A half smile spread across Tariq's lips as he pictured the bloody scene. "Two shots to the head apiece. I got the body bags in the back. We gon' toss them into the river right by the rest stop. It's a perfect setup. All head shots, got it?"

"I got you, man," the boy hissed. "We went over this a million times already. If you doubted my skills, then you shouldn't have put a nigga on, ya heard." Poppa was lightweight offended. Tariq going over the plan with him repeatedly made it seem like Tariq thought he couldn't handle his business like the big boys. Poppa couldn't remember how many times he had told these cats that age ain't nothin' but a number.

"Well, mu'fucka, I don't care how many times we have to go over this, li'l nigga. You got to hit they ass right, feel me? Any mistakes could cost you your life. Joe stay strapped, and I know Malek's ass is going to have his banger, so you just make sure you do the shit right. You gotta be quick. I don't want to have to pull out my piece and cover your ass," Tariq spat.

"Oh, nigga don't want to get his hands dirty, but wanna be the boss?" Poppa chuckled under his breath.

"What was that shit, man?" Tariq turned around and asked.

"Oh, nothing, man, I was just sayin', You the boss." Poppa smiled and then quickly erased it.

Tariq turned back around. That's when he saw Joe's car pull into the parking lot. He could feel his heartbeat increase, and the palms of his hands got a little sweaty. He wiped his hands down his pants and then calmed himself down, trying to look normal.

"It's showtime!" Tariq sang. "This is going to change both of our lives. We gon' be like Jerry Maguire and shit. We Tom Cruise and Cuba. I got some shit going on with Sweets, and we are all going to come together." Tariq told more of his full plan. "I'm going to run the North Side and make you my right-hand man, young gun. You ready to become a legend, nigga? This is where you earn yo stripes."

Poppa got himself into a comfortable position in the back, where his marks wouldn't be able to see him. "I'm ready."

Malek drove Joe's Lexus coupe into Atlas Restaurant parking lot and noticed that Tariq's truck was parked toward the back. He then looked over at Joe, who was sitting next to him. "You sure you want to roll out with him, knowing that it's a setup?" Malek parked the car.

Joe said, "Do you trust me, Malek?"

"No doubt," Malek answered. "You my man."

"Roll with me on this one then, fam. I got this under control." Joe grabbed his pistol from his glove compartment and tucked it in his

waist. He then gave Malek a look, as if giving him one last opportunity to break out.

Malek was skeptical and didn't know what Joe had planned, but he trusted him and was willing to have his back through whatever, especially if it meant seeing Tariq's head roll. Malek gave him a nod, letting Joe know that he was "ride or die."

As Joe and Malek got out of the vehicle, Malek's heart was pounding, not out of fear, but pure adrenaline. He didn't know what to expect, and he didn't see the logic behind Jamaica Joe walking into a setup. He guessed Joe didn't want to believe that his right-hand man would do him harm, and was hoping that he would have a change of heart and back out.

This nigga got balls, for real, Malek thought. *I'm keeping my hands on my banger at all times. That's my word.*

Joe instructed Malek to get the duffle bag from his back seat. Malek did as he was told, and then the two headed toward Tariq's truck. When Joe approached it, he opened the back passenger's side door.

"What up," Tariq said simply, looking over his shoulder at Joe.

"Handling this business," Joe replied. "That's what's up."

"Then let's ride out. Get in."

Joe hesitated for a minute. "I was thinking we ride out in my whip. You ain't really had a chance to roll in my new ride. Besides, I kinda wanna ride in the comfort of my own home, if you know what I'm saying."

Malek, who had one hand on the front passenger's door and the duffle bag in the other, paused to see what the deal was, whether they were going to ride in Tariq's vehicle or Joe's.

"Well, uh, you know I done, uh," Tariq started, with Joe trying to read the expression on his face and his body language, "I done got an oil change and shit and gassed up, you know."

Tariq, not wanting to look too suspicious, added, "But we can roll in your whip if you want to. It's all good." Tariq took his keys out of the ignition as if he were all gung ho about riding in Joe's car, but inside he was waiting for Joe to say the words that, within seconds, he eventually spoke.

"Nah," Joe said. "We can go on and take your shit. My shit almost on empty, and I ain't trying to make no stops riding dirty. You know what I mean?"

Breathing a silent sigh of relief, Tariq replied, "Yeah, I know what you saying."

Joe looked over at Malek and nodded for him to go ahead and climb in, which he did.

Malek and Joe hopped into Tariq's truck. Joe sat in the back, just like he always did. He never liked anyone to sit behind him. Malek sat up front with Tariq, who pulled off as soon as they were both in.

Tariq looked in the rearview mirror and addressed Joe. "What's good, fam?"

Joe nodded. "Like I said, just trying to make this money . . . *fam.*"

Joe, as hard as it was for him, maintained his composure toward this man who had for years called himself his right-hand man. Tariq had served as his confidant, his ace. Now it sickened him that he had to share the same air with him . . . but not for long. It was do or die. One of them was gon' do, and the other was gon' die. But which one?

Tariq looked at Malek and put his hand out to greet him. "What's good, Malek?"

Malek didn't even respond; he just kept his head straight.

Tariq's actions were a dead giveaway to Joe and Malek. Both Malek and Joe couldn't help but notice how out of character Tariq was acting already. Tariq never spoke to Malek. His jealousy of him had always been present. He displayed it by being silent and giving Malek the cold shoulder, but today he made an exception. That didn't sit well. If Malek and Joe hadn't known something was up before now, Tariq's actions tipped them off for certain

Malek watched Tariq pull his trembling hand back. *This nigga has got to be the dumbest mu'fucka in Flint. Look at this nigga.* It was obvious that Tariq's nerves were getting the better of him. It was written all over his face, and his uneasiness was evident.

Joe didn't want Tariq to sense that they knew something was going on, so he said, "Yo, fam, you sure this nigga is a hundred percent?"

"I'm sure. He is getting money out in the *D.* My uncle used to run with him back in the day. The nigga is one hundred percent, for sure. Square business!"

"If shit don't go down as expected, I'm holding you personally responsible, you feel me?" Joe told Tariq.

Tariq glared at Joe through the rearview mirror before saying, "Don't worry, boss. I promise that if things don't go as you expect them to, I'll be glad to take full responsibility." Tariq then turned his attention back to driving.

For the next thirty minutes, the three of them rode on I-75 without sound, everyone attending to their own thoughts. Poppa lay slumped in the back, trying to remain as quiet as possible. His heart raced a hundred miles per minute as he gripped his .45 automatic pistol. He was ready to go through with the plan. All he had to do was wait for Tariq to pull over at the rest area so that he could earn his stripes.

Ever since he was twelve, when he did his first hit, Poppa felt like he always had something to prove in the streets. He was tired of people taking him for some okey-doke Negro. Although his history had just been poppin' off niggas for pay, which was how he came about the moniker *Poppa.* This wasn't no ordinary work for hire. He was caught up in a situation with the king of the North, which would earn him

more street credit than he had ever imagined. Ready to make a real name for himself in the streets and shut niggas up from ever doubting his skills again, Poppa sat back and waited for his cue, which didn't take long to come

"Yo, I got to piss like a mu'fucka." Tariq squirmed in his seat. "Here's a rest area coming up," he said as they passed the sign. "I'ma pull over real quick."

"Yo, you can't wait until we handle this business, fam?" Joe asked, hoping that Tariq would change his mind and not go through with it. "I said I didn't want to make no stops riding dirty. Fuck, we could have taken my car if we was gon' be stopping any damn way."

"I got to go now," Tariq said nonchalantly as he frantically kept checking the rearview mirror.

Once they came upon the ramp and Tariq exited the highway, the tension in the truck grew, as everyone knew something was about to go down.

Tariq pulled into the rest area and threw the car in park. He looked around and saw that no other cars were at the rest stop. He knew this shit was destined to go down. Luck was on his side. Now he didn't have to worry about someone hearing the gunshots, or having to take out any extra heads. Hopefully Poppa would be quick about his business before any other cars pulled up.

"I'll be right back." Tariq turned up the music and yelled, "Y'all can just chill and listen to this new Scarface CD."

As Tariq got out of the car, Malek slowly slid his hand to his waist and waited for shit to pop off. He kept his eyes burned to Tariq's back. If his eyes could shoot bullets, Tariq would be full of holes the way Malek was glaring him down.

Tariq walked toward the men's restroom with a quick pace. He could hear his heart beating as he braced himself for the gunfire that he anticipated. He thought back to the time when he and Joe were as tight as blood brothers. He would have killed for Joe. As a matter of fact, he had killed for Joe on several occasions. Now the game had changed—well, at least the players were about to change anyhow. Tariq knew that there was no turning back now. He could only stand in wait to hear the gunshot blast come from the car, so that he could get it over with.

Tariq might have talked a good game, and as big as his talk was, one might've thought his bullet game would be just as big. Poppa had even asked him why he didn't save himself the money and the trouble and just pop Joe himself, but Tariq turned the tables on Poppa by asking him why he wanted to know. Was he scared to put in the work? Not one to back down from a test, Poppa ceased his questioning and accepted the job.

In truth, even though Tariq had popped off a couple of cats before,

he just didn't have the heart to kill his man and Malek himself, so he was content with letting Poppa handle it. Poppa had no idea that Tariq was planning on slumping him after he killed Joe and Malek. Tariq didn't want any connections to the murder, so he had to get rid of all links that involved him. He had one mission and one mission only, and that was to take over. He didn't need no little young-ass sidekick, like Joe obviously thought he needed. Although he had admired Joe over the years, he didn't want to walk in his footsteps; he wanted to walk ahead of him, to take the game to a whole 'nother level of making money.

Tariq approached the bathroom, planning to come out an entirely different person. Just before he reached the door, he heard it.

Boom, boom! Two shots rang out from the car. Then two more. *Boom, boom!*

Tariq stopped in his tracks at the sound of the gunfire. He couldn't help but exhale as he turned around and rushed to the car, glad that it was all over with. The closer he got to the vehicle, the quicker his pace.

When he finally reached the car, he opened the driver's side door, and his heart skipped a beat with excitement. Funny how sometimes death could make a nigga's dick rise quicker than a butt-naked dime-piece sliding down a pole. Tariq couldn't hold back the smile when he saw Malek slumped on the dashboard. He looked back at Joe, who was hunched over in the seat. Tariq's smile grew even wider as he saw Poppa, who had a sinister grin on his face with the smoking gun in his hand, hovering over Joe.

"Hell, yeah! That's how you dead a nigga. We 'bout to take over!" Tariq yelled over the music before turning it off. "Ain't that right, my man?" he said to Poppa, giving the bodies another look.

That was when Tariq had to do a double take because something wasn't right. Something was missing. The more Tariq observed the crime scene, he realized what was missing—blood. There was no blood on the scene. Not one single drop.

He immediately looked up at Poppa and began to back away, but before he could move, a smiling Malek had his gun pointed at Tariq's head.

Joe, without a scratch on him, slowly rose up, glaring into Tariq's eyes the entire time. "You look surprised, fam," he said. "Niggas was just catching some Z's while you went to take a piss." Joe chuckled, shrugging his shoulders. "What? You thought I was dead or something?" Joe leaned back in the seat, cool, calm, and collected. " 'Cause you look like you've just seen a ghost." He pulled out one of his pre-rolled blunts and lit it. He took a long drag and blew the smoke in Tariq's direction.

Malek, his pistol now pressed to Tariq's head, reached into Tariq's waist and relieved him of his strap. "You didn't even have the balls to

kill me yourself," Malek said through clenched teeth. "You had to hire a gun? What kind of shit is that, *gangsta*?" Sarcasm laced Malek's words. "You had to go and hire Poppa?" Malek looked to Poppa while still talking to Tariq. "Unlike you, Poppa is loyal."

Tariq locked eyes with Poppa, who fired a look back at him that said, *"Nigga, what?"*

Poppa shrugged. A nigga had to do what a nigga had to do as far as he was concerned. Poppa had to admit, when Tariq first presented him with the offer to put in work, he knew taking out someone with Jamaica Joe's status would give him major street rep. It was also the type of rep that would come along with it, one of a traitor, that made him change his mind and tell Joe what Tariq was up to.

"You's a dumb mu'fucka," Joe told Tariq. "How you going to recruit one of my soldiers to hit me? Huh?" Joe chuckled. "I mean, he may be on your team, but the li'l nigga know where his pay come from. Did you really think he was gonna bite the hand that feeds him?"

Tariq remained silent. He just kept staring at Poppa, not believing that he had double-crossed him, which was ironic, because that's the same thing Joe was thinking about Tariq.

"What the fuck you looking at, nigga?" Poppa finally spoke to Tariq. "Joe been letting me eat since I was sixteen. I'm a real nigga. I stay loyal. I saw what you were up to." Poppa pulled out the body bags that Tariq had placed in the back with him. "You brought three body bags with your stupid ass. What, you think just 'cause I ain't graduate, a nigga can't count? I knew what you was gon' do, bitch. Who the third bag for?" Poppa gripped his gun tighter.

"Fall back, man. I got it," Joe said as he looked over at a Lexus pulling up beside him.

Tariq heard company coming, and for a split second he was relieved. It might be an opportune time for him to get away. Surely Joe wouldn't do him in front of witnesses if he didn't have to.

Unfortunately for Tariq, the person in the car was no witness. It was one of Joe's henchmen, there to pick them up just in case Joe and Malek found themselves in a shoot-out or something.

Malek pressed the gun even harder into Tariq's head. The time was near, and he was itching to pull the trigger. He had long wanted to take out this punk-ass nigga anyway. He was just waiting on the word from Joe to pop off this coward.

Joe looked over to Malek. "It's time."

Malek smiled and cocked his piece.

"Look, Joe," Tariq spoke up, swallowing hard, "how can you blame me? You didn't let me grow. You let Malek come in and you gave him the block I wanted. The block I had earned after all I've done for you."

"After all you've done for me, nigga?" Joe sat up and snapped, spit flying out of his mouth with every word.

"You ain't did shit for me, nigga. You the one that had to eat. I just kept the mu'fuckin' cupboards full. Don't think for once you ever prepared my plate, nigga. Joe was gon' eat with or without you." Joe looked to Malek. "As you can see, and not that I like to quote bitches and shit"—Joe leaned back and pulled on his blunt—"but you ain't irreplaceable."

"I was supposed to be yo right-hand man, not him! Me!" Tariq shot back. "You let this nigga come in and take my spot!" The veins showed in Tariq's forehead, and tears formed in his eyes as he verbalized his jealous thoughts to Joe.

Joe was unmoved. "Are you done, nigga?" he asked, nonchalantly puffing away.

Tariq braced himself and took a deep breath, knowing his life was about to come to an end. He stuck his chin up bravely and answered, "Yeah, I'm done."

Just before a single shot rang out, Joe said, "Good night."

Boom!

Malek put a bullet through Tariq's temple, and the driver's window suddenly looked like it had red tint. Tariq's upper body lay across the front seat, while his legs dangled outside of the truck.

It was Malek's first time catching a body. He didn't know how it was going to make him feel after the fact, but it wasn't as bad as he had imagined. He had often wondered how dudes could just take another man's life and keep it moving day to day like it wasn't nothing. Now he knew. Taking Tariq's life was personal. He didn't do what he'd just done for himself; he did it for Halleigh.

"See you in hell, bitch-ass nigga," Malek spat. Then he put his gun back down in his waist.

"Clean him up, Poppa. Put him in one of them bags so we can toss him." Joe stepped out the car and casually walked to the ledge over the river. He stared at the water and continued to smoke as he thought about the turn of events that had just played out. He put his head down and shook it in disbelief. He never thought that Tariq would turn on him. In a matter of time, though, Joe knew he'd shake it off and keep things moving just as before. In spite of how tight and loyal he felt Tariq was, he also understood that backstabbing, murder, and lies were all a part of the drug game. It just hurt him that after all this time Tariq was the one who had betrayed him.

"Keep yo friends close, but your enemies closer," Joe whispered to himself as he tossed the blunt into the water. He looked back and saw Malek and Poppa carrying the black body bag with Tariq's corpse toward him so that they could throw it into the water.

Once they reached the ledge, they lifted and propped the bag full of dead weight, literally, onto the edge, preparing to push him over.

Boom! Joe put a bullet through Poppa's head, causing him to fall over the ledge and crash into the water.

Malek jumped, dropping the bottom portion of Tariq's corpse.

"Damn, Joe! What you do that for?" Malek asked. "You at least could have warned me."

"I had to take him out," Joe admitted. "I would have always wondered, if I hadn't found out about the setup, would he have gone through with it? Just what move might that little nigga have made in the end if he hadn't counted three body bags?"

Prior to rolling to Detroit, Joe had managed to catch up with Scratch again and ask him to describe the worker that Tariq had been boasting to about his intent to set him up. When Scratch described the young cat Tariq had been talking to at the crackhouse, Joe knew it was Poppa. It didn't take a brain surgeon to figure out that if Tariq was running off at the mouth to Poppa, he was going to try to recruit him to help. In spite of the fact that Tariq had always come through for Joe on any assignment he had ever given him, he knew that Tariq was smart enough not to try to pull this one off alone. The fact that Poppa didn't come to him never sat well with Joe . . . and it never would have.

Malek remained silent and tried to stop his heart from beating so fast. He tried to conceal his nervousness, but Joe noticed.

"Let's get the fuck out of here," Joe said as he helped Malek push Tariq's body over the ledge.

Malek didn't realize it, but he had just moved up in the ranks by default. He showed Jamaica Joe a lot of loyalty and heart in that situation, and Jamaica Joe took note. Malek and Jamaica Joe jumped in the truck, with Joe's henchman following behind, headed back to Flint, two snakes lighter.

Chapter Fifty-one

Mimi was on stage working the pole as she looked out into the crowd. As always, Wild Thangs was packed, and dollar bills were scattered all over the stage during Mimi's show. Mimi didn't dance at the club on a regular, so it was always a treat for the regular patrons when she did. Manolo knew it meant extra incoming funds when a feature was in the house; and Mimi was indeed a feature.

She was always sure to call up all of her regular customers and let

them know when she was going to be taking the stage so that they could be there to spread the love in the form of dollar bills and at least a twenty-dollar drink, but she was known to have dudes buy her hundred dollar drinks. Mimi had taken the liberty to insist that all her johns be in the house tonight for what she knew was her finale. The idea of extra pocket change didn't hurt either.

As Keith Sweat's song "Chocolate Girl" played, Mimi put on the show of her life, sliding down the pole upside down spread eagle. She slowly straightened her legs and kicked them down, rising into a standing position as she looked out at the clapping crowd of men who had enjoyed her little stunt. She watched as they marched by the stage like an army of ants, dropping dollars. She even allowed a couple to stick some down her camisole, allowing them to get a quick free feel of her breasts. A satisfying smile spread across her face as she looked out and spotted Manolo, who hadn't really been paying her a bit of mind. He was sitting in his VIP booth with Tasha, Halleigh, and his young killers, the Shottah Boyz.

Manolo was poppin' bottles as if he was the king of the city, and Mimi could tell that he was feeling himself. According to the plan Tasha had shared with her and Halleigh earlier, his night was going to go downhill from there on out, and Mimi reveled in the thought. She couldn't wait to see his downfall. After all the bad karma Manolo had put out into the world, he was finally about to get his.

Mimi reached high on the pole and gripped it with her hands. She wrapped her ankles around it, released her hands, and allowed her body to hang upside down once again. She then slowly slid down. This time, her little trick caught Manolo's attention. He loved when she did that move. She winked at him as she made her way down to the bottom of the pole.

Nigga, you better enjoy this night. It's gon' be your last free night for a while, Mimi thought as she reached her hands back up to grab the pole before her head touched the ground. Then she put her pussy in a customer's face and did a slow grind. The man stuck out his tongue and licked her slowly. He had full access to her because of the crotchless camisole she was wearing. The crowd went crazy when they saw the man feasting on her.

Mimi wasn't embarrassed or ashamed by her performance; she was all about her paper and was willing to do whatever it took to get it. She'd made a name for herself as one of the best dancers in Michigan. She wanted to give her loyal fans a good finale and fill her Crown Royal bag at the same time. She knew that tonight would be her last time stripping on anybody's pole. She was done with the entire ho business and was ready to get money in a new way. She couldn't promise herself that it would be in a legit way, but she'd put her best foot forward.

After her set, Mimi joined Manolo at his table. He was drunk and feeling good when she sat down beside him. "Hey, Daddy," she greeted as she grabbed a drink from his hand and took a sip.

"What up? You got my cut?" he asked, referring to his percentage of her night's earnings.

His comment pissed off Mimi. He always tried to pull his pimp card when he was around his niggas. She concealed her attitude as she reached into her camisole, pulled out her money, and handed it over to him. Since he had only been half paying attention to her, she knew that he missed a couple of times several men had given her cash. Ordinarily she would have held out on Manolo just a little bit, but she figured at this point in the game, she would choose her battles wisely. Besides, this fight would be over soon anyway. Tasha had told her that she would split her sixty percent from the safe with Mimi and Halleigh so that they would at least have something to get them started once they were no longer working for him. So Mimi wasn't tripping over the money she had just turned over to Manolo. Mimi looked over at Halleigh and Tasha, who were sitting next to Manolo, one on each side of him. Mimi observed their smug expressions. She could tell that they were feeling the same way she was—thick. They finally had the upper hand on Manolo, and he was so stuck on himself, he didn't even realize it.

Everybody was loose in the club, and Manolo was talking big as usual. They partied for a couple more hours, and by midnight, the club was popping off proper.

Tasha checked her watch and knew what time it was. She scanned her surroundings discreetly. If everything went according to plan, Troy and his boys in blue would be there any minute.

Just like clockwork, less than five minutes later, the club was flooded with uniformed police officers. They stormed into the club with their weapons drawn. A couple of screams erupted throughout, but very few people were scared. It was typical for the po-po to raid the local strip clubs, be it legit or a shakedown. That's just how the Flint PD got down. Everyone put up their hands and watched curiously to see how the scenario was going to play out.

"Everybody on the ground! Now!" Troy screamed as he made his way to the VIP section, his fellow officers following right behind him.

Manolo was enraged. He didn't know what was going on. All he knew was that Troy should have given him a heads-up that boys in blue would be riding through. That way he could have made sure the place was clean—especially if Flint PD was sending dirty cops.

I'm paying this mu'fucka to turn his head to my business and he coming in here on some bullshit? He stood to his feet. "Fuck is going on, man?" he spat as Troy approached. "Thought we had a deal!"

Troy grabbed Manolo's arm and twisted him around, forcing him to lean over the table.

The Shottah Boyz reached for their pistols, but decided against it. They knew better than to catch a case by trying to come to Manolo's defense.

Troy applied the bracelets to Manolo's wrists and then pulled a search warrant from his back pocket.

"Fuck is you doing coming up in here? Fuck you looking for?" Manolo yelled.

As the police squad spread throughout the club, Troy commanded, "Turn this place inside out."

Troy wanted to make it look good, so he didn't go to the safe right away. He searched the club for about twenty minutes before he discovered the safe that, of course, Tasha had already informed him of.

"Jackpot, boys!" Troy announced. "Let's take him in to be processed." He placed the bricks in a duffle bag along with the money and then headed out of the club.

Tasha looked at Halleigh and Mimi. The satisfaction on their faces was priceless, but now it was time for her to go collect their money. "Stay here and clear out the club. I'm going to get our cut now before Officer Troy gets any ideas. I'll come back in about an hour," she stated before leaving the club.

Tasha drove toward Miller Road and parked her car in the empty shopping center lot. Just as planned, Troy was waiting for her. She eagerly hopped out of the car.

"I got to take ten thousand and two kilos of cocaine back to the station so that I can log it in as evidence," he informed her as she approached.

"What? You didn't tell me that."

"Look, my ass is the one who has to build this case against Manolo for him to do jail time. There's twenty thousand in there for you. You can also keep the rest of the dope. I can't do anything with that."

Tasha's eyes lit up when he said that. She knew that the eight bricks were as good as gold, so she shut up and accepted the deal. "Nice doing business with you, Troy," she stated with a wink.

"Very nice." Troy licked his lips and eyed her up and down. "Let me know if you'd like to do *it* again."

Tasha smirked. The sex was good, but it wasn't that damn good. She still hated cops, and she knew that she wouldn't make it a habit of dealing with him. She hopped back into her vehicle and pulled away.

When she arrived back at the club, Mimi and Halleigh were waiting patiently for her. She was surprised that they had gotten rid of everyone so quickly.

"You get the money?" Mimi asked, the dollar signs practically forming in her eyes.

"Yeah, I got it. There are twenty stacks here and eight bricks," Tasha replied.

"What are we gon' do with some dope?" Halleigh asked.

"Don't worry about it. I'm gon' holla at my brother. He lives in New York. We're going to visit him there. We'll let things cool down before we come back . . . if we come back."

Tasha divided the cash by giving herself $8,000 and then giving Halleigh and Mimi $6,000 apiece. She figured she should get a little more for putting the plan together and fucking with Troy to carry it out. Mimi and Halleigh had no objections.

"Look, y'all, no one can know that we set up Manolo's arrest, so we just have to keep our mouths shut and let things die down. Then I promise you that everything will be fine," Tasha said.

Halleigh smiled and hugged Tasha tightly. "Thank you, Tash. Thank you so much."

Mimi was busy flicking through her money when she burst out laughing.

Halleigh frowned. "What's so funny?"

Mimi shook her head and giggled some more. "Did y'all see Manolo's face when the police blew up his spot?"

Halleigh and Tasha joined in on the laughter.

Mimi shook her head. "His ass was getting ready to cry when they put those handcuffs on him."

"What goes around comes around," Halleigh stated. "I hope he rots in the mu'fucka."

"Let's get out of here." Tasha rose from her seat. "We've got a long drive ahead of us." When she decided that she would take Mimi and Halleigh with her, Tasha had changed her plans from flying to driving to New York. Leaving them in Flint was too risky. If they were with her, they couldn't talk.

The girls exited the club with a burden lifted from their hearts. Manolo had taken advantage of each of them in their own way. As they pulled away from the club, they felt safe and secure, knowing that their betrayal would be a secret that would never leave those four walls.

Just as Tasha, Halleigh, and Mimi drove away, Keesha came walking out of the club with envy in her eyes. She'd just overheard the conversation and knew it had to be worth something. She just had to figure out how she would use it to her advantage.

Chapter Fifty-two

"Oh my God, can we stop and grab something to eat?" Mimi attempted to shift to a more comfortable position in the small car. "We've been driving for eight hours straight."

"We're almost there." Tasha looked at her watch. It was three in the afternoon. "We got like two hours to go. We've got all this shit in the trunk, so we got to keep it pushing until we unload the bricks. My brother will know what to do." Tasha had told the girls before they headed out that they were doing the thing in one straight shot, so if anybody had to eat or piss, they best do it before they hit the highway.

"I just want to get out of these clothes and take a shower," Halleigh added. "Does your brother even know we're coming?"

"No, I didn't tell him," Tasha confessed, "but it's not gon' be a problem. I haven't failed you girls yet, so just trust me."

The girls drove for three more hours before they finally arrived in Brooklyn, New York. They pulled up to a modest two-story home, and Tasha smiled when she thought of the familiarity she felt just being there.

"Let's go, bitches!" Tasha yelled excitedly at the thought of seeing her brother.

Halleigh and Mimi got out of the car and followed her up the walkway that led to the house. Tasha knocked lightly on the door and stood impatiently as they waited for an answer.

"I don't think he's here," Halleigh stated with a sigh as she leaned against the porch ledge.

"It doesn't matter. This dumb boy always keeps a key underneath his doormat." Tasha knelt down and lifted the mat. Just as she had predicted, her brother hadn't changed.

Leaving the key under the mat was a habit Tasha's grandmother had always had. That way if any of her children ever needed to come, they would always have a way in. That tradition had passed down to their mother as well. Even though Tasha's brother didn't have any children, he had picked up the habit too. Now Tasha could see why it was such a good habit after all as she scooped up the key and let herself into his home.

They entered the home and were greeted by a ten-foot foyer with a shiny hardwood floor.

"Damn, he's living nice," Mimi stated as she nosily walked around the house. It wasn't anything extravagant, but it was definitely better than what she had grown accustomed to. He was hood rich, with flat-screen televisions and nice leather furniture. A huge fish tank with ex-

otic fish took up an entire wall. Surprisingly, the house was clean, but you could tell that it was a bachelor's spot.

Halleigh, too, was impressed with the sense of style as she looked around the four-bedroom home decorated in brown earth tones.

"Make yourselves at home." Tasha walked down the hallway and into one of the rooms. "I'm crashing in here. Y'all can pick whatever room you want," she said as she went inside and closed the door.

"How this bitch gon' tell us to make ourselves at home and this ain't even her shit?" Mimi stated with a laugh.

Halleigh ignored Mimi's comment. "I'm going to lie down before I pass out," Halleigh stated wearily. "That shower can wait. I can't even stand up long enough to wash up anyway."

Halleigh looked inside the remaining three rooms and chose the one that didn't look occupied, assuming that it wasn't Tasha's brother's. She pulled her shirt over her head, took off her jeans, and released her hair from the tight ponytail, allowing it to fall freely to her shoulders. She was tired, and all she wanted to do was sleep. She needed to wrap her mind around the fact that she no longer belonged to Manolo. She was free, the owner of her body again. Although she could never take back the fact that she'd lain down with more men than she could count in the name of money and security, she could take back what was hers, and that was peace of mind.

Her body had been abused and misused for so long that she no longer viewed herself as a lady. She felt like a ho. It would take a while for her to learn to love herself again, but this was a start. The last two years of her life had been hell. Now all she wanted to do was move forward.

Serenity took over her body. As soon as her head hit the pillow, she drifted off into the deepest sleep ever.

Halleigh awoke and hopped out of bed. Her head was still cloudy, but she was grateful for the couple hours of peace that she had experienced while she slept. A note rested on the pillow beside her. She picked it up and read it.

Hal,

Mimi and I are going out to grab something to eat. We'll be back in a few. If you need anything, just call my cell. Your lazy ass probably won't even get up before we get back, but just in case, you know how to reach me. Oh yeah, make sure you get dressed. We're going out tonight to celebrate our new freedom.

Tash

"Damn! They could've woke me up. I'm starving," Halleigh crumpled the letter and tossed it aside. "And how am I supposed to get dressed when my bags are in her car?"

She walked into the attached bathroom, quickly shed herself of her bra and panties then stepped into the free-standing shower. She turned the handles and closed her eyes as the hot water streamed down on her. It felt so good against her skin, like she was washing all of her sins away.

All of a sudden the shower curtain was snatched back. Halleigh screamed in alarm as she tried to cover her naked body.

"Fuck is you?" a dude asked her.

"Do you fuckin' mind?" Halleigh screamed as she stepped out of the shower and searched for something to cover herself. "Get out!"

"This is my crib!" the dude responded. His eyes looked her up and down as a sexy smile crossed his lips. He reached over to his linen closet and grabbed a towel. "Here, cover yourself up, shorty."

She snatched the towel from his hands and wrapped it tightly around her body. Her hands were shaking, and he noticed how uncomfortable his presence made her.

"Now do you want to tell me who the hell you are and what you're doing in my house?" He made sure to calm down his tone because he could see that he'd frightened her. He followed her out of the bathroom and into his bedroom. He noticed that his bedsheets were wrinkled and looked back at her as he awaited an answer.

"I'm your sister's friend," Halleigh explained. "Tasha went out to get something to eat. I was sleeping, so she left without me."

The dude frowned his face and nodded his head.

"Okay, let's call her," he said, not believing a word she'd said. He pulled a BlackBerry off his waist and flipped through it until he found his sister's number.

"Yo, Tasha, what's good, baby girl?" he asked when Tasha answered the phone. "Where you at?"

Dripping wet, Halleigh stood with her arms folded across her chest, the cold draft making her nipples stand at attention.

"I'm around your way, big bro," Tasha replied. "Me and my girls came into town earlier. You weren't home, so we let ourselves in."

"Yeah, I see," he replied. His eyes scanned Halleigh's physique, and she rolled her eyes. "You could've at least called me to let me know y'all were in my spot. You know how I get down. What if I had something up in here I didn't want y'all to see?"

"Boy, please . . . you leave a damn key under your mat. Anybody in the city can see what you got. Besides, it ain't too much we haven't seen already. I'm shopping down on Canal Street. I'll be back in a couple hours," she replied.

Halleigh sighed loudly. "Can you please tell Tasha that my clothes and stuff are in her trunk?"

Tasha's brother ignored Halleigh's request and said, "All right, sis,

I'll holla at you when you get here." He disconnected the call and then said, "What's your name, ma?"

"Halleigh."

"I'm Maury," he said, walking over to his dresser. He opened a drawer and pulled out a white Prada button-up.

He tossed it on the bed. "You can put that on until Tasha gets back with your gear. I'll be in the kitchen."

"Thanks." Halleigh followed him to the bedroom door and closed it as he walked out. "I'm-a kick Tasha's ass for leaving me up in here by myself," she mumbled, putting on the shirt and buttoning it up. The material swallowed her tiny frame, and she rolled the sleeves up before she walked out of the room. She found Maury sitting in the living room, waiting for her. She stood in the doorway.

He looked up when he felt her presence behind him. "Make yourself comfortable. I ain't gon' bite you, ma." He patted the seat beside him. "Then again, looks like you didn't need me to tell you to make yourself comfortable at all, now did you?"

Halleigh rolled her eyes and took the seat next to him.

He smirked at how timid she seemed to be. "I don't know why you acting all shy now. You already slept in a nigga's bed and everything," he joked.

A smile graced her lips. "I didn't know that was your room. I wasn't trying to be all up in your space."

"I'm not complaining. A beautiful woman waiting at home for me ain't exactly what I would call a bad thing," he stated, admiring her lovely features.

Halleigh felt his imposing stare and pulled her legs in, tucking them underneath the oversized shirt. "Now here you go," she stated in exasperation. She could smell Maury's game from a mile away. His compliments came out as if they had been used a million times before.

"What? I'm not lying, ma," he stated, a mischievous grin on his face.

"Whatever." Halleigh stood because she didn't want to be so close to Maury. Men made her wary, and being alone in the house with someone she barely knew didn't sit too well with her. She didn't know what it was like to be at ease around a man. The only person she'd ever trusted was Malek.

"Did Tasha say when she'd be back? I'm not trying to put you out or nothing," she said.

Maury smiled. He could see that he made Halleigh nervous. "Why are you nervous?" he asked.

Halleigh frowned. "I'm not. I just don't like the fact that Tasha left me up in here knowing that I don't know you. I don't trust everybody, so this is kind of awkward for me."

"You can trust me, ma. I ain't gon' kidnap you or nothing." Maury

stood up and grabbed her hand, pulling her into the kitchen. "You ate?"

She shook her head and allowed him to lead her to a barstool that sat in front of the kitchen island. She sat down and watched him walk over to the refrigerator. She had to admit that Maury was fine. His baggy jeans and thuggish swagger made him sexy. He wore a red fitted hat, and a black Sean John hoodie. Halleigh's eyes followed his every move as he stood with one hand on his belt buckle.

He looked back at her and turned his mouth up in a half smile when he caught her staring. "What you want to eat, ma?" he asked.

"Whatever you have is fine." Halleigh tried to hide the fact that she was blushing.

Maury frowned as he stared into the refrigerator. "Let's see, I got old lettuce." He pulled out a brown head of lettuce and set it on the counter. "I got some Gatorade, some eggs, but I don't know how long these been in here."

"That's okay. I'm not that hungry after all," she stated, laughter in her voice.

"You want to go out and grab something?" he asked.

"I don't have any clothes to put on, thanks to your sister."

"Okay then, let's see." He rubbed his hands together and thought for a moment. "You eat Chinese?"

Halleigh nodded.

"We can have them deliver it, and I'll put in a movie," he offered.

"Yeah, that sounds good."

Maury retrieved a Chinese restaurant menu he had hanging on his refrigerator. After asking Halleigh what she liked, he placed an order for their food.

When the food arrived, Maury grabbed a blanket and two pillows from the closet. They sat on the floor watching movies and stuffing their faces. He noticed that Halleigh didn't say much, but she seemed to loosen up a little bit as they sat in each other's presence. They laughed at Martin Lawrence's *Runteldat,* and they seemed to be enjoying each other's company.

Before Maury knew it, it was almost midnight and Halleigh was asleep next to him. He picked her up, and as if she belonged in his arms, she rested her head on his chest as he carried her to his room. He didn't know why he didn't put her in one of the guest rooms. She just looked right in his bed, and since that was the room she'd chosen to sleep in earlier, he figured it was where she was most comfortable. After laying her down, he went back to the living room, plopped down on his couch, and finished watching the movies until he too went to sleep.

Chapter Fifty-three

M alek walked into his small apartment in Grand Blanc, a suburb just outside of Flint. He went straight to the back bedroom, where his safe was located. He emptied the contents of a brown paper bag into the safe. He'd just made a pick-up from the money spot. He placed the two stacks neatly on top of the others and stared at the stacks of money he'd accumulated working under Jamaica Joe. He would hit Joe off with his take at the end of the week, but nevertheless, he was still getting money. His life had changed so quickly over the past couple of years. He once was a role model in the community, but now he was a certified D-boy and running blocks.

Malek began to think about Halleigh. *I miss that girl so much. I can't believe she's out there trickin', though. That's not Halleigh. It's not her.* He walked into the living room and flopped down on his sectional sofa.

He thought about her constantly, but knew that the streets had a tight hold on her. Before Malek could even finish his thought, he heard a knock at his door. From the pattern of the knock, he instantly knew who it was. Also, he'd only let one person know where he lived, so he had a pretty good idea who was knocking. He got up to answer it, and when he opened the door, Joe was standing on the other side.

"What's good?" Malek slapped hands with Joe and walked into the back room to get Joe's cut. He'd planned to wait until the end of the week to break him off, but since he was there, might as well handle it now.

"What's going on, fam?" Joe asked as he walked in, closing the door behind him. He walked over to Malek's couch and took a seat. He looked around and chuckled. "Yo, you need to move into a bigger place. You getting money now. You gotta start enjoying it."

Malek, unlike other hustlers who were making paper, preferred to live modestly. What the hell did he need all that bling-bling for anyway? As far as he was concerned, all that flashy stuff did anyway was bring attention to him, which meant drama and trouble would soon follow. So he decided that he would stay low-key in the game. He'd seen enough black people get the things they wanted, yet end up begging for the things they needed. He wasn't going to fall into that trap.

Joe began setting up the chessboard that sat on Malek's coffee table.

A few minutes later, Malek emerged from the back room with a small duffle bag full of money, approximately $52,000. When he saw that Joe had set up the board, he immediately knew that Joe wanted to discuss something with him. Joe always played chess when he was

telling Malek something important. Malek placed the bag by Joe's feet and took a seat.

Joe stared at the board, deep in thought, contemplating his first move. He knew that this move ultimately laid the foundation for the last. "I've watched you become a man in such a short period of time. I think you're ready to step into the big leagues, fam." Joe moved his pawn up on the board.

"What you mean?" Malek asked, his eyes on the board, contemplating his first move as well.

"After the shit that went down with Tariq, and with the feds being on me and all"—Joe paused, observing the board—"I need to fall back for a minute. I need to get out of town to clear my head, ya know?"

Malek replied with a simple nod.

"With that said, I want to give you the opportunity of a lifetime." Joe made his move.

Malek's full attention was on Joe, not even realizing that it was his turn to make a move.

Jamaica Joe pulled out one of his pre-rolled blunts and lit it. He took a puff, exhaled as smoke rings rose above his head and then added, "I want to introduce you to my coke connect. I need someone to run the empire while I'm away, and you the only person I trust."

"Are you serious?" Malek knew that Joe was offering him a "key to the city," and he couldn't believe his ears. This kind of opportunity was every hustler's dream. He was offering him on a silver platter what Tariq tried to take. A smile covered Malek's face.

"I know you one hundred. I can't say that about most of the niggas in my circle. Tariq was proof that you can't trust niggas, feel me?"

"You sound like you ready to give the game up or something," Malek said, trying his best to read Joe, not sure whether he was taking a temporary break or if this was his way of weaning himself away from the game.

"I'm not giving up the game; I just want to take a little hiatus. Malek, I see a lot of myself in you. I see how you flip those bricks and run your blocks. You have cats twice your age respecting you, and you keep your whole crew happy. That's a hard task, family. You're a lot smarter than I was at nineteen, that's for sure. You got what it takes to be a great in this game. You just don't realize it yet. You got the 'shark complex,' just like I had."

"Shark complex?" Malek asked, totally puzzled.

Despite how anyone else on the streets saw Malek, he'd always pictured himself as just another member of the crew. Modest and humble in the game, he knew his place, which was actually why he was so respected. He didn't put on no act. What you saw with him was exactly what you got.

"Yeah, fam. A shark will die if it stops swimming. That's the way they

breathe, the way they keep living, Malek. They have to keep moving to survive. That's how I look at life. I have to keep moving, keep progressing and stay on my grind, or I'm no more." Joe took a puff of his blunt, held it in for a moment, and then exhaled. "Ever since I was your age, I been a hustler, but everyone knows that this game doesn't last forever. At some point the head man gets death or jail. I feel that my fate is nearing. I need to fall back and let the new breeds spread their wings.

"Malek, you are the future. You are a boss in the making. If I don't give you the opportunity, you are going to come for my spot and eventually have to kill me. You don't have to take the spot; I'ma give it to you." Joe looked into Malek's eyes. "I'm not going to make the same mistake with you that I made with Tariq."

Malek thought about what Jamaica Joe was doing. He was giving him something more valuable than money; he was giving him food for thought, and Malek was scraping the plate. What Joe was saying made a lot of sense to Malek, and he was soaking it in like a sponge. He was about to come into his own.

Jamaica Joe and Malek rode down Interstate 75 on their way to meet Joe's cocaine connect. Canada, just north of Detroit and only an hour and a half away from Flint, was their destination. Since the U.S. didn't allow planes from Colombia to land in the country, drug traffickers usually did business through Canada, so there was a lot of drug trafficking going on across the border.

Joe had been preparing Malek for this trip all week. He broke the game down to him and told him how the transactions went down. "I never ride dirty. I just go and negotiate the amount and price and then send a mule up to get the weight."

"So you drive all the way to Canada just to talk? Why wouldn't you just call?"

"That's not how we move, family. Drug transactions 101—no phones. Phones'll get you bagged. Every conversation and negotiation is made face-to-face with us—that's how you do business. Look a man in the face and handle yours. You have to use every precaution in this game, Malek, because you never know if and when them alphabet boys, the FBI and the DEA, are listening," Joe said as he reached the U.S.-Canada bridge.

The bridge was the only thing that separated Detroit from Canada, so they were in Detroit one minute and in Canada the next. Joe drove his black Ford Excursion into the public park just off the bridge.

Malek looked around in confusion, wondering why they were stopping there. He then began to look around, checking out the surroundings. He noticed a group of men sitting under a chess pavilion, paired off at various tables.

"This is where you find Fredro," Joe said, referring to his coke connect. He stepped out of the truck, closely followed by Malek, and they approached the pavilion.

Malek looked at the group of men they were walking up on, trying to guess which one might be Fredro. To Malek's surprise, Joe walked right past the group of men and approached the bench next to a raggedy-looking man wearing a dingy fishing hat. A slim-built African-American man in his fifties with a full beard, he was pulling bread crumbs out of his pocket and tossing them to the birds. With the name Fredro, Malek was expecting an Italian, a Latino, or something—not a black man.

"Fredro, good afternoon," Joe said as he took a seat next to him.

"Good afternoon," Fredro replied in a deep, raspy voice, without taking his eyes off the pigeons that flocked to his crumbs.

"I want you to meet Malek. He is my man I was telling you about."

Malek stepped up into Fredro's view. "Nice to meet you," Malek said as he extended his hand.

Fredro shook Malek's hand and gave him a small grin. "I've heard a lot about you, Malek. I hear you're the future." Fredro threw another handful of crumbs.

Malek smiled and then glanced at Joe. "Oh, is that what they're saying?"

Joe began to discuss business with Fredro. "I need you to introduce me to some of your girls."

"How many?" Fredro asked, continuing to toss the breadcrumbs.

"I'm having a party. I need twenty of them."

"Twenty girls? That's a lot of girls, Joe."

"Well, my man Malek over here, he runs through them, feel me?"

"Yeah, I hear you."

"How old are they?" Joe asked, referring to the kilo price.

"They are all twenty-two. They're the best showgirls in the business," Fredro replied, still focusing on the birds before his feet.

"I'll send for them tomorrow night."

"Good," Fredro replied with a wink.

To the trained ear, a major drug deal had just gone down. Malek smiled at how they had just negotiated drug prices and quantity without mentioning any drugs. Jamaica Joe had schooled Malek about always talking indirectly to avoid incriminating himself. Malek was witnessing professionals at work.

"Fredro, like I was telling you, I'm taking a small vacation. My man Malek is going to be coming to see you in my place." Jamaica Joe nodded his head at Malek. "This li'l nigga is one hundred percent."

Fredro's facial expression immediately changed as he stood up and

began to walk toward the lake. He was in obvious discomfort from Joe's news. Fredro had been pushing weight since the '80s and didn't like new people.

Jamaica Joe could read Fredro's mind. He whispered to Malek, "I'll be right back." Joe got up and went to catch up to Fredro.

Malek watched as the two men conversed in front of the lake. He couldn't make out what they were saying, but he was pretty confident about what they were discussing.

Malek, too, could read the look on Fredro's face, but he knew he could prove himself if given the chance. "This nigga got to let me in," Malek whispered as he continued to eye the two men.

Just as he finished his thought, the men shook hands, and Joe headed back toward Malek. Jamaica Joe approached Malek and whispered, "You're in," as he brushed past him and headed back to his truck.

Malek couldn't help but smile. He had just achieved what D-boys around the country dreamed about. He was connected.

Chapter Fifty-four

Two days after Jamaica Joe and Malek met with Fredro, Joe organized a meeting with his whole North Side crew to announce his absence, and also to introduce Malek as the head of the operations. He knew that he would ruffle some feathers with his street lieutenants by putting a nineteen-year-old at the boss position, but he had more confidence in Malek than any other worker.

Jamaica Joe sat at the head of the table in the back of one of the many businesses he owned, waiting to start. He watched Malek and observed his demeanor. *That li'l nigga right there is built for the game,* he thought as he lit a blunt.

Joe took his time before addressing his crew. Once he was ready, he stood up with Malek next to him. "As you all know, I'm taking a little break from the game. Before anybody gets it twisted, no, I ain't leaving the game. It's just like I said—I'm gon' fall back for a minute."

Joe scanned the room, looking everyone dead in the eyes to make sure they all got the point. The last thing he wanted was some false

rumor floating around about him being out of the game. Niggas still needed to know that he ran the North Side.

"Everything will be the same," he informed them, "and business will continue as usual. The rules of the game have not changed. The only thing that will be different is that from now on"—He looked over at Malek like a proud father—"you'll put all your orders in with Malek. He will be filling in for me for a while."

The mood of the room changed suddenly with Joe's announcement. You could see the skepticism in the hustlers' faces upon hearing that Malek would now be the head man. Everyone in the room expected Tariq to be next in command, but they didn't know that he was no longer breathing.

Rumors were flying about Tariq's sudden disappearance, though. Some were saying that he ran off to New York or somewhere with Jamaica Joe's money to start his own crew. Some were saying that he got caught up in a bad run.

The cops hadn't found his body yet, so Joe decided to just let the rumors fly. He didn't have anything to gain by slandering Tariq's name and letting everyone know that he was a snake.

Looking back on the situation, Joe was man enough to take partial blame for Tariq's betrayal. He figured that Tariq had felt his own loyalty to Joe had already been betrayed when Joe brought Malek in the game. So Joe felt that he at least owed Tariq that much, to just let the nigga die without spittin' venom. Still, he didn't condone Tariq's acts and would send him to his death all over again if he had to.

Malek took the silence for what it was—doubt. Although usually laid-back and quiet, if he was gonna be in charge, some things needed to change. He needed to let these cats know that he could handle the position. "I see how niggas looking at me . . . like I can't handle this position, but I'ma tell y'all like this"—Malek pulled out his gun—"Take silver or take lead, straight the fuck up!"

Jamaica Joe smiled as he witnessed Malek begin to implement the tactics he'd broken down to him on how to run an organization. He was telling them to take silver (get money with him) or take lead (take his bullets).

Malek continued, "So you have two options. You can leave right now and become my enemy"—He scoped out every soldier in the room with an intense look in his eyes—"or you can stay and get money with me. Honestly, I'm cool with either. Choose one." Once again, Malek scanned the room, individually looking each hustler in his face.

Joe looked in Malek's eyes and saw sincerity. Malek wasn't saying something just to be saying it. He was ready to get at any nigga who went against the grain. At that moment, Joe knew he'd made the right decision in handing the operation over to him temporarily.

Nobody in the room moved as a brief moment of silence took place. The torch had just been passed.

Finally, Malek broke the silence and said, "Okay, let's get it then." He reached under the table and grabbed the oversized duffle bag, plopped it on the table, and opened it up. Inside the bag was twenty kilos of pure "unsteppedon" cocaine. Malek began to distribute the weight to the hustlers for them to supply their sections of the North Side.

Once everyone left, only Joe and Malek sat at the table. Joe told his protégé, "Malek, this is a different game now. You are the man."

"I'm ready," Malek assured him, chin up and chest poked out.

Joe admired how Malek immediately put on the full armor of boss status, attitude and all. "I know you are, fam, but there are a lot of rules to this shit, and each one must be followed with precision. The last thing you need is for any mu'fucka to catch you slippin', 'cause, re-member, there's always gon' be another nigga out there who wants your spot."

Malek nodded his head and listened closely as Joe gave him the game.

"With your new position, there'll be new responsibilities. You can't show weakness at all. Weakness will get you killed. Never let a nigga slide with anything. If you gotta put yo murder game down, then so be it. Remember one thing—Fear is much more powerful than love. If the streets love you, they could use that love to eventually sabotage you. Love never lasts forever. The streets build you up only to bring you down. But fear"—Joe took a puff from his blunt, which had burned on its own more than he'd smoked on it—"fear lasts forever."

Malek listened to Joe and was surprised at how Joe had the streets down to a science. He spoke on the streets as if he were Socrates dis-cussing psychology.

For the next hour, Joe gave Malek a crash course on being a king-pin. He explained to Malek that it was his time, and informed him about the big birthday bash/farewell party he was going to throw.

"I want to celebrate with the city before my departure, ya dig?" Joe said as he finished up his blunt and conversation with Malek.

Chapter Fifty-five

Tasha awoke and went to her brother's room. She opened the door and noticed that Halleigh was still sleeping in his bed. *What the hell is she still doing in Maury's bed?* She was sure that by now Halleigh would have figured out that the room she'd been playing Goldilocks in was her brother's room, and copped one of the other rooms, but there Halleigh lay, sound asleep. Tasha shook her head and turned to leave, but found Mimi standing behind her, peering over her shoulder. "What are we looking at?" "Nothing. I was just checking to see if Hal was still asleep. Come on, let's go get some food." They walked into the kitchen to find Maury coming into the house with bags in his hands. "Maury!" Tasha yelled excitedly as she ran to hug him.

"Tasha, hold up, before you make me drop my food," he stated as he set the bags down on the countertop. He then turned around and hugged his sister warmly. "Why you didn't let me know you were coming to town?"

"I didn't even know I was coming. It was spur-of-the-moment, so I decided to surprise you."

"Umm-hmm." Mimi cleared her throat loudly as she eyed the sexy man before her. *Tasha ain't tell me her brother was so damn fine.* She put on her game face and stood sexily in the stretch pants and camisole she'd worn to bed.

"Oh yeah, this is my girl, Mimi. Mimi, this is my brother, Maury."

Maury licked his lips and gave Mimi a head nod. He'd already peeped the way she was checking for him when he first walked in. "What up, ma? It's nice to meet you," he said with a smile.

"It's nice to meet you too," Mimi replied sweetly.

Tasha rolled her eyes. She knew that Mimi was attracted to her brother when she heard her "get-'em" voice.

"You've already met Halleigh," Tasha interjected before Mimi could spark a conversation. She added, "And why did you sleep on your couch last night?"

"Because shorty stole my room," Maury replied with a sexy grin. He pulled two containers of food from a bag.

"You bought us breakfast?" Tasha asked.

"Nah, sis, you know your way around town, baby. This is for me," he said, backpedaling out of the room.

Tasha frowned when she noticed he had two boxes.

"Well, who is that other one for?" she asked.

"This is for your girl. Since y'all left her on 'stuck' last night, I decided to buy her breakfast," Maury replied.

"Uh-huh." Tasha knew that Halleigh must have worked her magic on Maury, because his nose was wide open. She shook her head and watched him walk out of the room. "Oh yeah, Maury, I need to talk to you about something. It's important, so make some time for me today!" she yelled.

"A'ight, I hear you!" he hollered back.

When he was out of earshot, Mimi tapped Tasha's arm. "What the hell was that all about? He's buying her breakfast and shit, like they fucked last night."

Tasha could hear the jealousy in Mimi's voice. She'd peeped Mimi eye-fucking her brother too and knew that Mimi had her eyes set on a prize.

"You know Hal don't even get down like that. It's nothing. I'm sure it's nothing at all."

Good, Mimi thought, *'cause a bitch like me sure can make something out of nothing.*

Maury knocked on the bedroom door lightly. He didn't want to wake Halleigh if she wasn't already up, but he entered the room anyway when he didn't receive an answer. He walked near the side of the bed and placed the food on the nightstand.

"Yo, shorty, wake up," he whispered, nudging her shoulder gently.

Halleigh heard the male voice, and in her head she imagined that it was Manolo. She'd just had a nightmare that Manolo was on top of her, smothering her with his body, his hand over her mouth as she tried to scream for him to stop. In her nightmare, Manolo was raping her, and had been, every morning, to teach her obedience. Maury's voice had managed to blend into her nightmare.

"Your food is gon' get cold," Maury said, shaking her. "Wake up."

Halleigh slowly opened her eyes, and a feeling of unfamiliarity crept into her heart. She felt a pair of strong hands on her neck, and she immediately jumped up, thinking that it was Manolo touching her.

"Stop it! Get off of me! Manolo, please stop! Don't touch me!" She scrambled out of bed and peered frightfully at Maury.

"Whoa! Calm down, Halleigh. You're okay. It's just me," Maury said in a low, soothing tone.

Halleigh looked around slowly and began to realize where she was. This was one of the first mornings she was able to wake up without worrying about Manolo's treacherous ways. "He's gone," she whispered as she collapsed onto the bed and put her face in her hands. "He can't hurt you anymore," she told herself as her tears came unwillingly.

Maury didn't know who "he" was, but he knew that whoever Halleigh was referring to had terrified her to the breaking point. He sat beside her. "You're good, ma. Ain't nobody gon' hurt you." He wrapped his arms around her.

Halleigh rested in his arms for a few minutes. It felt so safe and re-

assuring. There was only one pair of arms that ever felt like that around her—Malek's. Halleigh closed her eyes and envisioned Malek there rescuing her from the horrible life she'd been living. She never wanted him to let her go.

Halleigh put her arms around Maury and pulled him closer to her. *Oh, Malek,* she thought as she pressed her face against him. Just then she looked up and saw Maury staring down at her. She quickly pulled away from him and walked into the bathroom and closed the door behind her, leaving a confused Maury on the bed.

As she began to whimper tears filled Halleigh's eyes. "He can't hurt you anymore," she told herself. "You run your own shit now. Your life is in your hands, and you won't allow anyone to make you feel powerless again."

Halleigh got a piece of tissue from the toilet paper roll and wiped the last tear from her face, promising herself that she would stay strong. She needed to take control of her life, and she decided that today was the day she would start and never look back again.

She splashed cold water on her face, dried her hands, and then walked back out into the bedroom. Maury was still sitting on the bed. Halleigh saw that he had breakfast spread out on a small tray for her.

"I didn't know what you wanted," Maury said to Halleigh as he nodded toward the spread, "so I got you a little bit of everything."

Halleigh gave Maury a smile that said, "Thank you." She then lowered her head. She was sure that he would want an explanation for what he'd just witnessed from her a few minutes ago, but to her surprise, he didn't mention it. She was grateful for that as she stood there looking down at the food, wondering why he was being so nice to her. Nobody was kind for no reason, not at first anyway. They always wanted something. Halleigh wondered just what it was Maury wanted from her.

"Come here," Maury stated. He got up, walked toward Halleigh and grabbed her hand. "What's wrong? Never seen sausage and pancakes before?" Maury tried to lighten the awkward mood.

"Yeah." Halleigh nodded. "But what's it for?" she asked as she followed him toward the bed.

"What do you mean, what is it for? For you to eat." He pulled back the plush comforter for her.

She sat down, and he put some pillows behind her back.

"I mean, what's up with you bringing me breakfast in bed?"

He placed the breakfast tray on her lap. "Just enjoy it, shorty, but don't get used to it. I don't do this for everybody, you know, but you deserve it for putting up with me and my gangster movies last night."

Halleigh looked around the room. "Well, how did I even get in this bed last night?" she asked, knowing that he had to have carried her to bed. She couldn't help but appreciate the gesture. If she had been at

another point in her life, Tasha's brother could have easily had her open, but she could barely keep Malek off her mind, so she knew she didn't have the energy to spark something with Maury.

"I brought you in here after you passed out on me."

Her eyebrows rose inquisitively. "And where did you sleep?"

Maury laughed out loud at her facial expression. "Chill out, shorty. I crashed on the couch."

"Well, thank you for the breakfast, Maury, and for sharing your bed with me."

"You don't have to thank me, Halleigh." Maury grabbed the bag with his own food and left the room.

Mimi waited near the room she'd slept in until she saw Maury emerge from the room where Halleigh was. She was now dressed in tight jeans that showed off her apple bottom. She wore no bra, so her nipples peered at Maury through her thin halter top.

"Hey, Maury," she stated as he walked toward her. She grabbed his hand and stopped him from moving past her. She walked up close to him and blatantly rubbed her body against him.

"What up, ma?" He looked her up and down.

Mimi's body was on point, and he felt his manhood jump in excitement, but he had to check himself. This was one of his sister's peoples. Besides, he knew Mimi's type. She was out for a quick-dick fix. On top of that, he was almost certain that it would cost him some paper in the end, whether it was flat-out cash or an afternoon shopping spree. Mimi's type came with a price. She could never be wifey. Like any man, he'd keep his options open, but for now, he'd have to put her on reserve.

"You tell me what's up," Mimi said seductively. She could see that Maury's eyes were focused on her breasts.

"You want to touch?" she ran her tongue across her front teeth . . . slowly.

By now, Maury's dick was rock-hard, and her offer was tempting, but he shook his head. "Nah, ma, maybe some other time."

He tried to walk away, but Mimi pulled him back toward her and into the room.

"What you doing, ma?" he asked. His breath caught in his throat as he put his hands in the air to avoid touching her.

Mimi didn't answer, but she grabbed his hands and put them on her breasts.

"What, what you doing, girl?" Maury said, attempting to push her away.

Mimi knew damn well that Maury could overpower her any day of the week. If he really wanted her to back up off of him, he'd be using much more force than he was. She put her hands on top of Maury's and began directing them to caress her. She let out a soft moan.

Eventually, Maury couldn't help himself. He began massaging Mimi's D-cups without her assistance, circling his thumbs around her stiff nipples.

"Ummm," Mimi moaned in his ear. "I knew you wanted to touch them." Mimi took one of Maury's hands, removed it from her breast, and put it up her shirt.

"Damn, girl," Maury let slip out. He didn't want Mimi to know that he was that into it, but now the cat was out of the bag. Maury closed the bedroom door, lifted her shirt, and picked her up so that he could bury his head in her chest.

One by one, back and forth, forth and back, Maury plucked at Mimi's nipples with his tongue. Her nipples tasted like honey as he licked all over them, sucking them aggressively.

She reached down and felt his manhood and then pushed him against the door.

"Damn," he whispered.

Mimi got down on her knees while unzipping Maury's jeans. She released his penis from his pants and put it in her mouth. She didn't play with it or hesitate, but deep-throated him with passion as she cupped his balls in her soft hands.

"Oh shit," he stated as he gripped the back of her head and ground his hips into her as if he were fucking her pussy. He didn't want to fuck with Mimi like that, not now, but her seduction was irresistible as he looked down at his dick disappearing over and over again into her mouth.

Fuck what you've read, Superhead didn't have shit on Mimi, as far as Maury was concerned.

Mimi moved from his dick to his balls, pleasing him with her tongue, while she massaged her hand up and down his shaft.

Tingles shot from Maury's toes to his upper spine, and he curled his toes in delight.

Mimi had mastered the art of sucking dick a long time ago and was giving Maury her all.

Maury didn't know what it was that Mimi wanted out of all this when all was said and done, but any broad who could suck dick like a champ the way Mimi was doing deserved whatever the fuck she wanted.

"I'm about to nut, ma," he whispered. "Put it back in your mouth," he instructed.

Mimi followed his orders, and thirty seconds later, he let off.

"Ughh!" he moaned as his body jerked. Maury had expected Mimi to let his semen drip to the floor, but to his surprise, she swallowed every ounce of him and licked his dick clean before tucking it back into his pants where it belonged.

Mimi smiled proudly as she stood back to her feet.

She attempted to kiss him on the lips, but he discreetly turned his head, and she caught his cheek. *I don't know where this bitch mouth been,* he thought. He had to give her credit, though—she had a mean head game.

"You gon' get with me?" Mimi asked him.

"Yeah, I'll get with you," he lied. He instantly began to regret fucking around with Mimi. He knew he had no intention of getting to know her better, and he was hoping that he hadn't led her on. *Fuck it! We both grown as hell. Bitch shouldn't have put herself out there like that if she doesn't want a nigga to take advantage.*

He opened the door and headed to the living room to go eat his food, but then he decided that he wanted to take a shower. He'd just have to warm his food up in the microwave afterward. Maury headed toward his room and knocked, slowly pushing it open.

Halleigh smiled when she saw him poke his head in first and then step into the room.

Upon seeing her pretty, innocent-like smile, Maury's conscience immediately began to fuck with him. He was trying to get at Halleigh, yet he'd just let one of her best friends suck his dick. He decided then and there that he would keep Mimi at arm's length and try to get close to Halleigh, hoping he hadn't completely destroyed his chances.

"I need to get in here," he stated.

"It's your room." Halleigh shrugged as she chewed up the forkful of pancakes she'd just stuffed in her mouth. "Go ahead and handle your business. I need to go kick Tasha's ass anyway for not coming back for me yesterday like she said she would." Halleigh bit a piece of sausage and then hopped out of the bed and gathered up the mess she'd made. She walked toward the door, but before leaving the room she turned and said, "Maury?"

"What's good, shorty?" he replied as he looked at Halleigh, who immediately put her head down.

"Thank you for not pushing the issue this morning about how I acted and all, you know, when you came to bring me my food. I know I spazzed out on you. I'm sorry."

"It's not my place to push you to do or say anything that you don't feel comfortable with. When and if you're ready to talk, I would like to know more about you, including the reason why you spazzed out, and why you never look me in the eye when I talk to you."

Halleigh nodded and replied, "Maybe one day we can kick it, just not today." She left the room in search of Tasha and found her sitting on the living room couch, channel-surfing.

Halleigh plopped down beside Tasha. "What happened to you yesterday?"

"Girl, you know how Mimi is. Act like she ain't never been nowhere in her life," Tasha said, rolling her eyes. "Mimi's ass was dragging me

all over town. We did the whole tourist thing down on Canal, buying all the knockoff shit. Then we stopped off in this little spot and had a couple drinks. By the time we made it back to the house, it was late. Sorry, girl. We wasn't trying to leave you here by yourself."

"It's nothing. I was too tired to be going out anyway. Plus, your brother hooked me up with some dinner last night." Halleigh turned to face Tasha. "You know, your brother is real chill. I like him."

"What? You talking about another nigga besides that lame Malek?"

"I didn't mean I *liked* him liked him. I just meant that he's cool people, is all."

Halleigh's mood immediately turned somber, and Tasha regretted letting the words come from her mouth. "I'm sorry, Hal. I wasn't thinking."

"It's all right. I'm good." Halleigh leaned back against the couch and let out a deep sigh, her mind filled with thoughts of Malek. "I do miss him, though, Tasha," she confessed. "I just can't ever be down with him again. I mean, how could he be fucking with the niggas that raped me? Why would he do that to me?" Halleigh asked, her voice low. "Is this his way of paying me back for hooking up with Manolo? I mean, I know it hurts him that I ended up doing what I do for a living—"

"Stop it right there," Tasha said, sitting up on the couch and facing Halleigh. "What you *used* to do. You are not a Manolo Mami anymore. That shit's in the past, do you hear me?"

"Yeah." Halleigh nodded as Tasha relaxed herself back on the couch. "But even so, why would Malek do that to me?"

"I don't know, Hal. I don't know. But fuck him! You don't need that type of drama in your life. You have sixty-five hundred dollars to start a new life with, and once I talk to Maury about these bricks, you gon' have way more than that. Manolo's gone, fuck Malek. It's all about us."

"I know," Halleigh replied. "It is about us now, ain't it?" she said with a weak smile.

"Now on to more important things. What did you do to my brother?" Tasha quizzed excitedly.

Halleigh pulled back with a puzzled look on her face. "What are you talking 'bout? I ain't do nothing. He's just cool peoples, that's all. We're cool."

"Just cool, huh. Got my cheap-ass brother buying you dinner and breakfast and shit. The same brother who made me pay his ass back if I borrowed a nickel from him to buy penny candy, and you say, 'Just cool'? Humpf."

"Girl, I'm serious. Nothing happened," Halleigh assured her, nudging her on the arm playfully. "Unless you call me falling asleep something."

"Whatever. I know you lying, but that's okay," Tasha replied. "It's

time to handle this business anyway." Tasha threw the remote down on the couch and got up. "Where is Maury?"

"He's in his room, eating or getting something," Halleigh replied. "I'm not sure, but he was in his room when I left out of there."

Tasha shot Halleigh a mischievous look. "Mm-hmm, and nothing happened."

Halleigh laughed. "Will you cut it out already?"

Tasha walked toward the hallway and called out, "Mimi, bring the bag out here!" and then returned to the couch next to Halleigh.

Mimi came waltzing in the room with a smug expression on her face as she carried the bag in her hand. She handed it off to Tasha and sat down in the chair across from her friends.

Tasha took the kilos of cocaine out of the bag and spread it out across the table. "Look, let me do all the talking, a'ight?"

"Okay," Mimi responded, and Halleigh just nodded her head in agreement.

"Hal, go grab Maury," Tasha said.

Halleigh got up and headed down the hallway toward the back of the house. She knocked on his bedroom door.

"It's open," he yelled.

Halleigh opened the door to find Maury standing in sweatpants with no shirt on, his upper body still wet from his shower. Her eyes admired his chiseled chest and abs for a quick second.

He smirked. "What's up, shorty?"

"Um, we need to talk to you in the living room," Halleigh said, shaking her head and diverting her eyes from his body.

Maury grabbed his shirt from the bed and started walking toward Halleigh. As he approached her, he noticed that she began to tense up. As a matter of fact, it seemed as though every time he got near her she tensed up.

Malek had been the only man ever to cause this type of feeling to come over her, so Halleigh didn't know what to make of it. The closer Maury got to her, the more chills ran up her body, causing her to tremble slightly. She quickly allowed her eyes to roam from Maury's perfect physique down to the floor.

By that time, Maury was all up in her personal space, placing his index finger underneath her chin and lifting her head so that she was now face to face with him.

"I can't see this pretty face of yours if you're looking down at your feet all the time," he whispered.

Halleigh couldn't help but crack a smile as she looked into his eyes. "Is this better?" she asked with a corny grin.

He laughed and replied, "Yeah, that's better." He slipped his shirt over his head, keeping his eyes glued on her the entire time. He then reached out his arm and stated, "Go ahead, I'm following you."

Maury put his hand on the small of Halleigh's back as she walked in front of him. It was a slight gesture of affection that Halleigh didn't even really make notice of, but Mimi saw it as soon as they came into clear view.

What the fuck? Mimi's insides began to boil, she was so angry. She was the one who had just given up the goodies to Maury, been on her knees, pleasing this fool, and now he wanted to spit in her face by toting Halleigh into the room like she was Beyoncé and Mimi was Kelly or, even worse, Michelle.

She looked over at Tasha to see if she noticed it, but Tasha didn't seem to be fazed. Mimi straightened her shoulders with confidence, checked herself out, and refocused on the task at hand.

When Maury noticed his table filled with cocaine, he stopped dead in his tracks. "Fuck you get this from?" he asked, looking directly at Tasha.

"Manolo," Tasha replied.

"Manolo?" It was the same name he'd heard Halleigh say earlier when she panicked in his room. His brow creased in disapproval. He had a feeling that his sister had not come by the product on good terms with the original owner. "Who the fuck is Manolo, and what do his bricks got to do with me?"

"They're not his bricks anymore," Tasha answered. "They're ours." Tasha looked to Mimi and Halleigh.

"Yeah," Mimi said, "and we need you to get these off for us."

Maury looked at Mimi as if she were crazy, but Tasha quickly cut in. "Of course, we'll give you a cut, Maury. I know better than to ask you to work for free."

Maury looked at Halleigh, who was still standing by his side, and shook his head. He would never have guessed she was in the dope game. Her looks were deceiving, and he made a mental note of that.

"How'd you get 'em, Tash?" Maury asked, ready to get to the bottom of things. Whenever someone wanted to come out on top, there had to be a bottom somewhere. He was determined to find out just what it was, before getting himself involved.

Tasha didn't want to inform her brother of all the details surrounding how she'd come to gain possession of the bricks, but she didn't want him going in blind, setting himself up for the okey-doke. Tasha took a deep breath and then started. "I set the nigga up to get caught with the dope and then cut a deal with the arresting officer."

"You did what?" Maury asked, enraged. "You know the game, baby! Fuck is you doing?" He shook his head from side to side. "Fuck was you thinking? You out in the Midwest by yourself, but you want to stick a nigga for his bricks? If the nigga would have come back at you, what was gon' happen then?"

"I'm not even trying to hear all that you talking," Tasha said, folding

her arms like a pretzel, poking out her lips, and then looking away. She didn't want to hear what baby bro had to say because she knew it wasn't going to be anything other than what she already knew to be the truth. "Look, I didn't have a choice, Maury!" Tasha said in her own defense, hoping to get her brother to understand.

Maury just stood there shaking his head at his sister's stupidity.

"Don't look at me like that, nigga," Tasha spat. "By hook or by crook is what you always taught me, so don't be frowning your shits up at me now! And Manolo ain't coming back at me, 'cause his ass is sitting in somebody's jail cell right now!" Tasha yelled.

"I don't even know you right now, Tash. I know you know better. I know you know. And then you pull Charlie's Angels into your mess with you," he said, referring to Mimi and Halleigh.

The girls all just stood there in silence, waiting for Maury to finish up his rant so that they could hear his final word—was he going to help them unload the bricks or not?

Maury sighed and covered his face with his hands. He thought for a moment and then slid his hands down his face. "Look, sis, let me clear my head before I say some shit that I might regret," he said as he turned and left the room.

"Maury!" she called, but her voice was matched by the sound of a slamming door.

"Fuck is his problem?" Mimi asked. "He shouldn't be worried about how we got 'em. The point is, they sitting on his living room table. Is he gon' help us get this cash or not?"

"I don't know what he's going to do." Tasha threw her arms up in the air and allowed them to collapse to her side in defeat. "I can't even talk to him right now. I don't know what I was thinking. He never listens to me anyway. For some reason he's always thought that he was the oldest and could tell me what the fuck to do and how to do it."

Tasha thought back to their childhood and how people used to just assume he was the oldest because of the way he always had his stuff together. Tasha was just the opposite. When an idea came into her mind, she just did it and hoped for the best. It was pretty much the same reasoning she used in setting up Manolo. As far as she was concerned, her instincts had not failed her yet, so she was going to keep sticking to them, no matter how foolish her brother thought they were.

"Well, time is money," Mimi spat. "Either your brother is in, or he ain't. And if he ain't, time is wasting. We need to move on to someone who will help us. Or like the old saying goes, if we want the shit done right, maybe we need to do it our damn selves."

"You're right, Mimi. Time is money, and time is a-wasting, but I can't talk to him right now. He's fired up, so I know some slick shit is going to come out of his mouth, and in turn, something slick is going to

come out of my mouth. That's the story of me and my brother's life."
Tasha then had a sudden thought. "Halleigh, you go talk to him."

"Me? Why the hell I got to talk to him? He's *your* brother." The last
thing Halleigh wanted was to have to get close to Maury again. Be-
sides, she didn't know what to say.

"Exactly. He ain't gon' do nothing but yell at me and tell me how
disappointed he is for me snitching. But, hell, he likes you. He
brought you breakfast in bed, didn't he? So, who knows? He might ac-
tually listen to you. And if you ain't learned nothing else in these last
couple of years, it's the power of your pussy."

"Oh, hell no!" Halleigh started. "If you think I'm gonna—"

"That's not what I'm trying to say, Hal," Tasha told her. "Come on,
you know me better than that. I'm not telling you to sleep with him
just to get him to help us. I'm just saying that he likes you, and be-
cause he likes you, he'll probably listen to you. Okay?"

Halleigh thought for a minute and then nodded her head. "All right.
You've had my back on more than one occasion," Halleigh told Tasha.
"This is the least I can do."

"Thanks, Hal," Tasha said.

Halleigh headed back to Maury's room.

She knocked, but didn't wait for him to invite her in before she
opened the door and stepped into the room. "Can we talk?" Halleigh
asked Maury, who was lying on his bed, his hands behind his head.

He nodded, giving her the okay.

Halleigh closed the door behind her, walked over, and sat down on
his bed.

"What up?" he asked.

"I need to tell you something."

"Look, I don't want to hear all the details of this bullshit y'all done
let my sister talk y'all into."

"No, wait. It's not about that," Halleigh told him.

"Then what's it about?"

"It's about, it's about me. Well, really about all of us," Halleigh told
him. "I know you don't know everything there is to know about the
life the three of us were living in Flint. I know because it's something
that Tasha was too ashamed to tell you herself." Halleigh couldn't be-
lieve that she was getting ready to share her troubles with Maury,
whom she'd known less than forty-eight hours. She paused and took a
deep breath.

"I'm listening," he said, urging her to continue.

"Have you ever heard of Malek Johnson?"

Without even having to think about it, Maury replied, "Yeah, I heard
of dude. That nigga should have been the next LeBron James, but then
he turned around and got on some stupid shit." Maury shook his

head. "What a waste. He was supposed to be the number one draft pick, what was it, about two years ago, right?"

Halleigh closed her eyes and nodded.

"Well, he is my ex-boyfriend. We were supposed to get married right after the draft, but we never made it that far."

"It's a shame. He could have had millions, and he jeopardized it all for some chump change he pulled from a petty robbery. I don't care if they did find him not guilty. Everybody knows that nigga did that shit. He just happened to have the best criminal lawyer money could buy. Hell, if you ask me, they even paid for that witness he—"

"Look, that's not where I'm trying to go with all this," Halleigh said, putting her hand up to halt Maury's words. She proceeded to explain her life from the night she got raped up until they arrived at Maury's house.

Maury couldn't believe all of the things she'd been through. She told him how Manolo had starved her for days, beat her mercilessly, and degraded her often. Halleigh told Maury how she was about to kill herself, until Tasha promised her a way out.

"Tasha would've never snitched on Manolo if she wasn't trying to help me," Halleigh explained.

Maury looked into Halleigh's eyes. Tears had begun to flow down her cheeks, and he wiped them away. Her story might have turned off most dudes, because they would view her as nothing more than a ho. But he viewed her as a survivor and immediately felt a connection to her that he'd never felt for any other chick in his life. Even though she was only nineteen and he was twenty-five, he was drawn to Halleigh. She had already lived well past her years. She had seen much and been through enough to last her a lifetime.

"So, y'all really need me to move those bricks for y'all, huh?" he asked, his tone revealing that his answer was going to be yes.

She nodded her head. "Yes, Maury, we really need you to do this for us." Halleigh grabbed his hands and held them in hers. For the first time, she wasn't shaking or nervous. Her future, her girls' futures, relied on Maury turning that dope into cash so that they could start life over, a life that didn't include having to sell their bodies.

"Please . . . I don't ever want to live that life again, and neither does your sister." Halleigh thought for a moment and decided to break the tension with a little joke. "Now, Mimi, on the other hand . . ."

Halleigh and Maury shared a slight chuckle.

Maury got serious again. He stared into Halleigh's eyes. This time Halleigh saw a strong passion in his eyes. That made her nervous.

Before she could turn her head away, Maury leaned into her, and she tensed up again. He shook his head and said, "I'm not Manolo, Halleigh. I won't hurt you."

He kissed her lips softly, and she kissed him gently, until she realized what she was doing. Then she quickly pulled away.

"Wait, Maury," she said as she wiped her hands across her lips. "I can't do this with you right now. I still have mixed emotions about Malek, and I'm still trying to find out who I am as a woman. I was seventeen when my childhood was taken from me, but I never knew how to be a woman. Now I can finally control my own life and I don't know what direction I need to go in. I have to find myself before I can give you anything," she said sadly.

"No, you don't, ma. You don't have to find yourself. You are who you are, and I'm willing to accept you for just that. And I don't want anything from you. If anything, I want to be the one to give you whatever it is that you need," he replied. He kissed her lips again and then said, "But I'll respect you as a woman and wait until you're ready." Maury knew Halleigh was special from the moment he'd first met her, but now after hearing her story, he felt she was even more special. He had to admit that he felt sorry for her, for the life she'd been forced to endure. Something inside of him just wanted to make up for all the wrong that had been done to her.

Halleigh wrapped her arms around him. "Thank you," she said. She stood to her feet and wiped her eyes.

"Send Tasha in here," Maury said.

"Okay," Halleigh replied as she turned to leave the room. Having a sudden thought, she turned back around and said, "Maury, about what I told you about how we worked for Manolo and all—"

"Don't worry," he said, cutting her off. "If Tasha wants to tell me, then I'll let her, but if not"—He put his finger over his lips, letting Halleigh know that it would be their little secret.

Halleigh smiled and then exited the room. She felt that it was Tasha's right to tell her brother the life she'd been living in Flint. When she walked back into the living room, Mimi was sitting on the living room couch and biting her nails impatiently, while Tasha was pacing back and forth.

Mimi was the first to spot Halleigh. "Well, what did he say?" she asked eagerly.

Tasha stopped pacing. "Is he going to help us or not?"

Halleigh just stood there looking at both girls, each with her own look of desperation covering her face. She sighed deeply and then stared down to the floor.

Both Tasha's and Mimi's shoulders slumped as they, too, sighed. Tasha threw her arms up in defeat and went to turn around, but before she could do so, Halleigh said, "He said yes!"

"What?" Tasha said, making sure she'd heard Halleigh right.

"He said yes. He'll do it," Halleigh replied. "Gotcha." Halleigh pointed to both of the girls and laughed.

"Girl," Tasha said, play-hitting Halleigh.

Mimi gave a sigh of relief. "Damn it, Hal, you almost made my heart stop. Don't play like that." Mimi put her hand over her heart and sat down on the couch.

"Sorry, girls. I couldn't resist," Halleigh said. She looked to Tasha. "Tash, he wants to speak with you."

Tasha playfully rolled her eyes at Halleigh and then gave her a little nudge as she passed by her, heading to her brother's room. Before completely exiting the room, Tasha turned to Halleigh. "What exactly did you say to him to get him to help us out?"

Halleigh looked down and began to stutter. "I–I, uh, you know, just told him some things about me, the life I was living with Manolo." Halleigh paused and looked up at Tasha. "And, you know, how badly we need his help and all."

Without Halleigh saying another word, Tasha figured that if Halleigh told Maury the lifestyle she was living with Manolo, then he'd probably already put two and two together and figured out that she'd been living the same lifestyle. Tasha simply gave Halleigh a look of understanding and then headed back toward Maury's bedroom.

Chills went up her spine as she thought about what her brother would think of her now. Would he look at her the same? How would he feel now, knowing that his sister, the one he was supposed to look up to, the one who was supposed to set an example for him, was a whore?

Now Tasha just wished she had told him a long time ago when she first got into the game, and gotten it over with. Now here she was, officially out of every aspect of the game, and yet she felt ashamed and dirty.

Up until just a few minutes ago, Tasha's brother thought she'd been living in Flint, working for a contract cleaning company. Tasha had told him that she was in charge of the employees. Seeing that she was in charge of all of the Manolo Mamis, she didn't feel as though she had completely lied to her brother. In addition to that, she knew that with her brother living in New York and her living in Flint, Michigan, he'd never find out the real deal. Nonetheless, the truth was out now, and she wasn't even the one to tell him.

A part of her wanted to be the one to tell her brother who she really was. Then there was another part of her that was glad Halleigh had removed the burden from her shoulders and had done it for her. So many times she'd wondered exactly how she would tell her brother that his sister was a whore. Now she didn't have to wonder any longer.

Tasha walked into Maury's bedroom and saw the pained look on his face, further confirmation that he knew the truth about his big sister.

"She told you, huh?" Tasha asked as she walked in and sat down beside Maury, dropping her head and staring down at her feet. She made

a mental note that as soon as everything was smoothed over and business was taken care of, she'd treat herself to a pedicure.

"Yeah, but why didn't you tell me?" he asked.

Tasha shrugged her shoulders. "I guess I was just embarrassed that I allowed myself to get in that situation. I wanted to tell you so many times, Maury. Believe me, I did. But then I didn't know how to. I mean, how does a girl tell her brother that her boss is really a pimp?"

Maury shook his head and gritted his teeth. "The nigga better hope he get jail time, because I'ma get at his ass if he don't. I can't believe he was pimping my sister."

"If it makes you feel any better, and I know it probably won't, but he hasn't pimped me in years. I started out turning tricks, but then . . ." Tasha stopped as she thought about the brutal attack from one of her johns that put her in retirement from hoeing. "But then Manolo realized that I'd make him more money being in charge of the other girls, keeping them in line and straight."

"So you were, what, a madam or some shit?"

"Yeah, something like that."

"So did you know how bad he was treating the girls?"

Tasha remained silent, which was enough to answer Maury's question.

"I mean, some of the shit Halleigh was telling me went down . . . what kind of man treats women like that?" He continued shaking his head as he thought of the life that Halleigh had led. "I can't believe that monster treated shorty like that."

Tasha did a double-take. "Shorty? What about me?" Tasha asked with mock envy as she punched her brother's shoulder.

"Yeah, and you too," he added before his mind wandered off again to thoughts of Halleigh.

Tasha just came right out and asked her brother, "You like her, don't you?"

Blushing with embarrassment, Maury straightened himself up and said, "That's not important. Let's focus on getting this money." He held his fist up in a pound.

Tasha smiled and met his fist with hers. It was a handshake they had done since they were kids, and she knew that it meant he was down for the cause.

Tasha and Maury sat and talked about him unloading the bricks for them. Even though Tasha hadn't been the one to tell her brother the truth about the life she had been living, she did bring him up to speed with some of the other happenings in Flint.

Maury thought New York was off the hook, but he was beyond intrigued by what occurred in a little city in the Midwest, of all places. Who knew? In his opinion, Flint sounded more gutter than New York, and from what he was hearing, there were a few cats out in Flint get-

ting money. He could definitely see the opportunity that was present-
ing itself.

Robbery was Maury's profession. It wasn't like he was on the up-
and-up in the life he was living either, but he had never kept it from his
sister and had always shared everything with her. That's just how close
they were, coming up. Heck, they used to use the same toothbrush
sometimes. No matter what Maury got into, though, Tasha was always
going to love him, the same way he still loved her.

Maury took the game of robbery to another level. It was a passion
he had perfected. He had to be one of the most ruthless and notorious
stick-up kids in New York City. He went from borough to borough,
holding cats up for their paper. Ski-masking was his method, and he
was living nice off his gains. Flint sounded like just the city for him. It
was small and unsuspecting, just the way he liked it. *Yeah, I'm
definitely about to see what Flint has to offer,* he thought as Tasha
finished up her tales about the city.

"'Spite what it sounds like, I do like Flint. Hell, my life is there."
Tasha looked down at the clothes she was wearing, which were just
some plain-Jane type of garments. She just grabbed what was easy
when she and the girls had left town. "Hell, all my damn clothes are
there too." She chuckled. "I worked too hard to just leave my shit for
them other hoes to cop." Tasha thought for a minute. "Besides, I was
thinking, the girls and I need to go back to Flint anyway."

"Why?" Maury asked.

"No one knows I set Manolo up, but if I just stay gone and shit, peo-
ple are going to put two and two together. So I'm going to tell the girls
that we need to go back just for a minute, so that we don't look so sus-
pect. If people ask where we were, we'll just tell them we were laying
low in a hotel somewhere, hiding from the cops." Tasha looked to
Maury for a reaction to her reasoning. "So, what do you think?"

"Look, sis, I see what you're saying. I agree but I can't let you go
back to Flint by yourself, not after the hot shit you just pulled. As far as
you know, that cop done turned on you by now. You could already be
looking suspect. On the other hand, no one may suspect a thing and
there might be more money to be made."

Maury looked off greedily. It was an expression Tasha had seen
many times before in Mimi's eyes.

"I know that look," Tasha told him. "What are you thinking, little
bro?"

"What I'm thinking is, that nigga Manolo probably got more than
one safe." He looked at Tasha. "You said you set him up at the club?
The police got him for his safe at the club?"

Tasha nodded.

"I'm sure that nigga got a safe at the crib."

Tasha hadn't really thought of that. She shrugged her shoulders.

"Yeah, if that nigga was a player in the game like you say he was, then I know he didn't stack all of his eggs in one basket. Bet you any amount of money that nigga got a stash where he lays his head."

"Maybe so, but right now, one bird in the hand is worth two in the bush. I'm trying to get paid off of the shit we got."

"All right, all right," Maury said, putting the idea of hitting up Manolo's crib on the back burner to simmer. "Tell you what, I'm going to get the bricks off here, and then in a couple days, we'll go back to Flint. I'd never forgive myself if some shit popped off and I could've prevented it from happening, so I'm gon' stick around your city for a while, just to make sure you're straight. Then if you decide you wanna roll back to the NY with me, you know you always got a place to rest your head."

Tasha nodded and reached out to hug her brother before she left the room. She was elated. In a couple of days, she would be twenty thousand dollars richer.

Chapter Fifty-six

The next day, Maury hit the block to get the bricks off. Although the drug trade wasn't really his line of work, he knew a couple cats from around the way who were looking to buy some work, and he blessed them with the weight for $15,000 per brick. Since the going rate in New York was at least twenty-three G's, niggas flocked to the price, and the eight bricks were gone in a matter of hours. His pockets were $120,000 heavier, and after he split it with Tasha and her crew, he'd still have sixty stacks all to himself.

He made his way back to the crib. When he arrived, he saw Halleigh sitting on his front stoop. He grabbed the duffle bag from his back seat, checked his hip to ensure that his pistol was in place, and his rearview mirror before exiting the Lexus IS. He knew word had probably gotten out that he had moved some weight, and he was sure that somebody saw him as an opportunity to get paid. He may have been the most ruthless stick-up kid in town, but he wasn't the only one. He knew the game. Had the shoe been on the other foot, he'd be waiting in the cut somewhere for his mark.

That was another reason why he knew it was a good idea to leave town and head to Flint with Tasha. He'd need to lay low. That way nig-

gas would think he went on vacation and blew the money somewhere. His trip to Flint would give his hood a chance to settle down and forget that he'd ever made the large transactions.

Maury approached Halleigh and, as he walked past her, motioned his head toward the house. "Come inside. I need to holla at you about something," he told her as he stepped into the house.

Halleigh followed behind him until they reached the kitchen. Mimi and Tasha were chilling in the living room, and Maury quickly gathered them up too. He poured the duffle bag full of money out onto the kitchen table.

"Damn!" Mimi exclaimed. She had never seen so much money in her life. She jumped up and down excitedly. "I'm about to cop me a new whip as soon as we get back to Flint. I know Pookie who runs that car lot over on—"

"Stop talking stupid, Mimi," Tasha said, cutting her off. "Ain't none of us copping anything extravagant. What we look like, going back home with new cars and shit? That would make us look suspect as hell. We didn't have it before, so we ain't about to get it now. At least until we figure out a front that would explain us coming into some money. Besides, I don't plan on making Flint home again permanently. We need to stick around just long enough to make sure our names are good. You never know when you might need a muthafucka again. If for some reason we were to make Flint home again, we want to make sure it's all good. You got that?"

Mimi shrugged, but in her mind, she was picturing a nice new candy apple red convertible.

"Go make sure the front door is locked," Tasha suddenly stated.

"I locked it," Maury told her.

"Go double check," Tasha insisted.

Mimi went and made sure the door was locked and then returned.

"This is a lot of money." Halleigh stared down at it in disbelief.

Manolo had made sure that she never saw more than a couple hundred dollars at a time. The less money he let the girls run around with, the more likely they were to be dependent upon him. In addition to that, he never gave the girls anymore than they'd need for their essentials. That way they couldn't stack up a nest egg to try to run off on him one day.

So, to Halleigh, having more than a hundred thousand in front of her was crazy. She knew that her life had just made a turn for the better as soon as Maury started dividing it up.

He took his cut first, which left the girls with $20,000 apiece.

"I can really start over with this much money," Halleigh stated happily.

Maury noticed her mood had changed instantly. It was as if a huge

burden had been lifted off her shoulders, and it caused him to smile discreetly.

Tasha and Mimi peeped the way Maury was looking at Halleigh. Tasha smiled to herself. She'd never seen her brother react to a chick the way he was reacting to Halleigh.

Back when Tasha was younger, she would have kicked Halleigh to the curb, as her friend, before she could blink. She hated when she would bring her friends around Maury and he would get a little crush on them. What she hated most was when the girls tried to holler at him behind her back. It was just an unspoken rule that friends don't date their friends' brothers. With Tasha, being as protective of her little brother as she was, just wasn't having it.

One time in particular, she had a best friend named Kera, whom she'd been tight with since fifth grade. Kera had come to the house and had sleepovers with Tasha on many occasions. Maury had never paid the girl much mind. In tenth grade, when Kera grew titties and an ass, Maury couldn't help but notice his sister's friend.

It wasn't until Tasha and Kera were seniors in high school that she learned that Kera, during sleepovers, would sneak out of her room in the middle of the night to have sex with Maury.

She never would've known if Kera hadn't ended up sleeping with one of Maury's friends too, which caused Maury and dude to go to blows in gym class. Maury was suspended,but he wasn't the only one.

When Tasha found out the reason her brother got suspended, she mopped the math class floor with Kera and was suspended too. She felt that Kera had just been using her. Tasha hated the feeling of being used. Ironically, she never felt she was being used by Manolo, since that was a game she got herself into.

Looking at how Maury was feeling Halleigh didn't upset Tasha, though. She looked at Halleigh like a little sister or something. She knew she was good people, so it didn't bother her that Maury was feeling her girl.

Mimi, on the other hand, harbored jealousy. Right now, she wasn't about to trip over no dick, so she just rolled her eyes and collected her cash from the table.

"Fuck what y'all talking about." Mimi licked her fingers as she counted her dough. "I'm about to go shopping. I can finally throw all this stripper shit away," she said as she left the room.

Tasha collected her cash. "I better go with this bitch to make sure she don't go back to Flint just as broke as she left. You coming, Hal?"

Halleigh knew that she needed new clothes. Everything she owned was cheap and indecent, but she honestly had bigger plans for the money sitting in front of her. She shook her head and replied, "Nah, y'all go ahead. I'm good."

Tasha and Mimi grabbed their purses and headed out to hit the stores, leaving Halleigh and Maury alone in the house.

"Why you didn't go with your girls?" Maury asked Halleigh as they sat on the couch watching television.

"I wanted to, but I need this money. I can't afford to go blow it on clothes and handbags. Not right now. I'm really trying to change how I'm living, you know," she said as she looked up at him.

Her beauty was breathtaking, and Maury just stared at her for a moment. "Let me take you shopping. You don't have to spend none of your cash. Everything's on me."

"I can't let you do that," she answered. Halleigh knew better. No man had ever done anything for her unless he was getting something in return. She'd learned from Mimi that an expensive shopping trip from a guy meant she had to give up the booty, and she wasn't ready to do that.

"Yeah, you can, shorty. You got to let a nigga treat you sometimes." Maury figured spending a couple thousand on Halleigh couldn't hurt his pockets, and he wanted to see her happy. "And I know what you're thinking," he said, reading Halleigh's mind. "No strings attached. I'm not looking for anything from you in return. I just want to show you that there are some decent men out there who know how to treat a lady, and I'm one of them. Ya feel me?"

Halleigh thought for a minute before replying with a nod and a smile on her face. "Yeah, I feel you."

"Good. Now let's dip," Maury ordered.

He took out five stacks. The rest of his share he put back in the duffle bag and hid it safely in his bedroom wall safe. He got another duffle bag from his bedroom closet and gave it to Halleigh to put her money in. Then they headed out the door, Halleigh feeling like Julia Roberts being escorted by Richard Gere in the movie *Pretty Woman*.

Maury took her to Macy's in Manhattan and watched her have a field day in the store. He took her to designer stores that she'd never even heard of before, purchasing her high-end clothes, sparing no expense.

Halleigh was enjoying the time that she spent with Maury. He was attentive and protective. When she was with him, he made her feel safe. He walked beside her, his arm draped securely around her shoulder. She almost forgot about the hell that was her life. He made her feel special and didn't judge her or look down on her for the way her life had turned out.

"Can I ask you a question?" she said as he opened the passenger door for her.

"Go ahead."

"Why are you being so nice to me? I mean, you know everything about me. Things that I can't even see past you've disregarded."

"I don't judge people by the past. What's done is done. You can't change that, Halleigh. You can only look forward and do better in the future." Maury leaned into her and kissed her softly on the forehead before pushing her gently into the car.

Halleigh spent the entire day with Maury. He showed her everything that New York had to offer. They storehopped for most of the day and then did an early dinner. He even purchased last-minute theatre tickets for *The Color Purple*. Halleigh was so impressed with the hustle and bustle of New York City. It was completely different than her hometown, and she enjoyed being away from the grit of Flint.

By the time they arrived home, Halleigh was exhausted.

"Thank you for everything, Maury," she stated as they stood in the dark foyer. "No one has ever done anything like this for me. I had a really good time with you."

"You deserve it," he replied softly as he touched her face.

She gasped from the warmth of his hands and closed her eyes. Halleigh wasn't ready to be in a relationship, but the way she felt when she was with Maury gave her hope that one day she could be happy.

"Come here," he whispered as he grabbed her hand and pulled her to his room. Maury opened the door.

Halleigh reluctantly followed him inside, her heartbeat increasing with each step she took.

After closing the door behind him, he stepped toward Halleigh. Her body trembled slightly, and he smiled to himself. Even though he knew her past, he still sensed an innocent nature in her. He slid the straps of her summer dress off her shoulders, and the fabric dropped to the floor. He then undressed himself, down to his boxers.

Halleigh's breaths became shallow as he pulled her onto his bed. Against her better judgment, she felt the space between her legs become wet.

"Maury, I can't." Her words came out more like a moan than a whisper.

"I know," he replied.

The feeling of his breath on her earlobe sent shivers down her spine.

He pulled back the covers so that she could put her feet underneath and then lay on his back, pulling her head onto his chest. "Go to sleep, Hal. I want you to feel me next to you. I'm willing to be here for you when you're ready."

Halleigh found a comfortable space on his chest as her legs intertwined with his, and he kissed the top of her head and wrapped his arms around her. Then they both drifted into a peaceful slumber.

Chapter Fifty-seven

The next day, they headed back to Flint. Mimi and Tasha rode in Tasha's car, while Halleigh rode back with Maury. "What the fuck is wrong with you?" Tasha asked Mimi, noticing the twisted-up expression on her face.

"Nothing." Mimi stared out of the side mirror at the couple following closely behind them. She cut her eyes, pushed her seat back, and pushed her oversized knock-off Dior glasses up on the bridge of her nose.

Mimi sighed. She was sick of Halleigh playing the weak and innocent role, the role that always seemed to make it so that she was the center of attention. *Hell, if it wasn't for her ass, Tasha would have never made a way to get us from up under Manolo. Why'd it take this bitch to make her finally give a shit? I been there selling pussy and getting beat down forever and a day and the bitch ain't never try to do no prison-break type of shit when it came to my ass.*

In Mimi's eyes, with Halleigh all up in Maury's face all the time, it was a wonder he could even breathe. Mimi folded her arms over her chest and thought, *Fuck it. If he wants to ride with her ass, let 'em. But that nigga could have been getting the best blow job in his life while we rode.*

Halleigh had no clue about Mimi's brewing anger toward her. Had she known that Mimi was feeling Maury like that, she would have quickly fell back from the jump—not that she was leaning forward or anything like that.

Early that morning, she and Maury had gotten up to talk. After expressing her concerns to Maury, he agreed to give her time to get herself together. They both decided that it was best for them to be friends and let their relationship progress naturally instead of forcing it.

Being honest, Halleigh had to admit that she did like Maury. However, she knew that she'd made the best decision for herself. She needed some "me time," if ever anybody did.

Maury didn't seem to be upset with Halleigh's wishes, and his behavior toward her didn't change at all. In all actuality, he respected her more. That same respect he showed her was one of the reasons she liked him so much. No matter what the end brought, Halleigh was sure that Maury would become one of her most valuable friends.

Maury glanced over at Halleigh, who was staring idly out of her window. He knew that Flint was the root of all of her problems and that she wasn't thrilled about returning. He reached over and grabbed her hand and told her, "Everything is gon' be all right."

She looked over at him, giving him a weak smile and a nod. "I know," she replied, but her tone wasn't believable.

The frightened looked in her eyes made him glad that he was accompanying them back to Flint. If anything popped off, he wanted to make sure he was there to have the women's backs.

Maury put in Jay-Z's CD *American Gangster*, and Halleigh reclined her seat. They followed behind Tasha and Mimi and prepared themselves for the ten-hour drive back to the city of Flint.

The first thing the girls did when they arrived back in Flint was find a place to lay their heads. They eventually planned on checking in on the place they had just days ago called home, the roof Manolo had kept over their heads, but they knew it wasn't safe to rest their heads there.

After checking out two other places that had FOR RENT signs in the windows, the girls managed to rent a three-bedroom apartment on the outskirts of Flint. Spots like that didn't care about credit checks and all that mess. All those slum lords wanted was the cash required to move in. If they had to put you out on the streets and rent to the next, then so be it.

Maury moved into a one-bedroom spot nearby and told Tasha to lay low for another couple days, just to be on the safe side. Tasha agreed to keep her girls in line for a couple of days. Halleigh wasn't going to be a problem, that she could bet the farm on. Mimi, on the other hand, was back in her element, and Tasha didn't know how long she could keep her still before the desire to go get her hustle on in the old way kicked back in.

It was crucial that the girls stayed out of niggas' radars. Word could easily get back to Manolo that they were out kickin' it, doing them instead of seeing about him. That would be a red flag for sure, and it wouldn't take long after that for Manolo to put two and two together and figure out that they were the ones behind his arrest. If that were to happen, then they would have an entirely new set of problems on their hands.

With Tasha, Halleigh, and Mimi out of harm's way, Maury took the opportunity to familiarize himself with his new surroundings. Riding up and down the city streets, he immediately recognized the mentality of its hoods. He could tell that he was in a city that bred killers.

He couldn't be more right. Every nigga in Flint had the heart of a lion. If he didn't, then he had his gun to back him up.

Maury knew that scary dudes were the first ones to reach for their pistols when something popped off. Therefore, he would have to be on point, especially being in a town that wasn't his home. Dudes always recognized outsiders, and would often try to test them. He immediately decided that he needed to hook up with a Flint native, and knew exactly who he would go to.

Maury knocked on the door to Tasha's apartment. He needed to get at Mimi. He knew she could feed him the information he needed that would allow him to distinguish between the haves and the have-nots of Flint. Mimi had worked the streets of Flint much longer than Halleigh. Besides that, she was live in the game, so he knew that she knew all the players—the starters and the bench warmers. He knew he'd have to watch her though.

He could just as easily have gone to his sister to get information, but she hadn't been in the streets working them the way both Mimi and Halleigh had. Even though Halleigh had been out there on the grind, she was too low-key. Maury did know that eventually Halleigh's assets would be beneficial too. Since she was low-key, he figured she was the type who just sat back and observed a lot of stuff. Sooner or later he'd need to see Flint through her eyes too, but, for now, he needed to get at Mimi, and soon.

After Maury knocked a couple of times, Halleigh answered the door. She was wearing one of the outfits he had purchased for her. The BCBG jeans and a fitted black turtleneck sweater gave her a mature, classy look.

"Hey," she greeted, a smile instantly forming on her face upon seeing Maury standing there.

"What up, ma?" He responded with a smile of his own. Halleigh was the only chick he knew who could possibly distract him from making money. Her aura attracted him. When he was in her presence, he was always focused on her.

He leaned in and gave her a hug, trying his best to keep it friendly, as she'd requested. He had to keep his mind on the money if he was going to make the most of his little trip to Flint.

"Come on in." She stepped to the side so he could enter their apartment.

"You good?" he asked her. "You need anything?"

Halleigh laughed and shook her head. "No, I don't need anything. I was actually just on my way out. Tasha's not here." She grabbed her leather Hermes bag. "But she should be back any minute. She just ran to the grocery real quick to pick up a few things."

He looked Halleigh up and down and asked, "Yo, so where you headed, shorty? Matter of fact," Maury said as if a sudden thought had just popped into his head, "why is Tasha's ass even out anyway? I thought I told y'all to stay low. Hell, I could have gone to the damn store for her."

"Chill," Halleigh said, pressing her hands downward as if telling him to calm down. "We have been laying low for the past couple days. And Mimi's here. She's right in her bedroom." Halleigh pointed to the closed door toward the end of the hallway.

"Good. At least somebody has some sense to keep they ass in the

house," Maury stated. "There's too much at stake for any fuck-ups. The last thing y'all need is for Manolo to get a whiff of y'all's asses and try to come at y'all."

"That's not going to happen. Tasha made a few calls to a couple of people who keep their ear to the street. There's no word out there about what's up with Manolo. We called the jail. No bail is set, so he probably won't be on the streets for a minute." Halleigh shrugged. "So we figured we can't hide out in this matchbox forever. Besides, I'm just going to grab some lunch right at the little restaurant down the block. Is that all right with you?"

Halleigh could see the hesitant look on Maury's face. He didn't reply.

"What?" Halleigh dropped her arms to her side in defeat. "Since you're so worried, why don't you just come with me?" She hadn't spent any time with Maury since they had come back to Flint. She did miss being around him. She loved his listening ear.

"Yeah, all right." He tossed her the keys to his car and said, "Go on and wait for me in the car. I'll be right out. I need to use the restroom."

"I'm driving," she teased, knowing he would never let her behind the wheel of his Lexus.

"Yeah right, shorty. You know better," he stated as he watched her walk out the door. He turned and hurried down the hall to Mimi's room. He knocked lightly.

Mimi snatched open the door and put her hand on one hip when she saw Maury standing there. He hadn't said two words to her since she had given him head back in New York, and she was furious about all the attention he was giving Halleigh. She wondered when Halleigh had found the time to suck his dick, 'cause obviously she had done something to keep the boy interested in her.

"What up?" Mimi asked with an attitude.

"What's up with you, ma?" Maury asked as he entered the room and closed the door behind him. "I'm just coming to check up on you, make sure you're straight."

Mimi looked him up and down to find any sincerity in his words. Was he just fucking with her mind, trying to come back for seconds, or was he really trying to look out for her? Hoping for the latter, she loosened up. She took her hands off of her hips and crossed her arms across her voluptuous chest.

"I'm good," Mimi told him. "I've been trying to get to know you better, but you've been playing me to the left." She walked toward him and stood directly in front of him. Then she reached between his legs and took hold of his firm penis.

Maury had to admit, Mimi was one of the most aggressive chicks he'd ever met. He wished he wasn't feeling Halleigh so much, because

he would definitely twist Mimi out. He thought of Halleigh waiting in the car for him and quickly decided to keep things strictly business with Mimi. He saw potential in Halleigh and didn't want to fuck up his chances with her over Mimi.

He removed Mimi's hands from his body. "Nah, it's not like that. As a matter of fact, I got this business that I need to discuss with you."

"Business?" Mimi's ears stood at attention. She knew business always meant money, so she was more than willing to listen. She put money over dick any day, unless the dick transferred into USD.

"Yeah, business," he repeated. "I want you to show me who out this way is getting it."

Mimi shot back, "'Getting it,' as in, you're trying to take it from 'em? Or 'getting it,' as in, you're trying to see who the competition is around Flint?"

"You already know what's up, Mimi. Ain't nobody fucking with this dried-up-ass dope game out here. I'm trying to take a nigga for what he got."

"What's in it for me?" Mimi was always down for whatever, but something had to be in it for her. On top of that, it definitely needed to be worth her while.

Maury knew that he could easily manipulate her into giving him the information without giving her shit, but he decided against it. "I'll give you ten percent of the take," he offered. "You wit' it?"

Although ten percent didn't sound like much, it wasn't in Mimi's nature to turn down any type of profit. She knew that ten percent could mean a lot, as long as she handled her end of the deal right. "Yeah, I'm wit' it," she replied.

"Maury!" Halleigh called from a distance.

Mimi rolled her eyes at the sound of Halleigh's voice vibrating through the house. "Get with me when you get off your leash. I got some information that'll help you," Mimi said dryly. She opened up her bedroom door and let Maury out.

Maury had peeped Mimi's jealousy toward Halleigh a long time ago, but he dismissed it. *I did let her suck my dick and then toss her to the side to get with her girl.* The thought made him chuckle as he met Halleigh in the living room.

Halleigh stood in the doorway, her arms crossed. She asked sweetly, "Was you gon' make me wait all day?"

"You know it ain't like that, ma," he responded. He put his hand on the small of her back and led her out of the house.

Mimi watched from the living room window as Maury opened the car door for Halleigh. She couldn't believe how he tried to play her. *Yeah, nigga, I got some information for you.*

She decided to put Maury up on Malek, make him think that Malek was the biggest kingpin Flint had ever seen. Then, once Halleigh

found out about Maury's plans to rob Malek, she would never fuck with him.

Nigga think he just gon' play me. I'ma make sure Hal can't stand the sight of the nigga.

Tasha sat in the styling chair as the stylist worked in her hair. New Attitudes was buzzing with gossip, and everybody was talking about Jamaica Joe's going-away party.

"Yeah, that nigga is out of the game. Word is, he bought a house down South and ain't never coming back," a girl stated as she flipped through a hair magazine. "His party is gon' be jumping. You know everybody gon' come out to show him love."

Tasha smiled to herself as she thought about Jamaica Joe making a clean break from the drug game. They had known each other a long time and at one point meant a great deal to one another. Tasha knew that she would be attending Jamaica Joe's party this weekend. It was time for her to show her face again, to let it be known that she was no longer one of Manolo's hoes. After getting her hair finished in loose curls, she paid her stylist and prepared to leave.

As Tasha reached the doorway, Keesha entered the salon and made her presence felt by bumping Tasha harshly, causing her to drop her purse onto the floor. "Excuse you," Keesha said as she mean-mugged Tasha.

Tasha told her, "I know you saw me coming out of this mu'fucka. You better watch where the fuck you going. Now pick my shit up."

"No, *you* better check your tone before I tell your little secret," Keesha replied softly.

"Bitch, you better stay in your place." Tasha peered at Keesha in a threatening manner.

"I know about your little set-up, Tasha. You, Mimi, and Halleigh better stay in your places. Y'all bitches treated me like shit when y'all thought you were sitting on top of the world, always looking your nose down on a bitch because she wanted to get down with Manolo. It's funny how the tables turn."

Keesha pushed her luck with her last comment, and Tasha smacked the shit out of her, as if she were her pimp. The girls in the salon abruptly ended their conversations and focused on the scene unfolding before them.

Before Keesha could even react, Tasha grabbed her by the back of her weave and brought her head down onto her knee. Keesha screamed in pain and surprise as Tasha pushed her face into the floor. "Bitch, you better remember who kept your ass. I run shit. You can never be a boss bitch like me," she stated as she pushed her head into the marble floor forcefully.

Tasha stood up, collected her belongings, and straightened her clothes as Keesha rolled on the floor, moaning.

Tasha could hear the laughter and instigating comments break out inside the shop as she stormed out and hopped into her car. She had to get to Halleigh and Mimi. They had a problem to handle.

Halleigh sat across from Maury in Applebee's. They were talking and enjoying each other's company as usual.

"So, what have you been up to these past couple days? I haven't seen you since we got here," Halleigh stated as she picked at her food.

"Nothing important. I've just been getting to know your city."

"You still could've stopped by."

"You sound like a woman who was trying to see her man. You can't have it both ways, Hal. You're the one who said you just wanted to be friends."

"I know, I know, and I do want us to be friends. I just missed you, that's all," she admitted. "I've gotten used to spending so much time with you. Then when we got back here, it just stopped all of a sudden."

"I can see this 'friends thing' is gon' be hard already."

Halleigh laughed loudly at the look of distress on Maury's face. "Is it that hard for you?"

"Don't play, Hal. You know how I feel about you. You say you're not ready, but when we're together, it feels like this is where you want to be. You'll fuck a nigga head up, if he let you."

Halleigh smiled because of how strongly Maury felt for her. "I'm sorry. You're right. I can't expect you to act like my man if you're not my man," she replied. "That's not fair to you."

Maury shook his head. "You ready?"

Halleigh nodded and then hopped out of the booth, while Maury placed his hand on the small of her back.

"Did you pay the club owner for the party?" Jamaica Joe asked Malek as they pulled into the restaurant parking lot.

"Yeah, I took care of it," Malek replied as he parked his brand-new Lincoln Navigator. "Quit worrying about that mu'fuckin' party, fam. Everything is in line for this weekend."

Jamaica Joe and Malek exited the car and headed into Applebee's.

Halleigh stopped in her tracks as Malek crossed her path.

Malek noticed her, and a sense of jealousy overtook him as he saw her standing so intimately with Maury. He looked Maury up and down, and Maury returned his stare as he checked his hip to make sure he was strapped.

Halleigh's breath caught in her throat as Malek approached.

Maury leaned over and whispered, "You know this nigga?"

Halleigh nodded, but didn't say a word. She couldn't take her eyes off Malek. He looked so different. He'd put on some weight, and his

demeanor was hard. Tears welled up in her eyes as she put her head down and began to walk with Maury past Malek.

Malek reached out and grabbed her hand as she passed. "Hal, can we talk for a minute?" he asked.

Halleigh looked back and forth between Maury and Malek.

Maury thought he recognized Malek from the couple of times he'd seen him on television back in the day. He looked so different, but Maury still had a hunch that the dude standing before him was Malek Johnson, Halleigh's ex-boyfriend. She'd told Maury a lot about their situation. He leaned down and whispered, "Handle your business, shorty. I'm right in the car if you need me." He squeezed her hand in support and lifted her head with his fingertips before he turned to walk away.

Jamaica Joe nodded his head toward the restaurant. "I'm inside, fam," he told Malek.

Malek nodded, never taking his eyes off Halleigh.

The last time Halleigh had seen Malek, he was down with the nigga that had raped her. Her heart immediately filled with coldness. "What, Malek?"

Malek eyed Maury's car. "That's your nigga?"

"You know what, Malek? I don't have time for this. After everything we've been through, that's the first thing you ask me?" Halleigh turned to leave.

"A'ight, a'ight, Hal, wait. You're right. That's not my business." Malek looked at her appearance. The last time he'd seen her, her body was deteriorating from drug use, but now she looked good. She was back to the Halleigh he'd fallen in love with. Although there was a lost look in her eyes, she was still very attractive. She had picked her weight back up and was filling up her designer jeans better than ever. She looked healthy, and had transformed from a beautiful girl to a young woman.

"I see you still fucking around with the niggas that raped me," she stated.

"Look, that's handled already."

Halleigh was silent as she stared at Malek.

"I heard about your nigga, Manolo. You good? You need some money or something?" Malek pulled a wad of cash out of his pockets.

"I don't need your money, Malek, or your pity. I needed you." A tear fell from her eyes. She quickly brushed it away as she began to walk away.

"Halleigh, I'm trying to be here now," he said, halting her in her step.

"How do you know I want you here now?"

"Look, I know you feeling that nigga." Malek nodded toward Maury's truck. "I know you. I can see it in your face, Hal, but you don't

love that nigga the way that you love me. You know what we got. I'm trying to make it work with you."

"I've got to go, Malek," Halleigh whispered. Her heart was beating a mile a minute. Malek was right. She did love him. He did know her, but she didn't know if they could ever get past all of their demons to make a relationship work.

"Can we talk later?" she asked. She knew that they needed to talk, but she needed the right words to say. Right now, she was simply running on emotion.

Malek pulled out a VIP pass to Jamaica Joe's party and handed it to Halleigh. "Come by Celebrations this weekend for Joe's going-away party. Things are about to change in Flint, Hal. The nigga leaving everything to me. We'll do it big Saturday night, and we'll talk later that night. I'm trying to see you, Hal. Don't stand me up."

"I won't," she answered with a weak smile.

"I love you, ma," Malek whispered. "You know I do."

"No, I don't know, Malek. We'll talk later," she replied before walking back to Maury's car.

Halleigh hopped into the car and stared out of the window at Malek. She didn't know what to do regarding him. He had hurt her to the point where she thought she couldn't live without him. Now here he was in her face, confessing his undying love.

"Don't let the nigga break your heart, Halleigh," Maury stated as he started his car and pulled away. "You're too good for that."

Chapter Fifty-eight

Lynch, the leader of the infamous Shottah Boyz, passed the dutch to Sweets as they sat in the front seat of Lynch's Toyota Camry. The haze of the blunt filled the insides of the car, and the two were beyond high as they plotted their murder game.

"You know that bitch nigga Joe leaving town. The grimy mu'fucka know what he got coming to him. That's why he trying to skip out," Lynch stated. "He's throwing a going-away party down at Celebrations. A nigga like me trying to fall up in there just to light the mu'fucka up, nah mean?"

Lynch was still out to avenge the death of his brother. Jamaica Joe

had shot him at point-blank range a year ago, and Lynch had been try-ing to see Joe ever since. However, Jamaica Joe was hard to touch.

"Nah, fam, I got that handled. The only thing we got to do is sit back and listen to the gunshots ring out. The nigga Joe ain't ever gon' make it out of Flint. Him and his li'l nigga Malek gon' meet death that night." A smile crossed Sweets' face. He hit the blunt and held the smoke down in his lungs before passing it back to Lynch.

"Fuck you got doing the job? You know ain't a nigga in Flint who can put they murder game down better than your boy."

"That's why I got a bitch doing it."

"Whaat?" Lynch exclaimed in disbelief. "You's a lyin' mu'fucka." He shook his head.

"No bullshit, my nigga. They'll never see her coming. Like I said be-fore, it's curtains for the North Side and anybody who affiliated with 'em."

Lynch nodded his head. His focus was taken off the conversation when he noticed a short, light-skinned girl with curly hair approach Sweets' home. He tapped Sweets. "Ain't that the bartender bitch from Manolo's spot?"

Sweets peered through the window. "Yeah, that's her. Fuck is she doing?" he wondered as she knocked on his door. "How the fuck this bitch know where I live?"

Sweets rolled down his window, releasing clouds of haze into the sky. "You looking for something?"

When Keesha turned around and looked at him, he could see that there was a long gash across her forehead. He frowned at the sight. *Somebody fucked this bitch up,* he thought.

"Yeah, I need to talk to you," Keesha replied.

Sweets shook his head, figuring she wanted money or a place to stay. Manolo had only been locked up for a couple of weeks, but many of his hoes had come to Sweets looking for help. They figured, since Sweets and Manolo were partners, that Sweets would take them in. Sweets didn't bother with Manolo's bitches and only took a cut of their earnings. He could give a fuck if they were out on the streets.

"I ain't got nothing for you." Sweets hit the button to roll up his window.

"Wait!" Keesha approached his side of the car.

"Bitch is persistent." Lynch chuckled at Sweets' irritated expres-sion.

"What?"

Keesha said quickly, "I got some information about why Manolo's club was raided."

Sweets immediately changed his tune. "I'm listening."

"Tasha, Mimi, and Halleigh went to the police and told them what

Manolo had in his safe. After the raid, they met with the lead detective and split the bricks and the money. That's why nobody's seen their faces since it happened."

Sweets shook his head. "I don't know where you got your information from, but somebody told you wrong. Don't come around my block looking for me again unless you got something important to say."

A look of confusion spread across Keesha's face as she watched Sweets roll his window up and disappear behind the dark tint.

"How the fuck you just gon' pass on that valuable shit she just told you, fam?" Lynch asked, an annoyed look on his face. "The bitch info might be legit."

"It was legit. I just didn't want the bitch to think I owe her something for putting me up on game. That's why I don't fuck with these bitches. You can't trust 'em. I took a loss when the police confiscated what was in Manolo's safe. I'm gon' take care of them bitches . . . right after I take care of Jamaica Joe."

Chapter Fifty-nine

It was Friday night and Celebrations was jumping. Everyone from the North Side came out to celebrate with Jamaica Joe. The huge parking lot was filled to capacity, as cars continued to pile in. Sweets sat in his truck toward the back of the lot, along with the Shottah Boyz. He couldn't believe Jamaica Joe had practically delivered himself on a silver platter by throwing this party. Sweets had been lying low for the past couple of months, just waiting for Joe to resurface. Now here he was.

Ain't this nigga learned his lesson about throwing parties? Sweets thought. He shook his head. He said to his crew, "This nigga must've thought the beef was dead. He slippin' like a mu'fucka. He honestly believes that he can throw a big party without having to see me?" Sweets laughed and then cocked his automatic 9 mm pistol. "He got another thing coming."

Lynch asked, "So, we just busting in there shooting?"

"Nah, nah, that ain't smart. We going to clear that mu'fucka out. Then I got it from there. It's all taken care of. Tonight the North Side gon' feel Sweets, believe that!"

"So, we're just going to wet the whole place up? How are we going to get to Jamaica Joe? It's not going to be that easy."

"We're just going to cause a diversion to put my plan into motion. That's only the beginning, my nigga. Jamaica Joe and that li'l nigga Malek are dying tonight. That's my word," Sweets said boldly.

That comment was music to Lynch's ears.

"This is for Rah-Rah," Sweets said as he pushed PLAY on his dashboard TV. A homosexual porno began to play on the screen.

The Shottah Boyz hated it, and didn't approve of Sweets' sexual orientation, but they couldn't do anything because Sweets was the boss. They tried their best to avoid looking at the screen, but still, the sounds were almost too much to bear.

Lynch frowned. "Sweets, man, why can't you turn that gay shit off?"

Sweets didn't even acknowledge his henchman's comment. He just sat back and rested his hand on his gun, a small smile spread across his face. It was the middle of August, but Sweets and the Shottah Boyz were about to make it look like the Fourth of July.

Jamaica Joe and Malek walked through the back entrance of the club, surrounded by their whole crew. They were draped in all black, and everyone was shining with long platinum Jesus pieces and crosses. Joe wore a black linen shirt and Armani slacks, with none other than Stacy Adams gators on his feet. Joe was the only one who wasn't sportin' any jewels. He only wore a watch, which spoke for itself, since his watch cost more than all his henchmen's jewels put together.

Joe taught Malek that conservative is always better, so he took heed and did away with the flashy jewelry. Malek just rocked an all-black hoodie under a black Sean John leather jacket, his burner tucked in the front pockets. An oversized fitted cap covered his eyes, and the only facial features that could be seen were his perfect white teeth and his neatly lined goatee.

The crew mobbed into the club. They could hear the new Lil' Wayne song that had been blasting the airwaves, with all of the radio play it had been getting in Flint. Jamaica Joe, Malek, and their crew made their presence known. Joe's henchmen began to make it rain on their way up to the VIP section. The club went crazy at the sight of them entering the club. It was a fitting send-off for Joe. Malek couldn't help but glance around in search of Halleigh. He had a lot of things he needed to say to her, things she hadn't given him a chance to say before. He hoped that they could heal old wounds and make amends. This time, no matter what, he was determined to get the love of his life back once and for all.

Chapter Sixty

Tasha, Mimi, and Halleigh pulled up to the club, Foxy Brown blasting out of the speakers. They were all dressed to impress that night, determined to be the showstoppers of the party.

"Damn! It's jumping in there," Mimi said as she examined the people lining up to get in the club.

"I told you it was going to be popping," Tasha said as she maneuvered her car up to the valet.

Halleigh was consumed by her own thoughts. *I hope Malek is in there. I really need to see him. I miss that boy so much.* She had been looking forward to running into Malek ever since Malek had told her about the party. Even though a part of her couldn't understand why he was hanging with one of the men that raped her, she knew deep down inside that she had to give him the benefit of the doubt. There was a chance that he'd had no idea that was the man who'd raped her. By the same token, Malek could have very well known, and was secretly plotting his own revenge. Halleigh hoped for the latter. So many things went unsaid between her and Malek. Truth be told, Halleigh wanted to see if their love was still there. Hopefully, tonight would be her chance.

As the three women hopped out of the car, all eyes were on them. Everyone expected to see Manolo close behind, but to their surprise, he was nowhere in sight. All of the girls strutted in with a model's precision and went straight to the VIP line so that they could avoid waiting. It was double the admission price, but they were coming in with style.

Maury sat outside in his rental car, waiting for his plan to come into play. He'd rented a motel room two buildings down from the club and was about to show Flint how New York niggas got down. He just hoped that Mimi didn't back out on him. *I shoulda fucked her to get her head gone first,* Maury thought as he watched the people fill up the club. He wasn't sure if Mimi was as bold as she claimed to be.

He looked toward the valet and saw his sister, Mimi, and Halleigh hop out of the car, all of them wearing diva shades. When Mimi got out, she pulled her shades down slightly and looked over her rims toward the building where Maury was. The two of them locked eyes, and she nodded her head, signaling to him that the plan was still in motion.

Maury then looked over at an unknowing Halleigh and his eyes got stuck. She was so beautiful. The dress she wore hugged her curves, and the high heels enhanced her long, toned legs. Maury's joint began

to harden just at the sight of her. He quickly snapped out his brief day-dream and refocused. He, too, needed for his head to be right in order for everything to go down as planned. Halleigh entered the club along with her girls. She noticed a lot of commotion coming from the rear of the club and tried to get a peep of what was going down. A blizzard of money was being tossed in the air, and the women in the club were going crazy, scrambling for the free cash. A mob of men dressed in all-black began parting the crowd like God parted the Red Sea for Moses.

Halleigh stood on her tippy-toes, trying to get a better view. "Damn! Who is that?"

"Yo, that's Jamaica Joe and them," Tasha said, a smile spread across her face.

The girls made their way over to a table near the bar and settled.

"It's jumping in this mu'fucka." Mimi danced to the music while still in her chair. "Where the mu'fuckin' ballers at?"

"You know all the broke niggas are on the main floor. What we need to be doing is getting into VIP." Tasha waved over the waiter.

Halleigh looked at the group of men going up the wraparound stairs that led to the VIP section. As she took a closer look, she noticed Malek was ahead of the pack, and her heart fluttered at the sight of him.

Tasha noticed Halleigh's attention was focused on something or someone. Tasha's eyes shot to the crew also, and her vision fixed on Jamaica Joe. *Jamaica Joe is looking good tonight.* She licked her lips and fixed her freak-'em dress.

Mimi looked at the entourage. She had a totally different agenda than her friends. She wanted to get the attention of the biggest baller in the club so she could put her plan into motion.

She downed her rum and Coke and stood up. "Let's see if we can we get up in VIP, where the real party is at."

"That's what's up." Halleigh stood up alongside Mimi.

All the girls made their way to the VIP section, each with their own personal agenda.

Chapter Sixty-one

"This toast is to celebrate our family, a family of hustlers, a family of brothers. Flint is ours. No, fuck that, the world is ours!" Jamaica

Joe held up a champagne glass along with the other ten men in the room, including Malek.

"The world is ours," they all said in unison as they tapped their glasses and downed the Moët.

Malek smiled, but then it quickly disappeared at the thought of what he had become. He looked around and noticed he was in the midst of killers and hustlers, something his deceased mother and stepfather had forbid him to become. Everything in his life seemed to happen so quickly that he couldn't even remember changing into the person he was today.

Making his way away from the crowd, Malek walked over to the window that overlooked the main floor and noticed a group of women maneuvering through the crowd. He smiled as he saw Halleigh, looking beautiful, on her way up to VIP. "There my girl go," he said. He gripped the Moët bottle by its neck and took another swig.

Moments later, Tasha, Mimi, and Halleigh made their way to VIP. After being searched by one of the bouncers, they were let in. Immediately after entering the room, the girls noticed the more relaxed environment that the VIP offered. Nice, slow music was playing and the oval, oversized couches were full with people relaxing and drinking.

Halleigh and Malek were instantly drawn to one another. They locked eyes, and it seemed as if there was no one else in the room but them. They slowly walked toward each other, neither trying to seem too anxious. As they neared each other, Halleigh smiled, and Malek returned the gesture. They stood face to face, staring at each other, not knowing what to say.

"I miss you," Halleigh said.

"I miss you like crazy too," Malek replied.

The two kind of chuckled and then embraced. Just the three little words, *I miss you*, were the beginning of the mending of their relationship. So many words had danced through each of their minds about what they would say to each other once they met up again, but none of those words even mattered now. Everything was like water under the bridge.

Malek and Halleigh, still embracing each other, slowly rocked back and forth. The warmth of Malek's body and embrace felt so good to Halleigh. Malek led her toward the back where they sat on the couch.

Halleigh looked closely at Malek and noticed a lot had changed with him. It was the first time she'd noticed the tattoo on his neck. It had the name of his deceased mother, and on his forearm, the words *North Side* were embedded in his skin.

"You're all tatted up now, huh?" She gave him a sexy grin.

Malek looked down at his forearm and then back at Halleigh. "Yeah, a li'l somethin'-somethin'," he said softly, smiling back at her. "Look,

Halleigh, I gotta be honest. I'm still in love with you, and I think about you constantly, nah mean?"

"I feel the same way, Malek. I don't want to play games. I want to be for real with you, and my love for you is real. It always has been. You know that. And us being apart—"

"Look, I can't take this no more either, Halleigh. You supposed to be with me, girl." Malek grabbed her hand and looked deep into her brown eyes.

Halleigh had been waiting to hear those words come out of Malek's mouth for a very long time. She'd dreamed of hearing those words, and now her dream was becoming a reality. Under the control of Manolo, Halleigh wasn't able to be with her love, but with Manolo now out of the picture, she was ready to be where she belonged. "I want to be with you too, Malek."

"We've wasted enough time, Hal. A lot of things are going to change. I'm coming into big things right now, and I want you to be a part of it."

"What do you mean?"

"I want you to be my woman. I want us to look forward and forget about the past."

"Are you serious?"

"I'm dead serious. We've wasted enough time. The life you living is not for you. Let me take care of you. I'm about to be over all of this." Malek waved his hand over the room.

A confused Halleigh asked, "All of what? This club?"

"No," Malek corrected her, "this whole side of town." He looked around again. "The North Side is mine, baby." He looked into Halleigh's eyes. "It's ours."

Halleigh had to make sure she was hearing him correctly. "You taking over for Jamaica Joe?"

Malek nodded humbly. Now that he had Halleigh's attention, he wasn't going to let her slip away. He was ready to make her his main woman, and he wasn't taking no for an answer.

Tears started to form in Halleigh's eyes. Tears of joy. Halleigh had waited so long to be at that point with Malek. She'd finally linked back up with her soul mate and wasn't going to squander the chance. "Okay. Promise to always take care of me." Halleigh inched closer to Malek.

"I promise."

They embraced each other.

Malek wasted no time. He instructed her to go home and pack her stuff so she could be with him. He knew that she'd been through a lot. He didn't care what she'd done in her life before that point. From that moment on, she was his woman.

Halleigh asked, "What am I supposed to do about my girls? I came here with them."

"It's me and you against the world. You have to leave that lifestyle alone and turn over a new leaf. How about this? After I handle a little business, I will book us a vacation, so we can start this off right."

"Are you for real?" Halleigh said excitedly.

Malek nodded his head. "I always told you that I would take you away from Flint, didn't I? Even if it is just for a moment, a promise is a promise, right?" Malek smiled.

"Right." Halleigh smiled back.

Malek went into his pocket and pulled out a wad of money, nothing but large faces. "Go home and get your things. I will meet up with you after I drop Joe off at the airport." Malek gave Halleigh his cell phone number.

Halleigh couldn't believe everything that was happening to her right now. It was as if a prince had come and swept her off her feet. Manolo had treated her so bad, she forgot how it felt to have a man's love, but she was witnessing it firsthand.

Without even saying a word to Mimi and Tasha, Halleigh crept out the back of the club along with Malek. He walked to the curb and hailed a cab for her.

"Go 'head and get your things and wait for me. I will have one of my boys bring me to you." Malek opened up the cab door for her.

"Okay," Halleigh said as she got in.

"It's me and you against the world. I'm coming for you."

"I love you, Malek Johnson."

Malek smiled and closed the door for her. After he dropped Jamaica Joe off, he was going to get his woman. It was their time now.

Chapter Sixty-two

While Tasha was drinking and mingling, Mimi was doing just the opposite. She was playing the back, trying to see who had the deepest pockets so she could lure them to Maury. She watched as Tasha became the center of attention, and it was obvious that she was well known and respected. The men gave Tasha respect. They weren't on her like vultures. All seemed to be just enjoying her company.

Mimi looked around for Halleigh and didn't see her. She then looked around for Malek and didn't notice him either. *They must have ducked out for a minute*, she thought as she continued to scan the VIP room.

Jamaica Joe sat at the bar, talking to a fair-skinned woman with green eyes. She was by far the most beautiful woman up in the club, if not the city of Flint. Her island accent only added to her sexiness. They had been engrossed in deep conversation for the past hour. He'd just met her that night, and they clicked. Although the woman had a good conversation game, Joe was trying to see her without them clothes on. He sat talking to her, scoping her whole body out and stopping at her inner thighs. Her dress had risen up, slightly revealing her red lace panties

"You're a bad boy," the woman said in a sexy voice. "I see your eyes wandering down there."

"I'm sorry, but I can't help but look. You are a beautiful woman."

"Well, maybe we should go somewhere private after the party to show you how beautiful I really am." She licked her lips seductively.

Joe's manhood began to jump instantly at the sexy woman's advance. He hated that he had a flight out of town later that night. He wanted nothing more than to take her up on her offer, leave with her right then and there, but then he thought, *I can't leave my own party.* "I have plans tonight, but we will get it in soon." He couldn't believe what he was saying as he looked her up and down again.

He watched as she spread her legs, causing her dress to come up higher and expose her vagina.

"Very soon," he added, his manhood rock-hard.

"Well, let me just give you a little something to tide you over until you can find the time for me, *papi*." The woman stood up and began to sway her hips to the music.

Joe watched as the mystery woman seductively danced to a slow rhythm. He was totally in a trance. He didn't know if it was the liquor or his imagination, but she was looking more like a goddess than just a beautiful woman. She slowly wound her ass up against his now erect penis and was giving him a lap dance while he sat comfortably on the club's loveseat. He looked around for Malek and noticed that he had left the VIP section. *Where my nigga at?* He frowned up, but quickly focused back on the fat backside of the mystery woman.

Malek returned inside the club with Halleigh on his mind. He was ready to make it work for them. His entire life seemed to be about new beginnings right now. He thought about the sudden change in his life. He was about to become the boss, and he had finally gotten his woman back. He maneuvered through the packed club, trying to reach the VIP section. That's when he bumped into Mimi.

"Malek, what's good?" Mimi rested her hand on his chest.

"What's up with you? Cece, right?" Malek asked, trying to recall Mimi's name.

"No, boy! You know my name is Mimi." She playfully hit him, one hand on her hip.

Malek wasn't really trying to make small talk, so he smiled and began to walk away. Before he could leave, he felt her grab his arm. He turned back toward her to see what she wanted.

"I need to holla at you about something," she yelled, trying to be heard over the loud music.

"Maybe later." Malek freed his arm and began to leave.

Mimi knew she had to act fast if her plan was to go smoothly, so she said the first thing that came to mind that she thought would catch his attention. "It's about Halleigh. Someone is trying to kill her!" she blurted out, staring at Malek, hoping he would go for it.

"What?" he said as he frowned up and got closer to hear her better.

Mimi was smiling inside. She knew he'd taken her bait. "Let's go over here and talk." She grabbed his hand and led him to an empty table.

They sat down, and Mimi began to work her improvisation skills. She knew that Maury was outside waiting for her to bring a victim out so he could get them. Maury had told her to find a "get-money" nigga and he would handle the rest, explaining to her that he would kill whoever she put him on, so retaliation wasn't a worry for her.

She saw Malek as prey. *Why not get the next nigga in charge? This game ain't fair, and I'm out for self.* She waved the waiter over to their table. "Gimme two shots of Patron," she said, then focused her attention back to Malek.

"What the fuck are you talking about?" Malek asked.

"Well, it's this nigga that Halleigh used to trick with." Mimi paused and grabbed the drinks the waiter was handing to her. "One of her old tricks, he is after her. Malek, I think he's gonna kill her. He's nuts."

"What? Who?" Malek asked, growing more enraged at the sound of someone bringing harm to Halleigh. He had made a vow that he would never allow anyone to hurt her again, not under his watch.

Malek was so busy trying to figure out what was going on that he didn't see Mimi drop the crushed-up Rohipnol pills into his drink. She discreetly shook it up to hide the substance. Once Malek ingested the drink with the roofies Mimi would be able to do whatever she wanted with him.

"Here, take a drink. You need one for what I'm about to tell you," Mimi said, hoping that he would follow her instructions. She turned her head to make sure no one was keeping an eye on them. By the time she turned back around, Malek had downed the drink and was wiping his mouth.

Malek, wanting to know more about this person trying to harm

Halleigh, focused back on Mimi. "What the fuck are you talking about? Who got a beef with Halleigh?"

I got 'im, Mimi thought as she made up a false story.

Maury sat outside in the car, patiently waiting for Mimi to come out of the club with a victim. *This bitch bullshitting. I hope she don't back out.* He took a puff of the weed-filled blunt that hung out of his mouth. He saw the cars and bling that the men had on as they were coming in and out of the club, and he was like a fat kid at the candy store.

"I'm about to shake this mu'fucka up. Word to my mother!" he said to himself as he smiled sinisterly. Just as he finished his sentence, he saw Mimi coming out of the club with a man who seemed to be drunk.

"Bingo!" he said as he realized that Mimi had come through for him. *That's the nigga that Halleigh bumped into the other day,* he thought.

He knew that he'd hit the jackpot, because on that day, he saw that Malek was driving a Range Rover, one of the more expensive luxury SUVs. He also knew from the way the man was staggering that Mimi had slipped him the pills that he'd supplied her. He knew that a man with a hard dick and a blurred thought process was easy money. He just hoped that this nigga was a real baller and not some wannabe flashy punk, so he could lead him to a stash spot. Maury was a professional at what he did and was ready to introduce Flint to his honed craft.

Maury started up his vehicle and watched. Mimi had her arm around the man's waist as he openly groped her breasts. They walked two buildings down to the motel that Maury had booked earlier that day. He pulled the vehicle into the parking lot of the motel as Mimi practically dragged Malek into the room.

He cocked his pistol and caught a hard-on, something that happened every time he was about to hit a caper. "Let's get it," he whispered as he exited the car with a rolled-up ski mask on top of his head.

Chapter Sixty-three

Sweets and the Shottah Boyz loaded up the clips to their pistols and prepared to make it rain bullets inside the club where Joe and the North Side crew were getting their party on. They approached the

door, which was guarded by only one of Joe's henchmen. Before the henchman realized who was approaching him, Lynch sent a hollow-tip slug through his forehead, killing him instantly. They made their way into the club, about to set it off.

Boom! Boom! Boom!

Shots rang out one after another and sent Celebrations into complete pandemonium. Joe, by habit, reached for his pistol and got low. He pulled the mystery woman to the floor with him, and then everyone in the VIP followed suit.

Sweets and the Shottah Boyz stood in the middle of the club, letting their assault rifles go off. They weren't aiming at anyone in particular. They just shot at the ceiling to try to lure Jamaica Joe out of the building, so their scheme would succeed.

Joe looked onto the main floor and saw Sweets and his crew letting off rounds. "Yo, go get at them niggas!" he said as he grabbed the girl and ran to the private entrance through the back of the club. He had routed a getaway path just in case something like this went down. The woman Joe was with gripped his hand as he led her to his truck parked in the back right by the door.

Chapter Sixty-four

Mimi watched as Malek clumsily stumbled onto the motel's bed and lay flat on his back. He gripped his rock-hard dick and Mimi almost felt sorry for him. She knew that Maury would kill him after he got him to take him to his stash spot, but greed pushed her to let the scene unfold. She seductively walked over to Malek and dropped to her knees. She then began to unbutton his Evisu jeans as he tried to pull away.

"What you doing, ma?' he said almost incoherently, slurring each syllable.

"Just relax, Malek. Your mouth is saying no, but your friend down here is saying yes," Mimi said just before she took Malek's ten inches into her mouth.

She had purposely left the door unlocked so Maury could creep in. *Where this nigga at? He's taking all day,* she thought as she continued to go up and down on Malek's shaft. She grabbed his rock-hard pipe and began playing with the tip of it with her tongue.

She paused to look at Malek, and as she looked up, what she saw scared the living shit out of her. Malek was smiling with his pistol in his hand. His demeanor had totally changed. He no longer looked distraught and confused, like he had been moments before.

"You look surprised," Malek said just before he struck her in the temple, causing her to fly onto the motel's carpeted floor.

She gripped her bloody forehead in agony, and her vision became temporarily blurred.

"You thought I didn't see you try to slip me that spiked drink, ma? Huh? I ain't new to this, I'm true to this!" Malek yelled as he stood up and put his pipe back in his jeans.

Only moments before he'd pretended to drink the spiked liquor, but had quickly poured it on the floor when Mimi's head was turned.

He pointed his gun at Mimi. "Now look at you! That's why niggas can't trust these hoes out here! I know a nigga is about to come in here any second now. I saw yo dumb ass leave the lock unlocked, and I peeped you scoping out that blue car that followed us in here."

"Malek, wait! I—"

Malek struck her again in the head with the butt of the gun. He aimed the gun at Mimi's head. "Who is trying to hurt Halleigh? Were you telling the truth?"

Mimi, scared to lie, tried to tell the truth. "No, it was a—"

Before Mimi could get out her sentence, Malek sent a hollow-tip through her chest with his silenced pistol. He heard all he needed to hear. To his surprise, he wasn't even afraid of catching his second body. The rage inside of him made the situation easier. Now his only concern was the guy that was scheduled to come in the room any second.

Malek stood over Maury's shaking body as he watched him struggle for his life. Malek had caught him with four slugs to the chest the moment he walked through the motel door.

Malek held the smoking gun in his hand and began to tremble slightly. In his young years on earth, he had never killed anyone, but now in the past couple of weeks, he had caught three bodies.

He witnessed Maury take his last breath and then quickly fled the scene. He ran over to the club to put Joe on to what had happened.

For all Malek knew, Sweets had set this whole thing up as an attempt to take him out. On the other hand, it could have just been Mimi trying to set him up on her own. But either way it went, he needed to confide in his mentor. If Sweets was setting Malek up for the okey-doke, then chances were he was setting Joe up too. Malek had to warn him.

Malek's heart pounded frantically as he raced to the back entrance of the club. He noticed the large group of people running out of the club in a frenzy, and then he found out why. He heard the gunfire com-

ing from the club and quickly gripped his pistol tighter. He spotted Joe's car and then he saw Joe and the young lady he was with earlier jump into it.

"Joe!" Malek yelled as he ran to the truck.

"Come on, Malek. Jump in!" Joe screamed as he waved Malek over.

The girl took the back seat, and Malek jumped into the passenger's side.

"Joe," Malek said, nearly out of breath, "a nigga tried to set me up in the—"

Before he could say anything, the girl reached into her garter belt and pulled out a snub-nosed .22 pistol. She let off a shot to the back of Joe's head and then reached over and shot Malek three times to the chest. Joe's limp head rested on his horn, causing it to honk continuously, blood covering the front window. The girl that Sweets had sent for the job smiled. She loved what she did because she was damn good at it. She was one of the most prolific hit-hoes in the underground world. She could get to dons quicker than anyone could even fathom.

Just as she was about to step out of the car to meet Sweets in the front as he had instructed, a phone rang. It was Malek's cell.

"Hello?" the mystery woman said, trying to add salt to the wound. She always did menacing things like that. She got an adrenaline rush and laughter out of her bold, sinister act.

"Who is this? Where is Malek?" the female voice on the other end of the phone asked.

"He's sleeping," she said before letting out a big laugh and hanging up. She left the car, leaving Joe and Malek slumped.

Fifteen minutes ago Halleigh couldn't wipe the smile off of her face if she wanted to. She was so happy about Malek's proposition, she couldn't wait to move forward and leave her current lifestyle in the dust. She rummaged through her clothes, trying to stuff all she could into her luggage. Malek had made her feel like a new woman, and was ready to start her life with him.

It only took her thirty minutes to pack up everything. She called Malek's cell, but he didn't pick up, so she left a message that she was ready and told him where he could pick her up. She then sat on the porch, waiting for her Prince Charming to arrive. *Hurry up and get here, Malek,* she thought as she waited anxiously.

After fifteen minutes of waiting on Malek to pick her up, Halleigh tried calling him on his cell phone again, but when a woman picked up and told her that he was sleeping, she was dumbfounded. She just looked at her phone in disbelief. Her heart crumbled at the thought that another woman had picked up Malek's phone. He was supposed to be on his way to pick her up and yet he was with another woman.

I knew it was too good to be true. I knew it, Halleigh thought.

Tears began to flow down her cheeks. Once again, her heart had been broken in two.

Chapter Sixty-five

Malek woke up with an aching pain in his chest. He looked over to his left and saw his mentor, Jamaica Joe, slumped on the steering wheel. It all happened so fast that Malek couldn't believe it.

"Joe," Malek whispered. He tried to shake him, but it was to no avail; Joe was already gone. The bullet-proof vest that Malek was wearing protected him from the bullets that the mysterious woman had shot at him moments before, but there was still a nagging pain in his shoulder that wouldn't go away.

"Joe!" Malek managed to scream as he continued to shake him. He couldn't grasp the reality. Shock took over his reactions as he tried his hardest to wake Jamaica Joe. Blood trickled onto Malek's hand. That's when he noticed the small hole in the back of Jamaica Joe's head.

Seeing his big brother, mentor, and teacher gone was too much to bear. Malek let out a painful roar as tears welled up in his eyes, and his vision began to blur. Malek heard the sound of sirens as he looked in the rearview mirror.

As he reached for the door, an intense pain shot through his body. "Aghh shit!" he yelled out. He stumbled out of the car, and for the first time he noticed all of the blood on his own shirt. He patted his body frantically to see where he was hit. He was in shock and couldn't pinpoint where the pain in his body was coming from.

An ambulance and police cars pulled up simultaneously as Malek fell to his knees.

"Put your hands up where I can see them!" the police called.

"It ain't me! They got Joe! Joe in the car," he muttered as held his body up by placing one hand on the ground. "Help Joe!" he shouted as he began to cough up blood. The paramedics rushed over to him and immediately began work.

"We have a bullet wound to the shoulder. Get me some oxygen and let's start him on an IV," the medic called out to his peers.

Malek felt weak, and the taste of blood in his mouth frightened him.

"We're going to have to question him," one of the officers stated.

"You're going to have to wait until after he gets this bullet removed. If not, he's going to bleed to death," the medic stated sternly as he helped place Malek's body on a stretcher. Malek was slipping in and out of consciousness and was losing pints of blood at a time.

As Malek's head fell to the side, his eyes witnessed the police zip up Jamaica Joe's body bag. "Joe," he whispered faintly.

Anger ripped through Malek. Joe had been so close to his departure from the dope game. He had taken careful steps, crossing every *T* and dotting every *I*, to ensure that he made it out of the game alive and free. Unfortunately someone had other plans for him. On the night of his farewell party to the dope game, he said farewell to his life.

Malek knew that there was only one person who would be so bold to attempt a hit on Jamaica Joe. He knew exactly who was behind this hit, and vowed to make Sweets pay if he lived to see another day.

Halleigh sat by the window, staring blankly at the darkened city block, her heart aching at the fact that Malek was with another girl. She couldn't help it. She didn't care if he had a thousand other girls besides her; she had to be a part of his life.

Her heart beat rapidly as she impatiently waited for Malek to show up at her door. She was furious with him, but she needed him. She was so close to having him. *Where is he?* she thought solemnly as tears fell from her face. Her anxiety was eating her up inside. Every time a car rode down her block, she would go to the door and hope that it was Malek pulling up to get her. She thought it was Malek every time a headlight shone through her window. Every rumble of an engine could've been him.

"Why isn't he here?" she asked aloud. "He's probably fucking with some bitch." She checked the clock on the wall and noticed that it read 4:40 A.M. *He was supposed to be here three hours ago.* Her mind was telling her to give up hope, but her heart wouldn't allow her to.

Halleigh sat in front of the window until dusk turned to dawn and the nightlife gave way to the bright sunlight, signifying the start of another day. "He's not coming," she uttered as she finally came to terms with her reality. She had hoped that things would go back to normal and that Malek could look past all of the things that she'd done since she'd last seen him, but with daylight came the realization that things could never go back to the way they used to be. Too much had happened. She had changed in the most drastic way.

"He doesn't want me anymore," she cried as she dropped to the floor next to her packed bags. Tears fell freely. She didn't blame him for not showing up, since she wasn't the same girl that he'd once cherished. She had turned too many tricks, taken too many drugs and acquired too many demons. She was definitely not the innocent teenage girl that he had known.

"Why would he want me?" she asked herself.

Ring! Ring!

The screeching blare of the telephone startled her, and she staggered to her feet to answer it. She silently wished it to be Malek. She wiped her eyes and nose as she tried to calm down before picking up the phone.

"Hello?" she answered, her voice cracking in her attempt to sound okay.

"Halleigh! Oh my God, Halleigh, Maury got shot tonight! He's at Hurley Hospital. The doctors won't tell me anything!" Tasha screamed.

"What?" Halleigh responded in shock.

"Halleigh, just please come down here," Tasha pleaded. "I can't handle this by myself. He's all I've got."

The line went dead before Halleigh could reply, but she knew that she had to put her feelings aside so that she could be there for Tasha. Tasha had been the only person to stand by her side through her ups and downs, and she felt obligated to return the favor. Without hesitation she rushed out the door.

Tasha stood in front of the nurse's desk, impatiently waiting to receive news on her brother's condition. "Is he okay?" When she didn't get an immediate response, she yelled in frustration, "Why won't you tell me anything?"

"You really should wait for the doctor," the nurse told her. "He will help you understand what happened."

"Fuck you mean?" Tasha stated in exasperation. "Understand what? What happened? Please just tell me that Maury is okay."

"I'm sorry, miss, I can't," the nurse replied.

Tasha knocked all of the nurse's papers off the counter and stormed out of the hospital in a pained rage. Her head felt like it would explode. *I need to get some fresh air,* she thought as she rushed out of the double doors that led to the emergency room parking lot.

Just as Tasha was about to sit down on the curb, she saw Halleigh running toward her. She stood and hugged her tightly.

"What happened, Tash? Where is he?" Halleigh asked with concern as Tasha sobbed in her arms. Halleigh didn't know what to do. She had never seen Tasha like this. Tasha was the foundation of their friendship. She was the strong one, the leader. The roles had quickly reversed, and now Halleigh was the one trying to figure things out.

"I don't know, Hal. They ain't telling me shit. This is bad, Hal." Then she added in a whisper, "We should've just stayed in New York. If we had, he wouldn't be lying up in this hospital."

Halleigh knew that she couldn't cry. She had to be strong for her friend, but on the inside she prayed that Maury was okay. Halleigh and Maury had a relationship that only the two of them could understand. If she wasn't so hung up on Malek, she could've easily seen herself

falling for Maury, but her feelings for Malek were too strong for her to let go. Malek was a part of her, and she couldn't let her heart love another if she tried.

"Everything's gon' be all right," Halleigh said unconvincingly. "Come on, let's wait inside."

Halleigh and Tasha made their way back to the waiting room, where they both sat solemnly in silence, consumed with their own thoughts.

Ten hours had passed since Maury had been shot. Tasha had been in the hospital now for about three hours, yet she was still in the dark about her brother's status. She was more than thankful that Maury had her name listed under *Sister* in the address portion of his BlackBerry. That was the only way that the doctors were able to contact her to inform her that her brother had been shot. The unending wait to find out his condition was like torture.

Another hour passed before a doctor finally came out to see them.

"How is my brother?" Tasha asked as soon as she saw the doctor step into the room.

"I apologize for keeping you waiting this long," the doctor stated. "I don't know how to tell you this, but your brother was D.O.A. We called you down here because we needed a relative to identify his body."

Halleigh watched as Tasha broke down.

Tasha's body went numb as she looked at the man through glassy eyes. "D.O.A.? Identify his—No!" she cried. "No! God, no!"

"I'm sorry for your loss," the doctor stated out of routine. His tone held no sympathy, and he barely looked at Tasha as he delivered the worst news she'd ever received. "I'll give you a few minutes to cope with the information I've given you. I will still need you to ID the body." He walked out of the room without once looking back.

Tasha's screams could be heard through the entire emergency room. Tears fell from Halleigh's eyes as she wrapped her arms around her friend. Tasha clung to Halleigh, and the two girls sat down, rocking each other back and forth in an attempt to deal with their grief. Although Halleigh's pain wasn't as great, she was still hurt by Maury's death. He had treated her like she was worth more than gold, and she appreciated his brief presence in her life.

God, please take care of him. Halleigh looked toward the sky as she held onto Tasha. She let go when she looked up and saw the news flash across the waiting room TV. Malek's picture was on the morning news.

"Turn that up!" Halleigh yelled as she jumped up, leaving Tasha's side and rushing to the nurse's station. "Please turn that up!" she repeated. The nurse increased the volume on the TV, and Halleigh watched in desperation.

"Hi, this is Grace Stocker reporting live from Celebrations nightclub in Flint, Michigan. Last night this was the scene of a deadly shooting.

Two people were shot and killed. One was injured. These deaths bring the total to thirty-seven in Flint's murder count, making it one of the most violent cities per capita in America."

Halleigh shook her head in disbelief. "He didn't show up last night. He was shot," she whispered. "He was dying."

As Malek's picture was displayed on the screen again, the newscaster continued, "Malek Johnson was among those individuals involved in the chaos. Just years ago he had been deemed Flint's star and was expected to be the number one draft pick in the NBA. Now he is involved in yet another violent encounter.

"Viewers may remember the violence and chaos that erupted at Berston Park during a basketball game between rival drug dealers that turned deadly. Malek Johnson was shot at that event, and now here we have yet another incident where Malek Johnson has been shot. Just another indication of how bad things are in the city of Flint."

Halleigh tuned the reporter out and rushed back to the nurse's station. "Is Malek Johnson here?" she asked, knowing there was a good chance that he could be in the hospital somewhere. "Please tell me he's here."

The nurse typed in Malek's name and nodded her head. "Malek Johnson is in room eight-fourteen."

Halleigh looked back toward Tasha, who was still grieving uncontrollably over the loss of her brother. She ran over to her and kneeled by her side. "I'll be back, Tasha. I have to go check on Malek. He could be lying up in here dead and I wouldn't even know it. Are you going to be okay?"

Tasha nodded her head.

Halleigh rushed to the nearest elevator in search of Malek. She stepped inside and closed her eyes as she prepared herself for what she was about to see. *Please, God, let him be okay.*

Grateful that he was still alive, Malek, lay on the hospital bed. Something told him to put on his bullet-proof vest the night of Joe's party, and he was glad that he had followed his instincts. His vest was the only thing that saved him from certain death. One of the bullets had struck him in the shoulder, but most of them hit his vest, leaving him with some bad bruises and one gunshot wound. He would rather have bruises and a bad shoulder than holes any day.

Having seen Jamaica Joe get shot in the head, he couldn't help but feel that he had cheated death. The emotions that he felt for his man were overwhelming. Jamaica Joe had become Malek's family, and now Malek had been forced to watch him die.

The doctors had given him Vicodin to take some of his pain away, and the potent prescription drug had him woozy. He could barely keep his eyes open, but he was paranoid that someone wanted him dead, so he made an effort to stay awake. He also knew that the police

would have some questions for him. They would want to know how he had acquired a bullet-proof vest, but he wasn't going to stick around and wait for them to question him.

Malek focused his attention on the door as Halleigh walked into the room. The room was dark, but he still recognized her. He could tell by the way that she walked that it was her. Her steps were timid, and she was afraid of the condition that Malek could be in.

"They got Joe, Halleigh. She blew his brains out right in front of me," he stated without looking up in her direction.

"Oh my God, thank you," she whispered as she walked to his bed-side and kissed his cheek. Her mind wasn't on Jamaica Joe. She was just happy to see that Malek hadn't joined him in death. She sobbed as she kissed his face over and over again.

Tears from her face dripped onto his skin, and he reached out for her hand. "Why you crying, ma?" he asked.

"I don't know. I'm just glad you're okay. When you didn't show up, I thought . . ." She couldn't finish her sentence.

"I'm right here, Hal. I told you I ain't goin' nowhere. It's me and you against the world," he whispered as he graced her face with his fingertips. "Okay?"

She nodded her head with understanding.

"Now help me out of this bed," he stated. "I got to get up out of here before the police come through."

As Halleigh helped him out of the bed, he grimaced. She was careful not to touch his bandaged chest.

"Are you sure you're okay to leave?" she asked.

"Yeah, I'm good. I was wearing a vest, so the shots to the chest did-n't penetrate. I took one in the shoulder, though, and my entire arm hurts like shit," he answered.

Malek reached for Halleigh, and she helped him stand by putting one arm behind his back as he draped his good arm across her shoul-der. "Everything's gon' be good, Hal. I promise you, I'ma take care of you."

"But what about you? You just got shot. Who did this to you?" Halleigh stopped to look into Malek's eyes.

Malek sighed as he felt the throbbing in his chest. He grabbed the back of Halleigh's neck and brought her close as he kissed her on the lips. "Do you trust me?" he asked.

She nodded her head.

"Let me hear you say it."

"I trust you, Malek."

"All right then. Let me be your man and take care of you. You don't need to worry about anything."

Halleigh smiled slightly because she was finally where she wanted to be—with Malek.

Reminiscent of when the rapper Tupac Shakur had been ambushed and shot in New York City and then immediately checked himself out of the hospital against his doctors' wishes, Malek, fearing that his life was still in jeopardy, decided to "pull a Tupac Shakur," and checked himself out against medical advice. Halleigh held onto Malek, helped him into a wheelchair and then wheeled him out of the hospital without ever looking back. They were about to begin a new life together, with Malek as the boss and Halleigh as his wifey.

Tasha stepped into the cold room and stared at the bodies lying on the steel tables covered with white sheets. Her heart felt as if it would explode from fear. Deep within she knew that her brother was lying lifeless on top of one of the tables.

The coroner looked at the disheveled woman before him, and pity filled her face. A police detective stood in the corner of the room and watched her every move as the coroner led her to one of the bodies.

"Are you ready?" the woman asked as she put her hands on the white sheet.

Tasha wanted to respond, but the huge lump in her throat stopped her from speaking.

After a couple seconds, the coroner pulled the covers back, revealing Maury. Tasha's doubled over in grief and her hand flew to her mouth. "Maury! God, no! No!" she cried as she caressed her deceased brother's face. His skin was cold and held a blue hue. The four bullet holes in his chest were red, and dried-up blood had crusted around the wounds. The coroner nodded toward the detective, who then walked toward Tasha.

"Miss, when your brother was killed, he wasn't alone. We have another victim, a female, and we can't seem to find anyone that knows her. Would you mind taking a look to see if you recognize her?" the detective asked. He didn't even wait for her to agree before leading her over to another steel table.

The coroner followed and then pulled the sheet back.

"Mimi?" Tasha whispered. "Mimi!" Tasha couldn't stop the vomit that came up. She threw up all over the floor. The murder of her brother and her close friend was too much for her to bear. "Why would someone do this?" she asked as she glanced back toward her brother.

"I can't do this," she stated before racing out of the room. She could hear her heart pounding in her head, her breathing became erratic and shallow and her stomach was twisted in knots. *Maury's gone, Mimi's dead. What were they doing together? Who did this?* She couldn't contain her emotions. She didn't even make it down the hallway before she passed out on the hospital floor.

When she came to, she was in no position to deal with detectives,

but at the same time, she had to pull herself together because she wanted to help the police find the people who had done this to two of the people that she was closest to in this world.

"Tasha, we had several uniformed police officers taking statements after the violence erupted at Celebrations nightclub. Although Mimi and your brother were not killed at the nightclub, when we found out about their murders, we were able to go and re-interview some of the people who had given statements to the uniformed officers. At least three people have verified that they saw Malek Johnson leaving Celebrations with Mimi. So, before we question Mr. Johnson, we want to know from you if know Malek Johnson."

Tahsa's heartbeat immediately picked up, and while she ignored the cop's question, she wracked her brain, trying to think back to everything that had transpired the night before. Before she knew it, a light bulb went off in her head, and she could see the whole layout of the VIP area. Yes, she definitely remembered seeing Malek and Mimi talking.

What the fuck?

"Tasha, I know this is difficult, but if there is anything you can think of, it will probably help, no matter how small of a detail you may think it is."

"Malek? Yeah, who in Flint doesn't know Malek Johnson? He was damn near the LeBron James of Flint."

"Did you happen to see him with Mimi at Celebrations?"

Tasha paused; then she looked at the detective and shook her head. "Nah, to be honest, I seen Malek that night, but I never saw him with Mimi," Tasha lied. She didn't know what angle the cops were coming from, but she was street-smart enough to know to keep her fucking mouth shut, especially when it came to talking to "Jake."

Something the fuck ain't right! Tasha thought, but she just couldn't figure out what it was. She had to speak to both Halleigh and Malek to see if she could make sense out of Malek's name being in the police's mouth. If they had suspicions about Malek having something to do with Mimi's murder, then they also had to have suspicions about him being in on Maury's murder. *What the fuck?* Tasha couldn't help but notice how things seemed like they were quickly going from bad to worse.

Chapter Sixty-six

After she helped Malek into the backseat of the cab, Halleigh turned back toward the hospital. Malek could see her hesitation. "What we waiting on, Hal? Let's get out of here." Malek held out his hand for her.

"Tasha is in there, Malek. Her brother was killed last night. I have to go check on her," Halleigh stated. "Just wait five minutes for me."

Malek shook his head and replied, "Nah, ma, you've got to leave that life alone. All those chicks you were rolling with are dead to you now. I don't want you around anything or anyone that links you to that nigga Manolo, understand?"

"But, Malek, she's my friend and she needs me," Halleigh pleaded as she looked back at the hospital doors.

"So do I, Hal. I need you, and you can't have both worlds. You either with me, or you not. If you choose me, all that Manolo Mami shit and all the drugs you was fucking with got to be a thing of the past."

Halleigh looked back one last time at the hospital and then got into the cab with Malek. Her heart ached as the cab pulled away from the hospital. Malek was putting her between a rock and a hard place. Tasha was her closest friend, and now she was abandoning her.

She needs me, Hal thought as a tear slid down her face.

Malek quickly wiped it away. "This is a new beginning, Hal," he whispered as he pulled her head near and kissed the side of her face.

Halleigh gave him a weak smile as she reached out for his hand and intertwined her fingers with his. The warmth that generated between them was something that she'd wanted to feel for the past two years. Now that she had found her way back to him, she was never letting go. She told herself that she had to sacrifice her friendship with Tasha in order to save her relationship with Malek.

He's worth it, she thought.

Against Malek's better judgment, they pulled up to his one-bedroom apartment. She helped him out of the cab and up the steps to the third floor. Malek didn't let Halleigh know it, but he was feeling a bit paranoid. He wanted to avoid his South Side enemies, and at the same time, he wanted to avoid any questions from the police.He knew that going to his crib wasn't the best idea, but in the condition that he was in, he really wanted to avoid moving around too much.

When they entered the apartment, Halleigh helped him to the bedroom and sat him down on the edge of the bed. Malek looked up at her, and for the first time, he noticed a change in her, a sexy matureness. She seemed to have lost her girlhood innocence in a way that made her look and come across more mature, more sexy.

"You look good, Hal," he commented.

The two years that they had been separated had matured her, but they had also hardened her. She put her head down as she thought of all that she'd been through.

Malek immediately noticed her embarrassment, but didn't comment on it. He didn't want to make her feel worse than she already did. He was aware that she would have to rebuild her self-confidence. He only hoped that she would eventually be the same girl that he had known before her life was turned upside down.

Malek pulled her down onto the bed and she lay directly underneath him. The smell of her was intoxicating, and for the first time in two years, he felt whole. Halleigh was the missing piece to his life puzzle. Now that she was back, he was determined to never let her go.

"Hold up," he said as he eased out of the bed and went into a safe in his closet. He pulled out a .45 automatic and went to make sure that his apartment door was locked. After taking shots to the chest, he was paranoid. He knew that somebody wanted him dead and that he had to be on point until he got to the bottom of it.

He went back to the room, lay down next to Hal, and put the handgun beside his pillow as a precaution.

Hal snuggled closed to him, and he held her in his arms. It hurt like hell, but in spite of the physical pain he was feeling, he had to hold Halleigh just to have her close to him. The silence between them was a comfortable one. Eventually it transformed into the first comfortable sleep that either of them had experienced in more than two years.

The next morning Malek awoke to excruciating pain shooting up and down the left side of his body. He knew that his arm would hurt, but he had no idea how badly. He was careful not to disturb Halleigh as he got out of bed and made his way to the bathroom. He opened the medicine cabinet and retrieved some Tylenol. Taking five at a time, he hoped that the mild over-the-counter drug would relieve his pain.

His thoughts drifted to Jamaica Joe, and he gripped the sink in agony over the thought of losing his mentor. Now it was his time to step up to the plate, but it didn't feel right without Jamaica Joe by his side. Jamaica Joe had ensured that he'd learned all that he needed to know regarding the streets, but Malek knew that he had some big shoes to fill.

At twenty, he was in a position to be the king of the streets. The North Side belonged to him. He had managed to save $50,000 while hustling under Joe. It wasn't much, but it was more than the average hustler had in Flint.

He needed to come up with a plan. He already had the connect. Joe had made sure that he was in line with a supreme coke supplier, so that wasn't an issue. The problem was Fredro didn't deal in small quantities. He supplied Jamaica Joe kilos in bulk, and Malek's money

wasn't long enough to cop the usual twenty-five ki's. Fredro was giving up the goods for ten stacks a ki, but that price came along with the agreement that he would buy the same amount each time. Malek needed $200,000 more to make the deal happen, which meant he had to flip and re-flip his money in order to fuck with Fredro.

Malek looked in his bathroom mirror and saw Halleigh enter the room. She walked up behind him and wrapped her arms around his body, resting her face on his toned upper back.

"Hey, you," she greeted with a sincere smile. "How you feel?"

"I'm good," he replied as he turned around and kissed her on the forehead. "Just thinking about everything. I just can't believe I'm about to bury my man in a few days. That shit is fucking with me, Hal. You don't know. Joe been like family since the first day we met. I should've talked him out of throwing that party. He would still be here if I had been smarter."

"I didn't know Jamaica Joe that well, but I'm sorry that his death is hurting you, Malek. I do know that his death ain't on you, though. You can't control anybody else's destiny. If you could, none of this would've ever happened to us.

"I just want you to be okay. I want us to be how we were before all this bullshit sent us in different directions," she said. "Do you think we'll ever get back everything that we lost? I mean, time is something that you can't make up for. Two years have passed us by. We haven't spoken or touched one another. I'm not the same person that I was at seventeen. Do you think you can learn to love the new me?"

"I don't have to learn to love you, Hal. You a part of me, so I can never stop caring for you. We've got some issues that we need to work through, but we gon' be all right. I'ma make sure of that. I'm not the same person either. We all grow. Whether we grow for the good or bad is up to us. I'm about to be the king of this shit, believe that. All you gon' have to worry about is making your man look good, a'ight. Stand by your man and everything will be good for us."

Malek went into his room and into his safe. He pulled out two rubber-banded stacks of money and tossed them to Halleigh. "Go buy yourself some new gear. I don't want you in nothing some other nigga bought for you. Make sure you get a dress to wear to Joe's funeral."

Halleigh accepted the money. She had no desire to go to Jamaica Joe's funeral, but she knew that she had to go. Halleigh knew that the average person would never understand what it was like to not want to go to certain events out of fear, constantly wondering if you were gonna run into someone who had paid to fuck you. That was the main reason she didn't want to go to the funeral. She also knew that Malek expected her to go, and she didn't want to disappoint him. She wanted to be at Maury's funeral to pay her respects and be there for her girl, but she knew Malek would never allow it. She had been down

with the South Side for so long, it was going to be hard for her to adjust her loyalty. She was never loyal to Manolo or Sweets, but her girls were all she had, and she had grown to love them both. They had been her sisters. Just like Malek was connected to Joe, she was connected to them. Mimi and Tasha were the ones who'd helped her make it through their pimp's controlling and viciously abusive ways. They had also helped her make it through her drug addiction, which she had used as an escape from the emotional bondage that prostitution had held her in.

Now they were off-limits to her, and she couldn't help but feel like a traitor. She at least wanted to say good-bye to her girls.

"Malek, I know you don't want me to be around Tasha or Mimi, but I really need to go back and get some of my things. I don't need to bring my old clothes, but there are some personal items that I'd like to keep," she stated.

Malek looked at her skeptically.

"I promise it will be quick. I just need to pick up a few things," she said, trying to reassure him.

Malek agreed, and an hour later, he was driving her out to the suburbs of Flint to the apartment that she'd shared with her friends.

When Malek pulled up to the apartment complex, Halleigh saw that Tasha's car was parked in her normal spot. She looked over at Malek and said, "I'll be right back."

"Take your time and make sure you have everything you need. There's no coming back here after today," he stated seriously.

Halleigh nodded and took a deep breath as she exited the car and entered the building.

It was silent inside as she made her way back to Tasha's room. She knocked lightly before entering. "Tash," she called out.

Tasha didn't respond. Her back was toward Halleigh, and she was curled up in a fetal position on her bed. Her hair was all over her head, and she stared blankly at the wall in front of her.

Halleigh walked over to her bed, sat on the edge of it, and stroked Tasha's hair lightly. "Tash, I've got to talk to you about something, and I don't have a lot of—"

"She's dead too," Tasha interrupted.

"What? Who?" Hal asked in confusion.

"Mimi's dead," she stated through her cries. "She was with Maury when he got killed."

Halleigh's mouth dropped open. She whispered, "No, Tasha, please tell me you're lying."

Tasha didn't respond.

"Tasha! Please!" she begged, hoping that the news wasn't true.

"Halleigh, she's gone! They're both gone!" Tasha stated. "We're all we got."

Those words made Halleigh feel ten times worse than she already did. Tasha needed her, yet Halleigh was here to tell her that she was letting go of everything and everyone that reminded her of her past.

"Tash, we need to talk," she began. She tried to swallow the lump in her throat, but it wasn't going away. "I can't stay here, Tash. I have to move on with my life, Tasha. Malek doesn't want me to—"

"Malek? Hal, my brother and our friend were just killed. I have been here for you since the day I met you. You mean to tell me, just because you back with that nigga, you gon' act like I don't exist? You are like my sister." Tasha stood up from her bed.

"Tasha, it's not like that! I love you. You're my girl. I just can't afford to lose Malek again."

"The world doesn't revolve around Malek, Halleigh!"

"My world does! I met you in a whorehouse. You were the madame that was supposed to help my pimp keep me in line! Malek doesn't understand how you helped me. He doesn't want me around anybody that is down with the South Side. I have to respect it, Tasha. He's my man, and I love him."

"So fuck me and everybody who gave a damn about you when he left you for dead?" Tasha yelled, with one hand on her hip as she stared incredulously at her friend. "Fuck me, fuck Mimi. Fuck Maury too, Halleigh? My brother loved you. I've never seen him look at a chick the way he looked at you. Fuck him, though. Fuck that he came here to look after your skinny ass!"

"That's not fair, Tash!"

"No, you're not fair, Hal! And you know what else? I been sitting up here trying with everything I had to block some shit out, saying to myself, 'Nah, there's no way that Halleigh could do me like that.' But I guess I was wrong! Your nose is so far up Malek's ass that it doesn't even bother you that he murdered Maury and Mimi! Right, bitch? Tell me I'm lying and I swear on everything, I'll lay your ass out right here!"

Halleigh felt the tears coming to her eyes. "Tasha, what are you talking about?" Halleigh asked with a twisted and confused look on her face.

"Stop with the bullshit. You know what I'm saying is true, and that's why you ain't been around and that's why you running off! The cops told me what was up, and I played shit cool and covered for Malek's ass. Why? Because that's how I do for my people! And because I never in my wildest thoughts would have believed that Malek would do some shit like this!"

Halleigh burst out into tears.

"Halleigh, enough of the crocodile tears and all that fake shit!"

"Fake? Tasha, this ain't fake! You . . . I . . . I mean, I know you are hurting and going through it, but you're talking crazy. I'm dealing with a lot of conflicting shit too, and I don't even know what is going on."

"Halleigh, you wanna know what's the fuck is going on? Yeah, whatever! But I tell you what; you walk outta here, and I'll know what was up and what went down, and you won't have to say shit. And if you stay, then I'll be on my knees apologizing and forever grateful. But understand this: if you leave after all I done did for you, then it's on! On the life of my brother and on the life of Mimi, it's on!"

Halleigh was feeling beyond stressed out. She shook her head and stared at Tasha. Then she left the room and went into the one that she had once occupied. All of her things were as she had left them. She grabbed a small laundry basket and placed some of her items inside, including a few of the pieces that Maury had purchased for her while she was in New York.

She wouldn't tell Malek why they were important to her, but she had to have them. Maury had helped her rebuild her self-esteem in a way that Malek couldn't. See, she looked at Maury as a neutral person who didn't judge her or come down on her, and in the process, he helped to validate her. She was eternally grateful to him for that. With Malek, he didn't judge her or come down on her for anything, but he was someone that she'd loved and known and had history with. So, in her mind, she never really knew if Malek's actions toward her were stemming from a genuine place in his heart or out of pity for her.

More tears came to her eyes when she looked at the picture of herself, Mimi, and Tasha that sat on her night-stand. She wiped them away, took a deep breath, and picked it up. "Mimi," she whispered as her fingers graced the faces in the picture. "God, please take care of my girl."

Honk! Honk!

The sound of Malek's car horn made her jump. She put the picture in the basket and took one last look at her room before turning out the light.

Tasha was waiting in the hallway, leaning against the wall. With her arms folded in front of her, she looked defiant.

Honk!

"I've got to go," Halleigh stated reluctantly.

Tasha nodded and said, "It's on, bitch! I should whup your ass right now! Hmm."

"Take care of yourself, Tash," Halleigh stated through her tears. She took her house key off her key ring and held it out for Tasha.

"Get that shit out my face before I wear your ass out," she replied, slapping the key out of Halleigh's hand.

Halleigh left the house in tears and in shock and walked back to the car.

"You a'ight?" Malek asked. He saw that she was crying, and he reached out for her hand.

She gripped it tightly. "Let's go," she whispered as she looked up at the apartment building.

Malek put the car in gear and pulled away from Halleigh's past. "Halleigh, what's up? What's wrong? What happened in there?"

Halleigh slumped in her seat and blew some air out of her lungs. "I don't know . . . she talking crazy. It's like I go from Manolo and one controlling situation to another. Like she don't want me to leave, talking about if I leave, then it's on. *'It's on, bitch!'*" Halleigh said in a mocking tone. "I mean, I can't believe her."

"Halleigh, it's done! You outta here and you ain't looking back."

Halleigh didn't respond immediately to Malek.

"You trust me to take care of you, right?"

Halleigh hesitated, and then she looked at Malek and said, "Malek, you know I trust you, you know that. But I wanna ask you something, and I need you to be straight-up and completely honest with me."

"Definitely," Malek responded.

"Malek, did you kill Mimi and Tasha's brother Maury?" Halleigh asked with a frown and a concerned look.

Malek cut his eyes at Halleigh, trying to figure out how she could have known that. He was also wondering just how he should answer her, so he kept quiet. His hope was that through his silence, Halleigh would get the answer she was looking for.

Halleigh asked again, "Malek, did you kill Mimi and Maury?"

Malek reached forward and turned up the volume to Jay-Z's *American Gangster* soundtrack. He made sure not to answer Halleigh's question.

Chapter Sixty-seven

"**M**anolo's money is my money, and you fucked up Manolo's money. So that means you fucked up my money!" Sweets bitch-slapped Tasha, sending her to the floor of the beauty salon.

Tasha had reached out to Sweets, asking him to meet her at the hair salon. Her hope was that if she were to meet him in a public place, he wouldn't spazz out on her. With the loss of her brother and one of her best friends, she was really going through it, and she decided to return to the one thing that was familiar to her: selling pussy.

Sweets held his foot to Tasha's throat, completely cutting off her air. "Where the fuck was you?"

As Tasha was about to pass out, Sweets finally relented. He grabbed her by her hair and dragged her out of the hair salon and into his waiting Yukon Denali. "Get yo ass in that truck!"

Tasha got in the truck, and Sweets got in the backseat with her and instructed his driver to take off. He reached in his waistband and pulled out his 9 mm and pressed the barrel of the gun against her forehead.

"Bitch, you better start talking, and you better make that shit good!"

Tasha was so nervous that she was about to wet her pants. At that moment, she was second-guessing her decision to want to reach out to Sweets and Manolo.

"Sweets, I know how it looks, but as soon as I could reach out and say what was up without getting killed, that's exactly what I did. Officer Troy is a dirty muthafucka and snatched up me, Mimi, and Halleigh, and threatened to lock our asses up and to kill us if we didn't get down with what he was gonna do.

"We didn't know exactly what he was plotting, but now I know what was up. Halleigh and her snake ass had been down with Malek from the North Side, and she put Malek up on how Manolo was moving. Malek worked it out with Officer Troy to rob Manolo, which was all part of Malek and Jamaica Joe's plan to take over the South Side. Malek promised Troy way more than he could turn down, so Troy went with it.

"Then I find out people is dropping like flies. Mimi got hit, and my brother got hit, but meanwhile shit is looking good for Halleigh. So I put two and two together, and I find out that Malek done murked my brother and Mimi, and that's when I knew what was up.

"I said fuck Officer Troy and his bullshit threats, 'cause I knew that I was next to get killed. So it was either I get killed by officer Troy, I get locked up by officer Troy, I get killed by Malek, or I risk my life and reach out to you and Manolo and tell y'all what's up and try to get back on this madame grind! You feel me?" Tasha said all in one breath. Trying to come across as convincing, she was rambling nonstop like a chickenhead. That was because she was nervous and because she knew that her life was seconds from being snuffed out.

Still holding the gun to her head, Sweets squinted his eyes as he looked at her.

"Sweets, tonight I can get this ho shit back on and poppin'! I'll sell my pussy and I can get that chick Keesha who been trying to get down with Manolo from day one. Come on, just let me get this money for you, Sweets."

"Bitch, I should throw your ass out this moving car right now 'cause you playing me for a bitch-ass nigga."

"Sweets, I'll get Officer Troy on the phone right now. I'll put him on speaker, and you'll see for yourself that I ain't lying."

Tasha was lying through her teeth, but she was desperate. She just hoped like hell that Sweets didn't call her bluff because, if he did, she knew that he wouldn't hesitate to pop her ass.

Sweets, eyes still on Tasha, lowered his gun.

Tasha exhaled.

"So Malek is really trying to be Frank Lucas, American Gangster in this bitch?"

"Sweets, his ass is so lame! He running around like a gangsta, and meanwhile half the city done ran up in his girl that he's treating like wifey. And this nigga ain't never even screwed Halleigh yet? Bitch ass!" Tasha's words made Sweets chuckle to himself.

"That nigga must be waiting for me to bend his ass over and lay some pipe to 'im," Sweets said in a sinister tone. His dick actually began to swell at the mere thought of being able to do a tender young enemy like Malek.

Tasha, like everybody else, was disgusted with Sweets and his homo-thug behavior, but she would much rather see Malek get raped and killed by Sweets than to see herself laying dead in the streets at the hands of Manolo or Sweets. In fact, she knew that Sweets would be the one to avenge the death of her brother and Mimi, who was like a sister to her. Like she had told Halleigh, *It's on!*

Chapter Sixty-eight

Malek sat in the limo along with Jamaica's Joe's baby mother and their two young sons while on the way to the funeral services. Sobs and lost hopes filled the air. It broke Malek's heart to see Jamaica Joe's young sons, smiling and playing, not grasping that their father was gone forever.

Just the day before, Malek had found out Joe had a baby mother and kids. Joe always preached to Malek about keeping family and business completely separate. Obviously, Joe used to practice what he preached because Malek had no idea that he had a family.

Although Malek didn't know about Joe's family, Joe made sure that his wife always knew who to reach out to and what to say in the event of his untimely death or imprisonment.

Malek made a mental note to remember and utilize the game that Joe had given him during their relationship. A chill went through his body as he saw Joe's grieving woman sobbing while sitting across from him.

Kim, Jamaica Joe's woman, kept whispering while quietly crying into a handkerchief, "He's gone, he's gone."

Malek rested his hand on her shoulder and assured her that he would retaliate against her mans killer. She kept asking Malek what went on that night and he told her everything, leaving out the mysterious woman, not wanting to throw dirt on Joe's name. She had enough worries; Malek didn't want to reveal that Joe was cheating on her in the process.

"Everything is going to be all right," Malek said confidently. He looked through the window and noticed that they had reached the church. His heart dropped when he saw the pallbearers unloading Joe's casket from the hearse. The death of Jamaica Joe had the whole North side in mourning. The city had just lost one of its elite, and all of the hood legends, crackheads, workers, and community were in attendance to pay their final respects to Flint's fallen boss.

Joe had taken a page out of Mob boss John Gotti's life. Like Gotti, Joe would always throw neighborhood barbecues, give turkeys on Thanksgiving, gifts on Christmas, not to mention fireworks on the Fourth of July for the whole neighborhood to enjoy. Although the citizens knew that he was a dangerous drug dealer, they all loved him. Because of his constant benevolence, they always overlooked his misdeeds.

Malek and Joe's family stepped out of the limo onto the packed sidewalk, where people crowded the streets outside of New Jerusalem Church. They walked into the church to say their final good-byes. Malek took a deep breath. He patted his waist to make sure his gun was in place before he entered the church. He saw firsthand what could happen when you put your guard down, and he vowed to himself to never get caught slipping again. *I'm never taking any more bullets again. That's my word. I'm going to body a nigga before they body me,* Malek thought as he felt the tenderness in his shoulder from the gunshot wound.

Joe's funeral was littered with undercover cops and federal agents who likely wanted to question Malek, but he didn't care at that point, because everything was about Joe. With the way he was feeling, he would probably go to jail for murdering a cop with his bare hands if they were to be disrespectful and approach him at Joe's funeral.

The walk to Joe's casket seemed like it was three miles long to Malek. He looked down at Joe's body and was at a loss for words. Seeing a man that was so powerful lying in a casket taught him a lesson—nobody was untouchable.

After the service, Malek sat with the family at Joe's estate just out-side Flint, in the suburb of Grand Blanc. He knew about Joe's spot in Flint, but never knew that he also rested in Grand Blanc. With Joe being dead, Malek figured that it didn't matter anymore who knew where Joe lived. See, Joe was a certified gangsta from the old school. Once a player in the game was either murdered or locked up, the player's family was off-limits to his enemies at that point.

Only there to show moral support for Joe's family, Malek was quiet and to himself. He stared out of the living room window, thinking about how Joe took him under his wing. Joe showed him how to be a thinking man and to always plan his moves. That's why Malek was al-ready thinking about getting to Sweets. Retaliation was a must for him.

All of Joe's henchmen and former workers were scattered around the room, grieving in sorrow. Malek felt someone gently rest a hand on his shoulder, and he turned to see Kim.

"Hey."

"Hey. How you holding up?" Malek asked as he faced her.

"I can't believe he's gone. He was just talking about leaving here for good. He promised me that once he got you situated and prepared you to take over the empire, he was gone."

Malek dropped his head, as a wave of guilt overcame him.

Kim gently lifted his head with her index finger and stared him in the eyes. "It's not your fault," she said. "Joe was his own man and made his own decisions." She grabbed Malek's hands. "Look around this room, Malek. You got an army that's willing to do whatever you say. You have power by default. You are in charge now. But with this game comes death, jail, and sorrow. Don't let this game swallow you. Get out! Get out now, before it's too late."

Kim's eyes teared up. She saw firsthand how the game altered Joe's mind, so that even though he had enough money to leave the game, he didn't. She witnessed how the allure of the game kept him in the streets, which ultimately led to his premature demise. She felt oblig-ated to warn Malek of the flip side of the game; the cons of the drug game. Malek reminded her so much of Joe, and she saw the same glare in Malek's eyes that once was in Joe's.

Kim reached in her bosom and pulled out a small key and a small piece of paper that had a safety deposit box number on it. "Malek, I'm supposed to hand this key to you. It rips at me to do it because it's like me signing your death certificate."

"Whatchu talking about? Ain't nobody bringing death to me!" Malek said defiantly.

Kim shook her head. Malek had that gangsta ego, which was one of the worst kind. "Malek, listen, just tell me you don't want this key be-cause you're about to get out of the game and you won't need it."

Malek smirked. He looked down at the ground and then at Kim.

"Kim, I'm supposed to be in the NBA right now. I fucked that up and I didn't make it. In the process, I let my agent down, I let my fans down, I let my coaches down. You wouldn't believe how I let my moms down, but you know what? There isn't anybody that I let down more than myself! So for me to walk away from you right now and not take that key, a key that Joe wanted me to have, then I would be letting Joe down and proving how much of a fuck-up and a failure I am."

"Malek, I hear you. You know, you're about to make tears come to my eyes. You were gonna be the number one pick in the NBA and now you're about to be the number one hustler in Flint. What you're missing is that you could be number one in whatever you put your mind to. Start a business and you'll be bigger than Bill Gates. Go to law school and you'll be bigger than Johnnie Cochran. That's because you got something special in you just like Joe had. Don't follow in Joe's footsteps and waste that special gift that God put in you."

Malek paused and took in every word that Kim had said. He felt that she didn't really understand him and that she never would, nor would anyone else. He moved forward and embraced her.He whispered in her ear and told her to be strong. As he hugged her, he simultaneously took hold of her hand and the key that was his.

"I'll be smarter," he said to her.

She nodded her head, knowing that she was handing him death.

About a week after the funeral, Malek walked into the First of America Bank, the place where Joe kept his safety deposit box. It had been two weeks since he'd been shot, and he was ninety percent healed from his wounds. Malek wondered what was in the safe deposit box and why Joe had told Kim to give the key to Malek. *It seemed like he knew he was going to die early,* Malek thought as he walked up to the male teller.

"Hello, how may I help you?" the man asked with a cheesy smile.

"I would like to go into my safety deposit box," Malek said as he slid the teller the card with the box number.

"Follow me," the man said as he made his way to the back of the bank. Malek followed the teller into the spacious vault.

The teller stuck his master key in the safety box and began to head out of the vault. "Ring the bell when you are ready to exit," he said before closing the vault behind him.

Malek walked to the box and entered his key. He slowly turned it and pulled out the large steel box from the wall. He took the heavy box over to the table in the middle of the room.

Malek didn't know what to expect as he stared at the box. He took a deep breath and opened it up. His eyes lit up at the neatly placed Benjamin Franklins lined up in stacks. He flipped through the money, all hundred-dollar bills. "Oh my God," he whispered.

A note with Malek's name on it was in an envelope under one of the money stacks. Malek picked it up and opened it.

Malek,

If you're reading this, that means I'm gone. Every hustler's reign eventually comes to an end.

The lifestyle that we live doesn't come with any guarantees or pension plans. It's hard for a man to express his feelings to another man. It's just our nature. But I wanted to let you know that I love you like a younger brother. I see myself in you, and I want you to remember all the things that I taught you. I don't want to tell you what to do or anything, but my greed probably is the reason why I'm not alive anymore. Get your money and get out of the game, Malek. If you stay too long, you will end up like me or in somebody's jail cell. Start you a family and enjoy the good things in life.

I left you one million dollars to secure your well-being. I am the one who turned you out to the streets; I feel it's only right to give you this. I put the poison in your hands and cursed you with a hustler's mentality. I never seen a hustler as smart or as disciplined as you. I created a monster. I can't tell you what to do with it, but please be smart. Remember to keep business and personal completely separated. Take care of yourself, Malek.

One, "Jamaica" Joe Holland

Malek took a deep breath and put the letter in his pocket. He wasn't ready to leave the game alone so soon. He had to admit that he didn't expect to be reading a note like that from Joe, but it was what it was. Nobody knew what it was like to be destined for the NBA and then to have that pulled from under you. Nobody understood what it was like to have things at your beck and call from the age of twelve simply because you can play ball. It was like a drug to Malek, a drug that only a handful of human beings ever experienced. Malek had experienced it, and he got addicted to it. He wanted to feel that high again. He didn't want to fuck the beauty queen and not climax. He wanted to fuck the beauty queen and nut all over her ass. And he hadn't nutted yet. As far as he was concerned, he wouldn't bust that nut until he had totally dominated the drug game in the same way he'd dominated the game of basketball.

Yeah, Malek knew that he had unfinished business, like murdering Sweets on Joe's behalf, and also making more money than Joe had ever imagined. He was going to learn from Joe's mistakes and become bigger and better than him. It was Malek's time.

Chapter Sixty-nine

Malek had never seen so much money in his entire life. One million dollars lay scattered across his bed. He was giddy on the inside. When Malek had seen all of the cash inside of the safe deposit box, he almost came on himself at the sight of so much dough. He had to make three trips back to the bank in order to retrieve all of the cash. He didn't want to draw attention to himself, so each time he came back to the safe deposit box, he only carried a medium-size duffle bag with him to put the cash inside. He had been making money hustling, but Jamaica Joe had been "getting it," and the evidence of Joe's success in the game was right in front of him.

Malek had more than enough money to cop from Fredro. He was about to hit the streets hard, and no one, not even Sweets, was going to stop his rise to the top.

He counted the money for hours, verifying repeatedly that all of it was there. It wasn't a task for him. The money felt good in his hands. He knew that he couldn't act on his impulse to splurge frivolously. He was about to turn the one million into an empire and make his mentor proud. Without a doubt, Malek had to get back at Sweets, but he didn't want to move on him just yet. He first wanted to get his paper stacked as high as he could stack it, and then he wanted to catch Sweets sleeping. Halleigh was silent as she lay across the bed in just her panty and bra set. She couldn't believe the riches that were scattered around her.

Malek never let Halleigh in on his thoughts about why he was more than willing to be patient to sex her. He wanted to come across as if he was being patient for her sake, while he was really being patient because he was trying to come to grips with the fact that her pussy was no longer special. She could have been infected with some type of disease, and on top of that, he was trying to figure out how he could make her his top bitch after she had basically been the whole hood's bottom bitch.

Fuck it! he thought as he took off his LRG jeans and his shirt and lay next to Halleigh on the bed along with all of the money. Without warning, he began kissing on her.

Halleigh loved the way Malek kissed her, and she loved the way his tongue felt in her mouth. She began to kiss him more passionately.

Malek slid his left hand onto Halleigh's pussy and began to rub on it through her panties.

"Emmmmhhh," Halleigh sighed with pleasure.

Malek was actually surprised that she hadn't tried to push him away

or move his hand from her crotch like she normally had done. She usually ran a line on him that she wasn't ready to go there with him. Malek never pressured her, yet he never could understand how she would push him away as if she was a virgin, even though she had been with more dudes than Heather Hunter.

"I want you," Malek seductively whispered into Halleigh's ear as he kissed on her earlobe.

Halleigh didn't respond, so Malek took that as his cue to continue. He slid her panties off and quickly undid her bra, leaving her completely naked. He thought about going down on her, but then he decided against it. He just wanted to get to it before she changed her mind.

Malek was definitely turned on, and that was evident by the way his dick was standing at attention. He quickly slid out of his boxers and his shirt and stood there looking at Halleigh with nothing on but his Jesus piece dangling from his neck. Malek spread Halleigh's legs apart and slowly slid his dick into her pussy, which was soaking wet and throbbing at this point. Malek was kind of surprised that Halleigh's walls gripped his dick so tightly. He was expecting her to be as loose as a Ziploc garbage bag.

"Damn, baby, your pussy feel so good," he said as he began to pump his dick in and out of her.

Halleigh tried her hardest not to tense up and think about the brutal rape that she had endured. She wanted to relax, and she hoped that Malek would truly enjoy her more than any other chick that he had ever been with.

"You really like it?"

Malek nodded up and down and continued pumping. Halleigh felt so good, she knew that Malek was gonna make her cum. Without warning, tears began to stream down her face.

"What's wrong, baby?" Malek asked.

"Nothing," Halleigh replied as she wiped her tears away. "I just can't believe how much I love you and how good you're making me feel right now. I never felt this close to anybody before."

"I'm not going nowhere, baby," Malek said. "You trust me?" he asked as he pumped his dick harder and harder.

"Yes! Yes! Baby, I trust you," Halleigh replied as she began to gyrate her hips and contract her walls on Malek.

Malek had never had a chick contract her muscles the way Halleigh was doing. "Wow, baby, you're gonna make me cum! Oh shit! Your pussy feels good!"

Hearing Malek say those words to her was enough to make Halleigh explode.

"Oh, baby," Halleigh screamed. "I'm cumming!" She wrapped her legs around Malek and urged him to do it harder.

Malek followed her orders and pumped her so hard that he thought he was going to break the bed. Within thirty seconds, he pulled out and came.

"Whoa!" Halleigh said. "Malek, I never came so hard before! I feel dizzy!" She began laughing.

Malek laughed and told her how good he felt. He then went to retrieve a towel so that he could wipe off Halleigh's stomach.

Halleigh and Malek lay on the bed holding each other. Neither of them said a word, but both of them were thinking the same thing. Thinking just how good life could have been had their lives never taken such a crazy turn.

"What are you going to do?" Halleigh asked finally after hours and hours of counting money that they had just finished having sex on top of.

She was hoping that Malek would say that he was going to take the money and get out of the game, so that the two of them could live the way they had envisioned when they were still in high school. She knew that they had enough money to live the same way an NBA contract would have allowed them. They had just had great sex, which would definitely continue, so in her mind, she couldn't see why Malek would want to continue in the drug game.

Malek looked at Halleigh and smiled. He remembered a valuable lesson that Jamaica Joe had taught him while he was alive. "Keep your business and personal life completely separated," he whispered to himself. He had the potential to give her the world, just as he had always promised. She was finally his, and he was going to take every precaution to keep her comfortable and safe. At the same time, he also knew to trust absolutely no one unless he wanted to risk a downfall. He still had never figured out how Halleigh knew that he had killed Maury and Mimi, and he left that subject alone. In his mind, he had to be smart and keep his mouth shut so that he could protect himself, his hustle, and Halleigh.

He had to move Halleigh out of the hood. She needed to be untouchable, separated from his life in the streets. "I want you to go out and find us a house in a nice neighborhood. We can't stay up in here for too much longer. Niggas know where I rest at, and with this much money, I'm not taking no chances at becoming somebody's target."

"I can really pick any house I want?" Halleigh asked in excitement.

"Anything you want. You got a quarter million to play with," Malek stated.

"Two hundred fifty thousand dollars!" Halleigh exclaimed as she jumped up from the bed. Malek laughed at her and pulled her close, kissing her on the lips. "Yeah, but make sure you get everything we need with that. Furniture and all," he answered.

"Can I start today? Can you take me house shopping?" she asked.

"Nah, I got some things I need to take care of. You playing with some paper, ma. Go buy yourself a whip."

"Seriously?" she asked.

"Yeah, for real. You gon' need your own car, so go buy one. Leave the money here in the safe, though. I'll take you to the car lot so you can pick out a car. When you find a house you like, just call me and I'll bring the cash," he said. Malek knew that there was more to buying a house than just bringing the cash, but what he was trying to do was let Halleigh know that she didn't have to want for anything or worry about a thing, because he had it like that.

Malek drove Halleigh to every car lot in the city in search of a car she liked, and in three hours flat, she purchased a Nissan Maxima. Malek tried to talk her into buying a Benz, but she wanted to save the majority of the money for their house. She was satisfied with the $25,000 car because it left her with more funds to splurge on her dwelling.

Malek leaned into her window, and the smile on her face told him that she was worth the money he had put aside to take care of her.

"I'll call you when I find the house," she stated. "A'ight. Be careful," he replied before she pulled out of the car lot full speed.

The first thing that Malek did was find himself a lawyer. He needed to wash his dirty money so that his large purchases wouldn't draw any unwanted attention from the alphabet boys; the last thing he wanted was the IRS and the feds on his back. He reached out to Jamaica Joe's lawyer, told him his situation, and asked him if he knew of any attorneys that he could refer him to. He was referred to Jacob Hill, one of the best criminal defense and financial advisement lawyers in the city.

Malek made his way across town to see attorney Jacob Hill and walked into a two-story building in his Pelle Pelle jeans and red-and-white team jacket with the matching fitted cap. His thuggish appearance was out of place in the corporate office, and the secretary eyed him suspiciously as he stepped to greet her.

"I'm here to see Jacob Hill," he stated smugly as he adjusted the cap on his head.

"Did you make an appointment?" she asked snootily.

"Nah, but he want to take this meeting with me. I'm about to bring him a lot of money," he replied as he sat down and leaned back in his chair. Malek told her which attorney had referred him to Jacob Hill.

The receptionist picked up the phone, all the while looking at Malek with contempt. "Mr. Hill, a young man is here to see you. He says it's important that you meet with him." The woman was quiet for a moment as she listened to her boss respond. She hung up the phone a moment later and said, "He'll be right out for you."

Malek nodded his head and waited until the attorney came out.

Jacob Hill walked from the back of the office and extended his hand toward Malek.

Malek stood and shook his hand. "Hello, Mr. Hill, I'm—"

"Malek Johnson," the attorney stated, finishing Malek's sentence. "I remember you from your basketball days."

From the look on his face, it was clear that he also remembered all the headlines about Malek's fall from grace.

"Yeah, that was a long time ago. I'm here for another matter," Malek stated.

"Well, come on back to my conference room," Mr. Hill invited.

Malek followed him through the office and into a room that contained a large red oak table.

"What can I do for you?"

Malek took a seat and replied, "I'm going to be frank with you. I need an attorney that likes to make money. Do you like money, Mr. Hill?"

The attorney adjusted his necktie nervously. "Well, who doesn't?" he answered.

"I have some cash, a large amount of cash, that I need to show a source for," Malek stated. "And I need a good lawyer to make sure I don't encounter certain aspects of the law."

"Well, that type of service doesn't come cheap," the attorney stated, trying to see what type of wealth Malek was working with.

"Will a quarter mill take care of it?"

The attorney's eyes widened at the amount of money.

"I'm trying to put you on payroll. I need to rely on you to make sure everything stays legit and accounted for," Malek said.

"You've got a deal," the attorney replied.

The two men discussed Malek's options, and Malek also expressed his expectations to his lawyer. Jacob Hill assured Malek that by the end of the week, he would be the owner of several profitable small businesses around the state of Michigan.

Malek knew that the only reason things had flowed so smoothly for him was because of the relationship that Jamaica Joe had with his attorney. Jamaica Joe's attorney had hipped Jacob Hill to how profitable it would be to have a major drug dealer as a client.

The attorney guaranteed that he would provide the financial statements and legal documents proving that Malek had been a major shareholder in a thriving business for the past three years.

By having a solid, successful company, Malek was free to purchase whatever he wanted, whenever he wanted, without raising anyone's suspicions. Well, it wasn't actually free; it cost Malek a quarter of a million just to get in the door with Jacob Hill, as well as an ongoing 10% of the laundered money. The money he spent and would continue to

spend to make it all happen was well worth it. It ensured his freedom and gave him an ally that was skilled in the art of interpreting the law.

That same night, Malek put in the call to Fredro to pick up forty kilos of cocaine. He purchased the bricks at ten thousand apiece. After the house, the lawyer fees, and copping the coke, he would only have one hundred fifty thousand dollars left, but Malek was more than confident that he was about to come into his own.

The North Side had been in an uproar ever since Jamaica Joe's death. It had only been a couple days, but he had to take control over his hood. Niggas were getting money on what were once Joe's blocks, and Malek was about to claim what was rightfully his. He knew who he needed to see.

Mitch was a hustler on the North Side of Flint, a young nigga who was doing his thing, but could never do too much when Joe was alive. Mitch had taken advantage of the open market and put his young boys to work on the North Side. Malek respected his hustle, and wanted Mitch on his team. Recruiting Mitch was the first move in this big game of chess he was about to play.

He drove through the hood in his Lincoln Navigator and came up on some of Mitch's workers who were posted up in front of Mitch's dope house. Malek sat his burner in his lap, just in case one of the young boys wanted to jump stupid. Then he rolled down his window and tapped on his horn to get the crowd's attention.

"Yo, my man. Come here," Malek shouted to one of the workers.

The young boy's eyes shifted nervously as he debated whether or not to approach Malek. His friends looked skeptically in Malek's direction.

"Look, li'l niggas, I got five stacks for whoever can deliver a message to Mitch for me," Malek called out.

The boys still hesitated, but one walked out of the pack. His jeans were low on his behind, and one hand was on his belt buckle. Half of his hair was braided, while the other half was all over his head.

"Shit, I'll make this money," he commented as he trotted over to Malek's car. "Yo, you for real, fam?" the boy asked as he stood at Malek's window.

Malek tossed a rolled-up wad of money out of the window and said, "Tell Mitch that Malek needs to holla at him about something. Let him know it's all love, though. Tell him to get at me sooner rather than later too." Malek didn't wait for the boy to respond. He put his car in drive and cruised down the block.

When Malek entered the house at around three in the morning, Halleigh was sleeping soundly on her side of the bed. The feeling he experienced when he saw her assured him that he still loved her. She was like a breath of fresh air. He stripped down to his boxers, placed

his pistol on the nightstand, and slid underneath the covers next to her. He wrapped her in his arms, arousing her slightly.

"Umm, I found a house today," she whispered groggily.

"Oh yeah? How much is it?" he asked.

"One fifty," she responded without opening her eyes. "Can you come see it tomorrow?"

"Yeah, we'll go first thing in the morning. Get some sleep."

Halleigh didn't respond, and her rhythmic breathing indicated that she had fallen back to sleep.

The next morning, Malek fulfilled his promise and escorted her to the house that she had chosen. To his surprise, Halleigh had found a four-bedroom, two and a half bath in the prestigious suburb of Grand Blanc.

"Why is it so cheap?" he asked the realtor that was showing them around. He knew that houses started at $200,000 in that neighborhood.

"It's being foreclosed on. It was an older retired couple that lived here on a fixed income. They ran into some medical bills and decided to refinance their home, and after doing so, they couldn't keep up with the new payments. But, hey, this is really an excellent buy. Unfortunately someone else's pain will now be your gain. You may have to redecorate on the inside. Like I'd just stated, an older retired couple lived here, so the décor is a bit outdated, and the pool in the back needs some work, but everything else in the house is in mint condition."

Malek admired the spacious layout of the house. He looked down at Halleigh. "You want it?" he asked her.

She nodded while smiling and replied, "I do. I know it looks old and funky on the inside, but I can do all of the remodeling and decorating myself. I can make it ours."

"We'll take it," Malek stated. "I'll be paying cash. How soon can we get the keys?"

The realtor looked surprised and also excited about the prospect of a quick sale. "I can have the paperwork completed for you by the end of today.If you want, you can take possession of it first thing tomorrow."

"Yeah, okay. Let's do that," Malek stated as he held onto Halleigh's hand.

Halleigh clapped happily and jumped up and down in excitement. "I can't believe it. Now I have to go to Home Depot to pick out new carpeting."

Malek laughed at her rambling and guided her out of the house.

They spent the remainder of the day picking out furniture and appliances, and hiring contractors to update the house. By the end of the

day, the paperwork was signed, and they were packing up Malek's apartment.

The next day, Malek hired movers to relocate their possessions. Halleigh was directing the traffic that was coming in and out of the small apartment, while Malek oversaw the activities. He noticed an old-school black Monte Carlo with tinted windows sitting up the block. Malek had a feeling that there was someone in the car watching him.

After fifteen minutes of eyeing the car, paranoia kicked in. He didn't want to alarm Halleigh, so he didn't tell her what was going on. If somebody was watching his crib, then they were targeting him.

He walked into the house slowly as he continued to stare up the street at the parked car.

"Hal!" he yelled.

Halleigh walked toward him. "What up?" she asked.

"I'm about to go to the store. You want something?"

"Nah, I'm good, babe," she responded as she kissed him quickly and then went about her business.

Malek strolled outside, his five-carat Jesus piece glistening against his fitted white T-shirt as he jogged over to his Navigator. He reached underneath his seat and retrieved his burner. His temperature was through the roof. He couldn't believe a nigga had the nerve to plot on him. "I know they ain't trying to bring heat to my home," he said to himself as he took his gun off safety.

He pulled out of the driveway and drove in the direction of the idle car. He sped up until he was directly beside the Monte Carlo and then jumped out, leaving his car running. He snatched open the passenger side door and pressed the pistol to the passenger's head.

"Ohh shit! fam, hold up! Fall back, my nigga, damn!" he heard the driver state. "Malek, chill out!"

Malek aimed his pistol toward the driver and was surprised to see Mitch sitting there with a blunt in his hand.

"Fuck you watching me for?" Malek demanded.

"Fam, you came through the hood looking for me. I was just coming to check you out to see what was up. Damn!"

The passenger in the car was holding his face and groaning in pain.

"Nigga, you posted up the block from my crib like you lurking. My woman rests her head up in there. What the fuck were you sitting so long for?" Malek yelled.

Mitch held up the burning blunt that was still in his hand and stated, "We was getting blowed. Damn."

Malek finally tucked his gun back in his pants and shook his head. "My fault, fam."

"You got my man over here all shook," Mitch said. "What's good?

You came through the hood and paid my li'l man five stacks. You got them thinking you boss, fam." Mitch's tone was light and joking, but Malek could sense the seriousness in his voice.

"Come spin the block with me for a minute," Malek stated.

"I'll be right back," Mitch told the guy in his car, who frowned at Malek.

"My fault," Malek stated, finally acknowledging the passenger that he had roughed up. The guy didn't respond, but Malek didn't care. *He shouldn't have been posted in front of my crib,* he thought without remorse as a smirk crossed his face.

Mitch caught his expression and burst into laughter. "You wrong for fucking that nigga up like that," Mitch commented as he continued to laugh.

They hopped into Malek's car, and he pulled away.

"I know you know you hustling my blocks," Malek said, no malice in his voice, but his tone serious.

"I'm hustling. And I know you used to roll with Joe, but I don't know too much about them blocks being yours," Mitch responded.

"Look, I ain't against you getting money. What I'm against is you taking money out of my pocket and you pushing that bullshit-ass product on Joe's blocks—on my blocks. Now, I'm not trying to beef out with you. If we go to war, don't nobody make no dough, feel me?"

"Yeah, I hear that, fam," Mitch agreed.

"So why don't we just do this together?" Malek stated.

Mitch was reluctant. "No disrespect, but why would I split what I'm making?"

"Because I've got Joe's connect."

"Word?" Mitch said in shock.

"Look, I'm going to put it to you like this: You can get down or lay down. This is a movement what I'm about to do, and I want you on my team. If you not an ally, I'm going to consider you an enemy. I'm tryin'a give you a key to the world right now, fam."

"You actually got Joe's connect?" Mitch asked in disbelief. He knew that Joe had the best coke in the city for years and that no one could seem to match his product. On occasions, he'd even lied to some of his buyers, saying that he had got the raw from Joe, just to get the sell.

Malek smirked and replied, "Your tune sound like it done changed, fam. You in or you out? I need a right hand."

"I'm in, fam, I'm definitely in. Let's get this money," Mitch replied.

Malek nodded his head as he pulled back onto his street. He dropped Mitch off at his car and noticed that the passenger was still ice-grilling him. He got a bad aura from Mitch's man.

"I'ma get at you in a couple days," Malek said as he slapped hands with Mitch. "But first thing you need to do is get rid of that mu'fucka.

He got larceny in his heart. Nigga can't crank my product or be a part of nothing I'm doing."

Mitch nodded in agreement just before getting into his car.

Chapter Seventy

Over the next six months, Malek completely took over the city. He hadn't seen or heard from Sweets during his takeover. He got word from the streets that Sweets and his crew left town, and he was just waiting to hear from or see Sweets so he could send him to meet Joe.

What Malek didn't know was that Sweets had hired an excellent attorney for Manolo. The attorney was able to subpoena the police department's video surveillance tapes of the precinct where Officer Troy worked. On those tapes they were able to go back to the date that Manolo's club had been raided, and they saw Tasha going into Officer Troy's office.

With the threat of Tasha being able to testify and further expose corruption within the Flint Police Department, the department was willing and able to spring Manolo from jail on technicalities—the major "technicality" being that it was an election year and Flint's incumbent mayor didn't need any new police scandals landing on the front page of the newspapers if he wanted to retain the slim chance he had of being re-elected.

So, with Manolo being sprung from the joint, he and Sweets were planning to take out Malek. They were just laying in the cut, waiting to catch him out there, high off of his own rising status in the game.

Malek learned from Joe's mistakes and molded himself into a force to be reckoned with. One of those mistakes that Malek had seen Jamaica Joe make was his disloyalty to Tariq. Although Malek had benefited from the favor and found himself in with Jamaica Joe, he was smart enough to realize that Tariq, by right, should have been in his position. Jamaica Joe sort of passed Tariq over, and it brought problems to Joe that he wouldn't have had to deal with had he properly promoted the people who had been with him the longest.

Malek and Mitch were similar in more than one way, and they clicked instantly. Malek put Mitch in charge of the streets, while he

managed the distribution and business side. Malek had to keep Mitch's belly full, otherwise it would be Mitch who would soon be coming for Malek's crown the same way Tariq had been gunning for Joe's.

Malek had managed to do what no other hustler in Flint had ever achieved, taking over the North and South Sides. He offered the best dope and the cheapest price, and like any successful businessman, created a brand, labeling his coke "Joe Blow." Everyone craved for it. He was getting it so cheap, he didn't have to mark it up too high. Eventually the empire spread into Detroit, Lansing, and other cities in Michigan. Malek had quickly turned the $500,000 into $4 million in a small amount of time. His relationship with Halleigh was strong, and he had the streets on lock. Malek had recently purchased courtside season tickets to the Detroit Pistons, where he and Halleigh loved to spend their nights as a couple.

During the days, Halleigh was your typical kept woman. She wanted for nothing, drove high-end cars, and did a lot of shopping for clothes by designers with names that are hard to pronounce. In addition to being a diva, she was also very domesticated. She made sure she stayed on top of the numerous contractors that she'd hired to do renovations to their new home. She also found the time to cook on a daily basis.

Malek felt on top of the world at that point. He even managed to recruit some of Sweets' old workers and place them under his organization. Everyone wanted to get a piece of the American dream. With Malek's prices and high-quality product, they were more than able to.

Malek and Mitch were cruising down Clio Road in Malek's drop-top BMW, bobbing their heads in unison to 50 Cent's "I Get Money," which was blasting out of the subwoofers.

"Yo, I never seen this much money in my life, fam. We getting major paper, son!" Mitch clapped his hands together to emphasize his point.

"No doubt. We're going to continue to get it too. We have to just stick to the rules and keep a low profile. How is everything in the hood?" Malek asked as he pulled up into Popeyes.

"Everything is one hundred," Mitch answered. "Money is right, and everybody paying on time, everyone except Big Petey in Selby hood. He like a week late on that last brick I hit him with."

"Word?" Then Malek said into the intercom, "Let me get a two-piece meal."

"Yep, the nigga talkin' greasy too, like he don't gotta pay on time because he was Joe's man." Mitch nodded his head up and down.

Malek had recruited Big Petey months before, because he knew that he was a good customer to Joe when he was alive. *He thinks because Joe ain't around anymore that shit is sweet. I see I'm going to have to make an example out of him quick,* Malek thought as he retrieved his food and pulled off on his way to pick up his money—from Petey.

"There go his hangout spot right there," Mitch said as he pointed down the street to Rube's Bar. Malek pulled his new BMW on the curb and got out. He and Mitch strolled down the block where the small bar was located. Malek and Mitch entered the dark bar, and just like Mitch said, Big Petey was in there. There were only three people in the whole bar: Petey, an old junkie in the back, and the owner, who stood behind the bar.

"What's going on, Rube?" Malek said as he sat at the bar, wiping off the counter.

"Malek! My man! What's going on, youngblood?" the overweight Rube said. Rube had owned his establishment for years and was known and respected in the community.

Malek remembered when Rube sponsored his youth team's jerseys when he was in middle school.

"What's up, Big Petey?" Malek asked as he watched Petey down a shot of Hennessy.

Petey didn't respond. He knew that Malek came to his spot to ask him about the money. He also noticed how Mitch was ice-grilling him. Big Petey instantly felt disrespected. Without even acknowledging Malek, he signaled for Rube to pour him another shot.

Rube, sensing the hostility, looked at Malek and then went over to pour Petey his shot.

Malek disregarded the blatant disrespect from Petey and continued to attempt to converse with him. "My man Mitch says that you owe me a li'l something."

"You got some nerve, coming to my block with some tough-guy shit. I been hustling since you been pissing in yo diaper. Like I told that stupid mu'fucka, I'ma hit you off when I get it. Damn!" Big Petey said as he downed the shot.

"Well, when do you think you going to have it?" Malek asked cool, calm, and collected.

Mitch moved his hand to his waist, where his pistol rested, and Malek quickly shook his head, signaling Mitch to fall back.

"I'll get it when I get it!" Big Petey yelled in a drunken slur.

Malek slowly got up, reached into his pocket, and pulled out a wad of money. He gently placed a hundred-dollar bill on the counter, and then, without any emotion on his face, looked at Petey. He said, "I am going to pick up my money in one week. One week exactly. The drinks are on me." Then he signaled Mitch to follow him out.

Malek winked at Rube and began to walk out, but before he reached the door, Big Petey said something under his breath—"Ol' bitch-ass nigga"—just loud enough for Malek to hear him.

Malek stopped dead in his tracks and, without even turning around, said, "Yo, Big Petey, you don't have to worry about that little bread you owe me." Malek walked toward the door, not to exit, but to lock the

place up. He didn't want anybody to walk in while he was taking care of business.

Petey was so busy drinking his glass of Hennessy, he didn't notice Malek come back into the bar. Before Petey could react, Malek struck him over the head with a beer bottle. Petey awkwardly fell onto the floor. Without hesitation, Malek pulled out his gun and squeezed a round into Petey's face.

It was a new era. He was sending a clear message. There was a new sheriff in town. A sheriff with the balls to kill. Just like Malek had made it a point to up his street credibility by telling key street niggas that he had murked Mimi and Maury, he was sure to let the hood know that he had also dropped Petey. Malek knew he had to be careful because with too much bravado came snitches, murder investigations, and jail time.

Chapter Seventy-one

At the beginning of Game One of the NBA Eastern Conference finals between the Cleveland Cavaliers and the Detroit Pistons, it wasn't LeBron James or Rasheed Wallace who received the loudest applause from the sold-out Detroit Pistons crowd, but Malek Johnson.

Malek's face flashed on the big screen located inside the arena, and then the words *Michigan's Finest Is in the House* flashed underneath Malek's name, which was followed by highlights of dunks from Malek's sensational high-school career.

Malek loved every minute of the attention as he sat court-side with Halleigh. He had more than ten thousand dollars in cash in his pocket and was decked in jewelry worth upwards of one hundred thousand dollars. He and Halleigh were dressed in outfits that cost about two grand each. They looked like movie stars who had the money to make sure their skin, teeth, and hair were cared for by highly paid professionals on a daily basis. Malek nodded and raised his hand to the crowd and mouthed the words *Thank you.* An indescribable adrenaline rush consumed his body, and it felt so good. It reminded him of the high of being a superstar, a high that he hadn't felt in years.

As the players warmed up in preparation for the game, a player for the Pistons walked up to Malek and gave him a pound and a quick ghetto embrace. He shouted into Malek's hear, "You supposed to be out here. This is your house. Can't nobody on this court stop you."

Malek wasn't expecting such kind words of praise, and he definitely appreciated it.

"That's what's up!" Malek replied.

The crowd was still in a frenzy, screaming in anticipation of the game that was about to begin.

All throughout the game, Malek was constantly being tapped on his shoulder and handed a pen and a piece of paper and asked for his autograph.

"They always gonna love you, baby," Halleigh said to Malek as she kissed him on his cheek and snuggled close to him.

At halftime, an ESPN reporter and a cameraman came up to Malek and asked him if they could have a moment with him on camera.

"No doubt," Malek replied. By this time, Malek was buzzing from all of the Heineken he'd drunk.

"Malek, obviously you've had some bad breaks in terms of your career. Can you give the fans a little insight into the outlook on your future?" the reporter asked.

"Well, yeah, I mean I've had some unfortunate things happen to me, and I've come to grips with the fact that my career as an athlete is basically over," Malek said rather bluntly. "But don't get it twisted, and please understand that if I laced up some sneakers right now, I could go out and score fifty points against any team in this league."

"Wow! I see you still have the confidence that got you to be the most coveted player since LeBron James. But, Malek, how do you internalize that, and how does that make you feel?"

"I'm human, so obviously there's huge disappointment. So that's how it makes me feel. I feel disappointed. How I internalize it is, I realize that I'll always be number one at whatever I do and whatever I set my mind to."

"Well, give the people a little update as to just what you have been doing with yourself since you put down the ball."

Malek reached into his pocket and pulled out the huge wad of money he was carrying. He laughed and then he replied, "I been getting this paper! Word! That's what I been doing. And you see these courtside seats that me and my baby got; these were a gift. I purchased these for the season. A hundred and twenty thousand for the year is what these seats ran me. And from this vantage point, the vantage point of a fan, I realize that I can actually aspire to own a team of my own. That's what I want the public to know. Know that I won't be a tragic statistic. Nah, Malek Johnson is gonna be like Jay-Z. He went from hustling to owning a piece of the New Jersey Nets, and if he can do it, then so can I."

The reporter smiled and said, "Well, there you have it, folks, straight from the mouth of Malek Johnson, or shall I say soon-to-be NBA owner Malek Johnson."

Malek sat back down in his chair next to Halleigh and waited for the players to finish warming up so that the game could start. As Malek sat and thought, he realized that he actually could become an owner if he set his mind to it. He settled in his mind right then and there that he would indeed one day become an owner of an NBA team.

About a minute or so into the third quarter, Halleigh let out a sigh. "What the hell is that bitch doing here?" Halleigh asked as she saw Keesha walking toward her and Malek.

Keesha was sitting on the lower level of seats, about ten rows away from Malek and Halleigh. She began ice-grilling Halleigh as soon as she was able to get her attention. Halleigh kept listening to Malek and paid Keesha no mind.

As soon as there was a real raucous part of the game, Keesha took advantage of the commotion and rushed past security. She ran up on Halleigh, yanked her to the ground, and began wailing on her.

Halleigh tried her best to fight back and fight off Keesha, but she wasn't strong enough. Keesha's first blow had caught her real good and made her woozy.

"The fuck is you doing?" Malek shouted as he kicked Keesha and then pulled her off Halleigh.

It took the spectators some time to realize what was going on, but as soon as they did, the crowd went into an uproar. "You snitch-ass bitch!" Keesha screamed at Halleigh.

Some dude in a ski mask asked in a mocking tone, "Yo, Malek, can I have your autograph?" as he reached in his waistband and pulled out a gun and started firing in Malek's direction. The players were quickly rushed off the court, and security rushed to the fight in an attempt to break it up.

Malek didn't have his gat on him, so he couldn't return fire on the dude. He ducked and dove and grabbed Halleigh, and the two of them went crashing to the ground. With the sound of the gunshots, the entire arena went into a panic and headed for the exits.

"Baby, we gotta get the fuck outta here!" Malek shouted to Halleigh. "Come on! Stay low! Let's go!" He grabbed hold of Halleigh's hand, and the two of them rushed out of the arena amidst the chaos. All Malek could think of was getting to a safe spot so he could call his boys and tell them to strap up and get ready for war.

He knew that it was Sweets who had just sent a hitman to take him out in a very public place. Malek had to react and react quickly, especially since the whole world would now be talking about how Malek Johnson almost got killed at an NBA game.

Chapter Seventy-two

"You did good, baby girl! Real good!" Manolo said to Keesha as she slurped, sucked, and stroked his dick.

Keesha shifted her eyes and looked up at Manolo, to see if he was enjoying her skills. "You like the way I suck your dick, daddy?"

"Yeah, daddy likes it, baby. Superhead ain't got shit on you! You'll do anything for daddy, right?"

Keesha nodded up and down to indicate that, now that she was officially a Manolo Mami, she would in fact do anything for Manolo. She was even willing to kill if she had to.

Manolo stood up from the chair and had Keesha get up off her knees so that he could fuck her doggy-style. Manolo loved Keesha's pussy. He couldn't figure out why he'd waited so long to put her down with his stable of bitches. Then he remembered that Keesha was the loud, screaming type that hollered and moaned and carried on.

See now, this screaming and hollering shit is gonna be bad for business, Tasha thought. She could hear Keesha hollering clear from the other side of the new townhouse that Manolo had rented for his stable of women.

Keesha was exactly the type of chick that Manolo needed around. Not only would she make him money by selling her pussy, but by kicking Halleigh's ass at that Detroit Pistons game, she had shown how much heart she had. Just as Sweets had used a woman to kill Jamaica Joe, Manolo and Sweets both knew that thirsty-ass Keesha would be their triggerwoman that would take out Malek.

As Manolo screwed Keesha, he kept pressing rewind on the DVR remote control so that he could keep replaying the news clip of Keesha pummeling Halleigh. "You beat that snake bitch's ass!" he said, laughing at the sight.

He pumped harder into Keesha, and she screamed louder than a virgin.

"You gonna kill that nigga for daddy, right?"

Keesha turned her head and looked at Manolo and screamed, "Yes!"

"That's what daddy's talking about!"

Manolo and Sweets both knew that things would be real hot for the next few weeks, so their plan was to just chill for a minute. Then they would make their move on Malek.

Keesha had been fucking Mitch on a regular basis and Mitch was all about that almighty dollar so Keesha would be able to flip him and get him to help her set up Malek. In her mind, it was just a matter of time

before she would pull off the hit on Malek. She was certain that Manolo
would elevate her over Tasha to be his top bitch. Finally, Keesha's ship
was ready to come in.

Chapter Seventy-three

Halleigh lay outside next to her pool, her Chloe glasses covering
her eyes, and her two-piece Dolce swimsuit complementing her
gold stilettos. Despite the recent drama, she was living how she always
imagined she would.

Malek was wonderful and treated her with respect. The only thing
that she didn't like was the fact that they didn't have sex all day, every
day. Her body was aching in the worst way. She wanted Malek badly,
but she was afraid that he'd look at her differently because she had
been with so many men. His attitude didn't confirm her suspicions,
but her suspicions were right on cue.

Yet still, Malek was damn near perfect. He was attentive and he spoiled
her rotten. He was getting so much money that she was having a hard
time spending it. He gave her a weekly allowance of $10,000 and she
blew it on clothes, shoes, and jewelry. She had even saved up for two
months and bought herself another car, a cherry red BMW convertible,
which made her the envy of the town. She remodeled their entire
house from top to bottom, and now she felt like she didn't have any-
thing else to do. She was bored. With Malek being in the streets, she
was alone a lot. He kept late hours, which left her with a lot of time on
her hands. She had been forced to end her friendship with Tasha and
was lonely without her former partner in crime. Malek had literally se-
cluded her from anyone and everyone that she knew, but she under-
stood why. He had stepped into Jamaica Joe's shoes and was "that
nigga" in the streets. Every bitch wished they could get their hands on
him, and every nigga was trying to be down.

Being his woman made her a certified street diva, and she was play-
ing her position well. She had gone from a Manolo Mami that any man
could purchase, to a woman that no one could have. She was a hood
legend. She was respected and talked about, but rarely seen. She was
respected because Malek had upgraded her, and she was grateful for
her new lifestyle.

The only time she ever went to the hood was to get her hair done. It was her one chance to catch up on everything that was happening on the North Side. When she first started going to the salons, she experienced "shade" from the North Side girls. By being a Manolo Mami, she was automatically looked at as competition by all of the South Side chicks like Keesha, who were thirsty to get down with Manolo. Once they found out about her and Malek, the North Side girls warmed up to her. She had so many associates, she couldn't even count, but she wasn't naïve. She knew that they were not her true friends. If anything, they just wanted to get close to her so that they could get the inside scoop on Malek and one day take her place. Halleigh would never set up her own fall from grace, so she kept all those thirsty bitches on a leash, staying close enough to know what they were thinking, but not close enough for them to know her thoughts. "Keep your friends close and your enemies closer," was her motto when it came to the gold-digging chicks she met on her way to the top.

Halleigh grabbed her silk robe and put it around her body before walking into her house. It was almost time for her hair appointment, so she headed inside to get dressed. She wore a yellow halter sundress with a yellow satin bow that tied around her waist. Yellow Aldo sandals with the wood-colored heel adorned her French manicured feet. Her hair was thick and nappy. She was definitely in need of a touch-up. She pulled her hair up in a loose ponytail, left her glasses on her face, and stepped out of her house.

Driving into the city, she bumped Keyshia Cole out of her custom speakers. She bobbed her head to the soul-searching lyrics. It was the middle of the summer, so as soon as she entered the city limits, she saw everybody out riding around in their cars and chilling on the block. Halleigh loved the attention that she got as she sped down Clio Road. She parked in the parking lot to her favorite salon and hopped out, engaging her car alarm as she walked toward the building.

Halleigh was definitely living ghetto fabulous, but everything in life came at a price. In Halleigh's case, there was a price to being the first lady to the city's biggest hustler. For Halleigh, the price that she had to pay was dealing with enemies, and especially the jealousy and envy of those who wanted to have what she and Malek had.

Halleigh made her way into the salon, she realized that for the first time in her life she was literally a bit paranoid. She thought, *What if Keesha pops up again? Is Keesha now cool with Tasha, and if so, is Tasha gonna come at me for what she looked at as a lack of loyalty? Is Manolo still locked up, or is he out on the streets? Would someone try to kill me for just being Malek's girl?*

Yeah, Halleigh had stress to deal with, but she tried her best to pamper herself at home and away from home.

* * *

"Man, that young nigga ain't playin'. Scratch saw the whole thang, ya dig. I mean, he just blew that joker's brains out without even thinking about it. Now pass me the pipe, nigga. You always hoggin' the rock," Scratch said as he conversed with three of his crackhead friends who had huddled in the alley to split the twenty-dollar rock they had all put in on.

Scratch grabbed the crack-filled pipe from his associate and took a deep pull, letting the crack smoke rush down his throat and into his lungs. He noticed a person walking past the alley and jumped at the opportunity to hustle up on some more money.

Halleigh noticed a man coming from the alley.

When Scratch saw her approaching, he jumped up desperately. "Aww, pretty lady, pretty lady, can you give ol' Scratch some spare change?" he asked as he scratched the back of his small, dirty Afro.

"Scratch!" Halleigh yelled in excitement. Halleigh hadn't seen him in over a year and, oddly enough, was glad to see her old smoking buddy.

"Li'l Rina?" Scratch said, calling her by the nickname he gave her "That sho' is you. You look good, girl. Scratch heard you were messing with that young boy Malek. I heard he got you up in a big ol' pretty house in the suburbs somewhere. Ten bedrooms, twenty-eight bathrooms. Hell, even a golden shithole for the dog. You large, Li'l Rina! I'm proud of you."

Halleigh couldn't help but laugh at his exaggeration. She knew that the hood was talking about her if Scratch knew her business. "I'm doing real good, Scratch. I'm clean now, and I'm happy," she stated. She reached into her Birkin bag and pulled out her wallet. She peeled off three hundred-dollar bills. "Here you go, Scratch." She handed him the money. She knew how it was when you had a monkey on your back and you couldn't get it off. "Take care of yourself, okay."

Halleigh literally would have given Scratch the shirt off her back., That was because they had a connection that was formed in the gutter—a bond similar to the one soldiers form with one another when they're in a foxhole and enemy armies are gunning at them, trying to kill them. She knew that Scratch would use the money to get high. While she hoped that he would one day get help and get clean, she wasn't going to act holier-than-thou and forget where she'd come from. So, she helped him out with some of her blessings.

"Yeah, okay, Li'l Rina. You take care too," he replied as he watched her walk into the building. "My Li'l Rina, my Li'l Rina," he mumbled. He was happy that the young girl was clean and healthy. Scratch smiled, thinking about how Halleigh's life had changed for the better, and about his next stop, the nearest dopeman to get his next fix.

Chapter Seventy-four

Halleigh lay next to Malek. Her head rested on his chest, and their fingers intertwined as they sat back and enjoyed each other's company. It was the first time in a long time they had spent some quality time together. Lately, the only thing that Malek had time for was getting money. His constant hustling had caused her to spend many lonely nights in their new home.

"I've missed you," she whispered intimately.

"I know. I'm sorry I haven't been around much. You know what I've been doing. I've got to make sure that we want for nothing. A couple years of hustling and we'll be set for life. I'm doing this for us," he replied while he ran his fingers through her hair. He knew that he had been neglecting home, but it was for a good cause. He was making money in the hood. He had to be on point if Halleigh wanted to continue to live the lavish lifestyle that he was providing for her.

"I know, I know," she said. "It still doesn't stop me from being lonely sometimes."

Malek noticed the disappointed look on her face and sighed deeply. "Look, Hal, I'm here now, ma. Let's just enjoy this time together, a'ight. It's all about you today."

"Okay," she reluctantly answered with a light smile.

Malek pulled his T-shirt over his head in one swift movement and then turned her on her back. He kissed her neck gently, running his warm tongue across her skin.

Halleigh arched her back in anticipated pleasure, but before she could get into it, Malek's cell phone rang loudly. "Don't answer it," she whispered with lust in her voice as she turned Malek's head back toward her.

Malek kissed her distractedly as the phone continued to ring. "Give me one minute," he said as he rose from the bed.

Halleigh sighed as she watched Malek walk over to the dresser to answer the phone. She knew that his focus could never be on her completely. The streets didn't allow it.

"Hello?" Malek said as he flipped open his cell.

"Yo, fam, I got that for you. I just picked up the scratch, and it ain't what it's supposed to be, nah mean?" Mitch was on the other end of the phone, and the news he was delivering wasn't good.

"What you mean, fam?" Malek asked. His workers had come short on his money last month, and after a routine shakedown, he was confident that it wouldn't happen again. This was becoming a problem.

"Shit's like a hunnid thou short," Mitch informed heatedly.

"A'ight, fam, come through my spot. We got to figure this shit out, and we also gotta talk about handlin' them niggas, Sweets and Manolo. If I don't respond soon, then the streets is gonna start thinking I went soft. You feel me?" Malek said.

"I'm about fifteen minutes away from your crib. I'll be there in a minute," Mitch replied.

Malek allowed Mitch to know where he lived, simply because he thought about how Jamaica Joe had operated, never even letting his closest henchman know where he officially rested. Malek understood why Joe did what he did, but at the same time, he reasoned that if the closest people in your organization didn't know where you lived, then that would breed mistrust in them and cause envy and hate to build up in your top people.

Malek snapped his cell phone closed and looked back toward the bed. Halleigh looked disappointed as she got up then walked out of the room, shaking her head. Malek let her leave. He didn't have time to entertain her. No matter how much he wanted her, he had other things that were more important at the moment. His workers were coming short with his money, and he needed to figure out why.

He put his cell phone on his clip and put on a white Enyce T-shirt before joining Halleigh in the kitchen. He found her standing in front of their liquor cabinet. She poured herself a glass of wine as he walked up behind her and wrapped his arms around her waist.

"You upset?" he asked her, already knowing the answer to his question.

"It's all about me today, huh?" she replied sarcastically as she sipped her red wine. She knew that she loved her man, but she was feeling left out of his life. He made sure that she was taken care of. Halleigh literally wanted for nothing, but the thing she craved the most was his presence. They had missed so much of each other's lives. All she wanted to do was to make up for lost time. She wanted to get to know Malek again. Mentally they had grown, and physically they needed to become acquainted again.

"Don't be like that," Malek stated. "I love you, Halleigh. I just have to handle this, a'ight." He kissed the nape of her neck as she stood with her back toward him.

The feeling of his lips on her body sent shivers down her spine and left her vulnerable to his touch. She couldn't help but forgive him.

"Okay, Malek, but you need to make some time for me one of these days. She misses you too," Halleigh whispered erotically, referring to the yearning that she felt between her legs. She tugged at his earlobe with her teeth and slipped her tongue inside.

Malek's loins called for her. He picked her up by the waist, his hands firmly planted on her ass and her legs wrapped snugly around him,

their tongues entangled. Malek placed her on the kitchen counter as he took a position between her legs. He could feel the intense heat coming from Halleigh's body. Her desire obvious, he suddenly forgot about his duty to the streets. Ding-dong! The ringing of the doorbell interrupted their rendezvous.

Malek closed his eyes and rested his forehead against hers. "Hold that thought. We gon' finish this as soon as I'm done with business," he said.

"I hope so," she replied with a mischievous smile as she picked up her wine glass.

Malek went to answer the door and was greeted by Mitch. They slapped hands and embraced quickly before Malek invited him into his home.

Mitch looked around and was impressed by the interior of the expensively decorated living space. Malek was definitely doing well. "What up, fam?" Mitch asked as he took a seat on Malek's oversized leather sectional.

"This money, nah mean?" Malek replied, pacing back and forth. "What is up with these niggas? Them dudes you got out here playing wit' my money? I thought we already made an example out of Big Petey. Pour that on the table," Malek instructed, indicating the duffel bag full of money that sat at Mitch's feet.

Mitch unzipped the bag and emptied the contents onto the coffee table, covering it with wrinkled bills. They began to separate the bills by denomination, and when they were organized, they pulled out the money machine.

"What is this?" Malek asked as he looked at the bills going through the money machine.

"That's the take. That's what we made this week, fam," Mitch answered as he shook his head in disbelief.

Malek had noticed his paper was short in the Fifth Ward, usually his most profitable block for cocaine. For the past couple of weeks, he had begun to see his money decline in that neighborhood, and he began to grow suspicious. Malek stopped the money machine and calmly sat back in his chair, shaking his head from side to side, obviously disturbed. *Either niggas is skimming off the top or crackheads just stopped smoking rocks. That is the only explanation for the Fifth Ward not to do numbers,* Malek thought as he looked over at Mitch. Malek had been hustling with Mitch for months, and Mitch hadn't shown any sign of disloyalty up to that point.

"Why is the paper constantly coming short from the Fifth, Mitch?" Malek folded both of his hands and leaned back in his seat.

"Niggas saying it's hard to eat because of that new rehabilitation center that was built on Detroit Street. They built it right in the middle of the hood. They be having bullhorns and shit, protesting with signs.

No one want to be making their pay in that kind of environment. Feel me?" Mitch answered.

"Man, one rehab ain't shutting down an entire block—someone is putting they hand in the cookie jar," Malek stated.

"Nah, they ain't stupid. They ain't tryin'a see us. We just got product that ain't moving. I got workers that usually move three bricks a week sitting on 'em 'cause they can't get 'em off like usual because of that center, fam," Mitch explained.

"What's the rehabilitation center called?" Malek asked, confused.

"Um . . . The—" Mitch snapped his fingers, trying to remember the name of the place, and it finally came to him—" The Genesis, yeah, that's what the shit's called. Some reformed addict named Moses is in charge of it."

The Fifth Ward was the source of about half of Malek's drug income, so this was definitely a problem.

"How can a little-ass center stop us from making money?"

"It's just hard trying to sell drugs while someone is on a bullhorn telling people that it will eventually kill you. Li'l man that works for us said that half of his former customers are in their rehab. It's going to be impossible to do numbers while that center is there. They on some save-the-world shit, and it's costing us money."

"I mean, damn, you talking like everyone done stopped smoking. They still tryin'a get high," Malek said.

"Look, fam, that ain't the only problem," Mitch stated. "That faggot Sweets been causing problems on the South End too."

"Word is bond, Mitch. It's time to lay him down! How we gon' get at that homo-ass Sweets?" Malek asked in irritation. His tone indicated that he was obviously upset about the sudden change in profits, and even more so about Sweets and his annoying tactics.

"Man, Sweets can get got, and I know just how to get at his ass. According to the dudes we got posted on the South Side, Sweets been sending them young murderers he got to get his blocks back. You know Sweets be on that gay shit. Supposedly, he done already made an example out of a couple of our workers. They ain't trying to see Sweets like that, so they'll rather come short on our money than face him."

Malek was enraged. There was no way he was going to give up the South Side. He would rather go out in a blaze of gunfire than let Sweets kill his former boss and then muscle in on his territory. Malek was the first hustler to take control of both sides of the city, and Sweets wasn't going to stand in the way of his reign of power.

"We got to get rid of Sweets. I ain't tryin'a do this back—and-forth shit either, fam. I want him dead, nah mean?"

"Yeah, I hear you, fam. You know I'm with it, but that still don't handle our other problem," Mitch stated. He turned on the television and flicked to the evening news. "This rehab been all over the TV. They try-

ing to expand and everything. You think it's a problem now, wait until they spread those centers all over the damn city."

Malek focused his attention on the screen and listened to the news report:

> *"Here in Flint, the drug problem has plagued our city for over a decade. For the first time in years, a rehabilitation center has been able to reach out to those citizens who struggle with drug addictions. Genesis opened just thirty days ago, and with limited funding has been able to reach out to our city. Genesis offers drug rehabilitation programs that promise security once the program is completed. They have job placement agencies, and even hand out weekly stipends to their patients. Upon completion of the program, the participants are given a check for the stipends that they have earned, and are helped to find residence and employment.*
>
> *The organization was founded by none other than a woman who goes by one name: Moses. Moses is a reformed heroin addict and has been clean for more than twenty years. She has applied for federal funding, and the center is currently undergoing evaluation to see if it qualifies. The center has its first awards ceremony in exactly one week. The public is welcome to attend."*

Malek hit mute on the remote control and shook his head. He couldn't believe that one rehab center was affecting his cash flow. There was never money to open up a rehab facility in the city, and now all of a sudden this one was sent from heaven, or some miracle shit, and now it was healing more addicts than Jesus.

"What the fuck, fam? This one place got all the addicts going clean?" Malek asked in frustration.

Mitch nodded his head and responded, "Not all of 'em, but enough of 'em for us to feel it. Moses is relentless. She be coming onto the block to recruit the addicts. She even offers to reform the drug dealers. She's a problem, and if she gets that federal grant, she's going to really mess up our money."

"A'ight, a'ight," Malek stated as he sighed deeply. "We're about to settle this shit with Sweets. Then we'll focus on that center. Maybe we can convince them to relocate," Malek said as he pulled out his pistol and set in on the table.

Without Malek saying anything else, Mitch got the picture.

"Listen, there's this ho-ass trick that I know, and she be fucking with Manolo, so I know we can get at him and Sweets through her," Mitch stated. He was referring to Keesha, but he didn't let Malek know who

he was talking about, simply because he didn't fully trust Keesha and he knew that Malek had no love for her after she had whupped his girl's ass.

Malek didn't know it, but Mitch was doing a "Donnie Brasco" on him—He was playing both sides of the fence, and he was also a switch-hitter, down with that homo-thug shit. Right after Joe was murdered, Sweets had convinced Mitch to fuck with him, and they had a plan to not only divvy up the streets of Flint, but to also take over all of Detroit and split that down the middle as well. So although Mitch was telling Malek that the reason for the decline in money was due to the rehab center, he was just blowing smoke up Malek's ass. The real deal was that Mitch was robbing Malek blind.

Halleigh came walking through the living room on her way to her bedroom.

"Halleigh, come over here and meet my man," Malek called out to her as he outstretched his arm for her to take her place within his embrace. She wore pink pajama shorts and a matching wife-beater.

She walked over toward the men, but Malek blocked her view of Mitch.

"Halleigh, this is my man, Mitch. Mitch, this is Halleigh," Malek introduced as he wrapped his arm around Halleigh's shoulders.

Halleigh looked down at the man sitting on her couch and immediately recognized him. She felt as if she would lose the contents of her stomach, and her breaths became shallow as she stared at Mitch. The look in his eyes let her know that he knew who she was.

"I—it—it's nice to meet you," Halleigh said as she held out her hand.

Mitch, of course, knew exactly who Halleigh was. Keesha had been trying her hardest to describe her to Mitch, and when he saw the clip on the news of her getting her ass beat at the Pistons game, he immediately remembered paying to fuck Halleigh in the backseat of his car in the park on the day that Malek was shot.

He grabbed her hand gently and caressed it slightly. He wasn't going to bust her out, but he smiled and replied, "It's nice to meet you too, ma." He held her hand a little longer than needed, and she pulled it back to avoid Malek's suspicion.

Halleigh couldn't help but notice how good Mitch looked in his butter Timberlands, Sean John jeans and button-up shirt. His caramel complexion looked good enough to eat. She felt disgusted with herself for even feeling the tiniest bit of attraction to him, and so she averted her eyes to the floor.

Malek looked at her and peeped her nervous energy. "What you nervous for?"

Halleigh looked up at him, her mouth still dropped down in an O

of surprise. "I'm not," she replied. "I'll be in the room." She slipped from underneath his arms and high-tailed her ass out of the room.

Mitch's eyes discreetly followed Halleigh out of the room. He definitely remembered her tight-ass virgin pussy, and he knew that the only thing tighter than that was a nigga's asshole. She had the best pussy he'd ever had, and hoped that they would cross paths again. Now he was seeing her on the arm of his man. He looked up at Malek and stood to his feet. "I'ma get out of here, fam," he stated.

"A'ight, I'll get at you tomorrow, so we can get on that Sweets situation," Malek replied as he slapped hands with his boy. He walked Mitch to the door and sighed when he thought of all the problems that had suddenly arisen. He definitely had a lot to deal with, and he didn't have a lot of time to do it.

Halleigh couldn't believe that Mitch was Malek's right-hand man. She couldn't believe that she had run into him again. Her heart racing nervously, she contemplated what she should do. Should she keep her mouth shut, or should she tell Malek what the deal was? He had been the first trick she had turned, and she remembered it as if it were yesterday.

Malek could see the look on Halleigh's face and frowned. "You good?" he asked.

Halleigh knew that she must have been wearing her heart on her sleeve. Malek could always tell when something was on her mind. "Yeah, I'm good."

Malek climbed into the bed beside her and massaged her back. The feelings of his hand on her body caused moisture to form between her legs. She was yearning for him and couldn't wait to have him inside of her.

Sex had always been equated to money with her. For the first time ever, she was intimate with a man, and it was her choice to give herself to him.

Malek looked into her eyes as he slipped two fingers into her opening, which was now dripping wet. Their faces were so close that they could feel each other's breath.

"I'm sorry for everything," Halleigh whispered. She began to grind her hips as he fingered her.

"Shh!" he whispered. "You don't have anything to be sorry about."

Malek had no idea that Halleigh was actually apologizing for having had sex with Mitch, his new right-hand man. He showered her body with kisses, beginning at her neck and making a trail down. His tongue caressed her erect nipples, and he tugged on them softly with his thick lips.

A moan escaped her lips as he continued to go south. He lifted her hips and lowered his head, French-kissing her middle. He gave her clit attention that she'd never experienced, causing her to scream out in pleasure. His mouth was warm, and the heat felt good on her swollen

jewel. She began to grind against his face, her legs spreading wider as she came over and over again.

Malek's manhood hardened, and his ten inches grew. Halleigh's moans only intensified his hunger for her. His penis throbbed and pre-cum rested on the tip. He explored her lips with the tip of his dick, and the sensation of the wetness caused him to call out. "Shit," he whispered as he eased himself into her.

Halleigh tensed up out of habit. She'd learned to fear sex. Being forced to prostitute herself had given her a misconception of sex. She held her breath when Malek entered her. He looked down at her. Again, there were tears in her eyes. "Are you sure you want to do this?" he asked.

She nodded. "Yes, I'm okay. Make love to me."

"I would never hurt you, Halleigh," he whispered as he rocked inside of her. He maneuvered in and out of her, catching a slow rhythm as he thrust passionately. He felt her body relax beneath him, and she matched his pumps intensely.

Malek's manhood was thick, and it stretched her walls as he brought her pleasure. Sweat glistening on his chest, he leaned into her and kissed her on the lips.

Halleigh moaned loudly as he deep-stroked her. She had been fucked before, but never had she felt the intense emotion that was connected to her lovemaking with Malek.

Halleigh's toes began to curl, and her face twisted in contortion as she felt herself climaxing. "Malek!" she called out as her back arched. "What are you doing to me?"

"Loving you," he whispered as he watched her cum. The look on her face caused him to pump faster and deeper.

As the bed rocked and the headboard hit the wall, Halleigh could feel his manhood throbbing as he let off his seed inside of her, collapsing on top of her and kissing her forehead.

"I love you," he told her.

"I love you, Malek," she replied as she nestled in his arm and fell into a comfortable sleep.

Mitch couldn't believe that he had run into Halleigh again. After he fucked her, he had thought about her for weeks. He had even contacted Manolo to see how he could have her, but Manolo wasn't a fool. He knew that Halleigh was a hot commodity and wasn't to be sold. When he saw her tonight, Mitch was happy that she had managed to stop selling her pussy. Although Manolo was his man, Mitch knew instinctively that Halleigh never should have been selling pussy because she was a good girl and wasn't built for that shit.

He was saddened by the fact that Malek had gotten to her first. Halleigh was perfect. Her beauty was uncanny. He wouldn't hesitate to fuck her again if he got the chance. In fact, he was definitely gonna go

after her as soon as Sweets bodied her man Malek. Mitch wouldn't violate his man by coming at her, but if Malek ever fucked up, he would make sure to be there to pick up the pieces.

Chapter Seventy-five

Malek and Mitch sat in front of Big Al's, a local soul food spot. They had just ordered some food and were plotting on Sweets as they sat in the car and picked at their fried catfish dinners. They both had automatic pistols sitting in their laps and ski masks in the backseat. They had been staking out Sweets' house for hours, waiting for him to show his face. After seven hours of stalking, their hunger got the better of them, and they decided to call it a night. "You sure you trust that bitch? This is the crib, right?"

"Fam, I got this! Shorty wouldn't do me dirty. Let's bounce, but we gon' get this nigga. Trust me on this," Mitch said.

Malek put his food back in the bag and started his car. He looked in his rearview mirror to observe the block. A few minutes passed as they continued to pick at their food. Just as they were about to drive away, a white Denali pulled into the parking lot. Sweets exited the car, and an entourage of killers followed him into the restaurant. It was obvious that Malek and Mitch would be outnumbered if they approached Sweets on some beef shit.

"Ain't this about a bitch? We've been trying to catch up with this nigga all day and here he is," Mitch stated in mock disbelief, knowing that all the time that they had spent staking out Sweets' crib had been just a front on his part. He had known all along that Sweets wasn't home and that he wouldn't be home all day.

"We can't just rush up in there," Malek stated more to himself than to Mitch. His mind was turning as he tried to devise a plan to get at Sweets. Murder was his motivation, and he wanted nothing more than to avenge Jamaica Joe's death. He knew that if he took an attempt on Sweets' life and failed, it would spark a bloody assault, if not an all-out blood bath, on his soldiers in the street. If Malek was gonna make a move on Sweets, he had to hit him and kill him. He couldn't take a shot at him and miss or simply wound him. Anything less than killing Sweets would further fuck up his money, so he had to put his anger

aside and think strategically for a solution that was beneficial to everyone. Even if it meant giving Sweets a temporary pass.

"I know. He got them Shotta Boy niggas with him, and you know they stay strapped. We can't roll up in there with two pistols against all that," Mitch said.

"Fuck it!" Malek stated. "I'ma give Sweets a chance to save his own life. It's like I told you: a war keep everybody's pockets on E. I'll let Sweets have the South Side back if I'm getting forty percent of the take and if he cops his weight from me." Malek said that to test Mitch's response.

"You think he gon' go for that?" Mitch asked.

Wrong response, Malek thought.

If Mitch was really gangsta and riding with him, he would have been in fight mode and wouldn't want to be diplomatic about shit. Now Malek had to question just what was up with Mitch.

"Yo, fam, what was the chick's name who put you on to where Sweets rests at?"

Malek's question caught Mitch off guard.

"Eh? Oh, oh, Monica. The chick's name is Monica. She used to fuck with Sweets real heavy."

"Fuck with him like how?" Malek asked.

Mitch didn't answer the question. Instead he tried to change the subject back to what Malek had mentioned just a few minutes ago. "So, yo, you really think he gon' go for that deal?" Mitch asked again.

Malek didn't press Mitch on the name of the chick, but he knew right then and there that Mitch more than likely had been bullshitting him the whole time. He played along with it. "He ain't gon' have a choice. He can either take these bullets courtesy of Jamaica Joe or fall in line," Malek replied. He got out of the car and walked across the darkened parking lot.

Mitch reluctantly followed him. He knew that he could be walking into a potential death trap. If Sweets saw him with Malek, he would wonder if Mitch was really down with Malek. So Mitch strategically kept his hand on the handle of his chrome pistol as they headed into the restaurant.

Malek's adrenaline was pumping, and he could hear his heart beating in his ears. Malek walked in, and the bell above the door rang, causing Sweets and his entourage to turn around.

Sweets' face turned up in disgust at the sight of Malek. He pulled the red Blow Pop from his mouth as he placed his hand near his waist.

Mitch nodded to Sweets, to let him know that everything was straight.

"Look at this mu'fucka," Sweets said with a smirk, "living in Jamaica Joe's shadow and trying to run my side of town."

The sound of Joe's name coming from Sweets' lips sent rage through Malek's heart. "You might wanna keep my man's name out your mouth, nah mean?"

The Shotta Boyz sent glaring stares his way, and Malek sent them right back.

"You lucky I'm not coming in here to twist your shit back behind that stunt you pulled at the Pistons game, but I'm about my bidness," Malek said. "I hear that you're interested in getting your hood back."

"I never lost my hood, fam," Sweets replied with larceny in his heart. "Can't you tell? I mean, considering how you a businessman and all, ain't you curious why your money been so short lately?" Sweets winked at Malek and blew him a seductive kiss.

"See, I've got a problem with that 'cause them streets belong to me now. Ain't no North Side-South Side beef, 'cause all that paper coming to me. Now we can blaze out for them blocks if you want to—" Malek pulled his nine out of his waist and let it rest in his hand by his side as he continued. Sweets saw the move and removed his pistol as well— "But you and I both know that wouldn't be a good thing. If we out here killing each other, we ain't making no money. Don't nobody like to watch over they back every minute, nah mean?"

Sweets wasn't a fool. He could see that Malek was setting up some sort of negotiation. He wasn't against that, but the way he saw it, Malek had to really sweeten the pot. Otherwise, Sweets would be shorting himself, especially since he was already getting a piece of Malek's money through Mitch.

"So what's up? Speak to me, young'un," Sweets said.

"I'll give you your blocks back under two conditions," Malek said. "One, you cop your work from me, and two, you give me forty percent of your profit." Malek could see the anger behind Sweets' eyes.

"You must think it's a game, young'un. I run those blocks on the South—"

Before Sweets could finish his sentence, Malek raised his pistol and fired a shot into one of the goons standing behind Sweets.

Sweets' and Lynch's eyes bugged in anger. Lynch, the only remaining Shotta Boy, knew that he should've carried his pistol into the restaurant. Now he was naked and vulnerable, and they had no choice but to agree to Malek's terms.

"Uh-uh. Keep them hands up, baby," Mitch said as he waved his gun back and forth between Sweets and Lynch.

"Like I said, we can beef out, but if you want to live, you'll accept my offer," Malek added.

Sweets shook his head and laughed loudly. "A'ight, li'l nigga. You da man," he said in a mocking tone.

"Good."

Malek and Mitch backpedaled toward the door as they prepared to leave.

Before Malek was completely out of earshot, Sweets said, "Hey, Malek, how is your bitch doing?"

"What?" Malek asked, raising his voice.

Sweets snapped his fingers and said, "What's her name? Um, um . . . Halleigh, yeah, that's it."

Malek shook his head, knowing that Sweets had just made a threat on Halleigh's life. He walked out of the restaurant and ran to his car, where he pulled out of the parking lot, his tires screeching as he peeled off.

Scratch, fiending for a fix, looked at the garbage can where Malek's worker had hid his stash. There was nothing worse than being on E and not having any money. Scratch itched his arms as he schemed on the unsuspecting block hustler. He looked at the other fiend that stood beside him. They peeked around the corner, and their desperation caused them to devise a plan.

Scratch laid out the instructions to the woman he'd just met, and they agreed as they went about their get-high mission. "Okay, look," he said, "you go distract him with that ol' fish pussy you got, and Scratch will get the stash. Meet Scratch back in this alley, ya hear?"

Scratch watched with greed in his eyes as the raggedy-looking woman approached the young hustler on the block.

"Come on, daddy," she said, "let me get something. I'll give you something if you give me something." The woman dropped the dirty skirt and exposed her yellow- and brown-stained panties.

Scratched creeped up the block as the hustler responded.

"Bitch, get your ass out of here. If you ain't got the cash, you ain't got the coke," the hustler responded, keeping his hands in his pockets.

Scratch silently walked over to the trash can and picked up the bag of crack rocks.

Just then, the hustler turned around and noticed him. "Yo, you stealing my shit!" he screamed as he approached Scratch and snatched him up by his collar.

"Ah, nah, young'un, Scratch don't mean you no harm," Scratch explained nervously as he tried to shield his body from the hits of the young man.

The hustler raised his fist and brought it down over Scratch's face, causing his eyes to immediately swell.

"Aghh, man . . . wait!"

Scratch's cries didn't faze the hustler, but he was stopped by Halleigh's shouts as she ran up to the scene.

"Hey, what are you doing?" Halleigh screamed as she stepped out of her BMW. She was parked up the street from the busy salon when she saw Scratch getting jacked up on Malek's block. "Let him go!" she yelled as she stood back, her oversized Birkin bag hanging underneath her arm.

The hustler shoved Scratch away, out of respect for his boss' girl. He had never really seen Halleigh before, but he knew exactly who she was because of the car and expensive clothes that she sported.

Halleigh rushed over to Scratch and helped him up. His lip was busted, and he was bleeding as Halleigh led him to her car. "Are you okay?" she asked as she pulled away from the curb.

"Scratch is okay," he replied. "It take a whole lot more than some young'un to take me out the game."

Halleigh was worried. Scratch didn't look good, and she could tell that he hadn't been eating well. "Scratch, are you hungry?" she asked.

"A little bit," he replied.

Halleigh was going to miss her scheduled hair appointment, but looking at Scratch, she could tell that he needed her. She drove to Mc-Donald's and ordered Scratch some food. She watched as he scratched frantically at his arms, and tears came to her eyes.

"Scratch, you're breaking my heart," she said. "I know this is you, but do you ever think about shaking this shit?"

"Scratch think about it all the time, Li'l Rina, but once you're on it, there is no turning back. I've been on this dope for over ten years. Dope runs through Scratch's veins more than blood," he explained.

Halleigh didn't reply as she watched him stuff the food into his mouth. She knew that he needed help, and she was determined to get him off the drugs. She didn't care how much he protested, he was going to get clean.

Halleigh rolled down her window as the stench from Scratch's body hit her nostrils. She tried her hardest not to frown up, but the smell was too much to tolerate. The stink from his body was penetrating her leather seats, and she hoped that it wouldn't linger in her car after he was gone.

Scratch noticed Halleigh's twisted-up face and began to feel slightly embarrassed.

"It's okay, Li'l Rina. Where Scratch from, baths don't come easy. You can roll down ya winda. Scratch won't get offended." Scratch rolled down his own window and stared at the passing city.

Halleigh silently thanked God that Scratch let down his window, letting her off the hook. She released a forced smiled and tried not to hurt Scratch's feelings too much.

"It's okay, Scratch," she lied. "I just got a bad headache, that's all."

"Where we going anyway, Li'l Rina?" Scratch asked as he patted down his raggedy Afro.

"Scratch, would you do anything for me?" Halleigh asked, obviously trying to avoid his question.

"What kind of question is that? You know Scratch will do anything fo' you, girl," Scratch said, displaying his brown, buttery teeth.

"Scratch, I want to help you get better. I'm taking you to a rehab to get you clean," Halleigh said as she pulled into the Genesis Rehabilitation Center.

Halleigh had heard Malek express his dislike for the rehab center, which he thought was helping to dry up his business, and wanting to take Scratch to the rehab center was sort of like sleeping with the enemy. The way she looked at it, Malek would be good with or without the rehab center; Scratch, on the other hand, would be dead very soon if he didn't get his habit in check.

"Come on, Li'l Rina, I don't need help!" Scratch said, feeling slightly betrayed.

Halleigh put her car in park and placed her hand over Scratch's. "Look, Scratch, it might seem crazy, but you are the only family I got. I know we're not blood, but we family. You the only one who acted like they gave a damn about me when I was out in those streets. I don't want to see you like this anymore," Halleigh said, tears forming in her eyes.

Odd as it may seem, Scratch was like a father figure to her. He was the father that she'd never had.

Even though they'd smoked drugs together, Scratch always felt guilty and wanted to reject the high, but the monkey on his back was too heavy. He looked in Halleigh's eyes and could not help but surrender. Her big brown eyes got him every time. He noticed how much she resembled her mother, and his heart melted.

"Well, I guess, Li'l Rina," Scratch mumbled as he dropped his head. He didn't want to admit it, but he didn't like who he had become. Halleigh didn't know it, but she was Scratch's only family also. No one gave a damn about him, and for Halleigh to tell him that he was family meant the world to him.

"Yes!" Halleigh yelled as she hugged Scratch, disregarding the foul odor that reeked off of him. She felt obligated to help Scratch beat his addiction, like Tasha had helped her beat hers.

One of the most painful things she'd had to do was walk away from Tasha at Malek's request. Tasha had single-handedly gotten Halleigh off drugs, so she was grateful. She had no way of showing her gratitude to Tasha, so by helping Scratch get off drugs, it helped put her mind at ease. She looked at it as passing on the gift of unwavering concern that Tasha had shown her.

"But I ain't getting up in front of no folks talking about I'm a crack-head and all. I be seeing that on TV. Them folks make you get up and say what you did for a hit. I even saw a man say 'I sucked dick for crack. He had to be outta his cotton-picking mind. Scratch might be a junkie, but I never pulled any gay shit to support my habit. Scratch love the ladies too much fo' that. Hey, I might be ugly, but in my day I woulda gave them a run fo' they money," Scratch boasted, poking his chest out and patting his Afro.

Halleigh smiled and admired how Scratch could look like he did, but somehow could charm a lady with a couple of sentences. She exited the car and walked hand and hand with Scratch into the building.

Scratch squirmed and tussled in his dorm's bed, as his body tried to separate him from its addiction. Suffering from the worst of both worlds, Scratch was addicted to heroin and crack cocaine. Drenched in his own sweat, he clenched his aching stomach. The lack of heroin in his system caused his body to undergo complete agony.

The counselors offered Scratch methadone to help him wean himself off the drug, but he refused. He wanted to beat his addition cold turkey. He wasn't trying to shake his heroin addiction just to become addicted to methadone. No. He was going to shake it on his own.

Scratch stood up out of the bed and began to pace the room in attempt to ease the pain in his stomach muscles. Even his footsteps against the concrete floor sent pain through his body. The drug was calling for him.

"Come on, Scratch!" he said to himself as he frantically paced the small room. It took all of his might not to storm out of the rehab and hit the streets in search of a fix. The thought of Halleigh appeared in his head, and it crushed all desire to relapse. For years no one had shown that they cared for Scratch, but when Halleigh showed concern, he totally appreciated it.

"Scratch finally got someone in his corner!" he said, talking in third person as he always did. He balled up on the ground and clenched his aching stomach and cried himself to sleep. Scratch was taking this battle head on.

Scratch stood up in front of the group of fellow drug users. "Hello." he said. "My name is Marcus 'Scratch' Pipes, and I'm a mu'fuckin' crackhead."

The room burst into laughter at Scratch's brutal honesty. Halleigh smiled as she saw Scratch trying to better himself. She sat toward the back and just watched as he testified in front of the small group.

Scratch continued, "I'm forty-two years old, and I've been smoking, shooting dope, stealing, and robbing for the past ten years."

Halleigh wasn't supposed to be in the meeting, but the rehab center agreed to let her sit in just that one time, since it was the only way Scratch would have gone through with the process. The rehab center had to also first make sure that it was okay with the other addicts.

The mediator, Moses, said as she sat in the middle of the group, "The first step to recovery is admitting you have a problem. Marcus has done that. Please give him a hand."

"Uh, no disrespect, baby, but could you please call me Scratch? Crackheads do have dignity, ya know. I don't want everybody to know my government name, baby," Scratch said smoothly before sitting back down and crossing his legs. Even though Scratch dressed in shabby clothes and smelled like ass, he had a certain swagger about himself. You could tell that he was somebody in his heyday. He looked back at Halleigh, who smiled at him, and he winked his eye at her.

Halleigh smiled back and took a glance at her watch. "Oh shit!" she whispered as she realized that she was late for her lunch with Malek. She quickly gathered her purse and slipped out the door. She put on her oversized shades and discreetly slipped into the brand-new BMW Malek had purchased for her.

She knew she was playing with fire, being on one of Malek's blocks. She wanted to tell him about helping Scratch, but she had promised him that she would stay out of the hood for all reasons and leave her former life behind. She didn't want to disappoint him, so she kept it a secret. After she made sure Scratch was good, she would never step foot in her old neighborhood again.

Halleigh maneuvered her luxury car through the city streets, trying to rush to the Italian restaurant to meet Malek.

Attorney Hill walked into the Genesis Rehabilitation Center with an Armani two-piece suit on, carrying a briefcase. He stuck out like a sore thumb amongst all the addicts and counselors. Malek had sent him to give the president of the rehabilitation center an offer she couldn't refuse. Hill approached the front counter and set his briefcase on the desk.

"Hello, I would like to speak with the owner of this facility," he said with a smile.

"Just a minute. I'll get her for you." The receptionist picked up the phone and notified Moses that she had a guest.

Moments later Moses came out of the back, her dreads neatly pulled away from her face. She greeted Mr. Hill with a smile and an extended hand.

Like a gentleman, Hill stood when she entered the room and shook her hand.

"Hello, I'm Martha. Everyone around here calls me Moses, though. How may I help you?"

"Jacob Hill. Nice to meet you. I'm here on behalf of my client. I would like to discuss a few things with you."

"No problem. Follow me into my office," Moses replied and waved for Hill to trail her.

Once they entered the office, Moses sat behind her desk and offered Hill a seat.

"That won't be necessary, ma'am." Hill set his briefcase on the desk and popped it open. "I've researched the worth of this property. Since this is a non-profit organization, the revenue isn't that great. So, I say you gross about thirty thousand a year from the federal grants, correct?" Hill asked.

"Yeah, that's about right. What are you getting to?" she asked as a confused look formed on her face.

Hill turned the open briefcase toward Moses, revealing the stacks of Benjamin Franklins. Hill fixed his tie and smiled slyly. "My client wants to offer you one hundred thousand dollars. You see, he wants this establishment to close down immediately."

Moses closed the briefcase and gently pushed it toward Hill. She couldn't believe her eyes. She looked up at Hill in puzzlement. "I know what you getting to, Mr. Hill. This won't be necessary. Genesis wasn't established to be a profitable organization. We're here to clean up our community and help with the increasing drug use that's killing our residents."

"I thought you might say that. My client would like to offer you two hundred thousand dollars, double the amount."

"What are you trying to do, Mr. Hill? We are not going anywhere. You must work for a drug dealer. I can't stand people like you. You come in here with your fancy suit and blinging cuff links, trying to push people like me out of the community so you can continue to poison it. You can tell your client that I said no thank you," Moses said as she walked to her door and opened it. "Have a good day, Mr. Hill."

Hill closed up the briefcase and proceeded out of the door.

"Good day," Hill said as he exited the office.

Moses didn't know what she had just gotten herself into. Whether she liked it or not, that neighborhood belonged to Malek Johnson.

Chapter Seventy-six

Ever since Sweets had made that "girlfriend" remark, Malek was concerned for Halleigh's safety and was keeping constant tabs on her. He called Halleigh's cell phone and didn't receive an answer. He hadn't heard anything from Sweets, but the threat that he had made was still fresh in his mind. Yeah, he had been paranoid since seeing Sweets, and the fact that Halleigh wasn't answering her phone only irritated him more. His money had still been coming short, and as the rehab center grew more popular, his pockets grew shorter and shorter.

Malek had plenty of money saved up, but he wasn't ready to let go of the game. He loved the power and respect that he received in the hood. He was a boss, and he was going to hold on to that status until he no longer could.

His lawyer had called and informed him that Moses had denied his proposition, so he knew that he had to approach the situation differently. He was going to go to plan B. If Moses wouldn't leave his hood willingly, he would make her.

Halleigh sent Malek to voice mail for the third time. She hated ignoring his calls, but if he knew that she was in the inner city, he would trip on her. She couldn't handle his questions right now. She just wanted to help Scratch, and she knew that Malek would never understand why.

When Halleigh walked into the clinic, Moses greeted her with open arms. "Welcome, Halleigh," she said. "It's so good of you to come here as often as you do to check on your friend."

"It's really not a problem. I just want to support him. I know how hard this is, and I'm proud of him for trying."

As Moses nodded, her medium-length dreads, bounced up and down. She was the kindest woman that Halleigh had ever met, and Halleigh would've never guessed that the woman had once been strung out on drugs.

"Well, his body is still detoxifying itself. He's in a lot of pain, so be sure not to touch him."

Halleigh nodded and then made her way back to Scratch's room. She sat with him as he shook and trembled. He looked so weak, and seeing him like that reminded Halleigh of her own experience. Tasha had taken good care of her. She was there for Halleigh and had been such a good friend, and Halleigh missed her dearly.

She sat with Scratch for an hour and promised to come back later that week.

"Take care," she said when she left. She looked at her phone and

noticed that she had two more missed calls from Malek. She knew that she would have to come up with a good excuse because he was going to want to know where she was.

When she walked into her house, Malek and Mitch were sitting in her living room. Both men looked up at her, and she could see the worried expressions on their faces.

"Where you've been?" Malek questioned. "I've been blowing your cell up all day."

"I was at the mall." She felt bad for lying to him, but she couldn't tell him the truth.

"When I call you, answer the phone!" Malek yelled as he pointed his index finger in her face.

"Okay, Malek, damn it! You don't have to yell at me." It was the first time that Halleigh had seen him display that kind of aggression toward her, and tears came to her eyes.

"I'm sorry. I didn't hear you call. I probably didn't get service in the mall," she added, hoping that he believed her story. The last thing that she wanted was for him to become suspicious of her and think that she was cheating.

"You heard what I said!" He grabbed his car keys and put on his fitted hat. "Keep your ass in the house until I get back," he said as he walked out of the house.

Mitch rose from the couch. As he walked past Halleigh, he could see that she was on the verge of tears. He wiped away a single tear that had trickled down her face, and she tensed up from his touch.

"When that nigga fuck up, you got somewhere to go," he whispered in her ear.

Halleigh knew what he was getting at. She could tell that he was feeling her, but this was the first time he had verbalized his interest. Every time she was around him, she felt awkward, but she couldn't see herself jeopardizing her relationship with Malek to be with him. She turned her head to the side and walked to her bedroom as Mitch let himself out of the house.

Mitch had been spending a lot of time at Malek's crib, since the two of them were constantly talking business and trying to make sure that everything was straight. Ever since the second time that he had come over to the house, he would flirt with Halleigh with every opportunity that presented itself.

Halleigh thought back to the second time that Mitch had come over to the crib with Malek and what had transpired when Malek went to the basement of the house to use the bathroom.

Mitch spoke in a low, seductive tone as he moved in close to Halleigh. "That pussy still tight?"

Halleigh's heart began to beat from fear of what Malek would do

if he walked in the room and saw Mitch all up on her. "Mitch, what are you doing?" Halleigh said through gritted teeth. "Back up off me!"

"You ain't tell Malek that we fucked, did you?"

Halleigh's heart sank to her feet. "Mitch, you are really bugging right now! Do you know Malek would murder you in a heartbeat if he heard what you just said? No, I didn't tell him!"

Mitch smiled and then leaned in and kissed Halleigh on her neck and said, "Good. Then we still got our little secret."

"Mitch! What is wrong with you?" Halleigh punched Mitch and pushed him off.

"My bad, my bad," Mitch said, smiling a devilish smile and then backing off Halleigh just as Malek re-entered the room.

Halleigh's stomach turned sour at the thought of Malek not knowing that she had been with Mitch, and at the thought of lying to him. She felt like she had to throw up and rushed into the bathroom as the contents of her stomach came up.

Afterward, she ran herself a bath and prepared herself for bed. She was extremely tired. She looked at the clock on the nightstand beside her bed. It was only eleven o'clock, so she knew that Malek wouldn't be home anytime soon. She picked up the phone and dialed his number, but Malek's phone sent her directly to voice mail.

Halleigh left a message saying, "I love you, Malek," and she retired for the night, but she felt a huge amount of guilt as she lay in the bed tossing and turning.

She felt like she had to come clean with Malek, so she called his cell phone right back. She was actually glad when he sent her to voice mail once again, but this time she left a longer message:

"Baby, I feel bad about something, and I just gotta come clean with it. But please promise me that you won't get upset. Okay, well, I know how you feel about the rehab center cutting into your business, and I just wanted to tell you that when you was calling my phone and you couldn't get me, that was because I was really with Scratch at the rehab, trying to get some help for him." Halleigh winced as she said those words, as if she were bracing to get slapped by Malek. Then she added, "And, baby, there's something else that I wanted to tell you, but I have to tell you that in person. It's about Mitch, okay, baby. I love you. Be safe. Call me back."

Halleigh let out a huge sigh of relief, but she knew that she had to first wait for Malek's reaction before dropping the bomb on him that Mitch had fucked her. At least she felt like she could turn off the TV and sleep in some peace.

Halleigh felt Malek crawl into the bed with her at around four o'-clock in the morning. Her heart began to race. She was feeling nervous, not knowing whether Malek had listened to her voice mail. She still had no idea why he had tripped on her the way that he had. She

didn't know what was up with him and Sweets, and she was wondering if he was just stressed about his business.

Malek realized that by loving Halleigh publicly, he had exposed his weakness to those around him, and now Halleigh could be a potential target. Her back was against his chest as he held her tight. He didn't say anything; he didn't have to. She knew that he loved her.

Halleigh could feel his heart beating through his chest. Something inside of her glowed as she thought about Malek. She thought about all that she had been through and knew that she would do it all again, if that's what it took to find her way back into the arms of this man.

The next morning, Halleigh woke up with the same urge to hurl. Feeling nauseated, she lay in bed groaning from the horrible feeling.

"What's wrong?" Malek asked.

Halleigh realized that Malek must not have heard her message, so she decided to just not bring up the subject. "I don't know. I don't feel good at all."

"You need to go to the doctor so you can get checked out."

"I don't think it's that serious," Halleigh replied.

Malek sat up on his elbow and brushed Halleigh's hair out of her face. "Do it for me, a'ight. I just want to make sure everything's good with you, ma."

"Okay, but you're coming with me."

Halleigh's trip to the doctor revealed that she was four weeks pregnant. It was the happiest news of her life. Tears came to her eyes when the doctor told her.

She looked at Malek to see what he thought, but she had a hard time reading his emotions. "What are you thinking?" she asked.

Malek was silent for a minute, so she continued, "If you don't want me to have this baby, I won't." She let her tears fall at the thought of terminating her pregnancy, but she would do anything to keep Malek. If he wasn't happy about their situation, she would have no choice but to change it.

"You're having my seed," Malek whispered in disbelief as if the news was just now hitting him. He placed one hand on her flat stomach. "I can't believe I'm about to be somebody's daddy."

"So you're not mad?" she asked.

"Hell no," he said. "You're having my baby. I didn't think it was possible for me to love you anymore than I already did, but I do because you are the mother of my child."

Malek thought about his mother. How he wished she was still alive to be able to see her soon-to-be-born grandchild. Then his thoughts went to having a little boy. He visualized teaching him how to play sports, how to mack hoes. A huge smile came across Malek's face. He was about to be a daddy. *Life is so beautiful*, he thought.

Malek left the doctor's office that day with a new inspiration for life. He was about to be a father. He and Halleigh had made a lifetime commitment. Through their child, they were about to bond forever.

With his new responsibility to consider, Malek was determined to get on his grind even harder because he was going to make sure his family was taken care of. He wasn't going to let Sweets or Moses get in the way of his family's safety or financial security. He made a phone call on his way home.

Mitch answered on the first ring. "What's good, fam?"

"Have you heard anything about Sweets?"

"Nah, since that shit popped off at Big Al's, he's been laying low. Maybe he got the message," Mitch replied.

"For his sake, I hope so. I'm tying all loose ends. Hal is pregnant, and I need to get this money, nah mean?"

"Yeah, I hear you, fam."

"Ride out with me tomorrow, a'ight. It's time to take care of that rehab situation."

"No doubt," Mitch replied. He thought of the seed that was growing inside of Halleigh's womb and couldn't help but wish that she was his. "Congratulations, fam. Send Halleigh my love." He hung up the phone and tried to take his mind off Malek's woman.

Chapter Seventy-seven

Scratch sat through a lecture by a reformed drug addict and was proud of himself. He hadn't touched a drug in eight weeks. Today was the day he graduated from the twelve-step program. Scratch kept glancing at the door, waiting for Halleigh to walk in so that he could share his special day with her. She promised she would be here.

I know baby girl ain't gon' let Scratch down, he thought as he played with his fingers nervously.

As the motivational speaker spoke, Scratch saw something that almost made his heart stop. Sharina, Halleigh's mom, walked in. It had been years since he had last seen her, and she looked good. Scratch was so happy to see her. He had honestly thought that she was dead, that she'd suffered the same fate as many of his drug-addicted cronies. The crackhead's glare that was in her eyes the last time he had seen her was now gone. She came in and sat in the back of the crowded

room. He couldn't believe the resemblance she had to her daughter. Even at her mature age, she looked as if she could be Halleigh's sister.

Scratch was glad that he'd decided to shave that morning. Back in the day, he had a thing for Sharina, and clearly the attraction was still there. He sat up straight and patted his Afro, trying to look as presentable as possible.

"Yo, we outside of the building right now," Mitch said as he sat in the black Navigator with three of his goons. "We're just waiting for the go-ahead." They all had fully loaded semi-automatic assault rifles.

Malek was on the other end of the phone, watching as Halleigh pulled off to go to her doctor's appointment. "Is their kids there?" he asked, not wanting to hit any children.

"Nah, there aren't any children." Mitch took another glance to ensure that he was correct.

"Good. Wait until the majority of the people leave and do it. Hit it! We gotta send a message. They're fucking up the money," Malek said before he closed his cell phone and walked over to the couch. He didn't want to send a message that malicious, but Joe had taught him, when in the drug game, you had to be ruthless and detach all emotions from business. Malek took a deep breath. He never thought that he would be ordering the shooting of a building full of innocent people, but to keep his position of power, he had to do it.

Halleigh rushed out of the house. She hated lying to Malek, but she had to be there for Scratch. He had finally completed the program, and she wanted to be there in his final steps to leading a clean life. She had even put some money up so that Scratch would be all right. She had managed to save five thousand dollars for him, trusting that he would do the right thing with the money.

She glanced at her watch and noticed that she was late for Scratch's ceremony. She had promised him that she would be there to witness him receive his completion certificate from the drug program. *I'm so proud of Scratch for cleaning himself up*, Halleigh thought as she got in her car and headed toward Genesis.

Scratch's hands became sweaty as he approached Sharina, who was sitting in the back and listening attentively to the motivational speaker. It had been so long since he had seen her, and he wanted to reintroduce himself.

"Hey, beautiful lady," Scratch said.

Sharina looked at Scratch, and when she realized who he was, she looked like she'd seen a ghost. It had been years since she'd last seen him. "Oh my God," she said, placing her hand over her mouth. Scratch leaned over and gave her a hug.

"Look at you, all cleaned up," Sharina said as she took a good look at Scratch. She had been in the streets a long time and could tell that Scratch hadn't been using.

They just stared at each other for a brief moment.

Sharina continued to look Scratch up and down. "How long have you been clean?"

"It's been eight weeks now," Scratch said proudly as he played with his fingers.

"I'm proud of you," Sharina said. She placed a gentle hand on Scratch's shoulder. "I know how hard it is to get the monkey off your back."

"Thanks. You looking good, Rina. I can tell by your eyes you're clean."

"Yeah, I have been clean about a year or so now," Sharina said confidently. "I had to get away from Flint for a while. I've been in Detroit for the past year. That's where I got my rehabilitation at. Moses helped me out before she relocated down here. She invited me back to speak."

"Are you serious?"

"Yeah, I'm serious. I'm here to share my story with the group." Sharina's smile suddenly dropped, and she looked down before adding, "And I have some unfinished business."

"You talking about Halleigh, aren't you?" Scratch asked before he could catch himself. It just came out.

Sharina looked up with tears in her eyes. She was surprised to hear her daughter's name. It had been so long since she'd last seen Halleigh, and it ate at her daily. She had been preparing to come back to Flint to find her baby girl. She owed her so much explanation because of her bad drug problem. She had sold her daughter's virginity to the local dopeman just to feed her habit. She was ashamed, and she needed to find her daughter so that she could apologize. She knew that the words wouldn't mean much at first, but she was hoping that Halleigh would eventually forgive her.

Scratch smiled because Halleigh had promised him that she would show up for the program. He kept it to himself, so that Sharina would have a big surprise. *Scratch gon' make Rina's day*, he thought to himself as he stared at beautiful Sharina.

Halleigh couldn't stop smiling, knowing that she was about to bring a life into the world. She pulled into the parking lot of Genesis. *I hope I didn't miss seeing Scratch get his certificate,* she thought as her heels clicked on the pavement on her way into the building.

Halleigh walked into the building during the middle of a woman's speech and saw Scratch sitting in the front row. She immediately took a seat, so she wouldn't be a distraction. As she sat down, she heard a voice that she hadn't heard in years. She immediately looked at the podium, and anxiety took over her body. Standing there talking to the people was her mother. "Oh my God," she whispered as she sat there in disbelief.

 * * *

"Drive by slow," Mitch instructed as he and another henchman, both with semi-automatic assault rifles, hung out of the window. The Genesis building had a glass front, so they could see all of the people gathered inside looking at the speaker. Under Malek's orders, Mitch prepared to let it rain bullets inside of the building.

"Thank you all very much," Sharina said as she received a standing ovation for her touching speech. She walked off the stage and over to Scratch and gave him a hug to congratulate him on his recovery.

Scratch whispered in her ear as they embraced, "I got someone I want you to see." Then he led her to Halleigh.

Sharina's heart nearly stopped when she saw her only daughter. She had been anticipating their reunion for so long, and now that she was face to face with her, she was speechless. She had so much to say, so much to explain, but nothing seemed to come out. Tears ran down her cheeks as she began to speak. "Halleigh, I—"

Before Sharina could finish her sentence, bullets rang out, one grazing her neck.

The entire place broke out into complete pandemonium. Scratch dove for Halleigh and covered her to protect her. The sound of shattering glass and horrified screams filled the air as they dropped to the floor, trying to avoid taking any bullets. After ten seconds of non-stop shooting, the mayhem finally ceased.

"Baby girl, are you okay?" Scratch asked as he uncovered Halleigh. He noticed blood coming from her thigh and panicked. "You hit! You hit in the leg!" he said as he looked at the rest of her body to make sure that she wasn't hit anywhere else.

A woman screamed, causing them to look in her direction. It was Moses. She had Sharina in her arms. Blood was coming from her neck, but fortunately for her, the bullet hadn't hit her jugular vein. It had merely broken her skin.

"Nooo!" Halleigh screamed as she scooted over next to her mother and held her in her arms. She didn't even get a chance to tell her how much she loved her, how much she hated her, how much she needed her, and how much she had to go through without her. She disregarded her own bullet wound as she asked her mom, "You okay?"

Thankfully, her mom wasn't dead.

The sound of ambulance sirens sounded, and the paramedics rushed into the building to save the lives of the wounded.

Halleigh threw up, and the room began to spin, as she was losing an awful lot of blood from her leg. She looked down at her stomach, and for the first time she thought of the life inside of her. "Oh God, no, please no," she whispered. She put her hand over her wound and tried to stop the bleeding.

"You need to get to the hospital, Li'l Rina." Scratch waved a paramedic over to Halleigh.

Losing a lot of blood, Halleigh became light-headed and fainted. The last thing that crossed her mind was Malek and her unborn child.

"It's done," Mitch said to Malek.

"Good. Maybe now they will see it my way." Malek hung up the phone and looked at his watch.

"Halleigh should have been home by now. Where my baby at?" he asked himself as he stood in his living room with a bottle of wine. The wind blew open his white linen shirt as he took a sip. He pulled out a box holding a three-carat diamond ring. That night was the night he would propose to Halleigh. *From here on out, life will be good.*

"Come on, girl, where you at?" Malek flipped open his phone and dialed her number, but he never received an answer. Malek checked his voice mail to see if Halleigh had left him any messages, and that was when he heard the message that she had left him the other night.

Malek quickly called back Halleigh's cell phone, but again he got no answer.

Immediately he thought the worst about Mitch. "I'll cut that nigga's dick off and shove that shit in his mouth and then murder his ass!" Malek screamed. He had a sick feeling as to what was up.

"He snaked me! Don't nobody come in my crib and snake me and think they can live!" All of the veins in Malek's head began to bulge, and fire was ready to shoot out of him. He took hold of his cell phone and called Mitch.

"Yo," Mitch said, answering his phone.

"Yo, Mitch, swing by the crib. I just wanna talk about this rehab shit, so all our bases is covered and nothing comes back to bite us in the ass."

"You want me to come right now?" Mitch asked.

"Yeah, yeah, and come solo. I ain't trusting nobody right now."

"Okay, no doubt. I'll be there in about a half-hour," Mitch said and then hung up the phone.

Halleigh was slipping in and out of consciousness as she rode in the back of the ambulance. Scratch was right there by her side, tears in his eyes. "Come on, Li'l Rina, you'll be all right," he kept saying, hoping that she could stay conscious.

"She's lost a lot of blood!" one of the paramedics said as he tried to apply pressure to her wound.

Halleigh tried to whisper something, but Scratch couldn't make it out clearly. "What's that, baby girl?" Scratch asked, stroking her hair and placing his ear next to her lips.

Halleigh whispered, "My-my baby, my baby," just before losing con-

sciousness. Those were the last words that she uttered, and she slipped into total darkness.

Chapter Seventy-eight

M alek paced back and forth in his extravagant living room, while Mitch stood at the door watching his partner go crazy.

"Where the fuck is she, fam?" Malek asked, his voice a mixture of concern and anger as he dialed Halleigh's cell phone number for the millionth time. "Why she got a phone, if she ain't gon' ever answer the mu'fucka?"

Malek snapped his phone closed and grabbed his Sean John coat. His thoughts went from one extreme to the other as he tried to reason with himself about Halleigh's absence. Malek loved Halleigh with all that he was, and she had never given him a reason to distrust her or shown him any shade in the past, but just the simple fact that she used to trick with niggas had him going crazy. Under normal circumstances, he knew she would never step out on him, but because of her history as a Manolo Mami, he was worried. That old cliché about a man not being able to turn a ho into a housewife, was now haunting him. He didn't want her reverting back to her old ways. He made it a point to do everything he thought possible to keep her on the up-and-up, seeing to it that she lacked nothing, especially when it came to sex.

He closed his eyes and could picture Halleigh being pleased by another man. He could hear the moans escaping her lips, the same moans that blessed his ears every time he stroked her right. "I'ma murder a mu'fucka tonight, fam." Malek grabbed his car keys and stormed out of the house.

"Where you going, bro? Your chick ain't fucking around on you. Calm down and just think about it. We talking about Halleigh here, not some chickenhead off the street," Mitch reminded him. "She probably just lost track of time, kicking it with some of her girlfriends," Mitch added, trying to reason with Malek.

"Girlfriends," Malek whispered to himself. He knew Halleigh didn't rock with a lot of chicks. The only friend she ever mentioned was Tasha. Which didn't soothe any of Malek's concerns, seeing as Tasha was an ex-Manolo Mami as well.

I hope she ain't sliding back into her old ways, messing around

with Tasha, he thought. Out loud, he said, "Roll with me for a minute. I think I know where she might be."

Malek left the house, and with Mitch in the passenger's seat, he rolled to Tasha's apartment complex just outside of the city. He had only been there once, when he had dropped Halleigh off to pick up some of her things, and he was hoping Tasha still stayed there. He sped through the illuminated city streets, his brand-new 6 Series decorating the hood as he passed by. Malek hit a button on his panel, and a compartment slid out of his console, exposing various-sized money rolls, a blunt, and a pistol. He grabbed one of the money rolls and tossed it to Mitch.

Mitch caught the roll then looked up at his boy with confusion on his face. He had no idea what the money was for.

"For that work you put in on the Genesis center," Malek explained, "Good looking out on that. We shouldn't have no more problems from Moses or her cause. Niggas trying to fly straight hurts my pockets, nah mean?"

Mitch didn't respond. He merely nodded his head and counted out the five stacks Malek had just hit him with.

Moments later, Malek pulled into Tasha's apartment community. "I'll be right back, fam." He got out of the car and headed toward what he hoped was Tasha's place.

He approached the front door and almost knocked it off the hinges with his hard, police-like knock, more out of anxiety than anger. He couldn't fathom the thought of Halleigh backsliding and making a fool out of him. People already thought he was off his game by making a Manolo Mami his wifey. The old saying "you can't turn a ho into a housewife" resonated tough in the hood, so he knew his relationship with Halleigh was a topic for discussion around the way. Because of his soft spot for Halleigh, some fools had misinterpreted that to mean he was a soft nigga altogether, testing him on a daily. On more than one occasion, he had to prove himself to be anything but. Sometimes he didn't know who he was trying to prove it to, though: the streets or himself. Nonetheless, he wasn't about to let everything he'd risked for Halleigh be in vain.

He had disregarded her lifestyle once because he knew what had forced her into the streets. A bad set of circumstances had put her out there., Once she was reunited with Malek, she left that life behind—or so he thought until now, when he couldn't get a hold of her. If he found out she was disloyal now, there would be no excuse.

If she's on the other side of this door, I'm cutting her the fuck off, Malek thought as he banged on the door.

Tasha snatched open the door wearing sweatpants, a sports bra, and her hair wrapped. It was obvious that Malek had awakened her. "What the fuck?" she spat, her mug all twisted up.

She looked over Malek's shoulder, as if looking to see if anyone else was with him. She couldn't imagine why he would be on her doorstep. She knew this nigga had balls, but not this big to show up where she laid her head, knowing the loss he'd caused her.

"Why are you banging my shit down like you the police or something?" She folded her arms and stood waiting for an answer. She hated him for what he had done to her brother. If looks could kill, Malek would've dropped where he stood.

"I'm looking for Halleigh. She ain't been home all night. It's four in the morning. I know she been out tricking with you." Malek pushed past Tasha as if he were walking into his own house.

"Nigga, I don't know you like that. Don't come at me out the side of your neck. Your bitch ain't here. I don't rock with Halleigh as long as she's fucking with you." Tasha went to retrieve her phone.

Malek was paying absolutely no attention to the words coming out of Tasha's mouth as he walked all over the apartment looking for his girl. "Halleigh?" he called out, opening door after door.

"You need to get out! No, wait. As a matter of fact,"—A sinister smile spread across her lips—"you can stay. I got something for your ass." She picked up her phone and began to dial Sweets' number.

Just as she was about to click on her cordless, the phone rang in her hand. Only one person called her on her home phone, and that was Manolo. She answered the phone with a smirk on her face, not even looking at the caller ID. "Manolo, I—"

The voice on the other end of the phone line interrupted Tasha. "Hello, I'm calling for Tasha Smith regarding your sister, Halleigh."

"Halleigh?" Tasha's eyes then quizzically darted toward Malek.

Malek stopped in his tracks at the mention of Halleigh's name. He slowly walked toward Tasha as she turned her attention back to the caller on the other end of the phone.

"Uh, hello," Tasha greeted with a stammer.

"Yes, is this Tasha Smith?"

Taken aback, Tasha responded, "Uh yeah . . . yeah, this is Tasha."

"You are listed as Halleigh's emergency contact in our hospital records. Halleigh was shot today, and—"

"Shot? What? Hold on." Tasha put the phone on hold and looked at Malek.

She hated Malek and everything he stood for, but she felt an obligation to tell him the news she'd just received. She wasn't surprised that the hospital had reached out to her instead of Malek because, back in the day, Manolo had ensured that Tasha was the contact person for all of his working girls, just in case a john ever decided to get rough. Tasha wanted to be an asshole and leave Malek wondering where his girl was, but if Halleigh was dying, she didn't think she deserved to die alone.

She sighed from frustration at her hatred for Malek, but her conflicting loyalty to her old friend prevailed. Tasha took the phone off hold and continued her conversation with the caller, learning a few more details, including exactly what hospital Halleigh was at. Afterward, Tasha hung up the phone and turned toward Malek.

"Why you storming up in here accusing Halleigh of fucking around?" Tasha said heatedly. "She's laid up in the county hospital. She's been shot, Malek. Now see yourself out." She pointed at her front door.

The words hit Malek like a thousand darts to the heart, and he backpedaled out of Tasha's apartment without saying another word. He didn't know what to think. He closed his eyes and washed his hands down his face and shook his head. He hoped that once he opened his eyes, he'd be lying in bed next to Halleigh, waking up from what had to be a nightmare, but when he opened them, there he stood, right there in front of Tasha's apartment.

"Damn," was the only word that escaped Malek's mouth as he stood frozen in his own thoughts. *Is she a'ight? How did this happen?* He realized he was wasting time standing there, so he snapped out of it and ran and jumped into his car. He sped out of the parking lot like a bat out of hell.

"Whoa! Fam, slow this mu'fucka down," Mitch stated as he looked at Malek.

Malek, his mind fixed on thoughts of Halleigh, had forgotten all about Mitch even being out there in the car. "She's been shot, fam. She's pregnant and could be dying, and I thought she was out doing dirt," Malek whispered regretfully. He banged his fist against the steering wheel.

It was then that Malek knew he would have to fully forgive Halleigh and renew his trust in her. This "hard" role he had been trying to play wasn't becoming of him, nor was it by any means fair to Halleigh. He had no idea where the college-bound Malek who used to be the star of the high school basketball team had gone. He had to be somewhere underneath that hard-ass exterior Malek donned himself in on a daily. Halleigh, to this day, was still the same Halleigh he had fallen in young love with. So, if he was going to spend the rest of his life with her, then he had to be real about it. Living in the past wasn't going to get them anywhere.

Constantly thinking of what Halleigh used to do and who she used to do it with had clouded Malek's judgment and was making him go crazy. Halleigh needed him, and he was out wildin' over something she hadn't even done. Once again, he hit the steering wheel forcefully, his anger shifting to a new place.

"Whoever did this is dead. On my mother, I'm going to catch a couple bodies when I find out who hurt her."

"I'll put the word out," Mitch said as he shook his head in disgust.

Mitch secretly envied Malek because of his relationship with Halleigh. He'd heard the stories of the young couple's history and knew he could never break their bond, but he had been interested in Halleigh since the first time he'd seen her. The fact that he'd twisted her out in the back of his car when she was working for Manolo was his own private joke that he often chuckled at. Malek would be bragging about his lady, and silently Mitch would be thinking, *I know, nigga. I've had her.* But having her once wasn't enough for Mitch. He wanted her permanently.

He had tried his hand at Halleigh after she got back with Malek, but she was loyal to her man. She'd turned down every advance Mitch made toward her; still, the fact that she never told Malek always gave Mitch hope. He was just waiting for Malek to mess up. Then he would get him out of the picture for good and take the streets away from him, along with his woman.

Chapter Seventy-nine

The drive to the hospital seemed to take forever. He double-parked right in front of the entrance and hopped out, leaving Mitch in the passenger's seat.

"I'ma park your whip. I'll be up in a minute!" Mitch yelled as he watched Malek disappear into the building.

Malek approached the reception area and bypassed the line of people waiting in front of him, worry and concern plastered on his face. People mumbled and complained about Malek's ditching the line, but he tuned them out. All he wanted to hear was that his baby was all right—both of them. He said to the young white intake nurse who sat behind the desk, "My girlfriend was brought here for a gunshot wound. Her name's Halleigh. What room is she in?"

She rolled her eyes and then looked down at some paperwork in front of her. "I'm sorry, sir, but you have to wait in line like everyone else. There are sick people and concerned relatives waiting for information just like you." She looked past him at the line and yelled, "Next!"

"Look, lady, I'm next! I don't care about a line. I need to know what room my girl is in. She could be dying while I'm down here arguing

with you!" he shouted, more out of emotion than anger. He had to keep it together.

A doctor passing by heard the commotion and stopped. "Is there a problem?"

"Hey, my man," Malek started, "please, I'm just trying to get to my girlfriend. She was shot today and—"

The doctor cut him off. "Are you here for Halleigh . . ." The doctor flipped through the charts in his hands to find Halleigh's last name.

"Yeah, that's her name," Malek said before the doctor could finish his sentence.

The doctor looked down at the intake nurse. "It's okay. I'll take him to her." He began to walk, and Malek closely followed his lead. "We've been trying to reach someone for her since she was admitted yesterday evening."

"What happened to her? Is she a'ight?"

"She's okay. She's a very strong young woman. We had a lot of gunshot victims come in yesterday as a result of the Genesis shooting. She was one of the lucky ones. Why anyone would want to shoot up a rehab facility is beyond me."

Malek's heart hit his stomach, and he stopped walking. He had put in the order for the Genesis shooting, and Halleigh had gotten touched behind it.

She wasn't supposed to be there, he thought.

"Is everything all right?" the doctor asked.

Malek's eyes had watered over from guilt, but he continued following the doctor. "Yeah, everything's good, doc," he lied. "Can I see her?"

The doctor stopped at a closed door and said, "She's right inside. She's in some pain, but she'll be fine."

"And the baby?"

"The baby is fine," the doctor answered with a smile. "We were able to hear a very strong heartbeat."

Malek exhaled and rushed into the room, where Halleigh was lying, weak, tubes running into her arms. It killed him to know that she was in that state because of him.

He walked over to her bed slowly. Her face was so peaceful, so still, that if it weren't for the up-and-down movement of her chest, he would have sworn she had already left him behind. He placed his hand on her stomach and leaned his head onto her bedside. "I'm so sorry, Hal. I didn't know you were there. I didn't know you were at the rehab center. I swear to God, I'ma make this up to you. I'ma make it right."

He kicked himself for being so stupid. Before making a move, he should have made sure that she was tucked away safely, but he had no idea she would be at the center. There was no reason for her to be . . . unless she was using again.

He dismissed that idea almost as quickly as it formed in his mind.

He knew the symptoms of an addict, and Halleigh had none. No, she wasn't using, yet she had gotten aired out in the middle of the Genesis shootout. It didn't make sense to him, but he was just grateful that his lady was still breathing. He felt Halleigh's hand wrap around his, and he looked at her in surprise.

"Hey," she said quietly, her voice scratchy and weak.

"Thank you," Malek whispered, lifting his eyes to the ceiling, acknowledging God's work. He had never been a Bible-toter, but he was so grateful for Halleigh's safety, he knew a greater power had to be at work. It wasn't the first time that some type of higher power had stepped in and saved the couple from the angel of death. As far as Malek was concerned, there wasn't anyone else he could give credit to but God. It certainly wasn't just plain old good luck. He knew better than anyone that luck had never been on their side. Ever since fate separated them and forced them to survive on the streets, both of them had faced death more than a few times. They had definitely experienced more than their share of bad luck.

Halleigh felt so tired. The medication they had her on was weighing her down, making her feel as if she had gained a thousand pounds overnight. It was even hard for her to move her mouth to talk, but she felt like she owed her man an explanation.

"Malek, I'm so sorry for lying to you. I wanted to tell you I had been going to Genesis, but I knew you would try to stop me."

"Why, Halleigh? Why would you be going there?" He tried not to be angry that she had been going to the place that was killing his street trade. This was not the time to be thinking about business.

"I have a friend there . . . Scratch. I was trying to help him kick his habit," she explained. "I wanted to let him know that someone cared. I thought it would help him get better. You know, the same way I knew someone cared about me." She forced her lips to curve into a slight smile, her sign of appreciation for Malek always being there for her. "That's what got me through. But I had no idea something like this would happen."

"Hal, when you didn't come home last night, I went crazy. Hearing that you were hurt was like a bullet to the chest, ma. I'm in love with you, and I'm so sorry I put you through this."

"You have nothing to be sorry for, baby." Halleigh gripped his hand tighter.

"Yes, I do." Malek swallowed hard, debating whether he should tell Halleigh the real deal. Being the main one who insisted there be no secrets between them, he knew he had to fess up. He told her the miserable truth and hoped she could forgive him.

"Hal, I'm the one who gave the order to shoot up Genesis. I pushed the button."

"What?" she asked in confusion as she withdrew her hand from his.

Malek reached for it again. "Don't do that to me, Hal. I'm sorry. I had no idea you'd be there," he said.

"Why would you do something like that, Malek? How could you?"

"I didn't know you were there. I was stupid."

"And if I hadn't been there, the other people there didn't matter? There were kids in there, Malek! People who weren't bothering nobody. They were trying to get their lives together," she whispered harshly, tears filling her eyes.

It hurt her so bad to think that person she laid up with every night was responsible for the tragedy that had almost taken her life. Halleigh loved Malek to death, God knows she did, but he just seemed to be so hard and ruthless these days, nothing like the Malek who'd stolen her heart back in high school.

"I know, Hal. I know. Let's just focus on you getting better," Malek said, attempting to calm her down.

"No, Malek." Halleigh pulled away from his touch. "You don't understand. My mother was in there," she cried.

Malek was shocked to hear Halleigh mention her mother, especially in a caring way. She was the reason Halleigh ended up on the streets in the first place. If it hadn't been for Sharina and her drug habit, everything might have turned out different. Obviously, Halleigh didn't hold a grudge.

"Yeah, I've hated her for a long time," Halleigh said, "but she was there, and I don't wish death on her. And my friend was in there."

"Hal—" Malek started, but she shot him a look that cut through him like a knife.

"I don't even know you right now," she said as a tear freed itself from her eyes.

Malek knew he couldn't really say anything that would make this better. Everything Halleigh had said was well deserved. He was nothing like the man he'd once dreamed of becoming. The game was sucking him dry. Sometimes he didn't even recognize himself. He had come so far away from boyhood, but sometimes he still felt like he didn't know shit about being a real man. Back when he was headed for the NBA, he never imagined he could one day become a straight-up killer. But now, forced to survive on the streets, that's exactly what he was—and it had almost cost him everything.

"I know how you must feel, but please forgive me, Hal," he pleaded.

Halleigh shook her head as another tear fell. "I'm tired of this, Malek. I love you, but I don't know if I want my life to be like this. For so long I was living wrong, and you judged me for it. But who are you to judge anybody?" She closed her eyes and turned her head away from him.

Malek started to protest, but Halleigh didn't give him a chance to

speak as she turned back to face him and then continued, "You don't have to lie and deny it. I can tell you still think about my past. You look at me, and a part of you can't get over the fact that I was a Manolo Mami. I've been working hard to regain your trust, Malek, but you can't throw stones when you live in a glasshouse. You ain't living right either. You shot up a building full of innocent people, Malek! How fucked-up is that?" Halleigh shook her head and waited for Malek to say something, but he didn't.

"Malek, I love you, and I know this isn't you. This isn't the real Malek." She looked him up and down. "This person standing in front of me, this person I've been living with isn't the Malek I know. I mean, you act like you've got something to prove to somebody, when all that's supposed to matter is me and you."

Finally finding his words, Malek spoke. "You gotta believe me, Hal. You and me is all that matters."

Halleigh, through the pain, tried her best to sit up as much as she could. "Do you really mean that, Malek? I mean, if it really is just about me and you, then we have to leave this life alone."

A smile covered Halleigh's face, as if reminiscing. "Remember before, in high school, what our only goal was?"

Malek smiled and nodded.

"Me too. It was to get the hell out of Flint. So when did that all change? Why did it change?"

Malek shrugged.

"Then let's do it. Let's get out of this city before it swallows us whole. We can go somewhere and be us again. We can go back and be how we used to be before our lives spun out of control."

"Give it all up," Malek said more to himself than to Halleigh.

"Give it all up for me. You have enough money to be set for a while. Let's start over," Halleigh pleaded, getting worked up.

Malek stood over her and rubbed her head gently. "Is that what I have to do to keep you?"

A tear slid down Halleigh's face, and she shook her head. "This is what you have to do to save me, to save us. I can't live like this anymore."

Malek thought about her words for a minute. He couldn't say he really wanted to give up the streets—especially now, when he was just coming into his own. He was the king of the city, and he couldn't deny that he was becoming addicted to the power.

He let himself think about how big he could become if he stayed in Flint. He could give Halleigh and the baby everything they'd ever dreamed of, and everyone would know his name. Then he looked down at his woman, who'd almost died because of him. No amount of money or power would have been able to bring her back.

It was time to give away the keys to the city. If he wanted to keep his

woman safe, he'd have to give it all up and move on, whether he wanted to or not.

"Okay, Hal, I hear you. I'll get my affairs in order, and then we'll get ghost and kiss this city goodbye."

"Are you just saying that, or are you serious? Because do you know how many dudes from the street say they're gonna go legit but then turn around and let the streets keep pulling them back in?"

Both Halleigh and Malek let out a little chuckle. Then Malek said, "Girl, you been watching too much of *The Godfather*. Anyway, I'm serious. I mean it. I wouldn't lie to you, ma, about something like this." Malek bent down and kissed Halleigh on the forehead. "You gotta trust me on this."

Halleigh looked deeply into Malek's eyes. "Baby, I do trust you."

Malek smiled and kissed her again. "Get some sleep, and don't worry about anything. I'll take care of it."

Halleigh closed her eyes and shortly thereafter fell off to sleep. Malek sat with her until the nurses forced him to leave. When he finally emerged from Halleigh's room, he saw Mitch sprawled out in the waiting room, his coat thrown over his face.

Malek looked at the clock on the wall. It was nine o'clock in the morning. He had completely forgotten that Mitch was even with him. He had a new respect for his right-hand man. Mitch had waited patiently throughout the night without complaint.

He approached Mitch and kicked his foot gently. "Yo, man, we outta here." Malek rubbed his red eyes. He had a lot on his mind and needed to get some sleep so he could wake up refreshed and analyze his situation.

He wasn't going to say anything to Mitch about his plan to leave Flint until he had all his ducks in order. Since Mitch knew all of Malek's business affairs anyway, he'd be the one to inherit the throne.

"How's Hal?" Mitch asked as he stood up and stretched. "She a'ight?"

"She was in the fucking rehab center. I had the mu'fucka shot up with her inside. Now she's laid up on the fifth floor," was all Malek could say, his voice cracking from emotion. Admitting to himself that Halleigh's circumstance was his fault was like taking a bullet to the heart.

"What?" Mitch asked. "What was she doing there? You should've made sure she was in pocket before you put that order in, fam. You know that. She should've been right underneath you, just so you were sure she wasn't in harm's way." Mitch's tone was more that of a concerned boyfriend than a supportive best friend.

Malek didn't like the way Mitch was coming at him, but he couldn't really get mad, because everything Mitch was saying was right. He didn't appreciate another nigga speaking on his relationship with Halleigh,

but he was too tired to start anything. He held his tongue, unaware that Mitch had larceny in his heart.

"I know, fam, I know. Don't rub salt in it, my nigga." Malek extended his hand to Mitch.

Mitch embraced Malek and grabbed his coat as they began to leave. "I got to piss." Mitch tossed Malek his car keys. "Go grab the whip. I'll be out in a minute."

Malek nodded his head and exited the hospital.

Mitch headed over to the elevator. He looked around inconspicuously before pressing the call button, and then slipped into the space unnoticed as he headed to the fifth floor. He walked casually down the hall, peeking his head into each room until he saw Halleigh's silhouette in a darkened room. He knocked lightly but didn't wait to be invited in before he stepped into the room.

Both his slight knock and presence caused Halleigh to open her eyes from her light sleep.

"What's good, ma? How you feeling?" he asked as he walked over to her and sat on the edge of her bed.

Halleigh sat up and nervously fidgeted with her hair. She never felt completely comfortable around Mitch because of the history they shared. She looked behind Mitch, expecting to see Malek walk through the door behind him. When he didn't, she asked, "What are you doing here?"

"I came here with Malek to check on you. I just want to make sure you're straight." Mitch looked over his shoulder to make sure the coast was clear. He turned his attention back to Halleigh and began to speak in a whisper. "Malek went a little bit crazy, Hal. I don't know what's up with him lately, so be careful, ma. I know you're with him now, but I care about you, and I don't want to see you caught out there on some bullshit."

Halleigh's eyebrows furrowed, and a look of confusion washed over her face. "What are you talking about, Mitch?"

Mitch began his infiltration into his comrade's relationship with the girl he truly had desires for. "Malek thought you were stepping out on him, Hal. He had you followed and then gave the order to have the building you were in shot up."

Halleigh didn't speak. She just lay there shaking her head.

"It's true, Halleigh," Mitch said convincingly. "He knew you were inside. His jealousy over you is crazy. I don't want to see you hurt."

Mitch was manipulative. He was planting seeds to cause problems in their relationship. His lies might not do much now, but they would remain in Halleigh's head until they manifested into a bigger problem. He was going to chip away at Halleigh's trust for Malek until he could snatch her, and then take the streets away from Malek.

"No, he wouldn't do that," Halleigh finally responded.

Mitch stood up and nodded his head as if he understood her choosing to be in denial over her boyfriend's true intentions on her life. He kissed the top of her head, even though she moved away from his touch. "I hear you, Halleigh. You're loyal. I know that's your man, but I just wanted to pull your coattail and tell you to be careful. I don't want to see you hurt. My offer still stands too. Whenever you're ready to leave your situation, you have somewhere to go," he stated before leaving her to her thoughts.

Halleigh thought about what Mitch had just told her, but she refused to believe him. *Malek would never do me like that on purpose.* She dismissed the idea and let the drugs the doctors had given her take her into a mind-numbing sleep.

Chapter Eighty

M alek hit the streets with full force knowing that eventually he would have to let them go. Being a hustler was a full-time job, and although Halleigh was his wifey, the streets of Flint were his side bitch, his retreat. He needed them almost as much as he needed Halleigh. He knew he couldn't just cut things off cold turkey, or else withdrawal would be a son of a bitch.

His connection to getting money was something Halleigh would never be able to understand. It was the only thing he had to hold on to that would keep him sane. His focus became his hustle.

Now that she was back, she was asking him to choose. The hood life or Hal? Which one was it going to be? Malek's guilt over the role he played in her injuries made him lean toward her. He just wanted to be with her.

For as long as he could remember, Halleigh had been the girl of his dreams. Malek knew that Halleigh would be his wife before she'd ever agreed to go out with him. He felt that deeply for her, and the fact that she was a virgin was extra special to him. She was saving herself for him, but made it clear that he had to earn it. Halleigh never saw dollar signs when she looked at Malek; she saw love, and that's why he cherished her so much. Fate just dealt them a different hand and separated them for a while.

A lot of things had changed since his puppy-love days with her. He wasn't the same. She definitely was not the same, yet here they were in

the present, trying to make it work. Malek wondered if they could get back all they had lost, because neither of them was innocent anymore. Still, he had to give it a chance. He loved her, and if he had to let the streets go in order to make her happy, he would regretfully do so.

He reached over to his passenger's seat and moved the cocaine-filled duffel bag to the backseat. He'd come to the decision that he'd give up the streets for her, to make sure the two of them would be straight when they started their new life together elsewhere. First, though, he had to get a few ki's off. Even if he was on his way out the game, he wasn't taking any losses.

The doctors said that Halleigh's hospital stay would be around three weeks, which gave him three weeks to get papered up.

Hand-over-fist sales were a thing of the past for Malek. He was a duffel-bag boy, but he was anything but little. In the backseat of his car, he carried a life sentence with him—fifty kilos of cocaine. Jamaica Joe had already left him with a meal ticket, so he didn't have to work another day of his life if he didn't want to, but Malek wanted stupid money. Malek wasn't trying to ball out for himself. He was trying to build generational wealth that he could pass down to his children and his children's children. He wanted security and was willing to put his life on the line to ensure that his family would be able to eat without struggling. He had watched his own mother fret over money for years. She was always robbing Peter to pay Paul, and that was something he refused to make Halleigh do. Now that she was pregnant with his baby, he felt obligated to take care of her forever.

Malek didn't have time to distribute the bricks on the streets. He couldn't hit anyone with consignment. He only had three weeks to get the dope off, and if he gave a nigga anything on credit and didn't get the return on his money, he would have to kill him, and that wasn't no front. That was on the real. He couldn't risk it. He couldn't jeopardize himself like that, because he had a girl and a baby on the way, and they were depending on him. Halleigh had given him an ultimatum, if Malek didn't retire from the dope game, then Halleigh would leave him and take his seed with her. He couldn't have that.

He spun through the city streets, acknowledging his street fame, giving head nods to the corner hustlers who noticed him and showed love. He would miss the game, but not the treachery that came along with it. He had seen a lot of people murdered, trying to be boss, and he himself had taken a lot of lives on his way to the top. Now it was time to pass the crown, which he knew Mitch would be more than willing to accept—that is, after he helped Malek get off those fifty ki's.

"What's on your mind, Mitch? I've been trying to throw this pussy at you all morning, and you been brushing me off, acting all brand-new. What's up wit' you anyway?" Keesha fussed as she sat up on the bed in frustration and hit a strawberry blunt.

"Halleigh was in the rehab center when it got sh—"

Keesha didn't even let Mitch finish his sentence. She smacked her lips in disgust. "Halleigh? Why are you so concerned about Halleigh? I'm tired of every nigga in the city acting like that bitch pussy can't get funky. Let me remind you of something, baby boy: Halleigh is Malek's girl, and you work for Malek. You're like his little bitch almost," she said with a patronizing smirk. "That mu'fucka say jump, and you and the rest of these small-time-ass niggas asking how high." Keesha choked on her words because of the weed smoke. As she held her head back to let the smoke ease slowly from her lips, she closed her eyes.

SLAP!

Mitch slapped the shit out of her, causing her to fall off the bed, the blunt falling on top of her and burning the side of her face.

"Let me tell you something, ma." Mitch got on top of her and gripped his hand around her throat. "I don't know how you talk to Manolo or that faggot-ass nigga, Sweets, but you better bite your tongue when you with me. You hear me?" Mitch said, spit flying in Keesha's face with every syllable. All Keesha could do was nod as the fear of death filled her eyes. Mitch released her with a jerk and got off her.

Keesha humbled up real quick, picking herself up from the floor timidly and holding her burning cheek. "I didn't mean nothing by it, boo," she said. "I'm just frustrated because I hate to see somebody in a spot they don't deserve. You know Malek wouldn't be where he is if it wasn't for Jamaica Joe. After Joe died, it was supposed to be you. You're not a right-hand man, baby. You're a star."

She walked over to Mitch and rubbed his back as she continued to blow his head up. "You've got to take your hood back. Sweets don't care if you run the North Side, because you're about your business. It's something in it for everybody; but Malek is still on that North versus South bullshit, and Sweets needs that nigga done.

"After you take out Malek, you'll be boss. Everybody in the city will be on your coattail, and just to show his gratitude, Sweets will cop all of the dope he sells to the South Side from you. It's a win-win situation. All you have to do is get Malek out of the picture." Keesha went and picked up the smoldering blunt from the floor, took a puff, then passed it to Mitch.

As Mitch took a hit, Keesha added, "And you need to forget about Halleigh. If Malek goes, then she needs to go. She'll get suspicious, and she'll become a problem if you don't get rid of her up front, so forget about them wet dreams you been having about her."

Keesha walked around and stood in front of Mitch. Her red thong and bra didn't even distract Mitch as he absorbed what she had just said. Keesha walked into the bathroom and out of sight as Mitch continued to get blazed. Mitch didn't realize it, but the same way he'd at-

tempted to manipulate Halleigh, Keesha had just manipulated him. The only difference was when a woman does things, she does it right.

As Mitch stood there blazing on the blunt, his jealousy for Malek turned to animosity, and he began to formulate a plan to knock him off his throne. It was a tricky situation, trying to get rid of Malek, who had inherited a lot of love and respect off Jamaica Joe's strength. He couldn't just kill him and then expect the city to pledge their allegiance behind him. There would be uproar, and Malek's loyal soldiers and allies would always have revenge in their hearts. He had to do it quietly and make it look like the work of an outsider. That way, when Malek was out of the picture, everyone would follow Mitch, no questions asked.

DING-DONG!

Keesha came out of the bathroom with a bandage on her face after hearing the doorbell ring. She was still unclothed, but that didn't seem to matter. She rolled her eyes and said, "I'll get it." Her "fatty" swallowed the thong as she left the room.

Mitch put on a pair of Sean John jeans over the boxers he'd been sporting as he continued to smoke, his chiseled and tattooed upper body still showing.

Keesha appeared in the doorway just as Mitch was about to exit. "Your daddy's here," she said with a condescending look, referring to Malek.

Mitch stroked her burnt cheek and whispered, "You don't learn well, do you?" He gave her a hard pat, making her flinch in pain. "Don't worry. I'll teach you as soon as my company leaves." He smiled as he thought about the foot he would put up her ass later.

Mitch and Keesha had a love-hate relationship at best. They weren't a couple by any means. Sweets had put Keesha on Mitch to make sure that he remembered why Malek had to get "got." They both knew their relationship was about business, but as soon as Mitch saw Keesha's small waist and fat onion-shaped behind, he pictured himself hitting it. It wasn't long before he actually did. So now they fucked and plotted, plotted and schemed, fucked, plotted, and schemed all day.

She was seeking the grand prize. After he took over, she wanted to be wifey. *Never that,* he thought as he entered his living room and found Malek standing in the doorway. He forced himself to turn his frown into a friendly smile. "Bro, what's good?" he asked, approaching Malek and giving him some dap.

"I've got to talk to you about something," Malek said seriously. He nodded toward the back of the house and added, "In private."

"Yeah, a'ight. Let me grab a shirt and we'll go grab some food or something." Mitch walked away and disappeared into the bedroom.

Malek decided to go wait out in the car for Mitch. He didn't know if it was just his nerves, but Mitch seemed to be taking extra long to come

outside. He looked at the time on his cell phone and realized Mitch had kept him waiting for more than fifteen minutes.

When Mitch finally got inside the car, Malek cut him a look but decided against speaking on it. He just started up his ride and pulled away from the curb in silence as soon as Mitch closed his door.

Malek's focus was straight ahead, and he seemed distant, causing Mitch to be a little uneasy. *I hope he ain't heard nothing about the deal I made with Sweets,* Mitch thought as he shifted in his seat.

All of a sudden, the leather interior of Malek's car felt like hot coals on Mitch's ass, and he began to sweat as the silent seconds ticked by. As Mitch was sweating bullets, Malek was lost in his own thoughts.

Malek knew he couldn't get fifty joints off on his own in three weeks. He would need Mitch's help. Once he made his money, he planned on stepping down and giving it all to Mitch, but he would wait to tell him that news until after his work was already moved. Malek didn't need Mitch thinking for self while pushing his product.

"The duffel bag in the back got fifty in it," Malek stated.

Mitch finally let out a sigh of relief when he realized he wasn't busted. "Fifty? Why so many?" he asked.

"We got some moves we need to make," Malek replied vaguely. "We need to get 'em off in three weeks. You think you can make that happen?" Malek kept his eyes on the road and never even looked over at Mitch.

"I don't see why not," Mitch answered with a shrug. Inside, he couldn't help but wonder what the time frame was all about, why Malek was set on moving the dope so fast.

"Make sure all the spots get hit with double. All of them niggas need to be on post twenty-four hours. For the next three weeks, ain't no such thing as sleeping. Nobody gets work on consignment. For the loyal niggas that cop from us, lower the price. Tell 'em they can get the bricks for eighteen each, or two for thirty. Make it so they can't tell you no. Get 'em off however you can.

"Be smart, though. We ain't had no trouble from the police so far, and we don't want none now, nah mean?"

"Yeah, I hear you. I got it," Mitch replied, still puzzled by the sudden urgency in moving product. "What's going on? I mean, why is there such a hurry to make this move? What's going on in three weeks?" Mitch chuckled. "You got a ransom you got to pay or something?"

Malek remained serious, acting as if Mitch hadn't even asked him anything. "When they're all done, I'll bless you with something. I'm not gon' be out here like that because Halleigh needs me right now, so I'ma need you to be my eyes, ears, and pistols. You feel me?" Once again he looked over at Mitch.

"I feel you."

"I'm not going hard for nothing, though, bro. It's something in it for everybody. Everybody's gon' eat as long as it gets done," Malek promised as he pulled back onto Mitch's street after circling the block.

"I got you, fam. It's as good as done," Mitch replied. He frowned when Malek stopped in front of his house. "We ain't going to eat?"

"You got three weeks, baby. Time is money." Malek popped his car locks, signaling for Mitch to exit his vehicle. "We can eat later. Oh and, trust me, we'll eat, but right now, it's all about that paper."

On that note, Mitch exited the car, and was left standing there confused as Malek peeled off.

Chapter Eighty-one

Mitch hit the streets with a vengeance all right, but his motivation was greed. By giving Mitch free reign over fifty kilos of cocaine, Malek had given him the push he needed to put his plan into action. Mitch was going to sell the coke, but he had no intention of giving all that paper back to Malek, and he definitely wasn't planning on lowering the prices. There was a cocaine drought in the Midwest, and Mitch was going to take full advantage of it. Supply and demand was the only scale he set his prices to. In fact, he was taxing for the bricks by charging cats twenty-four stacks for just one. Malek's loyal customers were the only ones getting a lowered rate, only so that they wouldn't go back and complain to Malek. Everybody else was getting raped by his outrageous prices.

It was nothing for Mitch to blow through the dope, because he had Sweets on deck for more than half of them. By the time the three weeks was up, he would be close to a million dollars richer, and Malek would be closer to death.

Mitch, like a lot of other cats in the game, had always been "lightweight" jealous of Malek because of how he seemed to have come up in the game without putting in half as much work as some other cats did. It was as if all he had to do was grow into his inheritance. Mitch didn't care how hard Malek made himself out to be; he wasn't no true hood nigga. It made Mitch sick, especially when he recalled all those write-ups in the local paper about Flint's godson, the kid that was going to put the city on the map the same way LeBron put Cleveland

on the map. Now more than ever, Mitch was bound and determined to put his own self on the map.

He used to feel bad and disloyal at the thoughts of undermining Malek that would often cross his mind, but Keesha had kicked her "fuck Malek campaign" into overdrive. That, along with the fact that Mitch was getting crazy paid, helped to erase any guilt that remained. Malek's demise was an equal trade for Mitch's come-up. The day that Malek called to ask for the money would be the same day that he would be found leaking somewhere. There was no way Mitch was letting that much dough slip through his hands.

Malek made it his personal mission to visit Halleigh every day in the hospital. Her room was filled with flowers and balloons from him, and every day he was bringing her a new gift. He was just so grateful to have her in his life and so excited by the fact that he was about to be a father. The flowers, balloons, and gifts weren't bribes just to get Halleigh to forgive him for the part he played in her being in the hospital in the first place. He truly wanted to give Halleigh the world and show her in every way how much he truly loved her. Eventually, Halleigh did express her true forgiveness to Malek, although he had not forgiven himself yet. Every time Halleigh smiled at him, he would think of how close he had come to never seeing her smile again.

"I'ma take care of you. You know that, right?" he asked her as he held her hand.

"I know, Malek, but who's going to take care of you?" she countered. "I know you're not going to leave the streets alone."

"I am," he said abruptly and definitively. "By the time you walk out of here, I'll be out of the game."

"Yeah, right, Malek. You're just saying all of that, thinking it will make me feel better, heal better, and get out of here even faster. I don't know. But I do know how addictive the street game is. It's much easier to just say you're going to give it all up than to actually do it. Trust me, I know."

"But I'm serious, Hal. At the end of the day, a nigga's word is really all he got. My word is gold; it always has been, when it comes to you. You don't know that by now?"

The tone of sincerity in his voice let her know that he wasn't lying.

"I don't want to lose you. If I got to give up the streets to keep you, then that's that. Plus, you being in that rehab center has been eating me alive. I can't believe I did this to you."

Their intimate moment was interrupted by a knock at the door. They both looked up and saw Sharina walk through the door.

Malek stood up to leave so that he could give mother and daughter some privacy. Halleigh hadn't really told him what went down when they met each other at the rehab center, but he knew they must still have a lot to talk about.

Halleigh shook her head and said, "No, Malek, stay."

He sat down reluctantly, but held her hand tightly to give her his support. Seeing Halleigh's mother put a bad taste in Malek's mouth. He didn't have too much respect for her, considering all that she had put the love of his life through.

"You're so pretty," Sharina said almost in a whisper as she slowly crept toward Halleigh's bedside. She stopped before making it all the way over to Halleigh. Her eyes clouded over with tears, almost like she was seeing her daughter for the first time.

Halleigh was silent as she stared at her mother from the hospital bed. There was so much anger built up inside of her. As she looked at her mother, she tried to forget that it was Sharina's sin that had sent her world spiraling out of control. On that fateful night, Halleigh's life was forever changed for the worse. Looking at Sharina, it was hard not to also see the men she'd let rape her daughter for the sake of a hit.

"It's been a long time, baby girl. You're all grown-up now. You remind me so much of myself." Sharina stood at the foot of the bed nervously twiddling her fingers as she waited for Halleigh to respond. She seemed to be afraid to get too close. Two years ago, Sharina was frail and sickly-looking; but now, it appeared as though she had picked up some of her weight, and she wasn't high, which made her almost unrecognizable.

"Well, I'm not you. I could never be you," Halleigh shot at her. "Why did you come here?"

"I'm sorry, Halleigh. I'm so sorry. I've thought about you every day since then," Sharina said. She swallowed the knot in her throat, hoping she wouldn't have to elaborate. Her hopes were shattered when Halleigh sat straight up in her bed and spoke.

"Since when, Ma? Since the first time you pawned my Christmas gifts to get high? Since the time we got put out in the streets in the winter because you spent the rent money on dope?"

"I know, baby."

Halleigh almost jumped out of her bed and across the room. "No, you don't know shit! You have no clue what I've been through!"

Growing up, Halleigh had never disrespected her mother. Dope-fiend or not, Sharina was her mother, and Halleigh had always treated her as such. Right now, she could no longer control all of the bitterness that had mounted up against her mother. "See, I could've forgiven all of those things, Ma. I didn't want the Christmas gifts. I would have lived in a cardboard box with you. I accepted you for who you were, because you were still my mother and I loved you. You were the only one I had."

"I love you too, baby girl," Sharina pleaded as tears fell down her cheeks.

"No, you don't. I forgave you time and time again, Ma, but you did the unforgivable the day you sold my virginity to the dopeman!"

There, it had been said. Sharina always knew that decision would come back to haunt her someday. What she did to her daughter was the thing she wished she could take back more than anything.

"I know, baby. I have regretted that since the day I did it, baby. I'm so sorry. I truly am. You have to forgive me." Sharina took one step closer to the bed, as if the invisible wall that separated them was slowly being chiseled away. "I'm clean now, Halleigh. I've been clean for six months, baby. I go to meetings at the rehab center to stay clean. I'm going to do it this time, if not for myself, then for you." She looked down at Halleigh's small baby bump. "And it looks like for my grand-baby too. I just want to be here for you and make it right."

Desperate for her daughter's affection, Sharina was begging like Keith Sweat. She didn't know her daughter had changed, and was no longer the sweet, forgiving, naïve little girl she had somehow managed to raise during her sober moments. Halleigh might not have wished her mother dead in that rehab center shootout, but at the same time, she didn't have much love for her.

"I'm glad you're clean," Halleigh said with a nod before going back to rest in her bed. "Maybe now you're clearheaded enough to think about how you ruined my life." She glared at her mother.

"Do you know the things I've had to do because of you?" Halleigh spat. "You were so used up that you couldn't have paid a corner boy to let you fuck your way into a high, so you sold me. You pimped me out and let them rape me. That was mine to keep and give to who I wanted, but you took it from me!"

Malek could see the past stirring up fresh anger in Halleigh. As he thought about the role Sharina played in robbing him of the precious gift Halleigh had been saving for him, new anger began to rise up in him also. Seeing his baby's mother was getting all "rallied" and stressed, he wanted to tell her to just calm down, even ask her mother to leave the room; but he knew this moment was a long time coming, and something Halleigh probably needed to let go of. Who was he to stand in her way?

"I can never forgive you for that," Halleigh told Sharina.

Sharina finally realized her daughter wasn't the same anymore. It was evident from the look in her eyes that the streets had injected its DNA into her baby. Now she was as cold as a Michigan winter. "I know it hurts," Sharina cried. "I know I did wrong, but I'm your mother, Halleigh. You're my baby. I need you."

"Well, I don't need a mother. I'm a grown-ass woman now. There's nothing left to raise. The streets raised me, but you know what? You were good for something. You showed me how not to treat my child. So this baby I'm carrying in my stomach is lucky, because I'm deter-mined not to fuck up, just to avoid being like you."

Halleigh's words were so sharp they cut Sharina to the bone. Malek

could see her shivering in pain as she began to backpedal out of the room.

"I'm sorry, baby girl. Mama had a monkey on her back. You have to know that I would have never allowed those things to happen to you otherwise. I love you, and I only hope that you will let me back into your life one day so that, even if you don't want me to be a mother to you, I can at least be a grandmother to my grandchild."

"You will never be a part of my baby's life!" Halleigh said, throwing daggers at her mother's heart. She knew from the look on Sharina's face that she hit the bull's-eye. "We don't need you. Now, please leave."

While spitting those last words at her mother, Halleigh had managed to stay dry-eyed. Any tears she might have shed for her mother in the past were now long gone and long forgotten. Not one teardrop had even threatened to appear in her eyes. She was as cold as ice, her tears frozen solid and unable to form.

Halleigh had chosen her words carefully. They were calculated to inflict as much pain as possible. She knew that no words could ever hurt her mother as much as Sharina had hurt her, but still, it had been well worth the effort.

After speaking her mind, Halleigh had hoped to feel some sense of relief, victory even, but that wasn't the case. Just as soon as Sharina walked out of the room, the ice block around Halleigh's heart quickly melted, and she broke down in tears. She cried the hardest she had ever done in her life, heaving violently as she thought of her rape, of the woman she'd once loved and would have done anything for, and of how proud she truly was that her mother had gotten herself clean. With so many emotions taking over her mind, all Halleigh could do was cry.

She might never see her mother again after what she'd just said to her, and as much as she hated to admit it, it hurt. No matter how painful that was, though, she couldn't forgive her. Right now, forgiveness just wasn't in her. How she was even able to forgive Malek was beyond her own understanding. All she knew was that her heart had no more room for mercy. Not right now.

She was just now starting to piece her life back together, and that was only by the grace of God—and Malek's love. She refused to let her mother come and break up her happiness with Malek yet again. Even if her mother was sober now, there was no telling how long that might last. Halleigh didn't have time to let someone else's burdens become her own. She had to let sleeping dogs lie and move on with her life. Logically she knew this, but it didn't ease the pain she felt in her chest as she bawled like a baby.

Malek sat by her side, stroking her hair and rubbing her back, reassuring her that everything would be all right. He'd actually been shocked by how cruelly Halleigh spoke to her mother. Sharina had

done the worst thing a mother could do to her daughter, but a part of him still wanted to urge Halleigh toward forgiveness, because he knew what it was like not to have a mother at all. His mother was gone, and he would do anything to bring her back if he could; life was short and could be taken away at any second. He didn't force his opinion on Halleigh. Instead, he comforted her in her time of need, trusting her to handle the situation as she saw fit. He knew that she'd gone through some awful things as a result of her mother—some things that she probably would never even tell him—so he let her scream on her mother, and then comforted her as she cried herself to sleep.

As the cold, icy layer melted away from Halleigh's heart, it seemed to be doing the same for Malek. Perhaps things could go back to the way they were after all . . . just not so easily.

Chapter Eighty-two

After spending three weeks in the hospital, Halleigh emerged from the elevator in a wheelchair, which Malek was pushing. He leaned over to kiss her cheek. "I love you, Halleigh," he said, finally glad that his woman was coming home where she belonged.

"I love you forever, Malek," she responded as he wheeled her through the sliding glass doors to where his car was waiting.

Halleigh grimaced at the pain that shot through her whenever she moved. The doctors had been giving her pain medication throughout her hospital stay, but because she was pregnant, they couldn't give her anything too strong. She had lost a lot of blood when she was shot, and she had dropped a lot of weight, so her doctors were giving her high doses of vitamins to get her energy back to where it should be.

"I'm going to drop you off at home and then go fill your prescriptions," Malek told her as he climbed into the driver's seat and pulled off. "I have to swing by and pick something up from Mitch, too, so I may be gone for a couple hours."

Halleigh looked at Malek through disappointed eyes. In her heart she felt like he would never give up the streets. For the past three weeks, he had been making lifetime promises, assuring her that he was getting out of the game, but something was telling her that he couldn't give it all up, that the hold of the streets was far too strong on him.

She didn't feel sure about how important she was to him, and she

needed, more than anything, for him to know she was willing to commit to being a permanent fixture in his life. The game was temporary.

Noticing the look in Halleigh's eyes, Malek told her, "Don't look like that, Hal. I told you I'm through with the streets, and I meant it. All I'm going to do today is pick up my money that I got out there, and then I'm out for good."

Once in front of their spot, he opened his car door and helped Halleigh inside. She was so grateful to walk into her own home after her extended stay in the hospital. She couldn't wait to take a bath, get some real food, and then pass out in her own therapeutic Sleep Number bed. Malek suggested she lay down and get some rest first. He promised that he would help her with a bath once he got back, but she wanted to get cleaned up to lay in her nice, clean, freshly made bed. After getting out of the bath and slipping into some comfy pajamas, Halleigh made her way down to the kitchen, where Malek was fixing her something to eat before he headed out. Halleigh noticed a small box tied with a bright red ribbon on the countertop.

"Is that for me?" she asked Malek.

Malek didn't respond as he poured some canned soup into a bowl, but his smile was enough for Halleigh to get excited. She knew it was jewelry because of how small the box was. She walked over to it and shook it playfully before untying the ribbon and opening the box. Inside was a Mercedes key surrounded by red tissue paper.

"I upgraded you, ma. You and my shorty got to ride in the best," Malek said with a wink. He walked over to Halleigh and rubbed her belly.

"Where is it?" she asked excitedly, jumping up and down in spite of her pain.

Malek motioned his head toward the garage, and Halleigh sprinted through the door. She stopped dead in her tracks when she saw the custom, powder-pink 6 Series. It was just like Malek's, except it was super-feminine. "Oh my God! Malek, I love it, boy!" she screamed in delight as she rushed to admire the white leather interior.

"I thought you might." Malek checked the time on his phone. "Hal, I've got to spin the block for a minute. I'll be back before it gets too late, a'ight."

"Yeah, yeah, okay," she said distractedly as she messed with the gadgets on the inside.

Malek laughed. "Your soup is inside on the counter. Don't let it get cold."

Still, Halleigh paid him little attention.

"Call me if you need me," he said as he headed off to take care of his final business transactions on the streets.

When Mitch received the call from Malek asking him to meet up, he knew it was time. He'd been watching his calendar and counting

down to the day when the streets would be his. He had easily blown through the weight Malek hit him with, partly because he had supplied Sweets with a "butter" price. Malek didn't know his dope was going to his adversary, but after today, it wouldn't matter anyway. He would be a distant memory.

Mitch grabbed the two duffel bags full of money and the twin pistols for security. The bags were filled to capacity with all street cash, the bills dirty and crinkled. Dirty money. He laughed at how paid he actually was. It felt good to have so much money. He was on cloud nine, and on his way to get rid of the only person who could possibly bring him down from his high.

He made sure both of his chrome 9 "milli's" were off safety then stuffed them into his shoulder holsters, one tucked safely between each arm. He put on his black leather Pelle coat, which concealed the holster, and then went to meet Malek.

Malek had been waiting at his spare apartment for Mitch to arrive. He'd rented the apartment just to have an extra place to rest his head, but since he and Halleigh had started a life together, he rarely used it. It was convenient for the purpose he was using it for tonight.

When Malek called, Mitch had assured him that all of the coke was gone and they were sitting on a gold mine. One million dollars was a lot of money—more money than a lot of people saw in their entire lives. Malek had always been smart, and watching Jamaica Joe as he reigned supreme only helped him to perfect his own hustle. He had a nice chunk of change saved up already, and with the money Mitch was about to deliver, it would be more than enough for him and Halleigh to relocate and start fresh.

He wasn't no dummy, though. He knew he couldn't just let that money sit idle when it could be making him more. The only difference was it would be legal this time. He really wanted to link up with a financial advisor because he wanted to make some arrangements for Halleigh and his baby. Just in case anything ever happened to him, he wanted them to be set for life.

When Malek heard the knock at the door, he knew it was Mitch. He was the only other person who knew about the apartment. Malek didn't bother to check the peephole. He opened the door to find Mitch standing at his doorway.

"What's good, bro?" Malek asked. "Come on in." He stepped aside for Mitch to enter.

Mitch came in and looked around. Malek didn't notice the paranoia in his eyes because he was too busy thinking about getting paid.

"You got the bread, fam?" Malek asked, rubbing his hands together.

Mitch lifted the duffel bag.

"Nigga, what's good? You all silent and shit," Malek commented as he motioned toward his sectional sofa.

"Have a seat. There's something important I need to holla at you about."

Mitch made sure he kept the duffel bag near his feet and then took a seat on the couch. He could hear his heart beating rapidly in his ear as Malek walked over to the bar. Mitch knew this was his chance to do what he'd really come to do. Malek's back was toward him, so he could easily shoot him from behind and dip without looking back.

Mitch reached inside his jacket to retrieve one of his guns, but halted when Malek said, "I'm getting out the game, Mitch."

Mitch released the grip on his steel. "What you mean, out the game?"

Malek finally turned to stare Mitch in the eyes as he spoke. "I mean I'm through. Halleigh is pregnant with my baby, and I'm trying to be around to raise him and see him grow. I don't want to make my wife bury me the way Joe did with Kim. That's why I needed that weight moved so quickly. The day Hal walked out of the hospital, I promised her I would walk away from the streets."

"And that day is today?" Mitch questioned. He had to see what Malek intended for him, because if he thought he was taking all the money and leaving Mitch with nothing, then Mitch still planned on putting two in Malek and taking the cash to build an empire of his own. Before he moved forward with his plan, he decided to give Malek the benefit of the doubt and hear him out.

"That's right. I appreciate you, fam. You've been loyal since we decided to do this together, and now I've got to hand it all down to you, bro. The money you made off of them bricks, two-fifty of it is yours, man, to cop your own weight and do your own thing. I'll even plug you in with my connect. It's all love, baby, but I've got to get out while I still have air in my lungs."

Mitch smiled deviously and replied, "No doubt, baby. You definitely got an angel watching over you, fam. You've dodged a lot of bullets. You're a smart man." He couldn't help but chuckle inside at his personal joke. Malek had dodged bullets all right. Unknowingly, he'd just dodged two.

Mitch was satisfied with Malek's severance pay, and decided to kill his plan instead of his boy. Two hundred and fifty thousand dollars was enough cake to get up and running and stash some for a rainy day. If Malek was getting out of the game anyway, then he wouldn't be a problem to Sweets or anyone else, so the situation was fitting for everyone. How Mitch saw it, it was a win-win situation for every player.

"So I take it you good with that, fam?" Malek walked over to Mitch with two shots of liquor in hand and extended one to him.

A smile crossed Mitch's lips as he accepted the shot. "It's all good."

"It's been a short run, but a good run," Malek said as he held out his glass.

Mitch did the same. They clinked their glasses together and then downed the liquor in one swallow.

"Now, let's count this money so I can get back to wifey."

Malek headed back to the kitchen, nodding for Mitch to follow. Mitch grabbed the bags and did just that.

Malek went to his refrigerator, grabbed two Coronas out and tossed one to Mitch, who then poured all of the money onto the table. They sat down and went to work counting and dividing the money.

"Congrats on your family, man," Mitch stated, like he had never had larcenous thoughts on his mind.

"Thanks, my nigga. I'm about to take this money and take care of her, bro. She deserves it."

"That she does," Mitch replied. "That she does."

Chapter Eighty-three

After counting out all of the money and breaking Mitch off with a hefty percentage, Malek had $750,000 in the trunk of his car. He was overjoyed at the fact that he could now live comfortably with his lady for years to come. He still had $500,000 saved up from the money Jamaica Joe had left him, so he was indeed a millionaire, with a little bit of change to spare.

He'd lost track of time, sharing last drinks and thoughts with Mitch. He punched eighty on the speedometer, until finally he was sitting in the driveway at his home. He jumped out of the car in excitement, grabbed the duffel bags out of the trunk, and hauled them into the house.

"Halleigh!" he yelled as soon as he entered. He didn't care that it was three o'clock in the morning. He couldn't contain his excitement and wanted to share his departure from the game with her. He couldn't wait to let her know it was real, that he was truly a man of his word.

"Hal!"

"Malek, what's wrong?" she asked sleepily as she came out of the bedroom. "Why are you yelling?"

"This is why, Hal"—He emptied the contents of one of the duffel bags all over the floor.

Halleigh wasn't the least bit excited, and once again, a look of disappointment showed on her face. "I've seen your re-up money before,

Malek." She shook her head and then flailed her arms in defeat. "I thought we had an agreement that you were out of the game?" Hal asked, not out of anger but confusion. She really didn't want to see Malek get hurt or lose his life the way so many hustlers before him had done.

"This ain't re-up paper, baby girl. It's ours. All of this money belongs to us, and I'm going to spoil you and my seed for the rest of my life." Malek rushed toward the love of his life and scooped her in his arms.

Consumed with so much happiness, Halleigh didn't even flinch at the pain she was in as she wrapped her legs around Malek's waist and he held her securely under her bottom. He spun her around and kissed her passionately.

"I need a vacation," Malek said, imitating the popular rap song by Young Jeezy.

Halleigh laughed as Malek laid her down gently on the money-littered floor.

"We can go wherever you like, Halleigh. Just pick a place and we're out."

"I really just want to get out of Flint. That's all I've ever wanted from day one," Halleigh confessed. "Our history here ain't all that great. I just want to go somewhere and start over. Maybe even go back to school or something. I don't really even have to be far from here. Let's go to Detroit or Saginaw, just anywhere but here."

Saginaw and Detroit were just as ruthless and hood as Flint, but the way Halleigh spoke of them, one would have thought she was talking about going to Paris.

"I don't know, Hal. That's just a different hood, same shit. I wanna take you to the Bahamas or something, so we can live like rich niggas do."

Halleigh laughed at Malek's crass outlook on the world. "I don't care about being in the hood, Malek. I just don't want to be in Flint. At least in Saginaw no one will know us. We'll be regular just like everybody else. Since you wanna see how rich niggas live, you can take me on a vacation. We'll go to an island in the Caribbean."

Malek kissed Halleigh gently and replied, "Okay, ma, whatever you want. You handle the passports and everything. The money will be in the safe. You know the combination. My money is your money. Take care of everything and make arrangements for us to leave Flint when we get back from our vacation. Deal?"

Halleigh smiled. "Deal." She couldn't believe it was happening, that she was finally getting out of Flint once and for all. God willing, she was never coming back.

Halleigh handled all of the details regarding their trip and their permanent relocation after their return. She had decided that they would

move to Saginaw, a small city about a half-hour north of Flint. She decided against Detroit because, in her days as a Manolo Mami, many of her clients had been ballers from the D, and she didn't want to run into anyone who might remember her from her former occupation. She was trying to let her past go and focus on the present. At the rate she had been turning tricks for Manolo, she knew if she and Malek moved to Detroit, she would inevitably run into someone she used to do business with. She was also excited about her pregnancy. She was healing well from her gunshot wound. Fortunately for her, it was only a flesh wound, and although the bullet had been the greatest pain she ever felt, it hadn't hit any major arteries or organs. The doctors told her that ordinarily she wouldn't have been in the hospital for more than a week, but with her pregnancy and all, they didn't want to take any chances. She was very grateful to be alive, and she thanked God for the safety of her baby as well.

She booked an all-inclusive trip to the Turks and Caicos Islands and filled out expedited paperwork for passports for herself and Malek. They were scheduled to leave in two weeks, which gave her more than enough time to secure a place to live in Saginaw and move most of their things from their home in Flint. She didn't want to rush into purchasing another home, so she decided to lease a condominium and wait for their home in Flint to be sold first.

She didn't see Malek much in the two weeks prior to their trip, since she was always on the go, taking care of their trip, and he was always asleep, catching up on years of missed sleep from hustling. She didn't mind him taking time to rest. She figured his mind and body needed it after the non-stop hustle he'd been on ever since blowing his NBA shot.

The child in her stomach linked them together for a lifetime. She was beginning to realize that their relationship was bigger than the two of them. They were now a family.

Halleigh made it her personal mission in life to be there for Malek the way he'd always been there for her. As she thought about how much she loved him, she began to grow more and more excited about their vacation to the Turks and Caicos. She had been fantasizing about going to the burgeoning tourist location ever since she'd learned of LisaRaye marrying the island's premier. Fuck the Bahamas. If a black person owned the island, that's where she wanted to be.

Malek was all she needed. Just the fact that they would be off in some exotic place, secluded from everything else in the world, made her smile. She couldn't wait to have her man all to herself. A sexy smile graced her lips as she hit a U-turn in the middle of the street. *I've got to hit up Vickie's Secret because on this trip, I'm going to show Malek exactly how much I love him—all day and all night.*

Chapter Eighty-four

Halleigh shook her head and giggled while listening to Malek snore. They had been on the plane for five hours. Malek had been knocked out since he first sat down. Halleigh, on the other hand, was too geeked to sleep. She could already see the crystal-clear ocean water and sandy-white beaches. She could hardly contain her excitement as she gripped Malek's hand tightly and did everything in her power to wake him up without getting him upset.

She coughed loudly, but he didn't stir, which only irritated her. She turned on his overhead reading light, hoping it would shine in his face and cause him to awaken. Again, there was no response. She knew she was being selfish, but she needed someone to talk to. She sighed loudly and removed her hand from his to lean against the window.

The feeling of Halleigh pulling away from him finally made Malek open his eyes. Holding on to her hand had comforted him and put his mind at ease enough for him to close his eyes. As soon as he felt his connection to her cease, he instantly awoke.

"What's good, ma? How long we been in the air?" he asked as he rubbed the sleep out of his eyes.

"Five hours, and you've been sleeping the whole time," Halleigh said with an eye roll.

Malek laughed and replied, "I felt you trying to wake me up, with your big-head ass."

Halleigh smiled and punched his arm gently. "Shut up. I was bored. Our vacation started the moment we arrived at the airport, not when we land."

"Okay, okay, you big baby. I'm all yours for the rest of the trip. I'll make sure you have a good time." Malek leaned over and whispered in her ear, "Meet me in the bathroom in a couple minutes so I can really show you that our vacation has officially started."

Halleigh gave Malek a mischievous grin and nodded her head as she watched him get up and make his way down the narrow aisle to the bathroom in the back of the plane. A normal chick might have been nervous, but Halleigh lived for moments like this. She loved sex—not tricking and sex with random men, but sex with Malek. Since the first time he touched her, she had become addicted to him, and he could get it whenever, wherever.

She waited for just a couple of minutes and looked around the aircraft discreetly to make sure no one was watching her. After she was comfortable that no one was focused on her, she got up with her purse in hand and walked to the bathroom. When she got there, she

could see where Malek had left the door just barely open for her. She quickly snuck inside and closed the door behind her. She slid the lock, causing the *occupied* light to come on in the cabin of the plane. There Malek stood, pants down, and a huge smile on his face.

"You are so bad," she whispered to him.

Not in the mood for words, Malek turned her around and kissed her hungrily while his hands grabbed her behind. He pressed his groin against hers to show her how hard he was. He felt like he was getting ready to burst through the fabric of his underwear. His hands moved quickly and with expertise as he unbuttoned her skintight jeans. He knew she didn't have on panties. She never wore them, which only aroused him more. He lifted her up and put her on the tiny sink.

"Malek, this sink is going to break." Her protest was soon followed by a moan, as her man cupped her breasts.

"Shh," he whispered. He got down on his knees, spread her thighs, and dove into her wet pussy. He knew oral sex was her weakness.

Halleigh's head fell back in pleasure, and she closed her eyes as soon as Malek's tongue hit her pulsating clit. She began to grind her hips slowly, making love to his face.

"Ooh shit, Malek," she moaned. "Yes, daddy, eat this pussy."

Malek took orders very well and devoured her as he began to stroke himself into pleasure.

"Malek, I'm cumming," she whispered.

"I know," he replied as he continued to feast.

Halleigh trembled as her love came down. Malek arose then sat on the toilet, his dick sticking straight in the air. Halleigh hopped off the sink and rode Malek backwards. She would never allow herself to orgasm without pleasing him as well. She grinded her ass into his groin, and within two minutes, Malek was cumming inside of her.

Receiving double the pleasure, Halleigh felt another orgasm coming on, so she sped up the process by putting her fingers on her pussy and stimulating her clit into bliss. The rendezvous lasted only a few minutes, but it was some of the best sex they'd ever had.

Malek wiped his face, rinsed his mouth with a travel-size mouthwash that Halleigh had in her purse, and then kissed her lips before exiting the bathroom. He ran straight into a flight attendant who was standing there with her arms folded and an accusatory expression on her face.

"Excuse me, miss," Malek said smoothly. "Do you have any Vernors and crackers for my sister, or anything that may settle her stomach? She's pregnant and has been throwing up in this bathroom for the past fifteen minutes."

The flight attendant immediately wiped the angry look off her face and replaced it with a concerned one. "Oh, of course, sir. I was just

going to knock to see if you needed any assistance. Only one passenger at a time is allowed in the bathroom, but under the circumstances, I understand."

Overhearing the conversation outside the door, Halleigh smiled at Malek's wit and then leaned over the toilet as if she was going to heave. Before exiting the restroom, she sprayed two splashes of body spray to erase the smell of sex and then proceeded to her seat, her hand over her stomach. The flight attendant delivered the crackers and pop to Halleigh, who smiled graciously, still feigning nausea.

Halleigh flashed Malek a devilish smile and leaned back in the comfortable first-class seat. All it took was some good sex to put her to sleep. She closed her eyes and invited the darkness that took her under as Malek gripped her hand.

"I love you, Hal," were the last words she heard Malek whisper into her ear.

Chapter Eighty-five

The island was even more beautiful than either of them could have imagined. Coming up in a concrete jungle, neither of them ever thought they would see a place so grand. All they knew was what was presented to them growing up, which was death, destruction, and poverty. Everyone Halleigh knew was dead broke and robbing Peter to pay Paul. It was just a way of life for the folks of Flint, Michigan. It was a city of little hope, and according to many statistics, a dead city.

This is how I'm supposed to live, Halleigh thought as she followed Malek into their resort. She looked around the luxurious place in awe, feeling like a kid in a candy store. "We're a long way from the ghetto," she said to Malek with a warm smile.

"Yeah, we are. I ain't never seen nothing like this," Malek admitted, as he too seemed to be out of his element. As he looked around, he noticed some of the other patrons. Everything was so over-the-top— men wearing linen suits and women clad in designer swimsuits, not the trashy show-everything type of bikinis, either. These women could give Naomi, Tyra, and Giselle a run for their money.

All of a sudden, Malek felt insecure in his own skin, as if he were underdressed. He'd wanted to see what it was like to be amongst the

rich and the famous. Well, now he was experiencing it firsthand. Hopefully he'd soon adapt.

The couple checked into their beachside villa where they were greeted by their personal concierge. When they finally settled in, they remained silent, still absorbing the entire experience.

Malek finally broke the silence. "Damn, Hal! This is it, ma. We got a butler and everything."

Halleigh stuck up her nose haughtily. "You mean a concierge, good sir," she said in a horrible British accent. She burst out laughing, and Malek hit her with one of the luxury pillows that decorated the bed. He tackled her onto the bed, and she grimaced in pain. "Ow, Malek! Wait a minute," she said as she sat up and examined the scar from her gunshot wound.

"I'm sorry, Hal. I'ma make it up to you."

Halleigh smiled and replied, "Look around us, Malek. You already have." She leaned in toward him and kissed the back of his neck. "Now, let's get out of this room and hit the beach."

Malek frowned. "Hal, we just got off a six-hour flight. Can't we just get some rest tonight and start our day tomorrow? We're here for an entire week."

"Malek, one thing I've learned by being out in the streets is that tomorrow may never come. I live my life for today." She took his hand and placed it on her pregnant stomach. "We live for today."

Malek was extremely tired, but he knew Halleigh was right. Tomorrow was promised to no man. He nodded his head and said, "A'ight, let's live, ma."

Although most of the day was behind them, the couple enjoyed the rest of the evening together by taking a walk on the resort's private beach. They took the time to pay attention to the sunset for the first time and actually relaxed for a change. They lay on the beach, close to the water, and let the tide wash in on their legs as they talked.

They both felt brand-new, like they were in a whole other world. Flint bred a city of killers and shysters. Everyone who lived there seemed to carry the weight of the world on his shoulders, and had a swagger unlike any other region. "Fuck those who aren't like me and hate those who are" seemed to be the mentality of the entire city. With this attitude came misery, however, and it bred violence and anger.

In their hometown, the couple was always looking over their shoulders and watching their backs; in fact, the whole city was paranoid. But on the Turks and Caicos Islands, they were able to let go of all that. There were no rules, and for the first time ever in their lives, they felt able to breathe. It was even better because they were able to experience it with each other.

Malek caressed his woman, enjoying every single second that passed.

"I'm sorry. I fucked up, Hal," Malek said as he stared off. "We were supposed to be living like this a long time ago. You weren't supposed to go through what you did."

Halleigh sat up and turned to look at him. "We should leave everything here on this island, Malek—all of our baggage and anger and sadness. I know I've built a lot of that shit up over the years. I'm ready to let it go. I have you now. I have our baby. What else is there? I want for nothing, Malek, and it's not about the money. I just feel complete and safe. I have never been this secure in my life. I don't ever want to lose you."

"And you never will, Hal." Malek placed a soft kiss on her lips.

That ended their conversation, but they said so much more with their bodies. They made love right there on the beach until it was too dark for either of them to see.

Malek carried Halleigh up to their villa and watched her sleep. He wished his mother had lived long enough to really get to know Halleigh. She was the total opposite of what his mother had made her out to be—just another gold digger chick after his NBA money. Halleigh truly was the one person in his life who he would die for. She was his confidante above all else, and before he went to sleep, he sent a prayer up to God, thanking Him for bringing her to him.

Halleigh and Malek slept well into the afternoon. The 1000 thread count linens felt like a personal masseuse and just would not let either of them wake up from their peaceful slumber. When they finally awakened, they were well rested and ready to tackle another day.

"What do you want to do today, ma? It's all on you," Malek said as he removed his clothing and prepared to take a shower. He wrapped the plush white towel around his lean waist. He still had the body of a basketball player. Tall and toned, he was perfect in Halleigh's eyes.

"Glass-bottom boat," Halleigh replied excitedly as she jumped out of the bed.

Malek nodded his head. He wasn't much of a water person, not that he knew many black folks from the hood who were, but he had promised Halleigh her heart's desires while on this trip, and he wasn't going to let her down. "Glass-bottom boat it is," he said and then went into the bathroom to shower. He yelled, "Hal, get some money out of the lining of my suitcase. After you get ready and dressed, we'll dip."

"Okay. And I'll call the front desk to make sure we don't need an appointment or anything. If we do, we can just grab a bite of something to eat first."

Halleigh headed over to Malek's suitcase. She was surprised at the amount of money he had brought with him. He probably had

$100,000 stashed in there. She took the money stacks out of the suit-case and put them in the villa safe, taking out a few thousand for the day. Then she locked the safe and proceeded to contact the front desk. She was relieved to find that they didn't need an appointment, but the glass-bottom boat ride was on a first-come first-served basis. The front desk clerk informed her of the departure times.

Halleigh rushed to get ready. She didn't want to miss the next boat, which would be leaving in an hour.

"Mind if I join you?" she asked after removing her clothes and creeping into the bathroom to join her man in the shower.

"Do you really even have to ask?" Malek looked over at Halleigh's naked body. "I thought for sure that you'd had enough last night." He licked his lips. "But you know me . . . always ready to make things hap-pen." He reached out and helped Halleigh into the shower.

"Don't get any ideas, mister." Halleigh playfully smacked Malek's hands. "Although I could never get enough of you, we have a boat to catch. It leaves in an hour. I'm only showering with you to save time. So here." She handed Malek a rag. "Get to washing my back, will you?" She winked and smiled at her man then turned her back to him.

"Oh, so it's like that? You just using a brother for convenience?"

"Hmmm . . . something like that." She handed him the bar of soap.

Malek wet Halleigh's rag then lathered it up with soap. Just touch-ing her was turning him on, and his manhood stiffened. "Not even just a quickie?" he whispered into Halleigh's ear, brushing his lips against it.

Malek's soft breath blowing into her ear and just the mere touch of his lips sent chills through Halleigh's body. "Ummmm," she moaned. "Just a quickie, did you say?"

"Yeah, in and out. Nobody gets hurt." By now Malek had dropped both the soap and the rag and was rubbing his hands down Halleigh's sides.

Halleigh abruptly turned to face him. "Make it quick, daddy," she said, throwing her leg up around his waist. "We got a boat to catch."

Almost an hour later, Halleigh and Malek were running down the pier. The quickie had turned out not to be so quick after all.

"Wait!" Halleigh yelled as she ran toward the departing boat. "We're coming!"

The dock person held the boat for Halleigh and Malek. Halleigh smiled excitedly and boarded the boat first.

Malek, still on the dock, pulled out a wad of money and asked, "How much, my man?"

"We don't accept cash, sir," the attendant said.

"What? What do you mean, you don't accept cash? You don't accept American money or something?"

"You have to go back to the resort and set up an account," the man replied. "All excursion payments must be made at the front desk."

"But we'll miss the boat!" Halleigh exclaimed, wondering why the clerk she had spoken to didn't tell her that when she was on the phone earlier. "Can't you just accept cash this one time? It all spends the same."

"I'm sorry, miss. I will lose my job," the guy stated. "We are not allowed to accept any cash from guests. I would if I could, but it's grounds for immediate termination, whether you really turn in the money or not."

A man who happened to be passing by stopped and interjected, "It's okay. You can charge their boat passes on my account card." He was a blond-haired, blue-eyed man with a tan that looked like it was designed specially by God. He wore Dolce & Gabbana linen pants with a shirt and sandals.

He smiled at Halleigh. "Sounds like the lady here really wants to go on this boat ride." Still smiling, he looked at Malek. "Gotta give the ladies what they want."

"Thanks! We'll pay you the money," Halleigh said excitedly as Malek stepped onto the boat.

Malek immediately began to count out the bills to hand over to the kind stranger.

The white man shook his head. "No need. I have a house on the island. I'm a regular here, so I have a lot of resort credit," he assured them with the wave of his hand. "Don't worry about it."

Malek shook his head. "No, we'll pay you for it." If he hadn't learned anything else on the streets, he'd learned that everything came with a price. He'd always found it better to set his own price and pay it up front rather than receive the bill later with a much higher price than he'd been willing to pay.

Malek peeled off the exact amount of the boat ride plus an extra fifty for the man's trouble—sort of a convenience fee for him and Halleigh. He handed it to the man.

The guy smiled and nodded. "Okay, I understand. I like a man that pays his own way." He called a ship worker over and handed him the money Malek had just given him. "Bring us a bottle of your finest champagne, and please bring me and my guests menus up to the promenade."

"Right away, sir," the ship worker replied and then disappeared.

Malek watched the man give away the money as if it wasn't shit. *Back home, that would've paid somebody's rent*, he thought.

"I'm Gary, by the way," the man said as he extended his hand to Malek.

Malek shook his hand and introduced himself.

"I'm Halleigh."

The man took Halleigh's hand and planted a light kiss on the back of it. "Nice to meet you, Halleigh."

At first, Malek thought dude might be trying to disrespect him, you know, steal on his girl right in his face like he wasn't nothing, but then he had a change of heart when a gorgeous woman came up and stood next to the man. Her hair was blowing in the wind, and she wore huge designer shades on her face.

Halleigh admired the way the woman walked. She looked like one of the print models in a high-fashion magazine.

"Hey, I thought you forgot about me," the woman said to Gary, not even noticing the couple that stood with him.

"Um, Marie, I want you to meet Halleigh and Malek," Gary said. "They were having a little bit of trouble boarding. I've arranged for us to have drinks and lunch on the promenade deck."

"Well, it's nice to meet you both," she said with a nod. She rested her arms on Gary's shoulders, not bothering to extend them to shake either Halleigh's or Malek's hand. "Shall we?" she said. Then she led the way to the promenade deck.

Halleigh looked at Malek and made a face that let him know she was impressed with the lady's elegance. They were definitely out of their league, but each was carefully taking note of how Gary and Marie carried themselves. The young couple from Flint didn't know that only the richest of the rich frequented the Turks, but they'd made up their minds that by the time they revisited the island, they'd fit right in.

When they arrived at their table, Gary asked, "So, Malek, where are you guys from?"

"Flint. Flint, Michigan," he answered. "What about you and your wife?"

"Well, Marie is not my wife; she's the mistress." Gary said it like having a mistress on the side was a normal practice to just flaunt. Perhaps that was true where Gary came from, but in the hood, it was grounds for a nigga to get cut.

Gary kissed Marie's cheek. She appeared proud to bear the title of "Gary's mistress."

Noticing Halleigh's expression of surprise, Marie spoke up. "Oh no, sweetheart, don't look like that," she said to Halleigh in a comforting tone. "I'm not the mistress because I have to be. I'm the mistress because I *choose* to be." She looked over at Gary. "Isn't that right, love?"

Gary nodded in agreement, and then Marie turned her attention back to Halleigh. "You see, Gary's wife gets to play Susie Homemaker while I fly around the world, shop mercilessly, and fuck the shit out of her husband. I play my position very well," she stated with an arrogant yet confident smile.

Halleigh's eyebrows rose in amazement. She looked at Malek, who sat smiling. "Don't even think about it," she warned him playfully.

Gary laughed. "He wouldn't dare. I wouldn't need a mistress if my wife was as beautiful as you, Halleigh. You're a lucky man, Malek." He held up his champagne flute, and the rest of the group raised theirs as well before taking a sip.

"Halleigh, you are just glowing. How far along are you?" Marie asked.

Halleigh blushed and then removed some of the hair from her face. "Oh . . . um, I'm three months. I didn't know I was showing yet. Most people don't even notice." Halleigh looked down at her champagne glass, wondering if Marie was trying to be funny by asking her about her pregnancy. She began to feel a little guilty.

"Oh, not to worry," Marie said, noticing the look on Halleigh's face. "I'm sure a little sip of champagne won't hurt for now. But, remember, you got a little one in there to look out for."

"Yes, ma'am," Halleigh said, feeling strangely as though Marie was more like a mother figure.

"*Marie* will be fine. Save the 'ma'am' stuff for your elders." Marie winked and then took another sip of her champagne. "Besides, I can barely tell you're pregnant. You have a tiny baby bump, but your skin and hair are shining with only the vitamins that children can produce."

"You have kids?" Halleigh asked.

"Oh God, no!" Marie downed some more champagne. "I'm not the motherly type, if you know what I mean. I always get jealous when I see what pregnancy does to your complexion, hair, and nails, though. It's like the perfect tan. It's gorgeous. Still, I don't envy mothers the least bit when I see what pregnancy does to their figures. But you look as though you are going to carry yours well."

Halleigh couldn't help but laugh at how shallow the girl was. "Thank you, Marie," she managed to say between chuckles.

"So, where did you say you were from?" Malek asked Gary.

"Miami, but I have a home here as well. I try to visit as much as I can. It's really beautiful here." Gary leaned back and looked out over the water for a minute, then said, "If you guys aren't busy tonight, you're more than welcome to come and join us for dinner. There's this cultural tribe coming to play music for me at my home. You'll love it. You'll get to see and hear some real Caicos flavor," he explained with a charming smile. "What do you say? Does it sound like something you'd be interested in?"

"Of course they are," Marie stated, answering on their behalf. "It'll be fun. I'm glad we met some friends on this island who aren't ancient."

"I'll toast to that." Gary smiled and lifted his glass yet again as they drank to the newfound friendship.

The foursome really became glued at the hip for the remainder of the boat ride. They explored the entire ship, spending most of their time on the bottom of the boat watching the tropical fish through the clear bottom. The couples literally had nothing in common, but that's what made their interaction refreshing. Halleigh was proud of Malek for holding his own in his conversation with Gary. She noticed that Gary never spoke over Malek's head, and that Malek was speaking politics with Gary as if he had studied it like a science. Malek and Halleigh felt like they were entering high society.

Chapter Eighty-six

Malek and Halleigh took Gary and Marie up on their offer and joined them for dinner. Upon entering Gary's home they were practically speechless.

"Oh my God! This is so unreal. Your home is crazy." Halleigh admired the high vaulted ceiling entryway and marble-lined foyer. Entering the home was like entering paradise, its light-colored décor giving the effect of an indoor beachfront.

Gary laughed at her description and replied, "I hope that's a good thing."

"It is," she answered.

"Well, I want you and Malek to make yourselves at home for the remainder of your stay here. If you'd like, you can check out of the resort and stay here. There's plenty of room. The guest wing is like having your very own private quarters. Trust me, you won't be in our way. In addition, staying here will save you the cost of paying for a villa."

Halleigh and Malek looked at each other. It was a wonderful offer, and Gary's home made their villa look like something out of the projects, but they didn't want to impose.

Taking note of their hesitance, Gary said, "I have more than enough room here, and the resort allows me to access all of the amenities. Like I said, it's everything staying over at your villa has to offer and more."

"No, we can't, but thanks anyway, man," Malek decided.

"*No?* That's a word I haven't heard in quite some time," Gary said as he walked over to his white leather bar with a glass top and poured two glasses of cognac. "Malek, the first rule to getting rich is learning

when you're getting a great deal, and now is one of those times. Come on. It'll be fun."

"Yeah, Halleigh, you guys might as well stay put here. That way Gary and Malek can talk business while you and I take care of business."

Halleigh looked at Marie with a puzzled expression.

"Shopping, sweetheart," Marie told her. "You and I have a lot of shopping to do."

Halleigh turned to Malek skeptically and asked, "Should we?"

Gary walked over to Malek and handed him one of the glasses with the dark liquor. "Of course you should. The bedrooms are upstairs." Gary motioned his head toward the spiral staircase, which was covered with thick white carpet. "Like I said, make yourselves at home."

Malek finally nodded and shook hands with Gary. "Okay, I appreciate it, man."

"Fine. I'll call over to the resort and have someone pack up all of your things and bring them here. I'll also make sure you receive full credit for the unused portion of your stay."

"There, then it's all settled," Marie said. "Let me show you where you'll be staying."

Marie led Halleigh up the stairs to their deluxe guest quarters, while the men remained downstairs and drank up.

The couples enjoyed their cultural evening with the local band and danced the night away, just the four of them. Malek didn't really dance, but he watched Halleigh have a good time, and enjoyed sipping on the fine liquor.

Later that night, Malek and Halleigh held each other in their bed as they stared out of the open balcony window into the moonlight.

"Today was amazing, Malek," Halleigh said. "Marie and Gary are really cool. I'm so glad we agreed to stay here. And I can't believe the resort agreed to refund all of our money for the room," she added, amazed by the amount of pull Gary had on the island.

"I know, Hal. This is all more than I could have ever imagined, and you deserve it."

"No, Malek," Halleigh corrected him. "*We* deserve it."

Smiling down at his woman, Malek agreed. "You're right. We deserve it. Now get some sleep, ma. I love you."

"I love you forever, Malek."

They dozed off to the sounds of the waves hitting the shore beneath them.

Over the next few days, the couples did everything together, including gambling, sightseeing, and shopping. They dined in the finest restaurants and shopped in designer boutiques, some of which Halleigh had never even heard of. Gary took them to his office in the

Turks and showed them where he worked. From the look of the expensive office building and the mini-staff he had, Malek could tell Gary was a man of importance. He was intelligent, and was an excellent people person.

Malek was even more surprised to find that Gary was a high school dropout. Here this man had never even finished high school, let alone graduated college, and he was obviously a multimillionaire. To Malek, Gary was hope personified. He was evidence that a man could reach any heights he wanted to, no matter what odds were stacked against him. Malek couldn't wait to get to that level of professionalism. Once he was so far removed from the streets where he couldn't remember what gunpowder and crack cocaine smelled like, like Biggie Smalls said, "Sky was the limit."

On their fourth night together, Malek finally asked Gary something he'd been wondering all along. "How did you get all of this, fam? You seem to be pretty young to be this rich and successful. Your parents put you on or something?"

Gary had never volunteered just what type of work he did, and Malek had never asked, but now curiosity finally got the better of him. He had to know what it would take to reach this level of wealth, and whether he had enough money on reserve to invest in such endeavors. The ladies were gone out to dinner, so it was only Gary and Malek in the house. They were in the private theater watching an old Al Pacino movie, and Malek hoped that asking Gary about his profession with just the two of them present would make him more apt to share the secret to his fortune.

"I don't mind sharing at all," Gary answered. "I grew up in a trailer park. Everything I have, I got through hard work and making the right connections."

Gary paused for a minute and stared at Malek. Then he added, "Let me ask you a question, Malek. Do you have any credit cards, any 401(k)'s set up? A house? Don't mistake me. I know you are not stupid or broke, so please don't be insulted. I'm just saying I've seen you pull out wads of money all day, which leads me to believe that you are in a business that has no future."

Malek's silence confirmed Gary's suspicions. "Don't get me wrong, Malek, nor be offended, my friend. That trade you're dabbling in is a gold mine, but you have a girl and baby to think of. You say you're trying to get money like this? Then you have to allow your money to make money. I made my first million through connections and investments."

Malek nodded his head in agreement. "I hear you, G," Malek said, using the name he'd penned Gary with over the last couple of days. "I had this local lawyer working on my financials, but he couldn't handle the amount of paper I was bringing to him. Then he got greedy and

wanted to dip into the cookie jar, so I just said, 'Fuck it! I got a brain and two hands. I can count all this money myself.' Nah mean?"

"I hear you, Malek." Gary nodded.

"How can I get my paper up like this?" Malek looked around Gary's house, admiring all of the expensive furnishings. "I mean, look at all the nice shit you have. I want a piece of this pie."

Malek appreciated Gary taking the time to talk to him. He knew businessmen didn't like to share secrets. "I know you have no reason to do this for me, but I'm going to ask you anyway. I have more than a million in a safe at my house back home. I want to make that into two hundred million. I want to go into business with you. I know my money doesn't sound like much to you, but it's all I got, and I worked just as hard as the next man to get it."

"Whoa, Malek, slow down," Gary said, holding his hands up as if to halt Malek's words. "I'm not into the illegal thing. I don't want to jeopardize myself."

"I know. And I wouldn't even put you in that kind of position. My trip to these islands is kind of like a celebration of my retirement from the game. I'm not into that anymore. I just have this money sitting around, but it's not enough. I need stupid money. Any advice you can give me, I'd appreciate."

"Stupid money comes from stupid people. What you need, Malek, is legitimate and long money. If you're serious about staying out of the streets, then I'm willing to take a chance on you." Malek clapped loudly and stood up.

"Don't get too excited too soon," Gary told him. "It's a process involved here, Malek." Gary stood up with him. "Until I clean all of that drug money you have, you have to stay out of the spotlight. No large purchases, no more expensive trips, nothing. Even the things you've already bought may be in jeopardy."

"The only big purchases we've made is the house and our two whips, both six Series Benzes," Malek explained. "Nothing too big." He shrugged his shoulders as if the average Joe Blow could make those types of purchases.

Gary couldn't help but laugh at his new friend's nonchalant attitude. "Those are huge purchases, Malek. But don't worry. I'll draw up some paperwork to legitimize those purchases." He walked over to the liquor cabinet and poured them both a glass of cognac.

"Don't worry about it, Malek. I'll take care of it for you and, more importantly, teach you how to take care of it yourself." He handed Malek a glass then sat down in one of his twelve plush theater chairs.

Malek took a seat next to Gary. "Yo, G, you really don't know how much I appreciate you doing this for me."

"No need to thank me. You seem like a man who has put in enough

work in his own right to really be able to enjoy life. Besides, your inquiry only confirms what I knew from the moment I ran into you and your lady over at the pier."

"Oh yeah?" Malek asked, curious about just how Gary had perceived him. "And what is that?"

"That you are someone who, like myself, stays hungry to achieve more in life. That you are satisfied with nothing, and therefore strive for everything. It's that same thing that got me to where I am today." Gary looked at Malek. "And I was right."

"You certainly were." Malek smiled. This time he was the first to raise his glass for a toast. "To a new partnership."

"And a new friendship," Gary added.

The next day, Malek accompanied Gary to his office to set up accounts in the islands and to sign paperwork to legitimize the purchase of his cars and home.

"The accounts are through the Turks and Caicos Banks of the Caribbean. These accounts are set up so that only you and I can access them," Gary explained. "I cannot access them without you, and vice versa. I have made a deposit already with my own money to match what you said you have saved up. This partnership is contingent on a fifty-fifty split, so our initial investment is equal."

Gary nodded toward the statements Malek was looking over. "You can see proof of my deposit from the statement you have right there in your hands."

Malek looked over the statement and clearly saw the existing balance. "So how do I get my money to you?"

"When you arrive back to the States, you can call a friend of mine. Her name is Ashley Wagner, an accountant in Detroit. She can wire your money to the secure account I have set up," Gary explained. "I've already called her and explained everything to her, so she will be expecting you."

"Cool," Malek said with a nod, his blank facial expression masking his disbelief.

"Something wrong?" Gary asked, eyeballing the papers. "Did you find some type of discrepancy?"

Malek paused for a minute before he spoke. "No, it's not that." He paused once more.

"Then tell me. What is it?"

Malek took a deep breath then looked up at Gary. "It all makes sense, but at the same time, it doesn't. I mean, where I'm from, no way would cats share the wealth. The minute a nigga find out another nigga is seeking his wealth and riches, the last thing he does is bring him on board, because the first thing he does is arrange for his elimination from the game completely."

Gary put his hand on Malek's shoulder. "My friend, that's the difference between me and the men where you come from. I know that when I call myself helping someone out, in actuality, they are helping me out. We have each put ourselves in a position where one has no more to gain than the other, nor does one have any more to lose than the other. If for some reason our investments fail, then we both lose our money. You get me?"

"Yeah, but still, why me, some dude you just met and don't know from Adam? I mean, inviting me into your home was enough. Now you're inviting me into your finances."

"So you're a skeptic, huh?"

"No, it's not that. I'm just keeping it real. Back home, you have to prove yourself to get put on. I've done nothing, so I guess I'm just having a hard time understanding why you'd put me on."

"Like I told you, when I met you, I just knew there was something about you. You reminded me a lot of myself. My mother always said you know after one conversation whether you can really trust someone. Well, I knew I could trust you, Malek. Now all you have to do is trust me." Gary held out his hand.

Malek looked down at it, smiled, and then shook it.

"So, as I was saying, I am coming back to the States at the end of the month, and when I arrive, we will choose some investments to get you started in. We will invest aggressively because we want to make as much money as we can while we're young. I invested in Starbucks before it became such a huge brand, and now I'm sitting on piles of money, so we will look for companies that have future earning potential.

"I know you've said that the money is your savings, so if you reach a point where you'll need to withdraw money from the account, just contact Ashley. She'll be your personal banker, and will set up the transaction for you without the IRS getting wind of it. It also puts your home and cars in the name of a dummy corporation so that the IRS won't inquire about the attainment of your home."

"Sounds easy enough," Malek said, papers still in hand. "Let's make it happen."

"Good." Gary pointed to the paperwork. "All I need you to do is sign here and here." He pulled out a pen from his shirt pocket and handed it to Malek.

Malek exhaled then signed. "Thanks, man. You don't know how much weight this has lifted off my shoulders. I don't have to worry about having dirty money lying around for the government to take, or worry about someone trying to rob me."

"No problem. Just make sure you stay off the corner. Don't make me regret doing business with you."

"Never, fam," Malek responded.

"All right then, my friend, let's go enjoy your last night in the Caribbean."

Halleigh had been asleep for about two hours, but Malek just lay in the bed. He couldn't seem to get any sleep. He looked over at Halleigh and admired her beauty. It was true about the glow of a pregnant woman, because Halleigh looked even more beautiful. Pregnancy truly was becoming to her.

The couple had partied on the island all night, and Malek was exhausted, but his mind was racing. The endless possibilities of becoming successful the legit way had him excited. Players in the game always talked about giving up the street life and going legit, although few ever really could overpower the allure of the game. Looking at the success of his new friend, Malek knew his chances were much better than most.

Malek looked around the guest room. *This is just what I need,* he thought. *I can really establish a good future for my child and Halleigh.* Coming on this vacation and running into Gary had to be fate, as everything was falling right in line with his and Halleigh's plan to leave the hood life for the good life.

Feeling a little bit parched, Malek got up slowly making sure he didn't wake Halleigh, who was sleeping so comfortably. He headed downstairs. As he stood in the kitchen getting a drink, he heard voices in the living room. He put the glass down and headed toward the voices.

Malek crept into the living room, and what he saw blew his mind. A totally naked woman—for some reason, he thought she was Brazilian—was performing oral sex on Marie while they lay on a bearskin rug.

Marie moaned. She was resting on her elbows, her head thrown back and her legs opened wide. Gary was in back of the Brazilian-looking woman, sexing her while she partook of what Marie had to offer.

Malek was in the doorway, and they didn't see him. He wanted to leave and not watch, but his eyes couldn't come off the erotic escapade.

They all seemed to be on the same page as they sexed each other in perfect harmony. He watched as the perfect, perky breasts of the Brazilian woman swung against Marie's inner thighs every time Gary gave her a thrust. He then looked at Marie, who now lay flat on her back, massaging her own breasts while getting oral pleasure.

Malek was in complete shock. He had never seen anything so beautiful. It wasn't like some nasty porno tape. It all seemed so well rehearsed and orchestrated. It was as if he was in a dream state as he watched.

Marie sat up and turned around so that the woman could taste her

from behind. With her back arched like a cat, she looked under her, in order to witness the woman's tongue teasing her clit. That's when she got a glimpse of someone in her peripheral view. She quickly looked toward the entrance and saw Malek standing there. She was startled by his presence, but she didn't let the others know. She just continued to grind her body against the other woman's face while looking seductively into Malek's eyes. It seemed as though Malek's voyeurism was the icing on Marie's cake, as it turned her on even more.

Malek, though intrigued at first, was now totally uncomfortable, knowing that Marie was watching him watching them. He felt like a pervert. He tensed up and started to back away, but that's when Marie stood up and walked away from the woman, who was moaning and groaning in ecstasy from the treatment Gary was delivering to her.

Marie made her way over to Malek. Everything in him told him to continue backing away, but he was hypnotized by the vision before him. He looked at the long, slender body and admired the tantalizing view.

Marie, without saying a word, grabbed Malek's hand and guided him into the party. When Gary and the woman saw that they had a new participant, they didn't lose a step.

Marie dropped down on all fours and grabbed Malek's already rock-hard tool from the slit in his boxer shorts. Before he could refuse her offer, she'd taken him into her mouth. Malek quickly looked over his shoulder, making sure Halleigh wasn't coming, then turned his attention back to Marie and watched her go to work on him.

"Ohh, uhh, ohh," the Brazilian woman and Gary moaned as they climaxed together.

Before Malek knew it, the Brazilian woman left her position on all fours in front of Gary and joined in with Marie on the blowjob.

"Mmm," Marie moaned. The women were taking turns licking Malek and then each other's tongues.

"Oh shit!" Malek had never been more turned on in his life. He rotated his hips to the rhythm of the women's tongues as they took turns sucking harder and fondling him. He knew it was only a matter of time before he exploded in their mouths.

It wasn't long before Malek saw Halleigh's face. Not in the flesh, but in his mind. Suddenly a wave of guilt overtook him, and he pulled away from the two women, exiting the room the same way he had come. His conscience wouldn't let him indulge any further. There was only one woman he ever wanted to take him to such a level of ecstasy, and that was Halleigh, the mother of his soon-to-be born child.

Malek ran back up the stairs and got in bed with Halleigh, this time waking her.

"You're still up, baby?" Halleigh asked as she cuddled under his arm. She could feel his heart beating rapidly. "Are you okay?"

"Yeah, I'm fine. Go back to sleep," Malek said as he wrapped his arms around her. He couldn't believe what he'd just witnessed. Even more so, he couldn't believe what he'd just done. Although he felt guilt, he had to admit it was exciting. Gary was living the high life, and Malek definitely wanted a piece of it. All of it!

Chapter Eighty-seven

Halleigh and Malek hated to say goodbye to Marie and Gary. They had grown close in a short amount of time, but it was time for them to get back to the real world. Flint awaited them. Although it pained them to just think about landing on the soil that would take them back to that town, they felt better knowing they wouldn't be there for long. They had their new home to look forward to.

The couple wished they could pull strings like Gary had and just have someone go to their place, pack up all of their things, and deliver it to their new domain. But that wasn't realistic. Besides, Malek had a couple of loose ends he needed to mend. So, Halleigh and Malek packed up all their things and prepared to say farewell to their new friends.

Marie hugged Halleigh tightly and said, "Oh, take care of yourself, sweetheart." She rubbed Halleigh's stomach. "And take care of that baby too."

"I will," Halleigh assured her, returning the hug. "I had so much fun. You take care too," she replied. "Hopefully, once Malek and I get settled and situated after the baby is born, we can return."

"That would be great. Perhaps make it an annual thing."

"Sounds good to me," Malek said as he came down the steps with luggage in hand. "That's if Gary here doesn't mind." He looked at Gary, who was standing next to Marie.

"Of course I don't mind . . . partner." Gary winked and shook Malek's hand. "Farewell, my friend. We'll be in touch."

"Yes, we will." Malek nodded.

Gary and Malek shook hands. Their goodbye was less emotional than that of the women. For one, they were men, and two, they knew they would be seeing each other again soon.

"I've arranged a car for you. It's waiting out front," Gary told the

couple. He and Marie walked them out to the car and bid them one last farewell as the car pulled off.

Halleigh wasn't looking forward to the long airplane ride. It was much more exciting heading toward the destination than returning from it. Besides that, she was beat and needed the comfort of a bed. She'd told herself she would sleep during the entire flight. That way, maybe it wouldn't seem so long; but her discomfort wouldn't allow her to doze off. To make the time go by, she decided to strike up a conversation with Malek. Finding a subject matter wasn't difficult, since Gary had said something that piqued her curiosity.

"What did Gary mean when he referred to you as his partner?" Halleigh said to Malek just as he was about to finally doze off.

"Huh?"

"Gary called you *partner* and then winked," Halleigh told him. "He even said that he'd be in touch, like you have some business to take care of."

Just the thought of the business that he and Gary had to take care of put a smile on Malek's face. "I was going to wait to tell you, you know, once the money got flipped and everything."

Before Malek could say another word, Halleigh snapped. "I knew it. I didn't want to ask because I really didn't want to know. But I knew Gary was someone involved in the drug business. And now he's pulling you back in." Halleigh slammed her fist against her knee. "And I have no one to blame but myself, insisting we stay there and—"

"Halleigh." Malek chuckled, cutting her off.

"Oh, you think it's funny, Malek? You think it's funny that you broke a promise?" Halleigh's eyes began to water.

"Baby, listen," Malek said in a serious tone. "You've got it all wrong. Gary doesn't deal in the drug trade. He earned everything he has the legitimate way. He's into stocks, investments, and all that good stuff, and—get this—he's going to put me on. He's gonna teach me the tricks of the trade so that I can be in his shoes someday, and hopefully soon."

Halleigh paused for a minute, staring into Malek's eyes. "You serious?" she asked, wiping her eyes dry.

"As a heart attack, baby." Malek ran his hand down Halleigh's hair. "I told you that you could trust me, and that I'd always take care of you. Believe that, baby. It's happening. It's really happening."

Halleigh couldn't do anything but smile and picture their new life together as he explained to her the business deal he'd struck with Gary. Although she didn't quite understand all of the specifics, she was happy to hear it because now she knew for sure that Malek wasn't going back to the streets. No longer would she doubt her man's intentions. She could honestly say that for the first time, for real this time, she felt one hundred percent secure in her life and her future with Malek.

"I'm so proud of you, baby," she said.

"To tell you the truth, so am I . . . so am I."

Malek and Halleigh entered their home, and although it was nothing like Gary's, it was theirs and they'd missed it. The two never thought they'd see the day where they would miss anything about Flint, but they did.

Malek and Halleigh shed all of their clothing. They were too tired to even shower before they passed out in their king-size bed. The two slept through the night and well into the morning before they were interrupted by the buzzing of the clock alarm on Malek's cell phone.

"Shut it off," Halleigh moaned as she put her pillow over her head and returned to sleep.

Malek reluctantly got up and turned off the alarm. He didn't want to wake up yet, but he had business to handle that couldn't wait. He had to put the nail in the coffin that would seal his and Gary's deal. Malek got showered and dressed. Then he packaged all of his money from his safe into two briefcases. He kissed a sleeping Halleigh on the head before whispering, "I'll be back."

Halleigh didn't respond, but he knew she'd heard him, by the soft moan she released and the shift in her position.

Malek got into his car and headed for Detroit to meet with Gary's accountant, who would be his accountant, too, once he hit her with his million and change. As he drove, even though he hadn't profited a dime yet, for some reason he felt like he'd already accomplished something. He was going legit. He knew Jamaica Joe would have been proud.

"Mama," Malek said as he drove, "I know you'd be proud of me too." He smiled as his GPS system guided him directly to his destination.

Malek pulled into the parking lot of the accountant's building. It was a glass office building that sat in the middle of downtown. He picked up his cell phone and dialed Gary's number, wanting to make sure everything was still all good.

"Malek, how's it going?" Gary answered. "I'm glad to see you made it home safely."

"Yeah, thanks. I just wanted to let you know that I'm about to meet with your girl Ashley now. I'm outside of her office. Is everything still good?"

"It's all good, my friend. And so is Ashley. She's the best in the business. She'll take care of you. I've already faxed her all of the documents," Gary said. "She has everything she needs." Gary cleared his throat. "That is, with one exception, of course."

"Not to worry." Malek looked at the briefcases that rested on the passenger's seat. "I got it all here with me."

"Good."

"So, let me head on in here, and I'll talk to you later, fam. I don't want to be late," Malek stated, knowing that tardiness in the professional sector was frowned upon. Hell, even in the streets when a nigga was supposed to meet up with him at a certain time and didn't come through it was frowned upon. Malek just figured, when it came to money, shit always needed to be on time.

Malek closed his cell phone and proceeded into the building. When he found her office, he entered. The receptionist wasn't at her desk, so he stood and waited nervously. He didn't know why his nerves were getting the better of him. Perhaps he just felt that it was all too good to be true.

He didn't have to wait too long before an older white woman appeared from the closed door behind the desk.

"I'm sorry to have you waiting. My receptionist is at lunch. You must be Malek," she greeted with an extended hand. "I hope you weren't waiting too long."

"Actually, I just got here," Malek told her, shaking her hand. "I'm Malek, and it's nice to meet you, Ms. Wagner." He held up the two briefcases. "I have the money to deposit into my account."

"Right this way," she said as she led Malek to her office, back through the doorway she'd just come through.

The white walls and floor-to-ceiling windows gave the room a bright look. Malek sat in the chair across from her glass desk, on which a laptop sat, and she took her place behind it.

"How much did you want to deposit?" she asked.

"It's a million and some change," he answered. He opened each briefcase and revealed the money to her.

She closed the briefcases without even counting the money and put them underneath her desk.

"Now, if you need to access these accounts or need assistance adding up interest or dividends, just call me. You have my card. We can meet once a month to make sure everything is going smoothly, if that works for you."

"That's fine," he answered.

She removed some papers from her desk and handed them to Malek. "On the last page, please fill in the amount of money you are depositing, and then sign by the X."

Malek quickly filled in the information and put his signature on the paper. He was too busy thinking about how rich we was going to be to even read all the fine print on the page. He handed them back to Ms. Wagner.

"Thank you." She smiled. "Now, what day works best for you next month, so we can meet to talk about how much your investment has earned?"

"The first is good," he responded. "Pretty easy to remember."

"The first it is then, Mr. Johnson." She scribbled on her calendar. "How about one o'clock?"

"One o'clock is good."

Ms. Wagner stood, signaling that their meeting was over.

"Is that it?" Malek asked.

"That's it," she replied. "For now anyway."

The transaction was easier than Malek thought it would be. He was sure there'd be more paperwork for him to sign, but obviously Gary had taken care of absolutely everything. This made Malek feel even more confident about his partnership with Gary, a man, like himself, who handled his business.

Malek shook her hand once more and left the office feeling like a new man. He was now a businessman and was stepping into the majors.

Chapter Eighty-eight

Malek drove down I-75 on his way to his appointment with Ms. Wagner. It had been a month since he had turned over his money to the accountant to get cleaned. It was now the first of the month, which meant it was time to go check up on his investments. He was excited to see what dividends he'd made on his money. It had only been a short time, but he had learned that in the world of high finance, so much could transpire in a month. During one of his and Gary's discussion back at the island, Gary had hit him up on a time when he tripled his money in only one week. Malek would be more than satisfied to simply double his money.

Malek and Gary had been touching base on the telephone all month. They had arranged to meet up in Miami on the upcoming weekend to talk face to face. Hopefully, after his visit with Ms. Wagner, they'd be celebrating as well. Malek finally reached his destination. He pulled into the parking lot and stepped out of the car feeling like a million bucks. Over the past month, just the mere thought of going legit had him feeling ahead of the game and prepared for the future. He'd managed to stay free and clear from the game, with the exception of the couple of times Mitch had hit him up with a few questions regarding contacts and whatnot.

As he walked up to the office, he noticed something strange. It looked like there was no light shining through the vertical blinds covering the office window. From a distance, the place looked closed.

The closer Malek got, the quicker he picked up his pace, with a sick feeling growing in the pit of his stomach. Upon arriving at the double doors to Ms. Wagner's office, his concern grew worse. He turned the knob and pulled on the door. It didn't budge. It was locked.

Malek nervously looked down at his watch. "One o'clock," he said out loud. He was exactly on time. He tried the door again, hoping that maybe it had just gotten jammed or something and would open this time. Unfortunately, that wasn't the case.

Looking down at his watch yet again, Malek tried to ignore his nerves, telling himself that perhaps Ms. Wagner had just gone to lunch or something and hadn't made it back. As his blood pressure rose, so did his suspicions. As much as he didn't want to admit it, he was starting to understand the real deal. Hesitantly, he exited the building and walked over to the window. He pressed his hands to block off the sun's glare, and stared into the room where he and Ms. Wagner had done business—the room where he had handed over pretty much every dime he had.

With a clear view of the office, he quickly discovered that what just one month ago had looked like a well put-together accounting office was now a vacant suite. "No fucking way!" He went back inside the building and tried the office door again. "Fuck!" Malek spat as the thoughts he'd tried to suppress began to rise.

Malek's heart dropped when he looked down and saw a shiny piece of paper with a piece of tape on it. He picked it up and turned it over, only to discover that it was a sign that read: OFFICE SPACE AVAILABLE FOR RENT. It must have fallen off the door.

"Son of a bitch!" Malek yelled as he stormed away from the building.

As he made his way back to the car, he called the number he'd reached Ms. Wagner on before. He heard a recorded voice saying that the number was disconnected.

Malek began to panic. He looked down at the phone to make sure he had dialed the correct number. Although it appeared he had, he still punched in the numbers again. He got the same response from the automated operator.

"Fuck!" Malek yelled as he gripped the phone tightly and pushed the end button. It took everything he had not to throw the phone across the parking lot and through the vacant office window. Instead, he surfed through his phonebook contacts and retrieved Gary's number. Malek couldn't wait to tell Gary about the sheisty accountant. He knew Gary would be just as pissed. After all, he had deposited more than a million dollars with her as well.

As Malek waited for the call to go through, he tried to convince himself that everything was just a misunderstanding. "That bitch better had moved her office or something," he said to himself as he waited for Gary to pick up the ringing phone. But after a few seconds, an operator's voice notified Malek that Gary's number was no longer in service.

This couldn't be right. Malek had just spoken with Gary less than five minutes ago.

This time, Malek pulled up his calling log on his cell phone. Gary was the last person he'd called, so he simply redialed the number he'd just spoken to him on. When he heard the operator repeat her same spiel, the phone almost slipped from his hand.

"I promise to God, Ashton Kutcher's ass better pop out from somewhere and tell me I'm being punked or else—" Malek gritted his teeth.

Malek's hands began to sweat, and his heart was beating a thousand times per minute. He couldn't believe he had been swindled. *This can't be happening*. He scrolled through his phone and found Gary's office number. When he got the same recorded response, he knew for sure he'd been set up.

Malek jumped into his car, and out of frustration, pulled out his gun. He then got back out of the car, walked back toward the office, and emptied his entire clip through the office window. He stormed back to his car determined to be on the first thing smoking back to the island. He was about to go straight to Gary and see what was going on. Malek was racking his brain on the whole plane ride back to the islands. He didn't want to worry Halleigh, so he didn't tell her about the mishap. He'd simply told her that he needed to meet with Gary face to face to handle some business. He didn't want to stress her out until he found out for sure what was going on. It was probably nothing but a misunderstanding—at least, that's what he kept trying to tell himself. But it had been two days since he'd tried to contact both the accountant and Gary, and he hadn't heard from either one of them. Up until that point, he and Gary had pretty much talked on a regular basis.

Even if it turned out that Gary was on the up-and-up and had nothing to do with the accountant going MIA, Malek planned on holding him accountable, since Gary had hooked the whole thing up. He was going to get his money back, one way or the other. If Gary was behind this whole scam from the beginning, Malek had made up his mind that Gary would have to pay him back or else pay with his life.

His intentions were to pay Gary a surprise visit. He knew Gary would never expect him to pop up on him so quick, but he was about to bring the heat right to his front door.

Just hours later, Malek was at Gary's house. He banged on the front door after ringing the doorbell repeatedly and getting no answer. After a while, someone finally unlocked the door. Malek breathed a sigh of

relief, but was somewhat puzzled by the person who stood on the other side of the door.

"Hello, sir. Are you my one o'clock appointment?" the profession-ally dressed woman with clipboard in hand asked as she extended her hand for a shake.

"I'm looking for Gary Williams," he said as he frowned in confu-sion.

"Oh, I'm sorry. Gary Williams only rented this villa out for the month. This is the property of Prestige Rentals, sir," she said con-fidently.

Malek wasn't trying to hear anything she had to say. For all he knew, she was just someone Gary told to get rid of him while he relaxed in another room.

Before the woman could say another word, Malek brushed past her and entered the house. "Gary! Gary!" He stormed around the house furiously. "Where the fuck are you?" he yelled as he searched the placed. He noticed that the few pictures of Gary and Marie that he'd seen around the house before were now gone. That's when he finally admitted to himself that his suspicions were true—He had been got.

"Sir! Sir, excuse me," the woman said as she struggled to keep up with Malek's pace. "I'm not sure what's going on, but like I said, Mr. Williams is not here. This is not his residence. Never was. It's a time-share rental. Now, if you're interested in renting this property, then by all means we can talk business, but if you are here for any other rea-son, then I'm going to have to ask you to excuse yourself." Malek just stood there breathing hard, casting an evil glare on the woman. He hadn't meant to be intimidating to her, but he couldn't help himself. This wasn't like one of his contacts shorting him on some dope, or one of his corner boys shorting him on some change. This was more than a million dollars at stake. This was his life. This was his future. Not just his future, but the future of Halleigh and his unborn child.

"I'm sorry, sir," the woman said, trying her best not to show any fear, although her trembling hands were a dead giveaway. "You have to leave, or I am going to be forced to call the cops," the real estate agent said.

"Fuck the cops!" Malek yelled just before he stormed out the door. With no other leads on how to contact Gary, Malek decided all he could do was go home. But then he remembered the office Gary had given him a tour of. Only thing was, he couldn't remember the name of the facility, nor where it was located. He didn't know what to do next, but he knew he couldn't give up, not just yet.

Malek sat on the plane on his way home, still trying to understand the fact that he had just lost everything he'd worked for. He'd hired a driver to escort him around, looking for the facility which Gary

claimed housed his company. He was sure that they had covered every inch of the island, but it was to no avail. Malek was, once again, disappointed by his lack of results. At this point, though, he knew that even if he had found the building, it would most likely be vacated, just like the bogus accountant's office. Malek felt like he'd lost his mind. He kept replaying the scenes in his head, starting from the moment Gary showed up to save the day at the pier. He wondered how he missed seeing the snake in the grass. While he was worrying about why Gary would trust him enough to go into business with him, he should have been asking himself why he should trust that fool. How could he have been so stupid to get caught up in the entire fantasy of the good life?

Everything had seemed so real, like destiny was unfolding and Gary was a part of it. In those few days Malek spent with the millionaire, he hadn't detected anything shady. Nor did he sense anything strange during any of their phone conversations. Unfortunately, Malek had to blame his lack of experience in the "real world." Now he was paying for it.

Had it been just his future at stake, Malek would have simply chalked it up as a loss and kept moving, but that wasn't the case. He buried his face in his hands as he wondered how he would explain to Halleigh that he had been swindled, and that they now only had $10,000 to their names. He was grateful that he had kept even that little somethin'-somethin' to tide them over until his money made a profit. He had been tempted to put all of it in the hands of that accountant, and then he and Halleigh would have been penniless now.

How could I not see this shit? Malek threw his head back against the coach seat. Just a month ago he'd been enjoying the good life of first class; now he was back in coach. Just when he thought there was no place left to go but up, everything was going right back down. In the past, he had always managed to come out on top no matter what. Now, he just couldn't imagine how he'd be able to pull that off one more time.

Chapter Eighty-nine

As the moonlight shone into the room, Malek stood near the window and stared at Halleigh, who slept peacefully in their bed. He

couldn't manage to get any sleep, knowing he had no money to take care of her and their unborn seed. It had been a couple of days since he returned from the islands, and every time he thought about telling Halleigh that he was swindled out of their life savings, he couldn't go through with it.

A part of him wanted to take the ten grand he had left and go flip it on the streets to avoid ever having to tell her. The last thing he wanted to witness was the look of disappointment on her face when she found out they were broke. He knew without a doubt he could once again reach millionaire status by getting back in the game. Although he had already vowed to leave the streets of Flint alone, things had changed. That promise was made before he found himself back at square one. He slowly paced the room, trying to think of a way to make things right, but all of his ideas led back to the hustling. He didn't want to break his promise to Halleigh, but his back was up against the wall. His options were slim to none.

He clenched his jaws as he walked over to the night-stand and picked up his phone. He didn't want to do what he was about to do, but the way he saw it, he was between a rock and a hard place. Either way it went, he'd be letting Halleigh down. If there was a slim chance that he could grind without Halleigh ever finding out, he was more than willing to take that chance.

Slipping out of the bedroom with phone in hand, Malek scrolled through the contacts and dialed a number he never thought in a million years he'd be dialing. "Just a couple of flips and I'm out," he whispered to himself as he walked into the living room so his conversation wouldn't wake Halleigh.

Malek stood in front of the window as he listened to the ringing on the other end. Like Jay-Z, it was time for him to make one more brief appearance in the game. Yeah, he was about to dive back into the game, but with a purpose this time.

Mitch drove down I-75 on his way back from meeting Fredro, his coke connect. It was nearly two in the morning, and the highway was clear and calm, just the way he liked it. He was able to cruise free and clear while listening to his stereo pump out his famous tunes. This always made him feel as though he was on top of the world—as did the fact that he had just negotiated a deal to bring a hundred kilos of coke back to Flint. It was the biggest order Fredro had filled since he had been supplying the city of Flint. Mitch couldn't believe how major he had become, and how quickly. Mitch was preparing to take over the North and South sides of the city with an iron fist. Nothing or no one could stop him. He envisioned being the most notorious player Flint would ever know. Unlike Malek, it didn't matter how much money he banked; he wasn't giving up life on the streets. Even in corporate America, Mitch couldn't think of one millionaire who didn't want an-

other million. By any means necessary, he was going to make sure the money continued to flow.

Mitch didn't have a beef with Sweets like Malek did, and he was prepared to put the war aside to make money. *Violence only begets more violence, which means police.* Mitch thought about how much money he was about to get as he switched lanes.

Since Sweets had agreed to cop coke from him, Mitch could, and did, set his prices as high as he wanted in the streets, seeing that his main competition, the person who had kept him from being "the man" in the streets, was out of the game anyway. A smile spread across Mitch's face. Malek was no longer a threat to him.

Just as quickly as the smile had appeared, it was gone, thanks to thoughts of Keesha's antagonizing words resurfacing and echoing through his mind. He thought about all that time he'd worked under Malek, and about the number of people who must have seen him the same way Keesha did—just a flunky sidekick to Malek. Even though Malek was now out of the game and cats in the streets were dealing with Mitch, a trace of jealousy was still evident in his heart.

Mitch clenched his jaws just as his cell phone vibrated in his pocket. Keeping his eyes on the road and erasing thoughts of his predecessor, he answered the phone.

"Mitch, what's good?" the caller asked.

Mitch almost went left of center at the sound of the caller's voice. He wanted to kick himself for thinking him up. "What up?" he responded, instantly getting aggravated by the sound of Malek's voice.

"Shit all bad right now. I got caught up in some bullshit, and I need back in."

A huge lump formed in Mitch's throat. "What you mean, you need back in?"

Mitch hoped Malek didn't mean what he thought he meant, but Malek quickly confirmed his biggest fear.

"I need back in the game. I need to go meet with Fredro and get hit with something," Malek said, telling him more than asking.

Mitch didn't even have to think twice about his response. The game wasn't big enough for both him and Malek. "I don't think that's going to happen, homeboy," he said, hate in his voice.

"What? What you mean?" Malek asked, not believing what he was hearing.

"You heard me, nigga. It ain't happening."

Malek couldn't fully understand the sudden change in Mitch. The last they talked, everything was all good, so he couldn't imagine what had changed between then and now. "Mitch, what's the problem, fam?"

Mitch started, "I'm not the one with the problem! You—"

Malek cut him off, screaming through the phone, "Who the fuck is

you talking to, nigga?" Had Mitch forgotten just that quickly who put him on? Just in case he did, Malek felt the urge to remind him. "I put you in the position you are in right now. You sound like a damn fool, telling me what I can and can't do. What's got into you, fam?"

"I'm boss now. If you want in, you can work one of the blocks in the Fifth Ward."

"Work a block? I move bricks. I hit niggas that work on blocks. I'm not a worker, or did you forget? I don't know what has gotten into you, but all that shit gon' change when I get in Flint. Don't let the money go to your head, fam, for real."

"Fuck you! Come see me then, nigga. You know where I'm at, son," Mitch said menacingly, totally losing his cool.

"I see it's too late. Shit done already went to your head. I guess now your ass think you the king of Flint now, huh? Well, we'll see if you singing that tune later, homeboy!" Malek yelled then hung up.

Mitch smiled as he flipped down his phone, his ego fed, knowing he had just demeaned Malek. Hell, Malek should have been grateful that he'd even offered to put him on in any kind of way. When he turned over the reigns, it was a done deal. Mitch wasn't about to let Malek climb back up on his white horse and come riding back to Flint like some knight in shining armor. He had his chance at the top and had given it all up. Now, if he wanted back in, he had to start at the bottom. Mitch couldn't control his excitement. For the first time, Malek would know what it felt like to play second fiddle.

Malek was furious as he flipped his phone down, not believing what he had just heard. "I put him on. He got the nerve to think he's going to stop me from getting back in. I am Flint!" Malek said, talking to himself.

As Malek paced back and forth in anger, he saw a figure in his peripheral view. It was Halleigh in her nightgown, looking as beautiful as ever, as she yawned and stretched her arms out.

"Why are you still up, baby?" she asked, seeing the concerned looked on Malek's face.

"Just thinking," Malek said, still trying to figure out how to tell her that he'd just lost everything they had.Halleigh walked over to Malek and began to rub his shoulders. "Want to talk about it?"

Malek was burning on the inside, not only because of his situation, but because of the way Mitch had showed total disloyalty. Back to back, he had been completely wrong about the character of the people he'd decided to do business with.

"No, I'm good," Malek answered Halleigh. "I'll handle it. Just go back to sleep, baby."Malek headed toward the bedroom, and Halleigh followed behind him. She climbed back into bed, thinking that's where Malek was headed. Instead, he walked over to his dresser, opened drawers, and began slipping on some clothes.

"Where are you going?"

"I'ma take a ride just to clear my head, okay?"

Halleigh sat up in the bed, a worried expression on her face. "You sure everything is all right, Malek?"

Malek turned and looked into the eyes of the woman he'd die for. As much as he wanted to just crawl up in the bed next to her and tell her everything, he couldn't. He couldn't admit that he'd let her down.

"Everything is going to be all right, I promise." Malek nodded his head up and down, all the while putting a plan together in his head to try to make things all right.

Mitch watched his sweat drip onto the small of Keesha's back as he grinded her deeply and slowly. She had been waiting for him to return from seeing Fredro so they could live out their planned sexual escapade, and that's exactly what they were doing. Mitch watched as his pelvic area hit Keesha's behind, and a small wave went through her fat ass cheeks. He gripped her love handles as he dug her out, enjoying every minute of it.

"Mitch! Ooh, baby! That's the spot right there," she said as she gripped the bed sheets tightly and bit down on her bottom lip so hard that for a minute there, she thought she'd drawn blood. He was thrusting in and out of her so hard that it hurt so good.

"Who's the boss?" Mitch smacked Keesha's ass.

"You are," she moaned.

"Who?" He smacked her again.

"You are."

"I'm what? Say that shit! Say it!"

"You're the boss!" Keesha exclaimed as she climaxed.

Mitch pumped harder and harder as Keesha declared him the boss. That alone was turning him on more than the actual sex. He smiled as he thought about being the head nigga in charge. He had just put Malek in his place and he felt damn good about it. He pumped faster and harder as he thought about the demeaning comments Keesha had been making about him being under Malek, as if he wasn't boss.

Mitch was so busy trying to blow Keesha's back out, he never heard Malek creeping up behind him. The cold steel from the gun startled him as Malek pressed it to the back of his head.

"Surprise, mu'fucka!" Malek said from behind Mitch.

"Aghhh!" Keesha screamed as she turned around and scooted to the corner of the bed. She watched Mitch on his knees at gunpoint.

"Shut the fuck up!" Malek said to Keesha through clenched teeth, giving her a stare colder than the winter in January.

Keesha immediately stopped her yelling, knowing what was best for her.

Malek turned his attention back to Mitch. "Nigga, I can get to you anytime I want. Remember who the fuck I am. I'm cut from the cloth

of Jamaica Joe. Remember that!" Malek pulled back the hammer on his gun.

Mitch was frozen in fear, and it was written all over his face. He'd just forced Keesha to declare that he was boss. Now he sat in front of her looking like a bitch-ass nigga.

"Turn around and look at me in my eyes." Malek nudged Mitch in the head with his gun.

Mitch slowly turned around with his hands in the air and then looked in the eyes of the man he'd just betrayed.

"I can get to you anyplace, anytime. You can't push me out the game. I am Flint!" Malek said, getting louder with each word. He pointed the gun at Keesha and watched as she squirmed and her face became flush.

He released a small chuckle and then exited the room. He could have very well taken Mitch out right then and there, but that wasn't his intention. He was playing mental chess with Mitch, and just wanted to show him who was still boss.

Mitch's heart was beating double-time as he collapsed on the bed. It felt as if it would jump out of his chest. Not only was his heart racing, but his blood was boiling too. Mitch was furious. He hated that Malek just had his life in his hands and played with him like a cat did its prey.

Now it's war.

Mitch was breathing heavily. He heard the sound of his front door slam shut. Malek might have just slammed the door closed behind him, but he'd just opened up a new chapter to a novel—one that was sure not to have such a happy ending.

Chapter Ninety

Scratch sat with his old friend, Sharina, who was still pretty upset over the shooting at the rehab center. She had come back to Flint after getting sober, hoping that she could fix things with Halleigh. That never happened, because the shots rang out before they had a chance to talk.

After Halleigh was whisked away in an ambulance, Sharina had searched every hospital until she found her daughter. She still wanted to clear the air and apologize for everything that had happened in the past. Scratch, who held a special place in his heart for both of them,

was really hoping they could patch things up. He was almost as disappointed as Sharina when she came back and told him that she'd found Halleigh, who basically just told her to get the hell out of her life.

Scratch looked for her, but no one in the streets had seen or heard from Halleigh since she got released from the hospital. It was as if she'd fallen off the face of the earth. Scratch felt obligated to stay close by Sharina's side. He was afraid that if she got too depressed about Halleigh, she might start getting high again. That's why he hated to tell her the bad news.

"I tried to find her, but no one has seen her. I put word out that I was looking to get in touch with her, though." Even if he did find her, Scratch couldn't help but wonder if Halleigh would even want to hear about her mother.

Scratch put his hand on Sharina's shoulder. "I'm sure she's gonna come and see you sooner or later," he said, giving her false hope out of the pity he felt for her.

Sharina didn't mind grasping at every little bit of hope dealt to her either. "Yeah, I sure do hope so. I have so many things to ask for forgiveness for, ya know." Sharina sighed sadly. "I never was much of a mother to her, and I still have so much to say to my baby."

Scratch listened and nodded his head in complete understanding of Sharina's words. He, too, had some demons that he was battling. One in particular that he wanted to hide from Sharina was the fact that he was responsible for introducing her daughter to drugs. He felt so guilty, but knew that he would never tell Sharina. What good would it do to tell her? The whole thing ate him up every time he thought about it.

"Keep trying to find her, will you?" Sharina told Scratch, desperation in her eyes. Sharina then turned away in defeat. "Even though, if you do find her, she probably won't come racing to see me no-how." Sharina shook her head as her eyes watered.

"Don't talk like that. Li'l Rina will come around eventually. I'll make sure of it," Scratch assured her. Then he gave her a peck on the cheek and exited the room.

Scratch was going to find out where Halleigh was at, but he didn't know where to start. He'd looked under every rock in Flint to no avail. She had simply vanished, but she had to be somewhere. For the sake of Sharina, he wasn't going to give up.

Scratch walked down the street headed to the homeless shelter, where he planned on trying to get a place in line, so he could have a roof over his head for the night. He knew it was on a first-come, first-serve basis. They didn't hold a bed for nobody.

He walked with a pimp's swagger. Even though his bones were worn out, he still managed to have that same ol' stride he was once notorious for, before he allowed drugs to get the better of him. He

hummed the sounds of an Isley Brothers tune as he walked past the same block where he used to score his dope. It was hard being a recovering addict, but he promised himself he would fly straight and get the monkey off his back for good. Every time he got the urge to put the drug that once controlled his mind and body into his system, he quickly remembered how his inner demons took over when chasing the high. He would do any and everything just to score the drug. He learned firsthand that no matter what a dopefiend said he wouldn't do, when it all came down to it, he'd do it in a heartbeat. Scratch had been one of those fiends.

Ostracized by his entire family because of his addiction he was left with nothing and nobody. His family and close friends turned their backs on him, locking their doors closed when they saw him walking down the street. The days of being invited to family Thanksgiving and Christmas dinners had become a thing of the past. Although it hurt Scratch, he couldn't even be mad at his peoples. They had every reason to disown him.

Scratch would constantly scheme and swindle just to achieve his next high, even if it meant cheating and stealing from his own family. He remembered one time on Christmas, they were all having dinner at his mother's house, and his twelve-year-old niece had gotten a purse for Christmas with a hundred dollars in it. She wasn't aware that she couldn't just leave her purse lying around, even though it was only with family. No one explained to her that when one of the family members is a crackhead, the rules change. In all honesty, Scratch hadn't set out to steal from his family that Christmas Day. As a matter of fact, he'd been clean for almost a week and was quite proud of himself; but when he walked into the bathroom and saw that purse just lying there next to the hand towels, he couldn't resist the temptation. He knew it was just a kid's purse and probably didn't have any money in it, but, out of habit, he had to see for himself.

He picked up the purse, unzipped it, and to his surprise, five pairs of eyes were staring up at him—all belonging to Andrew Jackson. Scratch counted out the five twenty-dollar bills. That's when the tug-of-war within him began. He put the hundred dollars down in his pocket then headed to the bathroom door. Before he could even leave the room, he pulled the money back out of his pocket and stared at it. "I can't do this," he told himself. He headed back over to the purse. "I don't need this," he reasoned as he placed the money back inside the purse. "I'm not even gonna get high no more."

Once again he walked away, but then that little voice spoke to him, calling him a fool for not holding on to at least some of the money . . . just in case he felt the urge to get high. On that note, Scratch took twenty dollars, leaving only eighty in his niece's purse.

"I could have taken it all. At least I left her most of it," he told himself, which allowed him to sleep that night. By morning, the guilt had eaten him up to the point where only one thing could wash away the guilt—getting high.

Once the family discovered that there was a missing twenty-dollar bill, they didn't even have to think twice about how it had vanished. Stealing from a child was the ultimate low, as far as Scratch's family was concerned, and they let it be known to him by disowning him. Everyone cut him off, including his own mother. Today, after all these years of getting high, Scratch was determined to never go that route again. He was ready to turn over a new leaf. He knew it could be done. It just wasn't going to be easy. Although the homeless shelter wasn't a place he wanted to call home forever, it was a start. He'd have to prove himself to the world all over again that he could be trusted and that he wanted to change.

Maybe Scratch will even get a job 'round these parts. I still got swagger, he thought as he touched the tip of his brim and walked past the dope house he used to cop at, which Mitch now ran.

Malek sat back and watched as the crackheads and dopefiends went in and out of one of his old spots like clockwork. It looked as though business was booming. Not too long ago, he thought he'd never miss the game, but now he'd give anything to have a piece of the action.

Without Halleigh's knowledge, Malek had made a trip back to Flint, first to put Mitch in check, and secondly, to observe his old business. He thought about his woman, who waited at home for him miles away, thinking that their life was peachy. She didn't know they'd just hit rock bottom, and he was still trying to figure out a way so she'd never have to know.

How did I let this bullshit happen to me? Malek scolded himself. He knew the only person he could really be mad at was himself. He'd turned over his livelihood and put his trust in virtual strangers. When he thought about it, what did he really know about Gary anyway? He'd put in so much work to save the money, and then let some fast-talking guy sweet-talk him out of all of it, like a virgin on prom night being sweet-talked out of her panties by the prom king.

"Gary is a dirty mu'fucka!" Malek spat, shaking his head. *That's probably not even his real name.* When he got some money, he would figure out a way to find him. *When I catch him, I'ma make him suffer.*

Malek looked at himself through the rearview mirror and felt pure failure and disgust. As he was beating himself up verbally with a string of expletives, he saw Mitch pull in front of the dope house in a blue Benz. Malek knew Mitch would be on his p's and q's, since he had caught him slipping but didn't kill him. He almost wished he hadn't given the fool a heads-up, but his anger had been in control as he did

ninety miles per hour down the highway in the middle of the night to get at him.

Now, seeing the arrogant bastard rolling as if he really was boss, it took all of Malek's willpower not to step out of his car and blast that fool. He knew it wasn't the right time, though. Malek was outnumbered, as Mitch was accompanied by some of his goons. So, he just sat there and watched as they disappeared into the house. Now his thoughts of revenge were aimed toward Mitch, and it was the only thing on Malek's mind. Oh, by no means did he plan on letting Gary get away with stealing from him, but right now a bird in the hand was worth two in the bush. With Mitch refusing to let him back in the game, Malek was powerless. Nevertheless, with a baby on the way and a woman to take care of, Malek needed money. He came up with a plan. He was going to hit Mitch where it hurt the most, in the pockets.

I'ma hit all of his dope spots and take him for all he got. Malek glanced down at the pistol that sat in his lap. He knew his idea was not well thought out, but he was in extreme circumstances. The last time Malek called himself going to commit a robbery, his life went downhill after that. But the past was the past. Then he was a "virgin" on the streets, and it was his first time testing the waters. Now with his well-cultivated skills, he knew he had a better chance of pulling it off.

Malek wasn't no dummy, though. Having been away from the streets for a while, it was very possible that Mitch had changed up some things, so he needed someone who knew the ins and outs of the spots so he could rob them smoothly. That's where Malek's first problem surfaced. He had no idea who would know about Mitch's spots that wasn't loyal to him.

Malek noticed a man walking down the street with a 1980s pimp stroll, wearing raggedy clothes and a brown top hat with a feather. Although the man looked like a bum, his walk blared confidence. Upon closer observation, Malek realized it was Scratch, an old friend of Jamaica Joe. A bulb went off in Malek's head. He knew right then and there that Scratch could be just as valuable to him as he'd been to Jamaica Joe. No matter what, Scratch always seemed to know any and everything that was going on in the streets, and always willingly reported the goings-on to Jamaica Joe.

Chapter Ninety-one

"Yo are you game, old-timer?" Malek asked, his eye on the people going in and coming out of the dope house.

"Let me get this right." Scratch rubbed his hands together and thought long and hard about the opportunity Malek had just presented him. "Say, you want Scratch to help you rob Mitch's spots? I mean, I'm not a young gun like yo'self anymore. Scratch can't move like he used to, ya dig? Maybe I'm not the one you need to be recruiting for this here job."

When Malek first stopped Scratch as he made his way to the homeless shelter, Scratch thought he was about to get robbed.

"Yo," Malek called out, doing a light jog toward him, "hold up, my man."

Scratch had immediately raised his hands in surrender.

"Look, youngblood, I ain't got nothing for you. You got the wrong one. If you trying to stick me up, you'd just be practicing, because I'm on my way to the homeless shelter." Scratch nodded toward the shelter, which was only a few buildings ahead, making it a point to look straight ahead and not in Malek's eyes. He didn't want the young cat to kill him just because he'd witnessed his face, nor did he want him to think he was trying to challenge him.

"You got it all wrong, fam," Malek told him. "I'm not here to try to take something from you. As a matter of fact, I'm here to offer you something—the same way you used to always offer my man Jamaica Joe something."

Malek's words got Scratch's attention—especially the mention of Jamaica Joe's name. Scratch could recall the many times Jamaica Joe had broken him off some dough just for keeping his ears and eyes glued to the streets, so he assumed this kid wanted something similar from him.

Scratch lowered his hands and faced Malek. That's when he noticed the familiarity of Malek's face. "Hey, I know you. You used to run with Joe, his little prodigy or something. You was that kid that was supposed to go pro. You were supposed to be the American dream for all the people stuck in Flint, the example that there was a way out besides death or jail."

Malek should have been flattered at Scratch's words, but they only twisted the knife that he already felt was in his chest. Hearing that so many in the streets of Flint had put him on such a pedestal that his success would be a reflection of theirs only made him feel worse about his current predicament. Seeing the blank look on Malek's face, Scratch

continued, "So you said you got something for Scratch?" Like Malek, he knew that nothing in the streets came without a price. So now he'd just have to hear the youngster out and see if what he had to offer was worth it. "Talk to me, youngblood."

Scratch listened intently as Malek explained to him how he needed his assistance in seeing through his plan to rob Mitch's spots, and how after doing so, he could probably afford his own place rather than relying on the homeless shelter. Malek made it sound like an offer that Scratch couldn't refuse. "C'mon, man. You wanna spend the rest of your life sleeping in the homeless shelter? You help me with this and you won't have to worry about having money to get your own place." In all truth, Malek needed Scratch to keep him and his family from the homeless shelter.

"You're the perfect person for the job, actually." Malek could tell that Scratch was now seriously considering the proposal he'd hit him with. Malek turned toward Scratch, looking him directly into his eyes. "You know where all the spots are at. You can get in and peep the scene for me, ya know? You can let me know how many workers are in the spot and where the straps are at."

Scratch thought for a moment before replying. "No disrespect, youngblood, but I never cut you out to be a stickup kid. You and Jamaica Joe were tight. I thought y'all were cut from the same cloth, but a stickup kid Joe was not. So, if you don't mind me asking, why are you hitting his old spots? Seems like, if anything, you'd be on the same team as his crew."

"Shit happens," Malek told him. "I was on the same team. It was me who Jamaica Joe handed the operation over to, not Mitch. Eventually, I handed it over to Mitch. My intentions were to leave the streets alone, you know."

Scratch could empathize with Malek. That was his intention as well, to leave the streets alone. "So you've changed your mind?"

"No. More like, some things that went down didn't really allow me a choice. But that's beside the point. What matters is that when I called up Mitch, the mu'fucka who I put on, and asked him for one small favor, he forgot that I was the one that put him in the position of power. So if he wants to play it that way, I'ma take instead of asking," Malek said, getting angrier with every word that came out of his mouth.

Scratch nodded his head, completely understanding the game. He was once the head dope man in his heyday, so he knew where Malek was coming from. When he was on top, everybody wanted a piece of Scratch, but just as soon as he began to decline, no one wanted to reach out a helping hand. All they wanted to do was stick out a foot and kick him hard while he was down.

"I tell ya, youngblood, shit ain't like it used to be. I was in the game

when it began to change. These young cats nowadays have no loyalty. That's the difference between the game back then and the game now. These young'uns in the game playing fo' keeps."

"So you game?" Malek asked, trying not to beat around the bush any longer. He felt like he'd shared enough information with Scratch for him to be able to make a decision on whether he was down. "Like I said before, if you're in, then I'll definitely hit you with something for your help. And if all really goes well, I'll make sure to hit you off with a li'l somethin'-somethin'."

Scratch already knew what Malek was thinking, and he wanted to let it be known that he was flying straight. "It ain't like that, man. Scratch left that bullshit alone. Like yourself, youngblood, Scratch trying to leave these streets and everything they stand for alone."

"Then we can say fuck these streets for the last time together, but we need each other to do it. Some things we just can't do by ourselves, and some things we do ain't just for ourselves. I got a woman at home, and her future lies in my hands."

Malek's words jogged Scratch's memory. He remembered that Halleigh had expressed how crazy she was over Malek, and now he wondered if she was the woman at home he was referring to.

"Say, have you seen Halleigh?"

Malek saw the way Scratch's eyes lit up when he mentioned her name. At first he couldn't figure out why this crackhead would be so interested in knowing about his girl, but then it dawned on him exactly who Scratch was. He had been so caught up in his one-track mind, trying to get revenge on Mitch, he'd forgotten that Halleigh had explained to him how tight she and Scratch were.

Now Malek's eyes lit up. This was just one more thing he could use to his advantage. If Scratch wouldn't do it for Malek, then maybe he would do it for Halleigh. Malek would only pull that ace out of the deck as a last resort. He needed to make sure he could trust Scratch. Once upon a time, Jamaica Joe trusted him very much, but like Scratch had just said, the game changes, and he had no way of knowing if Scratch had changed.

"Oh yeah. Halleigh is doing good," Malek answered. "I got her set up out of town."

Scratch smiled. He felt better, knowing Halleigh was doing okay. "So that's why no one on the streets has seen her. Man, I been searching for her high and low. I need to get with her on some personal things."

Malek shot Scratch a quizzical look. He wondered why Scratch was so anxious to get at Halleigh. The only personal things those two ever had in common was dope. No matter how broke Malek got, he would never put Halleigh in a situation where she could go back to doing drugs.

As if Scratch could read the expression on Malek's face, he replied, "Youngblood, I told you I don't mess with drugs no more. It's not even like that. Li'l Rina is like a daughter to me. I would never . . ." Scratch's words trailed off. He couldn't finish his sentence without lying. Had it not been for him, Halleigh would have never gotten hooked in the first place.

Mistaking Scratch's sudden loss of words for him getting emotional and being sincere, Malek replied, "I tell you what. You help me, and I will take you to Halleigh. We got a deal?" Even if Malek didn't trust Scratch one hundred percent, he trusted Halleigh to make all the right decisions concerning her body and the health of their baby. After all, that was the reasoning he'd fed himself for the move he was about to make. It wasn't for him; it was for Halleigh and the baby.

"We got a deal," Scratch said without thinking twice. He extended his hand to Malek. With everything Halleigh had done for him in the past, showing him undivided loyalty, providing inspiration throughout his recovery at the rehab center, he owed everything to her. If helping Malek was going to put her in a good place financially, then Scratch was all for it. Maybe after she found out that he helped, she'd listen to him, and then he could reunite her with Sharina. Then, in Scratch's mind, everything would be right with the world.

Malek shook Scratch's hand. At that moment a partnership was formed, both sides offering something. Scratch was helping Malek seek revenge, and although he didn't know it, Malek was helping Scratch seek redemption. Malek only hoped that this partnership was the real deal.

"It's not going to be that simple, youngblood," Scratch said, keeping it real with the young'un. "Since Mitch and Sweets came together, they—"

"Sweets and Mitch? Together? What the fuck you talking about?" Malek's heart began pounding almost out of his chest, and his temperature began to rise.

"Well, from what I hear from the streets, Mitch and Sweets ended the North versus South beef to become one. It's all the same operation now. So you gotta know that if you hit Mitch, you also dabbling into Sweets' money," Scratch explained. "They got a lot of loyal cats up under them. You'd be starting a one-man war against two teams. I know you done seen the movie *300*. Though them soldiers put up a good fight, they lost in the end." Scratch was reminding him of the brutal outcome of the movie, in which the little army with a big heart got slain. In so many words, Scratch was trying to let him know that a big heart couldn't defeat a big army. Maybe in the olden days of the Bible it was possible, but not in the street game.

Malek had to get out of there. If he stood there any longer, he was

liable to say the hell with a robbery and just straight-out get to poppin' off that lead. "Look, let's ride," Malek ordered Scratch, turning away and heading toward his car.

Scratch followed, and they got in his car, where Scratch continued to discuss the beef between the two sides of town. Malek was even more furious at that point. Not only did Mitch betray Malek, but he had sided with the person who killed Jamaica Joe. Mitch was playing a dirty game, and Malek hated it.

That nigga has no morals, Malek thought as he pulled away from the block.

Scratch said, "Can I ask you something, youngblood?"

Malek nodded his head, maneuvering through the city traffic.

"Have you ever done this before?" Scratch asked, referring to robbery.

"No. Can't be that hard, though, right?"

"It's time for ol' Scratch to give you a crash course in this game here we like to call robbery." Scratch remembered the days when he'd resorted to being a stickup kid to get high. He remembered the year that he and a heroin addict– turned street lit writer robbed the dope houses throughout Detroit, Flint, and Saginaw in the late '70's. "You can't run before you walk, youngblood. We need to hit Detroit before we just bust up into one of Mitch's spots."

"What you mean, Detroit?"

"We need a little practice, ya know. Now, you may no longer reside in the city limits, but I live here in Flint. I can't just shit where I sleep, unless I know there's enough toilet paper on the roll to wipe up all the mess." Scratch got situated and turned slightly to face Malek. "I've been shooting dope since before you was born, and in my journey, I have run across many dope houses throughout the state. We need to hit one that's not so close to home first, to get your game up," Scratch said, beginning to feel more comfortable.

As far as Scratch was concerned, robbing dope houses was like riding a bike. It was something a person never forgets how to do once they learn how, but he still needed to go for a test-ride, especially now that he had a sidekick. In his day, Scratch had never needed an accomplice.

As Scratch schooled Malek, he felt like his old self in his old habitat. "If we gonna do it, we gotta do it right." He flipped down Malek's mirror and fixed his brim. Then he winked at himself and declared, "Scratch is back!"

Chapter Ninety-two

Halleigh sat in her living room reflecting on her life. She looked at the table, where Malek had left the note for her when he'd made his exit in the middle of the night. It read:

Good morning, Love
 Here's some money to go shopping and relax for the day.
 I'm going back into the city to handle some business, and I'll be home to you later tonight.

Malek

Along with the note was a stack of money that amounted to five thousand dollars, half of what Malek had left to his name. Every other time he'd given her money to hit the mall, it had never been anything less than that. He wanted to be consistent, to make sure that Halleigh didn't suspect anything regarding his recent loss. He wanted to carry the burden and handle it on his own. Besides, he didn't plan on coming back home broke. Halleigh was at a happy stage and was elated that her life was finally coming together. She had a good man, a baby on the way, and a beautiful home—out of Flint. Falling back onto the couch in what felt like the lap of luxury, she imagined that this was what Marie must feel like.

Thoughts of Marie caused Halleigh to pick up her cell phone and call the long-distance friend. She hadn't talked to her but once since returning from the island, and now was the perfect time to call her. With five Gs to spend, she hoped the classy Marie could give her some contacts for her next big purchase. Halleigh wanted to buy a diamond bracelet, and recalled Marie mentioning that she knew some jewelers in the Midwest with flawless diamonds for reasonable prices.

I know she knows someone, Halleigh thought as she held the phone to her ear.

When the call connected, she heard an unexpected recording at the other end. "This number is no longer in service. Please check the telephone number and try again."

Halleigh frowned and looked at her phone to make sure she was dialing the right number. The number was correct. "Her phone is turned off?" Halleigh said to herself, slightly confused.

Her game all fucked-up. She got a millionaire for a boyfriend and she can't keep her phone on? I'ma have to teach her a thing or two. Halleigh flipped down her phone and got up so she could get dressed.

"I guess I'll go ahead and do a little bit of shopping today," she said as she headed into the back room.

Halleigh opened her robe and let it fall to the floor as she walked into the bathroom and turned on the shower. As she stepped beneath the spray, she dropped her hand to her stomach and smiled, thinking about the life forming inside of her. She adjusted the water temperature, and the steam began to fog up the room. Halleigh let the water hit her face and cascade down her body. The feeling of the hot water was almost orgasmic. She closed her eyes and was enjoying herself as images of Malek popped into her head.

Halleigh was so deep in thought that she didn't hear the two masked men creep into the bathroom with her. All of a sudden, she felt a cold draft as the shower doors flung open. Startled, Halleigh opened her eyes and found herself staring into the eyes of a man with a ski mask. She tried to scream, hoping Malek would somehow come and save her, but the man grabbed her and put a rag over her nose and mouth. She could smell the chloroform. She tried to kick and scream, to release herself from the man's grasp, but his strength was too much for her.

After only a few seconds of trying to free herself from the man's hold, Halleigh began to lose her consciousness. The foggy bathroom made the scene dreamlike, leaving Halleigh disoriented and scared just before she finally blacked out.

A couple hours later, Halleigh woke up groggy, and still naked, the way she was when she was yanked out of the shower. She looked around the unfamiliar empty room. There was nothing in it except for a toilet and a soiled mattress on the floor.

Confusion and fear sank in and Halleigh began to do the first thing she could think of doing and the last thing she remembered trying to do—scream for help. "Help! Somebody, help me!" She stood up and ran to the steel door, the only exit in the windowless room. She figured she was in a basement because of the concrete walls and floor. The moist air had a damp, horrendous smell that made her nauseated. She pounded on the door, screaming and kicking.

After a couple minutes of no response, she dropped to her knees in defeat. She began to think about her unborn baby as she gripped her stomach. *Oh my God! Who would do this? Where am I?*

"Malek, where are you?" she whispered, curling up into a fetal position and crying her eyes out.

"Here it is right here." Scratch pointed at the big brick house on Nebraska Avenue. He had taken Malek to a small weed spot that the local Mexicans ran on the east side of Detroit. "They move heavy reefer out of this one right here," Scratch said as he and Malek looked on.

"How you know?" Malek asked, wondering how a dope-fiend knew about a weed spot. "Man, I know everything that goes on in this city," Scratch said with pride. "They've been making good money over here

for years. Big Poncho is over this one, and he runs a solo operation. He sells weed out the front and a small amount of smack out the back. He has a shooting gallery in his basement. He charges dopeheads to come use his gallery, and it's small, but this spot will give us practice."

Scratch looked at the house and shook his head. "Whew! I ain't did this in years, youngblood," There was a little nervousness in his voice.

His adrenaline began to pump as he continued filling Malek in on the spot. "He might have a couple of li'l niggas in there, but nothing serious. If we do it right, we can hit him and take him for what he got. He keeps his money under floorboards in the closet in the master bedroom.

"You say he doesn't have a lot of people around him?"

"That's right. Sometimes his little brother is in there with him, and sometimes his li'l honey dips, but for the most part, he never has a crew inside. He does keep a gun on his hip at all times, and I know he probably has a couple of straps stashed around the house."

Malek sat and listened intently as he put a plan together in his mind. *Maybe Scratch isn't as dumb as he looks.*

"I got a plan," Malek said as he cocked his gun back. He reached into his glove box, pulled out another pistol, and set it in Scratch's lap.

Scratch gripped the gun and examined it like it was a rare art piece. He cocked it back also, loving the way the cold steel felt in his palms. It had been years since he held a gun, and it felt damn good.

After Scratch finished schooling Malek on the scenario, the two got out of the car and prepared to proceed with their plan. Malek kneeled by a bush near Poncho's back door, waiting for Scratch to unlock the back door for his entry. Scratch had gone into the house through the front door with the intent to let Malek in. As Malek waited, it felt as though hours had gone by. He was beginning to think Scratch had chickened out. "I know I shouldn't have dealt with a junkie," he whispered as he remained in a crouched position. He gripped his black .45 and stared at the door. Then, he heard the sound of the back door being unlocked. Malek smiled. Scratch had held up his end of the plan.

Just as Malek rose and walked to the door, he saw something unexpected. A Mexican-looking female with long, flowing hair came walking out the door with a garbage bag, apparently to take out the trash.

They locked eyes and stared at each other in silence. When the girl saw that Malek was wearing all black and a ski mask rolled up on top of his head, she figured out he wasn't there for a friendly get-high visit. She tried to run back into the house, but Malek grabbed her by the hair and put his gun in her face.

"Shhh!" he ordered, quieting her before she even got the chance to scream for help. "Look, if you listen and do everything I tell you to do, then you won't get hurt," Malek said sternly. "But I promise you, if you

make one false move . . ." Malek didn't see the need to finish his sentence.

The girl nodded her head and began to tear up. Malek guided her back into the house as he pulled his ski mask over his face. He put his gun to the back of the girl's head and pressed her into the living room, where Poncho was weighing up ounces of weed. Poncho was taken by surprise. Malek pushed the girl toward him. Poncho tried to grab his gun, which was on the coffee table near him, but Malek swiftly motioned toward him, causing him to freeze.

"Don't try it!" Malek pointed the gun directly at his head.

Poncho instantly put up his hands and swore under his breath, knowing he'd been caught slipping.

"You already know what time it is, homeboy. Where the stash at?" Malek walked closer to him and put the gun to his temple. He cautiously looked around the room, making sure that no one caught him slipping, and hoping Scratch would surface.

Once again, he kicked himself for thinking he could trust a junkie. He was certain that thoughts of their plan had gone right out of Scratch's mind the minute he walked into the dope house.

"There isn't a stash, bro," Poncho said with a heavy Spanish accent.

"Oh, so you think I'm playing, huh?" Malek smirked. Without hesitation, he pointed the gun at Poncho's foot and let out a shot, leaving Poncho's Timberland boot smoking and pouring blood. Poncho's and the girl's screams echoed through the house as Malek watched him roll around on the floor in agony.

At that point, Malek was going for broke. He didn't care how he got money. His only concern was taking care of Halleigh and his child, and if niggas had to suffer for the happiness of his loved ones, so be it.

"So let's try this again. Where is the stash?" Malek said, more authority in his tone this time.

The girl didn't even let Poncho respond. She pointed to the back room and yelled, "It's all in the back safe, under the floorboards." She was crying hysterically.

Poncho knew he had to kiss his whole stash goodbye. "Stupid bitch!"

Malek smiled. He was about to tie them up, but before he got to Poncho, he felt a gun on the back of his neck and froze up. He slowly raised his hands, not wanting to turn around and cause Poncho's younger brother to shoot.

The gunman, his red bandana covering his forehead and sitting right above his eyes, said, "You fucked with the wrong *ese*, homes! Drop the gun!" He nudged Malek with the barrel of the shotgun.

Before Malek could obey the man's command, another familiar voice filled the air, a more smooth tone. "Naw, playa, *you* might wanna drop your gun." Scratch pressed his gun to the back of the man's head.

Malek smiled. Scratch had come through for him.

"Drop it!" Scratch yelled.

Poncho's younger brother dropped his gun and put his hands up. Poncho continued to shake his head, regretting that he wasn't more cautious. He couldn't believe that a junkie had set him up to be robbed.

Malek grabbed Poncho off the floor and guided him to the back. "Scratch, hold it down in here!" Malek yelled before he exited the living room with Poncho.

"I gotcha, youngblood." Scratch kept his gun trained on the woman and Poncho's younger brother, while Malek went back to get the money. Scratch smiled, feeling good to be a part of something. It gave him a sense of importance, and while the ride lasted, he was definitely enjoying it.

Chapter Ninety-three

A small smile formed on Mitch's face as he sat in one of his many stash houses and watched Halleigh on the monitor. She was balled up on the ground, crying. He, along with his henchman, Bugz, shared a weed-filled blunt while watching her like she was a star on a television reality show. Mitch had had a camera installed in the basement room where he held Halleigh.

Bugz smiled as he enjoyed every minute of the torture Halleigh was going through. He was tall and lanky with a neat Caesar haircut. Two huge front teeth had earned him the name Bugz, because of his close resemblance to the cartoon character, Bugs Bunny.

"How long are we going to keep her down there?" Bugz asked after he exhaled the weed smoke.

"As long as we need to. That nigga Malek thinks shit is sweet. He should have killed me when he had a chance. Now I'ma make that nigga suffer," Mitch said as he saw flashbacks of Malek holding the gun to his head.

Halleigh was Malek's weakness, and the best way to get back at him. It wasn't hard for him to get Malek's address. He had a computer geek on his team that could find out any information that he needed about Malek, so finding where he rested his head at was simple.

Mitch stood up and began to think about how he was going to kill Malek once he got to him. The only thing he had to do now was to wait. He was expecting a call from Malek sometime soon.

"I'm not going to just kill him. I'm going to make that nigga regret the day he woke up and thought he could put a gun in my face. I am the new king of Flint. Hands down!" Mitch yelled as he paced the room and his rage began to take over.

Malek and Scratch bolted out of the house with two bags full of weed and money. They left the three Mexicans gagged and tied up. Malek popped the trunk and tossed the goods inside while Scratch hopped in the passenger's seat. Malek snatched the mask off of his face, got in the driver's side and pulled off.

"That's what I'm talking about, youngblood!" Scratch said excitedly. "I haven't had that type of rush in years." He looked back at the house in his rearview mirror. "This shit was supposed to go down. Can you believe not another mu'fucka was up in that house?"

Malek was just as excited as Scratch that the two had pulled off the robbery, even though things hadn't gone exactly as planned. "Good job, Scratch," Malek said as he maneuvered the car through traffic.

"Thanks, youngblood. Scratch still got it, baby," Scratch said, talking to himself more than Malek.

"That's not the hit I wanted, though. This can't be any more than ten thousand in cash and about fifty grand worth of bullshit weed that probably won't even sell," Malek said, slightly frustrated but not completely ungrateful. The only thing on his mind was getting back the money that Gary had swindled from him. He would go after Gary later, but until that could happen, he had to make sure he had enough money to support Halleigh in the way he'd promised. There would be no scraping to buy groceries for his family.

"See, youngblood, this wasn't for the money. This was practice for the big hit. You did a lot of things wrong, and if that was one of Mitch's or Sweets' spots, you would have been dead."

Malek frowned up at Scratch's comment, not liking the fact that Scratch was pointing out his flaws. Something in Malek told him that he should listen to what the old G was saying. Wisdom was something no one could buy, so he allowed Scratch to continue without interference.

"The first mistake was, you didn't keep everything in front of you," Scratch told him. "You gave the other cat room to sneak up on you. You have to work from a corner, so that nothing can creep up behind you."

Malek knew Scratch was correct. "Is that right?"

"That's right. Another thing you did was underestimate the female. You had your gun just on Poncho, and all your attention was on him. If

that fox was smart and up on the game, she could have popped you with the gun that was hid in the seat of the couch. I guess she didn't know it was there, but Scratch peeped it as soon as he got in the room."

Malek listened close and soaked up the game that Scratch was dropping. Although Scratch was a raggedy has-been in the street game, there was definitely knowledge there that he had picked up through his rough journey. Malek was new to the stickup game. He only knew how to hustle and move bricks; but he was a quick learner, and now he had his sights set on Mitch's spots.

Malek thought about his former comrade's complete disloyalty and disrespect. "I'm ready to get at Mitch," he said under his breath.

"I don't wanna throw a wrench in your program, young-blood, but if you wanna hit Mitch, you might want to go in the middle of the morning. That way you can catch him unsuspecting. If we go now, he's gonna have young guns sitting around, waiting to pop off."

Malek nodded his head and got on the highway. "You right."

"So, if it ain't too much, can I see my girl Halleigh now? Scratch ain't seen her in a while," Scratch said like a proud father.

"I got you, baby," Malek said as he headed toward their home in Grand Blanc. He knew the close relationship that Halleigh and Scratch had. After all, he was the reason why she'd been at the rehab center during the shooting. He usually wouldn't bring anybody to his home, but he would make an exception for Scratch. He felt that Halleigh would appreciate being surprised by Scratch's presence.

"Just don't say nothin' to her about what we just did, okay?" Malek warned.

"No doubt," Scratch answered then leaned back in the seat, happy he was going to see his girl, Li'l Rina.

Chapter Ninety-four

Bugz watched Halleigh closely on the screen. Mitch had left to make a couple runs and had assigned him to stay at the abandoned stash house with her, so he was responsible for feeding and guarding her. Bugz watched as Halleigh kicked and screamed, trying to get help. The more he looked at her, the more he became fascinated by her.

Mitch was very adamant about telling Bugz not to mistreat or even interact with Halleigh while she was in their custody, explaining to him that she wasn't the enemy, just a means to an end. Halleigh's beauty was too much for Bugz to resist. He looked at her curvaceous body and wondered what it would be like to have a woman of her beauty. Her perky breasts and fat ass had him aroused, and he wanted to feel the inside of her. Although her hair was wild and she was distraught, she still was beautiful in his eyes.

Actually, he had gone to school with Halleigh, but she became too popular and out of his reach once she hooked up with the so-called basketball star. She never gave him a second glance. He'd always had a small crush on her and secretly envied Malek. Now that the tables were turned and her life was in his hands, it was sweet revenge for him. He walked over to the refrigerator, grabbed a TV dinner, and tossed it in the microwave. He waited for it to warm and then headed down the basement stairs with it.

Halleigh heard the creaking of the wooden stairs, and her heart began to beat fast. She didn't know who to expect to walk into the room, and hurried to the corner, as far away from the door as possible. She sat down and pulled her knees close to her chest as she waited to see who was coming. She heard the dead bolts being unlocked—there were at least four of them on the door.

Halleigh saw the tall, lean man step into the room. She began to breathe heavily as she stared at the face that had some familiarity to it. "Where the fuck am I?" she asked, trying to figure out how she knew the guy.

"Don't worry about it." Bugz tossed the TV dinner toward Halleigh then slowly approached her. As he got closer, he could see Halleigh tense up, trying to cover her naked body with her hands as best she could. Bugz was in awe at her physique.

"I'm not going to hurt you," he said as he stood over her.

She looked up at him and screamed, "Why in the fuck am I here? Why?"

"Look, I don't know why. I'm just—"

Before Bugz could finish his sentence, Halleigh gave him a power punch to his groin, sending intense pain through his body.

"Aghhh!" he yelled as he grabbed his nuts and bent over in agony.

Halleigh made a run for it. She jumped up and bolted, darting up the stairs, where she tried to open the door. It was locked. She pounded on it furiously and screamed for help, but it was to no avail.

Bugz limped to the bottom of the stairs and looked up at Halleigh, who was hollering and trying her best to open the door. "You can't go anywhere without these, bitch." He held up a set of keys that unlocked the dead bolts on both doors.

"Let me go, you sick bastard!" Halleigh screamed as she glanced down at him. Then she began to pound on the door again. She wanted so desperately for her man to come and save her and her baby.

She wondered why this man had her locked up in a basement in the first place. Who would want to do this to her?—Manolo. Maybe he had something to do with this.

"You can bang on the door as long as you want and scream as loud as you want, but nobody can hear you. You might as well come back down here, sit yo ass down, and eat this food," Bugz said, massaging his aching balls. "That was a good shot you got on me, but if you do it again, I'm not gonna take it so lightly." He pulled out his gun; then he grabbed the shirt that was hanging out of his back pocket and threw it at her. "Cover yourself up and come back down here."

Halleigh gripped her stomach, thinking about the safety of her baby. She picked up the shirt that landed at her feet and put it on. Realizing she had no choice but to abide by his rules, she walked down the stairs and hesitantly approached Bugz.

When she got close to him, he grabbed her by the hair and threw her back into the room. She fell on her side and quickly headed to the corner, trying to get as far away from him as she could.

Bugz was enjoying watching Halleigh suffer. He wanted to have a little fun with her. "Now, let's try this again," he said with a menacing smirk. He was about to take what she would never give to him willingly.

Chapter Ninety-five

Malek and Scratch reached the house. Butterflies formed in Scratch's stomach as he prepared to see Halleigh. He was happy he would finally be able to talk to her again, because he missed his friend, but also because he wanted to convince her to forgive her mother. He hoped it would mean something to Halleigh that her mother had finally gotten clean and was one hundred percent drug-free.

"Halleigh is gonna be happy to see you," Malek said as he approached his front door.

Scratch followed closely. He took off his hat and tried his best to pat

down his nappy 'fro. "Gotta look good for my girl," he said to himself as he tried to straighten up his 1980s-looking shirt.

Malek put the key in the door and noticed it was unlocked. "I told that girl about not locking up," he said as he pushed open the door. "We may not be in Flint, but hell, crime don't discriminate." He smiled as he raised the duffel bags containing the money and the weed. He was going to split everything from their caper down the middle with Scratch. It wasn't nearly enough to set him up financially, but it would help. He knew the big heist would be at Mitch's and Sweets' spots. Malek walked into the house and called for Halleigh. "Hal, come out, baby. I have a surprise for you." He dropped the bags in the middle of the floor and headed toward the back room.

Scratch sat on the couch and made himself comfortable. He looked around and admired the plush place. It had been a while since he had been in a home so nice.

Moments later, Malek came storming out the back, his gun drawn and a note in his hand.

Scratch saw the look of worry written all over Malek's face. "What's wrong, youngblood?"

"Man, they got Halleigh!"

"What?" Scratch jumped up, not knowing exactly what was going on.

"I'ma kill that nigga!" Malek dropped the note on the table.

Scratch picked up the note and read the sloppy handwriting:

If you want to see your whore again, come see me. If you try that brave shit, she's dead. Mitch.

"Damn!" Scratch dropped his head and shook it from side to side.

"This ain't for her. This is not for her, man," Malek said as he thought about the love of his life and how he put her in harm's way. She'd already had a rough life, and he was making it worse. The burden of guilt rested on his shoulders. Then the thought of his unborn child came into play. Malek got teary-eyed and began to clench his jaws and fists. He looked around and noticed a lamp on the floor and the phone off the hook. There must have been a struggle when they took Halleigh. The thought of it made him even more furious. He headed for the door, willing to sacrifice his life to make sure Halleigh and their child would be okay.

Scratch followed Malek out without thinking twice. He was ready to ride or die for Halleigh. They were on their way straight to Mitch's main "trap spot."

Chapter Ninety-six

Mitch, surrounded by his goons, was in his main trap spot in the 5th Ward. He was smoking a blunt at a table where ounces of coke sat in piles, ready to be cooked up for distribution. He was waiting for Malek to enter any minute. He knew he would be on his way, because Malek had been calling him constantly. But Mitch didn't want to talk over the phone; he wanted to tell him what he had to say to his face.

He felt bad for kidnapping Halleigh, but in his eyes, it was all a part of the game. Mitch was a strong believer in an eye for an eye, and Malek had violated.

Mitch still had a thing for Halleigh, and he had no intentions of hurting her. In fact, he always wanted to be in Malek's shoes when it came to Halleigh. That was a contributing factor to his disloyalty. Just like he didn't think Malek had earned his way to the top of the game, he didn't think Malek deserved Halleigh either. He smirked at the thought that once Malek was out of the picture, maybe he would make her his woman. Just as expected, Malek stormed through the door, along with Scratch.

Mitch stood up and smiled at Malek, as if they were friends. "Oh shit! Look what we got here—Dumb and Dumber." He laughed. "What? You running with dope-fiends now, son? Shit must be real bad, huh?"

He was the only one laughing. Malek was furious as he stood a few feet away from Mitch. All of Mitch's goons had their hands on their waists, by their guns, waiting for Malek to make the wrong move.

"I see you got my letter, huh?"

"Where is Halleigh?" Malek said through clenched teeth, cutting right to the chase. He stared at Mitch intensely, hatred in his eyes, and didn't blink once. He wanted to put a bullet through Mitch's skull right then and there.

Mitch had Halleigh, so he was in complete control. He pointed his finger in Malek's face. "I should be the one asking all the questions, my nigga. Pat this clown down."

Three men ran up on Malek and searched him. One of them found a gun in his waist and quickly gave it to Mitch.

"You can take me. Just let her go, man," Malek said, trying to reason with Mitch.

"How do you know she isn't already dead?" Mitch said, sending darts straight to Malek's heart.

The words made Malek's knees weak, but he stood firm.

Scratch had heard enough. He pulled out the gun Malek had given

him and tried to point it toward Mitch. He handled the gun like an amateur, fumbling it, and Mitch's goons quickly attacked him and gave him a beat-down. Two of Mitch's goons started striking Scratch on the head with their guns, causing blood to trickle down his face. Malek stood there helplessly as Scratch got beat down by the two men who were half his age.

"Let that bum up," Mitch ordered as they stomped out Scratch. The goons returned to Mitch's side and focused on Malek.

Scratch spat up blood and held his stomach in agony. He slowly got up, blood pouring from different gashes on his face and mouth; but he still managed to release his famous smile. "That's . . . all you . . . young punks got?" Scratch gasped and held his broken jaw.

Just as the words came out of Scratch's mouth, a goon gave him another hit for good measure, this time knocking him out cold.

Mitch looked at Malek and thought about how he ran up on him in his own house. He wanted to make him suffer before he eventually killed him.

"I got somebody I want you to meet." Mitch looked toward the back room. "Yo!" he hollered, calling someone.

Moments later, Sweets, the homo thug responsible for the death of Jamaica Joe, emerged from the back. He crooned in a singsong voice, "Malek, Malek, Malek."

Just months ago, the two had been at each other's throats over a turf war, and now Malek was face to face with him. He thought he would never see Sweets anywhere on the North Side of Flint. Mitch had sided with the enemy, which only made Malek feel more angry and betrayed.

"Fuck you, Sweets!"

Sweets sat nonchalantly at the table, buried his head in one of the blow piles, and used his nose as a vacuum. Then he threw his head back, smiling as he wiped his powdered nose. "No. Fuck *you*!" he said. "It looks like you have made yourself a li'l situation here," Sweets said, referring to Malek's beef with Mitch. "I would hate to be you right now," he said in an instigating tone. "Oh yeah, and just to let you know . . . I faithfully piss on Jamaica Joe's grave every day. You know, I got to keep the flowers watered. It helps them grow better."

Everyone in the room had a good laugh, except for Malek and Scratch, who was still out cold on the floor.

"Okay, okay, enough of the reunion. You thought you could get away with coming in my shit like that?" Mitch asked Malek.

Malek remained quiet, but stared at Mitch intensely.

Mitch, gun in hand, walked over to Malek and stood face to face with him. He lifted the gun and pressed it to Malek's lips. "Open up," he whispered.

Malek gritted his teeth and kept his mouth shut.

Mitch shouted the order again, this time cocking the gun, and Malek reluctantly opened his mouth. Mitch forced the barrel of the gun in.

Meanwhile, Scratch began to regain consciousness. He shook his head, trying to focus his blurred vision. Once he remembered what was going on, his only thoughts were to get Halleigh back. Still feeling light headed from his beat down, he could only sit there and watch the situation unfold.

Mitch stood right in front of Malek."I want a half-million in seventy-two hours," Mitch said, thinking about the dough that Malek had exited the drug game with. "If that money isn't in my hands by Friday, you can start picking out Halleigh's casket."

A rare tear slid down Malek's cheek. He thought about his woman. He had put her in harm's way, and hadn't been there when she needed him.

Mitch pushed Malek forcefully and smiled. "You better go get my money, bitch," he said, like a pimp talking to one of his hoes on a Saturday night. Mitch thought Malek had money put away. Little did he know, Malek was dead broke.

Scratch got up and followed Malek out the door. They had only three days to get a half-million dollars, which was next to impossible, considering any money Malek had planned on getting was from Mitch's spot. Malek had to do something to get his love back, and Scratch was going to do all he could to help. They had no plan and little hope.

Halleigh cried her eyes out in the corner as blood trickled down her leg. She ached all over after being raped by Bugz. Just when she thought her life was changing for the better, the streets of Flint had grabbed her. Now she was knee-deep in the game once again. The shirt she wore had been ripped, and her eye was beginning to swell because of the blow he'd delivered to her when she tried to resist. She'd told Bugz she was pregnant while he was degrading her, but he didn't care. It only made him go harder, as if it excited him.

Bugz exited the room breathing heavily, a devilish smirk on his face. He finally got a piece of the "devil's pie."

Halleigh became lightheaded and nauseous, owing to the odor of semen and blood. Feeling herself starting to lose consciousness, she cried out for Malek. He'd broken his promise to never let anything else happen to her. Now, she honestly didn't know if she could ever trust him again. The last thing that rolled off her tongue before she blacked out was Malek's name.

Chapter Ninety-seven

Halleigh's body was racked with violent shivers as she hugged her knees close to her chest and tried to hide in the shadows of the dreary basement. She had just come to, having no idea exactly how long she'd been unconscious. For a second there she'd forgotten about what had taken place just moments before she blacked out. When she looked down at her body, she was quickly reminded.

She looked around the room, her eyes darting from one corner to the next, almost as if she was on drugs, but drugs were a thing of the past. She had been drug-free for a long time. Although no one appeared to be in the room with her, she could feel eyes burning through her.

After a few more moments of scanning the basement, she finally spotted what she could sense was there—the eye of a camera. She could see the tiny red blink of a camcorder in the upper corner of the room. Once again, she felt violated. She reached out in an attempt to grab something to cover herself, but nothing was there. She had no choice but to resume her earlier position, knees to her chest and her arms curled around her legs as she rocked slowly. A sharp pain forced her to let out a gasp.

She buried her face between her knees as tears fell from her eyes. She didn't want whoever was watching her to be empowered by her tears, so she felt the need to hide them. She couldn't help but wonder if anybody had been watching her while she was being raped. Who had sat in front of the monitor and witnessed the horrible act without intervening? What type of person could do something like that? Whoever it was, she hated them. Their voyeuristic sin was cruel. She was desperate for an escape.

Replaying the events of her abduction in her head, Halleigh got a flashback and lifted her head. In the split second between her being snatched from the shower and a cloth being put over her nose and mouth, she'd looked into the bathroom mirror and saw something. Someone. Someone familiar.

"Mitch?" The name fell off her tongue as she realized that all of this was possibly his doing. Initially she thought it was Manolo trying to get revenge but her memory helped to correct that thought. "I need to see Mitch," she whispered to herself.

If Mitch was behind this entire thing, she knew she had a chance to survive after all. As far as Halleigh knew, she'd never done anything to Mitch to prompt him to do something like this to her, so she could only assume that this had everything to do with him and Malek. She

didn't know what had sparked a beef between them, but she did know that Mitch had been sweet on her at one point. She was hoping he still was. If so, perhaps she could use it to her advantage. His attraction toward her was probably the only way she could ever get out of the situation alive, and she was willing to do whatever she had to in order to ensure her baby's safety.

It had been a full twenty-four hours since she had been given any food, and she hadn't seen another face besides Bugz's. The thought crossed her mind that, now that Bugz had gotten what he wanted from her and she could identify him, she would be left for dead.

She shook her head in an attempt to erase those dreadful thoughts. She hoped and prayed that Bugz was gone for good, but that someone else would come see about her. Bugz wasn't in this alone; she knew that much. There had to be someone else assigned to keep guard over her, but who? Maybe her eyes had deceived her. Maybe it wasn't Mitch she'd seen before blacking out.

She closed her eyes and ran the scene through her mind. The scene had happened so quickly. She visualized the shadowy figure that stood off to the side. Unless her mind was deceiving her, it was indeed Mitch.

Opening her eyes, Halleigh wished to God this had all been just a bad dream, but the fact remained, she was still being held hostage. The torment of being locked in the basement reminded Halleigh of when Manolo had imprisoned her in his basement for weeks. It had been sheer torture, and she truly believed that a part of her had been forever locked in that basement. When she was finally released, she was a partial image of the person she used to be. She could only wonder what kind of emotions this time would bring upon her. How much of her soul would she leave behind this time, if she made it out at all? Everything in Halleigh just wanted to get up, go beat on that door, and cry out for help, but she was all out of screams. There was no fight left in her. All she really wanted to do was just go home. She would do anything to be back home, safe and sound in her bed, next to her man.

She closed her eyes once again, and instantly, Malek's face appeared behind her lids. Her heartbeat began to speed up as she thought about the possibility of never seeing him again. She couldn't understand, for the life of her, why it seemed as though the two of them were always teetering on the edge. Why was their love so hard to keep? Just when it appeared as though they'd picked themselves up and dusted themselves off again, they were being kicked back down. Something always seemed to be in their way, keeping them apart.

Halleigh thought, *Perhaps we're not supposed to be together. True love couldn't possibly be this hard to maintain, could it?*

Tears ran down her face as she kept her eyes squeezed shut. She could see him smiling at her. He was holding her baby—their baby—in his arms. A sob escaped from her lips as she imagined Malek staring

lovingly at her, rocking a baby boy back and forth in his arms. Halleigh had never seen that much joy in Malek's face, and she was mesmerized by the child he was holding. He was the most beautiful baby boy she had ever seen. His smooth chocolate skin was flawless, and his big buck eyes were innocent and sweet. She fell in love at first sight, even though it was just a dream. As quickly as she fell in love, grief took over. She saw Malek fall to his knees with the baby in his hands. His face donned a look of pain, as the front of his white T-shirt filled with crimson blood. Halleigh reached out for him, but she couldn't get to him. She heard her baby crying, but she couldn't move.

Halleigh's eyes shot open at the sight of her love dying, and she stared into space. "God, please help us," she pleaded.

She couldn't help but think that her vision was some type of premonition. *That's why he hasn't come for me yet,* she thought. *Please, God, let Malek be okay.* Her love for him was just that deep. Even while she was in distress, she prayed for his well-being. Even if a part of her was angry that he wasn't there for her, she still couldn't help but love him. Only death itself could keep her from loving him. She hoped, though, that wouldn't be the case.

Mitch entered the trap house, his authority causing his henchmen to straighten up and pretend as if they hadn't just been distracted from the game of NBA Live they'd been playing for some hours. Mitch stood in the living room in his Pelle jacket, black hoodie, and Sean John jeans, a styrofoam food box in his hand. "Turn that bullshit off," Mitch stated in his low, serious tone. He walked over to the TV monitors and looked at Halleigh on the screen. "She ate?"

Bugz continued to play the game. "Nah."

"Since when?" Mitch pulled his baggy pants up on his waistline.

"Shit, I don't know, man. Yesterday, I think," Bugz replied, refusing to turn his attention away from the game.

"Why not?" Mitch asked calmly as he went over to where Bugz and two other corner boys were sitting.

"The bitch ain't got no act-right in her." Bugz hit the blunt that was being passed around. He chuckled as he thought about his sexual tryst with the captive.

Mitch walked over to the game and snatched the cords out of the wall, interrupting their tournament. "Fuck am I paying you niggas for? Huh? Didn't I give y'all strict orders? Why didn't y'all feed her? She's pregnant!"

Bugz frowned and shot back, "Damn, fam! I didn't know we was running a luxury hotel out this bitch. We kidnapped that broad. So I forgot to feed her. I don't see why we hanging onto this bitch anyway. I say we pop her ass and pop that bitch-ass nigga Malek."

Mitch shook his head in disdain and then lunged at Bugz, hemming him up by his collar, and pointing a threatening finger in his face. "You

feed her because I say feed her, nigga. I'm boss. You don't need to know why we hanging onto her. I'm not paying you to be sitting around with these mu'fuckas glued to an Xbox. Understand?"

Bugz, embarrassed that he had been degraded in front of his peers, snatched away from Mitch. He humbled himself and replied, "Yeah, I got you, fam." He brushed his shoulders off as if Mitch had gotten dirt on him by touching him. "Damn! My fault, my nigga." Bugz headed toward the kitchen. "I'll go feed her now."

"I got it." Mitch started down the stairs with the food he had for himself, to give it to Halleigh. He mumbled to himself about how incompetent Bugz was as he made his way to the bottom of the steps.

The loud noise his Timberland boots made as he descended the steps sounded identical to Bugz's footsteps. Halleigh cowered in fear, huddling farther into the corner of the basement.

As Mitch reached the bottom of the steps he looked up and fumbled around before he pulled the string hanging from the ceiling to illuminate the room. A yellow glow shone throughout the basement, and a funky smell, like fresh blood, filled the air. Mitch immediately frowned up and walked toward Halleigh. "Halleigh, come and grab some of this food."

Mitch's voice caused her to turn around. "Mitch?" she called out weakly.

He didn't respond.

Halleigh blinked a couple of times, adjusting her eyes to the light. Once she could see clearly, she was able to confirm that she had been right all along. Mitch was the person in the basement with her. He was the second figure she'd seen after being snatched out of the shower.

"Mitch, please let me go. Why are you doing this to me?" she asked from the floor. She wanted to stand, but her body was in too much pain.

Mitch swallowed hard, coaching himself the entire time not to let Halleigh's sweet voice get to him. "Come eat." He squatted down near her and put the food on the floor.

There was a look of terror in Halleigh's eyes, and as guilt bombarded his soul, Mitch tried his best to avoid eye contact with her. It definitely wasn't the same look he'd seen her give Malek, the one he'd secretly longed for. The last thing he ever wanted was for her to look at him as a monster, the way she was now.

As Mitch looked downward, dodging Halleigh's eyes, he noticed dried blood between her thighs. He could smell sex and sweat in the air. He frowned as he lifted her chin and rubbed her hair gently, as if she was his woman.

Halleigh closed her eyes. She couldn't stand to look into his eyes like that. She could still feel him staring at her, though. She began to shake, thinking that he, too, would force himself on her.

Mitch observed the torn shirt as well. Between that, the blood, and the smell, he put two and two together in his mind. Mitch's hands began to shake. His eyes scanned Halleigh once more. Her once confident swagger was replaced with fear and an insecurity he hadn't seen in her since her days as a Manolo Mami.

Mitch thought about his hardheaded worker. *No wonder Bugz hadn't fed her. He was too busy trying to fuck her. Son of a bitch!*

"Mitch, please," Halleigh whispered, interrupting his thoughts, "I need to see a doctor. He raped me, Mitch. He hurt me real bad. I just need to make sure my baby is okay. That's all I want to do. Please, Mitch."

Too pissed for Halleigh's soft words to even penetrate him at that moment, Mitch clenched his jaw and rose to his feet. He emerged from the basement and stood near the door as he motioned for Bugz to approach him.

"Yeah, uh, what's up, fam?" Bugz stammered. He could tell by the menacing look on Mitch's face that Mitch wasn't too pleased with him. He'd already gotten on him about starving the poor girl, so certainly he was over that and on to something else.

Mitch stared Bugz straight in the eyes, daring him to try to lie. "Why is she bleeding?"

Bugz attempted to laugh the tension away. "I told you the bitch ain't got no act right, so a nigga had to put some up in her." He snatched at his crotch and turned to walk away.

Mitch called out to one of the other henchmen sitting on the couch. "Yo, Jake."

"What up?" Jake replied.

BOOM!

Out of nowhere, Mitch put a bullet through the back of Bugz's head. "Clean this mu'fucka up." Mitch glared from one corner boy to the other. The room was quiet. "Any of you other niggas who can't follow orders gon' find yourself in the same predicament. I said watch her and feed her, nothing more, nothing less."

Jake hopped up and did as he was told. He shook his head in shock as he began to dispose of the body, but he didn't dare say a word. He wasn't trying to see Mitch, and he definitely wasn't trying to be next. Just as quickly as Mitch's temper had flared, it settled, and he went back into the basement. He removed the coat he was wearing and covered Halleigh's body before picking her up and carrying her up the stairs.

Halleigh, her body limp in Mitch's arms, almost like a rag doll, hadn't the slightest idea where Mitch could be taking her, but she didn't even have the energy to protest anyway. Being in a damp basement, she knew whatever he had in store for her couldn't be worse than that. Besides, Mitch's arms provided her with warmth from his body heat.

The first thing Halleigh saw when she emerged from the basement in Mitch's arms was Bugz's dead body on the floor. She looked up at Mitch, who simply stepped over the body without a word then carried her up another flight of stairs. He took her to a bedroom and laid her on the queen-size bed.

"Look, Halleigh, this wasn't supposed to happen," Mitch finally spoke. "This wasn't part of the plan."

"Plan?" Halleigh asked, a puzzled look on her face. "What plan, Mitch? What's going on?"

Refusing to allow the tenderness in Halleigh's voice to get to him, Mitch ignored her queries. "I'ma call a friend of mine over here to check on you and make sure you and your baby are okay." He deliberately put some sternness into his voice to let Halleigh know that, even though he was about to get her some help, he still meant business. "Don't act a fucking fool up in here either, screaming and all that. Don't give me a reason to hurt you, Halleigh. I don't want to take it there with you, so don't leave me without a choice. Just chill out for a minute, and at the end of all this, you will walk out of here unharmed."

Halleigh shook her head in disgust. "I don't understand you, Mitch," she replied, her voice laced with hatred. Confused, hurt, and mad, Halleigh needed to get to the bottom of this and find out what was going on. Why would Mitch be doing this to his best friend's woman? "You were Malek's friend. He trusted you. I trusted you, Mitch. Why would you do this to us? Is this about you and me? I mean, I'm not blind. I've noticed the subtle ways you are with me. Believe me, Mitch, you are a good guy, but . . . I could never be with you."

Mitch laughed charmingly, rubbing his neatly trimmed goatee. He shook his head in disagreement. He gently rubbed the back of his hand across Halleigh's cheek. "It was good, ma, but it wasn't that good." He pulled his hand away. "I don't beef out over no broad, but let me put it to you like this: Maybe if you had chosen differently, you wouldn't be in this situation. This shit don't happen to niggas like me. Only niggas like Malek. He ain't a gangster; he's a ballplayer. He should've stuck to the game he knew best. Believe it or not, he started this war. Now I'ma finish that nigga."

Mitch walked over to the door. Before exiting the room, he turned to Halleigh and said, "Now I'ma have my niggas set up the cameras in this room. The windows are armor-guarded, and the door has a dead bolt. Don't be stupid, which means, don't try anything stupid." Mitch turned to leave, but then he walked back over to Halleigh. "Oh, yeah, and don't even bother wasting your time thinking about Malek. That nigga is as good as dead."

He looked down at Halleigh's stomach. "I suggest you better concentrate on keeping you and yours alive." Mitch reached to stroke Halleigh's face, but she smacked his hand away forcefully. He smiled. He couldn't help but admire her loyalty. He had known all along that her loyalty to Malek was stopping him from pursuing her, which was why he never really stepped to her like he wanted to. As long as Malek was still around Halleigh would never choose him. She loved that boy way too much, and although he didn't like it, he respected it. Any nigga in the game would have loved to have a for-real ride-or-die chick like Halleigh on their team.

Unfortunately, she'd never be on his, especially not now. With that final thought, Malek turned around and walked out, leaving her alone.

Although she'd managed to maintain her composure while Mitch spat all that venom about Malek her way, now that he was out of sight, she began to cry her eyes out. Although he had basically promised her she would be okay, he had also assured her that Malek was going to die. If that was the case, she didn't even care anymore whether she lived. She couldn't see herself living without Malek. *What am I going to do?*

She could feel herself hyperventilating. With each forced breath, her heart hurt tremendously. She could feel the pit of emptiness expanding in her stomach. She wanted to scream for help, but knew better than to test Mitch. Still, she couldn't just sit there, knowing that her baby's father was about to be introduced to death. She had to do something. She had to make a move. Everyone else seemed to have a plan; now it was time for her to come up with one of her own.

Chapter Ninety-eight

Malek breathed heavily, and his palms began to sweat profusely. He watched closely as the other people in the bank casually tended to their business unaware of what was in store for them. He tried to look composed as he began to fill out a deposit slip under a fake name. He took a deep breath and thought, *It's all or nothing.*

With that simple thought, he erased any hesitation that dwelled in his heart. He couldn't turn back. Halleigh's survival and that of the child she was carrying in her womb depended on it.

Malek looked around, inconspicuously casing the place. The bank was small, but under heavy surveillance. Malek had scoped out the cameras in each corner of the lobby and also those pointed directly at the tellers' drawers. Malek glanced at the middle-aged white security guard who stood in the corner. He noted the overzealous look in the security guard's eyes, as if he'd been on the job for so many years just waiting for something to jump off. He wasn't just a flashlight security guard either. Medium-built, and most likely a police officer moonlighting, this guy had a black .45 on his hip. He patted it every so often, to make sure it was there. The security guard wanted to be a hero, and was just waiting for the opportunity to pull that gun from the holster and shoot it. If anything went wrong with his plan, the guard would be a problem.

Malek knew he was taking penitentiary chances by sticking up a bank, but the only thing on his mind was getting Halleigh's ransom. He clenched his jaws and gripped the pen tightly as he thought about Halleigh probably being tied up somewhere, hoping he would come for her, or even worse, giving up on him completely for not being there to prevent it all from happening in the first place.

Malek's eyes began to water. He had failed in his responsibility to protect Halleigh and his unborn child and this wasn't even the first time he'd failed her. The guilt felt like a ton of bricks on his shoulders. What type of husband and father would he make if he couldn't keep his family safe?

The fact that Mitch had taken his most prized possession had Malek questioning his manhood. *How could I have let this happen?*

He glanced at the door as Scratch, acting drunk off his ass, stumbled into the bank. In actuality, Scratch was as sober as a preacher on Easter, so his demeanor was all a part of their plan. Scratch was to cause a distraction and draw the attention of the security guard, while Malek robbed the place. As long as Scratch stayed in character, Malek felt like it was all a sure thing. Scratch was staggering and talking loud, a brown paper bag in his hand. At first sight, you'd think it was a forty-ounce beer bottle in the bag, but Scratch, prepared to shoot, just in case he needed to clear a way for them to exit, already had his finger wrapped around the trigger of the pistol inside.

The guard, patting that damn gun as if it were a magnet and his hand was metal, kept a watchful eye on the bank's patrons. Just as planned, he immediately motioned toward Scratch.

That's when Malek, his fitted cap pulled low over his eyes and exposing only the bottom portion of his face, headed to the first open teller in sight. He took a deep breath and walked to the teller, whose eyes were focused on the ruckus by the bank's entrance.

"Where in the hell is the manager?" Scratch yelled.

By now everyone in the bank was looking at Scratch, standing in

the middle of the lobby, swaying back and forth as if he couldn't keep his balance.

"My damn ATM card just got stuck, and I want my damn money!" he yelled. "I'm almost out of my drinky-drinky, and I needs my money to get some more."

While Scratch played his part to the nines, Malek approached the female bank teller. He was so high on his own adrenaline, he felt as if he would throw up, but he still pushed forward. Malek reached into his hoodie pocket and slowly placed the chrome .45 on the counter, his finger on the trigger.

Finally pulling her attention away from Scratch, the teller attempted to greet Malek. "How are you to—" She stopped mid-sentence after she glanced down and noticed the pistol pointed directly at her midsection. She flinched and put her hand on her chest. "Oh my God," she whispered, her breathing becoming shallow.

"Just relax and keep your cool," Malek instructed in a low tone. "You know what time it is." Then he added in the most subtle voice he could muster, "And if you try anything funny, I'ma have to push yo shit back. Okay?"

The teller simply nodded her head in fear. Too afraid to do anything other than that, she stared down at the gun, praying and hoping it stayed right there in its place.

"Now, I want you to give me the unmarked bills in your drawer. Put them in that big envelope right there." Malek pointed to a money deposit envelope among the many stored behind the teller, the type of leather pouch businesses use to make deposits. "Give me all hundreds and fifties, ma." He cocked the gun. "And if you even think about triggering the silent alarm, I'm going to make sure you're the first person I kill before the police get here."

Once again, all the teary-eyed teller could do was nod, her chest rising up and down. Malek could clearly hear her inhaling and exhaling. Malek noticed the pictures of the teller and her children placed inside her space. "Give me the money, so you can go home to your kids. Now, just calm down and be smart," Malek said, trying to coach her through the robbery.

She fought back her tears, doing just as Malek had instructed.

"You're doing good." Malek briefly looked over his shoulder to make sure Scratch still had the guard's full attention.

Scratch almost came to blows with the security guard and was being pushed out of the bank.

"Get yo mu'fuckin' hands off me, man!"

Scratch tried to get back into the bank, but the burly guard wasn't having it. Scratch was putting up a hell of a fight and causing a scene, but the security guard was too big for him to muscle through. Even the bank manager had approached them.

With all of this going on, not one person was paying attention to Malek and the teller.

After tangling with Scratch for another minute or so, the guard finally decided to just pick Scratch up and toss him out of the building like Mr. Banks used to do to Jazzy Jeff on *The Fresh Prince of Bel-Air*.

Just as Scratch was hitting the ground, Malek was coming out of the building, the bank deposit pouch stuffed with money under his armpit, inside his coat. He even smiled at the guard on his way out.

Scratch got up from the ground, fussing and cussing all the way around the corner. He was sure enough putting on a scene, until he rounded the corner, flipping the security guard the bird as he walked out of sight, to where Malek was waiting on him in the parked car.

"Let's go, Scratch!" Malek yelled out of the window as he started up the car.

Scratch hurried into the waiting vehicle, and they sped off without looking back.

Before the guard even noticed that the bank had just been robbed, Malek and Scratch were gone. Malek thanked God that he had gotten out of the bank without falter. Locked up, he would be no good to anyone. He had just taken a major risk.

Even so, he knew that the bank envelope didn't hold all the ransom money he needed to get Halleigh back. So, as he drove, he tried to get his mental together, preparing for bank job number two.

Just minutes later, Malek and Scratch were at another bank not too far from the one they'd just robbed. Working with very little time, they couldn't afford to take a break. They had to do this thing guerilla-style. He had to go all out to get the half-million.

When he'd arrived at the bank, Malek had filled out a deposit slip, the same as before. He scoped the place out and noticed the security guard to be less alert than the one at the bank he'd just robbed. He was too busy checking out the females' asses to pay attention to Malek. The more Malek thought about it, he probably really didn't even need Scratch to perform his Oscar-winning role. The big-booty women were distraction enough. Still, if it wasn't broke, there was no need to fix it, so things went on as planned. Ironically, though, a cop came to the bank on his lunch break to cash his Friday paycheck. Just as he pulled up in front of the bank and was about to get out of his car, he heard on his police scanner about the bank robbery that had just taken place. He listened as the voice on the radio explained the manner of the robbery, one man causing a distraction while another man stuck up a teller.

At first he was going to drive over to the other bank location to see if they needed any assistance, but confident that his fellow officers had everything under control, he decided that since he was already at the

bank, he'd go ahead and cash his check and stop by the other bank afterward.

When the police officer got out of his car and entered the bank, he walked in and saw Scratch acting a fool. The security guard on duty was almost unable to contain the man. The officer shook his head, realizing that this security guard probably needed his help more than the officers down at the other bank.

"Where the damn manager?" Scratch yelled. "My fuckin' money didn't come out that raggedy-ass ATM machine." He walked over to the banker's desk in the middle of the medium-sized bank.

Malek was taking the money from the teller, while the security guard was trying to calm Scratch. Just like before, all eyes were on Scratch.

Except the police officer who'd just entered the bank.

At first, it was the officer's instincts to go over and try to help get the situation under control, but then he remembered the call that came over the radio describing the technique used to rob the bank earlier.

He looked around, wondering what the chances were of the same exact thing taking place just a few blocks away a few moments later. When he saw Malek and the teller—the only two people in the bank not distracted by the commotion going on between Scratch and the security guard—he knew the chances were greater than he'd initially assumed.

The police officer slipped his hand down to his gun and walked up behind Malek.

"Remember, just stay calm and everything will be okay," Malek reminded the nervous teller. He tried to keep his head low, his fitted cap yet again covering most of his eyes. He could see the teller slipping one hand under the counter as she gave him the money with her other hand. "What the fuck you think you doing?" Malek said in a harsh whisper. He pulled back the hammer on his gun, which lay on the counter pointed toward her.

She quickly put her hands where Malek could see them.

Before he could do anything else, he heard the voice of the police officer behind him.

"Put your hands in the air where I can see them, son," the officer ordered, his gun aimed at Malek. "It's over. You're not getting out of here with this money today," the officer said sternly, but without raising his voice.

The cop deliberately used a calm tone because he didn't know Malek's state of mind and didn't want his suspect to harm the innocent teller, who was already visibly frightened.

"Fuck!" Malek cursed to himself under his breath as he thought quickly about what to do. What could he do with a gun pointed to his

head? Still, that didn't keep his mind from racing for a way out—hopefully, with the money.

Within five seconds, Malek had weighed his options and decided to do what he had to do. "I'm not going to jail today," he whispered. He swung around, catching the unsuspecting cop off guard with his bold actions, and immediately began firing his gun, hitting the cop in the midsection.

The cop managed to let off a couple of rounds, but none of them hit Malek, who ducked, dipped, and dodged toward the exit, using people as live body shields to deter the cop from firing at him for fear of shooting an innocent bystander.

Immediately, the patrons in the bank went into a frenzy at the sound of the gunfire, and the eerie screams of a stampede caused by the panic echoed throughout the building.

Before the security guard could react, Scratch had grabbed the guard's gun from his waist and pointed it at him.

Malek saw the officer he'd shot gasping for air as he dropped his gun and held his midsection. "Damn, damn, damn!" Malek repeated, as it registered in his brain that he'd just shot a cop. Malek quickly exited the bank, and Scratch followed close behind, almost out of breath.

"What the fuck happened, youngblood?" Scratch's eyes were bigger than golf balls. He couldn't believe what had just gone down. It was a horrible misstep that was sure to make them wanted men, especially if the cop died.

The Flint Police Department was like a gang in its own right. When one of their own went down, they showed no mercy on the transgressor. Malek and Scratch would be hunted to no end, and when, or if, they were caught, they might not ever make it to the jailhouse. The Flint police might just deliver them to their graves.

"We weren't supposed to kill nobody. That was a fuckin' jake!" Scratch yelled as they hopped in the car.

Malek quickly sped off. His mind was so messed up over the shooting, he didn't even stop to to see if there were any cars coming. He almost hit a passing car as he pulled off.

As they weaved in and out of traffic, Scratch cautioned, "Watch it, youngblood."

"My fault." Malek looked through his rearview mirror to make sure they weren't being followed. He hit the steering wheel with his fist. "He just ran up on me, man," Malek yelled as he maneuvered through traffic and made the getaway. "I had to."

Scratch kept looking back to see if anyone was behind them as they sped away, trying to get as far away from the scene of the crime as possible. Malek periodically looked in his rearview and then focused back

on the road. "Fuck!" he yelled again, repeatedly hitting the steering wheel. Then he looked at Scratch, who looked more nervous than ever. They had just stepped into the big leagues. Not only were they bank robbers, but possible cop killers.

Chapter Ninety-nine

Halleigh cringed at the touch of the skinny white man Mitch had called over to check on her condition. Halleigh didn't know the man, nor was he dressed in a white coat, but Mitch kept referring to him as Doc, so she assumed he was some street doctor they used in the game whenever one of their crew members got hurt or something.

Halleigh felt very uncomfortable as this stranger examined the most intimate parts of her body, especially with Mitch standing there watching the entire thing. At first Halleigh kept her eyes shut tight, to keep from seeing him standing there, but then she thought maybe if she did make eye contact with him, he would help her out a little.

Halleigh tried to look in Mitch's eyes, hoping that his conscience would get the better of him and he would find it in his heart to let her go. Every time she tried to lock eyes with him, he would just look away and avoid eye contact with her altogether. After a brief exam that took all of five minutes, Doc put his stethoscope and other tools inside his small gray leather bag and stood up. "Mitch, she should be fine. She just needs some rest." Doc dug down into his leather bag and handed Mitch a bottle of pills. "Have her take a couple of these aspirin. She'll be okay."

Doc also avoided eye contact with Halleigh and never spoke to her directly, just to Mitch. He walked toward the door, where Mitch was standing, and then glanced back at Halleigh. He leaned in close to Mitch and whispered, "What do you guys have going on here?"

"Get the fuck outta here." Mitch grabbed Doc by the collar and escorted him out the door. "Jake will pay you on your way out," he said, as the doctor hurried down the stairs.

Mitch returned to the room and focused back on Halleigh, who was balled into a fetal position. For a brief moment, he wondered if he'd done the right thing, using her to get to Malek, putting her in the middle of a street beef, when in reality she had nothing to do with the mat-

ter. Nevertheless, his pride wouldn't allow him to admit that he was wrong, nor allow him to punk out and give Malek the win by letting Halleigh go without collecting a ransom.

"It's all just a part of the game," he whispered to himself, trying to ease the guilt that rested square on his shoulders. He walked over to Halleigh and tossed the bottle on the foot of the bed. He began to say something to her, to let her know that everything was going to be all right, but he couldn't think of any words to say. So, he didn't say anything at all. He just turned and left the room, not even offering her a glass of water to take her pills. Halleigh heard the sound of the door closing, followed soon after by the clicking noises of the locks being turned. She glanced at the camera that Mitch had made one of his goons put in the high corner of the room, and gave the middle finger to whoever was watching her. Although she could be the sweetest, most loving and forgiving person in the world, right now Halleigh was full of nothing but pure hate.,The object of her emotions was none other than Mitch. She hated Mitch with a deep passion.

Everything in her wished that she could kill him, but she wasn't a killer. She never had been and knew that she never would be. It just wasn't in her, but if ever she just snapped and lost her mind, Mitch would definitely be at the top of the list of all the people who'd hurt her in her life.

It was almost as if Mitch could feel the daggers of hate being shot at him by Halleigh. He'd tried to get her off of his mind by blasting his car stereo with Lil' Wayne's latest, but as he cruised down North Saginaw Street, his thoughts kept going back and forth to Halleigh being left locked up back at the spot. Something in him was urging him to go back to the spot and let her go free. "Fuck that! That nigga Malek gon' feel pain," he said, trying to justify what he was doing to Halleigh.

He hit his steering wheel out of frustration as he jumped on the highway to go over to Keesha's house. If anything could get his mind off his wrongdoings, it was Keesha's head game. A few minutes later, Mitch pulled into Howard Estates apartment complex, where Keesha lived, and parked his Land Rover in the handicap space. He checked his mirrors and his surroundings before he got out of the car to enter the building. He patted his hip to make sure he was strapped. After scoping the scene for a couple of seconds, he hopped out.

When he made it to Keesha's door, he noticed that it was slightly cracked. His antenna immediately went up, because he had taught Keesha to always keep her doors locked and closed, no matter what.

Mitch slowly pulled out his gun and crept into the apartment. Keesha's spot was a place he frequented, to get a shot of pussy from time to time. Anyone who knew Mitch knew this about him. They didn't have to hire a private investigator or anything to follow his trail to Kee-

sha's. Keeping that in mind, he wondered if someone, perhaps some-one like Malek, was inside waiting for him.

At that moment he wished he'd gone with his first instinct to put one of his boys on Malek, to watch him just as closely as his boys had been watching Halleigh. That way he could be sure of every move Malek was trying to make, just to make sure he didn't try something stupid. It was too little too late for all that.

Mitch slowly crept through the door, his gun cocked and loaded. He heard the sound from the television coming from the back room. As he passed each room, he quietly peeked in, his gun aimed and ready, but nobody was in any of the rooms. As he crept toward Kee-sha's room, he noticed that the door was just barely open. For some reason, Mitch was expecting the worst, and his heartbeat began to pick up pace as he prepared for what he might find behind the door. *Did Malek get at Keesha for revenge?* He slowly pushed open the door.

It would have made sense for Malek to try to pay Mitch back by pulling Keesha into this. The only problem was, as far as Mitch was concerned, Keesha wasn't anywhere near an even swap. There was no way he would come up off Halleigh for the likes of Keesha. Her head game was tight, but certainly not a half-mil tight.

Mitch, his gun pointed, swung inside the room, and what he saw blew his mind.

A naked Keesha was playing with her clitoris and looking at Mitch dead in the eyes, as if she'd been expecting him. She'd seen him pull up in front of her apartment window and decided to be waiting and ready for him.

Mitch, taken by surprise, breathed a heavy sigh of relief. He lowered his gun and watched as Keesha pleasured herself, her body shiny from the baby oil she had applied to herself. It was driving Mitch crazy.

Without saying a word, Keesha invited Mitch to join in on the fun with the mere expression on her face and look in her eyes. Mitch quickly took off his shirt and unbuckled his pants as he walked toward her, his eyes glued to her oversized pink clitoris as it stood up and pul-sated, barely peeking out of her juicy vagina lips. Mitch crawled on the bed and helped Keesha masturbate, using no hands and letting his tongue do the work. He loved the way Keesha always had something new for him, which was why he kept her around. She had a fly-ass mouth, which kept him coming back for more.

The same adrenaline Mitch had built up when creeping in on what he thought to be a bad situation was now being redirected to the sex-ual encounter he was about to experience. He slipped his index finger inside of Keesha's womanhood and simultaneously played with her cli-toris.

When Keesha removed her hands and let Mitch do what he did best,

loud slurps echoed throughout the small apartment and, mixed with the soft moans from Keesha, created a soundtrack to their sexual escapade.

Mitch got Keesha just right and was ready to feel her warmth. He pulled out his rock-hard tool that seemed to be harder than ever and rubbed the tip against her outer lips.

Keesha looked down at Mitch's nine inches. Every single vein in his rod seemed to be trying to burst out of his penis. She watched as Mitch's tool disappeared into her, and arched her back in pure pleasure as they both let out a grunt.

Mitch began to work his magic, going as deep inside of her as he could. The feeling of his balls slamming against Keesha's other hole was giving her heaven on earth. Mitch stroked her hard and slow as he took one of her nipples in his mouth and moved his tongue as if it had a motor.

Keesha smiled as she felt herself about to explode. "Stop, stop!" she said as she put her hands on his "chance." She didn't want to cum so quickly.

Mitch ignored her request and kept thrusting, and within seconds, a small squirt shot from her love box and onto his stomach, causing him to become more aroused. About to erupt, he stroked faster and faster. "Aghhh!" Mitch yelled as he exploded inside of Keesha, depositing a walnut-size glob. He could feel her doing "Kegels" while he was still inside of her. He collapsed on top of her, and they both lay there breathing heavily.

As Mitch lay there, he felt as though Keesha had made a liar out of him. Maybe she would have been worth the swap after all.

Chapter One Hundred

M alek's eyes were red from going without sleep. There was no way he could rest until he had Halleigh back. In deep concentration, he sat silently, his elbows on his knees, and his hands clasped together and propped underneath his chin.

Unsure of what to say, Scratch sat nearby staring at Malek. He, too, had next to no rest as he and Malek thought of ways to get Halleigh from Mitch's clutches. With the shooting of the cop on their hands,

their chances of getting away with another bank robbery were slim to none.

For the past couple of hours, Malek had been racking his brain while Scratch sat there in silence, not wanting to interrupt him. Fresh out of ideas, Scratch knew it was best that he just remain quiet if he wasn't coming up with a plan to make some money to get Halleigh.

With not a word spoken in the last couple of hours, it was obvious that both Malek and Scratch were at a loss. Scratch had a bad feeling about the entire situation. He knew that the amount of money that Mitch was requesting for Halleigh's ransom was damn near impossible to acquire in such a short period of time. Back in the day, if a man demanded an outrageous ransom then, nine times out of ten, he never really had any intention of giving the kidnap victim back anyway. Scratch hoped and prayed that this wasn't the case and made sure not to let Malek on to his theory. Malek felt Scratch's eyes on him. "What?" he asked.

Scratch simply cast his eyes downward, hoping that Malek couldn't look into them and read his mind.

"I know what you're thinking, man, but don't say it. I can't deal with that right now." Malek let out a sigh and wiped his hands down his face. "I promise that if Halleigh doesn't come out of this, I'm not going to be able to live, man." He shook his head in despair. "I can't live without her. I tried that before, and it doesn't work. Without Hal, there's no point in me being here, so she has to come out of this. She has to."

Scratch wasn't so sure himself, but he tried to assure his friend. He knew he needed to be the voice of reason right now. "She will. If she can survive years on the street with a cold-blooded muthafucka like Manolo, then she should be able to get through this. Halleigh's a smart girl. I'm sure she's playing the hand she was dealt, but still, we've got to get to her quick. There's only fifty-two cards in a deck, if you know what I'm saying."

"I feel you, but I'm not going to try to kid myself. A half mil in seventy-two hours? We were pretty much doomed from the start." Malek stood up and began pacing. "Perhaps we went about this all wrong in the first place. Instead of wasting time running up in banks, trying to get that paper, we should have been running up on Mitch's bitch ass."

Scratch had to "lightweight" agree with him, but it was too late for all that now. They had to come up with something else. "You've got to think, youngblood. There's got to be a way for us to get to Halleigh besides coming through with that ransom." Scratch looked at Malek. "You know Mitch. He was your right hand for a minute there. You know what makes him tick. You know what makes him soft. Whichever button we push, we need for him to be off his square. Everybody slips

up every now and then. It's just a matter of getting caught. So what it boils down to is that we need to catch that nigga slippin', plain and simple as that." Scratch spoke with so much confidence, the impossible now sounded possible.

Malek absorbed what Scratch was saying and realized he was right. He knew Mitch the same way Mitch knew him. The same way Mitch knew how to get at him, he could turn the tables and do the same with Mitch.

No longer pacing, Malek stood erect with confidence. *I put this nigga in the position that he's in now,* he thought. *The same way I put him in the game, I'ma have to take his ass out.*

Malek couldn't take on the streets by himself, not even with old faithful Scratch by his side. Mitch had the allegiance of most hoods in Flint because he allowed anyone to eat, no matter what side of the city they were from. He had united the North and South Sides. Although Malek had love and respect in the streets, he couldn't fuck with niggas that weren't from his side of the tracks. Sweets and the South Side would never come up on Malek's watch, which was why he was now at a disadvantage. He needed more players on his team. *I can do this, but I need help,* he reasoned. *I can't put Halleigh at risk by trying to be on some Rambo-type shit. If I make a wrong step, then she could get hurt. I can't jeopardize her like that. I've jeopardized her safety enough already. This shit is bigger than me and my ego. I have to think about her and my seed.*

"So," Scratch started after watching the invisible wheels in Malek's head churn, "what are we going to do, youngblood? 'Cause Scratch'll go out blazing to save Li'l Rina. So you just say the word and tell me the plan."

Malek shot Scratch a serious look before taking a seat. "We're going to rob Mitch!" he said, his voice low and his eyes focused as if deep in thought. "That's our only choice. He's the only person getting money like that in the city. Even if we hit another bank, it won't produce enough money. Besides, you know every bank in town is on lock right about now. We need to hit Mitch's stash spot. Fuck it! This mu'fucka want a half a million, then I'm gonna rob him and pay him back with his own paper. It's our only way to get Hal back."

"Okay, okay! Now you thinking, youngblood," Scratch replied as he stood and began to pace the room. He was pacing out of anxiousness. He couldn't wait to set it off. The thrill of the game had for certain crept back into Scratch's heart as a smile crossed his face, showing off his crooked, yellow teeth. "By hook or crook we gonna bring baby girl home," Scratch declared. "But there's only one problem that I can think of." Scratch stopped pacing and looked at Malek. "Now, I ain't been in the game in a good while, but the game don't change. I know

Mitch ain't the big man. He's running the city, but he don't own no boats. He's getting his product from somewhere. If we rob Mitch, then we might potentially catch heat from his connect."

"Then we'll go to his connect. I put Mitch on. I know Fredro through Jamaica Joe. I'm a man and I stand on my own two, but I'll do anything to get Halleigh back safely. If I got to get at Fredro to get at Mitch, then so be it. Hopefully we can avoid any excess drama if I can just call in a favor." Malek then added, "Fredro was close to Joe, so I hope he's willing to lend me a hand." Malek stood to his feet and walked out of the room. Before he stepped out of view, he said, "If Fredro becomes a problem, then he can get it too."

"Hold up now, youngblood. I hear you, and I'm trying to save Halleigh too, but this is a suicide mission. Our two guns can't go up against Fredro. Just think about it."

Malek nodded his head, let out a sigh, and then whispered, "You're right, but I've got to figure out what to do before it's too late."

Scratch just shook his head and shrugged his shoulders as he sat down to think. He didn't have a clue either. Although just a minute ago he was pumped up, he felt in his bones that this thing wasn't going to end well.

He walked over to the mirror and straightened out his crumpled clothes, popping his collar. He looked at the bruises and bloody lip that Mitch's goons had caused him and said, "That young boy Mitch got a thing or two coming, if he thinks he can fuck with good ol' Scratch and get away with it." Scratch turned from side to side, examining his profile. "We're going to get you back, Hal."

When Malek returned to the room, Scratch turned to him and said, "First thing we need to do is count up this money and see how much more we need to come up with."

That thought hadn't even crossed Malek's mind. He and Scratch began to count out the money from the two bank robberies combined.

"This is only fifty-two thousand, and we done hit two banks," Malek barked. "How do this nigga expect me to come up with five hundred thousand in three days? That shit is impossible, and he knows it." Malek noticed his hands shaking. He picked up a stack of money and threw it back down on the table.

He didn't want to think about what Mitch would do to Halleigh if he didn't come through with the ransom. Mitch had never had anything against Halleigh, as far as Malek could tell, but that didn't mean he wouldn't do something bad to her to get back at him. After all, Malek had made Mitch look like a bitch-ass nigga in front of Keesha, so it really didn't surprise him that Mitch would want to make him look the same in front of Halleigh. *Perhaps that's all he wants to do is to make me look bad in front of Halleigh.* It was possible that Mitch

never had any intention of hurting Halleigh at all. Maybe all he wanted was to just strip Malek down to nothing by getting him for all of his money. Malek's stupidity and naiveté had gotten him swindled and left his pockets on *E*. He was back where he had begun—at the bottom— but the only difference was, he didn't have Jamaica Joe to lean on. Now his right hand was an ex-junkie, a far cry from the powerful reach of Joe

Malek was grateful for Scratch rolling with him. Besides, he could- n't be choosy. Not a lot of people would rock with him right now, so he had to be grateful for Scratch's loyalty. He didn't know why Scratch was so loyal to Halleigh, but he appreciated it and began to respect Scratch and Halleigh's friendship.

Malek looked over at Scratch, who now appeared to have a worried look in his eyes. Malek could sense his pain.

Scratch looked up when he felt Malek looking at him. "This some bullshit, youngblood. We gotta get Li'l Rina back. This shit ain't fo' her, man. It ain't for her. She don't deserve any mess like this. The game done gone stone crazy. All you young ones don't know a thing about it. Women and children used to be off limits. Now you dummies are snatching 'em off the street as if they are the ones responsible for the chaos." Scratch shook his head and ran his fingers through his matted 'fro. He then sat back and began to think of all the avenues of getting money. There was a brief silence as Scratch looked to Malek. The look on Malek's face let Scratch know he was making sense. "Exactly, youngblood," Scratch replied to Malek's non-verbal response.

"What about that Fredro fella you was talking about earlier?" Scratch asked. "We go against Mitch, we might as well sign our own death certificates, because them Italians don't play."

"Dominican," Malek corrected.

"Italian, Dominican, Swiss and cheddar . . . whatever—you know what I'm saying, youngblood. We mess with Mitch's money, we gonna catch heat. Now, don't get me wrong. Scratch ain't no punk. I don't mind any heat it may bring. I'm willing to go all out, but you got to know what you are jumping into before you even take that first leap."

Malek was desperate, and although he knew Scratch had a point, he didn't see any other options. "Fuck it! Like I said before, if Fredro got a problem, then he can get it too," Malek said, putting all the pieces in place as if he were playing chess.

"We gonna rob that boy and pay him with his own paper, huh?" Scratch repeated more to himself than to Malek. He began to chuckle and nodded his head. "I'm in! We have to move fast though, ya dig?" Scratch sat up, leaned in over the table, and began to put together a plan as the seconds ticked by. "Yeah, yeah! We can hit Mitch's spots and give him his own money before word get back to him that his trap spots have been hit. We can get Li'l Rina back that way."

Malek didn't think the idea was the smartest way to go about things, but with only a day left to get the money, it seemed like the only option. "Mitch isn't dumb," Malek said, trying to look at the plan from every angle. "He probably changed up the whole operation since I left. I know he doesn't keep the money in the same spot that we used to. We have no way of finding out the main spot where the dough is. That shit isn't as easy as it seems, old man, and if I know anything about Mitch, it's that he ain't a stupid nigga."

"Well, in my world, nothing is a secret. In the smack-user circle, everybody knows something. Maybe we need to ask around and see what we can come up with. It might not seem like it, but users have their own little community, ya dig?" Scratch stood up. "Take Scratch to his old stomping ground and let's see what we can come up with."

Chapter One Hundred One

M alek held his nose as he followed Scratch through a walkway and under the overpass of the highway. The stench was horrendous, and the smell of blood and body odor was overwhelming. The Michigan snow didn't hit under the overpass as it did the rest of the city, so it became the safe haven for the city's underworld. There, bums and users, with their cardboard-box houses, huddled around barrels of fire, trying to stay warm.

As Scratch made his way toward the back, he was being greeted left and right, like a hobo superstar. Scratch's popularity reminded Malek of his own, back in his days of walking the hall at his old high school. Malek couldn't help but smile as he watched Scratch do his signature pimp walk through the slum. Not only was Scratch respected amongst the homeless, he was like their mayor. Malek was surprised at how influential Scratch really was, and how much he knew the ins and outs of the drug game in Flint. No wonder Joe had trusted him to be his eyes and ears on the street. Scratch was privy to stuff that even Joe's own crew didn't know.

Malek made a mental note. He would look at crackheads and junkies in a new light. He would no longer demean them, because through his interactions with Scratch, he realized they were people too. They were just fucked up and forgotten, but they were also valuable.

Scratch looked around. For some reason, he felt uncomfortable. He had never been sober while living on the streets, and for the first time, he was embarrassed about the lifestyle he used to lead. Scratch, because of his twelve-step program, hadn't been to the spot in months. He'd even promised himself never to revisit the place, but he felt this situation was worth breaking his vow. Halleigh was worth more to him than anyone else in the world.

Malek leaned in close to Scratch and whispered, "Who are we looking for?"

"We need to see Grady." Scratch continued to scan the surroundings. "Good ol' dirty-ass Grady. He's one stinky-ass muthafucka, but he knows everybody and everything that goes down on the north side of Flint. You think Scratch see all, hear all, and know all when it comes to the streets? Scratch ain't got nothing on Grady."

Scratch spotted Stuttering Ron huddled over a barrel of fire and dressed in raggedy clothes and a holy skullcap. "Yo, Ron!" he yelled, getting the homeless man's attention.

"Yo, Scratch! Wha-wha-what's happening, baby!" Ron headed over toward Scratch and Malek.

Scratch leaned into Malek and quickly whispered, "Watch yo pockets around this nigga, youngblood. He will steal yo drawers off yo ass, without you even knowing that they're gone until you go to pull them up after taking a piss."

Malek chuckled and watched as Ron approached them.

Scratch and Ron shook hands and hugged as they reunited. Scratch was happy to see Ron still hanging in there. He and Stuttering Ron used to get high together in that same area, where Scratch had watched many men get taken by Ron without even realizing it. He might have been strung out, but his pickpocketing skills were comparable to none. His hands were quick, and his tongue even quicker. Since he had nothing to lose, there was no one he wouldn't try to sheist.

"W-w-where you been at? We missed you 'r-round here. And who this green nigga you got with you?" Ron immediately recognized that Malek wasn't a user. A seasoned user could always tell when they weren't amongst their own kind.

Scratch glanced over at Malek, whose jaws tightened at the comment the junkie had just made. "Aw, he cool, man. This my potna." Scratch threw his head toward Malek.

Once Scratch vouched for Malek, he was good. Ron reached out his hand to greet Malek. "What's happening, my man?"

Malek looked at Ron like he was crazy and left his hand hanging in the air.

Scratch interjected and began to work his mouthpiece in order to

try to locate Grady. "Yo, where is Grady? I need to ask him a few things."

"He's over there catching a nod." Ron pointed to the far corner where a man was sitting down propped up against the wall.

Ron gave Scratch a parting hug and then did the same with Malek, who pushed him off real quick, giving him a mere "what-up" nod. Scratch and Malek headed over to the sleeping Grady.

"Well, it was good to see ya," Ron said as he watched them walk toward Grady. Ron smiled as he looked down at the cell phone he had just lifted from Malek. He was ready to hurry off toward the hood to see what he could get for it. *Thank you, young brother*. Ron chuckled to himself, thanking Malek for providing the means to his next high.

Scratch approached Grady and saw that he was deep into a dope fiend lean. He began to nudge him, trying to wake him. "Wake up, son-abitch." Scratch knew it was damn near impossible to take a dope fiend out of his nod, so he was going to have to take some drastic measures. He grabbed Grady by the collar and shook him.

"What this raggedy mu'fucka going to be able to tell you about Mitch?" Malek said, getting frustrated. Malek covered his mouth and nose as the strong odor of all the junkies became almost unbearable. The smell of blood from the heroin addicts and their body odor was enough to make any man vomit, but Malek tried his best to cope.

Scratch began to unbutton the man's pants. "He's going to be able to tell me anything I need to know."

"What the fuck you doing, Scratch?" Malek turned his head away.

"I am waking his ass up," Scratch said as he pulled down the man's pants, exposing his small tool. He then reached onto the ground and grabbed a handful of water from a puddle. He tilted his hand and allowed the water to pour from his hand and onto Grady's private.

"This is the only way you know how to wake a nigga up out of a nod?"

"Trust me, I know," Scratch said, trying to hurry up and get it over with. "I done had plenty of water, snow, and ice on my balls in the past waking me up out of a dope fiend lean."

Seconds later, Grady jumped when he felt the wetness on him.

"Wake up, Grady!" Scratch said as Grady was coming to.

Slowly, Grady opened his eyes. "Scratch, what's happening, playa?" he said in a slurred voice.

"What's up?" Scratch replied. "I need for you to wake up." Scratch grabbed him by the collar once again. When he saw Grady was about to nod again, he laid a powerful smack on the left side of his face, leaving a handprint on his cheek.

Grady's eyes shot open. "Damn, Scratch! Slow down!"

Scratch slapped him again, this time waking him up completely. "I

need some info about Mitch," Scratch said, getting right to the point. He knew he was messing up his man's coma-like high, but time was of the essence.

"North Side Mitch?" Grady sat up and wiped the slob drooling down his chin.

"Yeah," Malek chimed in, now that their source of information appeared to be wide-awake and alert to the questioning.

"What about him?" Grady asked.

"I know you know where his spot is at."

"His main spot," Malek added.

"We need to know where he stashes all of the dope and cash," Scratch continued, hoping Grady could tell him something.

Grady was a veteran junkie. Although Scratch had several years of being hooked on dope under his belt, Grady was up on him by a good ten years, and it showed in his appearance.

Scratch still had somewhat of a swagger, while Grady appeared worn, burned-out, and seemed to have no hope of rehabilitating himself. His hands were swollen five times their usual size from shooting so much dope into his veins. Some people on the streets call it "elephant hands," when a person's limbs swell up so bad from heroin.

Grady was a viable asset to major pushers. They would ask him to test the drug and its potency. If it was strong enough to get Grady high, it was strong enough for the public. Mitch had used Grady for that very reason on a few occasions, so Scratch knew there was a good chance Grady would know something that might be able to help them out on hitting Mitch's spot. Grady looked at Scratch, and for a minute, it seemed as though he was about to speak, but then his entire demeanor changed when he looked over at Malek after remembering he was standing there. Grady knew exactly who Malek was. He spat, "I don't know shit."

In the past, Grady had often approached Malek or some of his workers to ask them for a free sample, or to ask if he could get a pass on coming short. Grady would sometimes come with eight dollars instead of ten, or with change he'd scrambled up. It never failed that Malek and his other workers would deny him, embarrassing and humiliating him.

One time, after a half-hour of begging and pleading, Grady had just convinced one of Malek's workers to let him slide with being $1.50 short. The boy had stuck to his guns, refusing to let Grady slide, but Grady hung around so long agitating the boy with his presence, even begging from paying customers to make up for his shortage.

The kid finally gave in. "All right. Damn, old man!" the boy had said to Grady, sucking his teeth and rolling his eyes. "Give me what you got

and then get the fuck on. You bad for business, and you smell like shit."

Grady damn near danced a jig as he collected the eight one-dollar bills and two quarters from his pocket. He handed the money over to the boy, who counted it.

Shaking his head, the boy dug a ten-dollar cop from his pocket and dangled it in the air. "I promise on everything, old man," the boy said, "you better come up with my dollar fifty. And don't think you gon' make a habit out of this shit. You ever come at me short again, I'm just gon' shoot your ass on GP. I don't care if you only twenty-five cents short next time, you ain't copping. Now take this shit and be gone."

Just as the boy was about to hand over the dope, a hand tightened around his wrist, preventing him from doing so.

"What's this about somebody being short?"

The boy turned around to see his boss, Malek, standing there. "Oh, uh, nothing," he stammered, knowing he'd been caught breaking one of the rules of slinging.

Malek said to his worker, "I know you ain't trying to lie to me. Are you, fam?"

"Uh, no, it ain't even like that. I mean, it's no big deal. Home boy here just short a dollar fifty. That's all. He's good for it." The boy looked to Grady for reassurance. "Ain't that right, old man?"

"Uh, yeah," Grady co-signed, reaching for the dope. With a carrot dangling in front of him, he would have said anything.

Malek couldn't help but chuckle. "So you got a dope fiend vouching for you now?" he asked, still gripping the boy's wrist. "And I'm supposed to be cool with that."

The boy was at a loss for words, realizing how stupid he sounded.

"All right," Malek said, finally letting his wrist loose. "If he says he's good for it, then go ahead and let him slide."

At that point, Grady was dang near salivating over the dangling bag of dope and was glad to hear the boy granted permission to let him have it. Just as the boy went to hand Grady the dope, Malek snatched it from his hand, cold-cocking the boy with the back of his hand.

"Mu'fucka, what the fuck are the rules about letting niggas fall short?"

He cold-cocked him again when the boy didn't answer Malek quickly enough, this time drawing blood from the boy's bottom lip. "If you let one muthufucka come up short, then every broke nigga on the block gon' come to us like we the damn Salvation Army or something, giving shit away for free." Malek continued to scold the young worker. "Nigga, this is my product. This is my reputation. You got that, fam?"

"Yeah, Malek, man," the boy said, wiping the blood from his lip. "My bad. It won't happen again."

"You damn right, it won't happen again. Get the fuck out of here!"

Without asking any questions, the young'un left the scene, leaving only Grady, Malek, and a few bystanders standing there.

"So, uh, yo, can I get that?" Grady said, pointing to the bag of dope.

Malek spat, "If you don't get the fuck outta my face . . ."

"But yo boy got my eight dollars and fifty cents. Can I at least get eight dollars and fifty cents worth?"

Malek could feel the old man's pain, but business was business. He'd noticed a small crowd had formed, and he had a reputation to uphold on the streets. Unfortunately, Grady would become an example. Malek sent him on his way, via a kick in the ass and a string of expletives, causing the onlookers to laugh. As Grady stood there and thought back to the several humiliating encounters with Malek and his boys, he knew Malek didn't have a clue who he was. *Now this mu'-fucka needs my help,* he thought. *I'm not giving his ass nothing. Nada. Zilch!* Not even if Malek were to offer him all the free samples in the world right now would Grady consider helping the young punk.

Scratch looked at Malek and motioned for him to give Grady something. Malek reached in his pocket and tossed a twenty-dollar bill at Grady.

No matter who a dope fiend was beefing with, the possibility of getting a high always quickly made them forgive and forget. The sight of the twenty-dollar bill washed away every thought Grady had just been thinking, and as he examined the bill as best he could for authenticity, he suddenly began to remember some vital information regarding Mitch.

Grady quickly put the twenty in his pocket and reconsidered his earlier stance. *Well, maybe just helping him out with a little bit of information won't hurt. After all, he just paid for my afternoon snack. Now I won't have to be on E.* Grady licked his ashy lips and began to sing like a bird.

"Well, I'm not for sure if it's his main stash spot or not, but I do know he has a spot off of Welch Avenue where he keeps a whole lot of dope."

Malek looked at him, his eyes silently asking Grady,

How would you know that?

Reading Malek's unspoken words, Grady continued. "I know this because when he got a big shipment in last week, he told me to meet him over there. He didn't have time to take me to the known stash spots, so he let me taste the drug right there on the spot. It was some good shit too!" Grady thought about the potency of the drug and how good the high felt.

Grady had Malek's undivided attention. "Who does he keep at that spot?"

"I forgot." Grady glanced down at Malek's pocket then back at Malek. Just from the desperation in Malek's eyes alone, Grady could tell that the information was worth more than twenty dollars. He was sitting on the edge of his seat, like he'd been watching a whodunit for the past two hours and was only seconds away from finding out who had done it. Grady had to take advantage of Malek's vulnerable situation.

Taking note of Grady's wandering eyes Malek grabbed another twenty and tossed it at him. "Like I asked, who does he keep at the spot?" he repeated.

With Grady's memory suddenly refreshed, he told Malek exactly what he wanted to know. "As far as I know, his sister stays there and watches over the money. It's a hush-hush spot, and nobody is supposed to know about it. He doesn't do any business out of the house. He just keeps the dope there, and she does all the counting there."

"So it's just a female up in there, huh?" Malek was surprised to hear that the only thing between him and hitting up Mitch's main stash spot was a broad. He thought he'd taught his prodigy much better than that.

"A bitch is right. A female dog, for sure." Grady nodded his head. "She is a loud, crazy bitch too! Personally, I don't care for her ass at all."

Malek looked over to Scratch as if things just might turn out good for them after all. They'd taken on big, burly security guards. Surely the two of them could handle some chick.

Grady noticed the eye contact between Malek and Scratch. "Don't get it fucked up, though. She is as feisty as they come. Worse than some dudes. What are y'all trying to do anyway?" Grady decided to be nosy, see what information he could get out of Malek and Scratch. One never knows. He might be able to take some information back to Mitch and make some more get-high money.

Knowing just how much he could trust Grady, Scratch replied, "Thanks for the information, Grady. Good lookin' out." Scratch then looked up at Malek, giving him the signal that it was time for them to split.

"A'ight then," Grady said. "But know that Mitch ain't to be tested . . . if you know what I mean."

"Take it easy, Grady," Scratch said, ignoring his friend's comment.

"You take it easy too, and whatever happens, y'all didn't get that little bit of information from me either, because I don't want any trouble with that young man. He'll whup my ass all up and down the expressway." Grady thought about what Mitch would do to him if he found out he was giving away such valuable information.

"Fuck Mitch!" Malek said. "Scratch, let's go!" Malek did a 180 and began to walk away, and Scratch followed.

Mitch's sister was about to get paid a surprise visit by Malek and Scratch, who were both prepared to walk into a situation unknown. Desperate times call for desperate measures.

Chapter One Hundred Two

Keesha sat in Sweets' brand-new strip club feeling like the queen bee. Money was flowing lovely for everyone since Mitch had taken over the city. Due to this steady flow of cash, Sweets had upgraded to a new club. The old-school beef between North and South was dead.

Keesha was no longer a measly bartender. She was now a stripper and an official Manolo Mami. Her dream had come true, the same way little blonde-haired and blue-eyed girls dreamed of being Miss America.

Although Manolo was locked up, the name had stuck because of the girls' notorious reputation around Flint. The Manolo Mamis were the shit and were known for having the best head game in the city. Keesha was now the HBIC of the clique. Sweets had demoted Tasha for disloyalty and could no longer trust her, leaving room for Keesha to come up in the game and be his bottom bitch. Keesha didn't necessarily enjoy what she had to do to stay on top. With Sweets being bisexual, he usually liked to do things in the bed that she wasn't into, but she held her tongue to keep her spot. When he put her on Mitch, Keesha happily obliged, never objecting or even voicing an opinion. She simply did as she was told which kept her in Sweets' favor.

Keesha sat in front of the lighted vanity in the dressing room of the club as she waited for her set to begin. She looked at Tasha's reflection in her mirror and turned up her nose. She disliked everything about Tasha.

Keesha remembered the days when Tasha, Mimi, and Halleigh were official. *Those bitches had their heads in the clouds. Hating-ass hoes were always looking down on me like they were better than me or something. Now look who's laughing. The bitch came begging for her spot back, but it's taken. This shit is all me.* She rolled her eyes in the mirror as she watched Tasha open up her locker.

When Mitch had first told Keesha about how soft Malek really was now that he had his little Barbie doll in custody, she knew Mitch was

only telling her because he still felt embarrassed at the way Malek had made him look like a punk in front of her. This was Mitch's way of telling her to look at who the punk was now.

For a minute, she even doubted there was any truth to the kidnapping . . . until Mitch let her view Halleigh through the camera. Keesha almost felt sorry for the vision before her, but those feelings quickly disappeared as Keesha thought to herself, *If the bitch had treated me like I existed, I might have even tried to help her out. But fuck her!*

Keesha applied makeup to her face. She was a pretty girl, but she had a fucked-up attitude, which had gotten her fucked up plenty of times by girls from around the way. It wasn't just the Manolo Mamis who didn't really care for her, but pretty much every chick she encountered. She had a nasty disposition about her that made people not want to associate with her. Unfortunately, too busy making the rest of the world out to be the bad guy she didn't see this flaw in herself. She always had something to say about everybody, and now that she was in not only Sweets' favor, but Mitch's favor as well, she thought she was untouchable. *All these bitches can suck a dick.*

Everybody knew her new position because she made sure of it. Her mouth was always running, and today was no different. "Hey, Tasha girl!" she said, faking friendship. She looked Tasha up and down, admiring her tall, curvaceous frame, and hating on her at the same time.

Tasha looked toward Keesha and replied with a weak, "Hey." Her words were dry. She didn't have too much kick-it for Keesha. She never had. From day one, she'd always been able to read Keesha like a book and knew she wasn't to be trusted, so she dealt with her with a long-handled spoon.

"You all right?" Keesha feigned concern. She was really just doing what she always did—picking, just to see what type of beans Tasha might spill.

Keesha may run her mouth a lot, but her words were calculated. Other people, if she gave them a chance, would just run their mouths, not even thinking what they were saying, always giving her some type of ammunition that she could eventually use against them or somebody else. A prime example is the time she was giving a female a private lap dance in the back room. The girl was straight, as in not gay, and she and her friends had just decided to come to a strip club for the fun of it. Then when her friends dared her to get a lap dance, chipping in to pay for it themselves, after a few shots, the girl gave in.

In the back room, Keesha had no problem dancing on the girl for the two songs her friends had paid for at twenty-five dollars each. The girl giggled and laughed all the way through the first song, as Keesha rubbed on her and grinded on her. Keesha knew the girl wouldn't have been down for it if she wasn't liquored. It also wasn't hard for her

to detect that the giggling was a nervous reaction. In order to take the girl's mind off things, Keesha engaged in conversation while she danced the second song.

The song wasn't even halfway over before Keesha learned that ol' girl was the bottom bitch of a young baller coming up in the game in Detroit. She ran her mouth so much about dude, Keesha got enough information on him to set him up to be robbed. So, on top of the fifty dollars she'd earned for obtaining the information, she got five Gs from the proceeds of the robbery. Knowing just how much getting a chick to run her mouth could benefit her, Keesha tried to play nice with Tasha.

But Tasha knew better and could see right through Keesha's fake-friend role. *Bitch, please,* Tasha said to herself in her head. *Your mu'-fuckin' ass is as transparent as Saran Wrap. What the fuck you want?*

Tasha continued to dress for her set, not even giving Keesha the courtesy of pretending they were friends. "Can I help you with something, Keesha?" she asked as she put on her M.A.C. cosmetics.

Although Tasha could barely afford the high-priced makeup now that she had fallen off, she still refused to wear anything less. A part of her felt shame for going back to the life of a stripper. Sweets pretty much owned her and had a price tag on her ass, and whoever had the most money could get it; but she wanted so much more in life. She felt like she was selling her soul to the devil all over again. She had been here and done all this before. Now her life had come full circle and she was back to square one.

"I was just trying to check on you, girl," Keesha said. "I know you've been kind of distant ever since you came back. I know it's probably awkward with me being the head girl in this piece, but I want you to know you can talk to me, girl. We're peoples. So if you ever need to talk to someone, just know you can always holler at me," Keesha said, piling on the sweetness.

Tasha scoffed and shook her head. "Yeah, a'ight. We're people." Tasha knew Keesha was trying to remind her that she'd taken her spot, but Keesha didn't realize the joke was on her. *There ain't no fucking way in the world I would be fucking Sweets' gay ass. Shit, at least Manolo was fine. Sweets' ass is ugly as fuck, and the nigga is a booty bandit. Dumb bitch probably don't even make the nigga strap up.* Keesha heard the sarcasm in Tasha's voice. She lowered her eyes in a disgusted gaze. "Take it however you want. I'm just letting you know I'm here. From the looks of things, you can use all the friends you can get. Ain't none of these new bitches trying to fuck with you, because you snaked Manolo, and that reputation makes them not trust you. But I've been around for a minute. I know the deal. You're a real bitch, and us real bitches got to stick together."

"Um," Tasha simply said as she sat down and oiled her toned legs. *I*

wish this bitch would keep it moving. If she thinks I'm about to fall for her fake-ass bullshit lines, she's got another thing coming.

"I know after your brother died you've been less talkative. That's fucked up how Halleigh was all up in your face, and now she's laid up with the nigga that killed your peoples," Keesha said, adding insult to injury.

Tasha cringed at the mention of Maury. She wanted to smack the shit out of Keesha for bringing it up. Tasha had gone many sleepless nights thinking of her loss and Halleigh's betrayal. Tasha felt like Halleigh was fake for choosing Malek over their friendship. She would have never chosen a dude over one of her girls. Being in the business she was in, she knew dudes were all the same, and at the end of the day, they'd choose money over bitches any day. So why should a bitch choose them over anything else?

With Keesha bringing all that back to her remembrance, she was hurting inside, but not tipping her hand to Keesha, who was still standing in her face. "I'm good on that conversation, Keesha," Tasha said. "You didn't even know my brother, so it'd be best if you wouldn't speak on that . . . ever." Tasha hoped that Keesha took the words as a threat, because she certainly meant for them to be.

"I hear you," Keesha said, putting her hands up in surrender. "My fault, Tasha. I know that's a sensitive subject, but just so you know, that bitch Halleigh is gonna get hers. Matter of fact, she's getting hers now."

Before Keesha knew it, the tables had been turned without much effort on Tasha's part, and Keesha began to run her mouth, all in the name of trying to lure Tasha to run hers.

Tasha wondered what Keesha meant by, "She's getting hers now." It didn't take her too long to figure it out, as Keesha filled her in on the details of Halleigh's whereabouts.

"Mitch got that bitch tied up in the basement as we speak." Keesha leaned in so that the two other chicks who'd just entered the room wouldn't overhear her. "I don't know what it is about this ho, but she had that nigga all googly-eyed too. I put the work in, though, and switched that nigga's train of thought real quick—Malek is the enemy, and so is his bitch. She won't be breathing long."

Keesha rambled on, thinking it was safe to speak on the situation to Tasha. After the way Halleigh had played both Tasha and her now dead brother, Keesha assumed Tasha would just as well want Halleigh to die in that basement after her disloyalty. Little did Keesha know, she couldn't have been more wrong.

Although Tasha felt played by Halleigh, the two had been through far too much together for her to just flat out wish her dead. She and Halleigh had been like sisters, and a deep-rooted bond still linked the two of them in some crazy sort of way.

Tasha's heartbeat began to speed up as Keesha spoke, but she kept

her poker face on. "Damn, that's fucked up," she said with nonchalance. "I guess karma is a bitch."

"Yes, it is. I pick up money from that spot for Mitch every day and laugh every time I see her dumb ass on them cameras."

Tasha gave Keesha a slight smile and then cut her short. "All right, girl, let me get out here and make some of this money. You know how Sweets is if we come up short."

"All right then, girl. But remember what I said—if you ever need to talk, I'm here."

Now Tasha was the one painting on the fake smile, making Keesha think she'd gotten one step closer to her world. "Thanks, girl. I really appreciate it."

Tasha thought of Halleigh tied up and hurt somewhere as she exited the dressing room. A part of her wanted to smile inside and just say, "Fuck it! That's what she gets. What goes around comes around." But the part of her that had connected with Halleigh from years of friendship wouldn't allow her to do so. Tasha couldn't help but feel guilt, knowing Halleigh was caught up in a dangerous situation. Tasha had always been protective of Halleigh, and felt as though she should do something to help her.

Chapter One Hundred Three

As Tasha received her introduction and stepped onto the stage, the thunderous applause put her mind back on her money and off Halleigh's predicament. Besides, she was no longer Halleigh's keeper, so why should she care what happened to her?

A Plies joint cranked from the DJ booth, and Tasha began to wind her body slowly. She slowly removed the fishnet cover-up she had over her skimpy two-piece neon-green thong set. With every slow wind, the two-piece appeared to be dancing in mid-air under the lights. It looked like a magic show as men became mesmerized and enthralled and money flew onto the stage.

Tasha was tempted to work the pole. She hadn't danced since she was twenty years old and didn't want to risk looking crazy, but that didn't keep her from working it out. She knew sliding down the pole would land her even more money. Dudes loved it when females did

tricks on the pole. Now twenty-six, her body was just as flawless as it had been from the beginning. Even with all the dollars flying on stage, and all the whooping and hollering going on around her by the men enjoying her set, Tasha's mind still somehow managed to drift back to Halleigh. She tried closing her eyes and continued to move her body sensually, focusing on the music that the DJ was spinning. That worked for a minute, but Halleigh's face kept popping up in her head.

She tried desperately to shake the thoughts, but she just couldn't. She could no longer hear the lyrics to the music playing, but instead heard these words dancing around in her head: *Didn't Halleigh fuck Mitch back in the day? Will he really hurt her?* Tasha was trying to convince herself that Halleigh wasn't her business. She didn't even know why she cared after the snake shit Halleigh pulled, but she had to admit, she was worried.

After hearing stories of how Mitch got down in the streets, she knew Halleigh was in danger. Mitch could be outright ruthless when it came down to it. Tasha didn't even know if there was anything she could do without getting caught up and even landing her a spot in that basement right next to Halleigh.

Tasha continued to try to convince herself not to interfere with whatever Mitch had going on. She kept going back and forth. *Why should I put my ass on the line for her? She's a fake bitch, and I'm tired of playing captain save-afuckin'-ho. Where has she been since Maury died? When I needed her, she was ghost with Malek. Nobody matters to her but him, so let his ass save her.* Just the thought of Malek all of a sudden had Tasha wondering where Malek was at, and why he'd allow Mitch to pull off something like this. *Where's her knight in shining armor when she really needs his ass?*

Tasha was so busy thinking about Halleigh and Malek, she didn't even hear her song stop. Only after the second time the DJ called out to her, finally getting her attention, did she realize her set was over.

Keesha stood at the side of the stage, tapping her foot with an attitude, waiting for her to get off the stage so she could make her paper. "So you leaving all that for me?" Keesha asked sarcastically, motioning her head to the money Tasha was leaving on the stage what the men in the club had thrown her way.

"Oh, yeah, the money," Tasha said, somewhat in a daze as she went and scooped it all up.

"I should have let her ass keep it moving," Keesha said under her breath, not knowing why she'd brought it to Tasha's attention. Keesha knew sooner or later it would have dawned on Tasha, and she would have hated to have to kick her ass over a few dollars.

When Tasha had finally scooped up all of her money and made her way off stage, she went back to the dressing room to change into an-

other outfit. She still had to work the crowd, and most importantly, the VIP. She wanted to be fresh. A stinking bitch is a broke bitch in the strip club, so she carried feminine wipes and body spray to make sure she was always on point. *He's going to kill her,* she thought as she quickly changed, still thinking about Halleigh. She leaned her head against her locker and inhaled deeply. Tasha's pride didn't want her to intervene, but her heart was all in. She tried hard to side with her mind, but her heart prevailed. "Fuck it!" Tasha said out loud to herself. "That bitch is fake, but that's the difference between me and her. I'm a real bitch, and real bitches do real things." Tasha kept up the conversation with herself while she freshened up. "If I didn't know, then it wouldn't be my fault, but I have to help her now. I can't just do nothing. Now I just have to figure out how I'm going to get her away from Mitch."

At that moment, Keesha walked into the dressing room, her skin glossed with sweat. It was obvious she had just come off stage. "The ballers are up in this piece tonight," she exclaimed. She started counting out a mound of money.

Tasha didn't reply. Her mind was on figuring out a way to get to Halleigh.

"You a'ight?" Keesha asked Tasha. "Your mind seems to be in a whole 'nother world. It must be, for you to walk off the stage and leave all your loot."

"Yeah, girl, I'm good," Tasha replied in the nicest voice she could muster up.

As real as she liked to believe she was, she knew she had to play the role of fake friend with Keesha. Keesha was her only hope, the only link to finding out exactly where Halleigh was being held hostage, and how to get to her.

"You know what?" Tasha said in a perky voice. "It has been a rough day, but I need to get my mind right and go make this money. Hurry up and change, so we can work these niggas in VIP."

Tasha was no longer in bitch mode. She was in pimp mode. Working underneath Manolo for all of those years, she had learned a thing or two. Keesha had met her match. Tasha, about to pimp the information she needed out of Keesha like a pro, all of a sudden was best girlfriends with Keesha.

"Girl, you ain't said nothing but a word," Keesha said. "Let's go!" Keesha knew that Tasha would eventually come around and learn to accept that she was now top dog. Like the saying goes, if you can't beat 'em, join 'em. She was glad that Tasha realized the real and decided to climb on board. Keesha had no problem with Tasha's sudden change in attitude.

The two women exited the locker room. Tasha led the way to VIP,

dudes grabbing at her left and right along the way, trying to buy her a drink. Ordinarily, Tasha might have stopped and let a dude buy her a drink or two, considering she made even more money off the drinks. Whenever the dudes bought the girls a drink, the cost of the drink was split with the bar 60/40 in the dancer's favor. The drinks for the dancers started at a ten-dollar minimum.

Tasha was headed straight to where the ballers played. They would go deep, with their drink minimum starting at one hundred dollars. With VIP full, she wasn't looking for a nigga with shallow pockets. Not for her own sake this time, but surprisingly, for Halleigh. Tasha needed someone that could bait Keesha without hesitation. Money definitely couldn't be an object for that someone, which was sure to grab Keesha hook, line, and sinker. She knew Keesha needed to do the pickup for Mitch and Sweets, but if everything went as planned, Keesha would hand the job off to her and try to make a couple dollars out of one of the club's patrons.

Tasha knew that she had to attract the guy because Keesha wasn't "snag-a-hustler" material. Her body was nice, but came a dime a dozen in the hood. Her face was cute, but her nose was big as hell. She definitely wasn't model material. She was what one would call average. Nothing about her was extraordinary. Most girls with average faces made up for it with humongous assets like big butts, or nice breasts, but Keesha was lacking in both departments.

Tasha had to give the girl credit. She got her share of dudes. Tasha knew Keesha's appeal had a lot to do with the rumors that she would do it anytime, anyplace, anyhow—for the right price, of course. She had the same tag line as Burger King; the dudes could have it their way with her.

Upon arriving in VIP, Tasha quickly spotted her "vic" in the crowd. Actually, he spotted her, grabbing her by the waist as she walked by, catching his finger in her thong.

Tasha slapped his hands away playfully. "You've got to pay to play this game, baby, but it's the best ride you'll ever get. Worth every cent," Tasha said, Keesha right beside her.

Tasha didn't have to worry about Keesha jacking her game, because there wasn't a bitch alive that could game a nigga like she could. Her swag came from years of practice. She had been got by many a nigga before she flipped the roles and started getting them. When she first got in the game, dudes used to basically throw at whatever they felt like to her, because they could tell she was fresh meat. That didn't last long. She quickly wised up, and started taking dudes for everything they and their wives had. It was her suaveness, loyalty, and dedication that convinced Manolo that she should be top dog, pulling her from working the streets to being in charge of the other girls.

That was back then and this was now. Even so, Tasha was seasoned through and through, a thorough broad who didn't have to try too hard to get what she wanted. Her sex appeal was natural; she never had to force anyone's hand. Niggas flocked to her like flies flocked to shit, and it was all because of her confidence.

Tasha could be standing next to Buffie the Body, Melyssa Ford, or any other industry chick, and intimidation would still be foreign to her. If she wasn't the baddest bitch in the room when she entered, by the time she exited, everyone would know her name. It was all about her aura, the way she carried herself, and her confidence level—the make-up of a true diva.

She was always on top, and another chick could never outshine her. Tasha was wifey material on the outside. God had blessed her when he had molded her. But nobody was perfect, and she had her flaws about her. Flint was small, and her promiscuous past had tainted her. Even though Tasha may have appeared to be wifey material on the outside, no man wanted to turn a ho into a housewife. As notorious as a Manolo Mami might have been, in good old-fashioned street terms, she was still considered a ho. So instead of being wifey, she was always the side chick that niggas came to when they needed some relief from the nagging ways of their main squeeze.

Tasha resented the choices she'd made in her life. She wished she could have turned back the hands of time to the beginning of her adolescence, the time when her life got crazy and she'd slipped into the clutches of Manolo. She couldn't blame it all on Manolo, though. Even though he was her pimp, he had her head because she allowed him to have it. She had always been a strong, independent woman. That's why anybody who knew Tasha back in her high school days couldn't believe she was doing the things she was known for doing today.

Back in high school, Tasha ran with the popular clique, a group of chicks that was not only beautiful, but brilliant, and stayed on the honor roll. Her teachers never had a single problem with her. Co-captain of the drill team, she'd earned varsity letters for drill team competitions. She knew she was all that, and never needed anyone to tell her, especially a man. That is why she, herself, couldn't believe she was in the predicament she was in today, turning tricks for the VIP in a strip club.

"Yo, ma, money ain't a thing," the dude in VIP told Tasha. "I got it to spend, if it's worth it. I'm trying to see you tonight after everything settle down," he said, looking her up and down and licking his lips. "What's your name?"

Same line, different nigga. Tasha tried her best not to seem bored with his lame ass. "Tasha," she replied as she leaned in to whisper in

his ear in her attempt to be heard over the music. "And this is my girl, Keesha." Tasha motioned her head to Keesha, who smiled and winked her eye in what she thought was a sexy gesture. *Lame-ass bitch deserves this lame-ass nigga,* Tasha thought. *Leave the winks to the movie stars.*

"You and your girl trying to grab a room or something after this?" he asked.

"I don't even know your name, and you already asking to slide out after the club lets out?" Tasha answered with an infectious smile as Keesha played the back. "Can I at least get a name? And don't give me no nicknames. I want what's printed on your driver's license."

The handsome, thuggish guy in front of her replied, "Lamont."

"Nice to meet you, hon," Tasha said as she extended her hand.

Lamont had to laugh to himself as he accepted Tasha's hand inside of his and shook it. He usually didn't have no kick-it for strippers. They were there to do a job and help him to relax, but he found himself enjoying this back-and-forth banter with Tasha, who could see it in his eyes, too, that she already had him lured.

"Nice to meet you too, Ms. Tasha," Lamont replied. "You and your girl want a drink or something? Have a seat and chop it up with me and my niggas." He nodded toward his boys he was up in there with.

Tasha and Keesha shot them some smiles and head nods.

Lamont then went into his pocket and pulled out a wad of cash. He peeled off four hundred-dollar bills from his large money knot and handed two to each lady then motioned for them to sit down. Tasha sat down after stuffing the cash into her neon top, and Keesha followed suit, dollar signs flashing in her eyes.

For the next few minutes, although Tasha smiled at the gentlemen, danced seductively, and entertained effortlessly, her mind was still set on getting to Halleigh.

Tasha was still sipping on her same Sex on the Beach she'd had Lamont order for her, while Keesha was throwing back Long Islands like it was water. Tasha knew Keesha's intoxication would lead to loose lips, and would make it easier to get Halleigh's location out of her.

Keesha was overly sexual, if there was ever such a thing in a strip club, and was throwing it all in the ring to earn her keep, bouncing back and forth from one lap to another. Lamont and his friends seemed to be enjoying her show, too, because they were showering Keesha with different denominations of bills.

As the night came to a close, Lamont and his friends prepared to leave. "What's up, shorty? You and your friend rolling with us?" he asked.

"I'm down," Keesha answered quickly. "I just need to make a run real quick, though. I can meet y'all at the hotel in like an hour."

"Cool." Lamont looked Tasha's way. "What about you, Ms. Tasha? You with it or what?"

Tasha shook her head. "Nah, I'ma take a rain check. My head is bangin' right now."

Lamont sucked his teeth. "What? Off of that one little drink you babysat all night? I know your tolerance is higher than that, working in this place where your real money is in the drinks."

"Baby, I'd had my share of drinks earlier," Tasha lied, rubbing her forehead for effect. "I usually can hang better than this, but I don't know what the fuck is wrong with me tonight. I'm going to have to pass, though. Come check for me next weekend. You know where I'm at." Tasha looked to Keesha. "Keesha, you can go ahead and roll with them now if you want. I'll handle your business here at the club for you, make your run, or whatever it was you needed to do." Tasha was extra friendly, as if she and Keesha were BFF's (best friends forever), when, in actuality, if the bitch was on fire, Tasha wouldn't waste her spit to put her out.

Keesha was all game and excited to go make that paper, but she knew she had to take care of her business. "Good looking out, Tasha, but I don't know. I got to do that thing for Mitch too," she stated, hesitation in her tone.

Lamont, obviously irritated by the fact that Tasha wasn't joining them and Keesha was acting like she wasn't down with it either, said, "Look, you trying to make this paper or not? I don't got all day."

Tasha could see the wheels in Keesha's mind churning as she decided between the possibility of making all that extra money, or making the delivery. She couldn't help but smile. Her plan was coming to fruition perfectly. Just in case, she added that little extra push. "Girl, go ahead. Just tell me where I got to go, and I'll pick that up for you and take it to your boy."

After a few more seconds of consideration and that final bit of persuasion from Tasha, Keesha decided to take Tasha up on her offer and roll with Lamont. "Okay, girl, thanks. I'm not trying to miss out on this money these niggas about to throw my way." Keesha leaned in and gave Tasha two diva kisses, one on each cheek.

Here go this bitch with this ol' made-for-TV bullshit. Tasha returned the fake love with a smile. "Just text me the address to the spot, and I'll handle it," Tasha assured her. "Have fun, and call me when you get in to let me know you're safe." Tasha then pointed a finger at Lamont. "Take care of my girl."

Lamont nodded and winked at Tasha, then he and his boys slid out of the club with Keesha in the midst of them.

Chapter One Hundred Four

As soon as Tasha saw Keesha leave out of the club, she hightailed it back to the dressing room. "I've got to get to Halleigh," she whispered to herself as she threw on a pair of skintight jeans and a Dereon hoodie.

She hurriedly slipped her feet into a pair of black peep-toes and stalked out of the club. Security at the club usually walked the girls out, but Tasha was in too much of a hurry to wait on an escort. After making it safely to her car, she threw her Nike gym bag in her trunk and then got into her car. She pulled out her cell phone and checked her messages. No new text or voice messages. "Come on, Keesha, send me the address," she said impatiently as she sat in the car.

After waiting another five minutes, she finally got the text. "Bing!" she said with a smile. She put her car in drive and burnt rubber out of the parking lot as she headed to the north side of Flint. As Tasha drove through Selby hood, goose bumps formed on her arms, and the hair on the back of her neck stood up. The hood was too quiet, which wasn't normal at all. It was the middle of the summer, and no one was out. Even the streetlights were blown out, and the banging of dudes flossing their subwoofers was non-existent. The hood wasn't the only thing on Tasha's mind right now. She couldn't help but wonder how many of Mitch's goons were guarding Halleigh?

Why am I even putting myself out here for this girl? For a minute she wanted to turn the car around and hit the I-75, headed back to the South Side, where she was most comfortable, but she didn't.

After a few minutes, she located the house address that Keesha had texted her, and put her game face on. Although her insides were twisted in knots and her guts were like liquid fire, on the outside she was cool, calm, and collected. After taking a deep breath, Tasha got out of the car and headed toward the house, her heels clicking on the pavement as she made her way up the driveway.

In the text, Keesha had instructed her to use the back door, so that's exactly where she went. After opening the screen on the back door, she knocked and waited patiently for someone to answer. At first, no one came to the door, so she knocked again. When once again there was no answer, she reached for her phone to double-check the address on the text Keesha had sent her, to make sure that she was in fact at the correct house. Before she could even pull her phone out, the door swung open, and a dark-skinned guy with a fresh Caesar looked her up and down. "What's good?" He looked over Tasha's shoulder as

if he was expecting someone else to be with her. He then looked back to her and said, "You definitely ain't Keesha, ma. Who you here to see?"

"Yeah, Keesha got caught up, so Mitch sent me over here to take care of the pickup." Tasha watched the guy ogle her as he puffed the blunt between his dark fingers. "What the fuck, nigga? Is you gon' let me in or what? You staring, like that's gon' get you any closer to this pussy. Come off them dollars, and we might be able to talk about something. Other than that, let's keep it moving and handle this business."

Tasha made her way into the house and moved past dude, but just as she suspected, his eyes were glued to her behind. "Where everybody at?" she asked casually after scoping out the place.

"Whose everybody, baby girl?" Dude closed the door and locked it. "It's just me and you, so let's take advantage of this opportunity." He moved up on Tasha and put his hands around her waist, a sinister smile on his face.

At first, Tasha was thinking about kneeing him right in his nuts, but then she caught a glimpse of the monitor that displayed Halleigh on the screen. Now she had a sinister smile on her face, as her plan was working out better and quicker than she expected.

There was only one thing, though. She didn't expect to see Halleigh chilling in a bed. Tasha could have sworn Keesha had told her that Mitch was holding Halleigh in a basement. *Exaggerating-ass bitch,* Tasha thought. She could have kicked herself for believing Keesha's story. For all she knew, Keesha could have been setting her up.

As Tasha observed the monitor more closely, even though Halleigh wasn't being kept in a basement, it still looked as though she was being kept against her will. From what Tasha could see, Halleigh was crying or had been crying. Her eyes looked puffy, and her hair looked as though it hadn't seen a hairdresser in days. She lay in the bed almost in a fetal position. Back in the day, Tasha might have even figured Halleigh was up in there making some money, but she knew better, since Halleigh had left the game alone when she cut up her Manolo Mami card.

The dude's hands seemed to be slipping lower down Tasha's waist and onto her butt. Most dudes knew not to touch the merchandise without making a down payment. *Fuck it, Tasha! Do what you have to do to get your girl and bounce,* Tasha thought. She then began to grind her behind into his crotch seductively.

"Don't play," he said as he continued to get blunted.

Tasha took the blunt from his lips. "*You* don't play." She hit the hydro. "You got the money?"

"Oh, it's like that? You don't want to play a little bit? You know what they say about all work and no play."

"I know what they say about all play with no pay." Tasha winked.

"I feel you, ma. I got you." He once again looked Tasha up and down, releasing her from his clutch. "But I can see you are the type of chick that likes to handle her business first."

On that note, the guy opened a kitchen cabinet and pulled out a medium-sized canvas bag full of money rolls. He handed the bag to Tasha.

Tasha inconspicuously looked at Halleigh through the monitors but didn't speak on it. She simply acted like she belonged. The dude was so distracted by her presence, he couldn't take his eyes off her and didn't even confirm that Mitch had actually sent her.

"You see something you like?" Tasha flirted.

The guy nodded lazily as he tucked his bottom lip into his mouth. He approached Tasha and didn't hesitate before covering her lips with his own. His hands roamed all over her body.

Tasha didn't usually kiss niggas in the mouth, but she went for broke. He tasted like weed, and Tasha was hoping that his being high would work to her advantage.

Tasha began to reciprocate, moving her hands along his body. She made a mental note of the gun she felt on his waistline. His hands moved with experience as he undid the button on the top of her jeans.

She allowed his hands to touch her body because she needed him to trust her. She pulled his shirt over his head and then removed his pistol. She allowed him to strip her down to her bra and panties, while she removed all of his clothing. He stood before her naked as the day he was born, confident with what he was packing. She understood why, because he was blessed in every physical way.

She caressed his manhood and licked on his neck then whispered, "Sit down, daddy. I want to ride you."

Unable to conceal his excitement, he sat down in the dining room chair.

Tasha backed away slowly, as if she was about to dance for him. "I want to dance for you, daddy. Close your eyes," she instructed.

The potential to hit a chick as tight as Tasha made the dude lose his mind. He obediently did as he was told. That was a big mistake on his part.

Tasha grabbed his gun, and in one quick motion, knocked him out with the steel. She swung twice, both times hitting him as hard as she possibly could. He fell to the floor, blood on his temple, and he wasn't moving.

Tasha moved into action. Her heart was beating out of her chest. She didn't want to yell because she was afraid to awaken the guy on

the floor. Although she knew that she should shoot him, she couldn't. She wasn't a killer. So, she prayed that he'd stay out cold long enough for her to do what she had to do.

Tasha quickly began opening up doors and looking in rooms. When none appeared to be the room she'd observed Halleigh in, she immediately ran up the stairs to the second floor. "As she made her way around the second floor, constantly looking over her shoulder, she called out quietly Halleigh!".

Halleigh thought she was dreaming when she heard a female voice call her name, so she didn't reply. But then she heard it again and shot straight up in the bed. She recognized that voice.

"Halleigh!" Tasha called out again.

"Tasha?" she answered, her voice scratchy from not talking. "Tasha, is that you? Please, I'm in here," she yelled. She went to the door and tried to open it, but it was locked from the outside. "Tasha!" Halleigh frantically began to try the doorknob. Tasha tried to open the door from her side as well, to no avail. "Damn it! Hold on, Halleigh! I've got to go get the key!"

"Tasha, no! Don't leave me here!" Halleigh screamed.

"Halleigh, I'm coming back. I can't open this door without the key. Just sit tight."

Tasha crept back down the stairs with the gun aimed, ready to fire. Her arm was like spaghetti, and her hand shook violently. She had to take a minute to breathe in order to calm down before she walked back onto the first floor. As soon as she rounded the corner, she was bum-rushed onto the floor.

"Bitch! I'ma kill your ass!" The guy smacked the taste from Tasha's mouth, causing the gun to slide across the floor.

Tasha frantically crawled to reach it, but the guy pulled her legs so hard, her face hit the floor, and she instantly felt her nose burst and tasted blood in her mouth. "Aghh!" she screamed as she swung her fists with power and connected with his chin.

This only infuriated her assailant more. He started throwing blows her way, and she saw lights every time he cracked her head. Tasha couldn't overpower him. He was too strong, and if she kept fighting back, both her and Halleigh would more than likely end up six feet under.

"Okay, stop! Please stop!" Tasha pleaded.

"Bitch on that grimy shit," the guy said to himself. He pried Tasha's legs open. "You should've just gave me this shit. Now I'ma take it."

Tasha's eyes glazed over as she was taken back to the first time she had been raped. She'd never imagined in her worst nightmare that it would happen to her all over again.

She slammed her eyes shut tightly as her attacker violated her. She

told herself that she couldn't allow this to happen to her again. So, with the last little bit of strength she could muster up, she instinctively brought her knee up and hit him in the balls as hard as she could.

"Ohh, shit!!!" he screamed in pain as he grabbed himself and rolled off her. "Fucking bitch!" he said, panting wildly.

Tasha's eyes darted around the room until she spotted the gun. She scrambled toward the gun, crawling like a snake. She was only a good three inches from the gun when her attacker quickly rebounded, once again pulling at her legs.

"Noooo!" Tasha began to scream out in fear as she kicked as hard as she could, hoping she was doing some kind of damage to the guy. She could feel her body being pulled farther and farther away from the gun. "God, please help me!" She snatched one of her ankles from his grip and turned from her stomach to her side so that her other leg twisted in his grip. With a clear shot of the perpetrator, Tasha pulled her leg up and then flushed it down into his face with all her might. The powerful blow loosened his grip from her ankle, allowing her one more chance at freedom. Managing to get up on all fours, Tasha crawled over to the gun. As soon as her hand reached the steel, she could once again feel his hands wrap around her legs. Without even thinking twice about it, Tasha brought the gun up, closed her eyes, and then pulled the trigger several times. She didn't realize it was over until she heard his body hit the floor in a loud thump. When she opened her eyes, he was lying right beside her, his eyes wide open and staring into hers.

The crimson red blood poured from a hole in the side of his neck, and he twitched while his eyes pleaded for Tasha to help him. There was nothing she could do for him now. Not that she would, even if she could. He was the enemy, and there was no telling what he would have done to her if she hadn't shot him. Still, Tasha couldn't believe the man next to her would die by her hands.

She avoided looking him in his dying eyes and began to pat his body down until she retrieved the key that would set Halleigh free. After going through both front pockets and coming up short, she finally found one single key in his left back pocket. That had to be the key she was looking for.

Gripping the key in the palm of her hand, Tasha ran up the stairs full speed and put the key in the lock. Her hands were shaking so badly, she could barely unlock the door.

"Tasha, is that you?" Halleigh asked from the other side of the door. She'd heard commotion and screams coming from downstairs as she had waited with her ear to the door for Tasha to return. She prayed the entire time that whatever was going on down those stairs, Tasha would come out on top. Right when Halleigh spoke, Tasha finally managed to unlock the door.

As it opened, Halleigh backed away, hoping her prayer was answered and that Tasha would walk through that door. When Tasha entered the room, Halleigh was standing in the middle of the room, worry and fear written on her face.

"Oh, Hal," Tasha said as she and Halleigh ran toward each other. They hugged like the long-lost sisters they were. Any animosity Tasha once held for Halleigh was out of the window. "Are you okay?"

Halleigh, flooded with relief when she saw Tasha's face, was too emotional to respond, but she nodded her head.

"We have to get out of here," Tasha said. She knew there was a possibility someone could come to the house at any moment, and she didn't want to be there if they did. She didn't want to have to kill again. She would if she had to, but if she could avoid doing so, that would be better.

She quickly wrapped her arms around Halleigh and guided her down the steps and toward the door. "Wait," she said, stopping in her tracks before they exited the house.

"Tasha? Come on, let's get out of here," Halleigh pleaded.

Tasha went and grabbed the bag of money and took the gun she'd used to kill the dude. After taking one last look at the body, she ran to the back door, helped Halleigh to the car, and then got ghost into the night.

"Tasha, I have to find Malek. He's going to kill him," Halleigh said as she rode in the passenger's seat.

Tasha shook her head in disgust. She couldn't believe the only thing on Halleigh's mind right now was that nigga Malek. She was the one who had come to her rescue, not Malek. If he was all that, how did she end up being held hostage in the first place? There had to come a time when Halleigh got over her addiction to Malek, and how Tasha saw it, the time was now.

"Halleigh, tell me one thing. You know Malek killed Maury—I know you're not stupid. I've been here for you since I've known you, and you said fuck me, to be with this nigga. When you were trapped up with Manolo, Malek never came for you. He was doing it up with Jamaica Joe while you were being pimped all over the city. You were just kidnapped behind this nigga's bullshit, I'm sure, and when I come save your ass, once again, the first thing you say is not 'thank you, Tasha,' but you on some 'save Malek' bullshit. Why?"

"Because I love him. I've always loved him. You know that, Tasha," Halleigh explained. "I know you don't understand. I don't expect you to." Halleigh stared out of the window. "But it's always about him, from the beginning, and you know that. Nothing has changed. No matter what Malek and I go through, that will never change. My life without him equals death."

Halleigh's answer floored Tasha. She had never felt love like that

before, but it was at that moment she realized Halleigh, following the same script from the very beginning, hadn't changed up on her.

Unfortunately, Tasha had opened her heart and found a dear friend in Halleigh, only to be disappointed because Halleigh's loyalty lay with Malek first and foremost. Tasha felt it was impossible for her to ever love another person on the level that Halleigh loved Malek, but it wasn't her place to judge. The only thing Tasha had was her word, which she'd kept by getting Halleigh out.

"Just get some rest, Hal. We're going to go back to my crib, so I can grab some clothes and personal things. Mitch is going to come looking for me because Keesha will tell him she sent me to the house. It's not going to take him long to figure it out. So it looks like I'm going to be on the run again." A sad disposition took over Tasha's tone. "I just wish I had Maury to run to this time."

Halleigh looked over at Tasha and rested her hand on top of hers.

"I love you, Hal, but I can't forget or forgive what Malek did to my brother," Tasha told her. "I love you, not him. I'll help you get yourself together, but after that, you're on your own. I'm getting out of town as soon as possible."

Chapter One Hundred Five

"Aghh!" Keesha screamed as Mitch slapped her with brute force, sending her head jerking to the side.

"Bitch, what the fuck were you thinking? You don't change my play. You just play your fucking position." Mitch paced back and forth in a rage. "You told this bitch where my stash spot was? Are you out of your fucking mind? Now one of my niggas is in the dirt, I'm out of a hundred grand, and Halleigh escaped!"

Keesha could see the hint of red flecks of rage behind Mitch's eyes. She cringed as he raised his hand to her once more, knowing that this ass-whupping was not going to be a short one. "Please, Mitch," she said, attempting to block one of his blows.

"Please, Mitch, my ass!" he barked as he continued his pacing.

Keesha wiped the back of her hand across her lip and looked down at the blood from her busted lip. "I'm sorry. I didn't know. I was just trying to make us some money, baby. I was doing this for you," she lied, thinking quick on her feet. She had no intention of giving Mitch a

cut from any of the money she'd made with Lamont and his boys. She screamed, "I had no idea she was going for Halleigh!"

"It doesn't matter if you knew or not! Bitch, use deductive reasoning. It's fucking common sense!" Mitch put his hands around her small neck and squeezed tightly.

Her eyes bulged as she felt Mitch threatening to end her life. He wasn't choking her, but the threat of death was fresh. He pushed her against the wall and lifted her feet off the ground a bit, applying more pressure to her fragile neck. She instinctively brought her hands up in an attempt to get out of his hold.

"Bitch, you gon' work all my fucking paper off. You no longer come and go as you like. You belong to me until further notice. Halleigh may have gotten away, but, bitch, now you gon' take her place." Mitch let Keesha go, and she fell to her knees.

"Okay, daddy, I'll work it off for you right now," she whispered desperately as she grasped at his belt buckle. She would do anything to keep her spot. If she could just put her head game on him, then his anger would lessen, but the familiar language of "bitch slap" brought her back to reality.

"Bitch, get your hands off of me and get your worthless ass out there and make my fucking money. I don't give a damn if you got to get it penny by penny. You bring it all back here. And if I have to come looking for you, then that's your ass. I won't be doing all this talking next time. I'ma dead your ass." Mitch dragged her out of the house and slammed the door in her face. "Fuck!" he screamed, knocking a lamp off his end table. He collapsed on his couch and put his head in his hands. He couldn't help but laugh to himself. Halleigh had slipped out of his clutches, and now his hold on Malek was non-existent. Both his money and Halleigh were gone. Mitch wouldn't have even been as pissed if Tasha had simply just gotten him for the bag of money. With the ransom he would have made off Malek, he wouldn't have even missed that, but now he no longer had a "marker."

Mitch pulled the .45 pistol from his waist and set it next to him. He had to be careful. Even with Halleigh gone and probably back in Malek's arms, Malek wasn't going to let this shit ride. He'd started a war when he took Halleigh, so his intentions were to put a hole in Malek's head after he handed over the money anyway. He had to stay on his A game because he'd vowed to himself that he would never be caught slipping again. Especially not by Malek.

After a few more minutes of shooting off a string of expletives to himself, hoping this was all just a nightmare, that Keesha hadn't been so stupid, and that he'd wake up from it any moment, Mitch realized that it was all too real. Deciding that he wasn't getting anywhere by sitting around thinking about the situation, Mitch got up and headed

over to his spot on Seneca Street. He needed to drop off his re-up money. He also had the money that he owed to his connect with him.

Mitch called his sister on her cell phone and let her know he was on his way. He'd always made this particular run solo, never wanting anybody to know where he kept the mother lode at.

Mitch pulled up to the small brick house and hopped out with the bag full of money. He entered the house through the back and walked in. Hearing the sounds of the running money machines, he instantly got mad. His sister was slacking. He'd instructed her to have all the money counted up a week ago.

Mitch regretted paying her beforehand. He whispered to himself, "That's why I should have paid her after she was done." He entered the room, and the smell of the purple Kush graced the air. His sister and two of her friends were wrapping the one-dollar bills into rubber bands, passing the blunt around.

"I hate these damn ones," one of the girls said.

"You scared the shit outta me!" Ree took a deep tug of the blunt.

"What the fuck is going on? I thought I told you to have the money counted up days ago?"

Ree removed the blunt from her mouth. "Damn, bro! Relax." Ree exhaled and a ring of smoke floated from between her lips as she spoke. "You had so many damn ones in this batch! If you stop letting muthufuckas break into they kids' piggy banks to pay your ass, we'd get done a lot faster."

Mitch's two cousins chuckled.

Ree wasn't about to let him blow her high with his attitude. "But don't get your boxers in a bunch," she added, brushing Mitch off. "We are almost done." She smiled.

"Well, I got some more. I need it all counted up tonight. I have to go see Fredro this weekend, and I need to know where I am as far as the count. Got it?" He walked over to her and pecked her on the cheek. When it came down to business, he stayed hard on his sister, but he loved her more than anything and would do whatever to protect her.

"Got it, bro." Ree grabbed the duffel bag from his hands.

Mitch, a whole lot on his mind, left the house, not even acknowledging his cousins.

Chapter One Hundred Six

M alek and Scratch had on black masks as they tied up the three girls who they'd caught off guard inside Mitch's stash house. The girls never saw them coming as they crept in through an unlocked window in the back of the house. For Mitch to be as strategic and on point as he was in the game, Malek had anticipated more of a challenge. He thought for sure Mitch would have his main spot on better lock than that.

Both Malek and Scratch had scoped out the house, looking for any signs of cameras or whatnot. When they didn't notice any, they almost assumed that Grady had misled them. No way would anybody of Mitch's stature, with all the money he was making, not at least have cameras. Little did they know, Mitch purposely didn't have any cameras set at his stash spot, thinking that cameras would be a dead giveaway to someone who was trying to stick him for his paper. So, he made a business decision to try to make the house appear inconspicuous, as though it was just another house in the neighborhood. Once Scratch and Malek had made their way into the unlocked window, they caught the ladies slipping with ease, engaging in the latest street gossip, smoking blunts, and counting money. Now Scratch held them at gunpoint, while Malek ran upstairs to where Grady said the money would be.

"In and out, youngblood!" Scratch yelled out to Malek, reminding him about robbing etiquette.

Scratch had schooled Malek to stay focused in a robbery. "Don't let your eyes and your mind wander onto anything else that might be of value or worth taking," Scratch had told him. "Greed is the surest way to fuck up a robbery. If you plan on knocking somebody over the head and taking their wallet, do just that. Don't get distracted by that shiny gold necklace hanging around their neck or that watch on the wrist. Take what you set out to take and keep it moving. It's always that last split second that can fuck a nigga up."

Following his own advice, Scratch stayed focused on the girls, who were trying to get out of their restraints. He told them, "Just stay calm and let us do what we came to do. Don't try screaming or anything, and it will all be over before you know it."

They did what he said, but he could tell by the look of fear in their eyes that they had doubts about making it out of the situation alive. "Look, baby girls, we ain't here to hurt nobody, so relax," Scratch coaxed the women. "I'm pretty good at tying knots, so I don't think you can wiggle yourself out of them there ropes. So just relax, baby," Scratch said smoothly, as if he weren't pointing a gun at them.

"Do you know who the fuck you robbing? Huh?" one of the girls spat, not able to keep her mouth shut, even though Scratch was standing there with a gun to her head. "You are a dead man walking. You're not even going to get a chance to enjoy that money, nigga!"

Scratch figured that was Mitch's sister, Ree. Her mouth alone was indication enough. She seemed to be the oldest of the trio and had braids straight to the back and a gold tooth in her mouth. Obviously she was ringleader of the girls, as she was the only one who decided to be hardheaded and get to running her mouth.

"And you can pull off that damn mask, *Scratch*. I know that damn walk and voice!" Ree yelled.

"Whatever you say, baby." Scratch glanced upstairs and wondered if Malek had found the money yet. "You all right up there, youngblood?"

Just as the words escaped Scratch's mouth, Malek came running down the stairs, skipping two steps at a time and carrying a duffel bag almost too full to even zip up. Bills fell out of the side of it. Scratch smiled. They had hit the jackpot.

"Yeah, I got it. Let's bounce!" Malek rushed toward the back door, followed closely by Scratch.

Scratch knew he wasn't playing the game right, being a halfway crook. The girls they were leaving tied up should have been dead, because they knew exactly who he was. Back in his day, Scratch would have smoked them without hesitation, but he couldn't bring himself to kill the young girls, so he headed out with Malek, knowing everything he'd just participated in was going to come back to haunt him, probably tenfold.

Just before Malek and Scratch reached the back door, a loud gunshot erupted, startling Malek. He looked back and saw Scratch's eyes get buck and his lips shiver.

"Scratch!" Malek said, a confused look on his face. He was no longer confused when all of a sudden he saw blood seeping through Scratch's chest.

Scratch had taken buckshots to the back, and tiny holes began to appear through the thin material of his shirt as the tiny bullet fragments tore through his insides. Scratch's face told of his excruciating pain, and he fell into Malek's arms.

Shortly after that, another shot rang out. *BOOM!*

Malek ducked and moved Scratch to the side as he went for his gun. He had no idea where the shots were coming from. For a split second he thought maybe Mitch or someone had run up into the house, but it wasn't long before he realized that the loudmouth girl had freed herself.

Ree was now blasting at him with a shotgun that had been hidden under the couch. The petite girl tried her best to hold the large firearm

and point it at Malek. She was relentless, and it was obvious she was going for blood, trying to take his head off.

Malek quickly fired two shots into the girl's abdomen, and she dropped instantly and yelled out from the burning heat of her wounds. "Aghh!" she screamed.

Malek silenced her with another shot, this time to the head. Blood began to seep out of her mouth. Malek ran over to her and kicked the shotgun away from her body. He could hear the other two girls crying in horror as they'd just witnessed their girl shot to death.

Malek looked down at the body of the dead girl and shook his head. "Why did you have to do that?" he asked her, almost in a pleading tone. Like Scratch, the last thing he wanted to do was to kill any of those girls. All he wanted was the money, and now, because of her trying to play Rambo, two people were dead.

He looked back over to Scratch, who was lying on the ground in a puddle of his own blood. Malek rushed over to his side and picked him up. "Hang in there, Scratch. I'm going to get you to a hospital. Everything's going to be all right."

Malek knew he was telling Scratch a lie, giving him false hope, but he couldn't bring himself to tell him he would never make it. Nor could he just leave him there to die without even trying to get him help, not as long as he still had life in him. Scratch had become more than an accomplice in all of the madness. He was a friend who loved Halleigh.Because of that, Malek would always have endearment in his heart for Scratch.

Before Malek could even carry Scratch to the door, Scratch began to choke on his own blood, and his body began to tremble. Although dying, he still managed to unleash his infamous smile.

Scratch stared into Malek's eyes. "Youn-youngblood, I haven't felt this alive in years. You made this old man feel young again." Scratch, his life slipping away, took a swallow of his own blood and gripped Malek's arm. "You made Scratch feel important. Didn't even look down on me. You let me ride shotgun with you, baby boy . . . like a gangster, ya know. I haven't ridden in a front seat of a car in years," Scratch said reflecting on his life as a junkie. "I was yo potna." Scratch gasped and then began to shake even more. He still continued to smile, though he knew his life was ending. He could feel his body temperature dropping as a cold chill took over his body. Not even Malek's words could give him any hope now.

"Yeah, that's right, Scratch. You my mu'fuckin' partner." Malek's eyes began to water, but no tears fell. It was hard to look at Scratch dying, but he tried to remain strong.

Scratch said in almost a whisper, "Go get my baby girl and get her home safe. Hear me? Tell her that I'm sorry for everything and that I

never got a chance to tell her, but . . . I'm . . ." Then his voice trailed off.

"I'ma get her, Scratch. Just stop talking, man. Save your energy." Malek nodded his head up and down.

Malek felt Scratch release his grip and watched the old man take his last breath then look away aimlessly. Malek shook Scratch and called his name, but it was too late. He was gone. Malek closed Scratch's eyes and whispered, "I'll tell her how much you loved her, fam. I'll tell her how much you helped." With those last words, Malek kneeled down and laid Scratch's lifeless body on the ground and folded his arms over his chest.

Malek rose to his feet and left, leaving the other two girls tied up and alive. The same thoughts Scratch himself had had just moments ago about knowing better than leaving eyewitnesses alive crossed Malek's mind as he headed out. Too many people had already been hurt behind the bullshit, and Malek wasn't going to contribute to the death of yet another individual, unless it was Mitch or anyone standing beside him. The two girls' lives he would spare.

Making his way back to his ride, Malek knew he needed to go somewhere and get his head together. Plus, he would have to change his clothes to avoid suspicion, because he was covered in blood. He stopped at Hallwood Plaza and went into Champs to get himself some sweat pants, a clean T-shirt, and a hoodie. He then headed across town to check into a nearby hotel. He needed to get his head together and calm himself before he went to see Mitch. With or without the half-million dollars, he was going to get Halleigh.

Chapter One Hundred Seven

Tasha sat on the hotel bed counting the money she had taken from the stash spot, while Halleigh took a shower behind the closed bathroom door. They had agreed to split the money down the middle, so that each of them could have a chance at making an exit out of the city. Tasha figured that she was entitled to that little bit of extra paper for putting her ass on the line to help Halleigh in the first place. She hurriedly stashed a stack of bills into her bag before Halleigh got out.

When she heard the shower stop she zipped up the duffel bag and

sat across the room from it. Halleigh came out of the bathroom, her body wrapped in a towel. Tasha put her hand on her mouth as she looked at Halleigh's pregnant stomach. She was still small, but her slightly protruding stomach was a clear indication that she was with child. Tasha gave Halleigh a half-smile. "Wow, you're really about to be somebody's mother, huh?"

"Yeah, I know, right?" Halleigh replied with a slight laugh. "I still can't believe it myself." She looked down at her stomach. "I don't do that well taking care of me. How in the hell am I going to take care of a baby?"

Though Halleigh tried to make light of the situation, Tasha knew her concern was real. Tasha was skeptical of Halleigh's mothering skills because she knew how truly weak Halleigh was without Malek. Never the type of woman to go out and accomplish things on her own, Halleigh had always depended on someone else. It was almost like she had banked on being Malek's NBA trophy wife. When those dreams fell through, she was left on stuck. She went from depending on Malek to Manolo to Mimi to finally depending on Tasha. It was a never-ending cycle of bullshit. Tasha couldn't believe that after all these years, after all Halleigh had been through, she still wasn't self-sufficient or independent. Tasha shook her head in disbelief and sent a quick prayer up to God for Halleigh's child.

With a soft-ass father like Malek and a lost soul like Halleigh for a mother, that baby is going to be all fucked in the game, she thought. "Are you ready for all of that?" Tasha asked.

"Is anybody? I know I'm young, but I can't see myself not having this baby. Malek and I are always drifting in and out of each other's lives. This was one thing that fate couldn't change. I'll always have a piece of him with me through this baby. This baby is Malek and me. I'm scared as hell, but I know it's going to be worth it."

"Are you sure, Halleigh?" Tasha asked again, just for good measure.

"Yeah, I said I'm sure!" Halleigh screamed back, becoming agitated by Tasha's doubt.

"Okay, okay." Tasha could see that her line of questioning was getting to Halleigh, so she changed the subject. "Are you okay? You might want to go to the hospital to make sure your baby is okay. Did they do anything to you?"

"I'm fine, Tasha. Mitch brought a doctor over to check on me and make sure I was okay. Right now I'm just trying to find Malek. I have to get to him before something bad happens. I just have a gut feeling that something isn't right with him. I tried to call him three times when we first got here, but his phone went straight to voicemail," she said in a worried tone. "Have you heard anything? I mean, you must have heard something. How did you know where to find me, or that I was even being held hostage in the first place?"

"I haven't heard anything. I haven't really been in the mix like that either. I knew about what happened to you because Keesha was at the club putting your shit all out in the streets, bragging about how Mitch had taken you."

"The club? What were you doing at the club?"

Tasha didn't speak. She just put her head down, ashamed that her life seemed to be a never-ending cycle of bullshit too. Seemed as though both Halleigh and her had come full circle.

"You're back at the club?" Halleigh asked, surprised, reading the expression on Tasha's face. That was the last place she expected Tasha to return to, and the one place Tasha had vowed she never would. *But, hey, shit happens. Life happens.*

"What? Everybody can't live the high life like you and Malek, Halleigh! Any chance I had of being happy Malek took away from me when he killed my brother. Just like he is all you have, Maury was all I had. So, yeah, I'm back at the club." Tasha shook her head in disgust. "Damn it, Halleigh! You have no idea. You live in this shallow little Malek bubble. You need to wake up. That boy ain't a fucking saint. You and him sit up on a high horse and look down on the rest of the city like you're gods. That's why Mitch took you, Halleigh, because of him. That's why he is in so much shit."

"I don't care what he did to anybody else. I only know how he treats me. I have to find him." Halleigh rubbed her stomach. "For both of us."

Halleigh could hardly sleep. The next day, she was going to go back to their home, even though Tasha didn't think it was a good idea. Halleigh couldn't wait. All that night, she lay restlessly as she thought of Malek, praying over and over in her head, *God, please keep him safe.*

Halleigh didn't know if Mitch's threats were real, but she wouldn't put anything past him. One minute he was talking sweet in her ear, all the while disrespecting Malek, who was supposedly his business partner and friend. The next minute, he was snatching her from her peaceful home and turning her world upside down. She knew that the only person she could ever trust one hundred percent was Malek. Not even her own mother had been worthy of it or had earned it. She knew Sharina was the real problem in it all. She had started a cycle of hurt and pain for Halleigh.

Halleigh desperately wanted off the roller-coaster ride of violence and drama, but there seemed to be no way out. Tears came to her eyes as she thought of her predicament. Everything she had done in her past was now affecting her present and would undoubtedly affect her future.

I'm a fucking mess, she thought. *My life is like a bad soap opera.*

Her silent tears transformed to audible anguish. She hoped that Tasha was asleep and couldn't hear her muffled cries.

Halleigh knew that Tasha disliked Malek, and as bad as she wished she could repair her and Tasha's friendship, as long as she stayed focused on Malek, that wouldn't happen. Still, Halleigh had to make the effort. Tasha had saved her, after all. Halleigh really did have love for Tasha, who had helped her through so many hard times, although frankly, those were times she'd rather forget. She couldn't change the circumstances under which they met. *She was Manolo's bottom bitch. Her job was to keep me there,* Halleigh thought. She couldn't help but think that if Mimi and Tasha had been up front with her in the first place about what she was getting herself into when they took her in, she would have never chosen to stay with Manolo and gotten sucked into his web of manipulation and fear. There was no doubt in Halleigh's mind that she and Tasha would have never crossed paths if she had never gotten caught up in the streets. Over the years, Halleigh had become a product of the hood, but deep down on the inside, she wasn't built like Tasha. They were not the same type of women, never had been, and Halleigh was just now realizing that. *What type of woman would want to see another woman go through what I did? Was she ever really my friend? Yeah, she helped me kick heroin, but she was one of the many reasons why I felt like I needed the drug in the first place. Tash is my girl, but Malek is my man. He has never done me dirty. He's overlooked all of my flaws just to be with me, and he doesn't look down on me. He's the only person I've ever cared about that hasn't disappointed me, so if I have to make the choice, it will always be him.*

Chapter One Hundred Eight

Malek sat in his hotel room and counted the money, which was scattered all over the bed. He looked at his bloodstained clothes and kept seeing visions of Scratch struggling for his life just before taking his last breath. Scratch had courage although he was older and an ex-fiend. Malek respected and admired Scratch's heart. He was loyal to Halleigh and the reason Malek had gotten enough money to get his woman back from Mitch.

Once Malek finished counting, he realized he'd gotten just over what he owed for the ransom. He loaded up the big duffel bag with a half-million dollars and headed to see Mitch. Something in his stomach told him things were going to end badly for everyone involved. There didn't seem to be a winner in any of it. At the end, even if he got Halleigh back and was left standing, he would still be in trouble. It seemed like he was going from one problem to the next without any resolution. He exited the room with the money and headed over to Mitch's trap spot to make the switch, exhaustion plaguing his body and mind. He tried to push the thought out of his mind that Mitch, after realizing he'd been involved in the robbery of his stash spot and the murder of his sister, would retaliate by killing Halleigh.

As Malek drove through the city streets, his mind was not on vengeance, but it was on his entire life's struggles. Feeling defeated, he took a deep breath and hoped to God Mitch hadn't got wind of the robberies. He had to move quickly and get Halleigh before Mitch found out.

Once he arrived at his destination, he hopped out of his car, duffel bags full of money in hand. He approached the trap house that Mitch told him he would be at. As Malek approached the row house, he took a deep breath. Two young guns who once worked under Malek stood guard at the door. They couldn't have been any older than fifteen or sixteen.

They couldn't even look him in the eyes. They just looked past him and opened the door for him to enter. Malek looked at each boy in the face and made sure they felt his animosity. If they ever crossed paths again under any circumstances, he couldn't be held responsible for his actions.

Malek slid past them and entered the house, which was full of hustlers. It seemed like Mitch had called all of Flint in to witness the drop-off. Once again, Mitch was determined to prove to everybody that he was the boss. Malek's showing up let Mitch know that he had no idea Halleigh had escaped. Now he really felt on top of the world. Mitch wanted the whole organization to see Malek broke-down. He smiled as he saw Malek enter. "Check him," Mitch ordered as he stood from the table he was sitting at.

Three henchmen ran up on Malek and began to search him. Malek clenched his jaw as he lifted his arms, the bag still clutched tightly in his hands.

"He's clean," one of the men said as they walked away from him.

"You got my money?" Mitch gave Malek a menacing smile.

"Yeah, I got it," Malek said aloud, but in his mind he thought, *I got your money literally, nigga.* He dropped the bag and kicked it toward

Mitch. "It's all there. Now, where is Halleigh?" Malek demanded through his clenched teeth.

Mitch unzipped the bag and flipped through the money. "Damn, my nigga! You actually got the money, huh—a fucking half a million dollars in just a few days. You must really love that bitch."

Malek wanted to lunge at Mitch for the disrespectful comment, but he had to hold his tongue and keep his cool, at least until he had Halleigh back in his possession. After that there was no telling. The joke would be on Mitch anyway, once he found out he was getting paid with his own money. He took a couple of deep breaths. "Where is Halleigh?"

Mitch remained silent as he flipped through the money and took his time before answering Malek. "Where is Halleigh?" Mitch asked himself out loud, trying to be sarcastic. "She might be at a spot on the South Side, or maybe she's inside one of my spots in the projects." Mitch lit a cigar filled with weed.

Malek's fist involuntarily balled up, and he was heaving, his chest going up and down. His temperature was rising, and he wouldn't be able to contain himself much longer. Mitch was trying to play him, and he didn't have the patience to play games, not after all he'd been through.

"Look at this nigga . . . about to cry like a little bitch!" Mitch said.

The whole room burst into laughter at the comment, except for Malek, Halleigh's safety being the only thing on his mind at that point.

Laugh now, cry later, Malek thought as he anticipated getting his girl back and then going after Mitch for revenge. He hated leaving his gun inside his car, but he knew Mitch's boys would have patted him down and taken it from him.

Mitch walked over to Malek and stood eye to eye with him. He was so close, their toes were touching. It was an intense, silent moment as the two men stared each other down. What had once been love between brothers was now hatred. Mitch's jealousy had led them to this point. Neither of them had any sign of retreat in their eyes.

Mitch was the first to move. He pulled out an all-black .45 and raised it to Malek's face. "Open yo mouth," he ordered and then rested the barrel on Malek's lips.

Malek tightened his lips, looking Mitch in the eyes.

"If you want to see Halleigh again, you should do as I ask. Now, let me try this again. Open yo mouth!" Mitch yelled.

Malek's pride was diminishing by the second, but the shame was worth Halleigh's life. He reluctantly opened his mouth.

Mitch jammed his gun inside. "I'ma only say this once—Flint is mine! I advise you get as far away from here as you can. You are dead in Flint. Dead! Jamaica Joe is not here to watch over your soft ass any-

more; remember that. I can touch anybody in this mu'fuckin' city; believe that. Now, get the fuck out of my face!" Mitch struck Malek in the temple with the butt of his gun.

Malek dropped to one knee and cradled his throbbing face, blood trickling down.

Mitch stood over him smiling. He loved seeing Malek on his knees; it was pure satisfaction for him. He tossed a piece of paper at him with the address Halleigh was being held at, as if to say, "Go fetch," even though Halleigh was no longer there. In fact, he was surprised that Malek showed up at all. He was sure the first thing Halleigh would have done was find her way back to him, but since she didn't, he decided to have a little fun. He was sending Malek on a wild goose chase, just for the hell of it.

He can find the bitch on his own time, but he can still pay me this paper for his disrespect. Mitch truly had the big head regarding his reign. He was the king of the city, and every man in the city needed to respect it.

Malek picked up the paper and hurried out, maneuvering through Mitch's goons to get out the door. He just wanted to go get his woman. He prayed to God that she was alive and well at the given location. He would deal with his beef with Mitch later, because he knew just as soon as Mitch discovered the real, it was gonna be war for real. All this other stuff would be a chick fight compared to what would go down between the two. When Malek finally got to the house, he didn't know what to expect on the inside, All he knew was, he wasn't leaving without Halleigh. He kicked in the front door, and the sound of cracking wood echoed throughout the stash house. He peeked inside the house, his gun in hand, and saw a man shot dead lying on the ground. The living room was in shambles, with overturned furniture and glass from shattered lamps everywhere. Even the TV had been knocked out of the entertainment case. It was obvious that there had been a struggle. His first thought was the struggle involved Halleigh. He just hoped to God she'd been victorious, and was thankful it wasn't her body lying there dead.

Malek immediately panicked. Scanning the room, he noticed the small monitor that displayed another area of the house. He stepped over the man and rushed to the monitor. He examined the screen and saw an empty room with a bed inside. The window had bars on it, and the sheets on the bed were wrinkled. He ran through the house calling out Halleigh's name, desperation evident in his voice.

"Halleigh! Halleigh! Where are you?" he repeated loudly as he continued to rummage through the house. He reached the basement where he immediately shot off the lock, opened the door, looked around and saw nothing. His eyes focused on the bloodstained mattress, and his heart dropped at the sight. He fell to his knees and as-

sumed the worst. "Halleigh!" he yelled as tears began to pour down his face. A hollow feeling in his chest overcame him as he crawled over to the bed. He knew that was Halleigh's blood. He cried his eyes out as he thought about his woman and unborn child.

His sadness quickly became fury toward Mitch. "Muthafucka!" he yelled. He stood up and began punching the air as if he was punching Mitch in the face. "Son of a bitch knew Halleigh wasn't here and did this to torture me. He killed my baby." Malek broke down again, dropping to his knees on the mattress.

After a couple of minutes, he stood to his feet and, almost in a daze, walked up stairs, his head hanging low. He was a man possessed, and the only thing on his mind was murder. He was going to make any and everybody involved pay. As a matter of fact, he didn't care if they weren't involved. Anybody who had anything to do with Mitch or Sweets was as good as dead, just like his family.

Knowing the drug game, he was sure Halleigh was in the trunk of somebody's car, or in a dumpster somewhere. Every time he thought about her lying dead, it was like a dart to the heart. *This nigga made me go through all of this. He made me do all of this when he knew he was going to kill her. I should've known. I should've protected her.*

He slowly walked up the stairs. The first sight he saw was the man lying on the floor. Out of anger, he loaded another bullet in his body for good measure. As tears rolled down his cheek, he exited the stash house on a path of revenge.

Chapter One Hundred Nine

M itch couldn't believe the news he had just received as he spoke on his cell phone with his cousin, one of the two girls Malek and Scratch had left breathing. He yelled to his goons as he held the cell phone up to his ear, "Everybody get the fuck out!" He watched as everyone exited the house. No one asked what was wrong, knowing what was best for them. He took a deep breath and placed his phone back to his ear. After swallowing hard and trying to maintain his composure, he said into the phone, "What the fuck you mean? She can't be dead," he said, his voice cracking slightly.

She was telling him that his sister Ree was shot dead by a robber, and that one of the robbers was also lying dead in the house.

"I didn't recognize either one of them," she cried. "But I heard Ree say something about recognizing his voice and calling him *Scratch*, *Itch*, or something like that. The other one got away, right after he shot Ree." At that moment, Mitch knew exactly who the robber that got away was. Malek was responsible for his sister's death.

Just then, something else dawned on Mitch. He looked down at the duffel bag full of bills and realized that he had been paid with his own drug money. "Fuck!" he yelled as he hurled the bag to the floor in frustration. Here he was laughing at Malek, when in actuality Malek was having the last laugh.

Mitch closed his cell phone without saying another word. Tears streaming down his face, he picked up the bag and headed out the back door to where he always parked his car.

On his way out he called his other sister, who was in their hometown of Saginaw, to break the awful news to her. His sister Toy, Ree's twin, was in a league of her own. You couldn't mention her name if murder wasn't in the same sentence. Mitch was distraught as he waited for his only remaining sister to pick up the line. When she didn't answer, he flipped down his phone and rushed to the car, so he could head to his house.

Mitch was sick to his stomach, and his hands shook violently. His sister had been his responsibility, and because of his resentment toward Malek, she had been murdered. He never in a million years wanted her to get caught in the crossfire of his and Malek's beef. He imagined that's how Malek felt about Halleigh, but at least Halleigh was still alive. *How did he even know where my stash house was?* Mitch asked himself. *I was careful. I know I was careful. When I find out who let that shit out of their mouths, it's a wrap.*

His emotions, an equal blend of grief mixed with hate for Malek, were getting the better of him. He instantly regretted letting Halleigh and Malek live, and wished that he'd put a bullet in Malek's head when he dropped the money off.

Mitch was so busy putting his phone away, he didn't see Malek creeping from around his car with a gun. Before Mitch could even react, he was staring down the barrel of Malek's pistol.

Mitch had no fear, because Malek was just the person he wanted to see. Tears still on his face, he dropped the bag and intensely stared at Malek.

"Where in the fuck is Halleigh?" Malek asked.

Mitch smiled sadistically. "I sent her to the same place you sent my sister, mu'fucka!" he lied. He knew his words would incite retaliation from Malek, but at that point, Mitch didn't care. The only thing he knew was, his sister was dead, and Malek was the cause of it.

Malek pulled back the hammer on his gun. "We had a deal, you dirty mu'fucka."

"You killed my own flesh and blood. Your bitch is dead. Did you think I could let your people live after what you did to mine, you stupid muthafucka? Did you think I was gon' let your bitch live, with you trying to pay me her ransom with my own fuckin' money?"

Mitch knew that his words weren't true, but it was obvious that Malek didn't know that. He said it just to get under his skin. It was his only way to get a little bit of revenge before he went out. There was no turning back. Too much had gone down between the two of them. Someone had to die. From the looks of the scene at hand, Malek had the upper hand, so Mitch knew his seconds were numbered.

"You were supposed to be my nigga. I put you on."

Mitch responded with a smirk. He hawked up some spit and sprayed it right in the direction of Malek's face.

Malek immediately moved his head to the side, just missing the mouthful of mucus.

Mitch then reached for his gun on his waistline, but before he could even grip his pistol, Malek fired three rounds into his chest.

With Mitch confirming that Halleigh was dead a sadness Malek had never felt overtook him. As the bullets left Malek's gun, it was like therapy for him. He was tasting a full serving of revenge. He watched as Mitch's body fell to the ground and blood poured out of his chest, painting his shirt crimson. Malek stood over him and fired three more rounds, rocking him to sleep forever.

When Malek heard the distant voices of Mitch's goons as they came running from the front of the building, he grabbed the bag full of money and hurried over the fence onto the next block, where his car was parked.

Chapter One Hundred Ten

Halleigh and Tasha sat in the motel room, uncomfortable with each other's presence. There was a lot of tension between the pair of old friends, and there seemed to be a huge elephant in the room. Halleigh couldn't help but wonder why Tasha had come for her at all, if that's the way she truly felt about her. After reuniting with Malek and turning her back on her, Halleigh was surprised that Tasha was willing to put her life on the line for her.

"Thank you, Tasha," Halleigh said. "I really appreciate what you did for me. I thought I was going to die in there."

Tasha didn't respond. In her eyes, Halleigh's gratitude was long overdue. She remained silent while Halleigh continued to speak.

"I'm sorry, Tasha, for deserting you when you needed me most. I'm sorry about what happened to Maury." Halleigh genuinely was sorry about Maury's fate. Just as it was with everyone else in Halleigh's life, it seemed Malek was the only thing that stood between her and Maury eventually getting even closer.

"You just won't admit that Malek killed him, will you?" Tasha asked, emotion in her voice. "The man you love killed my brother, Hal. How am I supposed to know you didn't help set that shit up? I trusted you. I loved you like a sister, girl." Tasha looked Halleigh in her eyes. "And even more so, Maury loved you. I can only imagine how you treat people who don't give a shit about you."

"Tasha, I'm not going to lie to you. I had a lot of love for Maury. He made me feel special after Manolo had stomped me into the dirt and had my self-esteem at an all-time low. Maybe in another lifetime we could have had something good, but I couldn't fully invest in him, Tash, because Malek had the keys to my heart. Maury was a good guy, Tasha, and I feel so bad about what happened to him. I've never asked Malek about what happened that night, because a part of me doesn't want to know. I can, though, tell you that I didn't have anything to do with it." Halleigh paused for a moment in an attempt to try to read Tasha.

When Tasha gave her nothing, she went on. "Don't you find it a little ironic that Mimi died that same night? That was my girl too, and I loved her, but you know she was grimy. Did you ever think for one moment that whatever went down she might have had something to do with it and not me? I cared about your brother, and I love Malek, even if he is the man that killed him."

"That's fucked up." Tasha shook her head from side to side, unable to accept a half-ass apology. "You were my girl, Hal. Then you just forgot about me."

"Is that what you think? That I forgot about you?" Halleigh let out a chuckle. "You were the sister I never had. I love you so much, Tasha, and I am so thankful to have had you when I was going through all of the bullshit, but think about it. It's hard to get your man to understand that you used to be a ho. I used to trick myself out to some of the same niggas that be in Malek's face, Tasha. Think about how that makes my man feel. He doesn't have anything against you personally, but he didn't want me around the bullshit anymore. To tell you the truth, I didn't want to remember that life. I was running from it too."

"If you forget your past, you are bound to repeat it, Halleigh. I can understand where you coming from, but if I was on the same fake shit as you, then I would have left you in that house and never looked

back. I guess me and you are just two different types of people. If you're my girl, then that's it. There ain't a nigga in the world that can pull me away from you. I'm loyal, but that's not something that everybody respects. It's cool, though. I'm not tripping on it. Now I just know where we stand."

"Tasha, we will always have each other to lean on. You know if you ever really needed something and I had it, I would give it to you in a heartbeat," Halleigh said with a slight smile.

Tasha nodded and wiped a lone tear away. She knew Halleigh well enough to know she was being sincere and meant every word she was speaking. "Same here, Hal," Tasha said. "Just so you know . . . I forgive you."

"Thank you. That really means a lot to me," Halleigh replied and then initiated a hug between the two.

"Okay, enough of that mushy stuff," Tasha said, breaking contact. "Have you heard anything from Malek yet?"

"No, I keep leaving him messages. Every time I call, it goes straight to voicemail. I've left him like ten messages. I left him a message on his voicemail telling him where we're at, but he just won't call me back. I'm so worried about him. I don't know what I will do if something happens to him. I'm about to have his baby. I can't survive without him."

"You better learn how to, Halleigh, because even if he lives through this shit right here, in the lifestyle he's living, there will be other times like this. You've got to think about your baby. Even if you do it alone, you've got to do it. You already knew this was one of the consequences of dating someone in the game."

"But that's just the thing," Halleigh said. "He's not in the game anymore. He got out."

Tasha let out a laugh. "That's what they all say, Hal, that's what they all say. Even so, tomorrow ain't promised to no man. You still need to learn how to be independent and do things on your own."

"I don't know if I can."

Tasha could see that her words were getting to Halleigh, so she turned on the TV to change the mood. Even though she did not believe what she was about to say, she let the words come out of her mouth anyway. "Malek is a trooper, so you know he's all right, girl. We just have to find him, so he can get you out of town. Everything is going to be all right." Tasha scooted toward Halleigh and comforted her. She didn't want her to suffer alone.

"I know, I know. That's what I want to believe, Tasha, but something isn't"—Halleigh stopped mid-sentence as she saw a picture of Malek on the eleven o'clock news. "Tasha, turn that up."

Tasha obliged, and they listened to the news reporter.

"Former Flint Central High School basketball star was involved in a bank robbery. Here is a clip of him, along with another unidentified man, robbing Chase Bank and First National Bank early yesterday morning. Flint police officer, Robert Snell, was killed at the scene, and this incident has the entire police department on a manhunt. Police have yet to release any further details about the robbery, but surveillance video has confirmed the identity of one of the robbers as Malek Johnson. This is not Mr. Johnson's first time being involved in armed robbery. A few years ago he was charged and arrested for holding up a corner convenience store just months before he was expected to be drafted into the NBA. Authorities do not want the community to underestimate this suspect. He is armed and dangerous.l If you see this man, you should call the police department immediately. If you have any idea of the whereabouts of these men, please call 1-800-CRIMESTOPPERS. This is Anari Simpson, signing off from Channel Seven News."

Halleigh's mouth practically hit the floor when she saw a picture of her man on the screen. They had used an old high-school picture and put his face on prime-time TV. Halleigh knew that somehow, just like last time, she was the cause of his extreme measure. She could just feel it that her being held in that basement had something to do with Malek robbing those banks. Tears began to fall as she put her hands on her mouth and remained silent.

Tasha was also shocked as she looked along with her. Tasha didn't think that Malek had it in him to stick up a bank, let alone two. Obviously she was wrong. She had thought all of his balls came from the backing of Jamaica Joe.

I guess he's got a little bit of gangster in him after all, Tasha thought as she sat in shock.

Halleigh began to hyperventilate and was becoming short-winded.

Tasha placed her hand on Halleigh's back, trying to help her. "Are you okay?"

"I just need some cold water," Halleigh said as she placed her hand on her chest.

Tasha jumped up and ran into the bathroom to run Halleigh some water. "It's not getting that cold." She opened the door and went to the ice machine outside, leaving Halleigh in the room alone.

Chapter One Hundred Eleven

Malek couldn't believe what he was seeing on the TV. He watched as his high-school basketball picture appeared on the television screen. He shook his head as his heart began to beat fast. He had to get out of town, and quick. A part of him wanted to believe in his heart that Halleigh was alive, but he knew she was gone. Mitch's words wouldn't let him think otherwise.

Initially, Malek wasn't sure that the police officer he'd shot was dead, but the evening newscast confirmed it. He buried his face in his hands and began to cry. His life had fallen to pieces, and he had nothing. No Halleigh, no child, and no love. The drug game had consumed him and swallowed him whole. He wished he had chosen another path in life, but in actuality, he didn't choose the game, the game chose him. The guilt of Halleigh's and his baby's death was on his heart. He gripped his gun and put it to his head. He had nothing else to live for. Not even the money was worth living for. His eyes became bloodshot red, and his hand shook as he held the gun to his temple. He believed he was responsible for Halleigh's death, and the pressure was too much for him to bear.

Everything in the room was blocked out, and the only thing Malek could hear was the sound of himself breathing, as flashbacks of him and Halleigh making love in the islands appeared in his thoughts. He saw her pretty smile. The thought of never seeing it again was breaking his heart.

He quickly pulled the gun away from his head and tossed it on the hotel's bed. He couldn't bring himself to take his own life. That would be the easy way out. Malek's mother had always tried to teach him the right way was God's way. He didn't want to burn eternally for committing suicide, although he wasn't so sure that he'd go to heaven anyway, because of all the wrong he had done.

He stood up and began to pace the room back and forth. He had a bag full of money and didn't know what to do next. It seemed like every move he made was a bad move, so now he was just stuck and indecisive.

Afraid, confused, misguided, and alone, at that moment Malek realized he needed Halleigh. At first he thought she needed him, but without her, he had no purpose. The universal pull of soul mates was inevitable, but Halleigh had been pulled to a place where Malek couldn't follow. *Then how come I can still feel you, ma? It's like you're somewhere out there calling for me. I can feel your heart, Hal*, he thought as fresh tears came to his eyes.

He kept thinking about Halleigh's body lying somewhere and rotting. That thought alone was driving him crazy. He knew he had to get out of the room and make a run for it, but what then? Where would he go? Who would he turn to? Malek didn't have a clue, but he did have a bag full of untraceable dirty money, and that always did the trick. He would have to go far away and begin anew. Start a new life and try to move on from the chaos, death, and destruction. *I'll always carry you with me, Hal. There will never be another woman for me. You're mine, and I'm yours . . . in life and in death.*

Malek snapped out of his love funk and began to think of how to get out of town. He couldn't stay in the same spot for too long for fear of being apprehended. The entire police force was probably searching for him at that very moment. *I've got to get the hell outta dodge.*

He had checked in the hotel room under his name, just to get off the streets, and knew it would only be a matter of time before the cops found out where he was hiding. At first, he didn't care if the cops found him; that's just how messed up in the head he was, but now he was coming to his senses.

Malek's thoughts seemed to be disorganized and jumbled. It was the worst way to be when devising a plan. Scatterbrains made bad decisions and didn't think things through fully, but Malek's nerves were too bad to even consider that. He gathered the bag of money and his gun and headed outside so that he could start his car to let it warm up in the brutal Michigan winter weather. Just as he walked out, he saw what he thought was a familiar face brush by with a fur coat on. She pulled up her collar, trying to block the cold winds, but that prevented him from getting a good look at her. He was glad. He didn't need anyone spotting him, especially her, if it was in fact who he thought it was.

"Malek!" he heard someone call out.

Malek didn't pay the voice any mind as he continued his trek to his car parked toward the back of the parking lot.

"Malek!" she yelled again, her hands on her hips. "I've got Halleigh!"

At first he just looked around suspiciously as he made his way to his vehicle, but when he heard those last words come out of her mouth, he stopped immediately and turned around, hope entering his body.

Tasha couldn't believe the man she was looking for was right in her face. *What a coincidence*, Tasha thought at first, but then she remembered someone once telling her that there are no such things as coincidences. *Maybe, just maybe, this Halleigh and Malek thing was meant to be.*

"What did you just say?" he asked urgently as he began to head back toward Tasha. He was so wrapped up in what Tasha had just said, he didn't even notice the cop cars heading toward him.

"I said I have Halleigh," Tasha repeated. "She has been trying to call you. She's called like forty times. Haven't you gotten her messages?"

Malek patted his pockets to retrieve his phone, but felt nothing but empty space. *That muthafucking junkie.* Malek remembered Grady giving him a hug. "Where is she?" he asked Tasha, not pressed about the cell phone.

"She is in the hotel room going crazy over you. You have to go help her," Tasha said. Then she saw flashing lights whip into the parking lot just a few hundred feet away from them.

The police cars went around the building, giving Malek only a matter of time to make a decision on what to do. Malek couldn't believe what he had just heard. Tasha's statement gave him hope, but it was short-lived. Malek, at that point, didn't care if he got caught by the police. The only thing he was thinking about was his woman and if she was really alive, because for a split second, he wondered if Tasha was setting him up, trying to lure him into the hotel room so she could get some type of reward money for his capture or something. It was a chance he was willing to take.

Malek rushed toward Tasha with the bag in his hand. "Where is she? Where is she?" he yelled as he neared her. "Tasha, look, I don't have a lot of time. Take me to her." He grabbed Tasha by the shoulders and looked around to see if the cops had made their way back around.

"She's in the room," Tasha said, hurrying toward the motel room that Halleigh was in. Malek followed, holding the bag full of money.

When Malek got to the motel room with Tasha, he saw Halleigh sitting on the bed, gripping a blanket. When their eyes met, it was as if a magnet had drawn them together. Halleigh rushed over to him and grabbed him, squeezing him as tight as she could as tears began to flow freely.

Malek slightly lifted Halleigh off her feet and hugged her tightly as he buried his face in her neck, smelling her scent. "I have been going crazy trying to get you back." He looked into her eyes. "Did he hurt you?" Malek quickly thought about what she could have possibly been through. "Did Mitch hurt you?"

Halleigh looked into Malek's eyes and saw a look of deep concern accompanied by defeat.

Malek clenched his jaw tightly and gently placed his hand on Halleigh's stomach as he awaited her answer. Halleigh could see that Malek was blaming himself for what had happened to her, and she didn't want to bring him more pain. She wanted to tell him what they had done to her and tell him everything that she had been through, but she couldn't bring herself to add more stress to Malek's plate.

"No, Malek, I'm fine. I'm okay, baby. Don't worry about me. I missed you so much. I was so afraid that I was going to lose you, Malek," Halleigh said, refusing to let Malek go as she felt the tension and stress melt away from her body. Malek was like her savior. As long as he was near her, everything in her world was all right.

Tasha rolled her eyes at the sight. It almost made her want to vomit, but somewhere deep inside herself she wished that she could know a love so pure and true as the one before her. Malek kissed Halleigh passionately and got on his knees to speak to his unborn child.

"The baby is okay," Halleigh said, reassuring him as he wrapped his arms around her waist while still kneeling on the floor.

"Daddy's here now. I'm never going to let anything happen to you again. I put that on everything I love," he whispered to the baby.

Before Malek could say anything else, Tasha interrupted him. She was looking out of the window. "Police are everywhere!" she said as she looked on in amazement. Tasha quickly regretted helping Halleigh. She didn't sign up for any police trouble. The last thing she needed was a case for aiding and abetting.

"Fuck!" Malek rushed to Tasha's side and peeked out of the window.

Five police cars were spread throughout the vicinity. They seemed to have the entire hotel on lock. The flashing lights intimidated him. He was clearly outnumbered. "They must've seen me come in." Malek's mind began to race. The Flint Police Department was gunning for his head for killing one of their own.

"Is what they're saying about you on the news true?" Halleigh asked Malek, hoping he would tell her something different. Malek remained quiet, and his silence was her answer. Malek took out his gun, walked over to Halleigh, and kissed her like it would be his last time ever doing it.

Halleigh felt it and wasn't having it. "Whatever you are about to do, I'm doing it with you," Halleigh insisted without a drop of fear in her heart.

At that very moment, she reminded Malek of Scratch and how set he'd been on having Malek's back. "No! Just know that I love you." Malek gave her another hug and kiss. He was about to go out blazing with the cops because he knew they weren't planning on bringing him in breathing.

"I have an idea." Halleigh grabbed his hand.

Tasha looked on in disbelief, waiting to see what was to unfold.

Toy looked at the body of her dead brother Mitch as the paramedics put a white sheet over his body. She was infuriated and thirsty for revenge. With her long-braided cornrows and loose jumpsuit, she looked like one of the boys as she was surrounded by her goons from Saginaw. She had just gone to identify the body of her twin sister, and wasn't expecting to come bury her brother along with her.

Sweets walked up on her, and Toy's goons immediately reached for their guns.

Sweets put up his hands to signal there wasn't any beef. "Slow down. I'm Sweets. Mitch was my man. We did business together."

"I know who you are. You the faggot, right?" Toy said, hiding her green eyes behind the Dolce & Gabbana glasses that sat on her face.

Sweets clenched his jaw at her comment, not because she called him a faggot, but she was being blatantly disrespectful. He gave her a pass, since she had just lost two of her loved ones.

"Yeah, I'm the faggot," he answered sarcastically. He rubbed the front row of his teeth with his tongue.

"Set up a meeting," Toy said. "I want to talk to his crew ASAP."

Toy was a boss in her own right. She moved heavy heroin in the Saginaw area, and actually, she was homosexual also. Mitch had given her the rundown on Sweets months ago. She knew they'd been doing business together, but at this point, until she got to the bottom of the situation, everybody was suspect.

Toy watched the paramedics cart off her only brother. "Do you know who is responsible for this?"

Sweets slowly nodded his head and rubbed his hands together slowly. "Malek."

As soon as the name came out of his mouth, Toy knew exactly who he was talking about. Mitch had also talked to her about Malek when he and Malek were hustling together. At first when he told her about his new business partner, he sounded confident and happy, as if he had found his long-lost brother. Slowly, over time, his conversations regarding Malek began to change, and Mitch would tell her of Malek's arrogance and inability to lead his troops. Toy knew it was only a matter of time before Mitch took Malek's empire for himself, but she wasn't prepared for the young gun to come back with so much force, leaving her without her brother and sister. Toy's trigger finger began to itch as she prepared to light the city of Flint up on behalf of her slaughtered family. "Set up the meeting!" she yelled, rage and pain in her voice. Then she walked off, her entourage right behind her.

Chapter One Hundred Twelve

Halleigh put on an Oscar-worthy performance, screaming as if she were scared to death. "I will shoot this bitch!" Malek yelled. "Back the fuck up!" He pressed the gun to Halleigh's temple.

Malek inched his way to his car as at least ten police officers, partially hidden behind car doors, pointed their weapons toward Malek.

"Back the fuck up!" Malek jerked Halleigh closer to him. "Sorry," he whispered in her ear, trying to comfort her because he had her in an uncomfortable hold. "We almost to the car, baby."

Malek and Halleigh finally reached the driver's door, and Malek, with his free hand, opened it and stuffed Halleigh in. She scooted over, and Malek hopped in right after her.

The police officers tried to get a good aim, but Malek's tinted windows hindered them, and they didn't want to risk shooting the innocent hostage by just blindly shooting at the vehicle. Malek sped out of the parking lot with a trail of local police officers and state troopers on his tail.

Tasha remained back at the hotel room, tied up with sheets. Just in case the police questioned her, she'd appear as though she were a victim too.

Halleigh glanced back and saw the many flashing red, white, and blue lights. "Oh my God, Malek, they're on us!"

Malek hated that he had brought Halleigh along with him, but she had refused to let him go by himself and devised the hostage plan.

Halleigh saw the look in Malek's eyes as he pushed his whip just over ninety miles an hour on Pierson Road, trying to reach the highway. Lucky for him, Flint was not the type of city that harbored traffic jams. Mostly everyone in the city was broke and unemployed, so the streets were never packed with after-work cars. As if he were an Indy 500 driver, he floated through the few vehicles on the road.

The longer he drove and shook the police, the more police cars seemed to accumulate behind them.

"Oh, shit, Malek. It's like twenty cars behind us!" Halleigh yelled out. "You've got to go. Drive faster!"

Malek, disregarding all traffic laws, was going as fast as the car would take him. He barreled through intersections, knocking other cars out of his way, holding Halleigh back against the seat with one arm, trying to keep her from getting hurt. "Put your seat belt on, ma!" he screamed.

"I'm with you!" Halleigh braced herself against the door handle as he swerved through traffic. She was affirming that she was willing to ride or die with her man.

Malek gave her a forced smile and gripped the steering wheel tighter. This wasn't the way he envisioned life with Halleigh. If it was his time to go, then so be it. He was a man and he had gotten himself into the situation, but he wanted Halleigh to die an old woman. He wanted her to see things and go places he'd only dreamed of. He

wanted her to live and breathe. He wanted her to love and be free. Only after she experienced all these things did he want her to die; not right now. She hadn't done enough yet. In fact, she hadn't done any of it yet.

"I love you," Malek said.

"I love you too."

They jumped on the highway, police cars tailing them and spinning out of control as they turned onto the ramp without even touching the brakes.

Malek looked up and saw a news helicopter hovering just above them. They had managed to outrun the cops on the highway headed toward Detroit. The police cars began to fall back as if on command. Malek figured that for some reason they'd deemed the chase too dangerous to pursue, but he couldn't outrun the aircraft.

Malek had a souped-up car. His Benz engine was custom-made to outrun any car in the police department, but he didn't think there was a car invented that could outrun a helicopter.

They were approaching the tunnel that ran between Detroit and Canada. "I know they're going to have tire spikes to stop us after the tunnel," Malek said, sweat dripping from his forehead. He had watched too many high-speed chases on television to be green to their tactics. Even though they were crossing into Canada, he had no doubt they'd be stopped.

Malek looked over to Halleigh to see how she was doing, only to find her peeking over his shoulder like she was the lookout chick. Halleigh didn't care what happened, just as long as she was with Malek.

They entered the tunnel doing at least 130 miles per hour. Malek knew they only had about a minute or so before more cops got on them to catch them after flattening their tires. He stopped in the tunnel and threw the car into park.

Halleigh looked at him like he was insane. "What are you doing?"

Malek took a couple deep breaths and then looked at her. "I love you, Halleigh. I always have. You are the only person I got in this world. I want you to know that you are my soul mate."

"I love you too, Malek. You all I got too. Why are you talking like this is the end?" Halleigh tried to figure out what Malek was about to do.

"It is." Malek's eyes began to water, but he remained strong as he displayed his smile, trying to put Halleigh at ease.

They could hear the police sirens nearing the tunnel exit. Malek knew it was time to go through with his final plan.

"Let the baby know that I loved him or her, okay?"

"*Loved?*" Halleigh said, trying to understand why he was talking in past tense as if he was preparing to die.

"Look, Jamaica Joe used to use this tunnel to bring drugs in from across the border, so I know another way out. There's an old escape hatch that I'm gonna take you to. I'll distract the cops to give you some time to get out of the tunnel." He handed her the duffel bag full of money. "Take this and go to a bus station. Get the hell out of Flint for good. I want you to never look back. Understand?" Malek cupped her face and stared deep into her eyes.

"No, Malek, I am not leaving you. We're in this together. It's me and you against the world, remember?"

"Halleigh, go! We don't have much time." Malek revved up the engine.

Halleigh shook her head in defiance. "I'm staying with you."

Malek couldn't change her mind. He took a deep breath and prepared for what he was about to do. He gripped her hand tightly. "No one loves you more than me, Hal."

Chapter One Hundred Thirteen

E very local channel was covering the breaking story of Malek taking a hostage on a high-speed chase with the law.

Sweets and the Shottah Boyz were sitting in his living room, waiting for Toy to arrive. "Can you believe this shit?" Sweets asked as he watched Malek on television.

Sweets didn't want to admit it, but he was kind of glad that Mitch was dead. He was finally in total control of the city. *The North Side crew took each other out. Dumb niggas! It's my time now,* he thought silently as his crew watched the chase like it was an action movie.

One of Sweets' goons, who was glued to the television, said, "The camera lost him in the tunnel." Everyone waited in anticipation as the news helicopter filmed the police officers waiting on the other end of the tunnel so that the road spikes could slow Malek down; but Malek's car didn't come out.

"They're gonna kill that mu'fucka as soon as he come out of that tunnel." Sweets laughed. "Ain't no way out. He either got to come out, or in a minute, they gonna go in there after his ass."

After about two minutes of waiting, Malek's Benz appeared, speed-

ing wildly out of the tunnel. The car ran over the spikes, causing it to lose control and spin before it hit a railing and flipped repeatedly. Malek's car caught fire. Seconds later, the car exploded, causing a balloon-like flame to mushroom into the air.

A smile spread across Sweets' face as he imagined Malek burning to his death.

The news reporter was giving the viewers a play by play of the chaos, informing them that the chase had come to a tragic end. Seeing Malek's life crumble on television, all of the people in the house were smiling with satisfaction.

A knock at the door put a brief halt to their entertainment. Everyone reached for their guns, but Sweets told them to relax and put away their weapons. Mitch's sister was supposed to come and meet with them, so it was probably her.

"I hope this dike bitch don't think she's coming to fill her brother's spot," Sweets said. He had heard Mitch talk about her as if she was a street legend. From what Mitch told him, Toy had schooled him in the game. Mitch had also told Sweets that his sister was not to be underestimated. She was just as deadly as any killer walking the streets. Sweets didn't know what to expect, but he would soon discover what Toy was all about. One of the Shottah Boyz answered the door and let Toy and her people in.

Sweets stood up to greet Toy as she walked in with four men. Toy left her signature shades on as she walked into the room like she owned the place.

"Toy, these are the Shottah Boyz. They worked under your brother." Sweets threw his head in the direction of the couch, where they sat watching the news telecast. "That's Malek, the dude you don't have to worry about anymore." He nodded to the television. "Looks like he's burning in hell." Sweets chuckled.

Toy wasn't at all relieved. She still wanted to know what went down between her dead brother and his now dead killer. "What went down between that rat bastard and my brother?" she asked Sweets.

"Mitch had Malek's girl kidnapped and wanted a ransom, but everything went wrong. I don't know how all of this shit happened. Mitch was here one minute, gone the next. Feel me?"

"Who was supposed to have my brother's back when he got killed? Who was with him?" Toy asked coldly, not wanting to hear anything extra come out of Sweets' mouth.

Sweets looked at the Shottah Boyz, who were supposed to always have Mitch's back, and Toy's goon wasted no time loading up all three boys with bullets. Sweets was taken by surprise as he watched the young boys he had practically raised die from multiple gunshots.

Toy pulled out her gun and put it to Sweets' neck. She put her lips close to his ear. "Now that that's taken care of, who killed my family?"

In shock, Sweets couldn't fix his lips to say anything. He just stared at the boys as their eyes were rolling in the backs of their heads.

"Who is responsible?" Toy was ready to put her murder game down and take out all of the city of Flint to get to the bottom of things.

"What the fuck?" Sweets became frantic. He wanted to reach for the gun in his waist, but five people had their guns trained on him at that point. Sweets felt his knees get weak as his entire team had just been murdered. "Why did you have to do that?" Sweets asked, almost in a pleading tone. He looked at his young'uns, and his heart broke in two. "That nigga Malek killed him. Malek did it, bitch!" He pointed to the TV screen.

The room was silent, except for the voice of the news reporter. Malek's face appeared on the screen.

"This is a picture of Malek Johnson in his better years, when he was a superstar high school basketball player headed for the pros. Now this once promising life has come to a tragic end. . . ."

Toy asked, "That's him?"

Sweets nodded his head as he clenched his fists. He wanted to kill Toy, but was in no situation to act on his impulse.

Toy sent a single shot through Sweets' skull, reuniting him with his crew.

What Malek and Jamaica Joe had spent years trying to accomplish, she had come to town and done in literally a day. She had killed the infamous Sweets. Her main focus now was getting revenge for the death of her family members. She didn't care if Malek was dead. She wanted every trace of Malek Johnson wiped from the planet. She wouldn't rest until she saw everyone who had ever associated with him suffer and die.

Toy wiped Sweets' blood from her face. "Check the house and see what they got in here," Toy said. She was an opportunist, the exact kind Scratch had spoken of. She didn't want to leave any money in the house. Toy was a hustler first, killer second.

They stumbled upon the surveillance tape that Sweets had just retrieved from the stash house where Halleigh had been held captive. Toy and her crew examined the tape and saw a woman pacing back and forth in a room, looking scared. It didn't take them long to figure out that this was Malek's girl, the one Sweets had said was being held by Mitch. Hate flooded Toy's heart. The way she saw it, this bitch was part of the reason her brother was dead.

They kept watching, and witnessed the moment when Tasha broke into the room and rescued Halleigh.

"Who the fuck is that?" Toy asked. But it didn't really matter who the other woman was. Toy knew it wouldn't take her long on the streets to

ID this chick, and then she'd be dead. If she rescued Malek's woman, then Toy considered her an enemy. Anything and everyone connected to Malek or Halleigh was living on borrowed time.

Toy and her crew grabbed the tape and headed out, itching to kill.

Chapter One Hundred Fourteen

Sharina lay in her hospital bed, looking at the newscast and hoping that her baby was okay. She saw Malek's face on the television and listened as they described him as a ruthless, cold-blooded killer. They also kept showing video footage of Malek and an unknown robber sticking up a couple of banks. When Sharina saw the footage, she automatically knew it was Scratch. A small smile spread across her face as she watched Scratch do his infamous walk into the bank.

"Scratch ain't gon' ever change," she said to herself. Her smile quickly faded when her daughter's face appeared on the screen and the news reporter said she wasn't a hostage, but an accomplice on the run with Malek.

Sharina began to pray for her baby. Once she finished her silent prayer, she thought about how she'd never told Halleigh who her real father was. Back in 1984, Scratch had fathered her after a one-night stand. At the time, Sharina was dealing with another man, who was doing better financially than Scratch. She decided to go with that man because she thought he had a better future. How could she tell Halleigh that her father was a junkie and bum that stayed on the streets?

The man Halleigh believed to be her father died when she was five. He was a good man, so Sharina thought it would have been selfish to let Halleigh find out that he wasn't her father.

Sharina saw the door crack open and noticed an unfamiliar face. The woman had long braids and didn't seem to be a nurse.

Without saying anything, the woman walked toward Sharina, and the look in her eyes expressed pure hatred. The woman slowly closed the door and smiled at Sharina, but the smile wasn't a warming one. It was more like a sinister smirk.

Sharina could see the devil in the woman's eyes, and her fear filled the air.

The woman pulled out a gun with a silencer from her waistband and pointed it at Sharina. She took her time, so she could be precise and accurate.

Sharina froze in terror. Before she could reach for the nurse's call button, a hollow-tip bullet went through her skull, killing her on contact, splattering blood on the white bedsheets.

Toy held the gun and smiled. Her vengeance rampage had begun. Flint had never experienced a killer like Toy, but they were about to get put on game.

Tasha had nothing to complain about. She had the money she took from Mitch, and no police troubles. She had managed to free herself from the sheets and slipped out of the hotel room while the police gave chase to Malek and Halleigh.

Later, she discovered that everyone from the old crew was dead, even Sweets.

"Karma is a bitch." She smiled and licked her thumbs as she sifted through the bills. She thought about Halleigh, but those thoughts were short-lived. She was gonna worry about herself and herself only.

Tasha was so busy counting the money, she didn't notice the person creeping up behind her.

Toy and her crew had broken into the back of the house. Flint was small, so it wasn't hard for Toy to find out who was the woman in the video and then find out where she lived.

When Tasha felt someone was in the room with her, it was too late. Toy had an all-black TEC-9 pointed to the back of her head.

"Oh my God," Tasha whispered, taken by surprise.

"God can't save you now, baby girl," Toy said in a low tone, admiring Tasha's pretty hair.

"I came to talk to you about Halleigh." Toy pulled up a seat in front of Tasha, who was still in shock. Before she killed her, Toy had a few questions for this beautiful woman. The details were still sketchy, but talk on the street let Toy know that this chick was close to Halleigh. She probably had inside information that would help Toy understand exactly what happened to her brother.

Tasha didn't know the woman that sat in front of her, but she wasn't going to ask who she was either. "Please don't hurt me," Tasha said in a pleading tone. Her eyes never left the gun Toy was holding.

Toy smirked and then stroked her hand down Tasha's soft hair. She looked deep into Tasha's eyes, almost mesmerized by her beauty. Although she was about to kill her, she took a liking to Tasha. "You and me have some things to talk about. If you tell me what I want to know, maybe I'll make your death quick and painless."

A tear ran down Tasha's face. Her whole body was trembling.

"I'll even put this gun down while we talk," Toy said as she leaned

back in her chair. She kept the gun pointed at Tasha, but put it down in her lap. "So, let's start at the beginning. Tell me how the fuck my brother Mitch let himself get killed by this muthafucka Malek."

Chapter One Hundred Fifteen

ONE YEAR LATER

B altimore, Maryland had a different feel, a different vibe, and different people. It was a long way from Flint, Michigan, but Halleigh and Malek were happy. They were living in a quiet area just off the east side of B-more, far away from Flint's ills and their police. They had a newborn baby boy, and life seemed to be going good.

After Halleigh refused to escape from the Detroit tunnel without him, Malek had quickly devised another plan. Using a sand bag he had in his trunk, he placed it on the accelerator, causing his Mercedes to exit the tunnel at full speed. The resulting explosion was even better than Malek had hoped for. With the police and news helicopter crew distracted by the huge flames, Halleigh and Malek were able to get out of the tunnel undetected and make their way to the bus station. No one was looking for them at this point, because everyone assumed they were both inside the burning car. It was weeks before investigators discovered that there were no human remains among the ashes recovered at the scene. By that time, Halleigh and Malek were living in Baltimore under new names, while the bewildered cops were still searching for them on the streets of Flint. Malek used Mitch's money to buy a small brownstone, and invested the little he had left in a small coke operation. Malek didn't do it too big. He knew he had to make just enough money to get by and stay under the radar.

He thought for a minute about going legit, but he deemed it to be true what they say: The game pulls you in and never lets you go.

He watched Malek Jr. during the day while Halleigh went to her part-time job at a store at Mondawmin Mall. It worked out good, because the owner paid her off the books, so there was no record that she worked there. Malek had told her that was the only way she could work, since they couldn't risk being tracked down. Even though they

were living under assumed names, Malek still didn't want to take any chances. Although he wasn't in Flint, he still suffered from paranoia, and was always on the lookout for anything out of place.

One night, Malek came in late from doing his thing on the streets, and found Halleigh asleep on the couch with Malek Jr. on her chest. Malek locked the door behind him and peeked through the window with his gun in hand. When he was satisfied no one had followed him, he turned to look at his sleeping family.

He removed Malek Jr. from Halleigh's arms and held him to his chest. He got instant relief when he saw Halleigh's eyes slightly open up and a smile form on her face.

She then closed her eyes, the residue of the smile still on her face. It was something about her smile that made Malek feel warm inside. As long as he had that smile in his life, everything would be okay. If she was happy, he was happy.

He watched as the sun came up, and wondered what his life would have been like had he gone to college . . . if he had never gotten into the street life. What if Halleigh didn't have her innocence stripped from her?

All of these unanswered questions would remain that way, so Malek had to play the cards he was dealt. Those cards included a son he was proud of and vowed to do right by. He walked Malek Jr. into the bedroom to spend some time with him before putting him in his crib.

It was only a few minutes later that Halleigh woke up. She had been dreaming about Tasha, remembering the tight bond they shared during the years they worked together on the streets. Halleigh felt she owed her life to Tasha. If Tasha hadn't come to rescue her from Mitch's place, things could have turned out very different for Halleigh and Malek.

Although Malek had warned her to never make contact with anyone in Flint, Halleigh felt bad that she hadn't talked to Tasha. She felt like she at least owed it to her friend to let her know that she had a baby boy. He might never have been born if it weren't for what Tasha had done.

Thinking about Tasha had become almost a daily thing lately for Halleigh, and after tonight's dream, she felt like it was a sign. It was time for her to talk to her friend.

She heard Malek's voice in the bedroom, playing with their son. She peeked into the room, and Malek didn't even notice her. Feeling it would be safe to make just one quick call, Halleigh walked into the basement, where Malek wouldn't be able to hear her. She dialed Tasha's number, hoping it hadn't changed.

She smiled when she heard Tasha's phone ring. It had been a year since she'd talked to her.

"I forgive you, Halleigh. I've moved on, and I'm glad to hear that

you are doing good. I wish you well," Tasha said as she squirmed in her bed.

Moments later, without even saying bye, Tasha hung up and began to shake feverishly. She looked down at Toy, who was giving her the best oral sex ever. Toy worked her tongue like a professional and pleased Tasha better than any man had ever done. They had been lovers for about a year, and Toy had Tasha turned out and sprung on her.

Toy's pretty, wavy hair wasn't braided as it usually was, and with her clothes off, she was immaculate. Tasha watched as Toy pleased her, then moaned as she exploded all over Toy's face.

Toy came up and smiled, knowing she had just pleased her woman. "Is that who I think it was?" She wiped Tasha's juices off her face.

"Yeah," Tasha said, running her fingers through Toy's hair.

Tasha had been with Toy ever since the day Toy had come to kill her. Toy always got what she wanted, and she wanted Tasha. Toy was blown away by Tasha's beauty, and gave her an offer she couldn't refuse: If she became Toy's girlfriend, she would live.

Tasha wasn't gay and never thought in a million years she would go that way. Initially she agreed only so she could stay alive, but Toy had the swagger of a hustler, and Tasha eventually fell for it.

Aside from the sex, Toy kept Tasha around because she was sure that someday she would lead her to Halleigh, who would no doubt lead her to Malek. When the police finally figured out that there were no bodies in the burned-up Mercedes, the hunt for Halleigh and Malek was all over the newspapers. Toy wasn't even pressed to look for them, because she was so certain that one day they would resurface, and then she could get her revenge. It looked like that day had finally come, and Toy couldn't be happier.

She picked up Tasha's cell phone and looked at the number, noticing it was a Baltimore number. Then she smiled and went back down on Tasha.

One Hundred Sixteen

Halleigh sat at the front desk at the store typing into a laptop, since there were no customers. Ever since she'd called Tasha a couple of days earlier, she'd been feeling better. All of the loose ends were

finally tied back home in Flint. Tasha had forgiven her for being with the man that killed her brother, so Halleigh was at peace with herself.

Halleigh began to get teary-eyed as she thought about all the things that had occurred in her life. She often wondered about how her mom was doing. Although her mother had been nothing short of a bad parent to her, she just wanted to know how she was. Halleigh thought about her life of prostitution, hustling, and stripping at the hands of the game.

She looked at the computer screen, proud of what she had accomplished. She had just penned a novel, and her hard work had finally paid off. "I'm all finished," she whispered. She smiled and continued to reflect on her life. At the age of twenty-one, she had gone through more than most sixty-year-olds and lived to tell the story. That in itself was an achievement.

Halleigh scrolled to the first page and added the finishing touch to her book. It read:

> *This book is dedicated to good ol' Scratch. I know you're watching down on me. Love you.*

Halleigh closed her laptop, unaware that she had just dedicated her book to her father. She thought about Scratch's gap-toothed smile.

She was also unaware of someone standing in front of her at the counter until she looked up. "Whew! You scared me," Halleigh said. "I didn't see you come in. Can I help you find anything in particular today?" she asked the customer.

Halleigh looked at the butch female who stood in front of her. The woman wore dark designer glasses and long French braids to the back. "No, I don't need any help. I know exactly what I'm looking for."

Halleigh didn't understand what the woman meant by that statement, but she would soon find out. "I'm looking for the sequel to this joint right here." She handed it to Halleigh.

Halleigh felt like a fool for overreacting. *God!* She thought to herself. *Every gay girl with braids ain't Toy. Calm the fuck down.* She felt so foolish, her entire face turned red. She exhaled loudly and put her hand over her racing heart.

"Yo, ma, you a'ight?" the girl asked.

Halleigh nodded as she wiped away the tears that had accumulated in her eyes. "Yeah, I-I'm fine," she responded. "I thought you were somebody else."

"Somebody you not trying to see, obviously," the girl remarked with a smirk.

Halleigh didn't respond, ignoring the sarcasm in the girl's tone, and

then proceeded to ring her up. Once she left the store, Halleigh collapsed into her seat. "You've got to get a grip, girl. Get a grip."

Finally closing time came around, and Halleigh couldn't leave the mall quick enough. Gripping her Mace in the palm of her hand and checking her back as she walked, she hurriedly located her car. Once she was safely inside she clicked the locks and drove to the apartment she shared with Malek.

As soon as she stepped inside the door, she saw Malek lying on the couch asleep. The sight of him was the only thing that made her feel protected. They had been through the storm for one another, and she loved him more than anyone in the world.

She dropped her bag onto the floor and walked over to where her man was sleeping. She crawled directly on top of him, and without thinking twice, he wrapped his arms around her.

"Shh, I just put li'l man to sleep," he mumbled. He gave her a quick peck on the forehead and went back to sleep.

Halleigh smiled as she thought about how lucky she was to have Malek and their son. She nodded her head and remained silent as she laid her head on his chest. For the first time all day, she felt safe as she drifted off to sleep.

Chapter One Hundred Seventeen

A s Halleigh sat with her baby son, Malek Jr., in her arms, she watched his father get dressed.

"You're going out?" Halleigh glanced at the clock, noticing that it was eleven P.M. She raised one eyebrow at Malek as she awaited his response.

"Yeah, I've got to hit the block," Malek stated, not noticing Halleigh's attitude.

Halleigh shook her head in disappointment. She hated the mentality that Jamaica Joe had instilled into Malek. The streets had ruined their lives in the first place. It had destroyed their plans of the good life long ago, and after escaping Flint, she thought that Malek would finally let them go. But she was sadly mistaken because Malek had dived full force into the Baltimore drug trade, blaming it on their situation, saying that he was doing it to provide for them.

True, their finances had dwindled, and they were barely making it when Malek decided to get back into the game, but Halleigh didn't

care. The risk wasn't worth the reward. She had seen firsthand what that life could get you, and they had barely survived the first time. She wasn't sure they could deal with the ups and downs of the game again, but it was like Malek lived to hustle. It was in him like DNA. He acted as if he had never had a life before the streets began to raise him, and Halleigh felt like no matter how hard she tried to hold on, eventually she was going to lose him.

"I thought we came here to start over, Malek. I don't want you out there. This isn't our city. We don't know shit about B-more. We're supposed to be lying low," she reminded him.

"Don't worry yourself, Hal. I know what I'm doing. That li'l bookstore job you got ain't gon' pay the bills or put food in my son's stomach at night. I don't love what I do, but it's all that I got, so just trust me. I got you. I got us." He bent down and kissed his son on his head, then Halleigh.

Halleigh nodded and smiled a smile of uncertainty. She heard the words, but in her heart of hearts she knew Malek was moving all wrong. "I've just been feeling crazy lately. I'm constantly feeling like I have to watch my back. I have a bad feeling like something bad is going to happen or like someone is going to recognize us."

Malek shook his head and sighed. He knew the pressure of being on the run was getting to Halleigh. The stress was evident on her face. "You're just paranoid, ma. Relax. Nobody can hurt you from here. We're good. You're just thinking about the past too much. Let that shit go, Hal. Flint is miles away. And I know you don't like me hustling either. I hear you. Once I get my paper up, I'll stop. I promise."

Halleigh nodded. She walked Malek to the door and watched him until his car disappeared around the block.

She looked down at her son and cradled him gently in her arms. "Looks like it's just you and me today, baby boy," she whispered as she closed and locked the door.

As she looked around their small apartment, she couldn't help but think how their lives had come full circle. She had lived and seen it all. From the glamour and hood fame the game had to offer to the seedy side of life, she knew it in and out. Unlike Malek, she didn't miss it. She had a child to think about, and there was no way she was going to allow her child's life to be thrown off kilter the way hers was.

Halleigh sighed as she put her son into his crib for the night. Life in Baltimore was lonely, especially with Malek being constantly away from home. She had no friends, partly because she chose to keep to herself, but mostly because she didn't trust anyone.

But on nights like these when she had a lot of stuff on her mind, she needed someone to talk to. Someone she could relate to. Someone who had been through the same things as she, and would listen without judgment. *I miss Tasha,* she thought.

Although their friendship had been tested and stretched to its limit, it was the only one she had left. As she sat in the empty apartment, the loneliness that crept into her soul made her yearn for her friend's understanding. *Maybe I'll give her a call,* Halleigh thought.

Chapter One Hundred Eighteen

Tasha was feeding her nose the magnificent powder that Toy had introduced her to. She bent over the mirror and inhaled the lines of cocaine. She had never been addicted to anything in her life, but her new infatuation with white lines was slowly starting to grow on her. As she lifted her head, she pinched her nose and then snorted loudly, to stop her nose from running.

The ringing of her telephone interrupted her routine.

"Damn it," she mumbled as she stood to retrieve her cell phone out of her purse. Without even looking at the caller ID, she answered. "Hello?"

"Hey, Tasha."

When Tasha heard Halleigh's voice, she instinctively lowered hers. Toy wasn't even around, but she knew how long she had waited for that exact phone call. "Hey, um, hey. I know this ain't who I think it is," she responded.

"Yeah, long time no bullshit, huh?" Halleigh felt a sense of relief just from speaking with her longtime friend.

"What's up, Hal? I miss you, girl."

Tasha was making small talk in an attempt to keep her on the phone. It was just her luck that Toy would be M.I.A. on the day Halleigh finally decided to call. The average girl would have felt guilty about setting Halleigh up, but Tasha was tired of being captain save-a-ho. Halleigh wasn't a naïve little girl anymore. She was grown as hell, and it was no longer Tasha's responsibility to guard her.

"I was just thinking about you. I know we haven't talked in a while, and at first I was trying to cut all my ties to Flint, but you're all I got, Tash. You're my girl, and even though I know I have Malek, sometimes I just need my girl, you know."

Tasha could hear the sincerity in her words. She shook her head. *This bitch. That's why her ass always getting caught the fuck up. She's too fucking soft.* Tasha put her hand over her mouth and yawned,

bored with Halleigh's overemotional rant. "Yeah, I hear you, hon. Well, you the one who went into hiding. I feel you needing to leave the city because of your situation, but dang, girl, you didn't have to shut me out."

"I know. Everything just happened so fast."

"Well, where are you? We need to get together. I definitely want to see your son." Tasha could hear her indecision through the phone. She waited anxiously. She didn't want to seem too anxious about getting Halleigh's location, to avoid arousing her suspicion. She cleared her throat. "You know what, Hal . . . it's cool, babes. I understand why you don't want nobody to know where you are. I just thought we were better than that."

"Tasha, it's not like that. If you can get to Baltimore, then I'd love to meet up with you."

"Baltimore, huh?"

"Yeah. You got a pen?" Halleigh asked, not knowing she was about to give her enemy a one up on her.

Just as Tasha got up to scramble for a piece of paper and a pen, Toy walked into her home. She put her finger up to her mouth to signal her silence.

"Hold on, Hal," Tasha said, looking Toy in the eye. Toy smiled devilishly when she heard the name.

After finally locating a pen, Tasha said, "Okay, girl, where do you want me to meet you? Just say when, and I'll be there. I got a new man that'll give me the money to get there."

Halleigh arranged to meet Tasha that weekend at The Cheesecake Factory in downtown Baltimore. It was a public place, and she figured it was the safest way for them to reunite.

"Don't tell anyone you're coming to see me, Tash. Not a single person. Just get ghost," Halleigh stated seriously.

"I got you, Hal. I'll be there. See you Saturday," Tasha replied before hanging up the phone.

Tasha turned to face Toy and held the piece of paper up in her hand. "Who did that, mama?" she asked seductively, feeling proud that she was able to give Toy what she'd been fiending for.

Toy grabbed the paper out of her hand and looked at the rendezvous address. "You did that, ma." She planted a deep kiss on her lips, pushing her toward the bedroom.

Tasha had earned the orgasm that Toy was about to deliver. Now Toy could concentrate on the day she would face the bitch-ass nigga that killed her brother and finally bring him his fate.

Chapter One Hundred Nineteen

Scar Johnson and Derek Fuller sat across from each other in a small Italian restaurant just outside of Baltimore in a small town called Bowie. They always met there to avoid being seen together, which would be bad for their business arrangement. Baltimore was their stomping ground, so when they met, it had to be discreet.

Scar Johnson was a well-known kingpin throughout the inner city of Baltimore. He got the nickname Scar because of the long mark that went across his face. With his deep voice and built stature, the streets feared him, and the women loved him. All the makings of a street legend.

Fuller slid the rare steak into his mouth while listening close. He had a neat goatee and a lean build. He wore a leather coat and neat slacks, and looked like a cop. Maybe that was because he was one. Fuller was the head of the Baltimore Narcotics Unit and also partner in crime with Scar. Their operation was flawless. He was assigned to take down Scar, but in actuality, he was helping him, making Scar untouchable.

Scar said to Fuller, "Yo, I'm hearing a lot of noise about this new kid. He is fucking with my money. He's a out-of-town nigga trying to move in on my territory. He is selling coke at a cheaper price and taking away all of my clientele. My young boys are saying that our fiends are leaving our block to go fuck with him."

"So this li'l nigga is a problem, huh?"

"You damn right," Scar shot back. He had seen his money drastically slow up, and it became a problem that needed to be solved quickly. "Shake things up a little bit. Get the rundown on the nigga."

"I got you," Fuller answered confidently. "I'm on it today."

After discussing other matters, they exited the restaurant and headed back to Baltimore in separate cars.

Malek held Malek Jr. in the air as he looked into his son's eyes, seeing his own features. He glanced over at Halleigh as she sat at the vanity mirror combing through her hair, getting prepared for work. Halleigh didn't have to work by any means, but Malek let her because it kept her occupied and busy.

"You sure you don't want me to take Junior to the babysitter?" Halleigh applied some lipstick.

"Naw, I'm good, baby. I'm not going anywhere until you get back. He's cool here with me. Aren't you, li'l man?" Malek munched on his son's fat jaws.

Halleigh smiled and admired the way Malek was so close with his son. She knew he was a good man and would always protect them.

She was with the man of her dreams and wouldn't trade it for anything. But as you know, trouble always seemed to find Halleigh and Malek, so just because they had moved to Baltimore, shit didn't change. Just the scenery.

Chapter One Hundred Twenty

H alleigh sat in the busy Inner Harbor restaurant waiting patiently for Tasha to arrive. Her son sat in his car seat, which was atop the table. Anxiety filled her stomach as her foot tapped nervously on the floor. She was knocking at the devil's door by reopening the line of communication with Tasha. She knew the risks, but at the same time needed a friend, so she felt that it was a risk worth taking.

Like always, Malek was in the streets, but on this day she welcomed his absence. She didn't want to tell him Tasha was coming to town. He would flip if he knew Halleigh was meeting with her, so she kept this to herself.

Toy eased her car into the downtown traffic as she and Tasha approached the restaurant. "Don't be too pushy with her. Act like you are really here for a reunion between old friends. I don't need to make my move today. I just want to watch her and see if she leads me back to that bitch-ass Malek. When the time is right, I'll make my move."

"How long should I tell her I'm in town for?" Tasha asked as she pulled out a small baggie of powder cocaine.

"Slow down on that shit. I need you on point for this."

"I'm always on point." Tasha continued her get-high routine, vacuuming the coke up her nostrils. "Just drop me off at the corner. I'll call you before dinner is over, so you can be ready to pick me up."

Under normal circumstances Toy would have just snatched Halleigh and tortured her until she gave up Malek's location, but the young girl was a bit brighter than she had anticipated. As Toy looked at the crowded tourist area, she realized that Halleigh had chosen a place where nothing could go wrong. Too many witnesses.

Tasha emerged from the car and headed into the restaurant. Not a flicker of remorse crossed her mind as she stepped inside. It wasn't hard for her to spot Halleigh. Although her appearance had changed and she had put on a couple pounds of baby weight, Tasha could spot her a mile away. Her body language and gracefulness hadn't changed.

Halleigh breathed a sigh of relief when Tasha finally walked through

the door. The bad feeling that had been lurking in her heart immediately disappeared when she saw Tasha wave and smile. She stood to greet her with outstretched arms.

"Hal!" she screamed, not caring about the other patrons in the building.

"Hey, Tasha," Halleigh replied as they held one another and rocked back and forth affectionately. "It's good to see you, girl."

Tasha immediately focused her attention on Halleigh's son and her heart could not help but skip a beat at the innocent face. "Oh my goodness. He's beautiful, Halleigh."

"Thank you." Halleigh pulled him from his seat and handed him off to Tasha.

Tasha held Malek Jr. in her arms as she took a seat. The amount of love she felt from the baby boy surprised even her. She had to hurry up and get him out of her grasp before her conscience started eating at her. She was, after all, plotting on his mother and father. She handed Halleigh her son, and Halleigh put him back in his seat.

Halleigh discreetly zipped his diaper bag to conceal the .45 handgun she had taken from Malek's closet. She had brought it with her for protection, just in case, but now that she was face to face with Tasha, she didn't feel the need for it anymore.

She sat down, and after a round of drinks, they were chatting as if no time had passed them by. It seemed so genuine to Halleigh, and for the first time in months she felt normal. There was no need to peek over her shoulder every few minutes, no anxiety, no paranoia. She was relaxed and social. Finally she was able to let her guard down.

After sitting for hours, she checked her watch and noticed how quickly the time had passed.

"I've got to go, Tash. But how long are you in town for?"

"A few days."

"Well, we should get together again before you leave. I work at this mall out here called Mondawmin. I'm working tomorrow, but you can stop by if you want. I know you're always in the mood to do some shopping." Halleigh laughed.

"Definitely. I'll call you."

The two girls hugged once more before Halleigh wrapped her baby securely and left.

A bored Detective Maria Rodriguez sat back in her unmarked car and watched the restaurant. She hated to get stuck with the uneventful stakeouts. While the rest of her squad was busy tailing their mark, Malek Johnson, she had drawn the short stick and was instructed to follow his girlfriend. The only female cop on the task force of the Baltimore Narcotics Unit, she was used to being put on dummy missions and knew at first glance that Halleigh was a dead end. The girlfriends never lead you to anything. As she sipped her coffee, she knew this

stakeout was a waste of time. She picked up her squad car radio so she could two-way her partner.

"Hey, numb nuts. I hope you know you owe me dinner for this one. There's nothing going on my way."

"Just stay on the girl. There's a big reward in it for everybody if we stop this young boy in his tracks. Just play your position, Rodriguez," Detective Derek Fuller replied, reminding her who was in charge. "Everybody has a position."

She sucked her teeth and gave him a few choice words in Spanish before refocusing on the task at hand. Just as she was tempted to pick up the newspaper from her passenger's seat, she finally saw movement from the entrance of the building where the restaurant was located.

She watched as Tasha exited the restaurant first. The detective silently admired the glamorous clothing and jewelry. *These young girls walk around here with no job or education. All they have to do is snag a hustler or baller and they live the lavish life.* Here she was working a nine-to-five and could never afford the high-end designers that graced Tasha's body. That was the reason why she never felt bad about the drug dealers that she and the rest of her Narcotics Unit colleagues chose to extort. That leveled the playing field. And, unfortunately for Malek, he had come to town and stepped on the wrong toes.

She observed Halleigh as she retrieved her car from the valet. The detective started her own vehicle to prepare to set up her tail, but she fell back when she noticed a black Charger pull out behind Halleigh. She followed three car lengths behind, to stay undetected. She ran the plates and discovered that the car was a rental.

"Looks like somebody else is interested in this girl too. Maybe there is more to her than meets the eyes," the detective mumbled to herself.

She flowed with the traffic, making sure she made every light, to keep up with the two cars ahead of her. Something was up. She wasn't sure exactly what it was, but she didn't want to overplay her hand before she figured out what was going on. *This girl doesn't have people following her for nothing. What type of shit is she into?* Detective Rodriguez's instincts told her that Malek and Halleigh were into something other than the petty drug game.

To test her suspicions, she got off the highway and rode through the city streets, redundantly hitting for lefts. She hoped that the car behind her wouldn't follow suit, but her fears were confirmed when she made her first turn.

Detective Rodriguez fell back as she noticed Halleigh begin to drive in circles. *She knows she is being followed.* "She's not as dumb as she looks," the detective commented to herself.

She patiently waited at the corner to see how the situation would play out. Her stakeout had ended for the day, but she would start again

first thing in the morning because now she wanted to know who else was on Halleigh's trail, and why?

After realizing she was being followed, Halleigh jumped back on the expressway and headed in the opposite direction of her home. No way was she going to lead someone back to the place where she rested her head. She sped up, pressing her car to the max, hoping to shake whoever was on her ass.

"Fall back, Toy! She knows you're following her."

Toy, her eagerness for revenge making her foot heavy on the gas, ignored Tasha.

"You think she's going to lead you to Malek now that she knows we're behind her? Halleigh's not dumb. She's not going to put that boy in harm's way. She'll die herself before she lets anything happen to him! Fall back. I'm supposed to call her tomorrow. We can catch up with her then."

Toy reluctantly slowed her car down. She was too close to let her temper blow her plans now.

Chapter One Hundred Twenty-one

Scar and Fuller were set again to meet at the small restaurant in Bowie. On the way to the spot, as Fuller drove up, he began to feel guilt for playing on both sides of the law by being a cop and partner with a drug dealer. But Scar and Fuller had a relationship that went much deeper than what appeared on the surface. They were blood brothers. Derek Fuller thought back to how thier partnership came about.

"Mom!" Derek screamed, his small, angelic face turning flush red as he jumped up and down in sheer terror. His brother stood next to him and peed on himself as he watched too.

"I told you before, bitch. You don't play with my fuckin' money!!" a strange man screamed as he dragged their mother by her hair.

The man was so big, and his skin was so black; to Derek he looked like a giant monster. As the boys screamed, the man hoisted their mother in the air by her throat. Derek felt vomit creep up his throat, and his bowels threatened to release from the fear he felt. His mother clawed at the man's hands in a futile attempt to loosen his grip so she could breathe.

"Get off my mommy!"Stephon screamed the scar he was born with dragging the side of his mouth down, causing his words to slur.

Derek grabbed onto his little brother's shirt and pulled him back. He couldn't risk this monster harming his brother too.

"Please don't hurt my babies," their mother rasped, begging the man for mercy.

"Bitch, you should have thought about that before you decided to cross me," the giant said, hoisting her up and throwing her up against the wall.

She hit the wall with a thud and slid down, her body going limp like a rag doll. She continued to scream and beg for her life as the man pounded on her, his fist landing at will, each punch harder than the one before.

"You like to smoke crack? You like to steal from people, bitch?" the man growled as he lifted her weak body up so he could get to her face. With the force of a Mack truck he backhanded her, sending one of her teeth flying from her mouth. Blood covered her face and hugged the floor around her. "Now, I expect to get my money by tomorrow, or you and these bastard trick babies of yours gonna be dead." The man spewed a wad of spit on her crumpled form.

Five-year-old Derek and his four-year-old brother Stephon cowered in a corner, with Derek trying to shield his brother from harm, as usual. Although he was only five, Derek often acted as if he were ten or eleven. On the nights his mother disappeared or stayed holed up in her bedroom with different men, he would pour cereal or make a sandwich out of whatever was there for him and his little brother, who his mother had nicknamed Scar because of his misshapen head and the scar that dragged down one side of his face, making his head re-semble a boulder. He would make sure his brother washed his face and brushed his teeth before they went to bed.

"Rock-a-bye baby, on the tree top," she would sing to her younger son. She would call Derek her "baby genius" and tell him he was des-tined for greatness.

People often thought Derek and Scar were fraternal twins because they were the same size. Although Scar was a year younger, he was al-ways just as big as Derek.

When he was sure the giant was gone, Derek got up and went to his mother's side. "Mommy?" He nudged her frantically. He thought she was dead for sure. "Mommy!" he called out again, urgency rippling through his words.

Finally his mother shifted and winced in pain. Then she moaned and turned over. Struggling to get up and barely able to speak through her swollen lips, she rushed her boys to put on their coats.

Afraid and visibly shaken, Derek followed his mother's instructions and helped Scar into his coat and put on his own. Their battered

mother rushed them out of the apartment, looking around nervously the entire time. Once they were outside, she let her motherly instincts take over. She ignored the massive pains ripping through her entire body and walked at a fast pace to get her children far away from the potential danger. Derek could keep up, but Scar had a hard time, and he gasped for breath because he had to jog just to keep in step.

After walking for what seemed like an eternity, the trio finally came to a middle-class white neighborhood that Derek had remembered passing on numerous occasions and wishing he lived there.

"Go in there, and y'all stand right by that green dumpster. Don't move until I come back. You hear me, Derek?" his mother said, her words garbled and her face becoming more swollen by the minute.

"When you coming back?" Derek asked, shivering.

"Take care of your brother, okay? He is special, and don't you let nobody bother him about his face. You hear me?" Her body quaked with sobs.

"When you coming back?" Derek asked her again, an ominous feeling taking over him.

His mother shoved them along. "Just take care of your brother." As they started ambling forward slowly toward the dumpster, their mother turned and limped away, her heart breaking as she went farther and farther away from them. She knew somebody would find them there and take care of them. She feared that if she had kept them, her addiction would've eventually gotten them killed.

Scar began crying out, "Mommy! Mommy! Don't leave us."

"Shhhh! Mommy is coming back. I'm gonna take care of you until she comes back," Derek consoled, squeezing his brother's hand tight.

Derek took his brother and stood right where his mother had instructed him. They stood at the dumpster until the sun came up, and their legs throbbed. Scar whined and cried the whole time, between nodding from sleep deprivation. Derek refused to sit down or allow Scar to sit down. His mother had told him to stand there, and he would not let her down. Several people passed them and stared, but no one said anything to them. It was the trash truck driver who came to empty the dumpster that finally asked Derek why they were there.

"My mommy said she is coming back for us," Derek had said. After waiting with Derek and Scar for three hours, the trash man finally called the authorities, and Derek never saw his mother again.

When Child Protective Services workers and the police showed up, Derek still refused to move. "No! I'm waiting for my mommy! No!" He screamed and kicked to no avail.

They had to physically remove him from the dumpster, and he and Scar were whisked away to the hospital for a medical clearance and then off to foster care, where they remained for over a year.

With the mandatory expiration on parental rights, after eighteen

months, they were put up for adoption. Every Wednesday, Derek and Scar went to the agency along with about twenty-five other kids for display for prospective parents. Derek would always hold Scar's hand and secretly tell people that they were not going to be separated, and that if they wanted him, they would have to take Scar too.

With one look at Scar's disfigured face, the potential parents always turned away and found other kids to adopt. Derek's plan had worked for weeks, and each week he and Scar would go back to their foster home.

After a few weeks, the social workers couldn't figure out why at least one of the boys couldn't attract an adoptive family. The workers finally started sitting close to Derek and Scar and listening to what Derek was saying to the people shopping for children. When the workers got wind of what he was doing, the following Wednesday they put him and Scar in separate rooms, and Derek was picked immediately. He was seven, with the cutest dimples and the prettiest smile. Scar, on the other hand, had been overlooked again and again. The day Derek's new family came to pick him up—a father who was a cop and a mother who was a teacher—he refused to leave without his brother. He had fought and cursed and even locked himself inside the bathroom.

The social worker had lied to Derek to coax him out of the bathroom so his new parents could grab him and get him home. "Your brother will be coming along soon," she said. "Go ahead. You'll see him again."

Derek reluctantly went. He wouldn't see his brother for another fifteen years, by which time they had both landed on opposite sides of the law.

In Derek's new adoptive home, everything seemed to be perfect. His father fought crime, and his mother taught him everything there was to know in any book imaginable. They were a real family. They ate dinner together and had fun movie nights on Fridays, his father's day off.

Derek lived like a kid that had been born with a silver spoon in his mouth. He wore the finest clothes, had every toy before it even became popular with other kids, and most of all, he had a real family life with both parents.

But everything wasn't as peachy as it seemed. Derek's father worked the midnight shift, and when he left home at ten o'clock after tucking his son in and kissing his wife, things would take a dark turn in the house.

Derek's adoptive mother would creep into his bedroom at night and shake him awake, standing over him in a see-through nightgown. Longing for her husband's touch and affection, Ms. Fuller was lonely and desperate. She would climb into bed with her adopted son and

stroke his hair. Then she would tell Derek that she loved him more than anything in the world, and that if he wanted to see his brother again, he would have to touch her and she would help him find his brother.

At first it started out as touching. She'd take his little hands and guide them around her body. She would make him touch her breasts and put his fingers in her vagina. And by the time Derek was eleven, she had begun to make him have full-blown intercourse with her. She would always perform fellatio on him first then make him perform cunnilingus on her. Then she would take his still growing penis and force him to put it in her sloppy, oversized pussy. Most of the time Derek felt disgusting and dirty; sometimes he wanted to vomit.

But as the years went by, things changed and he felt differently. His body would betray him, and he started to experience sensations he didn't quite understand. Derek had conditioned himself to fight the good feeling that he started to get as he got older. He told himself the faster he got to that feeling the better, because his turmoil would be over. Derek would ejaculate after a few minutes, so he wouldn't feel so guilty. It was ingrained in him as a coping mechanism. "Come quickly, and it will be over," he used to tell himself.

Although at his adoptive home in the posh northern Maryland suburb of Bowie; Derek had every toy, private school education, went to church, and lived in a beautiful home, none of it was good enough. All he wanted was to see his biological mother and brother again.

Meanwhile, Scar remained in the foster care system in the hood of Baltimore. After years of enduring teasing and beatings at the hands of other kids in group home after group home, Scar grew angry inside. On most days he felt ruthless and often had visions of killing the social workers and the other kids with his bare hands. It wasn't long before Scar was on edge.

"Hey, ugly," a boy had called out to Scar one day, throwing a ping pong ball from the day room and hitting him in the head.

Scar bit down into his cheek and ignored his tormentor.

"You so ugly, we could probably win a world war just by showing your face to the enemies." The boy continued garnering laughs from the other kids sitting around. "Look at that scar and those saggy lips. I bet your mother must have fucked a gorilla to get something as ugly as you." The boy let out a shrill, grating laugh.

That was it. Scar snapped. His ear seemed clogged, and the room started spinning around him. He'd never tolerated anyone talking about his mother or his brother.

"Arrrggh!" Scar screamed out, suddenly lunging at the boy with a pocketknife he had stolen. Scar had buried the pocketknife deep into the boy's neck, hitting his jugular vein.

The boy's eyes popped open in shock. He didn't expect the "ugly monster kid" to ever fight back. Screams erupted in the room, and some of the other kids ran out into the hallway to get help, as the boy backed up from Scar's contact, holding his throat and gagging.

Scar stumbled backward at the sight of the boy's thick burgundy blood spewing like a fountain from his neck. Before any of the group home administrators could help, the boy bled to death within minutes, right at Scar's feet. And though Scar was scared to death, something inside of him felt powerful, almost invincible. The group home security quickly tackled Scar to the floor and held him there until the police arrived.

Scar spent two months in a mental institution because of that incident. After the psychiatrist cleared him, he was placed in a juvenile detention center, where he stayed until he was eighteen years old. It was at the detention center that Scar learned all of his criminal ways, so by the time he was released onto the streets of Baltimore, instead of being rehabilitated, he had become a ruthless dude with a nothing-to-lose attitude.

Derek went away to college and only returned to his adoptive home when his father was laid to rest after a long battle with cancer. When the funeral was over, he told his adoptive mother she would never see him again.

He had never forgiven her for years of sexual abuse, which had followed him like a looming nightmare. He always felt like he had no control over his own body or his own sexuality. When he began having sex for pleasure with girls his age, his body would betray him. His body would overpower his will not to ejaculate quickly.

Derek immediately moved back to Baltimore. Maybe, just maybe, he would run into his real mother or his brother.

After a year of looking for corporate jobs, he joined the Maryland State Police, hoping to become a state trooper. He had long since given up the active search to find his mother and brother again. In fact, he didn't know the first place to look. Checking the foster care system had turned up nothing on Scar. Those records were sealed on kids that aged out of foster care anyway.

Then one day, as a highway patrol trooper, he walked into the squad room of the Narcotics Unit to get a white powder test done on a substance he had seized during a car stop, and right on the wall was a huge poster with his brother's face and name plastered on it—wanted: STEPHON "SCAR" JOHNSON, REWARD $10,000 He stared at the picture for what had to be ten minutes. When it had finally sunk in that the man in the picture was really Scar, Derek got so nauseated and weak, he almost threw up.

"What's the matter, Fuller?" one of his colleagues asked. "You look like you saw a ghost in that mufucka, Scar Johnson."

"Nah, nah. Just looking around," Derek said, quickly pulling himself together before anyone caught on to his interest in Scar. After seeing that picture, Derek was hopeful again, and he set out to find his brother.

When he pulled Scar's criminal history, he learned just what his brother had been doing since he had last seen him at five years old. Scar had a rap sheet as long as a city block. Derek learned that Scar had become the founder of the notorious Dirty Money Crew, a crew of killers that had murdered their way to the top of the Maryland drug trade. Though Scar was on the other side of the law, being his blood, Derek was still determined to find him one day.

Derek worked hard to prove himself as the best trooper on the streets, just so he could get enough clout in the department to put in his application to join the drug team. He was a man on a mission. After six months, he made the Narcotics Unit, officially becoming a jump-out boy. Every time he went out on a jump-out operation to pick up the hand-to-hand street pharmacists, he was hopeful he would run into Scar or get some information on him.

Finally, Derek and his team jumped out on a set of corner boys, and it just so happened the little dudes they picked up were down with the Dirty Money Crew, and low men on Scar's payroll. It didn't take long for Derek to get one of them alone and promise him freedom if he told him where to find Scar.

At first, the little soldier was living by the street creed— No Snitching! But the longer the boy sat in a cell, unable to use the bathroom, get anything to eat, and with no phone calls, he finally gave in and provided Derek with the information he needed.

Derek had sat undetected outside of all of Scar's trap houses for weeks, but Scar never showed up. Being out there, he figured out every drop-off and pick-up time. He had numbered Scar's workers and tried to figure out who was a higher-up, which meant he was probably closest to Scar. Derek noticed one particular dude as the most consistent player at all of the trap houses, and he never stuck around long. Derek reasoned he was the lieutenant, in charge of bringing the re-up and picking up the profits.

Derek decided to tail him, and sure enough, one night he followed the dude right to his leader. His heart thumped wildly when he peeked out of his windshield and saw Scar in the flesh. There he was, his long-lost brother, all grown up and the leader of a crime syndicate. Derek could recognize that scarred face and huge head anywhere.

Both proud and sad, he wondered what their lives would have been like, had their mother not abandoned them that fateful night. He fig-

ured the big-ass man that had beaten his mother unmercifully had probably returned and killed her, and he had long convinced himself that she was probably better off dead than running the streets chasing crack.

Derek had watched Scar that first night without revealing himself, although he wanted to rush out of the car and embrace his brother with a big hug and a sincere apology. He didn't know how his brother would react to him, or if he would even remember him. Conflicted, Derek went home to his then girlfriend, Tiphani, and confided in her: He was a cop and his brother was a wanted criminal. Tiphani told him to do whatever would make him happy.

For two days Derek changed his car and disguise and watched his brother. Finally, he felt he had grown the balls to reveal himself to Scar. He walked up to Scar's bar and lounge, Katrina's (named after their mother), which also housed Scar's office in a secret room in the back. He was stopped at the door and asked what his business was, since it was a bit early for patrons.

"I just wanna get a drink, man," Derek said to the goons protecting the front door. Long fuckin' day."

The front door man surveyed Derek, trying to see if he could tell if this square was a cop or fed. Since he was dressed like a typical street dude, Derek was allowed entry.

Derek ordered a few drinks to build up his courage. "He's your little brother," he whispered to himself, "li'l Scar head."

Walking to the back of the lounge, Derek encountered yet another layer of security, a tall, muscular dude.

"Yo, man, I need to see Scar," Derek said to the dude, trying to sound as street as he could. Derek had lost that edge a long time ago, so it was a stretch for him.

"Who the fuck are you, nigga?" the goon asked.

"Tell Scar I got information on his family."

The goon crinkled his face in confusion. Everybody on the street knew Scar always proclaimed he was a purebred street nigga born from the concrete. No mother, no father, no family.

"Nah, Scar ain't got no family," the goon told Derek.

"Everybody got family. Now tell him I got information on his family," Derek said forcefully.

Scar's security guard reluctantly went behind the secret door, which was obscured with police grade double-sided glass. Two minutes later, the man returned and said to Derek, "Scar wants to know, if you got information on his family, where was his mother's birthmark?"

Derek swallowed hard as his mother's face came flooding back to his mind's eye. He could see her brown sugar–colored skin and straight white teeth so clearly smiling at him, but those memories were

from a time when things were so good for them. The last time he'd laid eyes on his mother, though, she was a gaunt skeleton with missing teeth and riddled with bruises.

Shaking his head left to right, Derek tried to get it together. "It–it was a heart-shaped, cherry-colored mark on her left cheek," he said, barely able to get the words out, "and she used to call it 'a mother's love' and tell us she got it from our kisses."

The man was really confused when Derek said "our kisses." He looked at Derek wildly and then disappeared. Within minutes the man returned, and Derek was allowed to follow him back to the secret office.

When Derek stepped into the room, it was like time stood still. Scar was sitting behind a huge mahogany desk like the CEO of a legitimate company, his face looking much improved. His scar actually made him look dangerous, instead of ugly and deformed like it did when he was a kid. Who would've thought an ugly birth defect could benefit him? Derek, thinking his eyes were deceiving him, was at a loss for words as he stared at Scar, and his legs grew weak, threatening to fail him.

"Ain't this a bitch! My big brother," Scar said, standing up and stepping from behind the desk.

Derek was still speechless. He didn't know whether to cry, scream, or say sorry.

"I know the cat ain't got your tongue, nigga. You ain't happy to see your little brother after a hundred years and shit?" Scar grabbed Derek for a manly hug.

"I'm just so fuckin' happy to see you, man," Derek, shaking all over, finally managed to say. "I'm so sorry I couldn't keep my promise at the time. I was a kid. They snatched me away from you. I had promised Mommy—"

"C'mon, man, I don't hold you responsible for nothin'. Them white people ain't care nothing about two black little niggas tryin'a keep whatever piece of family they had together. I ain't never blame you, my nig. Besides, if shit didn't happen the way it did, I wouldn't be the king I am today." Scar offered his dumbfounded brother a seat.

"I told Mommy I would always take care of you. I'm back and I will keep that promise," Derek assured his brother.

And he wasn't lying. Although he had pledged to uphold the law of the State of Maryland, Derek had another chance to keep his promise to his mother and he vowed he would forever be his brother's keeper—if his brother wanted to be kept. From that day forward he helped Scar stay one step ahead of the law. One step ahead of the jump-out boys and the narcs.

But when the heat got turned up on Derek to make some big busts, he spoke with Scar, and they agreed to put on their little show. Scar agreed to take a fall to help his brother look good in the eyes of the de-

partment and the public. That's why Derek Fuller would always be grateful to his brother and never forget the sacrifice he'd made for him.

Chapter One Hundred Twenty-two

Halleigh sighed in relief when she saw the car diminishing in her rearview mirror. Her heart was still pounding in her chest. She peered in the backseat to check on her son and saw that he was sleeping in his car seat. He had no idea what had just gone down, and frankly, neither did Halleigh. She knew this was more than her being paranoid. Somebody had tried to follow her home. She didn't know who it was, but she was sure she was in danger. She could feel it in her bones that something bad was lingering closely and she had to let Malek know.

"Malek!" she yelled as she raced into the house. "Malek!" She went through their apartment, turning on every single light in her home. Her distressed yelling caused her baby to begin to cry, and his wails filled the house. Realizing that Malek was nowhere to be found, she tried him on his cell phone.

"What's up, Hal?" he asked, upon answering.

"Malek, somebody tried to follow me home today!" she yelled, still in a panic.

"Halleigh, ma, we've been over this. Nobody is going to touch you here. Nobody's after you."

"Malek, I saw the car. I spun the block like you taught me. I'm sure—"

"Hal, baby girl, we'll talk about it when I make it home. You're safe. I'ma keep you safe, a'ight. I'm not going to let anyone hurt you again."

Frustrated, Halleigh hung up the phone. She wasn't as weak as Malek thought she was. Halleigh was hoping she could convince him to see things her way before things got bad and it was too late.

She securely locked the front door and checked every window before she staked out on the couch with her son lying on her chest, and waited for her man to make it home.

The next day Halleigh didn't even mention what had happened because she knew no matter what she said, Malek would simply brush her comments under the rug. She could feel him watching her with worry in his eyes.

"I'm fine, Malek," she said.

He stood and walked over to her, shirtless and sexy. "You've got to stop thinking that everyone is out to get you, ma. This is a new start for us, Hal. Nobody's gon' find us, and ain't nobody gon' touch you or my seed. I'll die first. I know Mitch fucked up your head when he took you, but I handled that. The nigga's a memory, but I can't fight your ghosts for you, ma."

Halleigh nodded as she rose out of their bed. "I've got to go to the bookstore today, baby. I'm working until close."

Halleigh left the baby with Malek and then dressed quickly before exiting the house.

Detective Rodriguez watched Halleigh emerge from her house. Today she was eager to follow the young woman. Whatever was going to go down with Halleigh, the detective didn't plan on missing it. She followed Halleigh to the mall. She knew she was in store for a long day of waiting. Work couldn't go by quickly enough for Halleigh, and as the mall closed down, she prepared to leave. The parking lot was dark when she stepped outside, and as she sped up her pace to hurry to her car, she didn't notice she had company. Toy and Tasha sat watching Halleigh, but they in turn didn't realize that Detective Rodriguez sat at the south end of the parking lot watching them too. Halleigh clutched her shoulder bag tightly, feeling the security of the .45 tucked inside. Her stiletto heels clicked against the pavement as she hightailed it to her car.

Feeling uneasy, she decided to make sure no one was following her before she headed home, so she pulled out of the parking lot and took the long way to her house, stopping to run a few errands on the way, all the while keeping her eyes on the same black car with Toy and Tasha.

"Fuck is this bitch doing? I'm getting real tired of playing cat and mouse," Toy stated.

Halleigh had pulled her card and was tired of playing games as well. She was done running and being the victim. It was time for her to find out who was behind the black tint. Her loaded courage was in her purse, and she figured that whatever they wanted, it was going to be handled tonight because she refused to bring the devil to her front door. She had a son to think about; it wasn't just about her. And whatever beef was looming in the air, she was about to cook it.

Her pounding heartbeat drowned out the sound of everything around her as she pulled into the deserted lot of a closed convenience store. Just as she predicted, the black car was not too far behind. Tired of being prey to this unknown shark, she got out of the car, clutching the gun from inside her purse.

The black car parked at the other end of the lot in an attempt to be

discreet, but Halleigh had already peeped game. There was no use in pretending. She wanted to know who was inside the car.

She began to walk across the parking lot, and when she was halfway to the car, she yelled, "Why the fuck are you following me?" She attempted to put some bass in her tone, but the quivering of her voice revealed her fear. As she stood her ground, she watched as the car before her turned off its headlights, and a car door opened.

"Get out of the car," Toy said.

"What?"

"She trusts you. Get her to come over to the car."

Tasha watched as Halleigh held her ground in the middle of the deserted lot. "And then what?"

"Then we make her take us to Malek."

Tasha had not planned on getting this involved. She had helped Toy find Halleigh and had even lured her out of her hiding place, but now Toy wanted her to basically help snatch her off the street. She started to say no, but the venomous look in Toy's eyes told her that it was do or die. She sighed as she climbed out of the car.

"Halleigh!" Tasha exclaimed as she walked over to her. "I've been following you for twenty minutes! Why is your phone going straight to voice mail? I've been trying to get you to pull over for miles."

"Tasha?" Halleigh yelled in confusion. She sighed a breath of relief. "What the fuck are you doing? Why are you following me?" She threw her arms up in frustration. "You scared the shit out of me!"

"I went to meet you at your job, but you were pulling out when I was pulling up. I tried to call you and let you know I was behind you, but your phone was going straight to voice mail." Tasha knew her excuse was flimsy, but she was hoping that Halleigh was still as naïve as she'd always been.

"Fuck, Tasha! You out here like a stalker. I didn't know who you were! Were you following me yesterday too?" Halleigh yelled angrily. She put her hand over her racing heart.

"What? Hal, of course not! Why are you spazzing on me? I just thought we could go out for drinks. You told me you worked at the mall, so I decided to meet you after work, but you got out of there like a bat out of hell. I couldn't keep up."

Halleigh nodded and calmed down a little, not wanting to overreact. She was the one who had invited Tasha to come to Baltimore to visit her. *She's your friend. Stop tripping.* She noticed the black Charger was still running. "Who's in the car?"

"That's my boyfriend. He flew in to surprise me last night. I want you to meet him." Tasha gushed. "Then maybe we can go for that drink?" She put her arm around Halleigh's shoulder. "It looks like you could use it, and someone to talk to. I know you, Hal. You're stressing about something."

Halleigh nodded and then stepped over to the car. It was comforting having her friend by her side. She began to doubt herself. *Maybe Malek's right. Maybe I am tripping.*

As soon as she stepped over to the car, Tasha pushed her from behind as the driver of the car stepped out and grabbed her neck violently. She looked into the eyes of the driver and knew she was in trouble. This was the girl she'd been running from. She didn't need an introduction. The menace behind her gaze told it all. Mitch's sister, Toy, was standing in front of her face, and she could see the rage, the hate, and the vengeance in her eyes.

"You bitch!" Halleigh yelled as she lunged for Tasha. "How could you! I have a son, Tasha! You dirty, grimy-ass bitch."

Toy slapped Halleigh across her face so hard, her neck snapped back, and stars appeared behind her eyes.

"Look, ma, I don't got time for this ra-ra shit. You know who I'm after. We could have avoided this entire li'l confrontation if you had just led me to the nigga, but you wanted to jump bad and play detective. Well, now you know who's behind the tinted windows, ma. Where's Malek?"

Toy spoke so smoothly, it almost sounded like she was trying to seduce Halleigh rather than threaten her. She did not need to raise her voice to get her point across.

Tasha said, "Halleigh, just tell her. You heard what she said. She ain't worried about you. She only wants Malek. That high-school love bullshit is played, and you know it. Stop being stupid, and think about what's best for you. Do yourself a favor and just tell her where he is."

"Fuck you! I'm not telling shit. You dyke-ass bitch, you'll never get to Malek."

There was no way she could tell Toy how to find Malek. That would be putting her son at risk, and he always came first. Toy punched Halleigh in the face with so much strength, it sent her to the ground. She popped the trunk of the car. "Get the fucking duct tape out of the back of the car," she told Tasha.

Halleigh held her face as she rolled onto her side. "Aghh! Shit!" She spat blood out of her mouth. She opened her eyes, and the first thing she saw was her purse lying next to her. Without thinking, she jumped at the opportunity. She reached inside the purse for the gun, wrapped her hands around the trigger, glad that she had left the safety off, and aimed at Toy's chest and fired.

Bang! Bang! Bang!

Chapter One Hundred Twenty-three

"Oh, shit!" Detective Rodriguez shouted as she watched gunshots erupt through the parking lot. The yellow flicker from the burst of the gun lit up the night like tiny fireflies. She knew she should have intervened when she first saw the situation get out of hand.

When she saw Halleigh aim her gun again at the other girl, she didn't hesitate to turn on her lights and swoop down over the lot. She sped up directly to the scene and hopped out of her car, her weapon drawn.

She aimed her well-trained shot at Halleigh. "Baltimore Police!" she yelled. "Put your weapon down! Now!"

"You dirty bitch! I trusted you!" Halleigh shouted at Tasha, who stood with tears in her eyes, and her hands in the air.

"Hal, don't do this. I didn't have a choice. She was going to kill me, Halleigh," Tasha lied. "You have to believe me."

"Halleigh," Detective Rodriguez said calmly, "I need you to put down your weapon. One person has already been hurt. Let's make sure everyone else goes home tonight." The detective could feel the animosity in the air.

"You were supposed to be my friend," Halleigh cried, snot dripping from her nose. She was hysterical, and her hand was shaking. Everything inside of her wanted to dead Tasha where she stood. *She deserves it,* Halleigh thought as her finger played with the trigger.

"Hal, it's me. I'm your friend," Tasha said. "You know I wouldn't do this to you unless I had no choice. She was threatening me."

"Friend?" Halleigh shouted. "Bitch, you call yourself my friend? Yeah, Tasha, you're my friend, my ace boon coon, bitch! The same friend who helped Manolo manipulate me when I was just an innocent teenage girl. The same friend who sat by and watched me self-destruct on heroin and cocaine? Yeah, bitch, you're my friend, and if that's how we do, then you deserve every one of these bullets. They all have your name on them!" It was obvious that Halleigh was letting out all of the resentment she'd held inside over the years.

"Halleigh, if you pull that trigger, then I have to pull mine. The first murder can be justified. It was self-defense; you were protecting yourself. I saw it. But if you kill this girl, there is no turning back. You will be a murderer, Halleigh."

Halleigh's resolve began to break, and she began to lower her arm, but just as she was about to drop the gun, she noticed the smile that came across Tasha's face. The smile enraged her. It was smug and arrogant, as if Tasha had never even expected her to be a threat. Halleigh

lifted her arm and fired a shot into Tasha's face, erasing her smile forever. Then she immediately dropped the gun and put her hands in the air.

"Get on the ground! Now!" Rodriguez yelled as she kicked Halleigh's gun away. "Face on the concrete!"

She shuffled over to Toy's body and checked for a pulse. After feeling none, she felt for Tasha's. Both women were clearly deceased, and now she had to clean this situation up. She didn't want Halleigh in jail, and she definitely didn't give a shit about the two dead black girls lying beneath her feet. Her and her team wanted Malek. Now she had leverage to hold over Halleigh's head to get her to help them get him.

She put a crying Halleigh in handcuffs and then pulled her forcefully from the ground. "You have the right to remain silent. Anything you say or do can be used against you in a court of law. You have the right to an attorney. . . ." The detective read Halleigh her rights as she pushed her toward the unmarked squad car and secured her in the back.

"Damn it!" Rodriguez slammed Halleigh's door shut. "Damn it!" she yelled again, hitting the trunk of the squad car. Now she had to figure out how she would clean up this mess she had allowed to happen.

Malek wasn't even an official case. It was one of their underground hustles, actually a favor to another drug dealer. Malek was competition, so he had to go, but things were going farther than they ever had before. Every cop bent the rules, but this was clearly breaking them. Two bodies would not be easy to cover up.

She trotted back over to the murder scene and discreetly picked up the murder weapon. She wrapped Tasha's dead fingers around it and shot the weapon once. She then did the same routine with Toy to ensure there was gun residue on the girls' hands so that when the coroner bagged and tagged them, there would be no suspicion of a third party being present. She definitely wasn't going to be the one to call it in. Someone would happen upon the bodies in the morning. For now, she had a hustler's wife to crack.

As Halleigh sat in the back of the squad car, being escorted to the police precinct, she knew Malek would be looking for her. *What have I done? My baby,* she thought. She knew she was on her way to prison for a very long time. She had shot two people in front of a police officer. She felt that today was her judgment day, and didn't think there was any way she was getting out of this one.

When they arrived at the police station, Rodriguez escorted Halleigh inside the building. Choosing to bypass processing, she took her to a private room where there were no two-way windows or video cameras. Whatever was said, only the two of them would hear, which was exactly the way Rodriguez wanted it. She pulled out a wooden chair and sat Halleigh down.

Halleigh winced when her bottom hit the seat. Her hands were twisted behind her back, and the handcuffs were uncomfortably tight on her small wrists. "Can you loosen these cuffs?"

Rodriguez obliged, knowing it wasn't going to take the bad cop role for her to get Halleigh to see things her way. Halleigh gazed at the floor silently, thinking about her fate.

Detective Rodriguez let Halleigh's imagination run wild and left the room to give the tension time to build. The more nervous, the more on edge, the more afraid she was, the better. This was the best type of informant to have, one that had something to lose.

Half an hour later, Rodriguez came back into the room. By this time Halleigh's eyes were red and puffy from crying. The left side of her face was swollen, and she had a busted lip from where Toy had punched her. Her bouncing leg let Rodriguez know that she was ready to crack. Rodriguez pulled out a chair and sat across from Halleigh. "You're in a lot of trouble."

Halleigh remained silent as she wiped her eyes with her hand. *I don't need this bitch telling me what I already know.* "I want a lawyer," she replied between sniffles.

"Even if Johnnie Cochran arose from the dead to represent you, he couldn't get you out of this one. You murdered two people, Halleigh, in front of a police detective."

"I didn't have a choice," Halleigh responded drearily.

"You have one now." Halleigh looked up at the detective and shook her head. She knew the look in Rodriguez's eyes well. She wanted something from her. It was the same thirsty look that Manolo had given her, that Mimi used to possess.

"You being there tonight wasn't a coincidence, was it?" Halleigh asked as tears built in her eyes. She felt like this entire situation was a setup.

"I have been following you for the past few days, Halleigh." Halleigh balled her fists and put them to her forehead. She knew she wasn't crazy. All this time her intuition was right. Running, hustling, surviving since she was seventeen years old, she was tired, exhausted at this point. Now here was one more person looking to use her in some way. "What do you want?"

"I want your boyfriend Malek."

"Malek?" Halleigh whispered back almost breathlessly. It was like no one in the world wanted them to be together. There was always a situation threatening to tear them apart. *What the fuck is this? National fuck over Malek day?* "What do you want with Malek?"

"That isn't a concern of yours. All you need to say is yes or no. You can help me and my people gather our evidence against him. I want to know where his money is, what type of business he's into, and who he is doing it with."

Rodriguez stood up. She put her hands in her pocket, revealing the gun and badge hanging off her belt. She circled Halleigh as she continued. "If you cooperate with us, I can make this predicament that you've gotten yourself in . . . disappear."

"Disappear?" Halleigh repeated skeptically.

"*Poof!*" Rodriguez opened her hand as if she were performing a magic trick.

Halleigh's heart ached as she closed her eyes. She loved Malek. There was no way she could turn her back on him now. They were soul mates. They were meant to be together. Their destinies had always been intertwined, and she could never see herself turning on him. They had been through everything together. The good and the bad, they had experienced it all, and still found their way back to one another. There was always treachery around them, and now this woman wanted her to create deceit from within. Obviously Detective Rodriguez didn't know their story. She didn't know their Flint tale and was unaware of the type of love they shared.

"I can't," Halleigh said. "I would never—"

"Why? Because you love him?" Rodriguez laughed as she removed a picture from a large manila folder she was holding. "We've been following him too, Halleigh. You want to know how he spends his days?"

The detective placed a picture on the table in front of Halleigh. It showed Malek going into the home of a young dark-skinned girl's brownstone. "You want to know how long he stayed?"

"About three hours?" Halleigh rolled her eyes.

Halleigh wasn't studying that photo. There was nothing that this cop could tell her about her own man. She knew the little broad in the photo was the girl who cooked up Malek's work. Malek had personally introduced the two and had sought Halleigh's approval before he even started doing business with the chick. Malek was always honest with her, and between them lay no secrets. She leaned forward and slid the picture back across the table.

"I'm not talking, so do what you got to do to me," Halleigh stated, remaining strong on the outside, but on the inside she was crying out. Detective Rodriguez had underestimated Halleigh's loyalty to Malek, but she had a trump card in her deck. She was sure her love for her son was much deeper than the one she felt for Malek.

"Are you really prepared to go to jail for life just to protect your boyfriend? Halleigh, what about your kid? Because if I turn you in, Halleigh, I can guarantee you will never see the light of day again." Detective Rodriguez could see Halleigh's heart breaking as her mind raced. If the world wasn't so cold, she would've felt bad about what she was doing. "I see a hundred girls like you every year, Halleigh. They stand by their drug-dealing boyfriends through it all. They give up their freedom, their children get sucked into the system, and for

what? For nothing, Halleigh. Even if we don't get to him through you, we will get to him eventually. He's in love with the streets, and they all fall. And when he does, we will be there to catch him. So you might as well save yourself now. If you don't care enough about freedom, care enough about your child to make the right choice."

Detective Rodriguez was plucking at the heartstrings of a good mother. As much as Halleigh wanted to be strong, the tears falling down her graceful cheeks were giving her away. This wasn't how things were supposed to go down. Their love story was meant to end in a happily ever after, not like this. No matter what decision she made, her son Malek Jr. would be losing one of his parents. Either she was going to prison for murder, or she was sending Malek in her place. "Why are you doing this to us? I don't know nothing about some king-pin bullshit. There is no money, no cars, no nothing. We're not even from here. We're just trying to live."

"You should have stayed wherever you came from then, Halleigh. This is Baltimore, and let's just say Malek has stepped on the wrong toes," Rodriguez admitted, finally feeling bad for the love-struck girl. Halleigh ended the conversation, refusing to speak to the detective any longer, but Rodriguez was patient and knew that time would crack Halleigh.

Hours passed before Halleigh realized she had been backed into a corner. She loved Malek and always would, but she couldn't see her-self leaving her son. It was no longer just the two of them. She had their son to think about, and he needed her.

She stood and went to the locked door that held her confined in-side the room. She kicked the door and yelled, "Rodriguez!"

Detective Rodriguez re-entered the room and waited for Halleigh to speak. Halleigh put her hands on top of her head. She couldn't believe what she was about to do. "Aghh!" she screamed in agony as she closed her eyes tight. She wished that when she re-opened them she would be awakening from a bad dream. "I'll do it," she said, barely audible. "Excuse me?"

"I said I'll do it!" Halleigh shouted.It was three o'clock in the morn-ing, and all Halleigh wanted was to go home. Malek had probably lost his mind with worry by now, because he had been expecting her hours ago.

"I need to call him."

Rodriguez leaned across the table. "You will tell him you were car-jacked. We brought you here to file a police report. That's the story you will tell him. We will return your car to you tomorrow and say we found it abandoned somewhere."

She began to break down the specifics of what she expected Halleigh to do, how she wanted her to record conversations that would help them take Malek down.

Halleigh barely listened. It was late, and she was overwhelmed, while exhaustion wrecked her. On top of that, her stomach was hollow from the blood on her hands.

"I can't do this right now. I said I'll do it, but I need to get my head together. I just want to go home," Halleigh whispered.

Rodriguez was eager to get down to business and irritated that Halleigh wasn't listening.

"Please," Halleigh pleaded. "We can meet the day after tomorrow at my job."

"Fine. But don't forget what is at stake for you. I'll still be watching you, so don't make this hard and try to run." Rodriguez stood. "I'll take you to use a phone."

When Malek raced into the police station with their son in his arms, Halleigh burst into tears. "Keep it together," Rodriguez mumbled as she watched Malek approach. Hal-leigh, unable to maintain her composure, ran to him and fell into his arms.

Malek held her face in one hand and caressed her cheek gently. "Did they touch you?" he asked, pain and anger apparent in his voice.

"No, no, they just hit me when I wouldn't get out of the car," Halleigh lied. "I'm so sorry."

"What are you sorry for, ma? This isn't your fault. The whip can be replaced; you can't. I love you, Halleigh. I would go crazy if anything ever happened to you."

Detective Rodriguez walked over to the couple. She had an inside-joke smirk on her face. "Halleigh, I will be in touch," she said. She handed her a card. "You can contact me anytime if you need me."

Halleigh nodded, feeling extremely uncomfortable. "Can we get out of here?" she asked Malek.

"Yeah, let's get you home," he said as he kissed the top of her head.

Halleigh grabbed her son out of his arms and cradled him closely as she allowed Malek to lead her out of the precinct. She could feel Rodriguez's eyes following her every move, burning a hole in the back of her head. She began to cry softly.

Malek tried to give her space, figuring she was just feeling vulnerable because of her experience. He was supportive and told her that things would be fine, but on the inside he was furious.

Derek Fuller and his crew stood in front of Malek's crack house, all of them wearing concealable bulletproof vests. They were about to ambush his spot and shut down his operation.

After Scar had given Fuller the rundown on Malek, they immediately began to plot. Scar wanted Malek's upcoming business to be stopped before it got too big, so Fuller grabbed his trusted squad and set up a raid to try to scare off Malek.

"One, two, three," Fuller said as he watched as his crew hold the battering ram, preparing to cave in the door.

On cue, they burst through the door and rushed into the spot, guns drawn.

"Everybody on the floor!" Fuller yelled as he rushed in.

What he saw blew his mind. The house was empty. Only a single card table sat in the middle of the floor. It had Fuller confused, and he and his crew stood there scratching their heads.

"Fuck!" Fuller turned around in a full circle, scoping out the room. "Bullshit!" He kicked over the table.

"Somebody must have tipped him off." He shook his head from side to side, his hands on his waist.

Malek sat in his crack house as he observed his youngsters cook, cut, and package the coke. He had set up shop in one of his many spots earlier that day. Malek never stayed in a spot for more than a week, and luckily for him he'd evaded the cops by the skin of his teeth without even knowing. Malek saw the money going through the cash machine and got a flashback to when he was getting money in Flint. He took a seat at the table and got a bad feeling. He didn't get into Baltimore's drug game to take it over. Just enough to stack a little paper and then retire from the game for good.

He went into the back room where his right-hand man, Dayvid, was at. "I got to let this shit go," he said to him.

"We just got started," Dayvid said, loading the duffel bag with money as it came out of the machine. "You going to let all of this shit go?" He looked at him with a furrowed brow.

"Yeah, I got a shorty to think about. I never wanted to stay in this shit. I'm just trying to stack a little paper and bounce. I'ma hand this shit over to you."

"Word?" Dayvid said, liking the sound of what Malek had just said to him. Dayvid was only nineteen, but by being under the wing of Malek for the past year, he grew up quick. Malek had taught him everything he knew and was molding him to be a kingpin.

"You ready for this?" Malek asked.

"I was born ready."

"Oh yeah, I almost forgot." Malek dug into his pocket and pulled out a small box and tossed it to Dayvid.

Looking up, Dayvid reacted quickly and caught the box with one hand.

"Happy birthday, my nigga," Malek said, releasing a rare smile.

Dayvid smiled. He was totally taken by surprise that Malek even knew it was his birthday. Dayvid had no family and never received anything for his birthday, so he never saw it coming. He opened the box and exposed the diamond pinky ring and slowly nodded his head in approval as he smirked.

"You want to be a boss, right? Well, you have to start looking like one," Malek said as he stood up. "Let's roll," Malek said as he headed toward the door.

Later that night Scar was lounging in the VIP section of the club with his crew as they did every Friday night, bottles of liquor and strippers surrounding them as they enjoyed themselves. They were on the top level, which gave them a clear view of the main floor, and the loud bass from the club's speakers had the club rocking.

Scar stood at the glass front and looked down at the floor, watching the stripper on stage shake her ass.

His goon squinted his eyes and noticed Malek in the corner of the club with his crew. They were showering the strippers with dollars, and all eyes were on them.

"Yo, Scar, I think that's the nigga that's been moving weight on our turf. The one with the black fitted hat on."

"You sure that's him?" Scar looked down at the man in question.

"I'm positive. There is his li'l man, Dayvid. The one that's making it rain."

"Send him a bottle of Mo and then tell him I want to holla at him."

Scar was a good businessman. He knew that beef wasn't good when making money, so he took the peaceful route, and decided to make Malek an offer to get down with his squad.

"Cool," Scar's goon said as he grabbed up a couple of niggas and headed down to confront Malek.

Scar rubbed his hands together. *Young stupid niggas always trying to make a come-up*, he thought as he smiled to himself.

Scar had learned earlier from his police informant that they had just missed Malek when they raided his spot, so he decided to step to Malek and offer him a position on his team. He'd been in the game too long, and he knew how to muscle people with his money. He was going to make Malek work for him and make him think he was a business partner.

Malek sat back and watched as his li'l man enjoyed his birthday. Although Malek was in the midst of half-naked women and his niggas, he was only thinking of Halleigh and his son.

Just as he formed a slight smirk, he noticed three men approaching the booth that he and his crew were sitting in, and immediately Dayvid and company stood up and went for their guns.

"Whoa, whoa! Hold on, fam. We come in peace, fam," the goon said, holding up the bottles of Moët in his hands.

Dayvid put his hand on the chest of the head goon as they were headed straight for Malek. "What the fuck is the problem?"

"First, get your fucking hand off my chest," the goon said to Dayvid as he looked down at his hand. "Second, we're not coming over here on no beef shit," he added in a non-confrontational tone. We just wanted to talk to your boss, that's all."

"Let 'em through," Malek said, sitting back and watching the scene unfold.

Dayvid stepped to the side and let the goon through, leaving Scar's other two goons standing at bay.

"What can I do for you?" Malek said as the goon sat across the table from him.

"Scar sent you these bottles of Moët and wants to have a sit-down with you."

"Sit down with me?" Malek then paused. "For what? We don't have anything to talk about," he said calmly.

"That's for you and him to discuss. I'm just the messenger."

"No, I'm good right here. Tell your boss he can keep those bottles too. As you can see, we have our own bottles." Malek grabbed a bottle of Dom and took a swig.

Malek didn't even give the goon a second look as he focused on the stripper on the main stage, and the goon slid out of the booth and headed to Scar to tell him the news.

Malek had heard about Scar, but didn't feel the need to make any new friends. He sat back and continued to enjoy himself.

Not even ten minutes later, he saw the same group of men approaching his table again, but this time they had another person with them. It was Scar.

Malek's crew all stopped partying and slid their hands down to their waists as the crew approached. Scar's crew was notorious for busting their guns, so Malek's squad wasn't going to take any chances.

But Malek knew who Scar was, so he immediately told his crew to fall back and relax.

Scar came humbly and stood at the table with both of his hands collapsed into each other, in a non-threatening approach. "Hello," Scar

said as he looked Malek directly in the eye with a small smirk. "I hear you're making a lot of noise in the streets."

"That's what you hear, huh?" Malek answered as he returned the stare. "I don't know what you're talking about, homeboy. I'm a working man."

"Please don't insult my intelligence, young brother. I'm not here to rain on your parade. I just want to give you a business proposal. I see you recruited my li'l man Dayvid, huh? I raised that nigga!"

Dayvid just stared at Scar with hateful eyes and never said a word. They'd had a past relationship that was a story of its own. Although heated by Scar's comment, he remained silent and played his position.

"I'm listening." Malek had already made up in his mind that he wasn't going to deal with Scar, but he would hear Scar out, so he wouldn't seem like he was blowing him off.

"I see you moving heavy coke. I know that I can beat your supplier's price. If you cop from me, I can keep the local police off your crew . . . and protection." Scar quickly grew a more sinister look on his face at the end of his statement.

"Protection?" Malek smiled as he sat up from his slightly slumped position. "Protection from who?" he asked, feeling the tension coming from Scar. "That sounded like a threat more than a proposition."

"You can take it how you want," Scar said, tired of playing games.

"Good day to you, sir," Malek said as he focused his attention on the stripper a couple of feet behind Scar.

Scar turned around to see what Malek was looking at. He chuckled, not believing Malek's arrogance. "You have a lot to learn, youngblood. Do you know who the fuck I am?" Scar asked, his jaws clenched tight.

Malek's crew acted accordingly to Scar's comment, and they all began to slide their hands to their waists, where their guns were, and Scar's crew followed suit.

Scar nodded his head slowly and stared at Malek intensely. He was growing more furious by the millisecond. He chuckled and then looked around at his crew, who all had ice grills and were ready to shoot on command.

"Let's go," Scar said, already having plans for Malek.

Scar turned around and left Malek and his crew alone. Scar's crew followed him. From the look on Scar's face, they knew what was to come next: *He don't want to get with the program, so he about to get shut down.*

"This is my city!" Scar mumbled as they made their way out of the door, cutting their night short.

Malek and his crew sat back and laughed at Scar's proposition and continued to have a good time.

An hour had passed, and it was approaching one A.M. Malek was taking shots with Dayvid, celebrating his birthday. Little did they know, Scar and his crew had no intentions of letting them leave that club alive on that night.

"This whole shit about to be yours, son," Malek said as he raised his glass and downed a shot.

"You're going to let all of this money we getting go?" Dayvid asked, not understanding how anyone could fathom an exit when business was booming.

"Yeah, I have been there, done that. I came to B-more to escape the street life, but it's so alluring, ya know. It seems as if the game just pulled me back in," Malek said, dropping knowledge on his young protégé.

"I'm going to buy this club and set up a legit life for me and my family," Malek said.

Just before Dayvid could respond, masked men ran into the club with automatic assault rifles and began to send shots at them. The sound of the bullets zipping out of the guns and shattering mirrors caused the whole club to go haywire.

Malek's crew quickly ducked for cover and returned fire, trying to defend themselves. Dayvid caught a bullet to the shoulder, but still managed to bust shots back while escorting Malek to the back exit.

Seconds later the rest of Malek's crew came bursting out of the back exit, and they jumped into the Suburban that they came in.

"What the fuck?!" Malek asked as he sat in the passenger's side, taken completely off guard by Scar's ambush.

"Get in!" Dayvid yelled, revving the engine as he waited for the other crew to jump into the truck. Once they were all in, he sped off, leaving tire marks on the back parking lot pavement. They had to leave and re-group. Scar had just started a war.

Scar sat back comfortably in an oversized Jacuzzi surrounded by three naked women, all sucking on different parts of his tattooed body.

The big plasma television that hung on the wall held his attention. He listened closely as the news reporter talked about the rising drug problem in inner city Baltimore.

Scar smiled, knowing he was the main cause of the drug problem in Baltimore, and by him having direct ties with the head of the Baltimore Narcotics Unit, he was untouchable.

He also knew shooting at Malek and his crew would lead to some sort of backlash, but he wrote Malek off as an amateur, which was a wrong move on his part.

Chapter One Hundred Twenty-five

The night was winding down, and Malek had just checked in on his sleeping son. Halleigh was lying in their bedroom, waiting for him. Malek had a lot on his mind, but didn't want to tell her about it.

He never wanted to bring his street business into his home, so he remained quiet about almost losing his life earlier that night. He instantly began thinking of ways to get back at Scar, but he was going to sleep on it, so he would make the best strategic move.

Malek walked in and looked at Halleigh and instantly wanted to make love to her. He sat on the bed, and she cuddled against him as he ran his fingers through her hair. He grabbed the remote and turned on the stereo. Classic Sade began to play.

Looking down at Halleigh as her head rested in his lap, all of his tensions melted away. Just being near her again felt good. He looked at her voluptuous figure and felt the swell of his dick rise against his jeans.

Halleigh sat up and straddled Malek, grinding her hips against his concealed manhood. She kissed him seductively, exploring his mouth with her tongue. Her body moved to the rhythm of the song, and Malek's hands gripped her breasts as they pressed against his chest.

Malek grabbed her backside firmly, and looked down at the thong that had disappeared in the crack of her ass. He pulled off the tiny thong and saw her fat lips soaked in her own juice. Halleigh sat up. She couldn't wait for her man to please her. She reached for his belt buckle, and removed his jeans. His thick ten inches stood at attention in her face, and she couldn't help but to taste him. She devoured him into her mouth, making him disappear and re-appear over and over.

Malek placed his hands on her head and gently guided her as she sucked him like a lollipop. Halleigh's head game was superb, as if designed just for him. She ran her tongue up and down his length and kissed the tip gently, causing his toes to *curl*.

He pushed Halleigh back on the bed, and they got into the sixty-nine position. He opened her lips with his tongue and tasted her wetness as he licked at her clitoris, his tongue flicking back and forth, fast and then slow.

Halleigh rotated her groin, making love to Malek's firm tongue. The better he made her feel, the better she sucked his dick. She couldn't help it; he was making her go crazy and she wanted to suck him until he exploded.

Malek inserted two fingers into her pussy and shoved them into her like it was a hard dick. Moans couldn't help but to escape her lips as he tickled her insides with his fingers and massaged her clit with his

tongue. She was riding his face like a cowboy, moving her head up and down like she was bobbing for apples.

Malek was large, and she wanted him inside of her, but she was feeling too good to stop him. He ate her out, and she hit him off until they both reached their climax. She swallowed his seed, leaving his dick spotless, arching her back as she came in his mouth. They both had reached ecstasy at the same time, releasing all of their pent-up tension.

Too exhausted to get up and do anything, Halleigh wrapped herself in Malek's arm.

"I'ma take care of you, Halleigh. You deserve the best, and that's what I'm gon' give you. That's my word."

"I already have the best. The world is ours, Malek."

Malek had to smile at her words. She was the perfect woman for him, and she would always hold him down.

"The world is ours, Halleigh. I love you, and after I get my dough up, we are going to relocate again. I am going to fly straight, I promise. No more hustling."

With those words they drifted into a comfortable sleep.

However, before he completely nodded off, Malek had figured out how he would strike back at Scar Johnson. He was going to hit him where it hurt the most. His pockets.

It seemed like the morning came too quickly because Halleigh was still groggy and exhausted from the night before. She felt the covers being lifted off of her and frowned as the draft of cold morning air caused goose bumps to form on her skin. She knew Malek wanted to pick up where they'd left off, but she was too tired.

"Baby, stop."

She felt him run his finger down her thigh.

"Malek, your hands are cold. Stop," she whined as she kept her eyes closed, not wanting to wake up fully.

It wasn't until Hal heard the shower running that she realized something wasn't right. The sound of running water sparked confusion in her mind. She sat up instantly to find three of Scar's goons standing in the room, one of whom was standing over her tracing the outline of her ass with a black .38.

"Ma—"

Halleigh tried to yell out to Malek, but before she could even get his name out of her mouth, a sweaty hand covered it, silencing her, and three pistols were aimed in her direction, the .38 pointed directly at her temple.

"Shut up, bitch," one of them calmly instructed.

Fear filled Halleigh's body, and her heart felt like it had sunk into her stomach. In any other situation she would have known how to react. She would have taken her chances and reached for the night-

stand where she kept her .22. She would have warned Malek that someone was in the house. She would have done something.

But this situation was different. She had been caught off guard, and the goon that had the steel pressed to the side of her head intimidated her. There was something about the way that he looked at her that told her he wouldn't hesitate to pull the trigger. For the first time in a long time she was afraid.

She instantly began to think about her baby in the next room. She was hoping he didn't wake up crying and let it be known that he was there.

She didn't know what was going to happen or even why they had come. As the men's eyes ogled her body, she wanted to pull up the covers but was frozen in place. Everyone in the room heard the running water stop.

The men cocked their weapons, and Halleigh's body stiffened when she heard the hammer to the .38 pull back. She did the only thing she could do and lifted her eyes to the sky and prayed silently.

Please, God, don't let them kill Malek. Please, don't let him come into this room.

Halleigh wasn't even worried about her well-being; the only thing she could think of was Malek. She didn't know what she would do if something happened to him.

Malek wrapped a towel around his waist and then made his way into the bedroom. He opened the door, and the sight of a gun threatening Halleigh's existence enraged him. He ran toward the bed but was halted by a bulky goon, who aimed a Ruger .357 Magnum in his direction.

"Malek!" Halleigh yelled out, afraid he would be shot. Her heart was beating like a drum, and tears began to swell in her eyes.

Malek's mind was focused on getting to her; he wasn't thinking about the hole that the Ruger would leave in his chest if fired. He grabbed the goon's wrist and punched him hard in the face, causing blood to flood from his nose.

"Aghhh! You muthafucka!," the goon yelled out in pain as he cupped his face with both hands and dropped to his knees in pain.

In one swift movement, Malek snatched the weapon from his hands and pointed it toward the bed where Scar stood next to a terrified Halleigh. Malek was working straight off of emotion and didn't notice the third goon, until he had his gun pressed against Malek's head.

Scar laughed as he jabbed his gun against Halleigh's head. "Malek, what the fuck are you doing? You're Superman now?" He continued to chuckle, and then firmly stated, "Don't be stupid! Put down the gun."

Malek hesitated as he looked at Halleigh, whose eyes were closed.

"What are you going to do?" Scar taunted. "You going to kill me,

Malek? Before you even move your finger, her brains will be all over the bedspread."

Malek dropped the gun and glared at Scar, who now had the gun on Halleigh's bare breasts, the cold steel making her dark nipples stand at attention, enraging Malek even more. He could see Halleigh trembling, and his jaw clenched as he gritted his teeth.

"Your girl has a nice pair of tits," Scar said as he stared Malek down.

Malek knew that Scar wouldn't hesitate to kill Halleigh, so he kept his cool.

"You got out of the club pretty fast last night. I didn't want to kill you, playboy. Just wanted to send you a message."

"If you touch her—"

"If I touch her, what? What are you going to do, li'l nigga?" Scar clenched his teeth together.

"This has nothing to do with her. Let's handle this amongst ourselves."

"I think she has a lot to do with this. I asked you if you wanted to get down; you told me no. I don't take rejection too good, as you can see. Maybe you need to reconsider your answer. Right?" Scar gave Malek a small smirk and then focused his eyes back on Halleigh's exposed body.

"Yeah, maybe I will reconsider," Malek said, telling Scar what he thought he wanted to hear.

"Great!" Scar smiled from ear to ear as if they were friends. "That's all I can ask for."

Scar and his crew headed for the door. He had no intentions of killing Malek or his family on that day. He just wanted to send him a message. Wanted to let him know he could be touched at any time.

Once they were out of the room, Malek rushed over to Halleigh and held her in his arms.

"Are you okay, baby?" he asked as he kissed her on top of her forehead.

Tears streamed from Halleigh's eyes as she nodded her head yes. She then rushed into the baby's room and checked on Malek Jr., who was sound asleep, resting peacefully. She scooped him and kissed him, glad to see he was okay.

Meanwhile Malek ran to the window in the living room and saw Scar's black Navigator pull off.

"Fuck!" Malek screamed as he paced the room. He knew he'd just put his family in the line of fire, and he couldn't accept that. Scar had just made it personal by invading his home, breaking all the rules to the game.

He returned to the back room, where Halleigh was crying and holding their baby close to her chest.

"Baby, I'm scared," Halleigh cried.

Malek stood in the doorway, not knowing what to say to her to explain the ambush. "I know, I know," he said, trying to soothe her. He walked over to her and gently hugged her, with the baby between them. He softly kissed her on the forehead and let her know everything would be okay.

Malek was going to let the beef stay in the streets, but Scar had crossed that line. He relocated that evening, and quickly put a plan in motion. Scar was about to regret the day he stepped to him.

Malek set his goons loose on Scar's crew, orchestrating the robbery of six of Scar's main trap houses. He already had planned on doing it, but now Scar had just pushed up the date for it.

Malek's crew, led by Dayvid, managed to take close to $100,000 from Scar's various establishments. Dayvid knew all of Scar's spots because he, at one point, had planned on robbing them anyway. So when Malek told him about the plan, he was well prepared and informed about Scar's spots.

Scar's squad never saw it coming. This only made the beef between them more treacherous and heated. They now hated each other.

Chapter One Hundred Twenty-six

Halleigh's secret was too much for her to handle. As soon as they entered their home, she put their son in his crib and began to pace back and forth in their living room.

"Hal, you're home now. Come take a shower with me. It'll relax you. You need to get some sleep. You've had a long day," Malek stated.

So many thoughts were racing through Halleigh's head, she barely heard him. She was used to them solving their problems together, but on this, she was on her own. She had to find a way to come out of this without taking Malek down. Everything she had ever done was for him. She couldn't bring herself to deceive him, even though in her heart of hearts, she knew she had no choice. The decision had been made for her when she'd pulled that trigger.

Malek frowned as he approached her. He knew her like the back of his hand. There was something heavy on her mind. He felt bad because, since they had escaped to B-more, he hadn't been there like he should have. He could no longer afford the luxury of sitting around and catering to Halleigh all day. No longer a major player in the game,

he had to rebuild his paper and his operation. That is why he spent so much time in the streets. He just wanted to give his girl and his son the best, but as he watched Halleigh stress herself out, he could see her falling apart at the seams.

"I can't do this," Halleigh whispered. She started getting choked up just thinking about it. She stopped pacing and stared at Malek. "Malek, I need to talk to you. Something happened tonight."

Malek went to her side and wrapped his arms around her as she buried her head in his chest.

"Aye, this is me, Hal. You can tell me anything. It'll be okay."

"Not this time, Malek. I need you to listen to me. I did something really bad tonight—"

Halleigh was ready to put it all out there, but before the confession could fall from her lips, a loud knock at the door interrupted them. It was the middle of the night, and they weren't expecting anyone.

Malek put his hand to his lips to signal for Halleigh to be quiet as he removed his pistol from his waistline. He approached the door and looked out of the peephole. He sighed when he saw it was the detective from the precinct. He handed his gun off to Halleigh, and she put it underneath the couch cushion.

"Who is it?" she whispered.

"It's just that lady cop that helped you out the other night," Malek said.

Halleigh started panicking, and her eyes got as big as saucers. "What! What is she doing here?"

Malek frowned and held out his hand. "I don't know, Hal. Just calm down. She probably forgot to tell you something at the precinct. Chill out." He opened the door and greeted the detective.

"I apologize for the late-night interruption," Detective Rodriguez stated. Halleigh left her bag and identification at the station. I was just returning it."

Halleigh walked toward the door, and Malek stepped to the side. Their son began to cry, and Malek excused himself to take care of him.

Once Rodriguez got Halleigh alone, she stepped in close. "Telling Malek would be a big mistake, Halleigh."

"I wasn't. I told you I was in . . . that I would do it."

Rodriguez reached into Halleigh's jacket pocket and removed the small listening transmitter that she had planted on her before she had left the station. She held it up for Halleigh to see. "This agreement is built on trust, Halleigh. I told you I would be watching you. Everything you do and say, we will know. If this happens again, all deals are off, and I'll take both you and Malek away from your precious little boy. Keep your mouth shut. Stick to the plan. I'll bring your car back to you in the morning."

By the time Malek walked back into the room, Rodriguez had departed, leaving Halleigh feeling even more stuck than before.

Rodriguez pulled out her cell phone and called her partner to update him. "Fuller," she said when he answered, "everything's a go. It shouldn't be long before this Malek kid is out of the picture. The girl's on board."

Halleigh watched out of their window as Rodriguez left. She wished she had the balls to pull the trigger a third time while she was at it. That way she wouldn't have been in the situation she was in now.

She couldn't believe that Rodriguez had planted a bug on her. If she had done that, there was no telling what other ways she was being monitored. For now, she couldn't tell Malek, but she had to figure something out because their fates were intertwined. Setting up Malek would be like setting herself up because she couldn't see herself without him.

"Hal?" Malek called out.

Halleigh turned around, and just seeing his worried expression melted her heart. He was holding their baby, and it was up to her to make sure that her slipup didn't destroy all three of their lives. If she had just played it smart and cut all of her ties to Flint, then none of this would have ever happened. Her mistake was trusting Tasha. Anyone born and raised in the murder capital of Flint, Michigan was larcenous, and she had risked everything just by inviting her to Baltimore. Their predicament was her fault, and she hated that Malek had to pay for her mistake.

"You good?" he asked.

Despondently, she nodded her head. "Yeah, baby, I'm fine."

"What did you want to tell me?"

"Nothing," she replied, "nothing at all. I'm just shook up, that's all. Let's go to bed."

Chapter One Hundred Twenty-seven

Derek Fuller got an inside tip from one of his snitches on Malek's new spot. That's why he was sitting outside of Malek's establishment and waiting to see if he would show up. Fuller had just left a rendezvous with Scar and found out that all of their spots had been robbed within a matter of twenty-four hours. Fuller instantly knew

that Malek was a bigger problem than he thought. He had to take him down if he wanted to keep his stake in Scar's drug business profitable.

"Come on, youngblood. What's taking you so long?" Fuller whispered to himself as he staked out the house and sipped on a cup of coffee.

Scar had requested that Fuller not only shake up Malek's business, but bust him and lock him up. Scar wanted Malek off the streets for good.

Fuller had been posted there for about six hours, and there was no sign of Malek, so he moved to plan B. He picked up his walkie-talkie and let his team know it was time to move in on the spot, although Malek wasn't inside.

"Fuck it! We can't wait on that son of a bitch any longer. Let's move in!" Fuller ordered into the transmitter.

"Roger that, captain," a man said on the other end.

Within seconds, vans whipped onto the block, filling the air with the sound of screeching tires. The side doors slid open on each of the three unmarked vans, and the narcs jumped out with bulletproof vests and their guns drawn, ready for action.

A crew held a battering ram and headed for the front door. On a three count, the police burst through the door, rushing into Malek's crack house. Women were inside cooking coke naked, while cocaine-filled tables and microwaves occupied the spacious studio-style house.

"Everybody on the ground!" Rodriguez grabbed up a girl by the hair when she tried to run to the back door. She yelled, "Don't play with me, dumb bitch!" and flung the girl to the floor by her hair. "Check the back!"

Meanwhile, Fuller drove around the corner, waiting to see if anyone would try to flee from the back of the house, and just as he thought, a man with a duffel bag jumped the gate and tried to get away. Fuller quickly put the pedal to the metal and headed straight for the fleeing man.

As he got closer, he saw it was Dayvid, Malek's little man. "Bingo!" he said, knowing he got a consolation prize by locating Dayvid.

Dayvid saw the car speeding toward him. "Fuck!" He instantly began to put on his best Carl Lewis impersonation and took off full speed. Fuller quickly whipped behind him and hit him, causing him to fly up in the air and onto the windshield. Fuller stopped, and Dayvid rolled off the car and hit the ground with the bag still in his hands.

Dayvid winced in pain from the extreme back pains the collision caused. "Fuck!" he said as he lay on the ground holding his back.

"Don't move!" Fuller yelled, his gun drawn and pointed directly at Dayvid's head. He snatched the bag and tossed it on the hood of his

car. He then flipped Dayvid around and placed handcuffs on him just before patting him down to make sure he didn't have any weapons.

Fuller then stood up and caught his breath. He peeked into the bag and saw nothing but rubber-banded money. "Damn, y'all over there getting it, huh?" he said.

"Fuck you, pig!" Dayvid yelled, showcasing his deep hatred for police.

Fuller chuckled at Dayvid's remark and then gave him a swift kick to the mouth, causing blood to spurt from it instantly.

"I know you. You're Dayvid Porter, right?' Fuller said, already knowing who Dayvid was because he had the whole rundown on Malek's crew. "Where is Malek?" Fuller bent down on one knee and grabbed Dayvid by the back of his neck.

Dayvid ran his tongue across his bloody teeth. "I don't know a Malek."

"Oh, so you want to play games with me?" Fuller nodded his head up and down, getting angrier by the second. He quickly bashed Dayvid's head into the cement, causing a bloody gash to form on his forehead.

Dayvid grimaced in pain, but shortly after, he began to smile, knowing he was getting under Fuller's skin by not giving up Malek's whereabouts.

"You can give your man up and tell me where he is, or go down to the station. It's all on you!" Fuller yelled as he began to grip tighter around the back of Dayvid's neck.

"I ain't telling you shit!" Dayvid spat out more blood.

Fuller had had enough and realized that Dayvid was loyal to Malek. "We will see how loyal you are." He yanked Dayvid off the ground and stuffed him into the back seat. They were about to take a little ride down to the station.

Fuller had Dayvid in a chair in the middle of the interrogation room of the police precinct. "You're looking at three to five, Dayvid." He rested both of his hands on the cold steel table. "You were maintaining a drug house, and I found thirty grand in your possession."

Fuller was itching to get Malek in the worst way, but Dayvid wasn't budging. He had a clean record, and he knew that he would only get a slap on a wrist for what Fuller was trying to pin him with.

Fuller continued to circle around the youngster. "Just give Malek up, and you can go scot-free. I will forget about what I found on you, and it would be as if you were never there."

"I don't know a Malek." Dayvid grinned. He would never in a million years cross his big homie. Never. He began to block out all Fuller was saying and began to think back to the first time he'd met Malek.

* * *

Dayvid sat sunken low in the tinted Grand Am, watching Malek closely. "I'm about to take all of that shit," he whispered to himself as he gripped the all-black .357 handgun. He had a ski mask rolled on the top of his head and was waiting for the right moment to ambush Malek.

Dayvid had been following him for days, and he was waiting until Malek led him straight to his home, because Dayvid thought that was where he most likely kept his stash. Dayvid needed that money in the worst way. The city was dry, and he was hungry. He had been watching Malek closely and knew he was an out-of-towner that came to B-more moving coke.

Dayvid had trailed Malek as he stopped at five different crack houses. It was the first of the month, so he knew Malek was picking up his trap from his spots. In Dayvid's eyes, that day was the perfect day to rob him.

The sun was just setting as Dayvid followed Malek to a nice-sized brick house.

"This must be where the nigga stay," Dayvid said to himself, as he witnessed Malek pull into the driveway and hop out of his car with the duffel bag in hand.

Dayvid was parked about a half a block down, but he still had a clear view of Malek getting out of the car. He made sure his gun was locked and loaded and got out of his car as soon as he saw Malek enter the home. There were no more cars in the driveway or on the curb, so he assumed Malek was there alone.

"He must be about to go count or stash the money inside," Dayvid said as he crept to the back of the house.

Dayvid's young mind didn't think logically, and he didn't care what he was getting himself into. He just knew Malek was getting money, and he wanted a piece of it.

He crept to the back, where there was a swimming pool and a glass patio. He quickly dipped into the back patio and saw the sliding double doors that led into the home. He slowly approached the double doors and glanced into the home, to see if the coast was clear.

After a few seconds of observing, Dayvid pulled out a lockpick, but when he gently slid the door, he noticed it was unlocked. *Hell yeah,* he thought to himself. It was his lucky day, and everything was going perfect.

He slowly stepped around the kitchen's porcelain counter and heard the sound of a money counter purring. Malek had to be dealing with big paper, a stickup kid's dream. He smiled as he pulled down his ski mask, thinking about how much paper he was about to get.

Dayvid crept to the room with his gun in hand. He saw Malek at the

table with his back turned toward him, putting the money in rubber bands as it came out of the machine. He slowly and carefully snuck up behind Malek, his gun pointed directly at Malek's head.

The money machine stopped, and the room grew quiet as Malek paused.

Without even turning around to face Dayvid, Malek said without an ounce of fear in his heart or shakiness in his voice, "I was wondering what was taking you so long."

What the fuck? Dayvid thought to himself. He wondered how Malek knew he was sneaking up behind him. "Come up off all of that dough, homeboy," he yelled, his hand shaking nervously.

"You sure you want to do this, young nigga?" Malek carefully swung around in his chair, so he could look the young robber in his eyes.

"Fuck all the talking, nigga! Put the money in the bag!" Dayvid said, avoiding eye contact with Malek.

"Look, you have two choices. You can rob me of this money and then deal with the consequences of taking money from a nigga like me." Malek folded his hands together. "Or you can put that gun down, and I will give you a job. I will let you work for me and show you how to get money rather than take it.

"One thing about robbing, once your stolen money is gone, you're right back to square one and broke again. But if you learn how to get money, you will never be broke." Malek looked the youngster straight in the eye and recognized the fear within them.

Malek's logic made a lot of sense to Dayvid, who wanted to get out of the robbing business desperately and get into the hustle game. He had always fantasized about moving up in the ranks and becoming a kingpin, so Malek's offer was very tempting. But the possibility of Malek just talking to get out of the situation had him hesitant.

"How do I know if I put the gun down, you won't try to kill me?"

"You are just going to have to trust me."

Malek spoke with a supreme calmness that had Dayvid petrified. All of Dayvid's instincts told him to just rob Malek and turn down the offer, but his heart told him otherwise. He used his free hand to pull his ski mask to the top of his head, and then he lowered his gun.

Malek instantly knew he had accepted his offer. "Good choice, youngblood." He turned around and began to rubber-band the money.

Dayvid stood there confused, as he didn't know what to do next.

Malek finally spoke up after a few seconds of silence. "Believe me, you made the right choice," he said. "I want you to take a look behind you."

Dayvid frowned his face up, not knowing what Malek was getting to. Dayvid did as he was told, and when he turned around, his heart almost dropped to the floor. There was a man standing there with a

Mossberg pump aimed directly at his chest. Dayvid flinched as he looked down at the steel that was now pressed against his chest.

"I knew you were coming. I saw you from a mile away. If you had tried to rob me, karma would have come instantly, and my man would've blown your brains out. But I respect your bravery, and I'ma keep my word." Malek pulled out the chair from underneath the table for Dayvid. "Have a seat."

The man holding the shotgun lowered his weapon, and Dayvid joined Malek at the table. That was the beginning of a relationship that would become closer than close. Since that day, Malek and Dayvid had become inseparable, and Malek showed his youngster how to get to the monster, molding him to be Baltimore's next kingpin.

Dayvid snapped out of his dream and focused on the present. Fuller was right in his face with an intense stare. "So what's it going to be? The ball is in your court." He waited for a response from the young Dayvid.

"Suck my dick!" Dayvid calmly said, looking through Fuller as if he weren't even there. Dayvid wasn't going to roll on his man.

Fuller became enraged, knowing that Dayvid was young and also that as a first-time offender, would get just a slap on the wrist, and that only infuriated him even more. He gave Dayvid a swift jab to the eye, for good measure, and stormed out of the room.

Dayvid took the punch like a man, and after the stars wore off, he thought about what Malek had taught him: stay loyal, which was exactly what he'd just done.

Within twenty-four hours, Malek was waiting for Dayvid outside of the jailhouse in a tinted car. He had sent his attorney in to bail Dayvid out, and just like that, he was on the streets again.

Malek's attorney had discovered that Fuller had raided the house without a warrant, so all the paraphernalia and evidence was inadmissible. Malek would just move his spot and would be open for business by the end of the day. Scar had his work cut out for him because Malek wasn't an amateur.

"What's up, kid?" Malek said as Dayvid entered the car along with one of Malek's workers that he'd sent in for him. A smiling Malek blew his horn at the attorney, who was getting into his vehicle across the parking lot. He knew he had outwitted Scar.

"What up, Malek? I'm glad to be out of that stink-hole." Dayvid got comfortable in the front seat and leaned back.

"Yeah. Tell me about it." Malek then reached over and playfully smacked Dayvid on the head. "You did good, you did good," and with that, he pulled off smiling.

Malek had his own little plan for Scar. It was obvious the man didn't know how he got down, and Malek fully planned on showing him.

Chapter One Hundred Twenty-eight

As Halleigh watched Malek sleep, she cried. There was no way she could stay in his life. After everything, their end had finally come. She leaned down and kissed his lips. He was a heavy sleeper, so he didn't stir.

"I love you, Malek," she said as she arose from their bed. She couldn't stop staring at him. Even though she knew she could never forget one detail about him, she wanted to burn his image in her brain because this was the last time she would ever see him again. She had to put distance between them. She had become a liability and was doing what was best for everyone involved by disappearing.

If Rodriguez knew she planned on skipping town, the shit would hit the fan, but by the time anyone realized she was gone, it would be too late. All she had to do was make sure that no one saw her leave and that she wasn't followed.

She pulled a suitcase from the closet, moving as quietly as possible, and began to pack some of her things. She didn't need much. A few clothes would do. She then went into Malek's petty cash stash and clipped five Gs from it. She had never stolen a thing from him in her life, but she needed this. Five thousand dollars was going to buy her a way out of town and hopefully be enough for her to start a new life.

She went into her son's nursery and checked on him. The last thing she wanted was to walk out of her baby's life, but she couldn't take him with her. She just hoped that one day he would understand, that both her child and Malek would understand. She kissed her fingers and placed them on his forehead then left the room.

She penned a note before she left because she would be ceasing all forms of communication. She didn't even want to take her cell phone with her because she knew she could be tracked down if she did.

Dear Malek,

I love you and have always loved you. I know that I always will, and because I love you so much, I have to leave you. I know you will never understand why I am doing this, but I need you to trust me the same way I have always trusted you. I'm doing this for our family because, even though we all won't be together, it is the only way to keep all of us safe. Don't forget about me, Malek, and please don't let our son. Tell him every day that I love him. Tell yourself that every day. I will always be thinking about you. I will never move on, and I will never forget what we have.

You were made for me, Malek. We both made a lot of mis-

*takes over the years that caused us to stay apart. This is just one
more of them, but you will always have my heart. Raise our son
right, Malek. He needs you, and you can't be there for him if
you're in the streets. I don't want him to end up like us. I don't
want him to have to see what we've seen.*

*We've been to hell and back. Protect him. Open your eyes,
Malek, and watch those who are watching you. You are all he
has. I love you.*
Always Yours,
 Halleigh

She placed the letter on her pillow, knowing he would find it when
he awoke, and then reluctantly she walked out on the people she
loved the most.

Halleigh peered out onto the street. There were always cars sitting
on the block at night, but tonight they all looked suspicious. Ro-
driguez had said that the police would always be watching, so to be
safe, Halleigh went out of the back of the building.

Creeping like a cat through the back alley, she walked until she was
on the next block and then ran until she was able to catch a cab in the
early morning hours.

"Where to?" the cab driver asked.

"BWI," she stated. She never looked back as the cab pulled off to-
ward the airport, afraid that if she did, she may not go through with
her plan.

Malek awoke the next day to the sound of his son crying. He was
used to Halleigh waking up with him, so he wasn't used to all of the
screaming.

"Hal? Baby girl?" he called out from underneath the sheets. When
she didn't respond, he sat up. She never let their son cry for too long.
He got up and walked into their son's nursery. "Hey, li'l man. What you
crying for?" he asked as he picked him up, and his crying stopped in-
stantly. "Where's your mommy?"

Malek went into their living room and saw that Halleigh wasn't
there either. She never left the house without telling him her plans, so
he found her absence odd. "Hal!" he yelled, but she was nowhere to
be found.

He didn't begin to worry until he called her cell phone and heard it
ringing inside of their house. Malek followed the ringing of the phone,
which led him back to their bedroom. Her phone was on the night-
stand on her side of the bed, and as he sat down, he noticed the letter
she left behind.

With his son in his arms, he picked up the note and read it. Reading
the good-bye letter that Halleigh had left for him broke him down.

Tears accumulated in his eyes as he gripped his son tight. He wasn't ashamed to cry.

Losing a woman like Halleigh would break any man. He loved her endlessly, unconditionally, and couldn't believe this was happening. His heart felt broken. He had never felt this much pain. When they had been separated before, it didn't hurt this bad because other people had kept them away from one another in the past. This time Halleigh had chosen to leave him.

She left me, Malek thought in anguish. He didn't understand. For so long they had fought to be with each other, and now she had packed her bags and given up on them. He couldn't help but feel like this was his fault. He had made a lot of bad decisions, and he hadn't kept her safe over the years. He thought maybe she was beginning to regret all of the heartache she had suffered just to be his girl.

A knock at the door caused Malek to gain hope. *Maybe Halleigh has come back.* He stood and raced to the door, practically snatching it off the hinges as he opened it. Disappointment filled him when he saw Detective Rodriguez.

"Now is not a good time, detective," he said.

"Well, then I won't take up much of it. I came to return Halleigh's vehicle. We located it on the south end of town. Whoever mugged her left it in an abandoned parking lot," Rodriguez said as she held out the keys for Malek. "Is Halleigh home? I would like to speak with her for a minute."

"Halleigh's not here."

"Is there a better time for me to stop back?" Rodriguez pushed. *Where the hell did she go? I had a car sitting on the building all night,* she thought angrily. She had a gut feeling that Halleigh had run, and she was infuriated.

"I got her keys. There really isn't a need for you to stop back," Malek replied. He began to close the door. He hated the police, and his patience with her had expired. He had more pressing issues on his mind.

"I have a few more questions for her," Rodriguez insisted.

Malek sighed. "She has your card. If I see her, I will have her contact you." He shut the door in her face.

Rodriguez stormed out of the building and immediately put in the call to her partner, Derek Fuller. Without a vehicle, there were only a few ways out of town, so she put a police detail on every bus station, airport, and train station in the city. There was no way she was going to let Halleigh escape. She would call out the entire Narcotics Unit of Baltimore before she let Halleigh slip through her fingers.

Malek's suspicion was aroused by the detective's interest in Halleigh. She seemed to be too persistent in her effort to speak with

Halleigh. Her sudden disappearance didn't make sense, but his gut was telling him that this lady cop had something to do with it.

That was the only thing he could attribute Halleigh's sudden change of heart to. They hadn't been having problems; in fact, he, had never loved Halleigh more. After almost losing her back in Flint, he cherished every moment that he spent with her now, and he knew that she felt the same. *Something is up,* he thought, now sure of himself that Halleigh needed his help.

Something was nagging at him. He returned to his bedroom and read her letter again, trying to read between the lines.

One line of her letter stuck out to him the most. "Watch those who are watching you," he whispered as her warning jumped out on the paper.

And like a light bulb coming on in his head, he thought, *The cops are watching.* He rushed into the hallway and down to the window that peered out over the street.

For the first time, he noticed the unmarked squad car that was hawking his building. *Fuck!* He cursed himself. *How long have they been on me? What the fuck they watching me for? A nigga ain't moving bricks. And how long has Halleigh known? What do they have over her that will make her skip town?*

Malek was beginning to think that more had happened that night than a carjacking, and as he raced back to his apartment, he tried to figure out where Halleigh had gone. *Think like her. Where would she go?*

Halleigh sat in the airport eagerly and nervously waiting for the delayed flights to resume service. She didn't have time for this. A security breach had caused the entire airport to shut down, and she had been waiting for hours for them to resume ticket sales. She figured that Malek had gotten her letter by now, and she was wondering how he had reacted. She wished she could go back home and make everything nice, but it was a wrap for her life in Baltimore. As soon as she was able to, she was purchasing a one-way ticket out of the city. She figured she would go down south to North Carolina, where her mother was from and where her grandmother still lived. Even though Halleigh had never met the woman, she knew her name, and was hoping they could get acquainted once she arrived. If not, then she would just have to do what she did best: survive.

At least down there she would be out of hot water. *Maybe one day I can come back for my son,* she thought. She felt herself becoming emotional at the thought of everything she was leaving behind. She went to use the restroom. Her eyes were red and puffy. She looked a hot mess. She couldn't wait to get out of Baltimore, so she could have peace of mind.

As she emerged from the bathroom, she looked toward the front counter. Her heart skipped a beat when she saw Rodriguez question-

ing one of the airline employees. Halleigh automatically knew that this was no coincidence. She was there looking for her. She knew that if Rodriguez was there, it was a good possibility that more cops were on the scene as well.

Halleigh quickly ducked back into the restroom. Creating a commotion at the airport was the last thing she wanted to do, but she had to get out of there. She peeked out of the door, and while Rodriguez was distracted at the ticket counter, she slowly eased out, keeping her head low to remain inconspicuous. Walking as quickly as possible out of the airport, when she finally emerged outside, she ran to the first cab she saw.

"Hal!"

She stopped mid-step and looked up in disbelief when she heard Malek calling her name. She had one foot inside of the cab as she saw him pulling up behind her, blowing his horn urgently to get her attention. Shocked, her mouth dropped open in surprise.

"Get in, Halleigh!" he shouted.

She rushed over to his car and jumped inside. She ducked low, keeping her eyes on the side mirrors.

Just as Malek pulled away, Halleigh saw Rodriguez emerge from the airport. "Go! Go!" she yelled.

When she was sure they were out of any police radar, she sat up in her seat. Her son was crying from his car seat in the back, and his cries affected her, causing her tears to flow too.

"You wanna tell me what's going on now, Halleigh?"

"How did you find me?"

"I know you, Hal," he said as he drove with one hand and touched her chin gently with the other. "You are me, ma. You ran, and I knew you wasn't riding no bus or train. You think you're too good for that." He smiled mockingly.

She shook her head and wiped her eyes. "You should have let me go, Malek," she said softly. "You don't know what's going on."

"Then why don't you tell me? I know the cops are watching me. Your letter told me that. But what is it that you are not telling me? We're better than this, Halleigh. Your burden is supposed to be my burden."

"I'll tell you everything. Can we just go somewhere, to a hotel room or something, so I can get my head together? Then we'll talk, and I'll tell you everything."

Malek and Halleigh checked into the Courtyard Marriot in Linthicum, and once they were safely inside with their child, it was time for her to fess up. Malek waited patiently for her to find her words.

"You can tell me, Halleigh. Whatever it is, just say it."

"I fucked up," she began. "When we first came here, you told me over and over again to let the past go. You told me that everything and everyone in Flint were dead to us, but I didn't listen. With you in the streets all the time, I felt like I had nobody to talk to, no friends, no real life in Baltimore. So I called Tasha." She paused to see what Malek would say, but he remained silent. His facial expression was blank, so Halleigh couldn't read his emotions.

"Keep going," he said.

"I invited Tasha to come to Baltimore about a week ago, and we met for lunch downtown. I thought she was my friend, Malek. I would have never told her where we were if I ever thought she would put us in jeopardy."

"Stop talking in circles, Hal. Just tell me," he stated seriously.

"She came to town, but she brought Toy with her. They followed me from the restaurant, but I shook them."

Malek closed his eyes because he remembered Halleigh had specifically tried to tell him that someone had followed her, but he thought she was paranoid and overreacting.

"That next night they followed me from my job, and I refused to lead them back to you and the baby, so I just pulled over. I found an abandoned lot and I got out. I had started carrying one of your guns because I was terrified. I've been terrified since the day we got here, but I was tired of running, tired of being followed. I was tired of being the victim. They tried to get me to lead them to you. I refused, and Toy hit me. I just reacted and I shot her, Malek. I killed her, and then I killed Tasha for setting me up."

"And the cop saw it," Malek finished, putting two and two together.

Halleigh nodded. "She saw everything. She said if I didn't help her get you, then she would throw me in prison for the rest of my life. I could never bring myself to harm you, but I can't go to jail either, Malek. So I ran. I just thought if I got as far away from here as possible, it would fix things."

"Come here, ma," he said as he pulled her onto the bed he was sitting on. He wiped her tears away. He could only imagine how Halleigh felt. Having taken many lives himself, he knew Halleigh wasn't built for murder.

She broke down in his arms. "What am I going to do?" she asked.

"You're going to do exactly what they want you to do. You're going to cooperate with the police," he said in a low but sure tone.

"What?" She looked up at him in confusion. "Malek, they'll throw you in jail."

"Look at that little boy over there," he said, pointing to their son. "He needs you, Halleigh. You're his mother. You didn't ask for any of this. You just took on the role of being with me. I would never make

you pay for that. I love you too much to ever see something bad happen to you. I can handle whatever the cops have coming my way. You just promise me that you'll always take care of my son."

Halleigh was hysterical crying and snot running down her nose. "I can't, Malek. I can't do that to you. This isn't supposed to be how we end. I need you."

"And I need you, Hal. I need you to be strong, baby girl. You're my world, and I need you to trust me. This is the only way. I'm a man, and I can stand behind all of the decisions I've made in my life, but before I let them take me, I need to know that you can hold things down for me while I'm away."

She nodded as he held her face. "I will try for you, Malek. I will do whatever you need me to do."

"I've got some money put up. It's not a lot, but it's enough for you and the baby to live for a couple years. Nothing extravagant, but it will pay for rent and food for a while until you can get on your feet."

"I don't want to do this, Malek."

"You have to, Halleigh." As Malek schooled Halleigh on how to survive without him, she almost tuned him out. She didn't want to believe this was happening, but this was real and there was no avoiding the inevitable. She was grateful she had a man like Malek, who was willing to take responsibility for the situation, but it didn't stop the sadness that plagued her.

Chapter One Hundred Twenty-nine

So many thoughts went through Malek's head as he drove down the highway along with Dayvid. They were just getting back from visiting the coke connect, and Dayvid was officially plugged. Malek had introduced him to the "birdman" and put him in a position of power, just as his deceased mentor, Jamaica Joe, had done for Malek when he was younger.

He kept visualizing Halleigh's face when she told him Rodriguez was blackmailing her. The hurt in her eyes was like daggers to his heart. He never second-guessed his decision to give himself up for his girl's freedom. He knew that when he walked in his own house it could be wired, starting off a domino effect that would land him in jail for a very long time.

Malek's heart began to ache as he thought about his son growing up without him. Nevertheless, it was better than his son growing up without both mother and father. He'd always told Halleigh that he would keep her out of harm's way when they relocated to Baltimore, but he'd failed to do that, and the guilt was weighing heavy on his soul.

"Remember everything I have taught you," Malek preached to his protégé. "You are too smart to stay in this game long enough for it to consume you. Don't be like me and let the allure of the money keep you in. Make money and exit. That's the key. Timing is everything."

Dayvid just sat back and listened closely as Malek hit him with a few last words of encouragement and instructions. Malek dropped Dayvid off to his block and watched as he exited the car. He grabbed him just before he got completely out and hugged him tight. Dayvid was confused and didn't know why Malek was acting so funny.

"I love you, my nigga," Malek said as he held on to Dayvid for a couple of extra seconds.

"Love you too. What's up, nigga? Why you acting all different?" Malek released him. "Don't worry about it. Just be safe out here, all right? And one more thing."

"What's up?" Dayvid looked at Malek dead in the eyes.

"If I'm not around, I want you to look after my son and Halleigh just as I did for you." Malek looked forward, avoiding eye contact with Dayvid.

"I got you," Dayvid said as he exited the car. Dayvid was taken off guard by Malek's comments, but he decided not to say anything about it. He noticed that Malek seemed to be stressing lately, and decided to address it at a later time.

Just before Malek pulled off, he caught a glimpse of the pinky ring he had given Dayvid and smirked. He knew Dayvid would hold it down in the streets and carry on his legacy properly. With that thought, Malek smiled and pulled off, headed home.

Malek knew that the next time he talked to Halleigh, she would be wearing a wire, and he would have to incriminate himself to get her off the hook for murder. He prepared himself mentally as he was about to voluntarily walk the path of self-destruction. Halleigh sat in the unmarked van on her block, three houses down from her and Malek's home. She clenched her jaws tight, and water filled her eyes as Rodriguez put the wire on her. She was shirtless, with nothing on but a bra, as Rodriguez applied tape on her chest to position the microphone right.

"Nice rack," Fuller said as he stared at Halleigh's plump breasts.

"Fuck you!" Halleigh said as she gave him a cold stare. If looks could kill, Fuller would have been circled in chalk.

"You wish," Fuller said with a sinister grin. "Look, you have to get

him to say something about him supplying kilos of dope to his runners. If he doesn't say that, the deal is off."

"I know what the fuck I have to do! I hate you!" Halleigh said as she continued to give Fuller a deadly stare.

"Yeah, yeah. Just remember what I said. If you don't follow through with this, you will never see your son, except through steel bars. It's your choice."

Halleigh knew Malek was sacrificing himself for his family, and the fact that she was about to help Fuller put him behind bars made her sick to her stomach. She had left Malek Jr. with a babysitter, not wanting him to be around when this disaster went down.

"Okay, you're done," Rodriguez said as she tapped the microphone to make sure it was on.

Halleigh snatched her shirt from the seat and began to put it on, shaking her head from side to side. She knew the countdown to Malek's demise had begun. If she had to sacrifice herself for Malek, she would have. But Malek Jr.'s well-being was at risk. So, with the permission of her man, she had to do what she had to do. It was show time.

Halleigh stepped out of the van and slammed the door as hard as she could. As she walked to her house, so many different emotions began to run through her body as she felt the burden of the situation weighing heavy on her soul—hatred for Fuller, and guilt for herself.

"How did I get myself into this shit?" she whispered as she entered her house and waited for Malek.

Malek pulled up to his home and turned off the ignition. He took a deep breath and prepared for what was ahead. He was determined for his son to have a normal life and not have to go through the hardships that he himself had encountered. And to do that, he had to give himself to the law.

He stepped out of the car and glanced down the street. He noticed two vans with plumbing advertisements. He already knew the vans held policemen waiting to move in on him. He quickly focused on his house and headed that way.

"Hey, baby," he yelled as he stepped through the door. "I'm home!"

Halleigh appeared from the back with tears in her eyes and her hands over her mouth, trying to stop from crying aloud. She ran into his arms, and he embraced her tight.

Malek kissed her on her neck. In the lowest tone he could muster, he whispered in her ear, "I love you, Halleigh. Always have and always will. Let's get this over with, okay." He stepped back from her.

Halleigh let her tears flow freely down her cheeks as she nodded her head in agreement.

As soon as Malek nodded his head, giving her the green light to start the rehearsed conversation, she did.

"Malek, you have to stop selling drugs. I'm tired of this life," she said just as he had instructed her to the night before. Halleigh's voice began to crack, and she ran her fingers through her hair in frustration. She mouthed silently to Malek, "I can't do this."

But he smiled at her and put his hand on her shoulder, helping her through it. "I have to flip a couple more kilos, and then I'm done," he said. "My dope connect, Scar, wouldn't like if I just stopped buying from him. It's not that simple." Malek smiled inside, knowing he had just incriminated Scar by saying his name. If he was going to go out, he was going out with a bang.

Detective Fuller sat in the van, earphones on, listening to their every word. He chuckled to himself at Malek's remark about Scar.

"That nigga think he's slick," Fuller said to himself. He immediately thought about how he would edit that small portion out of the wiretap before turning it in as evidence.

Fuller was patiently waiting for the right time to rush in with his squad and put Malek in handcuffs. He looked down at the duffel bag that contained four kilos and stepped-on cocaine that he would eventually pin on Malek. With the drugs and the wiretaps indicating that he was a heavy drug supplier, Malek was sure to spend a long time behind bars.

Scar's money had slowed up drastically, which meant that Fuller had seen his cut from the drug business slow up too, and he wasn't having it. Fuller wanted Malek off the streets just as bad as Scar wanted him off the streets.

"Come on, Malek, tell on yourself a little bit more."

"I just hit my spot off with a kilo a piece." Malek clenched his teeth tight, knowing he was telling on himself. But when he thought about what he was doing it for, he had no problem with doing so. Malek would tell on himself a thousand times and serve a million years, if it meant that his son would have a good life and Halleigh stayed free.

Halleigh cried as she stood there looking into Malek's eyes. Malek had said enough to satisfy the police, so he grabbed and hugged his woman and kissed her. "I love you with all my heart, and you are the love of my life."

"I love you too, Malek." Halleigh gripped him tight and buried her face into his chiseled chest. She tiptoed and whispered in his ear, "Let's just leave town. Let's run," trying to exhaust every possible option to change the inevitable.

Malek quickly shook his head no. He would've considered it if they didn't have a baby to bring along, but he knew that being on the run

with a baby was immoral. He couldn't bring himself to have his son caught up in the web of the treacherous street life he had created.

"I'm tired of running, Hal. I got us into this, I'ma get us out." He looked deep into Halleigh's eyes and added, "Tell my son that I will always love him."

Those words broke Halleigh's heart, knowing that Malek wouldn't be able to tell Malek Jr. that himself without being behind bars. Malek pulled his gun from his waist and placed his other hand on Halleigh's cheek. It was the most difficult thing either of them ever had to do.

"We will be together again," he said. Malek flashed back to years ago when they'd first met in high school. He thought back to a time when she was pure and innocent. He would trade his life to give Halleigh back her innocence. The ills of their hometown Flint had forced them to move to Baltimore, and even there, trouble found them.

He walked out of the door with gun in hand. "Bye, Halleigh," he said.

Halleigh saw the look in Malek's eyes, the pain that was embedded deep within. She didn't fully understand what that pained look meant, but she would soon find out. Scar sat back smoking a kush-filled cigar and thought about how business would pick up, now that Malek was on the road of destruction. Fuller had just phoned him and let him know that the master plan was in motion, and that Malek would be behind bars before the night's end.

Scar already had his goons in place to rush Malek's block and give his old workers an ultimatum: Get down or lay down. He had just checkmated Malek after a long battle of mental chess. The only thing left to do now was to wait for Fuller's call to confirm the arrest.

"Victory feels so good," Scar said as he watched the young lady go up and down on his shaft, making it disappear and reappear over and over again. "Damn, Mrs. Fuller, that feels good," he crooned as his toes began to curl.

He looked at her shapely naked body and admired her smooth skin while she pleased him. He reached over and smacked her buttocks, making a small wave flow, enticing him even more. The view was mesmerizing and made his pipe even harder.

While Scar's partner was handling business for him, he was banging out Fuller's wife. Scar, at that point, felt on top of the world. He had a dime piece sucking him off, bringing him to the brink of an orgasm, while his main rival was about to be nonexistent, making him the king of Baltimore.

"Move in! He's coming out of the house," Fuller yelled into the phone. He smiled. He was about to lock Malek up for a very long time. He was satisfied with the recordings he had and was ready to snatch Malek up.

Fuller looked closer at Malek stepping off of the porch and noticed that he had a gun in hand. "He has a gun!" Fuller screamed into the walkie-talkie as Rodriguez slid the van's door open.

Fuller's squad had already rushed Malek with their guns drawn, but Malek had his gun drawn also and pointed at the oncoming crew. Fuller jumped out of the van along with Rodriguez, their guns out.

"Drop the fucking gun!" one of the policemen said as they slowly approached Malek.

"You drop yo mufuckin' gun! I'm not putting down shit!" Malek yelled as he pointed his gun at each officer.

Fuller cautiously approached his crew and put his red beam on Malek's chest, ready to blast at any sudden movement by Malek.

Malek gripped his gun tight. He had no intentions of going to jail that day. He had planned to go out blazing, just like Jamaica Joe would have. Malek was about to go out like a gangster, no doubt.

Fuller closed one eye and aimed straight for Malek's head. "Drop that gun! You don't want to do this!"

"Fuck you!" Malek screamed, spit flying out of his mouth. His trigger finger began to itch. He saw Fuller's face and locked his aim on him, feeling deep hatred for him. The cops had blackmailed his girl and caused all of the pandemonium. He hated him deep down in his soul. The more he thought about leaving Halleigh and his son, he grew more irate.

A single tear dropped from Malek's left eye—a tear not of sadness, but of pain. "I'm from Flint, Michigan, mufucka!" Malek's grip grew even tighter, his index finger resting on the trigger. "Do y'all know who the fuck I am? Huh? I'm cut from the cloth of Jamaica Joe! Fuck all y'all!" Malek screamed, ten guns pointed at him.

"Malek! No!" Halleigh yelled as she stepped out of the door. Her heart dropped as she saw the police standing in front of the love of her life. As Halleigh stepped off the porch trying to get to Malek, he looked back, and that quick movement by him made Fuller fire a shot at him. That started a chain reaction among the other narcs, and the bullets started flying one after another, hitting Malek in the chest, jerking him from left to right.

As Malek lay there dying, all Halleigh could think of was that not only did she just lose the love of her life, but it was the end of an era.